The
DEATH'S HEAD
CHESS CLUB

John Donoghue

Atlantic Books
LONDON

First published in Great Britain in 2015 by Atlantic Books,
an imprint of Atlantic Books Ltd.

10 9 8 7 6 5 4 3 2 1

A CIP catalogue record for this book is available
from the British Library.

Hardback ISBN: 978 1 78239 645 1
Trade Paperback ISBN: 978 1 78239 311 5
E-book ISBN: 978 1 78239 312 2

Printed in Sweden by ScandBook AB

Atlantic Books
An Imprint of Atlantic Books Ltd
Ormond House
26–27 Boswell Street
London
WC1N 3JZ

www.atlantic-books.co.uk

THE DEATH'S HEAD CHESS CLUB

CONTENTS

THE DEATH'S HEAD CHESS CLUB

1.

The Latvian Gambit

1944

Konzentrationslager Auschwitz-III, Monowitz

It is late afternoon and the camp is quiet. The biting February wind blows from the east and prowls along the alleys between the wooden barracks, waiting for the return of the inmates, an enemy in a long list of enemies. Everyone knows that the wind in Auschwitz speaks its own strange language. It does not speak of the outside world, of the sun on distant mountains, or snow falling lightly on city streets. It speaks only of what it witnesses within the electrified wire that surrounds the camp, of hunger and privation, of solitude among the multitudes that live there, and of death. Arc lights cut through the gloom to flood the parade ground with an unnatural brightness, creating sharp shadows between the fence posts that surround the camp. The camp is hungry. Hunger is another enemy, ever-present, heavy and gnawing, a ravening emptiness in the pit of every stomach that neither the bread ration in the morning nor the thin soup at noon can remedy.

Weariness is another enemy, but the camp cannot rest. Constant vigilance is needed to guard against possible infractions of the rules – rules that are unwritten, unknowable, unfathomable; rules which can be made up on the spot; rules where the only purpose is to increase the opportunities for misery. Each and every rule, whether written or unwritten, known or unknown, is another enemy: the camp is at war, and for each inmate the only measure of victory is that somehow they have managed to survive another day.

In his warm office in the *Kommandantur* building overlooking the camp, SS-Obersturmführer* Paul Meissner gazes out of the window, a cup of coffee in hand. The coffee is good quality, not the ersatz that the soldiers at the front get, for duty in the camps is arduous and essential to the wellbeing of the Reich. Meissner raises the cup to his lips and savours the richness of its aroma. It is a moment of quiet. His gaze lifts to the sky: iron-grey clouds fill his horizon. His leg aches: a sure sign – it will undoubtedly snow before morning.

Meissner is tall, even for a German. His hair is dark, but his eyes are a shimmering blue, disconcertingly so. He is a rarity in the camp – Waffen-SS; his collar bears the double lightning rune in silver on black, not the death's head emblem of the camp SS, the Totenkopfverbände.[†] He walks with a pronounced limp – a parting gift from a Russian tank. It is a badge of honour: few others in the camp have seen service at the front. Now he spends his days in Abteilung I, responsible to the camp Kommandant. His duties are concerned with overseeing the many satellite labour camps that fall under the umbrella of Auschwitz, mainly the old *Zwangsarbeitslager für Juden*, Fürstengrube and Blechhammer and others even further afield. He is responsible for the SS personnel, and two Scharführers and their teams work daily miracles for him with rosters of men and transport.

---

* See appendix for a table of SS ranks.

† The SS was divided into three main branches: the general or Allgemeine-SS; the military or Waffen-SS; and the concentration camp guards, the Totenkopfverbände, or Death's Head Units. Uniquely, the Totenkopfverbände wore a death's head emblem on their right collar tab.

Meissner's biggest headache is the IG Farben *Werke*, the labyrinthine Buna industrial complex that the Monowitz camp was built to serve. Its capacity to produce synthetic oil and rubber from the surrounding coal fields is crucial to the war effort, yet construction is months behind schedule; so far not a single drop of oil or gramme of rubber has been produced.

Without warning, the quiet is broken. The camp orchestra* has struck up a tune, a jaunty marching song. He searches his memory for its name but it eludes him. He glances at his watch. Where has the day gone?

Minutes later, their day at the factory over, the inmates start to enter the camp. The scene is almost comic in its absurdity: ghastly wrecks of men in filthy, blue-striped uniforms marching in time to the cheery melody of the orchestra. Some of the *Kapos*† have even got their men singing. They are led straight to the parade ground where they line up in columns, five abreast. The early arrivals will have to endure the cold while they wait. There are over 10,000 inmates and it will be a while before they are all assembled and the roll call can begin.

---

* An orchestra made up of inmates was established in the main Auschwitz camp as early as 1941. Others were subsequently formed in Birkenau and Monowitz. The orchestra played when the inmates left, and returned to, the camp each day. According to one account, the orchestra was required to play 'at all official occasions – for the camp commander's speeches, for transports and for hangings. It also served as the entertainment for the SS and the inmates in the medical barracks.' The women's orchestra in Birkenau was the most famous. Its leader was Alma Rosé, a well-known musician, who died in Auschwitz in 1944.

† The SS used selected prisoners, the *Prominenten*, to run the camps for them. They were usually Germans sent to a concentration camp for a criminal or political offence. *Ältesten*, or elders, managed the living quarters; *Kapos* supervised the labour squads, or *Kommandos*. They were given privileges, providing they kept control of their fellow prisoners. In order to maintain their privileged status the *Prominenten* often acted with frightening brutality: there are numerous accounts of prisoners being beaten to death for some minor or imagined infraction.

Among the inmates is a recent arrival, from France. He has not yet acquired the haunted, hollow-eyed look of the camp, and, although he has lost weight and his uniform hangs loosely on his frame, his health is still good. He used to have a name, but that was in another life, a life that made sense beyond the daily struggle merely to survive. His name was Emil Clément, and he was a watchmaker. Now he is simply *Häftling** number 163291.

In the eyes of the Reich, Emil is guilty of a crime for which there can be no pardon: he is a Jew.

A hush descends on the parade ground. Roll call begins. The inmates must stand to attention and ignore the bitter fingers of cold that pinch at their emaciated limbs. The camp waits, gripped by numb anxiety. If the numbers do not tally, roll call will have to begin all over again. But not tonight. The Rapportführer† is satisfied and they are dismissed. One might expect to hear a collective sigh of relief, but no – the inmates simply move from one ordeal to the next. They do not have the energy to waste on sighing.

Emil collapses onto his bunk. Normally he spends his day in a machine shop, crafting tiny mechanisms for the repair of the many technical instruments that measure and regulate the processes that are the lifeblood of the Buna factory, much as he would once have created them for the workings of a fine watch. But today there was no electricity and he was reassigned to a labour *Kommando* unloading sacks of cement from railway wagons and stacking them in a warehouse. In his life he has never been so tired; every muscle and sinew hurts and his feet are raw from the

---

* Prisoner or detainee.

† An SS NCO responsible for conducting the roll call.

ill-fitting wooden clogs that the inmates wear so that even the constant clamour of his hunger is subdued.

He shares the bunk with another Frenchman, Yves. They arrived in Auschwitz on the same transport from the internment camp at Drancy, though they did not know one another before being assigned the same bunk. At first, Emil felt disgust at the thought of sharing his bed with another man, a stranger. Now he knows he is fortunate: it is the only time he is warm. They have become firm friends and look out for each other. If one of them is lucky and is able to organize some food – the most precious commodity in the camp – they share it, not like the other inmates in their block. Emil has noticed that most of them keep to themselves; their existence is so marginal, they cannot bear the thought of sharing anything. This solitariness is the source both of their weakness and of the strength of those in charge. Auschwitz is a camp divided against itself.

Yves climbs up to the bunk. They are on the top tier. 'Move over,' he says. Emil groans as he makes his tired limbs obey. Yves grins. 'I had a good day today.' He pushes something towards Emil. It is a hunk of coarse black bread. 'One of the Poles left a woollen jacket lying around. When no one was looking I organized it.' *Organize* is the camp slang for stealing. The inmates are forced to organize if they are to survive. And, in accordance with the absurd rules of Auschwitz, organizing is encouraged, but punished severely if the thief is caught. 'I smuggled it back under my jacket.'

The garment is a great prize, but risky. It would be difficult to keep concealed for any length of time: better to trade it. In the washroom in the corner of the camp that is furthest from the barracks of the SS men there is a thriving market. Every day, as soon as the roll call is dismissed, hundreds of inmates rush there, some to sell, some to buy. It is a buyer's market, for every stomach is empty, and the currency of the camp is bread. Those whose eyes are brittle with hunger can be persuaded to sell for the lowest prices amid the chaotic uproar of barter. Spoons and knives: each prisoner needs one, but the camp authorities do not provide them. They must be purchased. It is here that other items, that various prisoners have managed to organize, are also exchanged.

'What did you do with it?' Emil asks.

'I sold it to the block elder in Block 16. I got two bread rations for it.'

It is a fair price. They eat the bread in silence, savouring every morsel, even though they are painfully aware that every other inmate in their block is hungry. They will not be disturbed. It is a code among the inmates. They would all do the same if they had the chance.

Soon it is lights out and the camp settles into an uneasy slumber; in only a few hours its toil begins again.

Yves is thankful he has been paired with Emil. He is a gentle, cultured man. They talk endlessly about France before the war. Yves is also curious about Emil's passion for the game of chess.

'Explain to me again,' he says quietly in the darkness, 'about the Latvian Gambit.'

2.

THE DUTCH DEFENCE

1962

Grand Hotel Krasnapolsky, Amsterdam

The interview was approaching its conclusion. Still the interviewer, an old hand who knew how to wring the best and the worst from his guests, had not asked the question. At last, with the deftness of a conjurer, he slipped it in: 'What many of our listeners would like to hear about is your time in Auschwitz.'

The man sitting opposite him adjusted his lanky frame in the armchair and sighed. He glanced at the tape recorder as if he hoped that the spools might stop turning. Again, someone had asked the question; again, the hard stamping on the brakes, bringing the course of his life to an abrupt standstill. Auschwitz: after nearly twenty years, still it followed him every-where. Bearing witness to the horror was a duty, but a heavy one. He had not expected to be confronted with it here. He raised his head to look at his tormentor. His eyes were a thin murky grey, like a sky threatening rain. They were eyes that seemed to look past the object of their attention, to depths and secrets that were best kept hidden.

The interviewer suppressed a shiver. Realizing that a silence had fallen between them, he felt compelled to break it. 'Your reluctance to speak about this is, of course, completely understandable...'

'Reluctance?' The word came out sharply, as if the man had been

7

caught in an untruth. 'No, not really. It is not so much reluctance, rather, it is not knowing what I ought to say. So much has been said already that there is perhaps little left to tell. It is complicated. If I start, where will it lead? And, of course, at the back of my mind I wonder what it is you really want.' Unconsciously, the man's long, slender fingers gripped the arms of his chair. 'Do you want to know what it was really like in an extermination camp, or do you want to hear lurid tales of what one had to do in order to survive?'

The interviewer knew his listeners would not want him to appear insensitive; he changed tack. 'In your book you wrote that you did not believe that any German who lived through the war could be untainted by what happened in the death camps. Guilt by association, you might say. Do you really believe that – that all Germans are guilty? Were there no good Germans?'

The question did not elicit the hoped-for response. The man bowed his head and ran a hand through his thinning hair.

The interviewer felt the need to prompt him. 'Mijnheer Clément?'

'It seems that everyone wants me to spend the rest of my life looking for a good German. Why? So he can apologize? There is no apology. You want a good German? Let me tell you, I saw none. Not one.' Clément enunciated the last words slowly and clearly.

Sensing there was something more, the interviewer persisted. 'You didn't mention it in your book, but isn't it true that it was a German who saved your wife's life?'

Clément looked sharply at his interrogator. 'Yes, it's true, after a fashion. I didn't include it in my book because I was writing about my experiences, not hers. But I will tell you what happened to her, if only to dispel the myth of the good German.' His voice had become harsh and tight, as if he were struggling to keep it under control. He took a sip of water before continuing.

'We both survived the camp, though neither of us knew that the other was still alive. It was months before I found her. Her registration card in Auschwitz said she was dead – "Shot while trying to escape" – usually a euphemism for dying under torture. But she wasn't dead; she was in Austria, in Mauthausen. She was in hospital. She had scarlet fever. If she hadn't been so weak…' His voice caught, and he coughed to clear it. 'All she wanted was to ask for my forgiveness. "What forgiveness?" I said. "You have nothing to be forgiven for. You are blameless." But she was insistent and, bit by bit, she told me what she had had to do to in order to live.

'Her life was saved by a note. Yes, a simple note. A note of the kind that could be written by anyone, for any number of reasons – a shopping list, a reminder, an apology, a demand for payment, an assignation – a tight little ball of paper that struck her lightly on the back of her head and fell to the floor. She knew it must have come from one of the guards. She covered it with her foot and glanced round to see who might have thrown it. There were two SS men nearby – it could have been either of them. She stooped to retrieve it and asked to be excused to go to the latrine. It contained three words: *Are you hungry?*

'It was a German, one of the guards. Yes, he saved her life, but at the cost of her dignity and self-respect. He saved her life, but it would have been better if he had not done so, for she felt she had betrayed not only me, but the memory of our children. How could she deserve life when they had perished? No more than me or any other survivor could she resist the instinct that called on her to choose life, but she could not forgive herself for surrendering to it.' Clément shifted in his chair, leaning forward and raising a forefinger to the other man as if to admonish him. His voice took

9

on a hard, bitter tone. 'You ask if he was a good German—? Well, if it is good to take advantage of the helpless, those who have nothing, those who have been cast adrift without hope, then he was good. But as far as I am concerned, what he did was an abomination.'

Emil Clément wandered back from the Grand Krasnapolsky and the bustle of Dam Square to his own hotel, a humbler affair overlooking the Singel Canal. It wasn't far. His room overlooked a small bridge, over which cyclists seemed to glide in the dreamy way that the dwellers of Amsterdam had made their own.

Emil wondered at the persistence shown by the interviewer. He had not expected it. It wasn't as if he was a politician or a famous entertainer; he was a chess player, nothing more. He felt unsettled. Perhaps he should not have come straight back to his hotel. He stood at the reception desk, lost in thought.

'Is there anything I can do for you, Mijnheer Clément? Would you like your key?'

Emil glanced at the man behind the desk, a portly man in his sixties. 'Yes, maybe there is. Is there anywhere in the city where people play chess? You know, a city square, or a park, perhaps?'

The man smiled. 'Of course. You should go to Leidseplein. I'm sure you'll find a game there. It's quite a way, but you can take a tram from Dam Square; it's easy to find. '

Clément shook his head. 'Thanks. I'll walk. I could do with some fresh air.'

Lijsbeth Pietersen walked as quickly as dignity and high heels would permit along the gilded corridors of the Krasnapolsky. She held in her hand a piece of paper that was important, very important: it had the potential to wreck the World Chess Federation Interzonal tournament – due to start in two days' time – before even the first pawn was played. Lijsbeth took her responsibilities seriously. The Interzonal was important: its leaders would progress to the candidates' tournament and from there to the world championship.

At the door of the room that had been allocated to the tournament's chief arbiter she paused to compose herself before knocking. Inside, a man in a dark suit was standing by a window, idly watching the comings and goings of the people on the square below. He turned as she entered.

'Miss Pietersen,' he said, with a thin smile. 'To what do I owe the pleasure this time?'

With studied care she placed the piece of paper on the desk that stood between them, smoothing it onto the polished surface. 'I know you've seen this, Mijnheer Berghuis,' she said, her voice tight with suppressed anger. 'I would like to know why you didn't feel the need to inform me, and what you intend to do about it.'

Harry Berghuis slid his spectacles from the breast pocket of his jacket. In the past week Lijsbeth Pietersen had become something of an irritation. It was he who was the chief arbiter of the tournament; she was merely the administrator, a fact she seemed to find difficult to grasp. He seated himself at the desk and picked up the paper.

It was a copy of the draw for the first round of the tournament. He glanced at it, then let it fall back to the desk.

'I don't understand what you're so upset about,' he said. 'As to what I "intend to do about it" – I intend to do nothing. The games will proceed according to the draw, as they always do.'

THE DUTCH DEFENCE

She gave him a look that spoke much of her opinion of his intelligence. Taking a pen, she circled two names. 'Look.'

He looked again and shook his head in bewilderment. 'What?'

'Emil Clément and Wilhelm Schweninger will play each other in the first round.'

'You know, Miss Pietersen, you really are going to have to learn to express yourself better. You're not making any sense.'

'Emil Clément is the contestant from Israel. He's a survivor of Auschwitz. He wrote a best-selling account of his experiences in which he said there was no such thing as a good German.'

'And Schweninger is a German.' He gave her a dismissive look. 'So what?'

'Schweninger isn't just any German. During the war he worked in their Ministry of Propaganda.'

Berghuis sighed. 'And?'

Lijsbeth pursed her lips. Was Berghuis really so dense? 'To work in the Propaganda Ministry, he had to have been a member of the Nazi Party.' She took a step towards the desk and placed her fingertips on its surface, leaning over him. 'Am I starting to make sense now?'

Berghuis did not like her tone. He felt his face getting hot and reached for his collar, trying to loosen it, hoping that a reason to ignore what she was telling him would present itself. 'Lots of Germans were members of the Party,' he countered. 'Was he convicted of war crimes?'

'It doesn't matter whether he was or whether he wasn't. If the press get hold of this, they're going to have a field day.'

Berghuis picked up the piece of paper again, as if by looking at it the means to resolve the problem would leap out at him. 'Damn,' he said quietly. 'What do you suggest?'

12

'The only thing to do is to re-run the draw, making sure that the two of them do not meet unless it happens in the final.'

'No.' Berghuis shook his head. 'We can't do that. Notification has already gone out to all the contestants.'

'We can tell them there's been a mistake, that it needs to be re-done.'

'What kind of mistake? The draw was done in front of at least twenty people.'

Lijsbeth could not resist saying, 'Perhaps now you understand why you should have entrusted the job of doing background research on the contestants to me. There's more to it than creating happy family biographies for the press.'

Berghuis lowered his head. 'Yes, all right,' he acknowledged. 'But that's not what's important now. We have to work out what we're going to do. If we do a re-run, someone is bound to smell a rat, and then the press will definitely stick their noses in. No, we'll have to go with what we've got and pray for a minor miracle.'

'You mean do nothing and hope that nobody puts two and two together?' Lijsbeth rewarded her boss with a condescending smile. It was a small victory, but satisfying. 'Well, I'm sure you know best. You're the boss.'

At fifty, Emil Clément was tall and spare, with dark, receding hair and a closely cropped beard that hid the lower part of his face. Going down the hotel steps, he turned up the collar of his coat. Though it was April, a chill wind was blowing off the North Sea, bringing with it flurries of rain, somewhat different from the weather he was used to now.

He followed the canal southwards, almost to its terminus. He was looking for a street called Leidsestraat, and on reaching it he turned right

– after crossing three canals, he would reach his destination. He flinched as raindrops spattered on his face. Dark clouds were looming: he would be lucky to find anyone foolhardy enough to be playing chess in the square.

By the time he reached the eastern edge of Leidseplein it was raining heavily. The square was indeed empty, apart from a few hardy people hurrying across, some struggling with umbrellas or sheltering in shop doorways. He ducked into the nearest café.

The barman was wiping the counter top with a cloth that had seen better days. '*Nog regent het?*'

'I'm sorry,' Emil said in English. 'I don't speak Dutch. Do you speak French, or German?'

The barman smiled. '*Ja, Ich kann gut Deutsch sprechen.*'

Emil ordered a coffee and said, 'I was told I might be able to find a game of chess around here.'

The barman jerked his thumb in the direction of the parlour at the rear. 'You'll probably find a couple of games going on back there. They're regulars, mind, so you may have a bit of a wait before you get a turn.'

The coffee was placed on the bar and Emil handed over several coins. 'No matter,' he said. 'I'll be happy simply to watch.'

3.

THE POLISH OPENING

November 1943

Oświęcim, German-occupied Silesia

Amid clouds of steam the train from Kraków groaned to a halt in the station in the small town of Oświęcim. SS-Obersturmführer Paul Meissner pushed open the door of his carriage and peered along the platform. There should be somebody there to meet him.

The stationmaster was about to put his whistle to his lips to send the train on its way when he saw an SS officer limping towards him. 'A moment, if you please,' the officer shouted. The whistle was lowered. 'I should be very grateful if someone could get my baggage off the train.'

SS officers were a common sight, constantly going to and from the camp, usually insufferable and demanding. But as the officer stood leaning heavily on his walking stick, the stationmaster detected a little humility in his bearing, and his eyes took in the Iron Cross on the officer's breast pocket.

'Of course,' he said. 'I'll see to it at once. Won't you have a seat in my office?'

Nearly an hour later, a shame-faced Rottenführer entered the stationmaster's office and stamped to attention. Meissner was not impressed by what he saw: the remains of a meal halfway down his tunic, collars that were curling upwards.

'Compliments of Hauptsturmführer Hahn, sir. I'm to take you to the officers' quarters.'

For long moments, Meissner did not speak.

'Your name, Rottenführer?'

'Eidenmüller, sir.'

'Well, Eidenmüller, let me tell you – you wouldn't last ten minutes in the Waffen-SS. A man who takes no pride in his appearance is unreliable. Next time I see you, I want you in a tunic that is clean and pressed, understood?'

The man stood ramrod straight. 'Yes, sir.'

'Good. Now pick up my bags and get me out of here.'

Ernst Eidenmüller had been in the SS for nearly two years. At first, his progress through the lower ranks had gone remarkably well. He was like a cat that always landed on its feet – 'Midas', his comrades called him: everything he touched seemed to turn to gold. He'd taken pride in his appearance then.

In June 1940, when the newsreels across Germany showed Hitler sightseeing in newly occupied Paris, Eidenmüller was not on the streets joining in the rapturous celebrations with his fellow countrymen: he was in a Leipzig police cell for possession of a stolen bicycle. His protestations of innocence availed him nothing: his accuser was a minor Party official. A year later he was charged with black-marketeering. Nothing was proven, but, with a previous conviction hanging around his neck, all it took was a word in the judge's ear from the local Gestapo chief and he was sentenced to eighteen months in a labour battalion. He braced himself for a tough time: everyone knew how hard life could be in the road gangs; instead, he found himself in an agricultural brigade.

His father was a Lutheran pastor, a severe man whose orbit he had been glad to escape, but he had given his son one sound piece of advice: 'There are three things you must never allow to control you – women, money, or the Nazis; above all, the Nazis.' Women had never been a problem: the kind of women he liked never seemed to be the kind that wanted to stay. As for money – Eidenmüller never had enough to be controlled by it. He had a taste for gambling. He was hooked on the thrill of it and never worried about whether he won or lost. That left only the Nazis.

The army wasn't keen to take convicted criminals into its ranks, no matter how minor the offence, but the SS was a different proposition, as long as recruits could demonstrate impeccable Aryan ancestry. Early in 1942, all the men in his barracks were ordered to assemble for a lecture in the dining hall. Waiting to address them was an SS recruiting officer. 'Healthy young men of German blood, your Führer calls you to do your duty...' He had harangued them in this vein for nearly an hour. They listened unmoved to the officer's words until he added that nobody would be allowed to leave the hall until they had pledged to join the SS – the first ten would be given the best postings. It was obvious there was no escape, so, with a shrug, Eidenmüller stepped forward. Along with nine others, he was assigned to the Totenkopfverbände and sent to Dachau for training; the remaining fifty were inducted to the Waffen-SS.

Eidenmüller soon realized he'd been lucky; life in the SS training barracks wasn't exactly a plate of *Zwetschgenkuchen** but neither was it backbreaking. The men were bored, they had money in their pockets,

* Plum cake.

17

and Eidenmüller had a way about him. He became the one who always knew how to obtain the myriad small items that would make life in the barracks easier. It wasn't that he delved or poked around or made lists; he simply had the knack.

He was appointed squad leader. He never had to bawl at the men. Because he always seemed able to find the things they wanted, they tried to please him – most of the time. At the end of training his promotion was made official, and Rottenführer Eidenmüller was posted east.

In Auschwitz, he was assigned to the pharmacy as a driver. He would collect medical supplies intended for the SS in the camp from the rail depot in Kraków, and, when required, make deliveries to the satellite camps. Medicines for the civilian population were in short supply and he set about getting friendly with one of the camp pharmacists and then acted as a go-between with a pharmacy in Kraków. His duties were light and soon he was running all sorts of errands for officers and senior NCOs. Collecting, carrying, delivering; his easy-going manner and his unerring nose won him friends in high places. Even Kommandant Höss had him collect packages from a warehouse in Birkenau to be delivered to an address near the railway terminal in Podgórze. Within months he had been promoted to Scharführer and more and more doors were opened to him.

When, late in the summer of 1943, Obersturmführer Morgen arrived, Eidenmüller knew the sleigh-ride was over. This was no ordinary SS officer, but an official of the criminal police, sent to investigate corruption in the camp. He ordered a raid on the NCOs' barracks. Eidenmüller's locker was crammed with soap and tubes of toothpaste. His explanation of how they had come into his possession was dismissed out of hand.

An SS court was quickly convened with the officer in charge of the

Auschwitz-I camp, Sturmbannführer Liebehenschel, as its president and Morgen as the prosecuting counsel.

Liebehenschel had already heard two cases that morning. One of the NCOs brought before him had had over a dozen expensive fountain pens in his locker. Collecting them was his hobby, he had insisted. It was obvious they had been pilfered from the possessions confiscated on arrival from the Jews sent to Auschwitz, but – Liebehenschel asked the prosecutor – was it important enough to require a court hearing? He ordered that the man should be disciplined by his commanding officer, with no further action. The next case involved the discovery of foreign currency. This was far more serious. The NCO was demoted to the ranks and transferred to the Eastern Front.

Then it was Eidenmüller's turn. Liebehenschel struggled not to laugh at the 'suspicious items' found in the NCO's possession.

'Soap, Herr Obersturmführer?' he asked Morgen. 'Suspicious? Really?'

The prosecutor drew himself up to his full height. 'Indeed, Herr Sturmbannführer,' he replied, his tone edged with astonishment that he should be asked such a question. 'Such a quantity could not possibly be for his own personal use. It is clear evidence of black-marketeering; a low crime, I'm sure you'll agree. Besides, the soap was of the type used by women and' – he looked pointedly at Eidenmüller – 'homosexuals.'

Eidenmüller winced. He was doomed.

Liebehenschel addressed him directly. 'The evidence against you seems pretty damning, Scharführer. What have you got to say for yourself?'

'Beg pardon, sir. The soap wasn't for me. It was for my girlfriend.'

'Your girlfriend? Just the one?' The officer was tempted to wink at the accused. Liebehenschel could not find it in him to send a man to the Eastern Front for possession of perfumed soap, but he ordered

Eidenmüller to be demoted and reassigned to a job where he would no longer be in temptation's way.

Later, as Eidenmüller packed his kit to go back to the troopers' barracks, somebody said to him: 'Look on the bright side – at least you didn't get sent to fight the Bolshevik swine.' That much was true, but for days afterwards Eidenmüller could not stop hearing his father lecturing him in the gloating voice he had hoped never to have to listen to again: '...above all, the Nazis.' He had been so right – the smug bastard.

'Fuckin' bastards,' the driver mumbled under his breath.

'What was that?' the officer beside him asked, sharply.

'Nothing, sir. I was thinking aloud, that's all. Beg pardon, sir.' Eidenmüller kept his eyes firmly on the road ahead, but his muttered imprecation seemed to have woken the officer up.

'Where exactly are you taking me?'

'To the *Stammlager*, sir. That's where officers are quartered. They're expecting you,' he added.

'They were expecting me an hour ago.'

'Yes, sir. Sorry, sir.'

'Out of interest, Rottenführer, why were you so late picking me up? Did you have an assignation over lunch?'

The driver reddened. 'No, sir. It was the motor pool, sir. Always having problems with it, we are, sir. If there's a big *Aktion* in Birkenau, they get priority.'

'And was there a big *Aktion* in Birkenau this morning?'

'Not that I know of, sir. Lack of spare parts is what I got told today. Still, you'll see how hand to mouth we have to live once you get there, sir. The military gets priority for most things, and we have to make do and mend as best we can.' When the officer did not reply, the driver continued: 'If I'd left it to them, sir, you'd still be waiting. As it happened, the Scharführer in charge of the motor pool owed me a bit of a favour, if you know what I mean. A quiet word in his ear and this car suddenly became available. Cost me a couple of packs of cigarettes, though.'

Meissner did not seem convinced by the driver's explanation, but said nothing more. It did not take long to reach the main camp, and the officer was pleasantly surprised at his accommodation: it was far more spacious and well appointed than he was used to. A servant had been assigned to him too, a short man with a shaven head. He wore a baggy, blue-striped uniform with a violet triangle sewn on its front.*

The small man lifted the baggage from the car and led the way to a small day room.

'With your permission, sir, I will unpack and put your things away.'

'What is your name?'

'Oberhauser, sir, though it's usual in the camp to use my number. I answer to 672.'

'You're German.'

'Yes, sir. From Elsdorf.'

'Really? I'm from Köln myself. It's a small world, isn't it?'

'Yes, sir.'

'Why were you sent here, Oberhauser? Political crimes?'

'No, sir.'

---

* The status of prisoners in the camp was denoted by coloured triangular badges worn on the breast of the tunic: green was for criminals; red for political prisoners, usually Communists; pink for homosexuals; violet for Jehovah's Witnesses; and, until the second half of 1944, a red triangle superimposed on a yellow triangle to create a makeshift Star of David was for Jews.

'You're not a Jew?'

'No, sir. I'm a Jehovah's Witness.'

'A Jehovah's Witness? I had no idea they were so dangerous.'

'Me neither, sir. May I carry on now?'

'Please do.'

An hour later Eidenmüller reappeared, this time in a clean uniform. 'Compliments of Sturmbannführer Liebehenschel, sir. The Kommandant asks would it be convenient for you to come to his office?'

The Kommandant's office was large but devoid of any personal effects, as if its occupant had only recently taken possession of it. Meissner brought himself to attention, raising his right arm stiffly in salute. '*Heil Hitler.*'

The salute was returned with rather less enthusiasm; Sturmbann-führer Liebehenschel held out his right hand. 'Welcome to Auschwitz, Meissner. Please take a seat. Let me tell you I'm glad to have you here. I can use as many good officers as I can get.'

'Pardon me for mentioning this, sir, but my orders are that I should report to Obersturmbannführer Höss.'

'The Obersturmbannführer has been recalled to Berlin. He's been appointed deputy to Gruppenführer Glücks in the Concentration Camps Inspectorate. I have taken his place, with immediate effect.' The Sturm-bannführer pushed his chair back and stood. 'But I am forgetting my manners. Allow me to offer you some coffee.'

The coffee was poured from an ornate silver pot, by another prisoner wearing a violet triangle. The Kommandant did not acknowledge the prisoner's presence, but spoke as he withdrew. 'Jehovah's Witnesses. The enlisted men call them "Bible-worms". We use them as servants. What else can you do with them? They could all walk out of here tomorrow if only they would sign the *Gottläubig*. We don't even expect them to believe it – just sign the bloody form that says they have no religious belief.'

'Are there many of them here?'

'No. A couple of hundred perhaps. The vast majority of the prisoners are Jews.'

'Is there any special reason why you use them as servants?'

'Well, for a start, they're good Aryans, but, to be honest, it's because they're the only ones in the camp who can be trusted not to rob us blind.' He laughed. 'I'm serious, Meissner. Probably the best advice anyone could give you is not to leave anything where it could be found by a prisoner. Turn your back on it for a second and it will disappear, I promise you.'

The Kommandant picked up a file from his desk and opened it. He struck Meissner as an affable sort. 'You're younger than I thought you would be, Meissner – I was expecting a hardened veteran after reading your service record. Most impressive. It says you single-handedly destroyed three Russian tanks with a disabled Wespe field howitzer.'

It was Meissner's turn to smile. 'That's not quite how it happened. It wasn't single-handed, the Wespe wasn't damaged, and the third T-34 was actually killed by one of our Tigers that joined the action in the nick of time. If not for them, I wouldn't have lived to tell the tale.'

'Still, you got an Iron Cross for it.'

'And this—' Meissner raised his walking stick.

The Kommandant closed the folder. 'Modesty. I like that in a man. I think you'll fit in well here, Meissner. In fact, I think I have the perfect challenge for a man of your obvious tenaciousness.'

'Which is?'

'I need someone to oversee the satellite camps. Not the day-to-day running of them – they're spread too far afield for that – but we have constant problems with personnel and transport; in fact, it's a bloody nightmare, a nightmare that we've been doing our best to ignore. Up to a few months ago our main concern was to increase capacity in Birkenau, but that's no longer a problem – we've got it running as smoothly as the Swiss railways. But now my orders are to increase armament production, and that means getting more out of the labour camps.' Liebehenschel stood and beckoned for Meissner to follow him to a map pinned to the wall. He tapped his forefinger on a particular point. 'Our biggest problem is here – the IG Farben *Werke*. It's one of Himmler's pet projects and it's months behind. I need people in place who will teach the Jewish scum what hard work really means. And that's where you come in. I need someone who's prepared to be single-minded, who will ignore the egos and tantrums of his colleagues – someone who will get the job done. This has top priority and you'll have my full backing. What do you say?'

Meissner's reply was immediate. 'I say yes, naturally.'

'Excellent. If you do only half as well as I think you can, you'll be a Hauptsturmführer by next summer – you have my word on it.'

4.

THE BENONI DEFENCE

1962

Amsterdam

The note was waiting in Emil's hotel pigeonhole when he returned. He understood immediately what had lain behind the interviewer's question.

He had been paired with Schweninger.

Emil waited until the next morning before seeking out Miss Pietersen at the Krasnapolsky. She sympathized, she told him, but the rules were the rules. If he wanted to play in the championship, he must face Schweninger. He insisted on speaking to Berghuis. With a small, self-satisfied smile on her face, she accompanied him to the chief arbiter's office.

'Mijnheer Clément,' Berghuis said smoothly, 'I agree it is a most unfortunate situation, but we cannot change the rules because one contestant has personal difficulties with another. Think of the precedent it would create. No, I'm afraid that you must go ahead with the match or forfeit it.'

Before Emil could reply, a fourth person burst into the tournament office. Red-haired and overweight, he stood for a moment in the doorway to catch his breath, eyeing Berghuis accusingly. That he was furious was obvious.

'Did you hear the radio this morning?'

'No.' Berghuis cast an alarmed glance at his assistant but her eyes were

25

fixed on Emil. Berghuis swallowed anxiously. 'Why?'

'Clément was interviewed by Piet de Woert on his culture show. He was asked if he maintained his view that there were no good Germans. He said that not only did he maintain it, but he gave his reasons why. It is an outrage!'

Lijsbeth Pietersen could see a disaster unfolding before her very eyes. Standing stock-still, her lips compressed into a rigid smile, she felt compelled to interrupt. 'Herr Schweninger, may I present Monsieur Clément?'

Her words had an effect similar to a car being driven off a cliff at high speed: they seemed to hang silently in mid-air while the people in the room struggled to understand what had happened.

Emil was the first to recover. He addressed the German in his own language. 'An outrage, you say, Herr Schweninger? If you consider freedom of speech an outrage, then I suppose you are right – what I said is an outrage, though I should have expected no less from one such as you.' He shook his head. 'But let me tell you what an outrage *really* is. It is when millions of people are murdered for no other crime than being born a Jew, including my mother and my children. That is what *I* consider to be an outrage, Herr Schweninger.'

'Perhaps it—' But Lijsbeth Pietersen did not get to finish.

'How dare you?' Schweninger bellowed, then turned on his heel and stormed out, slamming the door behind him.

The arbiter, the administrator and Emil Clément looked at one another.

'Well, I suppose it might have been worse,' Berghuis remarked.

'How?' Lijsbeth asked, shaking her head. 'How could it possibly have been worse?'

'Twenty years ago he could have had us sent to a concentration camp,' Emil said, acidly.

Berghuis could not hide his exasperation. 'Will you please stop saying things like that?'

Emil turned to face him. 'Why? Because they are true?'

'No. Because it is 1962. Hasn't anyone told you – the war is over. It is time to move on.'

Only Lijsbeth Pietersen remained calm. 'What is important is what we do about the situation. Mijnheer Clément, is it your intention to withdraw from the competition?'

Something had changed in Emil: minutes before he had been on the verge of quitting, but not now. 'Certainly not. I will play him and I will humiliate him and it will serve him right.'

Emil hurried back to Leidseplein, not seeing anything or anyone as he pushed his way past shoppers and office workers, not slowing his pace until he arrived, breathless, at the café.

The barman recognized him and smiled. 'Good morning, mijnheer. Coffee?'

'No. Something stronger. Cognac.' The barman glanced at the clock but said nothing. 'Is there anyone in who will give me a game this morning?' Emil asked when he had recovered his breath.

'I think so. By the way – did you know there is a big chess tournament in town? It was all over the radio this morning.'

Emil took the brandy and swallowed it in one. 'Yes, I knew.'

In the parlour a board was already set up, with an elderly man seated behind it, waiting.

'May I?' Emil asked. The old man nodded and, taking a white and a black pawn in his hands, held them out for Emil to choose. 'If you don't mind,' Emil said, 'I would like to play black.'

'Not at all.' The old man turned the board so the white pieces were on his side. He advanced his queen's pawn two squares.

Emil did not make a move but closed his eyes, allowing his hands to fall to his lap as if in prayer. He was still for a moment. 'Forgive me,' he said, when he opened his eyes. 'It's a little ritual I must go through before every game.' He moved his king's knight so that it stood in front of its bishop.

The old man immediately moved his queen's bishop's pawn forward two squares. Emil responded with the same move. The old man ignored the gambit and moved his first pawn forward one square. Emil moved his queen's knight's pawn forward two spaces. The old man took it.

'If you don't mind my saying so,' he said, 'that is a most unusual defence. I don't think I've seen it before.'

'No,' Emil replied. 'It is called the Benoni Defence. It means "Son of Sorrow".'

5.

A Queen's Pawn Game

January 1944

Solahütte, SS country club, German-occupied Silesia

Despite the chill, Meissner did not feel quite ready to quit the veranda and go in for dinner: he had wanted a few moments of solitude to add a brief observation to his journal. His fellow officers enthused constantly about the SS country club and what a fine place it was for winding down after the rigours and stresses of camp duty, but this was the first time he had visited it. They had not exaggerated. Set on a hillside with spectacular views of the surrounding hills and forests, it was a haven of tranquillity; at least until the evenings, when, inevitably, after a few drinks, somebody would start on the piano, or an accordion, and the songs would begin. It put him in mind of happier days, before the war. There were even women here, SS-Aufseherinnen, supervisors in the women's and family camps. Meissner smiled to himself. They had taken quite a shine to him: his Iron Cross was like a magnet. He wondered if they would be quite so enamoured of his wooden leg. Taking a last drag on his cigarette, he flicked it over the balcony and went inside.

Dinner at Solahütte was informal, and he took a place at a table with Vinzenz Schottl, the Monowitz Lagerführer, and Erich Weber, one of the SS doctors. To their surprise, they were joined by the Kommandant, recently promoted to Obersturmbannführer. They stood as he pulled out a chair, but Liebehenschel insisted they should not stand on formality.

'Gentlemen, please. Here we are all comrades in the SS, no?'

Dinner was served by ranks of Polish waiters in immaculate white jackets. The dinner service was Königliche porcelain and the glasses Bohemian crystal. Afterwards, cigars and cognac were served.

A relaxed Paul Meissner exhaled a stream of grey smoke, appreciating the exquisite flavour. 'Where on earth do these come from?' he asked.

'Havana, I believe,' Weber said, whose father was in the diplomatic service. 'Via Portugal and Spain.'

'One of the privileges of serving in the Totenkopfverbände,' Schottl broke in. 'After all, there have to be some compensations for what we are forced to put up with.'

Meissner had heard such observations before. This time he demurred. 'I must say I find life here rather easy compared with fighting the Russians.'

'For you, maybe,' Weber said, tapping his cigar and letting the ash fall to the floor. He fixed Paul with a supercilious smile. 'My duties are perhaps a little more... taxing than yours.'

The hours Paul had spent in the field hospital were burned deep into his memory: the dirt, the blood, the cries of pain, and the ever-present sound of gunfire. 'Really? You are a surgeon, are you not?' The doctor nodded in assent. 'I wonder,' Meissner continued, 'when you last performed surgery under fire?'

Weber reddened and shot the Waffen-SS man an angry glare.

The Kommandant intervened. 'Gentlemen, please. Let us have no harsh words here. We are all doing our duty in the different ways that are demanded of us. Let us leave it at that, eh? Obersturmführer Meissner has not been here very long. It takes a while to get used to our ways, especially after the privations of the front.' He stood and raised his glass. 'I'm afraid

I can't stay, as much as I would like to, but before I go, a toast.' He pinged his glass with a silver teaspoon. Officers at every table rose to their feet and raised their glasses. 'The Führer.' He drained his glass.

Walking past Meissner, he placed a hand on the junior officer's shoulder. 'A quiet word before I leave, if I may?'

The Kommandant waited in the empty bar next door for his subordinate to catch up.

'I apologize, sir, if I...' Meissner jerked his head in the direction of the dining room.

The apology was waved aside. 'That? Don't worry about it. Weber is a patronizing ass. No, Meissner, all I wanted was to say is that even though it's been only a few months since you took over their administration, I'm aware of the improvement that has come about in the performance of the labour camps. Well done.'

A smile of relief crossed the junior officer's face. 'Thank you, sir. I'm glad to hear it.'

The Kommandant fished in his tunic pocket and pulled out a piece of paper. 'There was something else.' He handed the paper to his subordinate. 'As director of Abteilung I, your duties include responsibility for morale. I received this on Friday.' He indicated the slip of paper in Meissner's hands. 'It is a directive from the Reichsführer-SS himself, stressing the importance of morale and instructing that it should be improved. He is of the opinion that SS officers should take an active interest in higher culture.' He paused as an orderly approached with his greatcoat and cap. 'Now, I'm not suggesting that we go so far as to try and create an interest in opera or anything like that,' he continued, draping the coat over his shoulders, 'but we must do something to demonstrate that we have taken these orders seriously. I'll leave it in your capable hands.'

31

Meissner limped back to the dining room reading the orders. He resumed his seat. 'Look,' he said, looking at the men around him. 'I'm sorry if I, well... if I said anything out of turn before.'

Schottl clapped him firmly on the back. 'Forget about it. You'll soon learn. What's that you've got?' he asked, pointing at the paper in Meissner's hand.

'Bloody WVHA.'*

'What do they want?'

'Seems the Reichsführer-SS is worried about morale in the camp system. We've been ordered to improve it... *I've* been ordered to improve it – in Auschwitz, at least.'

'How?'

'Culture, so it would seem. We've all got to become more cultured. And I'm the one that has to make it happen.'

Schottl started to laugh. 'And you thought life here was rosy, didn't you? That'll teach you.'

Meissner could not help a sheepish grin. '*Touché*. But if either of you has any ideas, I'm open to suggestions.'

'I have one,' Weber offered. 'How about a chess club? The idea struck me some time ago. I play myself, but I never got round to asking if anyone else did.'

Meissner was doubtful: he had been thinking more along the lines of a choir. After all, singing seemed to be very popular at the country club. He turned to Schottl. 'What do you think?'

'Well, it's certainly cultural, no doubt about that.'

---

* *Wirtschafts und Verwaltungshauptamt*, the SS Economic-Administrative Main Office, which included the Concentration Camps Inspectorate.

'Do you play?' Weber asked.

Schottl shrugged but said, 'Of course. Who doesn't?'

Meissner pressed him: 'But do you think it would catch on?'

Weber was already warming to his suggestion. 'Yes, yes. The more I think about it, the better it gets. Officers who already play' – he indicated himself and Schottl – 'could take those who don't under their wings and show them the ropes. It could even be opened to the lower ranks. That would definitely be good for morale, wouldn't it – officers getting to know their men better?' He leaned back and took a mouthful of cognac. 'What could be better than chess? Wasn't it invented by a German?'

On Monday morning, Meissner was in his office at seven. Eidenmüller was there before him, a pot of coffee bubbling on the stove. Meissner had sensed that the Rottenführer would be useful to have around, and he had been right: he was a born fixer, a wizard at acquiring all sorts of items that were otherwise difficult – if not impossible – to obtain.

Meissner greeted his orderly by saying, 'What do you think about us starting a chess club, Eidenmüller?'

The Rottenführer kept his face deadpan. 'What, here, sir? In the office?'

'No, you idiot. I mean a camp chess club, for all the SS.'

'Officers *and* men, sir?'

'Yes. All ranks.'

Eidenmüller thought for a moment before replying, 'Well, I suppose it depends, sir.'

'Depends? Depends on what?'

'On whether we would be able to lay a few bets on it, sir.'

'A few bets?'

'Yes, sir. If the men were able to lay a bet or two on the games, I'm sure they'd be all for it. If they weren't, I wouldn't think there'd be much interest, to be honest.'

Meissner suppressed a smile. 'This is supposed to be adding to the cultural life of the camp, not creating opportunities for more of your shady dealings.'

Eidenmüller's features remained impassive. 'No, sir.'

'So, let me get this straight – if I allow betting on the games, you think a chess club would be popular?'

'Very popular, sir.'

'And who exactly would run this gambling enterprise?'

'I might know one or two people here and there, sir. I could ask around – with your permission, of course.'

Meissner merely grunted and sat down.

The orderly picked up the coffee pot and, filling a cup to the brim, placed it on the officer's desk. He turned to go.

At the door, Meissner called him back.

'Eidenmüller, while you're asking around, find out how many chess sets you can lay your hands on, will you?'

Eidenmüller smiled. 'It will be my pleasure, sir.'

6.

ZUGZWANG

Tuesday, 11 January 1944
Auschwitz-II, Birkenau

It is night and the train has stopped in the middle of a forest. Packed into fifteen cattle trucks, over a thousand people wait anxiously. There is no sound, apart from the wind howling through the trees and the freezing rain that gusts along the sides of the train. In every truck people are huddled together for warmth, for the wooden-slatted sides offer little protection from the biting cold.

It is still dark when the train resumes its journey. The regular *clack-clack* of the wheels, which has been a constant companion for close on a week, lulls nearly everybody back to a fitful sleep.

Less than half an hour later, the train stops for the final time.

Bright lights come on, assaulting the numbed senses of the passengers even through the wooden sides of the trucks. With a crash that has the quality of an explosion to those inside, the doors are thrown open and from the unnatural brightness outside comes the harsh, angry barking of orders shouted at people who do not understand them.

Beyond the opened doors is a long concrete platform. The passengers are forced out and herded away from the train. Possessions must be left where they fall. Now the passengers can see their tormentors: dark figures in the grey military uniform of the SS.

In one truck there is hesitation. A hand reaches up to the nearest person – an elderly man – and pulls at him roughly. He falls heavily onto the concrete below and rises uncertainly. He looks like he has broken an arm. One of the uniformed men calmly unholsters a pistol and holds it to the old man's head. A shot rings out. A woman screams. Her cry sounds disembodied, as if some banshee is shrieking in the dark beyond the floodlights. The body is kicked off the platform to fall beneath the wheels of the train.

It is as if a spell has been broken. To cries of '*Raus! Raus!*' the remaining passengers surge out of the trucks knowing that their lives depend on it.

On the platform an SS officer asks, '*Wer kann Deutsch sprechen?* Does anyone speak German?' Emil raises a reluctant hand. 'Come with me.' He is led to where several other officers are standing with an air of impatience, as if waiting in the cold for a bus that is late. A few more prisoners arrive. Each of them is told to go with an officer and translate orders.

Men are told to stand to one side and women to the other. The SS men separate out the elderly and children. Emil is anxious about his two boys, but the officer tells him not to worry: adults of working age will go to a work camp and the children will be sent to the family camp, where they will be cared for by those who are too old for manual labour. He says it with the weary calmness of a man who has given this reassurance a hundred times before.

It has the ring of normality, of truth. But it is the first of many lies in the land of liars. 'Family' is a word the Nazis have violated so that it has lost its natural meaning. In Auschwitz, 'family' means death.

With Emil interpreting, the officer sorts through the men who are fit for work. How old? Any special skills? It seems they have a quota to fill for able-bodied workers. Those with skills are an added bonus. Emil is lucky. He can speak German and is a master watchmaker. Emil sees that his wife, Rosa, has been told to stand in the column of women who have been selected for work. Their children, Louis and Marcel, are on the left with their grandmother.

All is now silent. One shooting is enough to subdue any resistance until one woman sees her children and breaks from the ranks to go to them.

A single blow from a rifle butt puts her on the ground.

'Stupid bitch,' one of the officers says as she rises unsteadily to her feet, wiping at the blood that runs down her face, then: 'Fine – let her go with them.'

The left column is marched away and disappears into the maw of the misty darkness that surrounds the area lit by the arc lamps.

Emil mouths a quiet, '*Au revoir*,' to his children. 'Be good for Granny.'

He does not know he will never see them again.

Emil is shaken awake by Yves. He was shouting in his sleep. Now he is crying, inconsolably. 'My children, my children,' he wails.

Yves tries to comfort him. If Emil does not quieten, the night guard will report him to the *Blockältester* and he will be punished for disturbing everybody's sleep.

'My beautiful boys...' Emil weeps. 'I don't even have a photograph of them. I can't remember what they look like.'

7.

ELOHIM AND THE
POWER OF JUDGEMENT

1962

Grand Hotel Krasnapolsky, Amsterdam

Friday morning saw the official opening of the World Chess Federation Interzonal tournament, to be followed by a formal lunch.

Rumours were rife that the German Grand Master would not show up for his opening match against the Israeli. At a hastily convened press conference, Harry Berghuis had answered all questions concerning the matter with: 'We shall have to wait and see.'

The vast hotel ballroom, with its spectacular high glass ceiling, had been cleared, and rows of tables set up, each with two chairs, a chessboard and a game-clock. There was an atmosphere of high expectation as a gaggle of arbiters stood opposite the entrance, waiting for the contestants to take their places.

All eyes were on table 7, where the game between Clément and Schweninger was to take place. Outside the entrance, the corridor was jammed with reporters and photographers. Rarely did the press show so much interest in a game of chess.

Wilhelm Schweninger pushed through the crowd, using his bulk to force people out of the way. To a shouted question: 'So, you won't be withdrawing from the competition, then?' he had roared, 'Of course not! What do you take me for – a coward? I'm not frightened of him or of any of the rubbish he spouts.'

There had been several notes in Emil's pigeon-hole at the hotel from journalists requesting interviews, and a telegram from his publisher. He had ignored them all; he had a game to prepare for. He had chosen to make a more discreet entrance than Schweninger, cutting through the hotel kitchens, arriving at the service entrance to the ballroom just before time.

At the appointed hour, the doors to the ballroom were firmly shut: no more contestants would be admitted. This created a buzz of expectation among the press outside, who assumed that the Israeli was a no-show. Inside, the tension was even greater as, without a word of greeting to one another, the two at the centre of all the attention took their places. An arbiter held out her hands concealing a black pawn in one, and white in the other. With a contemptuous shake of his head, Clément indicated that the German should choose.

Schweninger touched the arbiter's left hand. It opened to reveal white. Without ceremony he advanced his king's pawn two spaces and started the clock.

As he had in the coffee house, Clément composed himself in an attitude of prayer. He ignored the ticking of the clock, which seemed unusually loud. When he opened his eyes, he peered searchingly at his opponent for several moments, then moved his king's knight to sit two spaces in front of the bishop. Schweninger smiled. As he had expected, Clément's opening move was defensive, conceding the initiative to his opponent. He advanced his pawn one more space to attack the solitary knight. The knight moved to sit beside the pawn. The white queen's pawn moved forward two spaces. The black queen's pawn advanced one, offering itself to the white king's pawn. The German refused the gambit and attacked the knight again, this time with his queen's bishop's pawn. Clément allowed his knight to retreat to sit two spaces in front of its brother.

Harry Berghuis sidled up to the arbiter and whispered, 'How is it going?'

'Unbelievable. The German is using a three-pawn attack, and Clément is employing the Alekhine Defence.'

Berghuis raised an eyebrow. 'We might have expected Schweninger to be aggressive. But the Alekhine? That's reckless, surely. I don't think it's been seen in a major tournament for nearly twenty years. What is the Frenchman playing at?'

'Perhaps he knows something we don't.'

The night before the tournament, Emil Clément had retrieved a small velvet bag from his suitcase. It contained ten ivory tiles onto which were etched the first letters of the Hebrew alphabet. He emptied them onto a table, face down, and arranged them in the shape of the Sephiroth, creating the structure of the ten attributes through which the Divine Essence of Infinity is revealed. He turned the seventh tile, Netzah. He had chosen it because its significance was ambiguous: it could denote either 'victory' or 'eternity', and it lay beneath Hesed, the promise of mercy and healing. He turned the tile to reveal the letter ה – He – representing the sword of the Almighty and the strength that flows from the limitless power of God.

So be it: victory, not compassion.

His path now clear, Emil slept. When he discovered the next day that his game was to be played on table number 7, his faith in the power of the tiles was confirmed.

*

Emil's refusal to be drawn perplexed his opponent. Schweninger's attacking opening meant his pawns were now sitting in the centre of the board, to little purpose.

Having succeeded in unbalancing his rival, Clément set about his destruction with seemingly effortless calm.

His victory caused uproar. Schweninger's defeat had been accomplished in less than an hour.

8.

The Réti Opening

March 1944

Konzentrationslager Auschwitz-III, Monowitz

It is a Sunday, one of two rest days that are permitted each month. Warmer air is coming from the south and the chill of winter is fading. Though the warmth of the morning sun is slight, it is still pleasant, for the mosquitoes that plague the camp in summer have yet to emerge.

Emil is squatting on the bare earth beside the dormitory block, leaning back against the wall, enjoying the all-too-brief respite from work. He has been up for a while; on rest days, the inmates are permitted to use the washrooms, if there is any water available. He was one of the first into the showers and to go for lice control and have his head shaved. Now he is eating his morning bread ration slowly, trying to remember what it was like not to be hungry.

Time has no meaning here: it is too painful to contemplate the past and impossible to conceive of any future. There is only now, which is seared, like a brand, upon the consciousness; the struggle for this day, this hour, this minute, is all there is.

Yves settles beside him. He has lost much more weight than Emil, which is to be expected, for he works outside in a construction *Kommando*, while Emil has an indoor job that does not involve heavy physical labour. He eyes Emil's bread covetously, feigning indifference but failing.

42

Emil offers him some, but he shakes his head. 'One of us,' he says, 'has to live to get out of here, if only to tell the rest of the world what is happening.'

Emil holds the bread out again, but Yves pushes his hand back firmly. 'You're a good man, Emil, but if you have too many scruples you won't make it.'

'And if you end up a *Muselmann*,* it will help neither of us,' Emil objects, pushing the bread into Yves's hand.

Yves smiles. '*D'accord* – but only this once. And if anything comes my way…' He pulls a knife from under his jacket and cuts a chunk off before giving the rest back.

Yves's knife was a gift from Emil. Making knives has become Emil's métier in the camp. In the workshop to which he has been assigned, he has access to sheets of steel from which he fabricates and repairs various instruments for the Buna factory. The factory is a vast maze, as large as a town. Unknowable thousands toil here, coming and going constantly. In Buna, Emil sees the fable of the Tower of Babel, for many different languages are spoken, from across Europe and the East. In this shapeless tangle of concrete, iron and smoke it is in the nature of things to be insignificant and unnoticed, like an ant, and so it is easy for Emil to organize a small piece of steel, shape it and add a crude handle to make a knife. He manages one or two a week and sells them in the market. The going rate

---

* Slang used in Auschwitz to refer to prisoners who were so debilitated by starvation and abuse that they had lost the will to live: little more than skin-covered skeletons, wrapped in tattered blankets, they would sit or stand and stare vacantly, unaware, lost in the emptiness of their wretched existence, drifting aimlessly in the place between life and death, impervious to shouts or truncheon blows from *Kapos* to make them move. The word is thought to have come from a supposed resemblance to the kneeling posture adopted by Muslims in prayer.

43

is half a bread ration. It is something, but it is not enough, not for Yves. He is slowly starving to death.

Yves coughs, a long, laboured rasp, before saying, 'I have some news for you.'

'What sort of news?' Emil prays daily for news of his wife. He has heard nothing since they were parted during the selection on that first night. He harbours little hope for his mother and his children. He is certain they went up the chimney the day they arrived.

Yves hears the faint stirring of hope in Emil's voice. 'Nothing very important,' he says quickly, 'but something I think you'll be interested in. The *Blockältester* in Block 46 has a chess set. I'm told he plays every night.'

Emil leans forward eagerly. 'Whom does he play?'

'I don't know. But there's only one way to find out.' Yves finishes his bread and stands. 'I'll come with you.'

'No. I can manage by myself. You should rest.'

The blocks in Monowitz are all built to the same pattern: at the front, the door opens to reveal a small day room, furnished with a brick-built stove that offers some meagre warmth in the winter if wood can be found to fuel it. The day room leads to a much larger dormitory with rows of three-tiered wooden bunks in which the inmates huddle together to sleep. At Block 46 Emil stands respectfully at the entrance to the day room, cap in hand, and asks if he may speak to the *Ältester*. A short, stocky man comes to the door. He looks well fed, which is not surprising, for the block elder is a German and wears the green triangle of a convicted criminal on his uniform.

'What do you want?' The man draws on a cigarette. Even though it has probably been made with *Mahorca*, the dreadful adulterated tobacco that circulates in the camp, Emil eyes it enviously. He has not had a cigarette in months.

Emil clears his throat. 'I have heard that chess is played in your hut.'

'What if it is?'

'I like to play chess. Before I came here, I was quite a good player.'

'And you think you're good enough to join our little circle, eh?' The block elder belches, takes another puff of the cigarette and flicks the still-glowing butt at Emil's feet. 'What's in it for me?'

'I make knives.'

The elder glances at the red and yellow Star of David on Emil's chest. In an instant he weighs the value of what Emil might bring to his little fiefdom. 'No Jews,' he says, with a tight little shake of his head, and walks back inside.

Emil concludes that if he wants a chance to play chess he must do something extraordinary. Walking back to his block, he decides what he will do. It is risky, but it is worth it.

Yves cannot understand why Emil would take such a risk. 'If you are caught bringing it into the camp,' he says, 'you could get a dozen lashes, or more. I don't understand why you would do such a thing just for the sake of a game.'

Emil cannot make Yves understand the divine nature of chess. It is much more than a game. It is a connection with the intangible Wisdom of Creation; sublime; the possibilities limitless. It is the game created by the Ophanim to please God.

Emil would rather die than never play again.

The following Monday, he puts his plan into operation. At his work-place, he makes an offer to the civilian supervisor. Wartime shortages mean that items like watches are difficult for civilians to obtain, apart from cheap, unreliable ones. Emil asks if the supervisor has any watches or clocks that need mending. In return for one broken watch, Emil will mend two others, using scraps and tools from the instrument workshop. He does the work during the break that the prisoners are allowed for lunch. The supervisor is delighted with the result. Word gets around quickly, and it is not long before Emil is asked to repair watches for others.

Two weeks later, he returns to Block 46. Again he asks to speak to the *Blockältester*. When he comes to the doorway Emil shows him the watch he has repaired. 'I forgot to say that as well as making knives, I'm also a watchmaker.'

The *Ältester* is bemused. 'You'll give me this if I let you play?' He can hardly believe it – the watch is worth a lot of bread. 'Fucking Jews,' he says. 'I'll never understand them as long as I live.' But he stands aside and lets Emil in.

SS-Obersturmbannführer Liebehenschel leaned back in his chair and put his feet up on the desk, the chair teetering on two legs. Eidenmüller, newly promoted to Unterscharführer, having deposited two cups of coffee on the desk, came to attention, about-turned smartly, and marched briskly out of Meissner's office.

Meissner opened a filing cabinet and took out a bottle of Armagnac. He poured a generous measure into each cup.

Liebehenschel smiled as he watched the NCO's retreating back. 'I must say, Meissner,' he said, as a cup was passed to him, 'you've wrought quite a transformation in this place. As for that fellow, I thought he was incorrigible, but he's a new man. I've never seen him looking so smart. I don't suppose you've managed to put a stop to his thieving, too?'

'One thing at a time, sir, one thing at a time.'

The Kommandant laughed. 'Fair enough. Rome wasn't built in a day.' He took a sip of his coffee. 'Now, about this chess club. When you suggested it I thought you were mad, but I'm amazed at the way it's taken off. Everywhere I go there are people playing – according to my orderly, even the enlisted men and NCOs. It's extraordinary. How did you know it would be so popular?'

Meissner thought back to the confrontation he'd had with the Kommandant over the idea for the chess club. His suggestion had been met with a frosty response: *'When I asked you to take this on, Meissner, it was because I had gained some respect for your abilities and devotion to duty. And you come to me with this? A half-baked notion about some chess club? This is the SS, not the Boy Scouts. I passed you a serious order, endorsed by Himmler himself, and this is how you respond? Did you know that at Majdanek they have started a choir? Next time the Reichsführer visits, they'll be able to regale him with a bit more than the fucking Horst Wessel song. Here, he'll be able to watch a game or two of chess – if doesn't fall asleep.'*

But as the Kommandant had already observed, one of the young Obersturmführer's qualities was tenacity. He had stood his ground: *'With respect, sir, the order was to improve morale, not to provide entertainment for the Reichsführer.'* He had been dismissed with a dire warning that it had better work.

And it had – not least because of the widespread and sometimes heavy betting that went on.

'It was Obersturmführer Weber who convinced me, sir,' Meissner replied. 'After all, what could be more German than chess?' Now Meissner wanted to speak to the Kommandant about how the idea could be augmented by instituting an annual camp championship. Eidenmüller had come up with the suggestion, inspired – Meissner was sure – by the fact that it would greatly increase the turnover of his gambling monopoly.

But although pleased at the initial success of the chess club, the Kommandant needed convincing that a competition was a good idea. 'How exactly would it work? I'm not keen on the idea of the enlisted ranks getting cosy with their superiors over a chessboard.'

'No, sir. I thought we could run two parallel championships – one for the enlisted men and NCOs, and one for the officers. We could have a supreme camp champion, with the winners of the two competitions playing in a grand final.'

'What about prizes?'

'I think there should be prizes, yes, sir.' Meissner had already worked out what the prizes should be: for the runner-up, a five-day pass to Berlin, and, for the champion, two weeks' home leave.

Now he added the final twist, which he was sure the Kommandant's vanity would find irresistible. 'Once we have our two Grand Masters, we can issue a challenge to the other camps. The SS-Totenkopfverbände Chess Championship could become an annual event, hosted by K-Z Auschwitz. Would that not more than fulfil the directive to boost morale?'

9.

Bishop's Opening

1962

Amsterdam

Apart from the first-round games that had yet to be concluded, Sunday was a day of rest for the contestants. Emil had a late breakfast and went out for a walk.

He had never been to a place like Amsterdam before. Its canals gave it a tranquillity that he had not expected – a quiet presence that had crept up on him, especially when the wind was still. The last flourish of winter was past and the trees that lined the canals were coming into bud. The sun peeked through the branches, throwing dappled shadows along the banks. People were up and working on house barges, giving them an airing and a fresh coat of paint, and the stalls at the flower market were full of daffodils and tulips.

Emil's walk led him further than he had been before, to Vondelpark. There, he rested for a while on a bench, watching the city go by. The young people on their bikes seemed particularly attractive, so carefree and full of life. It was well past noon when he decided to resume his journey, heading back towards Leidseplein.

The café, where he had become a regular visitor, was full of people out for a drink before Sunday dinner. On a row of tables outside, games of chess were in full swing. The old man he had played a few days before was standing by one of them, in animated conversation with a priest, a tall man with silver-grey hair.

When the old man saw Emil he waved. 'Good afternoon, my friend,' he said affably. 'We were just talking about you – about the strange defence you played, you remember? The Son of Sorrow.'

The priest turned. His face was drawn, its complexion sallow. Emil's first impression was that he looked tired, that he was somebody who had become old before his time. But a smile transformed his features, making it warm and welcoming.

The priest pulled off a black woollen glove and extended a bony hand. 'Hello,' he said, in a voice that was unexpectedly soft. No, Emil realized almost immediately, not soft – sickly. 'I was hoping I might meet you. Old Marius here has been telling me all about you, and the game you played. You made something of an impression on him. And your picture was in the paper – did you see it? Your victory over the German Grand Master made quite a splash. I'm a fan of chess, though I'm not much of a player. I think it requires a mind with more subtlety than mine.'

Emil took the proffered hand, but his greeting died on his lips. He had met the priest before, he was certain of it. His eyes were shockingly familiar: a blue as deep as the summer sky over Tel Aviv; clear as crystal.

'Hello,' he stammered finally, speaking in German without thinking. 'Emil Clément.'

A waiter was taking orders and the priest beckoned him over. 'Have you tried the advocaat?' he asked. When Emil shook his head he said, 'You should. They make their own here – a family recipe. If it were not sacrilegious, I should be tempted to say it was divine.'

He ordered three glasses.

'Forgive me,' Emil said, 'but I am sure we have met before.'

'Yes,' the priest replied, in a tone that suggested this was something he did not wish to discuss, 'we have. But, if you'll permit me to say, I think that this is not the time nor place to talk about it. For now, let us enjoy our drinks and perhaps watch a game or two of chess.'

'My parish is where the bishop lives,' old Marius announced proudly. 'He was sent here to convalesce – from the missions,' he added.

'Bishop?' Emil raised an eyebrow. There was no hint of exalted rank in the priest's apparel, which was plain black with the usual clerical collar.

'Here it's purely an honorary title,' the priest explained. 'My see is a long way from here – a province in the Belgian Congo.'

There was something in the priest's manner that Emil did not like, while his admission that they had met before was like an itch that he could not resist scratching. 'You said we had met before—? I know for sure I've never been to the Belgian Congo. Have you ever been to Israel?'

'No – but I think you might like the Congo if you were to visit. Leopoldville can be quite lively, and the interior has a reputation it tries hard to live up to.'

'Reputation?'

'Africa – dark and mysterious.' The waiter arrived with the advocaat. The priest raised his glass in a toast. 'To Africa.' He sipped appreciatively. When Emil left his untasted, the priest continued, 'I'm sorry – is it not to your liking?'

Emil set his glass down on a nearby table. 'No. What is not to my liking is a pointed refusal to answer a perfectly straightforward question.'

'I'm sorry,' the priest replied. 'I didn't intend to give offence. I thought it was for the best. It was a long time ago.'

'But where?'

'Auschwitz.' The word was like an electric shock. Their eyes locked and suddenly Emil knew. He barely heard the rest of what the priest said: 'My name is Meissner. Paul Meissner.'

Memory can play strange and sometimes unfortunate tricks. For Emil, the name was like a key that unlocks a door that leads to another, which in turn leads to another, then another, and so on, back, year after year, to the point in time before which his memory could not bear to travel: the spring of 1944. He saw the bishop as he had seen him then; and again, before he had disappeared. He remembered the crystalline blueness of his eyes, the certainty of his superiority, his imperturbable confidence. And now he had reappeared, as if the illusionist who had made him disappear nearly two decades ago had, at this very instant, decided to bring him back. Time stopped, anticipating the applause that would surely follow such mastery of the art of conjuring. And he was wearing the garb of a man of God – surely another trick? If Meissner had turned up wearing his SS uniform, it could hardly have been more shocking. Meissner had been a prince in the kingdom of liars, so this new identity also had to be a lie. No other explanation was conceivable.

Emil froze. He looked uncertainly from the bishop to the old man, to the other people milling around the front of the café. His brain sought frantically to find the words he had wanted to say to this man for nearly twenty years, but they would not come. Instead, he felt light-headed. The pavement seemed to take on the properties of a fairground mirror pulling his vision in and out of focus. He put out a hand to steady himself on a table edge but it slipped and with an almost inaudible gasp he fell, knocking drinks and plates from nearby tables onto the paving stones. At the edge of his consciousness he was aware of shouts of alarm, but they were distant, not part of his universe, from creatures that inhabited a dream world whose cries were foreign and unintelligible.

He heard again the lamentation that was the cry of Auschwitz.

10.

The Destiny of a Poisoned Pawn

April 1944

Kommandantur building, Konzentrationslager Auschwitz-I

Eidenmüller drove the *Kübelwagon* through the entrance to the *Stammlager*, passing beneath the blackened iron arch wrought with the words '*Arbeit Macht Frei*', before turning left to follow the road to the *Appelplatz*. He stopped to allow Obersturmführer Meissner to step down outside a two-storey building above which flew the emblem of everything the camp stood for: a black swastika in a white roundel on a scarlet banner.

The officer leaned heavily on his walking stick to push himself out of the car. 'Wait for me,' he said. He had an appointment with the Kommandant. He did not expect it to take long.

Inside, Meissner got quickly to the point: 'I have a suggestion to make, sir, that some may find shocking. Some might consider it disloyal but, please believe me, my motives are purely to do with the efficiency of the camp.'

Liebehenschel was intrigued. 'Shocking *and* disloyal? And all in one day. I can't believe that of you, Meissner.' He smiled and opened an intricate silver box that stood on his desk. 'Cigarette?'

Meissner took one and lit up. He exhaled a cloud of smoke upwards. 'The thing is, sir, that in order to sustain an acceptable work output, a certain amount of food is necessary. This holds true whether the worker is a German, a Russian, a Pole or a Jew. I'm afraid that the physical condition of many of the prisoners is poor at best, and this affects their ability to do strenuous work.'

Meissner's words prompted a searching look from his superior. 'You are quite right, Meissner,' the Kommandant replied. 'That is why our doctors work tirelessly to identify those who are no longer capable of doing what is required of them and have them eliminated.'

Meissner drew deeply on the cigarette. 'You'll forgive me for saying so, sir, but that approach is inefficient. It means that at intervals – which occur far too frequently – new workers must be inducted who have to learn skills that their predecessors had already acquired.'

'I take it you have a suggestion?'

'Yes, sir. I propose that the food ration be increased. That way we could get more work out of them for longer. It would be much more productive than the present system.'

The Kommandant flicked at the sleeve of his tunic, removing specks of ash that had fallen from his cigarette. 'You were right to bring this to me, Meissner,' he observed. 'With food at home strictly rationed, some of your colleagues would undoubtedly consider the idea of giving more food to Jews to be disloyal, and would be shocked that it had been suggested by a fellow SS officer. But I fully appreciate your motives.'

Meissner nodded, but did not tell his commanding officer what had brought about this sudden interest in prisoner rations. He had been taking some air a few days before, at the same time that the prisoners were being marched back from the Buna factory. A man had stumbled and fallen. The *Kapo* in charge had halted the squad and kicked and beaten the fallen man unmercifully.

Meissner had intervened. 'You won't get any work out of him if you kill him,' he'd said.

The *Kapo* had removed his beret and stood to attention. 'With respect, Herr Obersturmführer,' he had retorted, the sneer in his voice imitating that of many of the SS NCOs, 'that's all they're fit for. He's nothing but a dirty, lazy, idle Jew. Plenty more where he came from.'

Meissner had stared at the *Kapo*, his eyes drawn to the green triangle on his jacket: a criminal. So serious were his crimes that he had been sent to Auschwitz, where, in accordance with the perverse rules of the camp, criminals were put in charge of honest men and women.

Meissner had addressed the prisoner. 'What have you had to eat today?'

The prisoner had hung his head and not replied.

'He doesn't speak much German, sir,' the *Kapo* said. 'Italian.'

'Then translate, goddammit.'

The prisoner's voice could barely be heard. He'd had a ration of bread and a bowl of soup. No doubt the soup had been taken off the top of the cauldron and was thin, not like the thick soup at the bottom, where the chunks of potato and turnip settled. The *Kapo* and his cronies kept that for themselves.

Meissner had been furious. He had been charged with increasing the output of the labour camps but the poor food and capricious brutality were working against him all the time.

Now, Liebehenschel steepled his fingers thoughtfully. Meissner had a point, but the system for feeding the prisoners was long established – calculated to induce slow starvation among the Jewish slave labourers. There was nothing he could do to change it, no matter how much it might improve productivity. But he had to give the appearance of taking Meissner's concern seriously.

'Very well, Meissner, I'll speak to Dr Wirths about it. More than that, I cannot do.'

'He's the *Standortarzt*?'*

'Indeed.' Liebehenschel gave his subordinate a look that said he was dismissed, but Meissner did not move. 'There's more, Obersturmführer?'

'I've been checking the documentation relating to the acquisition of food. The records indicate that, in fact, enough food is purchased every day to provide an adequate number of calories for each prisoner. If the food isn't going to the prisoners, where is it going?'

The Kommandant sighed. Meissner was certainly tenacious, like a dog with a bone. Rather than answer immediately, he stood up and walked to the door, gesturing for Meissner to follow. In the doorway he paused and, turning to face the junior officer, said: 'You've never been to Kanada, have you, Meissner?'

April 1944
Konzentrationslager Auschwitz-III, Monowitz
Alarm is spreading through the camp. Typhus. It skulks in the shadows at every door looking for a way in. It is a pestilence feared by all. In the washrooms, there are signs in many different languages: *One louse is enough to kill you* – for that is how typhus ensnares its victims and spreads its foulness through the camp. The signs are among the many absurdities of Auschwitz, because the procedures for the prevention of lice are laughable. For the inmates, hot showers and soap are as rare as a visit from the Pope, yet lice are a deadly enemy, so when the inmates have time, they scour each other's bodies for the tiny creatures, squeezing the

* Chief garrison physician, with authority over the twenty or so other SS doctors in the Auschwitz complex.

life out of them between two fingernails. But now, it seems, there is an outbreak in Block 51.

Of course the camp is better informed than the SS doctors: all the inmates know the outbreak started two days ago. A man from 51 went to the infirmary after evening roll call. At first the symptoms are inconclusive. A day later, there were two more men from 51 with the same symptoms.

The SS doctors take no chances. On their command, the fate of the men is sealed: all three are sent to the gas chamber. This is to be expected. The sick men are resigned to their fate, and nobody lifts a finger to help them.

And now heavily armed SS men are marching through the camp, many of them with dogs. The camp bell is ringing, a sound that drowns out the camp's own frantic warnings. When the bell rings before sunrise it means: '*Out of bed. Rouse yourselves. Up, up, up!*'; when it rings at any other time of day, it is a command to return to your block and stay there.

In every block the inmates cower.

Emil is playing chess in Block 46 when the bell rings. He is winning but that is hardly surprising: since the *Blockältester* deigned to allow him to play, he has won every game. Nobody says a word when he leaves and walks like an automaton to his own block. Widmann, the *Blockschreiber*, is conducting a roll call. His pencil marks a tick against Emil's number. Inmates crowding around the door keep watch. It is the same in every block. The watchers shout into the block, reporting what is happening. The SS men march past without a glance in their direction. 'They are going past, they are going past.' The shouts are almost jubilant with relief. Bit by bit, more information trickles in from the door.

'They have stopped at Block 51.'

'They have sent the dogs in.'

'Now everybody is coming out.'

'They are marching them away.'

The SS doctors outside Block 51 come not as healers, but as executioners. Without regard for whether they are infected or healthy, all the inmates in the block are sent to Birkenau. Only the *Blockältester* and the other criminals who run the block for the SS are allowed the luxury of going to the infirmary. They will have to take their chances, but at least they are not going up the chimney.

The other inmates start to breathe again. They do not care whom fate has selected for death on this day, as long as it is not them. It is not because they are naturally cold-hearted. It is simply the way of things in Auschwitz. They deceive themselves, telling one another: 'It was their time; it is going to happen to us all eventually. Who has the strength to think about when it will be our time, as long as it is not now?'

A deep sense of shame runs through the camp. It has witnessed another barbarity. Its very conscience is defiled by what it has seen. It can no longer tell good from evil: there is no good, there is no evil – only life or death. Over 200 men are put into trucks and taken away. They will be forced into one of the gas chambers or shot. A day later their cold ashes will be scattered over the surrounding fields.

Emil finds Yves. Never before have they seen an entire block taken away to be murdered.

'It is an act of depravity,' Emil says, in the privacy afforded by their bunk space. 'Those were good men, healthy. These SS – some of them are doctors. Do they feel no shame?'

'Of course not,' Yves replies. 'If they did, they could not do what they do; it would be intolerable to them.' He is silent for a short while, then adds, 'Somebody must remember this day, to be a witness to it.'

Emil puts his head in his hands. He starts to weep, silent sobs shaking his body.

'What is it, Emil?'

The watchmaker searches his friend's eyes, as if hoping for forgiveness. 'I am scared that I have been infected by their corruption...if I were to look back on this day, it would be to say it was a day I played chess. This – *horror* – is too much to ask me to remember.'

Yves takes his friend's hands in his own. 'You mustn't think like that. This is not *your* shame to bear, but theirs. They do it because we are nothing to them. We are worthless. We are no longer even human beings. We are less to the SS than sacks of beans or potatoes. That is the truth of this place.'

But Emil is not satisfied. 'How did we become so worthless?'

'Have you not understood, Emil? Are you so caught up in your mystical other-world of pawns and kings that you have not seen that we are on a journey to nothingness?'

April 1944

Kanada, Konzentrationslager Auschwitz-II, Birkenau

Meissner surveyed the scene before him with seemingly calm detachment. He was in a large warehouse. Inmates scurried in with heavily loaded hand-carts, emptied their contents onto a large pile in the centre of the floor, then out again to return with a fresh load. An army of people, mostly women, some in camp uniforms, others in ordinary civilian clothes, delved into the pile, sorting it into a variety of categories: shirts, trousers, coats, dresses, jackets, hats, shoes, underwear, spectacles, suitcases, handbags – the last gleanings of the loot stolen from Jews from across Europe. Around the edges of the warehouse were mountains of these goods, waiting to be redistributed.

It was difficult not to show amazement at the scale of the plunder that was taking place before his eyes.

'Trains arrive daily,' the Kommandant said, in a low, matter-of-fact tone, 'sometimes two a day. Typically we can expect a thousand to fifteen hundred head on each train. They are compelled to leave their belongings on the unloading ramp. When they are inducted into the camp, they are relieved of their clothes and small possessions, like wristwatches or jewellery. Everything becomes the property of the Reich. It is all brought here to Kanada. All sorts of things find their way here. There is one Scharführer who spends every day doing nothing but sorting foreign currency. Every month it is sent to the Reichsbank where it is exchanged for Reichsmarks and the proceeds come back to the SS. Another is an expert jeweller who picks out choice items and grades precious stones. Gold and silver items are melted down.'

'Why is this place called Kanada?' Meissner asked.

Liebehenschel responded with a world-weary sigh. 'Because Kanada is a place of untold riches.'

'Why are you showing me this, sir? Does it have something to do with the discrepancy between the food that is purchased and the food that is distributed?'

The Kommandant stood aside to let a hand-cart pass. 'I'm afraid to say, Meissner, that not all members of the SS are as incorruptible as you. Some months before your arrival, the Concentration Camps Inspectorate initiated a commission of inquiry into corruption. Theft on a grand scale by SS officers was suspected. Some had their hands so deep in the honey pot that they were unable to get themselves clean again in time.'

He looked at Meissner. 'What I'm trying to say is that I'm sure there is still plenty of thieving going on, but it's more discreet, and on a considerably smaller scale. We try to control it by not allowing junior ranks to spend long periods of time here, but even officers are not always as trustworthy as they should be. Some of them collude with the prisoners – as you might have guessed. Valuable items that the prisoners find among the clothes and baggage are traded for food or privileges. What is happening with the rations in Monowitz is insignificant in comparison.'

April 1944

Technical workshop, IG Farbenindustrie Buna Werke, Monowitz

It is the day after the cleansing of Block 51. One of the Polish civilian workers brings a watch for Emil to repair. In return, he offers Emil a portion of his *Zivilsuppe* – the food prepared for the civilian workers – for the next two weeks. The watch is small and elegant, with a delicate movement. 'It belonged to my wife's mother,' the man tells him. 'She passed away a few weeks ago. It would mean a lot to my wife if I could get it fixed.'

Two words plunge deep into Emil's consciousness: 'wife' and 'mother'. He wants to shout, 'What about my mother? What about my wife?' He must keep such thoughts to himself. All morning, Emil keeps his thoughts locked in the vault of his mind, until the events of the previous day force their way in.

Everyone knows there is a camp for women. He hopes Rosa is there, but typhus is everywhere and the SS would have no more scruples over eliminating a block in the women's camp than they had had in Monowitz.

In an unguarded moment, these thoughts rush to the surface and Emil reveals his bitterness to the men at the nearby work benches. 'Did you see what happened to the men of Block 51 yesterday? It's only a matter of time before they do it to the rest of us. The SS are depraved,' he says. 'All of them.'

It takes only one to denounce him. Perhaps he is envious of Emil's newfound status with the civilian workers; perhaps not. Most likely he is simply starving. His reward is two rations of bread, riches beyond temptation to one suffering the hunger of Auschwitz.

As the men queue for the midday soup ration, the *Kapo* orders Emil to report to the Buna Rapportführer, SS-Scharführer Gessner.

Emil stands rigidly to attention, his cap held firmly in his hand, not looking at the SS man, eyes fixed on the wall ahead. The Scharführer is seated at a table eating his lunch: white bread and sausage. The rich smell of the sausage is torture.

The SS man seems to be in good humour. 'So, you are 163291.' For a moment he says nothing more, picking with his fingernail at a bit of sausage between his teeth. Then he reveals the depth of Emil's betrayal: 'The watchmaker.'

He pauses to let his words take effect. 'You thought I did not know about that, didn't you? Well, let me tell you, nothing happens in this camp that I do not know about.' He waits for Emil's reaction. When there is none, he continues: 'I have been informed that you said the SS is depraved.'

Emil feels his bowels constrict. His mouth goes dry and, instinctively, he swallows.

There is no point dissembling. Besides, he has made a promise to himself: he will not add to the lies on which the camp is built. 'Yes, Herr Scharführer.' His reply is not defiant, merely truthful.

The Scharführer leans back in his chair and slaps his thigh as if Emil has told him a great joke. A broad grin appears on his face and he laughs uproariously. There is a riding crop on the table. With great deliberateness, the Scharführer picks it up and, still laughing, comes from behind the table and strikes Emil viciously with it.

Emil falls to the floor, but he has seen what happens to prisoners who do not immediately get up: invariably, their punishment intensifies. Some are beaten to death. He picks himself up and stands to attention again. The skin on his face is split and blood runs from it, dripping over his chin onto his uniform. The pain is excruciating. Tears form in his eyes.

The Scharführer seems to approve. He walks in a circle around Emil, stopping once or twice to peer closely at the rough material of his tattered striped uniform.

Emil says a silent prayer that he has the correct number of buttons on his jacket and that there is not too much mud on his trouser bottoms. Although there are no facilities for the washing of clothes, punishments are frequently inflicted for having a muddy uniform. Emil tenses, expecting a second blow, but not knowing where or when it will fall.

The Scharführer speaks again. 'Your supervisor tells me you are a good worker. Can you believe he called you his "good Jew" and asked me not to beat you too severely?' Emil does not reply. The German continues: 'It astonishes me that you Jews do not understand the danger you pose to the Fatherland, especially after the Führer made it so clear. How can you be so ignorant?' He indulges himself with a second blow with the riding crop. He raises his hand to inflict a third but relents. What is the point? It is foolish to expect a Jew to understand – in fact, in a way, for a Jew to say the SS is depraved is a compliment. Everyone knows that in the twisted way that Jews think, everything is back to front: good is bad, rich is poor and depraved means heroic.

The Scharführer looks closely at Emil's face before dismissing him. 'If there could be such a thing as a good Jew, *Watchmaker*, I am sure you would be the one.' He laughs again. It dawns on him that what he has said without thinking is very funny. *A good Jew?* It is hilarious. But his humour quickly cools. 'Now, you stinking Jewish turd,' he says, his voice menacing and angry, 'get out of my sight before I change my mind and give you the beating you deserve.'

11.

Queen's Gambit Accepted

1962

Kerk de Krijtberg, Amsterdam

Emil awoke in a darkened room. Heavy curtains were drawn across tall windows. He was on a leather couch, with a blanket draped over him. Beside it was a small table on which stood a glass of water. As his eyes became accustomed to the gloom he was able to make out the features of the room. Opposite the couch was a heavy stone fireplace, above which was a large painting of the Madonna and the infant Christ. The picture was old, blackened from its proximity to the fire. The wallpaper was similarly smutted, adding to the impression of age. On either side of the fire sat tall, leather armchairs, their armrests rubbed to a shine, and horsehair stuffing peeking out in places where fingers had drummed times beyond counting. The hearth was home to a set of antique fire-irons. Against the wall opposite the window was a bookcase stuffed with ancient volumes and, above the door, a simple wooden crucifix. On the mantelpiece stood a clock in a brass case; as Emil tried to focus on it to see the time, it chimed four. Moments later, the door opened. Emil sat upright.

'Watchmaker,' the bishop said, his voice hushed. 'Welcome back. How are you feeling?'

Shocked, Emil struggled to make sense of what he had heard. 'Watchmaker? Nobody has called me that since...'

'No. But you didn't answer my question – how are you feeling?'

'I don't know. Awful.'

'You fainted. I suppose we could have called an ambulance, but on a Sunday it would have taken ages. The presbytery was not far, so I got a couple of volunteers to help bring you here. You've been out for quite a while. I was worried about you. I was about to call a doctor.'

Emil inhaled deeply, catching unfamiliar smells of incense and wax polish. 'Worried? Why would you be worried? You're not my keeper.' He got unsteadily to his feet. 'I should be going.'

The bishop barred his way. 'I don't think so. You should be resting. Let me help you – you've had quite a shock.'

Emil shook his head. 'Is that what you want – to help me? Why? So you can congratulate yourself that you came to my rescue again? No. I don't need your help, and I'm not staying.'

'I hoped we might take some time to talk.'

Emil was incredulous. '*Talk?* What could you possibly have to say to me that I would want to hear?'

Meissner retreated a little and bowed his head in an attitude of contrition. 'I thought perhaps I could start by saying I was sorry.'

'Sorry?' Emil found himself shouting. 'You are...' He stopped, unable to find words to express what he felt. 'We meet again after a gap of nearly twenty years and you think you can wipe away all that passed between us simply by saying *sorry*?'

'No, no, of course not. But it would have been a start.' The bishop moved aside, gesturing towards the door. 'Leave, if you wish,' he said, gently.

Emil's bitterness had been quick to erupt but Meissner's response had taken him by surprise. He had expected his anger to be met with more anger but, instead, the opposite had happened. His rage melted away; in its place he found the smouldering coals of what his life had become.

His anger could not always be trusted, but the coals could.

'Look,' he said, his voice becoming calmer, 'there is nothing we can say to each other that can possibly be worth saying, and as there is no changing what passed between us, I really do think it best if we go our separate ways.'

Meissner looked at him. 'It's for you to decide, naturally, but if you'll permit me to say, I do not agree with you that it would be best to go our separate ways. I think we have many things to say to one another, things that may be hard to say, but which nonetheless need to be said.'

Emil stood unmoving, casting his gaze around the room, taking in the odd variety of the knick-knacks that filled it, his mind seeking reasons to leave other than the bitterness with which he was filled.

'I would consider it an honour if you would stay to share my supper this evening,' Meissner said, breaking the silence.

'Why?'

From habit, the bishop's fingers strayed to the cross on his breast. 'Do you remember what you once said to me in Auschwitz? "There is no why. The outside world does not intrude here. We have been inoculated against it." For now, all I can tell you is that "Why?" is too complicated a question for me to understand.' He shrugged. 'For years now I have answered to an inner compulsion. I have tried to resist it, but without succeeding. I have told it I am not worthy, can never be worthy, but it does not listen to me. In the seminary they told me it was "my vocation", but I can't see it that way.' His voice took on a tone of almost desperate yearning. 'It is *more* than that. It is God's love working its way into the world,' taking as its instrument something – someone – that once served evil, but moulding it to its own divine purpose. So to answer your question "Why?" in perhaps a simplistic way – because I am a sword that has been beaten into a ploughshare.'

1947

Kraków

In his prison cell, Paul Meissner was waiting for his lawyer. Meissner did not like the man. He was possessed of a colossal sense of his own importance.

For his part, Meissner's lawyer regarded his client with cynical disdain. That the German was a war criminal was obvious. The state was wasting its money appointing a lawyer to conduct his defence.

As usual, the lawyer had been late. 'If it were possible to find even one Auschwitz prisoner to testify on your behalf, that would make all the difference,' he now said, not bothering to suppress a yawn.

An exasperated Meissner retorted: 'Have you listened to anything I've told you? I had nothing to do with the prisoners. Why would I? I was an administrator with responsibility for the SS personnel in the satellite camps.' Angrily, he banged his fist on the table. 'I told you there was only one prisoner I had dealings with. *He's* the one you have to find.'

The lawyer made a show of consulting his notes. 'Ah, yes, "the Watchmaker". But you say you can't remember his name, only his number.'

'It's not a question of remembering or not remembering. Everybody called him the Watchmaker. But you must be able to trace him from the number.'

The lawyer was sceptical. '*If* the records were preserved, and *if* he survived.'

'Yes,' Meissner agreed, dejectedly. 'If he survived.'

But no trace had been found of *Häftling* number 163291. He had not been included in any records of inmates who had eventually turned up at other camps, like Mauthausen or Bergen-Belsen.

The lawyer yawned again. The case was hopeless.

The president of the court addressed Meissner's lawyer. 'Before the verdicts are read out and sentence is passed, does the defendant have anything to say?'

The lawyer stood. Drawing himself up to his full height, he adjusted his robes, grasping them in his right hand in a pose he imagined to be reminiscent of Cicero addressing the courts of ancient Rome.

'With the court's permission, my client would like to read a statement.'

In the dock, wearing trousers without a belt and a collarless shirt, ex-SS-Hauptsturmführer Paul Meissner rose to his feet. Only weeks before, his ex-commanding officer, Arthur Liebehenschel, had been condemned to death by hanging in this same court-room. But when Meissner spoke, his voice was clear and unwavering.

'I have not attempted to hide from the court the nature and extent of my activities in Auschwitz. Terrible crimes were committed there – unforgivable crimes. I do not seek to diminish the part I played, nor do I seek to evade my responsibility. I acknowledge that I am guilty of grave crimes, but I would like to put on record that I believe I did what I could to maintain my honour. Before I went to Auschwitz, I had no idea of what was going on in Birkenau. I learned about those events only gradually. I had nothing to do with anything that occurred there. I never set foot on the unloading ramp, and took no part in any of the *Selektionen*. Not one prisoner in Auschwitz died because of me. Once I realized I had no ability to change what was going on, I took what I considered to be the only honourable course of action – I requested a transfer back to active service, even though my old regiment was at that time fighting on the Eastern Front. All of this was recorded in my personal journal, which the court has graciously acknowledged. Many thought I was going to certain death, but that was preferable to being an accomplice in mass murder. When I surrendered, I did so as an SS officer and, unlike others, made no attempt to hide it. That, too, was a matter of honour for me. I did my duty. I do not ask the court for clemency and I am ready to accept whatever sentence is deemed fitting.'

It took only minutes for the president of the court to deliver the verdict and sentence: 'On the charge of genocide – not guilty; on the charge of complicity in genocide – not guilty. However, on your own admission, you are guilty of the hideous crime of slavery. You administered a system in which tens of thousands, mainly Jews, were used as slave workers, and although they did not die at your hand or at your command, still many of them perished. This is a crime that demands exemplary punishment.'

Meissner braced himself. The court did not have a history of leniency.

'You are sentenced to six years' penal servitude with hard labour. The sentence is to commence immediately.'

1962

Kerk de Krijtberg, Amsterdam

'Six years with hard labour. Little enough reparation for the part you played,' Clément said, breaking chunks of white bread into a thick vegetable broth.

'Little enough,' Meissner conceded. 'But not easy, especially with an artificial leg.'

'Not easy? Is that what you tell people? You should listen to yourself.

Not easy?' Emil stared at him in disbelief. 'Easier than we had it every day in Auschwitz, that's what I would say. Did they feed you sawdust bread and pig-swill? You should be grateful you had a wooden leg.'

'The leg lasted less than two months. The best craftsmanship German engineering could produce, and it fell to bits.'

Clément held his spoon before him, like a weapon, punctuating his sentences with it. 'You know what this sounds like to me? It sounds like you're feeling sorry for yourself. Did you know that when the Russians liberated Auschwitz, they found thousands of artificial limbs from Jews who were killed in the gas chambers? *Thousands*. Maybe you should have asked for one of those.'

'How could I? I had no idea they were there. Besides, the Poles had no intention of finding me a replacement. And it's pretty nigh impossible to do hard labour on crutches. They did try, of course, but no matter how often they beat me, I kept falling over. After a while the beatings stopped. In the end they put me in the kitchens. I was given a stool and a knife and I spent my days peeling and chopping vegetables. I got pretty good at it.'

'How the mighty are fallen.'

Paul did not respond to Emil's irony and they finished the soup in silence. Afterwards, the bishop busied himself clearing the dishes from the table.

'Six years,' Clément mused. 'It's no time at all. Who decided on six years? Not a Jew, I think.'

Meissner resumed his seat at the table. 'Actually, in the end I served only four years in prison. I think they were tired of me. I was unceremoniously deported to the British occupation zone, where I had to undergo de-Nazification.'

'What did that involve? Making you wear *tefillin* to see if you were struck with apoplexy, or eat matzos to see if you choked?'

Meissner sighed. 'No. They made me complete the *Fragebogen* – a questionnaire – and a series of interrogations. The British were suspicious of me. By then, relations between the West and Russia were at a low and they suspected I was a Communist plant; it was months before I got my *Persilschein* – my official exoneration. Only then could I look for work. I was offered a job in a ticket office on the railways, but I had already decided what it was I wanted to do. I asked to train as a priest in the Catholic Church.'

'So you swapped one organization that would look after you and tell you what to do, for another. Not exactly a hard life, it seems to me – being a priest.' Emil turned in his chair. 'Take this place, for example. You're not exactly living in ruinous poverty, are you? Quite the opposite, in fact.'

Meissner demurred. 'You can choose to see it that way if you want to, but that's not the reason I wanted to become a priest and I think you know it. If I'd wanted an easy option, I could have spent my days punching tickets at the Köln Bahnhof.'

'No.' Emil's fist came down hard on the table. 'For your information, I *don't know*. I don't know anything about you. For nearly two hours you've been parading your self-justification but without answering the most important question – *why*?'

The bishop shook his head. 'The same question as before. And I only have the same answer – the inner voice that will not be denied.'

'And such a voice – that only you can hear. Does the Church have no qualms about accepting convicted war criminals into its fold?'

'Of course it does. But the very foundation of the Church is in forgiveness.'

'Father forgive them...' Clément intoned.

'Yes. The Church rejoices in every sinner who repents.'

'Is that why you wanted me to come here, so you could ask my forgiveness? Let me tell you right here and now – you won't get it.'

The bishop reached across the table to grasp Emil's hands. The Frenchman pulled away as if fearing to be contaminated. 'Your forgiveness cannot help me, Watchmaker,' Meissner said. 'For me it is too late. The only forgiveness that counts is my own, and after nearly twenty years I am still unable to forgive myself. I tell myself better that I had been put in front of a firing squad than I should have stood by and done nothing. I know that I have God's forgiveness, but that is not enough for me. You must think me arrogant, but I promise you I am not. I am guilty. I am ashamed. And I will carry the guilt and the shame to my grave.' He looked keenly at Emil. 'What I hope is that I can help you to understand that the power of forgiveness will bring healing for *you* – not me, not anyone else.'

Clément's face soured. 'You sound suspiciously like all the people who have wanted me to find a good German, who insist that the war is over, that it is time to forgive and forget.'

'I am not here to tell you to forget. Nor do I want you to find a good German. But I beg you to listen to me when I tell you it *is* time to forgive – if you can find it in you.'

Emil found Meissner's reasoning impenetrable. 'You say I must forgive, but if it's not you I have to forgive, then who?'

'You must learn to forgive yourself.'

Again a silence fell between them. The bishop rose. 'Please wait here. I will bring coffee. That is one thing the Dutch are very good at.'

Emil surveyed his surroundings. The kitchen was large, with a big refectory table that would easily sit ten. It was true it was not exactly luxurious, but it had everything that might be needed to serve a large household, and it was spotlessly clean. On one wall was a photograph of a pope, though he had no idea which one; on two others, portraits of saints: he could tell by the golden halos that adorned their heads. He could find no connection between these representations of sanctity and Meissner's stubborn insistence on forgiveness. The priest clearly had little understanding of what Emil had gone through, still less of why he might think the very idea repellent. And yet... He was both intrigued and irritated: irritated that he had been put in a position where he felt he was not in control; intrigued despite himself to know more of what Meissner had done since being freed from prison. He wondered what he could have been doing in the Belgian Congo.

Meissner returned bearing an earthenware coffee pot decorated in garishly coloured tribal motifs, and matching mugs. 'I brought these back with me from Africa. If I have any prized possessions, it's these.' He set everything down and poured two cups of thick, dark liquid.

'Many Nazis escaped after the war to out-of-the-way places, mostly South America,' Emil observed. 'You fetched up in Africa. Some might see that as more evidence that you were trying to evade responsibility for what you had done.'

Meissner sipped his coffee, closing his eyes briefly, thinking. 'Some might, I suppose, if they were in an ungenerous frame of mind. But it wasn't my idea to go there, not at first. I was sent to a leper colony.' He paused, then continued softly: 'I was happier there than I have ever been. In Africa, where the people have so little, where one's grip on life is so tenuous, where ignorance kills more than any disease and famine can pounce without warning, there is a joy that has to be seen to be believed – the simple joy of living, of loving, and accepting the Lord's gifts without question. I didn't want to come back. I wanted to live out my days with those people.'

Emil had listened without interruption. Now he said, 'Why *did* you come back?'

'Malaria. I tried to accept it as a trial sent to me by the Lord, but it was so severe I was incapable of doing anything. I was sent back to Europe to recuperate. But once I was here, it became clear that I have something more serious than malaria.' The bishop leaned forward, his face earnest. 'Watchmaker, I am dying. I have been sent home to die, and this is not even my home. I have leukaemia. I don't understand it fully, but it is a cancer that affects the blood. I have a matter of months, perhaps less, to live. But I still believe that God has a definite purpose for my life. Watchmaker, that purpose is you.'

12.

ALEKHINE'S GUN

April 1944

Konzentrationslager Auschwitz-III, Monowitz

The evenings are lighter now and Yves has taken to sitting on the ground outside the entrance to the block, not coming in until it is almost time for lights out. The poor food and strenuous labour have reduced him almost to a walking skeleton. He is staring at the sky, fearing he may not awaken to see it again.

Inside, the *Stubendienst** finds Emil rocking slowly back and forth, praying, as he often does when he is alone.

'Watchmaker,' he says. 'Bodo sent me to find you. He wants to speak to you.'

Watchmaker – the name has stuck. Emil does not like it: it singles him out when his best protection from unwanted attention is anonymity.

Bodo Brack is the *Blockältester*, a thick-set man who is serving a life sentence for murder. He has never shown any interest in Emil before.

'What does he want with me?'

His errand done, the *Stubendienst* shrugs. 'What am I – his secretary?'

Emil walks slowly to the day room. He can't think what Bodo could possibly want with him, but it can't be anything good.

* Block orderly: a prisoner responsible for keeping the block clean and tidy. He was not expected to work outside like his fellow prisoners.

Emil removes his cap and stands to attention before the block elder. Brack has been in the camp for over two years, longer than anyone else. Everyone knows he is the kingpin among the *Prominenten* – the favoured prisoners who run the camp for the SS. He can arrange better food and even the vouchers that can be used to visit the brothel that the SS runs for the *Blockältesten*, *Kapos* and even the *Scheissministers*.* But not Jews. Brack does not like Jews. Ten minutes pass before he deigns to notice Emil.

'Watchmaker,' he says, pausing to lick his fingers after chewing on a lump of cheese. 'Is this block not to your liking? Do I not see to it that your every need is provided for?'

'Yes,' Emil replies anxiously, wondering where this is leading. 'This is a good block and you are a most considerate block elder.'

Without warning, Brack springs to his feet and with a back-handed blow to the face knocks Emil to the floor. 'You lying Jewish pile of shit,' he yells.

Emil struggles to his feet. 'Please,' he says, 'what have I done?' A second blow falls. Now Brack signals to his cronies who are standing nearby and they lay into Emil, kicking him repeatedly. All he can do is curl into a ball and try to protect his head with his arms. After a while the kicking stops and he is dragged to his feet. He stands unsteadily. Blood is flowing from his nose, and from the wounds inflicted by the Scharführer only days before.

'That,' Brack says menacingly, 'is only the beginning – unless you start to cooperate.'

'Yes. Of course I will cooperate, only please – tell me what I have to do.'

'Where were you the other day when Block 51 was cleansed?'

* Latrine superintendents.

'I was in Block 46.'

Bodo exchanges a knowing look with one of his cronies. 'And what were you doing in Block 46?'

'I was playing chess.' Emil looks beseechingly at his tormentor. *What harm can there be in chess?*

But Bodo is oblivious.

'Who did you play?'

Emil shakes his head. 'I don't know. The game was arranged by the *Ältester* in Block 46.'

'I happen to know the elder in Block 46. He's not as tolerant of Jews as I am. Yet he lets you play chess. What did you give him so that he would let you play?'

There is no point trying to lie. Brack already knows the answer to the question or he would not have asked it. 'I gave him a watch.'

'And where did you get the watch?'

'I did a favour for one of the German technicians in Buna. He gave me an old watch that was broken. I fixed it and gave it to the *Blockältester*.'

The German brings his face to within inches of the Frenchman's. 'But you forgot something, didn't you, you stinking Kike?'

Emil shakes his head. 'I don't know.'

The *Blockältester* hits him again, though this time with less force. 'Don't fucking lie to me, you Jewish pig-fucker.'

'Please. Tell me. What did I forget?'

'You forgot that before you make a gift to a *Blockältester* in another block, you must first make a gift to your own.'

One of Emil's teeth has been loosened – when he touches it with his tongue, he can feel it move. 'I'm sorry,' he says. A distant, fleeting thought occurs to him of how perverse it is that he should apologize to the person

79

who has just inflicted a beating on him. 'How can I make amends?'

If he hopes that this will serve to mollify Brack, he is disappointed. 'I think you already know what you need to do,' Brack says, his words laden with contempt.

'Yes,' Emil acknowledges. 'May I go now?'

'You'll go when I say and not before. I haven't finished with you yet.'

Nervously, Emil swallows the blood that has pooled in his mouth and waits for the next blow to fall.

'From now on, you will not play chess unless you have my permission.'

Emil is not expecting this. It is as if a death sentence has been passed. But to protest would be to invite another beating.

Brack senses the effect of his words. 'I did not say you could no longer play chess. I said you could play only when I give my permission. From now on, you are playing chess for me.'

April 1944
Ministry of Public Enlightenment and Propaganda, Berlin
With a flick of his fingers, Wilhelm Schweninger launched the still-glowing butt of his cigarette into the street and pulled open the door to the Propaganda Ministry. His level of seniority did not entitle him to enter the building through the imposing portico of the Leopold Palace on Wilhelmplatz; instead, he passed beneath one of the tall, stone doorways that opened directly from Wilhelmstrasse.

With a nod in the direction of the uniformed doorman, he headed for the stairs that would take him to his office on the second floor.

For nine years, Schweninger has worked in Section III under State Secretary Hermann Esser, his every working day taken up with the propaganda opportunities offered by tourism. Unlike most of his contemporaries, a career in the armed forces or the SS had never been open to Schweninger. His father, Otto, was a farmer. At fourteen years of age, helping with the harvest, Wilhelm had trapped his hand in a baling machine. It had been so badly injured that amputation had been the only option. With a future working on the land impossible, the young Wilhelm had been encouraged to study, and he had gone to university in Heidelberg, where he had studied English. It was there that he had discovered his true calling: chess, giving himself over to the game so completely that he failed to complete his studies.

In order for any chess player to compete at a higher level, it was necessary to become a member of the Nationalsozialistische Deutsche Arbeiterpartei. Wilhelm's Nazi Party membership had proved doubly useful when, in 1935, in the run-up to the Berlin Olympics, the Propaganda Ministry had been looking for young Aryan men with a flair for languages to brief the foreign press. It had seemed the perfect solution for the twenty-two-year-old, who was already gaining a reputation as a fearsome chess player. The Propaganda Ministry was the biggest of the Reich ministries, so he had seemed set for an interesting career.

Even the war had not dampened his ambitions to become an international chess champion – not at first. Working in Section III afforded ample opportunities for travel, and having a position in the ministry meant that his talents in chess were encouraged, if only for their value as propaganda. Before he was thirty, he was the undisputed champion of Germany and had beaten several national champions from countries occupied by, or allied to, the Reich. But then had come the Allied landings in North Africa and the reverse of Germany's fortunes at Stalingrad. The work of Section III had become much more limited in its scope, as had international travel.

Of all the institutions in the Reich, the Propaganda Ministry was the most intolerant of defeatist talk and attitudes. But even so, now, at the beginning of 1944, the writing was on the wall for any but the most stubbornly myopic to see.

Wilhelm had never given voice to any of this, but, just lately, had decided that his career needed a new direction – one that would stand him in good stead after the war. He had learned that Herr Schweitzer, the graphic artist so favoured by Reichsminister Goebbels, was looking for an assistant. Under the pseudonym 'Mjölnir', Schweitzer's work could be seen all over Germany – striking posters that urged ordinary Germans to heroic feats, whether at the front or at home. The artist was held in the highest regard by all in the ministry. If Wilhelm got the job, it would transport him to the giddy heights of Section II, with its myriad opportunities in radio, film and the arts. His interview had been three days ago; he expected to hear the outcome today.

There was a definite spring in his step as he entered the office he shared with Georg Wetzel. Georg was in his fifties, a dour widower whose wife had been killed in a bombing raid. He now lived in constant dread of a letter from the army to tell him his son had been killed in action; so much so, his hair had gone completely white. Still, he saw himself as a father-figure to Wilhelm, and tried, in his clumsy way, to nurture his protégé's career.

With the insouciance of a circus performer, the younger man threw his hat on the stand and took his seat.

Georg spoke. 'Late again, Willi. It won't do. If Falthauser gets wind of it...' He jerked his head in the direction of the supervisor's office at the end of the corridor.

Wilhelm had heard it all before and shrugged it off. 'Couldn't be helped, old man. It was the bombing again. Tramlines are gone all along

Hohenzollerndamm. Anyway, I won't be having to worry about him for much longer.'

'If things carry on like this, there'll be nothing left to bomb, soon.' Georg looked longingly at the photograph on his desk of a woman and a teenage boy. 'If only the damned Luftwaffe did what they're supposed to do. It's every night now – every fucking night stuck in a cellar waiting for the one that's got your name on it and next day we're still expected to be at work on time. It's ridiculous.'

Wilhelm shot a warning look at Georg. 'Be quiet, you old fart, or you'll get us both in trouble. You know what the official line is.'

'I know what fat fucking Hermann's official line is … and he can stick it up his fat fucking arse.'

Schweninger made a show of opening his diary and going through it.

'And I don't know why you're bothering with that, either,' Georg continued. 'Word is, the Allies will be landing in France before the summer's out. How long do you think we'll be able to hold out after that happens?'

'Stop it, will you?' Wilhelm looked up in exasperation. 'You'll end up in a bloody concentration camp the way you're going. I heard the speech Doktor G gave from the Sportspalast. You should have too. "Total war is the demand of the hour," that's what he said.'

Georg snorted at the mention of Goebbels. 'Yes, and he also said that workers in government offices will work longer hours so that more of us can be sent to the fucking front.'

'Well, there's no chance of you being sent to the front – or me, for that matter. Anyway, as the Doktor said, it stands to reason that once the British and Americans are in France, they'll join with us and turn on the Russians – or face the prospect of Europe being overrun by the Bolshevik swine.'

The older man shook his head. The entire staff of the ministry had congregated to listen to Goebbels' New Year's speech on the radio, supposedly an act of solidarity. It had been a Friday and, instead of closing early, as it usually did, the ministry building had remained open; food and drink had been laid on, and wireless sets placed throughout the building so that everybody could listen. Timed to perfection, the dramatic final words of the speech had come only a minute before church bells across Germany started to ring in the New Year. The enthusiastic applause of the thousands of staff had changed to embraces, kisses and handshakes and cries of 'Happy New Year!' Georg had had to admit that the Reichsminister was very, very good: he had almost been convinced himself. The applause seemed genuine and spontaneous, though it was not always easy to tell.

Now, with bitter irony, Georg quietly echoed the Doktor's final words: 'Now, people, rise up and let the storm break loose!'

April 1944

Konzentrationslager Auschwitz-III, Monowitz

The camp is in darkness. All the doors are locked and the SS patrol the perimeter with their dogs and machine guns. In the bunk they share, Emil asks Yves what he thinks the *Blockältester* is up to.

Yves is more worldly-wise and astute than Emil, but he is completely exhausted and falls asleep mid-sentence. Emil prays he will make it to summer. Now that the biting cold of the Polish winter is past, he might have a chance.

Emil has an idea. It is common knowledge that Bodo has contacts with the SS. Emil will offer to repair their watches in return for extra food, which he will give to Yves. It seems a good plan, but Bodo is sure to want something in return.

Sleep comes slowly to Emil. He is aware of the night sounds of the block, the stirrings of his fellow inmates, the heavy, breathy sighs of hungry men sleeping, snoring; the occasional cry and the continuous to-ing and fro-ing of men to the toilet bucket. Emil needs to go to the bucket too, but waits. By now it must be nearly full, and he does not want to be the one who fills it and is then sent by the night guard to empty it into the latrine. At last he hears the sound of the door opening and the clang of the bucket against the doorframe as it is lifted out. In ten minutes he will be able to use it safely.

When the camp bell rings in the morning, it is still dark. The night guard switches on the light.

Although he has not slept well, Emil feels better. He has a plan, and he is sure it will work. He knows this because of the rules of Auschwitz: those who run the camp for the SS are all corrupt. They will agree to almost anything as long as there is something in it for them.

13.

A CLOSED GAME

April 1944
Solahütte, SS country club, German-occupied Silesia

Obersturmführer Paul Meissner stood on the veranda looking out over the valley and inhaled deeply. He loved this time of year, and, standing there in the midst of the pine forest, it was difficult to imagine there was a war on.

Officers and NCOs were already arriving for the grand final of the camp chess tournament. Competition in the heats and the two semi-finals had been intense. Even Eidenmüller had tried his hand: 'I know what the moves are,' he had said. 'How difficult can it be?' Fortunately, he'd had the good sense not to bet on himself. Meissner had made an amusing entry about it in his journal. As far as he could tell, his Unterscharführer had made a killing, but this final game was more difficult to predict.

To everyone's surprise, among the officers, Otto Brossman, the taciturn Hauptsturmführer in charge of the first and second guard companies, had excelled. The SS had a reputation for being anti-intellectual, so Meissner had been surprised when Brossman had confessed that he had read widely about chess theory, and at Heidelberg in the 1930s had even taken lessons from the university champion.

'It's all about tactics,' he told Meissner. 'Attack, defend, entrench, retreat. Have you read von Clausewitz's *On War*?' Meissner admitted that he had. 'It's as he says – "War is very simple, but in war even the simplest things are very difficult." Chess is the same. The individual moves are very simple, but combining them to create a winning strategy is a different matter. And,' he continued, 'no two games are alike. Each one has its own personality, as individual as the players pitted against one other. It's so intriguing.'

Meissner was impressed. He liked Brossman. 'You'll make a worthy champion of the SS,' he said.

The other contestant, from among the non-commissioned ranks, was an even greater enigma. Oberscharführer Hustek was in the Gestapo, in the camp's political section. About forty years of age, with dark, greased-back hair and a heavily lined face, he had swept all competition aside. Little was known about him other than his reputation for brutality with the prisoners and his hatred of Jews.

'He's an evil bastard, that one,' Eidenmüller told Meissner.

The officer raised an eyebrow. 'Is that so? That's probably an advantage if you're in the Gestapo,' Meissner replied.

'And another thing – he's a sly one. You'll never know what he's thinking. I wouldn't trust him as far as I could throw him.'

Eidenmüller's judgement proved to be a sound one: Hustek had chain-smoked his way through every game, unnerving his opponents by staring at them unblinkingly until they made their move.

'I reckon that's something he's learned from interrogating prisoners,' Eidenmüller opined. 'More effective than any torture, I'd say.'

'Well, I think he'll find Hauptsturmführer Brossman a somewhat different prospect,' Meissner replied. 'He puts chess on a par with von Clausewitz.'

'Sorry, sir – von who?'

Eidenmüller was offering odds of two to one against Brossman. For the first time, Meissner bet on the outcome – a week's pay. *That will teach Eidenmüller a lesson when he's forced to pay up*, he thought with a grin.

The game was due to start at 19:30 hours. Twenty minutes before the appointed time, Brossman eased his way through the ranks of SS who had made the trip out to the country club. 'Hustek not here yet, then?' he asked Meissner.

Meissner shook his head, but before he could reply, the Kommandant entered the room, followed by a visiting senior SS officer.

Liebehenschel called out, '*Achtung!*' The hum of conversation ceased as the men in the room snapped to attention.

'Gentlemen,' the visitor said, 'please be at your ease. No need for any formality on my account.' The hum of conversation quickly resumed.

He surveyed the occupants of the room. 'You are to be congratulated, Liebehenschel,' he said in a confidential tone. 'I had my doubts that your chess club was really as popular as you had said, but now I'm here, I'm most impressed. The effect it's had on the morale of your men is obvious. I will tell the Reichsführer myself what a success it is.'

'Thank you, sir.' The Kommandant inclined his head. 'But credit must go to Obersturmführer Meissner. It was his idea and he is the one who organized everything. An excellent officer, if I may say so; it's a pity we do not have more like him.'

'I'd like to meet him.'

'Of course.'

Moments later the Kommandant was making the introductions: 'Herr Gruppenführer, may I present Obersturmführer Paul Meissner, head of operations for the satellite camps and the organizer of this competition.'

The Gruppenführer appraised Meissner. 'You are Waffen-SS? How is it that you ended up here?'

Meissner raised his walking stick. 'I was wounded in action, sir. Sadly, I'm no longer considered fit for active service.'

'And your Iron Cross. Where did you get that?'

'Kursk, sir. The Voronezh front.'

'Meissner rarely talks about it, sir,' the Kommandant interjected. 'He's far too modest. He took on four Russian tanks with only a Wespe field howitzer, and killed two of them before our Tigers came to the rescue. His action saved the other two Wespes that were under his command, one of which had already been hit.'

The Gruppenführer extended a hand. 'Well done, Meissner. It is a privilege to shake hands with you. You are a credit to the SS.'

'Thank you, sir. I did my duty, no more.'

'Gruppenführer Glücks is head of the Concentration Camps Inspectorate,' the Kommandant explained. 'He has travelled all the way from Oranienburg to watch the final, and I have asked him to present the prizes to our champions.'

Meissner smiled and glanced at his watch. 'With your permission, Herr Gruppenführer, the final match is due to start shortly. May I invite you and the Kommandant to take your seats?'

As Meissner spoke, Hustek arrived. Without acknowledging anybody, he took a seat at the game table that had been set up in the centre of the room.

Meissner was indignant – Hustek's insolence was insufferable. 'Oberscharführer Hustek,' Meissner barked, in his best parade-ground voice. 'Attention!'

Slowly Hustek raised his head and looked coolly at the officer. 'I don't have to take orders from you, Herr Obersturmführer,' he said. 'I'm Gestapo.'*

The room fell silent. Meissner's knuckles turned white as his hand tightened on his walking stick.

A voice came from the side. 'Really? Then perhaps, Oberscharführer, you'll take orders from me.' All eyes were on the Gruppenführer.

Hustek sprang to attention and saluted. '*Heil Hitler.*'

'Don't "*Heil Hitler*" me. You dare to insult a hero of the German people? Where's *your* Iron Cross, eh? I've half a mind to have you sent to the Russian front. Then we'll see what you're made of.'

Hustek swallowed. 'No, Herr Gruppenführer. I beg your pardon, sir. My behaviour was unacceptable. It won't happen again.'

The Kommandant glowered at the Oberscharführer. Everything had been going so well. 'Herr Gruppenführer,' he said, in a voice that was menacingly quiet, 'I would consider it a personal favour if you would permit me to deal with the Oberscharführer myself – after the conclusion of the competition.'

With a final glare at Hustek, the Gruppenführer took his seat. The game could begin.

---

* The Gestapo had a presence at Auschwitz because there were many political prisoners there, mainly Communists. In practice, the Gestapo operated above and outside the German legal code and were accountable only to themselves.

14.

Two Knights

April 1944

Konzentrationslager Auschwitz-III, Monowitz

After roll call, Emil needs the latrine. Yves goes with him. The arrangements are primitive – a plank rigged above a pit, on which the *Häftlinge* must sit, shoulder to shoulder – and the stench is foul.

Yves settles beside Emil. He is worried about his friend after the beatings he has taken. 'Your face is a bit of a mess.'

Emil explores the scab on his cheek with his fingertips. 'I've been in better shape,' he admits.

Yves laughs hollowly. 'Haven't we all.' He holds out a bony hand for inspection. 'Look at me – I'm fading away to nothing. Jacqueline wouldn't recognize me if she saw me now.'

'Jacqueline?'

Yves looks away. The hurt inside had settled to a constant ache but now, in an unguarded moment, it has risen to the surface. 'My daughter.'

Emil finishes emptying his bowels. He pushes himself away from the plank and pulls his trousers up. He steps over to the tap to wash his hands. There is only a trickle of water but it will have to do. He is wiping his hands dry on his shirt when Yves joins him.

Gently, Emil puts a hand on Yves's shoulder. 'Jacqueline – it's a lovely name,' he says quietly. 'I wish you would tell me about her.' He squeezes the shoulder, every bone shockingly sharp under his hand. 'You know, here we are – we even share a bed...you would think we would know everything about one other – but we don't, do we? Not really.'

'She was...' Yves stops, an agonized travesty of a grin on his face. 'I can't.'

'It's hard to talk about them, isn't it?' Emil makes a point of looking his friend in the eye. 'But we must, otherwise they will be forgotten.'

Together they walk back towards the block. Their progress is painfully slow. Haltingly, Yves tells Emil something of his life before Auschwitz. 'My wife's name was Annette. We would have been married ten years in September. Jacqueline was our only child. She was eight when we got picked up in one of the mass arrests. There was only the three of us – no other family, you understand – Annette and I were both orphans. Funny that, isn't it? Both of us, orphans, I mean.' He pauses for breath; the simple effort of speaking is telling on him. 'Jacqueline was a beautiful child. Clever, in a quiet sort of way, and caring – always helping her mother. And then we got taken to Drancy. Annette was pregnant. The Germans didn't give a damn. We were put in a room with I don't know how many other people. And then Annette went into labour, about two months too soon. She haemorrhaged.' Yves runs a hand over his face. 'A doctor came. He said perhaps if she had been in hospital, she might have been saved. He was terribly sorry, he said. The baby didn't make it either. It was a boy – not that it makes any difference. So that left me and Jacqueline. She became very quiet after her mother died. It was like she had died too, inside, but was somehow managing to carry on, on the outside. I think she did it for my sake. After that, we were inseparable.

'Then there was the transport to Auschwitz. She was asleep when we arrived. When the SS bastards started hammering on the doors and yelling at us like mad people she got very frightened. Then we were sep-arated. Jacqueline was screaming to stay with me until one of the guards went over with a dog that started snarling and barking at her, which only made it worse…' Yves stops. He cannot find the right words. He collects himself and continues, his voice hoarse: '… until an old woman came and said, "Don't worry, monsieur, I will take care of her until you can come for her." *Don't worry.* The most stupid thing I have ever heard in my life. How could I have let them take her away?'

Emil stops walking. His friend's anguish is raw, as if everything had happened only yesterday. 'Yves.' Once again he takes his friend by the shoulder. 'You can't allow yourself to think like that. There was nothing you could have done: they would have killed you right there.'

'Maybe.' Yves's face is a picture of inconsolable pain. 'But the thought of my little girl going to her death with nobody to comfort her is unbearable.'

'I know, but it's not your fault. You can't blame yourself for what happened.' Emil almost goes on to say: 'It was God's will,' but he stops himself.

'I hate them,' Yves continues, his voice hardening. 'When most people say they hate someone, they don't really mean it, but I do. We have had the most perfect instruction in the art of hatred, Emil, and we have a duty to put it to good use. One day, if God gives me the strength, I will pay them back for what they have done.'

The story is not so different from Emil's own, and he wonders how many of the men in Monowitz have a similar story to tell, of families torn apart, of women left to die, of children murdered in their thousands.

Bitterly, Yves goes on: 'You know how some of the prisoners suck up to the *Kapos* and the block elders, trying to curry favour? Mostly they do it for nothing more than a crust of bread or an extra ration of soup. But

I've promised myself – no matter what, that's something I will never do. It would be a betrayal. I would rather make a pact with the Devil. If there was a way to get back at the SS and the scum who run this place for them I would take it, and to hell with the consequences.'

Emil is silent.

'What about you?' Yves asks.

'Me?' replies Emil. How can he tell anyone about what he has lost, when the full depths of his grief are still unknown to him? *But Yves is my friend. My only friend*, he reminds himself.

'My wife was called Rosa – *is* called Rosa. When we arrived at the unloading ramp I saw she was selected for work, like me. She may still be alive. I pray she is. We had two boys, Louis and Marcel. The Germans took them away too, but at least they were with their grandmother. As for what became of them...'

September 1939
Paris

The word on everyone's lips was 'war'. Only last year, Britain and France had both fallen for Hitler's bluff over Czechoslovakia, and now the German Chancellor was making threatening noises over Poland. Emil was sure there would be no second climbdown, but surely Hitler was astute enough to see that? However, such thoughts were far from his mind as he walked briskly along the Rue Cambronne on his way home. Sometimes Rosa would put Louis in the pram and walk to meet him. He loved it when she did that.

Looking up, he saw her walking towards him in the shade of the trees that lined the street; she seemed lost in thought. He ducked into a doorway until she drew level with him, then jumped out to surprise her.

Smiling, she punched him lightly on the chest. '*Fripon*,' she said. Rosa linked her arm in his as they strolled homewards.

'Where's Louis?' he asked.

'At home with your mother.' She looked at him coyly. 'I've got something to tell you.'

'Really? What?'

'Oh, no, not so fast. You've got to guess.'

'Guess? You know I'm no good at guessing.'

Rosa laughed.

'All right...I know. Le Quintette du Hot are playing at Le Chat Noir.'

'No, silly, you know they only ever play at Le Grosse Pomme, and anyway, they're in England at the moment.'

He grinned. 'I knew that. I was testing you.' He turned serious. 'War hasn't been declared?'

'Not yet.'

'I give in then. Come on, tell me.'

She smiled. 'We're going to have another baby.'

'Another baby?' Emil's face lit up with joy. 'When?'

'In May, the doctor says.'

Laughing, he took her hands and swung her round as if in a dance, all the way back to the apartment.

'*Maman*,' he yelled, running up the stairs to their door. 'Has Rosa told you the news? We're going to have another baby! In May! Isn't that wonderful?'

His mother greeted them not with joy but with foreboding. 'I take it you haven't heard the other news, then – France has just declared war on Germany.'

*

1962

Amsterdam

With a start, Emil woke. It was dark, and for a moment he could not remember where he was. His breathing was rapid and his heart was pounding. He must have been having a nightmare but he could not remember it. He lay back on his pillow and tried to settle again to sleep. But he could not get comfortable. The hotel pillow, which had been so soft earlier, was now solid and unyielding, despite the pummelling he gave it, and his limbs felt awkward no matter how he positioned them.

There was a reason why sleep had become so elusive: the conversation with Meissner and his ridiculous notion that the only way Emil could find peace was through forgiveness. And, more ridiculous still, that the person in need of forgiveness was himself. Emil rejected the suggestion. It was not he who had perpetrated such unspeakable evil. He was its victim. He turned again in the bed, his frustration and indignation mounting, but his attempt to relax was futile. Angrily he cast off the covers. Damn Meissner. To hell with him and his unassailable faith.

But there is no escaping the rules of Auschwitz. Everything is back to front. In Auschwitz the good are punished, the evil flourish, and the victims, not the perpetrators, are the ones who feel guilty. It is incomprehensible but true.

Emil had long ago lost hope that he would find anything to cleanse the past. And now Meissner had turned up, with his promise that hope could be rekindled ... But hope was mocking Emil because it knew, as the priest did not, that the price of forgiveness was too high.

Forgive? He could not do it.

*

At breakfast, Emil found his appetite had deserted him. Coffee and two cigarettes left a bitter taste in his mouth as he headed to the Krasnapolsky and his next game in the tournament. He did not notice anything of his walk. He was preoccupied with the thoughts that had refused to let go of him during the night.

Could it be that he was denying himself the redeeming power that the universe had to offer because he could not forgive? Or, as Meissner would have it, that he was refusing to forgive? If there was the smallest grain of truth in what Meissner had said, he would be a fool not to pursue it. But *was* Meissner right? Where did his authority come from? It was true the Catholic Church preached a doctrine of forgiveness, but its actions gave the lie to this: to be a Jew was to be acutely aware of the harsh treatment they had received at the hands of the Church over the centuries, right to the present day, and all in the name of their loving, *forgiving* Saviour. 'Forgive' – it was an easy word to say. Too easy. The promise of hope that Meissner was holding out to him was an illusion.

Unable to sleep, and in an effort to see a way forward, Emil had cast the ten tiles on the points of the Sephiroth again, but the results had been unclear. A shadow seemed to have fallen over his powers of discernment and there was nothing he could do to see through it. The tile that was revealed when he turned it face upward was א – Aleph – which denoted the inaccessibility of the Divine Light. It told him there were some things that were beyond his understanding, and that for these he must have faith: but in what? He was a Jew, and despite all his searching of the Kabbalah, the religion of his fathers had done little to answer the questions that had raged in his soul for nearly twenty years. Surely it could not be telling him to have faith in the easy and convenient dogmas of the Catholics? Over the years, Emil had built for himself a subtle series of fortifications to protect the few certainties he had left. It was the only way he thought he could survive. Now Meissner had succeeded in planting a seed of doubt inside this fortress. Emil steeled himself to make sure it would not take root.

In the second round, Emil had been matched against Lopez, an Argentinean. Emil had researched a number of his past games, won and lost, looking for his strengths and weaknesses. The South American played in a traditional style, attacking through the centre of the board, like Schweninger. If playing white, he favoured the English Opening; if black, the Queen's Indian Defence.

Emil felt equal to either challenge, and he won comfortably. As Lopez congratulated him, he remarked: 'You surprised me, Monsieur Clément. You didn't use any of the defences you have employed at the top level in the last three years.'

Emil smiled a victor's smile, gracious but not condescending. 'That's the point, Señor Lopez – to be unpredictable.' The result of the match registered by the arbiter, and their moves recorded for posterity, Emil made for the exit.

Meissner was waiting for him at the door.

'Good morning,' he said, warmly. 'You won, of course?'

Emil nodded. He was not sure he wanted to talk to Meissner again. He tried to walk past, but the cleric fell into step beside him.

Emil stopped. 'Look,' he said, 'I don't want to appear rude, but I think we probably said enough yesterday.'

'You think we said enough?' Meissner looked appraisingly at Emil. 'Perhaps you're right. Who knows? I have spent quite some time since thinking about what we said. I wondered if you had.'

Emil hesitated before replying, but then said, 'I've been thinking about it for twenty years.' He strode off, leaving the other man behind.

'There is someone I should like you to meet, and, in the circumstances, the sooner the better,' the bishop called after him.

Emil stopped and half turned his head. 'Who?'

Smiling, the bishop limped forward to place a hand on Emil's arm. 'It's a surprise, but I think it will do you good.'

'I'm at that time in my life where surprises are rarely enjoyable.'

The bishop dropped his smile. 'I did not say it would be enjoyable. I said I thought it would do you good. Will you come?'

'I'd rather not. I need to spend some time reviewing the games of my next opponent.'

'Indulge a dying man,' the bishop replied softly.

Emil sighed. 'Very well. But I don't want it to take too long.'

'Not take too long?' Meissner shook his head. 'Watchmaker, this is likely to take the rest of your life.'

15.

WINDMILL

April 1944

Solahütte, SS country club, German-occupied Silesia

The game started. Hustek drew black. Every officer sneered at the Gestapo man for his boorish behaviour, willing Brossman to win, while every NCO winced with embarrassment but could not set aside their conviction that Hustek would triumph.

Meissner felt torn. As the game's arbiter, it was his duty to be even-handed but, by God, he hoped that the Oberscharführer would get his comeuppance.

For ten or fifteen minutes, the game progressed with little advantage to either player. Then Meissner spoke quietly. 'I should be obliged if you would stop doing that, Oberscharführer.'

'Doing what?'

'Staring so menacingly at Hauptsturmführer Brossman while he decides what move to make.'

'Don't worry about me, Herr Obersturmführer,' Brossman growled. 'I don't scare so easily.'

So intent were the spectators on the game – including the Gruppen-führer – that the exchange was heard by everyone.

'I thought this was supposed to be a fair game, sir,' Hustek remarked, in an aggrieved tone. 'Is this how it's going to be – officers cosying up with each other to keep the lower ranks from winning?' He spoke quietly, but he knew his words would carry. He raised his face to stare defiantly at Meissner.

Hustek had castled to protect his king, and now Brossman brought up his queen to threaten the rook. If he moved forward one square he would take a pawn and have a direct diagonal route to his target. It took all Hustek's willpower to suppress a smile. The officer had walked into his trap. He moved his own bishop one space diagonally, threatening check, a move Brossman had to defend. However, Hustek's move also exposed his own queen. Brossman smiled, thinking Hustek had made a fatal error. He changed his tactic of attacking the rook to take the queen instead. It was Hustek's turn to smile. In three successive moves, he forced Brossman's king to move to avoid check, taking a pawn, a rook, and finally Brossman's queen.

The exchange greatly impaired the officer's ability to dominate the centre of the board. Minutes later, Hustek followed with a second windmill combination, this time taking a pawn, Brossman's remaining rook and a bishop.

Meissner was aghast. Would peasant cunning win out against an intellectual appreciation of the game? It seemed so. Brossman held on for another fifteen minutes, but his fate had been sealed the moment he had taken Hustek's queen.

April 1944
Ministry of Public Enlightenment and Propaganda, Berlin
As usual, Schweninger was late back from lunch. In the canteen he had met an attractive young secretary who had been impressed by his stories of foreign travel and international chess championships. She had been

wearing a V-necked woollen dress that exposed her cleavage enticingly whenever she leaned across the table. Standing over her, Wilhelm had not even tried to conceal what he was doing, taking full advantage of his height to peer down at her. That was what tourism was all about, wasn't it – taking in the sights? She had agreed to meet him for drinks and dinner on Friday.

In the office he found Georg in a sour mood. 'Late again, Willi. It really won't do, you know.' Schweninger rolled his eyes but said nothing. 'Falthauser's looking for you,' Georg went on. 'He didn't look happy.'

'Does that mean it's good news or bad news?'

The older man shrugged. 'Who can tell? He's such a miserable bastard.'

That was certainly true, Wilhelm thought to himself as he made his way from their cubbyhole to the large office at the end of the corridor.

'Come in,' was the crisp response to his knock on the door.

Wilhelm entered. It did not occur to him to be nervous. It had to be about his interview, and he was confident he had done well. 'You wanted to see me, Herr Falthauser?'

The supervisor looked up from a stack of papers piled on his desk. He seemed his usual, joyless self. 'Yes. It's about your application for the post of Herr Schweitzer's assistant.'

Wilhelm was aware of a change in Falthauser's demeanour. He seemed pleased. That could mean only one thing.

'I regret to inform you that your application was not successful.'

'Not successful? But…' Wilhelm was shocked. 'Are you sure there's been no mistake?'

Now the supervisor smiled. 'No mistake, Willi. You're here for the duration – better get used to the idea.' He turned back to his work.

Still stunned, Wilhelm turned to leave. Before he reached the doorway, his supervisor called after him: 'Who do you think you are – the second Max Amann?'

Wilhelm stopped. 'What? What do you mean?'

Falthauser looked up. 'Don't worry, you'll work it out – eventually.'

Wilhelm took his time walking back to the cubbyhole. He had been so *certain*.

'You look like you've just been given the sack, Willi,' Georg said.

The younger man slumped onto his chair. 'I might as well have been.'

'What did Falthauser have to say?'

'He asked me if I thought I was the second Max Amann.'

For moment Georg did not understand, then, with a sigh and a shake of his head, he gave a wry chuckle.

'It's not funny.'

Georg suppressed the laughter that was building inside him. 'Fucking Falthauser. What a fucking comedian. He couldn't be funny if his life depended on it, but this time...'

'Well, I'm glad you think it's so fucking hilarious.'

'Don't you see?' Georg said, grinning. 'It's his cock-eyed way of telling you why you didn't get the job.'

'No, I don't see. Tell me.'

'Because you're a one-armed cripple. Goebbels doesn't like cripples. It reminds him that he's one himself. It's not so bad if you're stuck down here out of sight in this hole, but anything else – forget it. Max Amann is the only exception.'

'What's so special about him?'

'Him and the chief go back a long way – and he publishes *Das Reich*.'

Understanding dawned on Schweninger. *Das Reich* was the weekly paper for which Goebbels wrote the editorial. 'And he's only got one arm?'

'He's only got one arm. Lost it in a hunting accident in the thirties. Some say Franz Ritter von Epp shot him deliberately.'

Wilhelm shook his head in disbelief. 'How the hell do you know all this stuff?'

The older man smiled. 'Well, when you've been around as long as I have…'

Scowling, Willi glanced around the cubbyhole. 'Christ, I'd rather be fucking dead.'

April 1944
Solahütte, SS country club, German-occupied Silesia
Summoning his reserves of dignity, Gruppenführer Glücks presented the awards – first to Hustek and then Brossman. He decided it was an opportune time to say a few words. He disliked speaking in public, fearing to say the wrong thing or to have his words misrepresented by a rival, but here he was on safe ground. Something big was about to happen to Auschwitz, and it was important to bolster morale in advance. Luckily, Himmler had recently made a speech on the same subject. Glücks had no qualms about plagiarism: the Reichsführer would take it as a compliment.

'Gentlemen,' he said. 'It is most gratifying to see such good spirits among our fighting men for – make no mistake – every man here is fighting a war every bit as much as any soldier of the Wehrmacht on the Eastern or the Italian fronts. Only our war is against a foe more wily, more insidious, more vicious than any Russian or American or Englander. Our foe is the Jew who, given the slightest opportunity, would betray our people and take from us our birthright. We must be stern – not only with our enemies, but with ourselves. We cannot permit ourselves to relax our vigilance for an instant, for to do so would invite disaster.

'It is a crime against the blood of the German people to be concerned for Jews in labour camps, or to make concessions that would make things still more difficult for our children and grandchildren. If someone says to you, "It is inhumane to use women or children to dig ditches or work in factories; I can't make them do it because the exertion will kill them," then you must reply, "If that ditch is not built, or if those armaments are not made, then German soldiers will die, and they are sons of German mothers. You are a traitor to your own blood."

'As for the difficult work you do here in Auschwitz, this is a page of glory in our history that can never be written, and the heroic part you have played will never be acknowledged. But *we* know how difficult it would be for Germany today – under bombing raids and the hardships and privations of war – were we still to have the Jews in every city as secret saboteurs and agitators.

'We have the moral right' – he paused – 'no, more than that, we have a *duty* to our people, to our blood, to destroy this race that wants to destroy us. It is no different to a doctor who exterminates a germ because if he does not eliminate the infection it will kill his patient. The Reichsführer-SS has said that any infection must be eradicated *without mercy* before it is able to gain a hold.

'This work is not easy, but it is our duty. We did not ask to be given this duty, nonetheless we take up the burden willingly. Despite all the difficulties we face and the enemies that would destroy us, we can be proud that we have carried out this most arduous of tasks in the spirit of love of our people, and that the work we do will cause no harm to our soul, our virtue or our honour.'

He raised his right hand. '*Sieg Heil!*'

The roar that followed was deafening. The men gathered round him must have shouted '*Heil!*' three, five, ten times.

With the clamour resounding in his ears, the Gruppenführer left the room, followed by the Kommandant.

Meissner waited until the noise abated before offering a hand to Brossman, saying, 'My commiserations.' He turned to Hustek. 'Oberscharführer,' he said, his voice curt, 'come to my office on Monday and I will make the arrangements for your leave.'

'Thank you, Herr Obersturmführer,' Hustek replied in a sneering tone. 'I can't tell you how much I'm looking forward to it.'

Meissner exchanged a glance with Brossman. 'Indeed, Oberscharführer,' he said, not bothering to disguise the irony in his voice, 'it must be almost as much as we are.'

Hustek froze. With studied insolence he placed his cap on his head and, without saluting, walked away.

The two officers watched as he made his way through the crowded room. Among all the NCOs present, only one congratulated the Oberscharführer, and left with him.

'The insolence of that man,' Meissner seethed.

'Gestapo,' Brossman replied, as if no other explanation were necessary. 'Don't let the bastard get to you. And if you want my advice, I would start watching my back if I were you. I think you've just made yourself an enemy.'

Meissner reached into his pocket for his cigarette case. He offered one to Brossman. 'I can take care of myself,' he said. 'Besides, after the Kommandant has finished with him, I think Hustek will want to keep a low profile for quite some time.'

*

The Kommandant enjoyed the use of a large house close to the main entrance of the *Stammlager*. That night, he hosted a dinner party for his senior officers, with Gruppenführer Glücks as guest of honour. Liebehenschel apologized for the poor quality of the food but, in reality, the fare was sumptuous compared with what most Germans enjoyed.

Glücks, who prided himself on being an instant judge of character, found the Kommandant a difficult man to assess: Liebehenschel was too familiar with his senior officers and Glücks sensed he was not a man to inspire much in the way of loyalty among his subordinates. But he could not fault his hospitality: wine flowed freely, followed by cognac and cigars, leaving the company in a relaxed mood.

When it was time for the officers to take their leave, the Gruppenführer asked the Kommandant's deputy, Sturmbannführer Richard Bär, to stay behind. While two orderlies cleared the dinner table, the three SS men retired to the sitting room.

Bär was the first to speak. 'I trust you feel your visit has been worthwhile, sir?'

The Gruppenführer rested his cigar in an ashtray and held out his snifter for a refill. 'It's always worthwhile to meet front-line officers and get from them the true picture of what we're up against. But I must confess that I had another motive in coming here. Your chess tournament merely gave me a convenient reason.'

'Oh?' The Kommandant poured a generous measure of spirits into his own glass.

'Yes. I've been putting it off, but I can delay no longer. Something quite extraordinary is about to happen, and I must make sure that all the pieces are in place to ensure its success.'

The two Auschwitz officers exchanged a glance. 'I'm sorry, sir,'

Liebehenschel said, 'I'm afraid I don't understand.'

'I want your honest opinion, Liebehenschel. Tell me – what's your position on the Jewish question?'

The Kommandant frowned. 'The Jews? I'm surprised you should ask me that, sir. Like any good German I think they're a menace and a blight on humanity.'

'Yes – but what do you think we should do with them?'

'I think we should make the swine work for the good of the Reich, like we are already doing here and in other camps.'

'But you don't think they should be exterminated?'

'I didn't say that, sir. Once they've outlived their usefulness, what else can one do with them? But I think it's inefficient simply to kill them out of hand. Surely it's better to get as much as we can out of them first?'

The Gruppenführer cleared his throat. 'It's being said in Berlin that you're not the right person to be the Kommandant of Auschwitz, that you're too soft on the Jews.'

The Kommandant sat bolt upright. 'And who is saying that?'

Glücks registered Liebehenschel's alarm. 'It doesn't matter. What matters is that it has reached the ears of the Reichsführer-SS.' He sighed heavily. 'Look, Auschwitz is the most important of the camps in the east. It embodies everything we're trying to do about the whole Jewish problem. The Kommandant of Auschwitz has to be like Caesar's wife – above even the slightest hint of suspicion. We simply can't have someone in charge who's soft on the Jews, or who is perceived as being soft on them.'

The Kommandant was affronted. 'Sir, if I have been soft on the Jews in Auschwitz, it is only because I had orders to increase the productivity of the factories. And it was only a few hours ago that you were telling me what a good job I had done.'

'Yes, but at the same time, the numbers being sent for *Sonderbehand-lung** in Birkenau have fallen noticeably.'

Liebehenschel leaned forward, eager to explain. 'But if we want to keep the work camps operating at full capacity, we have to send fewer people to the gas chambers. It's simple arithmetic. Since the beginning of the year, all arrivals who are physically fit have been selected for work, and the results speak for themselves. It is on my orders that we have begun construction of an extension to the Birkenau complex to house them.'

The Gruppenführer's voice took on a conspiratorial tone. 'I am here to inform you that the situation has changed. There are plans to send many more Jews here – far more than will be needed for work in the labour camps. Capacity for special treatment at Birkenau must be increased dramatically.'

'Many more Jews?' Bär asked. 'But I thought we had practically emptied Europe of them.'

The Gruppenführer shook his head. 'Not quite. The French are dragging their feet, and it seems that in Denmark the Jews disappeared overnight. But these new arrivals are from elsewhere.'

'Are we permitted to know where?'

'Hungary. According to Eichmann, there are at least a million Jews there, and it has been decided to get them out before Horthy and the rest of his pack of cowards go over to the Russians.'†

---

* The SS rarely referred openly to the extermination of the Jews. Instead, the euphemism *Sonderbehandlung* – 'special treatment' – was used.

† Admiral Miklós Horthy was the regent of Hungary, effectively its ruler since 1920. Although an ally of Germany, up to this point in the war Hungary had permitted only limited persecution of Jews. In the spring of 1944, fearing that Hungary might surrender to the Russians, the German army was sent into Hungary, swiftly followed by SS units led by Adolf Eichmann, determined to round up the

Liebehenschel could hardly believe what he was hearing. 'And they are all coming *here*? It will take a year to process that many, at least.'

'We don't have a year. Eichmann says he can send us twelve thousand a day.'

Liebehenschel frowned. He thought he was used to the unreasonable demands of his superiors, but this—? 'No,' he said. 'It's not possible. Even with all the crematoria going at full tilt, we simply don't have the capacity to process so many.'

The Gruppenführer drained his glass. 'I thought that's what you might say. I'm sorry to have to tell you, but as of this moment you are relieved of your command.'

'What? Relieved of my command? But... *why*? You said I was doing a good job. Surely...' Liebehenschel realized he was gabbling and stopped speaking. A moment later, he resumed, his voice calmer. 'Naturally, I will follow whatever orders I am given, but... who is to take my place?'

The Gruppenführer indicated Bär. 'You will be succeeded by your deputy. He will take over responsibility for the day-to-day running of the camp, but it was felt in Berlin that a more experienced hand should take charge of processing the Hungarian Jews. Obersturmbannführer Höss will return temporarily, specifically for this purpose. The operation is code-named *Aktion Höss* in his honour.'

Bär raised his glass in salute. 'Thank you, sir. I will do my best to live up to my new responsibilities.'

'And what is to become of me?' Liebehenschel asked, quietly.

The Gruppenführer reached across to squeeze the ex-Kommandant's

Hungarian Jews and transport them to Auschwitz. There were far too many for them to be assimilated into the labour camps: the vast majority were sent to the gas chambers immediately on arrival.

arm. 'No need to look so downcast. You are to be the new Kommandant of Majdanek. You'll have a fortnight's home leave, then take up your new position on your return.'

'And when does all this start?'

His task done, the Gruppenführer permitted himself a small smile. 'Tomorrow.'

16.

FIANCHETTO

1962

Amsterdam

In his hotel near the Oude Kerk, Wilhelm Schweninger was packing to go home. He had hoped his return would be triumphant, but it was not to be. He was not sorry to be leaving: the hotel's attempt at modern décor merely made it look drab, and he was still smarting from his defeat by Emil Clément. In his wallet he had a ticket for the 16:17 train from Amsterdam Centraal to Berlin, where he intended to get numbingly drunk.

There was a knock on the door. He looked at his watch and sighed. The porter was too early: check-out wasn't until 11:30. 'I'm not ready yet,' he called in German, knowing the porter spoke it fluently. 'Come back in a quarter of an hour.'

'I'm sorry, Herr Schweninger,' a voice replied, also in German. The long narrow corridor beyond the door gave it an odd echo. 'But could you spare a few minutes of your time? It's rather important.'

Schweninger dropped a shirt on the bed and opened the door. 'Oh,' he said, surprised. 'I wasn't expecting a priest.'

'I must ask you to forgive the intrusion, Herr Schweninger. Allow me to introduce myself. My name is Paul Meissner.'

Schweninger did not stand aside to let the priest in. 'What can I do for you, Father?'

'It's more what I can do for you,' the priest replied.

'And what is that, exactly?'

'I offer forgiveness for your sins.'

Schweninger shook his head. 'I'm sorry, Father, I'm no longer a believer, and you've caught me at a bad time. I am about to leave Amsterdam.'

'I know. That's why it's important that I speak to you now.'

'You're talking in riddles, and I've got a train to catch. If you don't mind—?' Schweninger tried to close the door.

Meissner put his shoulder against the door and spoke quickly: 'My SS number was 1214958 and my Party membership number was 6374971. You joined the Party in 1934 and your membership number was 1265409. Although you held a position at the Propaganda Ministry, you were never inducted into the SS because of the injury to your hand.'

Schweninger paled but then grew angry. 'What is this? Are you trying to blackmail me? Well, you can forget it – I have owned up to my past and put it all behind me.' He pushed at the door again.

Meissner put his foot against it. 'It would be a strange sort of blackmail, attempted by a priest, would it not? I revealed my own history to you to show that I too am tainted by a previous life that will not let me be.'

'Look, I don't know how you know all these things about me, but I don't respond to threats. Now if you don't go, I'll call reception and have you removed.'

'I'm not here to threaten you, Herr Schweninger, far from it – I'm here to help you. If you'll allow me to buy you lunch, I will tell you everything. Afterwards, you will be quite free to catch your train, I promise.'

There was something in the tone of Meissner's voice that made Schweninger hesitate. He stepped back from the door, allowing it to swing open.

'Let me be sure that I understand what you are saying, Father Meissner,' he said. 'If I listen to your story, you will buy me lunch and, afterwards, you will not try to stop me from getting my train.' Meissner nodded. 'In that case, why not? But I warn you – I have a healthy appetite.'

Schweninger picked up a jacket and stepped out into the corridor. Followed by the priest, he walked along it to the door to the stairs.

'What exactly is all this about?' he asked, as they walked.

'There is someone I would like you to meet. He's waiting for us in a restaurant on Oudekerksplein.'

May 1944
Konzentrationslager Auschwitz-III, Monowitz
Meissner had a letter, from France. The envelope was creased and thumb-print-stained. It had clearly taken some time to reach him. It took him some moments to recognize the writing.

I Abteilung

SS Panzer Artillerie Regiment 2

2nd SS-Panzergrenadier-Division Das Reich

Montauban, 12 March 1944

My dear Paul,

I'll bet you're surprised to hear from me. You must have thought I was dead! To be fair, that wouldn't be so far from the truth, but you know I'm not given much to writing. I tried to see you when you were still in the field hospital but they told me I was too late and that you had already been sent back to Germany. Nobody seemed to know where you had ended up and there were still many Russians to fight. After you went on your little holiday they counter-attacked in force. You probably saw something of it in the newsreels but you can't get the sense of what it's really like from them, can you? You know what I'm talking about. You don't get the smells – the earth burning around you, the tightness in your belly when you see a squadron of T-34s heading towards you, and the elation when you're surrounded by a dozen burning tanks and you've come through unscathed. You'll be pleased to know that old Schratt is still making life hell for the junior officers. In case you didn't know, he was the one that pulled you out of the Wespe after you were hit...

Meissner looked up and stared out of the window. *Old* Schratt? Not so old. He couldn't have been more than three or four years older than he was himself. He could picture him clearly: his helmet pushed back on his head and a chin like a rifle butt. It was good to know he was still well. He was one of those soldiers that every regiment needed – he had probably been born wearing jackboots. He had terrified Meissner when, as a young officer, he had arrived to take command of the unit. The Scharführer had taken him to a quiet corner and made it clear that it was he who was in charge – not some wet-behind-the-ears Untersturmführer foisted on them by a tin soldier in headquarters who had nothing better to do. What Schratt taught Meissner was far more important than anything he had learned in officer training. He had taught him how to keep himself and his men alive. 'How much you care for your men every day is exactly how much they'll care for you when it really counts.' And the Scharführer had been right, as he had been about everything else. And now it seemed that old Schratt had saved his life.

...Well, the good news is that now we're on holiday too. The division was pulled out of the line and as a punishment for not fighting hard enough we have been sent to France. We are stationed in Montauban, about 50 km north of Toulouse. I must say the French make a bit of a change from the monumental stupidity of the Ukrainian peasants. Most of them don't like us, of course, but it doesn't stop them trying to sell us their cheese and wine. And the women, Paul – you should see the women. Real beauties.

You probably won't have heard that Knocken and Ernst Bock are both dead. Knocken was killed in a bombing run by some half-blind Stuka pilot who couldn't tell the difference between the Ivans and his own men. Of course that lunatic Hempel ordered us not to shoot at the stupid fucker, but what the hell, we did anyway. And Ernst got caught in the open when we came under mortar fire. I yelled at him to get down but he kept on running. Stupid bastard.

But that's enough bad news for one letter. The good news is that I have been promoted to Sturmbannführer. Can you believe that? If war is crazy this is surely all the proof you need. So here I am. The Das Reich is to be refitted as a full Panzer division and I am on holiday enjoying the French sun and wine and women. Whoever said war is hell got it completely wrong – if this is hell, all I can say is I'm glad I spent my life as a sinner. You'll also be glad to hear that Schratt has managed to keep most of your old unit together. On the odd occasions I bump into him – incidentally, he's a Sturmscharführer now – he always asks whether I have any news of you.

You're still missed here, Paul. I ought to say it's despite the way you used to go on at us about duty and honour, but I think it's probably because of it. If you ever manage to get some leave, try to get down here and visit your old comrades.

Sincerely,

Your brother in arms

Peter Sommer

1962

Amsterdam

Emil had taken a table at the rear of the restaurant, telling the waiter that he was meeting a colleague – possibly two – for lunch. He could not stop himself from looking at his watch. Twenty minutes, Meissner had said, and it had been nearer thirty. He still wondered why he had allowed the priest to convince him to come but, he had to admit, Meissner could be very persuasive.

While he was waiting, he tried to recall the first time he had met Meissner. To his surprise he found his recollection imperfect. He had thought it etched deeply into his memory, and it was a shock to find how elusive it had become.

The door to the restaurant opened and two men entered. With the light behind them it was difficult to tell whether it was Meissner or not, but then Emil saw the walking stick. With a start, he realized who was with him.

Angrily, he stood up. 'You have misled me,' he said. 'I knew I shouldn't have trusted you. What you thought you could achieve by bringing *him*...' He raised a finger to point at Schweninger.

'Do not worry,' Schweninger replied in frosty recognition. 'I have no more wish to be here than you.' He directed a curt nod at Meissner. 'I think it best if I forgo your offer of lunch, Father. I will bid you good day.'

'Please,' Meissner said. 'Enough of this ridiculous posturing, both of you. If you won't even talk to one another, how can you expect anything to change?'

'I never said I expected anything to change,' Emil said.

'And as far as I am concerned,' Schweninger said, 'Herr Clément and I have nothing to say to each other.'

'Nothing to say? Are you so determined to be enemies? It is my belief that you both have much more in common than either of you realize or would care to admit. Is the idea of talking to each other really so terrible?'

Behind Schweninger, a waiter was hovering hesitantly. 'I have a suggestion,' Meissner said. 'Let us at least have lunch and I will tell the beginning of a story that I pray will bring us to at least a little common understanding.'

Emil and Schweninger exchanged a mutually suspicious look. Schweninger shrugged. 'What the hell,' he said. 'I've come this far and, anyway, I'm starving.' He looked directly at Emil. 'How about you, Herr Clément? Is the promise of a free lunch enough for you as well?'

Emil frowned. There was something that did not feel right about sitting down calmly to lunch with two former Nazis, and the memory of his angry exchange with Schweninger was still fresh. How could Meissner think there could be any rapprochement between them? It would be easy to walk away. And yet, last night, when he had cast the tiles, they had told him to have faith; in what, he still did not know. For a moment he hesitated but then, quietly, he sat down again.

Relieved, the waiter stepped forward. 'Would any of you gentlemen like something to drink?'

They ordered beer. Meissner and Schweninger seated themselves.

Meissner spoke first. 'This is a long and complicated story,' he said, 'and Herr Schweninger has a train to catch later this afternoon, so we must try to keep to the point. I don't think any of us knows the full extent of it, so we will all have something to tell. Let me start by saying that Herr Clément and I knew each other during the war. We were both in

Auschwitz – I was an SS officer and he was a prisoner. In normal circum-stances, it would have been extremely unlikely that our paths would ever have crossed, but in Auschwitz nothing was normal.'

The drinks arrived.

'So what was it that brought you together?' Schweninger asked.

Meissner made no attempt to respond. He looked to Emil.

Emil sighed. 'Chess,' he replied. He lifted his glass to his lips and drank deeply.

Schweninger seemed unconvinced. 'Chess? In Auschwitz?'

'Yes. It was played among the prisoners. Apparently I was one of the better players.'

A smile played fleetingly on Meissner's lips. 'One of the better players? Come now, I never took you to be one for false modesty.' He turned to Schweninger. 'The perception of the other prisoners was that he was so good it seemed he had almost magical powers. He was their talisman, their unbeatable champion. I can't begin to tell you about the problems he caused me.'

'This is fascinating,' Schweninger said, dropping his pretence of dis-belief. He took a sip of his beer. 'Did you know that late in 1944 I was approached by the SS and asked if I would play a chess match in Auschwitz?'

Meissner smiled. 'Yes, I did know. The request came from me. But then I was transferred back to my old unit. I never found out whether the game took place.'

Schweninger's eyebrows lifted. 'From you? Then you would know who my opponent was to have been.'

Meissner looked from Schweninger to Clément. Understanding dawned on both men.

'Are you gentlemen ready to order?' the waiter asked.

17.

Ruy López

May 1944

SS Officers' quarters, Konzentrationslager Auschwitz-I

On Sunday evening, Meissner was in his quarters in the *Stammlager* half listening to a programme of light music on the wireless. The music was doing nothing to improve his mood. *I ought to be celebrating*, he thought. Before leaving, Gruppenführer Glücks had commended him both for his efforts to improve morale and for the results of his work with the satellite camps. Added to this, Liebehenschel had been as good as his word and had recommended him for promotion to Hauptsturmführer, which Glücks had been happy to confirm. He had also been given a week's leave.

If it had been longer, he might have attempted to get to Toulouse to see his old comrade, Peter Sommer. The truth was, he was ambivalent about going home. He felt changed by the war, tempered and reshaped in its furnace, and the old certainties that he had once happily shared with his parents and his fiancée now seemed distant and unimportant. All the same, he felt he should spend a few days with them. It worried him that he hadn't heard from them for a couple of weeks, though with the bombing, disruption of the postal service was becoming more frequent.

On top of that, he was sure somebody had been looking through his journal. It could only be Oberhauser. His servant denied it, of course, but Meissner could not shake off his suspicion, despite the reputation for honesty that the Bible-worms enjoyed. In future, he would make sure to keep it locked away.

Now, Oberhauser was folding his clothes prior to packing them. Knowing that it was practically impossible for his servant to write home, Meissner had offered to take a letter back to his family for him. His servant was such an odd character; Meissner could not understand his stubborn devotion to his incomprehensible religion. 'Why,' he had asked, 'do you not simply say that you no longer hold your beliefs? That is all that is required for you to be able to go home. Nobody will care if you continue with your beliefs, as long as you do it in private.'

But Oberhauser had been adamant. 'Jehovah's Witnesses are commanded to live in the truth,' he had replied. 'If I did as you suggest, it would be a lie. Better that I should lose my life in the service of Jehovah than to even pretend to turn my back on Him.'

Oberhauser was sewing the insignia of Meissner's new rank onto his uniforms when Eidenmüller arrived to inform his superior that Oberscharführer Hustek had departed for Berlin earlier that day. Meissner took it as a subtle reminder that it was time for him to make good on the wager he had made on Brossman to win.

'It all went so well,' Meissner observed, 'until the end.'

'You mean the wrong man won, sir?'

Meissner smiled wryly. He wondered where Eidenmüller's unconscious knack of lightening an atmosphere came from. He went into the bedroom to retrieve his wallet, passing Oberhauser on the way. 'Did you hear about our little tournament, Oberhauser?' The servant nodded. 'No doubt you disapprove that Unterscharführer Eidenmüller made so much money out of it?'

121

'It's not my place to approve or disapprove, sir.'

Meissner returned to the sitting area and counted a number of notes into Eidenmüller's hand.

'Did you know, sir, that chess is also played in the camp by the prisoners?'

Meissner regarded his servant with surprise. It was rare for Oberhauser to volunteer anything without being spoken to directly.

'By the prisoners? No, I didn't. Where on earth would they get a chess set from?'

The servant held his sewing up to the light to check the stitching. 'I couldn't say, sir.'

'I assume it is the *Blockältesten* and *Kapos* who play?'

'No, sir. It's mainly the politicals and some of the Jews.'

'The Jews? Really? I wouldn't have thought they'd have the strength.'

'No, sir, I suppose not. But they say that one of the Jews is so good his talent is unnatural. I heard one of the *Blockältesten* say he was unbeatable.'

'Unbeatable, eh?' Meissner found the idea highly amusing. 'What do you think of that, Eidenmüller? It wouldn't be too healthy for your gambling enterprise if there really *was* a player who was unbeatable, would it?'

Eidenmüller smiled broadly. The chess tournament had indeed made him a lot of money. 'Oh, I wouldn't say that, sir. Nobody's unbeatable, especially not a Jew. After all, it's us who're the master race, not them.'

'Sounds to me like you think we ought to issue a challenge.'

'Definitely, sir. Can't have a Jew going round thinking he's unbeatable, can we?'

'No,' Meissner agreed, 'I don't suppose we can.'

*

1962

Amsterdam

The conversation over lunch was polite, if reserved. Schweninger said little as the other men talked about their time in Auschwitz, but ate heartily.

'I always wondered,' Meissner said, as the waiter cleared their plates, 'why people called you "Watchmaker".'

Emil looked at him, surprised. 'Because I made and repaired watches. Before I was sent to Auschwitz, I had a shop in Paris. Then, at the camp, because I had those skills and could speak German, I was put to work in a technical workshop. Word got about, and before long I was repairing watches for the SS guards and the civilian supervisors.'

Schweninger's disbelief resurfaced. 'You spoke German?'

'I grew up in Metz.' Emil took a swallow of beer. 'It was only later that I moved to Paris. Although my family was French, until I was six, Metz was part of Germany. In the 1930s, there were many in Metz who wished they were still under German rule and who wanted to follow the example of the National Socialists regarding how they treated the Jews. He paused. 'One day my mother was knocked to the ground by a group of men wearing swastika armbands. They screamed at her that she was a filthy Jew and that the time when the Jews got what was coming to them was fast approaching. Even though the men were arrested, my mother was very frightened. We decided it was time for us to leave.'

His words were followed by an awkward silence. Neither German could meet Emil's gaze.

Schweninger mumbled, 'Yes, I suppose it could not have been very easy for you, but things were worse in Germany.'

'Worse?' Emil snapped. 'Worse for whom?'

Schweninger bowed his head, embarrassed. 'For the Jews. Things were bad for everyone, but for the Jews…'

Gently, Meissner tried to steer the conversation. 'I can imagine things must have been awful. But still, it must have been a difficult decision to pack up your entire family and leave.'

'It was not such a difficult decision. My father had died in the war, fighting for the Kaiser. He even won an Iron Cross. My sisters both died from influenza after the war. There was only myself and my mother. We sold the family pawnbroking business and I set myself up as a watchmaker in Paris, near the Gare Montparnasse. It was there that I met my wife.'

1935
Paris

Emil adored Paris. After the dour, narrow streets of Metz it was open, bright and exciting. He and his mother had taken an apartment off the Boulevard Garibaldi, with its overhead Metro line, not far from the shop he was renting in Montparnasse.

After two years, the business was starting to take off, and an expanding coterie of discerning clients was sending family and friends to buy watches made by the young master craftsman from Metz. Emil was also gaining recognition in Parisian chess circles. That had not been so easy – there were some who did not welcome Jews, but his uncanny brilliance won many people over.

But, for once, chess was not the centre of his life. The twenty-three-year-old Emil had become a regular at Le Chat Noir, a jazz club off the Place d'Anvers. Jazz was not the only attraction. There was a girl, Rosa. She was like no woman he had ever met before. She was intelligent, witty and overflowing with a simple, infectious joy. Emil was in love.

Le Chat Noir was not like its bigger rival, Moulin Rouge, with its extravagant burlesques and tableaux. Patrons of Le Chat went there for two things – the heady beat of jazz, and to dance as if their very lives depended on it.

One night in September, dripping with the joyous perspiration of dancing, Emil ordered champagne for his circle of friends.

'Champagne?' Rosa said, her eyes sparkling. 'That's extravagant.'

'Tonight I feel like being extravagant,' Emil said, smiling first at Rosa, then at everybody else. 'Tonight is the most important night of my life.'

'I agree that the news that Duke Ellington is coming back to Paris is a reason for champagne,' somebody said, 'but surely that doesn't make it the most important night of your life.'

'It's my birthday, too,' Emil said.

'Your birthday?'

A waiter arrived with two bottles of champagne, another with a tray of glasses. With a flourish of gushing froth the waiter poured until all had a glass. Somebody began to sing 'Happy Birthday'. In an instant the entire audience had taken it up, then a clarinet and a muted trumpet, and within moments the whole band was playing it. Everybody was laughing and cheering and toasting in pure, hedonistic rapture.

Rosa pulled Emil to her and kissed him. 'You never told me it was your birthday,' she said quietly, her lips against his ear. 'I didn't get you a present.'

Eyes bright with happiness, Emil said, 'The best present you could give me would be to make me the happiest man alive.'

Rosa's eyes widened as Emil went down on one knee. The band was still following its own unfettered variations of 'Happy Birthday' and he had to shout over them: 'Rosa, will you marry me?'

She took his face in her hands. Tears started, tears of joy. She couldn't hold them back. 'Marry you?' She pretended to hesitate, until she saw uncertainty playing on his face. Her beautiful, full lips parted in the widest of smiles. 'You idiot. Yes, of course I'll marry you.' She laughed.

Emil got to his feet. He waved at a waiter. 'More champagne,' he shouted. 'Listen, everyone! We're getting married! Rosa has no idea what she's letting herself in for, but we're getting married.'

The next day he had told his mother. He had expected her to share his enthusiasm.

'Married?' she said, as if she couldn't believe it. 'You're getting married?'

Emil was so excited he couldn't keep still. He smiled and nodded and played with his place setting, unfolding and folding his napkin. 'Yes, Maman. Married.'

But his mother did not share his excitement; she did not leave her place to kiss and congratulate her son. Instead, she said, 'And who is this girl you're getting married to? What do you know about her?'

'Only that she's the most beautiful woman I have ever seen. I love her, and she loves me. That's all that matters.'

His mother tut-tutted and shook her head. 'But what do you know about her family? Is she Jewish?'

With that question the joy inside Emil seemed to shrivel away. 'No, Maman, she's not Jewish. She's a Catholic.'

'A Catholic, you say? And what do her parents say about her marrying a Jew? What if they disapprove? How will you marry her then?'

Emil tried to smile but he had not expected his mother to take this attitude. 'She doesn't need her parents' permission to marry – she's over twenty-one. Besides, she doesn't live with them. She's from the south.'

'So you are going to marry this girl, a Catholic from the south who's

THE DEATH'S HEAD CHESS CLUB

gone past the right age for marrying and who doesn't live with her parents. Please don't tell me you've picked up some dancer in a cabaret and made her pregnant.'

The disapproval in his mother's voice was hard to bear. 'Maman, please don't be like this. She's not a dancer, and she's not pregnant. I hoped you would be happy for me. We're in love.'

'Hmph,' his mother snorted. 'So much in love that you couldn't bring her home to meet your mother.'

'I'm bringing her home to meet you today, Maman. I beg you, please don't be difficult, for my sake. Once you get to know her you'll love her as much as I do, I promise.'

His mother reached a hand across the table to touch his. 'You are my son, all I have left in the world. Naturally, what I want is for you to be happy. But there are so many things that need to be sorted out. For starters, where will you get married – will it be in a synagogue or in a church?'

'You are right, of course.' Emil took his mother's hand and squeezed it reassuringly. 'There are many things that need to be sorted out. But for now let us put them all to one side while you and Rosa get to know one another.'

In the end, their union was blessed in neither church nor synagogue: they settled for a civil ceremony followed by a small reception in a restaurant owned by one of Emil's friends. His mother's reluctance thawed over the months and her fondness for her daughter-in-law seemed genuine.

For their honeymoon, Emil took Rosa to Switzerland, to Basle, where he introduced her to Walter Nohel, now in his late sixties, to whom Emil, at the age of fourteen, had been apprenticed.

'Meister Nohel taught me to play chess,' Emil told her. 'Most people think that chess is merely a game, but it is more than that. It was created by the angels to please God.'

Nohel had also introduced Emil to a deeper understanding of his own religion, to the Kabbalah; something Emil had never spoken about, even to his mother. It was in his contemplation of the Kabbalah that he had found the most profound revelations about the game of chess – how it connected him with the divine thoughts of angels and how he could draw on their strengths when he played.

That there was a close bond of affection between apprentice and master was plain to see. One evening, at dinner, Nohel said, 'I have been thinking about retiring. I have had a reasonable offer for my business from Adolf Boeckh. You remember, he has that place on the corner of Koenigstrasse.'

Emil remembered it only too well. Its windows were always brightly lit and the merchandise festooned with trinkets and gewgaws, 'lacking in taste and decorum' his master had always said, calling it 'Boeckh's Bazaar'. And now it seemed that Nohel's elegant establishment would suffer the same dreadful fate.

It seemed obvious that his master was tempted by the offer, but was most reluctant to see his life's work come to nothing. 'How are you finding Paris?' Nohel asked. 'Is your business prospering?'

'Better than I could have hoped for. I have an excellent location in Montparnasse, and a clientele that is growing steadily.'

'And a reputation,' Rosa added.

'Of course,' Nohel agreed sagely. 'But would you not consider coming back to Basle? I would much rather hand the business over to you than to that nincompoop, Boeckh.' He regarded his former apprentice hopefully. 'It is well established and profitable, and I wouldn't expect you to pay me out all in one go – you could buy the business in stages, over a few years.'

He was smiling now, warming to the idea. 'Don't give me an answer now; take time to think about it. Come back and see me again before you return to Paris, eh?'

Later, Emil and Rose talked about it. It was tempting, but Basle was no match for Paris.

'Is there even a Le Chat Noir in Basle?' Rosa asked.

'If there is a Le Chat Noir in Basle, it must be well hidden,' replied Emil. 'So well hidden that I was here for seven years and still I could not find it. Basle is probably the dullest city in the world. After Metz,' he added.

1962

Amsterdam

'It seems quite extraordinary that in the midst of so much privation you managed to play chess.'

Schweninger's words brought a sharp look from Meissner. 'I assure you it's quite true.'

'Please don't misunderstand me. I'm not questioning the veracity of Herr Clément's story. All I'm saying is that it's extraordinary, that it seems almost an extravagance, in a place where there was no room for such things.'

'I don't think it's possible to understand unless you were there,' Clément said. 'Everything was extraordinary. The mere fact of survival was extraordinary. The depths of deprivation we suffered were unbelievable. Many times I have asked myself the question, "How can men be so lacking in pity that they can subject their fellows to such brutality?" Yet it happened every day.' He shivered. 'Different people did different things to survive. I played chess.' He looked at the German. 'I wonder what you would have done if it had been you instead of me.'

'Since I was not there, it is hardly a fair question. I'm sure I would have been able to find something.'

'Find something? Like what?' As Schweninger shrugged, floundering, still Emil pressed him: 'No, I really want to know.' His voice took on a commanding tone. 'Tell me – how exactly do you think you would have survived?'

Schweninger coloured. 'You're not the only one who managed to survive,' he retorted. 'You ask me what I would have done – I would have conformed. Followed the rules. Kept my nose clean.'

Clément smiled. 'Followed the rules?' He shook his head. 'Like I said, it's not possible to understand if you were not there.'

Schweninger appealed to Meissner. 'Well, I was not there and that can't be changed. Herr Clément says it's not possible for me to understand.'

Meissner signalled to the waiter to bring coffee. 'I'm not sure it's possible for anyone really to understand the paradox of Auschwitz. Even those who were there.'

'The paradox? What paradox?'

'The conditions in Auschwitz were appallingly degrading, yet prisoners and guards alike came to accept them as normal. It was as though we had entered another world, where the normal rules of civilization were suspended. The prisoners were utterly at the mercy of those in any sort of authority. You might expect there would have been some sort of solidarity among them as a result, but that was not the case. The need to survive was so acute that some prisoners would prey on their fellows without giving it a second thought. And yet . . .' The priest paused while the waiter placed cups before them.

'And yet?' Schweninger urged.

'And yet there were places where the human spirit continued to burn brightly. That was why the Gestapo were there in force – to extinguish all hope before it could take hold. But they could never put it out completely.' He lifted a cup to his lips but put it back down without drinking. 'And that is why I think Herr Clément played chess in Auschwitz, because, for him, it was an affirmation of his humanity.'

Schweninger turned to Emil. 'Is that true?'

Emil sighed. It seemed plausible, but was it true? With a shake of his head he replied, 'I really don't know.'

Schweninger frowned, and ran a hand through his hair. 'Tell me,' he said, 'how it was that the two of you came to meet.'

'You need to be a little more patient,' Meissner replied, 'or you won't understand the extraordinary circumstances that brought us together.'

18.

AHLHAUSEN'S OPENING

May 1944

Konzentrationslager Auschwitz-III, Monowitz

Bodo Brack had not merely survived in Auschwitz for two years; he had
thrived.

During the Weimar years,* Brack had made a good living organizing
muscle for the Social Democrats for their brawls with both the Communists and the Nazis. He did not care for politicians and their posturing; all
that concerned him was what he could make from them. In 1929, sensing
a bigger game was to be had in Berlin, he had left Hamburg for the capital.
Joseph Goebbels had been appointed Gauleiter† for the city – an entirely
unofficial position until the Nazis came to power – and had immediately
started a vendetta against the chief of police, Isidor Weiss. Misjudging the
mood in the city, Brack had decided the greatest profit was to be made
from the Communists, who were being bankrolled by Stalin.

---

* The period of democratic government in Germany from the end of the First
World War to the enabling Act in March 1933 by which the Reichstag granted
dictatorial powers to Hitler and, as a democratic body, voted itself out of existence.
† During this period, when the Nazis were aiming for electoral success, a Gauleiter
was no more than a regional Nazi party leader. The Gauleiter of Berlin was a key
position if the Nazis were to make inroads in the capital. Nazi tactics included
attempts to discredit every element of the Weimar government, including the
police, who would often try to prevent Nazi actions against their political rivals.

In the summer of 1931, the Communist *politburo* in Berlin decided that a deliberate provocation would tip the balance in their favour. The police were thought by many to be the puppets of the Social Democrats and were unpopular in Communist areas. An example was to be made. In August, a car stopped outside the Babylon Cinema near the Bülowplatz. Two men got out and gunned down three policemen.

The Communists waited for the popular uprising to happen, but they underestimated Goebbels' ability to use the crisis to his advantage. He put on the mantle of righteous outrage: it was intolerable, he said, that law and order had so declined that policemen doing their simple duty of protecting the citizens of Berlin could be gunned down with impunity. He promised swift justice.

The full weight of the Nazi network of informers was put behind discovering the identities of the killers. Within days, the newsstands proclaimed that three men were wanted for murder: Bodo Brack, Erich Mielke, and a third, as yet unnamed, man. The reward for information leading to their capture was huge.

Mielke, a high-ranking member of the Communist Party, was spirited out of Berlin to Moscow. Brack had no such luck.

It was not the police who found him, but Nazi Brownshirts. While relations between Goebbels and the police chief might have thawed over this matter, the Gauleiter was not prepared to share the credit for apprehending one of the killers. Brack was in an apartment in the Fischerkiez district. In twos and threes, the Brownshirts made their way there, their uniforms concealed under overcoats. Despite the hot weather, nobody noticed how strange this was. When the building was stormed, Brack received a brutal beating, but was nonetheless delivered to police headquarters alive.

In court, the prosecutor demanded the death penalty, but the judge was a Communist sympathizer. Brack received a life sentence with hard labour.

When the Nazis came to power, they proved to have long memories. In 1936 they established a concentration camp north of Berlin where their political opponents could be incarcerated away from public view. One day, Brack was brought from his cell and handed into the custody of two men in black SS uniforms. He was taken to Sachsenhausen. There his head was shaved and he was given new prison clothes: a coarse, blue-striped uniform with a green triangular patch on the breast and a prison number beneath: 11442. He still wore that number.

The SS understood that the most efficient way to operate a concentration camp was to get selected prisoners to run the camp for them. They created a system of *Ältesten*, or elders, who would manage the living quarters, and *Kapos*, who would supervise the labour squads. These *Prominenten* would be given privileges but would keep them only by maintaining an iron control over their fellow prisoners. They would do anything to avoid losing their positions. If ever they were returned to the status of an ordinary prisoner, their lives would be short indeed as their fellow inmates exacted revenge. The system resulted in extremes of violence as the *Ältesten* and *Kapos* competed to curry favour with their SS masters, who imposed few limits on their brutality.

If the Nazis thought that incarceration in Sachsenhausen would be the end of Brack, they were mistaken. He discovered that among the prisoners, those with a green triangle could prosper. Greens were convicted criminals. They fared much better than prisoners with red triangles, the Communists, or homosexuals or Jews. In the camp, Brack discovered his natural milieu. It was as if somebody had been able to enter his mind and, on finding his greatest aptitude, had created for him the perfect playground. Instinctively, he knew how to make the system work for him.

Where the Communists refused to cooperate with the camp authorities on principle, and the SS loathed the homosexuals and Jews, criminals like Brack became natural collaborators, and he rose rapidly in the camp's perverse hierarchy. In 1942, in return for a promise to commute his sentence from life to fifteen years, he agreed to be moved from Sachsenhausen to Auschwitz.

Brack started as a *Kapo* in the original Auschwitz camp, the *Stammlager*, but things did not turn out as he had expected. Brack's record – suggesting Communist sympathies – had come with him. In the Nazi pantheon of hatred, this was almost as bad as being a Jew. He was taken to an interrogation room in the punishment block.

Like most of the buildings in the *Stammlager*, the punishment block was brick built, and two storeys high. Brack was taken up unlit stairs to the upper floor. Dark stains on the bare walls and concrete floor bore witness to what he could expect. Two SS men strapped him into a heavy chair.

He had been there for about twenty minutes with a single guard for company when the door opened and a man entered: a dark, thick-set man with a heavily lined face, and thick, greasy hair. Klaus Hustek was Gestapo, and a Communist-hater of the highest order.

As soon as Brack saw him, he recognized someone with as little regard for his fellow man as he had himself.

'How is it,' Hustek asked, in a hushed voice, 'that you have managed to insinuate yourself into this camp as a Green, when you are a known Communist terrorist?'

'Herr Scharführer,' Brack replied, trying to keep his voice calm, 'I was convicted of murder. I did not kill because of any political convictions, but because I was paid to do it. I have no interest in politics,' he added.

His response earned him a hard slap across the face. 'No lies, Brack. Understand? I can tell when you're lying. Now tell me, who did you bribe to get the green triangle?'

The Scharführer seated himself and lit a cigarette, all the while staring at the prisoner with unblinking, heavy-lidded eyes.

'Nobody, Herr Scharführer,' Brack protested. 'How could I bribe anybody? What would I have that anybody would want?'

Hustek made the slightest of gestures and the guard hit Brack from behind with a cane, raising an angry weal on his right cheek. A nod, and the blow was repeated; then again, and again.

Brack tried to pull away from the blows, but it was futile. In under a minute, his face had become a bleeding, purple mess.

'That's enough.'

A bucket of water was thrown over the prisoner.

Hustek took short, thoughtful puffs on his cigarette as he gazed at his prisoner. Brack's attention flitted between the guard, who now stood beside the Scharführer, and the window that looked across to a similar barrack block perhaps twenty metres away.

The Gestapo man's voice brought him back. 'You know, it does not do to make an enemy of me.' His voice was quiet. In different circumstances it could almost have been mistaken for being friendly.

Brack tried to speak but his throat was thick with fear and his mouth full of blood. Fearing to spit it onto the floor, he had swallowed. Forcing a cough, he replied, 'Please believe me, Herr Scharführer, I have been in Sachsenhausen since 1936, and nearly four years in Spandau before that. I am not a Communist, and I have not bribed anybody.'

Hustek ground out his cigarette butt beneath his jackboot. 'Today is your lucky day. Today I believe you.' He raised his face to look directly at the man strapped to the chair. 'But I want you to be very clear about something – from now on, you belong to me. Every breath you draw in this camp will be at my pleasure. I will permit you to live, but in return you will do something for me. You will be my eyes and ears wherever you go in this camp, and you will report to me everything you see and hear. Is this understood?'

'Yes, Herr Scharführer.'

Hustek held a hand out to the guard and was handed the cane. With a back-handed swipe he brought it across Brack's already battered face. 'I did not hear you properly, Brack. What did you say?'

Brack spat a gobbet of blood onto the floor and shouted, 'I said yes! I will do anything you ask.'

'Good.' Hustek stood and walked to the door. Opening it, he said to the guard, 'Have him assigned to Block 14. It is a rat's nest of Polish Commu-nists.' He turned to Brack. 'I want results, and I want them fast.'

Delivering the results Hustek had wanted was easy. Brack's reputation as a Communist who had killed three police stooges and the obvious evi-dence that he had been badly beaten meant it was not difficult to get the Poles to trust him. Within a fortnight, six of them were lined up against the wall outside the punishment block and shot.

Brack did not lose any sleep over it. For the next year it became his task to work his way into the confidence of new Polish prisoners as they entered the camp. He was not looking only for Communists: Hustek wanted information about the Polish underground, the black market, smuggling rings – anything, and Brack delivered. Yet there was no respect between him and the Gestapo man. Brack had a nose for how people felt about him and he knew that Hustek considered him scum. His opinion of Hustek was the same. He hated Hustek for the hold he had on him, and in the long darkness of winter nights he schemed endlessly about the day he would get his revenge. When Hustek was promoted to Oberscharführer, he gave Brack one of the vouchers that the *Prominenten* could use in the camp brothel. Brack got an hour with a Polish whore and cursed Hustek savagely for it.

In August 1943, while the Battle of Kharkov was at its height, Brack was transferred to the Monowitz camp. He was surprised at how far it was from the *Stammlager* and he calculated that Hustek would never bother to make a special trip all the way to the other side of Oświęcim to find him.

Despite being in thrall to the Gestapo man, Brack had not done badly, and he was determined to do even better for himself in Monowitz. Better than any of his fellow Greens he knew how to organize a gang of thugs and, before long, his status as unofficial Führer of the camp underworld was secure.

Nearly a year later, one of Brack's fellow *Prominenten* told him about a Jew who had given him a watch so he could play chess. At first, Brack was merely curious, but when he learned the Jew was from his own block, he became angry. He could not allow such a slight to go unpunished: the Jew had to be taken down a peg or two. He deserved the beating he got. But now the Jew puzzled him. Brack could understand that people would want something to distract them from the constant misery that existence as a *Häftling* entailed, but chess? The Poles played it, he knew, and some of the politicals, but a Jew? He should have been too exhausted at the end of every day. In truth, Brack's refusal to allow Clément to play had been more about asserting his control over the Frenchman, but he had soon started to wonder how he might make a profit from this foolish game.

Like himself, many of the *Prominenten* spent much of their time in idleness, desperately bored, amusing themselves by baiting prisoners and occasionally getting a ticket for the brothel. Now, he wondered if it was possible to get them interested in chess.

If he had been in the *Stammlager* he could have organized items from Kanada to give as prizes, but the camp economy in Monowitz was confined within such tight boundaries that, apart from brothel tickets, it was hard to think of anything that his fellow Greens would value enough. The *Häftlinge* were another matter: almost anything was of value to them as long as they could exchange it for food, but that wasn't going to be much use to him. No, try as he might, he could think of no way to turn the game to his advantage.

He sent for the Watchmaker. 'Give me the watch you promised and you can play your stupid game.'

The Frenchman held out something wrapped in a piece of cloth. 'I was already on my way,' he said.

Brack opened it slowly. It was a pocket watch. 'You gave Muckermann a wristwatch,' he snapped.

Emil knew he had to choose his words carefully; he had been dreading this moment. 'I beg your pardon, Herr Brack. I assumed a man of your eminence would prefer something more fitting to his stature.' His heart had sunk when the Polish foreman had given him the ancient timepiece. But it had polished up quite well, and although the case was brass, not gold, it had a handsome crest engraved upon it, and a pleasant chime that Emil had managed to restore. Emil reached across to demonstrate. 'It chimes every hour,' he said, turning the hands to make it sound.

Brack actually smiled. This set him apart. It also told the other *Prominenten* that the Watchmaker belonged to him. And it was then that it suddenly occurred to him how he *could* benefit from chess: the *Häftlinge* were all slave labourers – slaves without owners, but that would change. There must be many good chess players in the camp. He would make it his business to find them, and then he would set them against one another, like fighting cocks – no, not fighting cocks, something more refined than that…like *racehorses*. And the games would become entertainments that he, Bodo Brack, would put on, an affirmation of his dominance.

1962

Amsterdam

Schweninger leaned forward, puzzled. 'Let me be sure I understand,' he said. 'The prisoners who played chess were slaves, playing at the orders of this brute, for the entertainment of his fellow criminals…like the gladiators of ancient Rome?'

'Precisely,' Emil admitted.

'I would have refused to play,' the German stated flatly.

Meissner rolled his eyes. Emil said, 'I have not the slightest doubt that that is exactly what *you* would have done, but it would have changed nothing, and I would most likely have been killed.'

'Then I would not have played as well as I could have. I would have ruined their sport.'

Emil looked hard at the German. 'I was not playing for their pleasure. I was playing for *me*. I was playing because chess was something the SS could not take from me. With or without chess, we were slaves. This way, at least, I got to play the sublime game.'

Schweninger sniffed and shook his head dismissively. 'This Brack.

Do you know what happened to him after the war?'

'Yes. But that would be getting ahead of myself. You said you wanted to know how the bishop and I met for the first time.'

Meissner raised his hand a little as he shook his head. 'Please. I would be most grateful if you would stop calling me "bishop". My name is Paul.'

'And my name is Emil, though you persist in calling me "Watchmaker".'

Meissner winced. 'Yes. You are right. I am sorry.'

Emil nodded curtly. 'So, I first met *Paul* in late May or early June—'

'I can tell you the date exactly. It was a Sunday. The twenty-first of May 1944.'

'How strange that you can remember so precisely.'

'Not really. It was my mother's birthday.'

'My mother was killed in Auschwitz. Did you know *that*, Paul?' Emil's voice cut through the café; several diners turned to stare. 'She celebrated her last birthday in 1943,' he continued, more softly.

A silence fell between them.

The exchange had made Schweninger feel uncomfortable. At a loss for something to say, he glanced at his watch. 'My God,' he said. 'Have you seen the time? I've missed my train.'

Instinctively, Emil and Paul checked their watches. 'Dear Lord,' the priest murmured, distractedly.

Schweninger scratched his cheek thoughtfully. 'Herr Clément...' His voice thickened and he coughed to clear it. 'Would you be offended if I offered my condolences?'

Emil's eyes were now closed, but he gave a slight jerk of his head.

Schweninger's chair scraped on the floor as he pushed it back from the table. 'I'm sorry, but I must leave. If I don't get back to my hotel, they will let my room go.'

Meissner reached across the table to touch Schweninger's sleeve. 'Don't worry about that. It's my fault. I insist you stay with me at the Krijtberg.'

'Is that a hotel?'

The question provoked a surge of anxiety in the priest: he wanted Schweninger to remain in Amsterdam, for now, at least. 'No,' he replied. 'It's a place run by my order. It is a church with a house attached, which is usually occupied by priests like me, home on leave from the missions. There are only two of us there at the moment – the parish priest and myself. Most of the bedrooms are empty. It would be no trouble to put you up.' He breathed a quick prayer that his powers of persuasion would prove to be as strong as ever. 'The rooms are perhaps a little spartan compared with your hotel, but they're clean, and the housekeeper gives us a hearty breakfast each morning. What do you say? Will you give it a try?'

19.

The Najdorf Variation

Emil made his way back to his hotel. Meissner had asked him to meet them later, but he was not sure he wanted to.

The late afternoon sun was bright, but gave little warmth as Emil stood on a bridge over the Singel Canal, wondering what he was doing. Schweninger and Meissner had both been Nazis, committed to the dream of a German Empire lording it over the rest of Europe. Slavery had been the least of many crimes, and yet Schweninger had immediately protested that he would never have submitted to it, as so many had.

Did he have a point? For the life of him, Emil did not know. The realisation shocked him: *he did not know.* Until today there had been a sharp clarity in his consciousness, especially in his hatred of the Germans, that he had nurtured, as a parent would a child, until it was almost the only thing that gave him any meaning. Hatred and chess: was that the sum total of his existence? *Meissner is right*, he thought grudgingly. *What kind of a life is that?*

He stared at the water below him, and saw a stranger staring back at him from its murky stillness. He heard the voice of Yves, as clearly as if he were standing beside him: 'One of us has to live to get out of here, if only to tell the rest of the world what is happening.'

Well, he had done that. He had fulfilled his duty to the thousands who had perished in Auschwitz. Nobody knew for sure how many they were:

143

at his trial, Kommandant Höss had claimed the death toll ran into millions; so many that the numbers were distant, abstract – they were not real people, they were figures to be entered into a calculating machine, like an exercise in accounting. And Emil had done his duty. He had testified. He had written his book. He had borne witness to the horror... Still it was not enough. Nothing he did could free him from the aching loss and guilt. Meissner was right about that too, he realized now. It was not enough to bear witness. He had to make people understand the truth of existence in a death camp; how it penetrated every consciousness, poisoning every experience, twisting every thought.

Painful as it was, Emil decided he would tell his story to Schweninger. Then perhaps the German would understand. And perhaps he, Emil, would find some peace.

Perhaps.

Tuesday, 6 June 1944
Konzentrationslager Auschwitz-II, Birkenau
Something terrible is happening. The camp senses it but cannot see it. It is hidden, concealed in unknown depths. The camp has felt this pulse of pain and terror before, but never with such intensity, repeating over and over. The camp is searching for the source, determined to find it, frantically extending tendrils of consciousness along the pathways and between the many huts of Birkenau. It is transmitted through the concrete posts that have their roots deep in the earth, and along miles of electrified wire; there is a whisper of it in the railway siding where, every day now, the cattle cars unload their human cargo.

We follow the rails inwards from the arch, beneath which the trains enter the camp. Ahead, there is a grove of birch trees. Their silvery trunks reflect the sun to make patterns on the grass below. We listen. All we can hear is the rustling of the leaves and the sigh of an early summer breeze. Then we see them: a column of people standing quietly in the birch grove, queuing outside a low, red-brick building dominated by a large chimney. Thick smoke pours into the sky, a black stain on its pristine summer blue. There is an unfamiliar smell, cloying and unpleasant. Around the building, sheltered by the trees from prying eyes, are grassy lawns, and the people are there: men, women, and children, patiently waiting their turn to descend into a stairwell that takes them below ground.

They proceed in a calm, orderly fashion, with no pushing or jostling. They have been told they have been brought to this place to take a shower.

'A shower?' a voice asks incredulously. It is a woman. Her nervousness makes her voice a little too loud. She did not intend for the SS men who stand around with dogs and machine guns to hear her. She is suspicious of the Germans. They are not known for their good treatment of Jews, and the set-up seems rather elaborate for something as simple as taking a shower.

Smiling indulgently, an officer calls to her. 'Where have you come from?'

'Debrecen.' The officer's eyebrows lift as if to repeat the question. 'In Hungary,' the woman explains.

'And how much time did you spend on the train?'

'Six days.'

He nods sagely. 'Six days cooped up with I don't know how many other people and you don't need a shower?'

Despite all that their experience has taught them about the SS, people nearby cannot help but smile.

'We are not barbarians, you know,' the officer continues. He looks more closely at the woman, who wishes now she had never opened her mouth.

She is young, in her twenties, and beneath the dirt and matted hair, she is quite attractive. 'What did you do before you came here?' he asks.

'I was a seamstress.'

'A good one?'

She blushes. 'Of course.'

'Men's or women's clothes?'

'Women's. Mostly undergarments.'

Again she is on the receiving end of his indulgent grin. 'Well, here you'll learn to make men's clothes. We are short of *good* seamstresses.' When he says 'good', he catches her eye and winks. 'We need as many as we can get to make uniforms for our troops.'

She does not seem convinced so he addresses the people nearby: 'Are there any more of you who are skilled at making clothes?' A couple of hands are raised.

The officer points at a man who is cradling a young child in his arms. 'How about you,' he says. 'What did you do?'

'I was a shoemaker.'

'Can you make military boots?'

'Of course.'

'Then you'll do well here.' The officer spreads his arms wide as if to embrace the people around him. 'We are not fools,' he says. 'We know good work when we see it, and we reward it. So let's be practical. Put away your doubts. You are in a work camp. After your shower, you will be given your assignments. I give you my word as a German officer.'

His speech is reassuring, but the people do not know that they have entered the kingdom of lies, and it is thus that the camp finds them, shuffling down concrete steps into a long underground chamber, where they are told to undress: men, women and children all together.

There are pegs with numbers where they hang their clothes. They are told to remember the number so they will be able to find their belongings afterwards. Many try to cover their nakedness with their hands as they shamble along the corridor to the shower room. There are very many of them and they are crammed in tight – too tight. Suddenly, the doors are slammed shut and there is the distinct sound of heavy bolts being shot home.

The lights go out.

Voices are heard in the darkness: 'What is happening?' Some call to their loved ones. Some start to weep. Children cry and cling to their mothers and fathers. Then there is a harsh, scraping noise from above, and a shaft of light penetrates. It reveals fearful faces staring upwards at the noise.

Above, SS men wearing gas masks have removed grilles from ducts that lead down to the shower room. In their hands they hold tins marked with a skull and crossbones. From the tins they pour granules of a powdery substance into the ducts. It falls lightly on those standing below – a fine, soft grit. It gives off a sweet, sickly smell.

The grilles are put back. Below it is dark again. Then somebody gasps: 'I can't breathe!'

Then another: 'Gas. Poison gas!'

People start to yell. Those nearest the doors hammer on them frantically, begging to be let out. There is a surge of panic towards the doors. Children and old people are crushed. Now many are screaming, especially the women and children. For a few short minutes the noise is deafening. When it abates someone can be heard saying Kaddish, the Jewish prayer for the dead. Some succumb to the poison less quickly than others, but in a matter of minutes, they are all silent, all dead.

Afterwards, the mouths of many of the victims remain open, as if their screams continued after death.

By the end of this summer day, nearly 4,000 lives have been extinguished. The only concern among the SS who have orchestrated this murder is that the corpses must be removed and burned before the next consignment arrives the following day.

All that is left in the underground chamber are the last traces of gas and rows of empty clothes hanging mute, in accusing ranks. Those, and the silence of a thousand absent voices.

A wail of grief passes through the camp at the horror it has just witnessed; a long keening wail that nobody hears: not the SS men who run the camp; not the thousands of prisoners who yet endure; not the camp orchestra which plays its absurd, cheerful tunes at the start and end of each day; not the birds that have deserted the trees that surround the camp; not the earth itself on which the camp lies.

Only the wind hears it, but it is only one cry among many, and before it can be remembered, it is lost.

1962

Kerk de Krijtberg, Amsterdam

Dinner in the presbytery was a frugal affair: onion soup followed by boiled potatoes and fried herring.

'I do enjoy herring,' Meissner said good-naturedly, 'but why did the good Lord have to give them so many blasted bones?' He grinned at Emil, pleased that the chess player had decided to return.

Schweninger was silent, chewing stolidly; as always, his appetite came first, conversation, later.

Afterwards, they retired to the same gloomy lounge where Emil had woken from his fainting spell.

'I think perhaps it's my turn to take up the story,' the priest said, offering cigarettes to his guests. 'There are two sides to every tale, after all.'

He held a taper to the glowing coals in the fireplace to get a light, then settled into an easy chair, inhaling deeply on his cigarette before starting to speak. 'You might be surprised to hear that I was not brought up to hate Jews. My parents were staunch Catholics and it was only when I was inducted into the Hitler Youth that anti-Jewish sentiments were demanded of me. But my parents never took the rhetoric too seriously, so neither did I. When I got to Auschwitz, as far as I could see, the work that the Jews were doing was badly needed by the Reich, and it did not occur to me that the new Kommandant, Sturmbannführer Bär, would object to the idea of pitting this "unbeatable" Jew' – he gestured at Emil – 'against our SS chess champions. After all, as my orderly, Eidenmüller, would have said, we couldn't have a Jew thinking he was invincible, could we?'

When neither Emil nor Schweninger commented, he continued. 'I was due to go on leave back to my family in Cologne, but when I got to the station in Oświęcim I learned that Allied bombing had severely disrupted rail traffic from Silesia to Germany, so I had to put off my journey. The following Sunday was a rest day in Monowitz, so I summoned Eidenmüller and told him I wanted to take a look at this Jewish chess marvel for myself.'

May 1944
Konzentrationslager Auschwitz-III, Monowitz
It was the first time that Meissner had entered the section of the Monowitz camp in which the prisoners were confined. At the administrative office, he learned the number of the block where *Häftling* number 163291

had his bunk. Accompanied by the *Blockführer* – an SS NCO – and Eiden-müller, he walked briskly through the camp.

At the *Blockführer*'s shout of '*Achtung!*' the inmates in the block sprang to attention.

At the rear, a small man slipped unseen into the dormitory. His eyes lit on a boy, perhaps fifteen years old, said to be Brack's *Piepel*,* though nobody mentioned it openly. The man grabbed the boy by the scruff of the neck.

'Where's Bodo?' he rasped.

'Block 39.'

'Not so loud. What's he doing there?'

'The Watchmaker is playing the one they call the Flying Dutchman.'

'Right. I need you to get him. Tell him I sent you and that there's an SS-Hauptsturmführer in his block. What he wants I don't know, but Bodo better get back here fast. Got it?'

In the day room, Meissner looked around, amazed. He had not real-ized how primitive the interiors of the blocks were. He had imagined them to be somewhat like the barracks of the SS enlisted men: basic, func-tional, but not completely bereft of any comfort. What hit him instantly was the smell. He knew that in the Buna factory many of the civilian workers used the word '*Stinkjude*' when they spoke of the camp inmates; Meissner had thought it a term of derision. It was not. It was a reference to the sickly sweet stench of men who lived packed tightly together and who had not had a proper wash for months.

'Where is the *Blockältester*?' the SS NCO roared. Nobody seemed to know.

* Teenage boys were used as personal servants by some of the *Prominenten*. Some were exploited for sexual gratification.

'Send somebody to find him,' Meissner said, before jerking his head to Eidenmüller to follow him back outside. 'Jesus Christ Almighty,' he spluttered once they were out. 'How do they manage to live like that?' The officer fished in his tunic pocket for his cigarette case.

His orderly struck a match, cupping his fingers to protect it from the breeze. 'Thank God we get plenty of fags, eh, sir? They're the only thing that makes the smell bearable.'

Before they had finished their cigarettes, they were approached by a clean-shaven prisoner. He stood to attention, pulled his cap smartly off his head and announced himself: '*Häftling* 11442, *Blockältester* Brack, Herr Hauptsturmführer. At your service.'

Meissner was astonished. It was the first time he had ever seen a prisoner wearing an immaculately clean uniform. The green triangle looked as if it could have been sewn on that morning.

Before Meissner could say anything the SS NCO joined them. 'Where the hell have you been?' he yelled. Brack did not flinch. This was another first for the officer. He had only ever seen prisoners shrink with fear whenever they were addressed by an SS man.

'Beg pardon, Herr Unterscharführer. I was…watching a game of chess.'

'*Chess?* What the fucking hell are you talking about, chess?'

'It's all right, Unterscharführer,' the officer said. 'That's why we came. I wanted to see this particular game of chess myself.' Smiling, he let the still-glowing remains of his cigarette fall at his feet and gestured for Brack to lead the way.

They followed the immaculate, blue-striped uniform for about 200 metres. Meissner noticed that Brack had well-polished boots rather than the rough wooden clogs that the rest of the inmates had to wear.

The *Blockältester* stopped at a block with a small plate bearing the number 39 nailed to its front. He pulled open its rickety wooden door. Meissner peered inside. What he saw was identical to the block they had left moments before, with a brick stove offset from the centre, and a narrow window set in the roof to let in a little light. The only difference was to his right, where a chessboard had been placed atop a wooden crate, with two men seated on smaller crates, one to either side. Crowded around them were perhaps thirty or forty men: some on the floor, some on makeshift chairs, some standing.

With a groan of rusting hinges, the door opened, flooding the interior with light. Brack held the door open for the SS men, shouting '*Achtung!*' as he did so. All eyes turned to the door. At the sight of Meissner's uniform, the prisoners sprang to their feet.

The SS NCO pushed his way to the front. 'What's the meaning of this?' he screamed. 'I'll have you all flogged!'

Meissner stood watching the scene in an almost detached way. Most of the spectators bore green triangles on their jackets, with one or two red triangles among them. The two men at the chessboard each had a red triangle over a yellow one – Jews.

The players stood rigid, eyes straight ahead. Senior officers rarely entered the prisoners' barracks. When they did, it was usually SS doctors come to make a *Selektion* of the sick and exhausted to be sent to the gas chambers. No Jewish inmate ever thought such a visit might be for their benefit. The presence of an SS officer was always an occasion for fear.

'Unterscharführer,' Meissner said crisply, 'thank you for your assistance. You have been most helpful, but I'll take it from here.' He paused and turned to Brack. '*Blockältester*, I see there is a game of chess under way. I'm a great admirer of chess, and I would like to watch the rest of the game. Tell these men to carry on as they were and to pretend that we are not here.'

1962
Kerk de Krijtberg, Amsterdam
'Is that how it happened?' Emil said. 'I had forgotten.'

Schweninger could not help himself: 'Forgotten? How could you forget something like that?'

Shaking his head slowly, Emil turned to the German. 'Only someone who had not been in Auschwitz could say such a thing. When an SS officer came to the block, the important thing was whether they were there for a *Selektion*. Fear drove all other considerations from your mind.'

Schweninger frowned. 'I do not understand what you mean by "*Selektion*".'

Keeping his eyes on the hearth, Meissner spoke in a low monotone. '*Selektionen* were how the SS carried out their mandate to maintain production in the armaments factories, while at the same time keeping the gas chambers operating. At regular intervals, SS doctors, accompanied by squads of soldiers, would be sent into the camp to pick out those who had been debilitated by ill health or starvation and who could no longer carry out the work that was required of them. They were sent to the gas chambers in Birkenau. There were so many Jews coming in on transports from all over Europe that there was never any problem replacing them.'

'And you knew about this?' Schweninger asked.

Meissner nodded, his eyes fixed on the red-glowing coals. 'Not at first, but eventually I came to realize what was happening. How could I not?'

'And you went along with it?'

'What else could I do?' Meissner shrugged, then looked up. 'At one point I tried to persuade the Kommandant that the arrangement was inefficient, that if we improved conditions for the prisoners, the productivity of the arms factories would improve. But it was made clear to me that if I persisted, I would be labelled as a Jew sympathizer and things would go badly for me.'

'Badly for you?' Clément was appalled. 'We were starving. Freezing. Exhausted. We were outcasts. The suffering inflicted on us is beyond my ability to describe. Yet you thought things could go *badly* for you? What would they have done – take away your brothel privileges?'

'I never visited the brothel,' Meissner said, stiffly. 'I tried to do what I could. Not one prisoner was sent to the gas chamber because of me. Not one.'

'How noble of you,' Clément mocked, his lip curling. 'You were still part of a system that sent innocent people to their deaths. You have blood on your hands as surely as if you had herded them into the gas chambers yourself.'

'Do not presume to think, Herr Clément, that I have not reproached myself for my failings.' The priest's voice was brittle with shame. 'And I will continue to do so for the rest of my life.'

'But still,' Schweninger said, after a pause, 'was there nothing you could have done?'

'I managed to save one life, and for me, that had to be enough.'

'And whose life did you save?'

The question was answered by Emil.

'Mine.'

20.

The Albin Countergambit

May 1944

Konzentrationslager Auschwitz-III, Monowitz

The result of the match was a foregone conclusion – the Watchmaker had defeated the Dutchman even before the arrival of the SS men, but was stringing it out for the benefit of Brack and the other *Prominenten* who had started to follow the games that were now being played.

Everyone knew that the Watchmaker belonged to Brack, but he had let it be known that he had no objection to other block elders or *Kapos* taking an inmate under their wing to pit them against his champion. But it was not Brack who had spread the word that the Frenchman was unbeatable: that was Pasinski, a Pole who claimed to have beaten the German champion in the 1936 Chess Olympiad in Munich.

Pasinski had been in the camp since the liquidation of the Warsaw ghetto in 1943. He had a gift for scrounging, and it was this that enabled him to survive when most of those who had entered the camp with him perished. Before the war, he had harnessed his natural shrewdness into a formidable talent for chess, and he had been looking forward to playing the upstart Frenchman he had heard about.

Pasinski had drawn white and made a conventional enough opening move: advancing his queen's pawn two spaces. The Watchmaker copied his move, blocking the pawn. The Pole had then advanced his queen's bishop's pawn two squares, offering a sacrifice to black. Clément had ignored the gambit and moved his king's pawn two places, to stand beside its brother. The Pole had taken this second pawn, allowing the first black pawn to then advance one place to stand before the white queen, creating a wedge in the white defence.

In only six moves, Pasinski had lost the initiative and, with it, the game. Later, he claimed to have known of the countergambit the Watchmaker had employed, but it was unheard of for it to be played at senior level – if any other player had made the same move, he would have lost, the Pole had insisted.

According to Pasinski, the Watchmaker had an insight into the thinking of his opponent that was uncanny. That was what made him unbeatable.

When the game with the Dutchman was over, Eidenmüller told Brack to have the Watchmaker brought to Meissner's office. 'But get him shaved and showered and in a clean uniform first. Is that clear?'

It was an hour before *Häftling* number 163291 found himself standing nervously to attention in the office of an SS-Hauptsturmführer.

The aroma of coffee in the room was tantalizing. The SS officer was stretched out in his chair, his feet up on the desk, watching the smoke from his cigarette as it rose slowly to the ceiling. An Unterscharführer poured coffee for the officer then took up position by the door.

After surviving nearly five months in the camp, Emil Clément knew better than to utter a word to an SS man until he had been directly addressed, and so he stood, rigid, his eyes fixed on the wall behind the officer, with a strong urge to scratch where the rough cloth of his new uniform was making his armpits itch.

1962

Kerk de Krijtberg, Amsterdam

'So you remember being summoned to his office?' Schweninger asked, indicating Meissner with a tilt of his head. 'But you had no idea why. Amazing.'

'Not so amazing,' Clément countered. 'It was merely another of the absurdities we faced every day. I guessed – after the elaborate cleansing I had been forced to endure – that it was not to inflict any punishment on me. I assumed it was probably to do with my skill at repairing watches.'

'Were you afraid?'

'Of course.' Emil shook his head in disbelief at the naivety of Schweninger's question. 'Always. Everyone who had not lost their senses was afraid. Every time you were spoken to by an SS man, it was like a game of cat and mouse. You weren't supposed to look at the SS man, but you had to, to try and guess what he wanted. You tried to work it out from how he was looking at you, or the way he was holding himself, or the way he spoke. If he was shouting you knew he was angry over something and that you were likely to get a beating. And while a beating on the spot could be painful, it was not as bad as a whipping.'

'Presumably for serious infringements of the rules?'

Clément spread his hands. 'Of course. Some men were so careless as to get mud on their trousers or lose a button from their jacket. I saw men flogged for that.'

Schweninger winced. 'But you didn't think that was what was waiting for you this time?'

The Frenchman nodded. 'No, but it was always a possibility. You feared even to speak. Anything you said could be twisted and used against you. You listened hard to try and work out whether there was some hidden meaning that you needed to understand so that you could give the answer the SS man wanted to hear, but it was almost impossible – anything you were told could be a lie, and the SS man was like a rottweiler, eager to pounce on any unguarded word and punish you for it.'

'And that was how you felt the first time we spoke?' Meissner asked, his voice barely audible.

Emil nodded.

'I'm sorry,' the priest said hoarsely. 'I had no idea.'

May 1944
Konzentrationslager Auschwitz-III, Monowitz

The Hauptsturmführer took his feet from the desk, stubbed out his cigarette in an ashtray fashioned from a shell casing and addressed the prisoner: 'Your name?'

'Clément, Herr Hauptsturmführer. Emil Clément.'

'And where are you from?'

'France.'

'I'm told you are an excellent chess player. Is that true?'

For a moment Emil's guard faltered: instead of staring at the wall, he let his gaze fall to look at the officer.

'Chess player? I'm sorry, Herr Hauptsturmführer, I don't understand.'

'It's a simple enough question. Are you a good chess player – yes or no?'

'I think so. I mean – yes, Herr Hauptsturmführer.'

'You speak good German for a Frenchman.'

'Yes, Herr Hauptsturmführer. Originally I was from Metz.'

'Almost a German, then, eh?' Grinning, the officer reached across his desk for his cup and took a sip of coffee.

Emil fixed his eyes once more on the wall.

The coffee seemed to help the officer get his thoughts in order. 'How long have you been playing chess?'

'Since I was about fourteen years old.'

'And have you ever played at national or international level?'

'No, Herr Hauptsturmführer, I have not.'

'Are you sure? That seems hard to believe, when I'm told that you have beaten at least one international-level player here in the camp.'

'Who told—?' Emil checked himself. 'It should not be so hard to believe, Herr Hauptsturmführer. Before the war it was not so easy for a Jew to get onto the French team – after the fall of France, impossible.'

'Did you know that we hold a chess tournament among the SS personnel here in Auschwitz?'

'No, Herr Hauptsturmführer. I did not know that.'

'How would you like to play against the SS?'

The question did not make sense; Emil struggled to understand it. There was always a trick question; everyone knew that. Perhaps this was it, the question that would lead to a flogging, or worse. What was the right answer? If he said yes, they would tell him he was an uppity Jewish turd and beat him for sure. The correct answer was surely no. It would show them that he knew his place; that he was not so stupid as to think of challenging the established order, even if invited to do so.

'Well?'

'It is not my place to think I could play against the SS, Herr Hauptsturmführer.'

Meissner leaned forward. 'Not play? Are you quite sure? I could make certain privileges available to you if you did.'

Emil licked his lips, his mouth suddenly dry. 'May I have permission to speak frankly, Herr Hauptsturmführer?'

The officer looked surprised that he should even ask the question. 'Please do.'

'Your privileges have no meaning for me, Herr Hauptsturmführer. How long do you think I would be able to hold on to them? And if I beat one of your SS men, I do not think I would survive for long – I would be pulled out of my work *Kommando* and beaten to death, or there would be a *Selektion* and I would be one of those sent up the chimney.'

Meissner frowned. He had not anticipated such a flat refusal of the chance of better treatment. 'So you refuse to play?'

'Respectfully, Herr Hauptsturmführer, I must.'

'What if I give an order that you must play?'

'Then I will play, Herr Hauptsturmführer, but not to win.'

Exasperated, Meissner stood. 'Are you really so deluded as to think you have a choice in this matter?'

But *Häftling* number 163291 stood his ground. 'One always has a choice, Herr Hauptsturmführer, if you are prepared to accept the consequences.'

1962

Kerk de Krijtberg, Amsterdam

'So you did refuse, after all. That took courage. Well done.'

Schweninger's words brought Emil up short. Was it approval he heard in the German's voice? 'It was not a matter of courage, Herr Schweninger,' he replied coolly, 'merely survival. I did not see how I could comply with this incredible suggestion and live.'

The German reached across and patted Emil's forearm. 'Please,' he said, his voice unexpectedly warm, 'enough of the "Herr Schweninger". Call me Willi – everybody else does.'

The clock on the mantelpiece chimed ten. Meissner looked at Emil.

'Do you have a match tomorrow?'

'No. Not until the day after.'

'Then may I offer you gentlemen a nightcap?'

His offer accepted, Meissner left the room and returned minutes later with three glasses and a bottle of Kümmel. 'It's Dutch, I'm afraid,' he said. 'Not as good as German, but not undrinkable.' He poured three generous measures. '*Prosit*,' he said.

Meissner and Schweninger clinked glasses. They held their drinks together, waiting for Emil to join the toast. Emil did not stir; instead, he stared at the colourless liquid in his glass. Meissner and Schweninger exchanged an uneasy glance.

Slowly, Emil raised his hand. '*Prosit*,' he murmured.

The men drank deeply, appreciating its satisfying warmth as it went down. 'So, where were we?' said Meissner.

Schweninger used his glass to point at Emil. 'Our friend had just refused your kind offer to play chess against the SS.' He took another sip of the liqueur. 'For which I congratulated him.' He winked at Emil then took a pack of Camels from his pocket, put one between his lips and offered the rest to his companions.

'Yes,' the priest said, taking one. 'But it was not long before he changed his mind, was it?'

21.

THE BALTIC DEFENCE

May 1944

Konzentrationslager Auschwitz-III, Monowitz

Unterscharführer Eidenmüller was furious; he could not remember the last time he had been so angry. The gall of that stinking Jewish piece of shit. Christ, no wonder everybody hated the ungrateful swine. He had stood listening to the exchange between the Hauptsturmführer and the filthy pig-fucker with growing disbelief, wanting to march across the office and give the little prick a good beating right there and then. But he knew the Hauptsturmführer wouldn't have stood for that, so he had been forced to let the bastard go. For now.

Eidenmüller made himself calm down. His boss wanted a game of chess. He would see that he got it.

He waited a week before returning to the block where the Jew had his billet. The day room was empty apart from the *Stubendienst*, who was slowly pushing a brush across the uneven floorboards. The brushstrokes quickened when the man saw who had entered.

'Where's Brack?'

The prisoner stopped what he was doing and came to attention, holding the brush pole like a rifle. The sight almost made Eidenmüller laugh. 'Block 19, Herr Unterscharführer.'

At Block 19, Eidenmüller pulled the door open and looked in. Brack

THE DEATH'S HEAD CHESS CLUB

was engaged in a desultory conversation with three other Greens. 'Brack,' Eidenmüller called. 'A quick word, if you don't mind.'

The obsequiousness Brack had shown in front of Meissner was gone. 'Yeah? What about?' he said, blinking as he came out into the bright sunlight.

'Let's go for a little walk.'

Curious, Brack fell in beside the SS man as they sauntered towards the parade ground.

'Tell me about this Jewish chess player of yours,' Eidenmüller said.

'The Watchmaker?'

'Is that what they call him? Why do they call him that?'

''Cause that's what he does. He fixes watches.'

'For the prisoners?'

Brack gave him a *Don't be so bloody stupid* look. 'What do you think?'

They continued a few paces without speaking until Eidenmüller said, 'You know, my boss wanted to set up a game between the Jew and some of our SS chess players.'

Brack stopped, astonished. 'Why would he want to do that?'

'Word's got out, Brack – know what I mean? I'm not saying it's your fault, but it's a funny thing, word getting out. Once it's out, it won't go back in again.'

'What the fuck are you talking about?'

'"Unbeatable", Brack. That's the word. Your Jew chess player. Fucking "unbeatable". Can't have that, can we? A fucking unbeatable Jew? So someone's got to beat him, only it can't be a put-up job. Everybody would know straight away if it was. So my boss wants to put him against some of our best SS chess players and, believe me, there's a couple of really good ones. Only there's a problem, isn't there?'

'A problem?'

'Yeah. The stinking little Kike doesn't want to play, does he?'

They walked on a little further.

'What is it, exactly, that you want me to do?' Brack asked.

'He's a decent sort, my boss, you know,' Eidenmüller said, ignoring the question. 'So he wouldn't take too kindly to it if he thought I had done anything to frighten his precious little Jew boy into playing. So I won't tell you what to do. You know your business. Just make sure the ungrateful little fuck agrees to play.'

'What's in it for me?'

Eidenmüller smiled broadly. 'Well, first, you get my undying gratitude. Second – when was the last time you had a decent drop of Schnapps?'

Emil and Yves are walking back to the block after evening roll call. Their progress is painfully slow. Yves has returned from the Buna factory completely spent. Every night, some prisoners are carried back by their fellows. Most of these will be earmarked for *Selektion*.

For days now, Emil has been expecting his friend to be one of them.

'Let's try to get you into the *Krankenbau*,'* Emil urges Yves. 'You can say you fell and twisted your ankle and that it can hardly support your weight. They won't be able to prove otherwise. The doctors are Jewish. They'll take pity on you. All you need is a few days of rest, and you'll be a new man.'

His words are hollow and he knows it, but, to his surprise, Yves agrees and joins the long queue outside the sick bay. For days, he has spoken of nothing but food; he dreams constantly of feasting. Yet when Emil offers him half his bread ration, Yves will not take it.

* Infirmary.

Emil helps his friend to sit on the ground and lean back against the wooden wall. 'Give me your bowl,' he says, 'and I'll fetch your soup ration. I'll be back before you know it.'

It is not far from the K-B to their block. As Emil gets to the front of the line, however, the prisoner doling out the soup calls out: 'Here he is. Tell Bodo.'

Emil is pulled out of the line and into the day room. At a word from Brack everyone clears out, leaving only Emil, Brack, his pimp, Widmann, and half a dozen heavies.

It is obvious that something is wrong.

'You've got a fucking nerve, you ungrateful piece of Kike shit,' says Brack.

Emil does not reply.

'Who the fuck do you think you are?'

Still Emil gives no answer.

Brack shouts, almost screaming. 'I said – who the fuck do you think you are, you stinking stupid Jew!'

And Emil knows he is going to die.

1962

Kerk de Krijtberg, Amsterdam

The housekeeper put her head round the lounge door. 'If you don't need me for anything else, Father, I'll be off.'

'Of course. Did you make up the bed for Mijnheer Schweninger?'

'Two beds, Father, I made up two beds – I thought you had two guests staying. And I've laid breakfast out ready in the morning for you.'

'Thank you.'

'Only I won't be in tomorrow, as it's my day off.'

'Thank you, Mrs Brinckvoort. I'm sure we'll manage splendidly.' As the housekeeper closed the door behind her, Meissner turned to Emil. 'You heard what she said – there's a room for you if you want it. Why don't you move out of your hotel and stay here for the rest of the tournament? You and Willi would probably enjoy picking over the games together.'

'Just a minute,' Schweninger interjected. 'I only agreed to stay here for one night, not for the duration.'

'As you wish. It was just a thought.' Meissner picked up the coffee pot. It was empty. 'More coffee, anyone? It won't take a minute.'

The two chess players contemplated the glowing coals in the hearth while they waited for the priest to return from the kitchen. He seemed to be taking a long time.

Eventually, Emil broke the silence. 'For years I've wondered,' he began, haltingly. 'I mean, I've read about it in books, but I've never asked someone who was there, somebody who was part of it…' His voice tailed away.

'What is it that have you wondered, Herr Clément?'

Emil took a deep breath. 'How could intelligent people like you and Paul have allowed yourselves to be so hoodwinked by Hitler that you ended up criminals?'

Only yesterday, this question would have caused great offence. Now Schweninger took it philosophically. 'What a question,' he replied. 'I've asked myself the same question many times, and the truth of it is very disheartening. People have talked about the failings of our politicians and the terrible effect on Germany of the Depression and the war reparations, but the fact is that too many of us *wanted* to say "Yes!" to Hitler. We knew he was dangerous, but he promised to lead us to our rightful destiny. Who could say no to to that?' He sighed, heavily. 'At first there was no real shape or form to the danger, but then the Nazi Party wormed its way into

THE DEATH'S HEAD CHESS CLUB

every nook and cranny of our lives, watching us and controlling us: the Brownshirts, the youth movements, the artistic societies, the propaganda machine – even the postal service, and, later, the Gestapo. It was like you were facing a colossus that was willing you, inciting you, imploring you to say "Yes!" without knowing what "Yes!" meant. But despite the undercurrent of fear, it was exhilarating, liberating. The Führer knew what needed to be done and all we had to do was to leave everything in his capable hands. Then all would be well and we would be strong again – one people, one blood, united in a common purpose, marching together to a marvellous future where the old uncertainties would be banished. If you had been part of it you would understand. It was irresistible.'

Emil shook his head slowly. 'No, I could never have been part of it. I was a Jew.'

Meissner returned. 'Coffee?'

'No, thank you,' Schweninger said, pushing himself up from his chair. 'I think I'll go to bed.'

'So early?'

But the mood in the room had soured; the feeling of fellowship that had been growing was gone.

'What about you, Emil, will you stay the night?'

'No. I think I should go back to my hotel.' He stood and stepped past Paul to the front door, retrieving his coat on the way.

Meissner followed him. 'Will we see you tomorrow?'

Emil stopped in the open doorway. 'I don't know. Perhaps. I need time to think. It's been a long day. Things might seem different tomorrow.'

'I'll pray for you.'

'Thank you. But I'm not sure what value the prayers of a Christian have for a Jew.'

'Christians and Jews both pray to the same God.'

'So it is said.' Emil turned away. 'Goodnight,' he called back.

As always, Meissner awoke early. He washed, put on a cassock and hobbled down the short flight of steps from the presbytery to the deserted street. He eased himself onto a bench overlooking the canal. With only birdsong for company he lit a cigarette, but it tasted bitter in his mouth and he threw it into the water. He twisted around to face the church with its double doors and twin spires and its dedication to St Francis Xavier. The Jesuits had been there for over three centuries – clandestinely for two of them. He usually took inspiration from their tenacity in keeping faith with Dutch Catholics after Holland had become avowedly Protestant, but not today. He sighed, spent a moment longer in the company of the birds and then stood.

Taking a key from his pocket he unlocked the church door and went in. He wondered whether he had done the right thing in bringing Emil and Willi together. It had gone better than he had expected until he had left them alone. Then something had happened, but what? He limped to the altar rail. The smell of polish and candle-wax usually made him feel he was coming home. He knelt, joining his hands in prayer, but he found the words that were supposed to bring serenity had become mechanical and bereft of meaning. He looked at his watch. It was still not seven o'clock. He decided he would say Mass.

In the sacristy he put on an alb and draped a stole over his shoulders. From a cupboard he took a little wine and a single communion wafer. He went back into the church and stood at one of the side chapels, dedicated to the Virgin. 'Holy Mother of God,' he murmured, 'please help me to do the right thing.'

He put the cup of wine and the wafer down on the altar cloth, genu-flected and crossed himself. '*In nomine Patris, et Filii, et Spiritus Sancti*…'

Meissner returned to the house feeling better, as he often did after saying a solitary Mass. *Ask, and it shall be given unto you.* Well, he had asked. Now it was in the good Lord's hands. Schweninger was still not up so he busied himself making coffee and frying bacon. The smell would surely wake his guest.

Within minutes Willi entered the kitchen, rubbing his eyes.

'I thought I heard the front door open before,' he said.

'It was me. I went into the church.' Quickly he changed the subject. 'Coffee?'

Over breakfast neither of them spoke about the previous evening. When they had washed the dishes and settled down for a smoke, Schweninger said, 'You never said what made Herr Clément change his mind.'

'No. And if it's all right with you, I think it would be better to wait for Emil to tell you himself.'

Schweninger leaned across the kitchen table to tap the ash from his cigarette into an ashtray. 'Fair enough,' he said.

They fell into a companionable silence until, after a while, the priest said, 'Why don't you tell me about what you did in the war. Ministry of Propaganda, wasn't it?'

Schweninger nodded. 'That's right. Section three – Tourism.'

'And you spent all your time in the ministry in the same section?'

'Yes. I liked being there at first, it was quite glamorous, especially during the Olympics, and there were opportunities for travel. But after a while I came to realize I was going nowhere. Even when I applied for a transfer, for which I was well qualified, I never got it. I was a bit slow working it out, but eventually it dawned on me that I had a stain on my record that I would never be able to erase.'

'You think somebody had it in for you?'

Schweninger stubbed his cigarette out, so hard that the butt disintegrated in his fingers. 'It's the only explanation.'

'Do you know who it was?'

'Oh, yes. I'm convinced it was the Malicious Dwarf himself, though naturally he considered himself above telling me to my face.'

'Malicious Dwarf – you mean Goebbels?'

Schweninger nodded. 'Yes, the old club-footed devil.'

'What happened?'

August 1936
Munich

It was a disaster: complete, unmitigated and humiliating.

Berlin, 1936. Germany was hosting the Olympic games. The year before, there had been a flare-up of anti-Jewish agitation which had led to the passing of the Citizenship Law and the Law for the Protection of German Blood and Honour, the so-called Nuremberg Laws, which robbed Jews of their citizenship and barred them from participating in civic life. When the German Chess Federation – the Grossdeutscher Schachbund – proposed a chess Olympiad to coincide with the Olympic games, the International Chess Federation, FIDE, announced that anti-Semitism in Germany meant they could not take part in a German Olympiad. In a cynical move, Germany agreed to suspend its ban on Jews being allowed to compete and the FIDE General Assembly voted to leave national federations free to decide for themselves whether to participate.

Although the *Schach-Olympia* 1936 was an entirely unofficial event, more teams competed than in any previous Olympiad, and the Nazi authorities considered it a great propaganda coup. Jewish masters from many countries took part, including Boris Kostić, Lodewijk Prins, and the young Polish genius, Mendel Najdorf.

Making his first appearance on the German team was a young player, Wilhelm Schweninger, whose daring – some said reckless – play had brought him rapidly to national attention. He seemed to embody the fever of optimism that had infected Hitler's Third Reich. Since the Nuremberg Laws had barred Jews from membership of the German Chess Federation, Germany had fallen in international rankings. Schweninger, convinced of his innate superiority, used his new connections within the Propaganda Ministry to tell the home audience that things were about to change: he was hailed as the face of the resurgent German chess movement which would soon take its rightful place at the forefront of the world game.

The young Schweninger's play was as swaggering and aggressive as everyone expected. In the first round he was paired with a similarly callow Jewish player from Latvia. Schweninger won convincingly and was lauded in the German press as living proof of the superiority of Aryans over the Jews. In Munich a dinner was quickly given in his honour, and he even received a congratulatory telegram from Goebbels. Schweninger allowed himself to imagine a meteoric rise within the ministry. He would be courted by the rich and famous, and beautiful women would hang on his every word.

He was able to enjoy his new-found celebrity for exactly one day.

In the second round he was matched against another Jew – the legendary Najdorf. The Pole had given his name to a variation on the Sicilian Defence. Naturally, Schweninger expected his opponent to make use of his famous move and was taken by surprise when, instead, Najdorf opened with a simple Queen's Gambit and proceeded from there to terrorize the young German, bringing the game to its inevitable conclusion with astonishing speed. At checkmate, Najdorf gave his opponent a cold look of contempt.

Utterly demoralized, Schweninger tried to maintain his dignity. 'Congratulations, Herr Najdorf,' he said, extending a hand to his opponent.

Najdorf ignored it. Without a word, he turned his back and walked away.

Simmering with resentment, Schweninger shouted after him: 'The time is coming, Herr Najdorf, when Jews will get the same treatment that they like to dish out themselves. Then we'll see whether you think you're too good to shake my hand.' But the victor merely continued his progress to the exit. Furious, Schweninger yelled after him: '*Heil Hitler!*'

But that was not the worst of it. Two countries, Poland and Hungary, fielded teams made up entirely of Jews. The German team was beaten comprehensively by both of them.

Goebbels was said to be incandescent with rage. It was a propaganda disaster and Wilhelm Schweninger was its centre.

1962

Kerk de Krijtberg, Amsterdam

'So Goebbels would not forgive you for being beaten by a Jew?'

'To be fair, I think it was probably more than that.'

'Fair? To the man who ruined your career?'

A ghost of a smile crossed Schweninger's lips. 'It was never much of a career, really. I did a good job shepherding the English journalists around the Berlin Olympics, but that was pretty much it. After that I was never much more than a glorified pen-pusher. I think that what so enraged

Goebbels was that I had used my contacts in the ministry not so much to create good propaganda for the German team, but to aggrandize myself. If I had been successful, all would have been well. As it was, I had the misfortune to come up against Najdorf.'

'He's here now, you know, in Amsterdam.'

'Najdorf? Yes, I know. I had thought I might introduce myself, and apologize for my boorish behaviour all those years ago, though I doubt he'd remember now.' Schweninger stood. 'Excuse me, I need the bathroom.'

When he returned, Meissner was at the sink, washing the dishes. 'What happened after Munich?'

Schweninger leaned on the counter, watching as the priest scoured a frying-pan. 'I was determined not to let a single setback define my career as a chess player. By 1940 I was the undisputed champion of Germany, but by then Goebbels had more important things to occupy his time than a chess player who had allowed himself to be beaten by a Jew. I further developed my attacking style, which I had based on the writings of Spiel-mann, even though he was also a Jew. If I could have played against him there would have been no argument about my being champion of both Germany and Austria, but he fled to Sweden.'

'It seems you were fated to have your career shaped by Jews, and now you get beaten by another one. Does it make you feel bitter?'

'No. If I'm honest, I had only myself to blame for what happened in Munich. I was arrogant and simply not good enough. But in my defence, I was only twenty-three. What I can't explain is how Clément managed to beat me so convincingly here in Amsterdam. I thought I was better than that. It's quite chastening to discover otherwise.'

'You should have seen him in Auschwitz.'

173

*

By midday, Emil still had not turned up, so Meissner suggested they walk to his hotel.

'I'm afraid Mijnheer Clément is out,' the receptionist informed them.

'I think I know where he'll be,' Meissner said.

22.

THE MUNICH GAMBIT

1962

Leidseplein, Amsterdam

It was a bright spring day. The two men retraced their steps along the Singel Canal. Dodging bicycles and trams, Meissner guided his companion over several bridges until they reached the open square that was the Leidseplein. Under trees that were coming into bud, a number of tables had been set out with chessboards. Meissner pointed to one that was opposite a café. 'There he is,' he said.

They walked across. 'I thought we might find you here,' Meissner said, smiling broadly.

Emil looked up from the chessboard, squinting into the sun.

'May we?' Schweninger asked, pointing to a chair.

Emil didn't answer; instead, he looked questioningly at his opponent. He was playing against a teenager who seemed a little anxious at the intrusion.

'Please don't mind us,' Meissner said. 'We are simply admirers of the game. If we're putting you off please say so, and we'll leave you alone.'

'No, Father, that's fine,' the youth replied.

The game proceeded slowly. With each move – both his own and his opponent's – Emil explained what was happening. The key to winning, he explained, was to anticipate what your opponent was going to do four moves ahead, but to make your own moves unpredictable.

After a while, the youth said, 'In four moves you are going to win.'

Emil smiled. 'Excellent, though that's not quite what I had in mind when I said you should think ahead. But may I say well done – you are thinking like a chess player already.'

The teenager started to rise, but Schweninger reached out to grasp his arm. 'Do you know who it is you're playing?' The youth shook his head. 'Herr Clément is the champion of Israel, though he's really French. In a week or so he is going to win the international championship.' He looked at Emil meaningfully. 'Some say he's unbeatable.'

The teenager was impressed. 'Really? If I'd known, I wouldn't have...'

Emil chuckled. 'Then I'm glad you didn't know. Thank you for the game; I enjoyed it.'

A waiter arrived. 'That walk has given me an appetite,' Meissner announced. 'Shall we have some lunch?'

Over a lunch of bread, cheese and beer, Schweninger said, 'This morning I asked Paul why you changed your mind about playing chess against the SS. He said I should ask you.'

Emil frowned. 'Did he?'

June 1944
Konzentrationslager Auschwitz-III, Monowitz

'You've changed your mind?' Meissner looks closely at the *Häftling* standing to attention before him. His face is discoloured and when he opens his mouth, a tooth is missing. He looks like he has taken quite a beating. Meissner sighs. This is decidedly not what he had wanted.

'Why?' he asks.

The reply astonishes him. 'Pardon me, Herr Hauptsturmführer,' Emil replies, 'but last time we spoke you mentioned certain privileges that you could arrange if I agreed to play. I do not ask for anything for myself, you understand. I ask on behalf of a friend.'

'A friend? And who would this friend be? Not *Blockältester* Brack, by any chance?'

Emil shakes his head. 'No, Herr Hauptsturmführer. It is the man I share my bunk with. His name is Yves Boudeaud. His number is 162870.'

'And what do you want for this friend of yours?'

'Something very simple. He is in the *Krankenbau* at the moment, recovering from an injury. The truth is he is starving and exhausted. He will die if nothing is done to help him. He is a good man. All I ask is that when he is discharged from the sick bay he is assigned to work in the kitchens. There the work will be lighter and he can get better rations.'

Meissner shakes his head, puzzled. He had been expecting a request far more extravagant – this is too small a thing to ask. There has to be something more.

'Is that it? Nothing else?'

Emil hesitates before answering. When he speaks, his voice betrays him by cracking. 'My wife and children, sir. I don't know what has happened to them but if they are still alive, I would like similar arrangements to be made for them.'

Meissner pauses, weighing his reply. 'I'm afraid I can't promise that. If they are alive they will be in Birkenau; I have no jurisdiction there. But I will grant your other request – your friend – on one condition.'

'Certainly, if it is within my means.'

'Oh, I have a feeling that it is well within your means. The condition is that you must win.'

Emil takes a moment to consider what the officer has said. 'I don't understand. Why is it so important to you that I win?'

'You mistake my purpose. It is not at all important to me that you win. However, it is essential that you *play* to win. Otherwise it would not be a true contest and the outcome would not be valid.'

Emil finds the officer's reasoning difficult to fathom. Surely the SS would want a Jew to be beaten? But does it matter? To him, it is simple: if – when – he wins, Yves will live; otherwise he will surely die. 'I see,' he says. He doesn't see: what the officer has said makes no sense. Frantically, Emil's brain rearranges the officer's words, as if they were pieces on a chessboard, looking for some hidden meaning, a move he must see through. 'But *if* I win,' he continues, choosing his words deliberately, 'Yves will be assigned to the kitchens – permanently? And you give me your word that he will not be selected to go up the chimney?'

'That's an additional condition,' Meissner points out. 'What you are saying now is that you will be playing for your friend's life. That is a heavy responsibility.'

'Maybe so,' Emil concedes, 'but still I must do it. He would do the same for me.'

'In that case, I will do as you ask. Your friend will be assigned to work in the kitchens and I will have it marked on his *Häftling-Karte** that he has been designated *Schutzhäftling*† and exempt from the *Selektionen*.'

'Then I will play.'

The prisoner bows and walks out of the room.

As soon as he is down the stairs, Meissner shouts for his orderly.

'Did you have anything to do with that?'

---

* Prisoner card.
† Prisoner in protective custody.

Eidenmüller's face, as he stands in doorway, becomes home to an expression of pained innocence. 'Me, sir? What, sir?'

'The prisoner, Eidenmüller. He's been beaten. I sincerely hope it had nothing to do with you.'

'The prisoner, sir? You mean the one who was in here just now? The Watchmaker?'

'"Watchmaker"?'

'That's what they call him, sir.'

'Well, then, yes, you idiot, the Watchmaker.'

The orderly gives a theatrical shake of his head. 'No, sir. Definitely not, sir. It must have been that *Blockältester*, sir. Brack, I think his name was, sir. Nasty piece of work. Didn't like the look of him, sir, not one bit.'

'Well, do something for me will you, Eidenmüller? I want you to go and see this Brack yourself. I want you to tell him from me that from now on, this Watchmaker is to be left alone. He's under my protection, and if anything happens to him I will make it my business to see that exactly the same thing happens to Brack. Got that?'

'Yes, sir. Got that, sir. Loud and clear, sir.'

1962

Grand Hotel Krasnapolsky, Amsterdam

Emil's next game in the tournament found him pitted against a Hungarian who was playing on the American team. Emil drew white and started the game by moving his queen's pawn forward two spaces on the board. The Hungarian responded by bringing out his king's knight so that it sat two squares in front of its bishop. Emil advanced his queen's bishop's pawn to stand beside its brother. The Hungarian moved the corresponding pawn to block it, offering it as a sacrifice to white. Emil ignored the gambit and advanced his first pawn one space, offering a countergambit to the black knight. The exchange of a knight for a pawn is not equitable, so the Hungarian advanced his queen's knight's pawn in a third gambit. Emil took the pawn. His opponent moved his rook's pawn one space and Emil took that too. The Hungarian fianchettoed* his queen's bishop to take Emil's pawn.

Watching from the sidelines, Schweninger whispered to Meissner. 'What is he doing? Doesn't he see he's been led into a trap?'

'A trap? How? He's a pawn ahead in the exchange. That's good, isn't it?'

'No. White always starts with the initiative but now he has lost it. Look how much more developed the Hungarian's position is, and the threat his bishop poses along the diagonal.'

Emil, however, was fully aware of what his opponent was doing. He was playing a variation of the Benoni Defence that Emil himself favoured when playing black. He had seen this variation before, in quite different circumstances, when there had been far more at stake.

June 1944

Konzentrationslager Auschwitz-III, Monowitz

Emil has to wait until he has finished work for the day before he can visit Yves in the K-B to give him the news. Yves is still weak, but he is more alert and his eyes have lost the dull sheen of desperation. Emil tells him he looks better already, before excitedly telling him of the deal he has made with the SS officer.

'So,' Emil says, feeling easier than he has for months, 'when it is time for you to be discharged you will be assigned work in the kitchens, and

---

* The fianchetto is a developmental move where the pawn in front of a knight is moved forward one or two spaces and the bishop occupies the space behind it, giving the bishop freedom to move on the long diagonal that the move has opened.

if there is a *Selektion*, you will not be among those sent up the chimney.'

But Yves's response is not what Emil expected.

'And what if you lose?'

'I will not lose.'

'But you might. What you are saying, Emil, is that if you lose, in all likelihood I will be in the next *Selektion*, and if you win, I will owe my life to you.'

'Yves, trust me – I will not lose.'

With a fervour that Emil has not seen for a long time Yves says, 'I do trust you, Emil, but that is not the point. Do you not understand? My life is not yours to bargain with. I am not a piece on a chessboard for you to play with.'

Emil is shocked at his friend's reaction. 'But you said one of us had to survive to tell people about this place.'

'I meant you, Emil, not me. I did not – do not – expect to survive. Look at me. I can't go on for much longer. A few days, a few weeks, maybe.'

'No. Yves, please. Listen to me. This will work. It will.'

'No, Emil. I will not let you do this thing. I do not wish my life to be saved because of the whim of some SS officer. What he gives today he can just as easily take back tomorrow.'

Emil is distressed by his friend's stubbornness, and his fingers pluck unconsciously at the fraying hem of his sleeve. 'I do not think he will take it back. He gave me his word.'

Yves is incredulous. 'He gave his word? To a Jew? And you believed him? Surely you know by now that none of the Germans can be trusted. They are liars, all of them. He is probably laughing at you as we speak.'

Emil pleads with his friend: 'Please, Yves. Let me try.'

'No. I forbid it.'

Emil is caught in a trap set by the kingdom of lies: to save his friend's life he must abandon the truth, something he promised himself he would not do. He tells Yves he will do as he asks, that he will play for his own life. By the time Yves is out of the K-B it will be too late for him to do anything about it.

Back at Emil's block, Bodo Brack has been summoned by the *Blockführer*. He is handed a piece of paper.

'What is this?'

'Notification of a change of status of one of the *Häftlinge*. Prisoner 162870 Boudeaud has been designated *Schutzhäftling* on the orders of Hauptsturmführer Meissner. Your *Blockschreiber* will amend his record accordingly.'

'Why has his status changed?'

'I have no idea. All I have are my orders.'

Back in the block, Brack hands the paper to Widmann. 'Who is this Boudeaud?' he asks.

'He's a Frenchie. Him and the Watchmaker share a bunk. Thick as thieves, the pair of them.'

'And what's so special about him?'

'Nothin' 's far 's I know. He's in a bad way, though, has been for weeks. Not long for this world, I wouldn't think. He's been in the K-B for the past few days.'

Later, when Emil returns to the block, Bodo grabs his collar and pulls him outside.

'What the fuck have you been playing at?'

'Playing at? I don't know what you mean.'

'Your bum-boy. Don't pretend you don't know who I'm talking about.

The one who shares your bunk. Are you so stupid you thought I wouldn't find out?'

'I still don't know what you're talking about.'

That earns him a slap across the face. 'Don't mess with me, you stupid cocksucker,' Brack screams. 'How the hell did you manage to get your arse-fucking friend designated *Schutzhäftling* on the orders of an *SS* fucking Hauptsturmführer?'

Emil explains, bracing himself for a beating, but when he finishes Brack simply dismisses him. Emil does not know what to make of this but takes his opportunity to get away. 'Scheming little bastard,' Bodo says under his breath, to Emil's retreating back.

The game takes place two days later. Yves is still in the infirmary. Emil is cleaned up and taken in a truck to the *Stammlager*. He sits in the back with an SS guard. The driver does not seem to care and drives recklessly, throwing his vehicle around with no consideration for their wellbeing. Emil is shaken and nauseous when he arrives. He is marched to the enlisted men's barracks, where a large room has been set up with a table and chessboard at its centre.

Emil is left waiting in a corridor where he is told to remove his cap and face the wall. As people pass, some make a point of shoving him into the wall or punching him. He is on edge, not knowing when the next blow will fall, and time passes painfully slowly. Eventually, he hears a voice he knows.

'Watchmaker.' It is Hauptsturmführer Meissner. 'Come with me.'

The room is full of SS men, mostly NCOs, but there are one or two officers. Emil does not recognize any of them. He is led to the chessboard. 'Your opponent will be here shortly,' Meissner tells him.

Emil has never been among so many SS men. He stands to attention and fixes his gaze on a wall.

Somebody brings a stool. 'Sit,' he is told, as if he were a dog. Holding his cap in both hands, Emil sits.

His opponent arrives, an SS NCO. On his collar he has the twin pips and bands that signify he is a Hauptscharführer. He is a heavy-set man with a wart on his chin and piggy eyes peering out from deep folds of fat.

'Must I go through with this, sir?' the NCO asks Meissner.

'Yes, Frommhagen. This must be a meaningful contest and you were a finalist in the enlisted men's championship. It is your duty to uphold the honour of the SS.'

The NCO rolls his eyes. Meissner is called away and Frommhagen appeals to Eidenmüller. 'Just 'cause someone said the Kike's unbeatable? Doesn't look that special to me. Why not just have him shot and have done with it? Happy to do it myself, if your boss is too squeamish to do it.'

Meissner rejoins them. 'Let's get on with it, shall we?'

Meissner holds out his hands in the usual manner of choosing which colour each player will get. Frommhagen chooses. He draws black. Emil starts the game by advancing his queen's pawn two spaces.

Emil's confidence has withered away. The knowledge that he must win or Yves will almost certainly die weighs heavily. The stool is uncomfortable and after he has shifted his weight nervously for the third time his opponent growls, 'Keep still, goddammit, you stupid Yid.'

Emil recalls perfectly his words to Yves: 'Yves, trust me – I will not lose.' Now he is frightened he will not be able to keep his promise.

After ten moves Emil is one pawn up but his opponent's position is better developed and his bishop threatening Emil along the diagonal greatly limits the unpredictability that is Emil's greatest strength.

1962

Grand Hotel Krasnapolsky, Amsterdam

Emil watched blankly as his opponent pushed down the tab on the game clock. The Hungarian's opening moves had been unconventional and disconcertingly effective. Emil peered at him, half expecting to see a resemblance with an SS-Hauptscharführer with a wart. He felt unsettled; no doubt because of all the time spent with Meissner raking over the past. Well, if he got through this stage, he would have to put a stop to that, at least until after the interzonal was over. Progress to the world championship was at stake. But first he had to beat the Hungarian.

The night before, when Emil had cast the tiles, he had uncovered ח – Heth – which signifies the Benelohim, the Sons of God. He had taken that as a sign of God looking benevolently on him, and he expected it to mean that he would win again. Now he was reeling at how easily he had fallen into to his opponent's trap. Luckily, progress from this stage in the tournament did not depend on the outcome of a single game, but on the best of three; still, he racked his brains for a way out of the position the Hungarian had created. The clock was ticking. If he advanced his king's pawn, black would bring his bishop across to take the white bishop. Emil would take it with his king but that would leave his king exposed, which would concede the initiative to his opponent still further. He could bring out his queen's knight, but that would still leave him without any immediate attacking options. Theory told him to play safe, but every fibre of his instinct told him that was what his opponent wanted. Without making a conscious decision, his hand settled on his queen's bishop and moved it kingside to threaten the black knight still nestled on the back row. It was not a conventional move, but it might make his opponent hesitate. If he could just gain a little space, he might at least salvage a draw…

Somewhere a floorboard creaked. In the hushed atmosphere it was surprisingly loud. The sound brought him back to another game.

It was the last thing he wanted to be thinking of, but the memory sprang into his mind unbidden. He could see again the bright red tributaries in the nose and cheeks of the SS man; he could smell the sauerkraut and beer on his breath and hear the shouts as his comrades urged him to see off this nuisance Jew.

The Hungarian saw the threat to his knight. He moved it, taking the lone white pawn in the middle of the board, but it was a fundamental error.

With a silent whoop of delight, Emil advanced his queen to capture the knight. The exchange left him dominating the centre of the board. It was not the way he liked to play, but his chances of winning had improved markedly.

Afterwards, Schweninger was voluble in his praise for Emil's victory: 'Such clever opening play by black,' he said. 'So unconventional. I can't ever remember seeing it before. Respond to it as you ought – as Emil did – and you're in trouble before you know it. Almost impossible to get out of it without a major concession. What Emil did was a master stroke: bold but eccentric; your opponent thinks they've missed something, and you're able to take the initiative back.'

'I've seen it before,' Emil said. 'It's called the Volga Gambit. I never expected to see it here. It caught me by surprise.'

'Where did you see it?' Meissner asked.

'In Auschwitz. In the first game I played, the Hauptscharführer used the same opening. I've no idea where he might have come across it. It took me by surprise then, too. It was the first time I had seen it and I remember thinking what a clever opening it was and wondering what I was going to do about it. There was an awful lot riding on that game.'

'Fascinating,' Schweninger said. 'You know, it's just occurred to me – I have an idea where he might have seen it.'

Emil responded with a sceptical look. 'Really? Where?'

'1936. In the Munich chess Olympiad. I'm sure it was Thorvaldsson who played it, though it was taken up afterwards by Eliskases. It was called the Munich Gambit then.'

23.

THE FRENCH DEFENCE

From the journal of Hauptsturmführer Paul Meissner

SUNDAY, 11TH JUNE 1944 It seems I have made something of a mis-calculation. Sturmbannführer Bär is quite furious with me. He is adamant that I should have consulted him before pitting a Jew against a member of the SS. He wanted the Watchmaker shot out of hand for having the temerity to win. He was not mollified when I explained that I had put the Jew in a position where he could not afford to lose. Nor was he impressed when I tried to convince him that the game was essential because of an idea that has sprung up among the Jews in the camp that one of their number is unbeatable. An idea cannot be defeated by shooting bullets at it, I said. Hauptscharführer Frommhagen was the weakest of the finalists in the camp championship, and the Watchmaker had trouble beating him. It seems likely that if he is pitted against our stronger players he will meet his match, and the 'unbeatable' Jew will soon be forgotten. The thought of the Jew pitting his wits against the likes of Hustek almost makes me want to pity him. At least the Kommandant agreed that we now have to go ahead with the further games – though he is still not happy about it. I told him that if he finds what I have done is so objectionable, he could arrange to have me transferred. He said that with *Aktion Höss* running at full tilt there was no question of a transfer. It seems I am indispensable, at least for now. Even so, I will write to Peter Sommer to see if there is any chance of my old regiment taking me back. It seems likely they'll soon be in the thick of the fighting in France – if they're not already. Goebbels vowed the enemy would be pushed back into the sea within a week, but there's precious little sign of that happening. The Führer promised Germany would never have to fight on two fronts again, and now we are fighting on three. Is this defeatist talk? If I knew what was good for me I would destroy this journal, but there is something that stops me from doing that. I tell myself it is the voice of reason. Heaven knows, that is a rare commodity these days, especially here. There is no reason, only orders. As for this Jew, I am reluctant to admit it, but there is something about him that is unsettling. His chief concern was for his friend, not for himself. That is what I might have expected from comrades who have faced death together in the heat of battle, not from a Jew mired in the filth of avarice. I begin to wonder whether all that has been said of this race is true, or whether, like Lot in the city of Sodom, the Watchmaker is the one good man among an evil multitude.

1962

Amsterdam

Narrow though Emil's victory had been, Meissner insisted they celebrate. He told them of a small, family-run restaurant on the Oude Turfmarkt that served marvellous Italian food. It was not far, perhaps a ten-minute walk. He would buy them dinner.

Walking through the lobby of the Krasnapolsky they encountered Lijsbeth Pietersen.

'Good evening, Mijnheer Clément,' she said. She had a book in her hand. 'I bought a copy of your book. I wondered if you would mind signing it for me, if it's not too much trouble—?' Her eyes lit on his companions. 'Oh. Mijnheer Schweninger. I wasn't expecting to see you. I thought...' Lijsbeth trailed off.

'You thought what, Miss Pietersen?' Schweninger enquired.

'I just thought... the two of you...' Lijsbeth flushed.

'Perhaps you thought that Herr Schweninger and I did not have so much in common that we would seek out each other's company?' Emil suggested gently.

'No – that is, I mean...'

'Let's just say that we have reached an accommodation,' Willi said. 'We have found that it is better to talk to each other than shout at each other.'

'So you...'

'We are talking, Miss Pietersen, and that will have to do for now,' Emil said, extending a hand for the book. 'By the way, have you read it?'

'Yes. It's very moving. It's hard to believe that people could have done such terrible things.'

'Yes, it is, isn't it?' He wrote something on the first page and handed it back. '*Au revoir,* Miss Pietersen.'

The three men descended the steps of the hotel and crossed Dam Square, going through the archway that led on to Rokin. The streets thronged with people and the air was filled with the tinkling of bicycle bells as their riders threaded their way through the crowds. The evening sun reflected off the windows of the bars, which were full of people having a drink after work.

'It's quite amazing, this city,' Emil said, ignoring for a moment Willi's discourse on the merits of an attacking style. He stopped to gaze at a row of ancient gables opposite. No two were the same. The occasional modern building intruded among them, looking clumsy and conspicuous. 'Why would they do that?' he asked, pointing at one. 'You know – put such ugly concrete blocks like those where they don't belong.'

'It was the air raids,' Meissner said. 'If one of the old buildings was destroyed, the Dutch saw no point in trying to hide it by creating a replica. The new constructions are monuments to what they went through during the war.'

'Makes sense, I suppose,' Schweninger said, walking on. 'As I was saying,' he continued, 'in my opinion, Capablanca will probably prove to be the greatest player of this century. The simplicity of his attacking play and the speed with which he made his moves were really quite…' He realized he was talking to himself and stopped. Looking back, he saw Meissner doubled over, holding onto a lamppost for support, and Emil, concern etched on his face, standing beside him, a hand on Meissner's shoulder.

'What's the matter?' Willi said, walking back as quickly as his bulk would allow.

Meissner waved a hand. 'It's nothing,' he said. His face was contorted with pain and his voice little more than an agonized whisper. 'Only an affliction that comes on me from time to time. Don't worry about it – it will soon pass. Malaria,' he added.

But it did not pass.

They were not far from a bar with its ubiquitous green-and-white 'Heineken Bier' sign, so Willi went in to borrow a chair.

Meissner smiled weakly. 'So, "Watchmaker",' he said. 'Now I am the one in need of help. I wonder, do you think we could forgo dinner? I would be grateful if you could help me to get back to the Krijtberg.'

Despite the coolness of the evening, beads of sweat stood out on the priest's forehead.

Willi returned with a chair. 'I'll find us a taxi,' he said.

Back at the presbytery, it took both men to help Paul from the taxi to the door. Willi rang the doorbell repeatedly. They could hear footsteps in the hall and the housekeeper calling, 'All right, all right.'

'Dear God,' she said, when she saw them. Quickly she stood to one side so they could move past her. 'What's happened?' She crossed herself.

'He's really not well,' Emil said. 'I think you should call for a doctor.'

By the time they managed to get him to bed, his nose had begun to bleed. Having summoned the other priest in the Krijtberg, the house-keeper had taken up station at the side of the bed and was tearfully trying to stem the blood. Father Scholten, a dour Belgian, stood at the foot of the bed praying, his lips moving soundlessly as he passed a set of beads slowly between his fingers. When the doctor arrived they all moved downstairs to the kitchen.

It seemed as if he was with his patient for a long time.

'How is he, Doctor?' the housekeeper asked when he came down, her voice tremulous with worry.

'I've given him some laudanum and he's resting now. You should let him sleep. What he needs is a bit of peace and quiet.' He took one of the housekeeper's hands in his own. 'He's very ill, Mrs Brinckvoort, but you knew that,' the doctor said gently.

'But he'll make a full recovery, surely?' Willi asked.

The doctor shook his head slowly. 'That's highly unlikely. Of course, we all pray for a miracle, but I'm afraid there's little more that medical science can do.'

'For *malaria*?' Schweninger's voice had in it more than a little outrage.

How could doctors in Holland be so far behind their counterparts in Germany?'

A look of comprehension crossed the doctor's face. 'Is that what he told you? Yes, I can understand that. He would not want your sympathy.'

'If it's not malaria, what is it?'

'It's leukaemia,' Emil said. 'He's dying.'

June 1944

Konzentrationslager Auschwitz-III, Monowitz

It is two weeks since the Allies landed in France. After hard fighting, the British have advanced as far as Caen and the Americans have succeeded in reaching the western side of the Cotentin Peninsula, isolating Cherbourg. Hitler has forbidden the local commander, von Schlieben, to retreat to the fortifications of the Atlantic Wall, leaving him no option but to stand and fight until his men are exhausted or dead.

Although it is isolated in the coalfields of Silesia, the camp is aware of what is happening over a thousand miles away: news is brought by Polish workers in the Buna factory. The camp is jubilant. In the years since it was established, it has not known a moment like this. In their compound beyond the wire, the British prisoners of war can be heard jeering at the guards.

The inmates do not know how to celebrate but there is no stopping the slender seedlings of hope from germinating. The prisoners have an unaccustomed spring in their step as they are marched off in their work *Kommandos*, and the jaunty tunes played by the camp orchestra no longer seem so ludicrous. Emil is one who has already broken the rule that says hope is forbidden in Auschwitz, and for him the news adds substance to his optimism.

Still, for some days he has been unhappy. When Yves was discharged from the K-B and assigned to the kitchens, he knew immediately that Emil had not been true to his word. Angrily, he accused Emil of betraying his trust. It was a strange form of betrayal, Emil told him, that saved the life of a friend, but Yves would not listen.

There is a rift between them and Yves has moved his bunk. Emil now shares with an Italian, a tall, taciturn man who does not respect Emil's space.

The companionship that Emil shared with Yves is gone. Emil prays that his friend will soon forgive him. The news coming from France buoys him and he decides that when he gets back from the factory this evening, he will seek Yves out and ask again for his pardon.

On their return from the Buna complex the prisoners sense a change. The camp is fearful. Dread and foreboding stalk its pathways as the inmates are made to wait on the parade ground after evening roll call.

At the head of the *Appelplatz* is a gallows. Three empty nooses hang from its cross-beam. Several SS officers stand watching. The Watchmaker recognizes the tall form of Hauptsturmführer Meissner, leaning on his walking stick and looking distinctly like one who wishes he were somewhere else.

The roll call is completed unusually quickly. The Rapportführer tallies the count. It is three short. Instead of ordering a re-count, he reports to the Lagerführer who responds with a curt nod. With a flourish, the camp orchestra strikes up Mozart's 'Rondo alla Turca'. They play well, and some of the officers standing around the platform smile appreciatively.

There is a stirring among the men massed there, as three bruised and bloody inmates are led out, their hands tied behind them. They have ropes around their necks and they are pulled along by SS troops like dogs. The Lagerführer gives a sign that the orchestra should cease playing and mounts the steps to the scaffold. He shouts at the assembled thousands. Though only the front ranks can hear him, he knows that before the parade ground has emptied his words will have been repeated a thousand times.

'These men are thieves,' he yells. 'They have been caught stealing food. This is a crime against the generosity of the German Reich, which sees fit to provide you with your daily bread. It is also a crime against *you*. The food they took was your food. By filling their bellies there is less for *you*. Such a monstrous crime calls for exemplary punishment.'

Emil is frantic. Yves was not present at the roll call. The SS men force the prisoners to lift their heads. Emil thinks he is going to be sick. The prisoner on the right is Yves.

The Rapportführer reads aloud the names and numbers of the three men. The nooses are put in place and pulled tight. The orchestra resumes its obscene parody of jollity. Stools are kicked out from underneath the condemned men and the camp watches helplessly as they kick and writhe, choking in their death throes.

Tears stream down Emil's cheeks but he is no longer sure whether he is crying for himself or for his friend.

And all for a few rotten potatoes.

Meissner is angry. Walking away from the executions, he catches up with the Lagerführer and pulls him around. 'Was that absolutely necessary?'

Obersturmführer Vinzenz Schottl regards the superior officer with a disdainful smile. 'Of course it was. They were caught stealing food. They said they had some ridiculous notion of doling out an extra ration to prisoners who were starving. An example had to be made.' Schottl tilts his cap back and puts his hands on his hips in an attitude that, in an enlisted man, would be considered insolent. 'But why would you care about the fate of a few worthless Jews?'

'One of them had been designated *Schutzhäftling* – on my orders.'

The Lagerführer sees his superior in a new and unflattering light. 'Really? Why would you do that?'

'I had my reasons. Why did you not respect his status, or at least speak to me about it?'

'I had no idea. I assure you there was no note of it on his *Häftling-Karte*.'

Disgusted, Meissner turns and walks away. The junior officer calls after him. 'Herr Hauptsturmführer, you should take care that people do not start to call you a Jew-lover.'

24.

The Torre Attack

1962

Amsterdam

A man is standing on Gerard Doustraat, outside the synagogue. He has a *kippah* on his head but hesitates to go inside. The building's purpose is obvious from the Star of David set in the window at the top of the gable, yet still he hesitates. He feels he has no business there. But he has an overwhelming urge to pray, and has learned that it was in this very synagogue that Rosh Hashanah was celebrated in 1943, before the last Jews of Amsterdam were deported to Auschwitz.

He senses a connection with this place, but he wonders whether it is because of the time he spent in Auschwitz, or whether it is because he is simply a Jew who cannot escape his people's history.

A man comes out. He has an iron-grey beard and wears the wide-brimmed hat of an Orthodox Jew. 'Good morning,' he says, in Yiddish.

The man in the street has not spoken Yiddish for nearly twenty years. 'Good morning,' he replies in Hebrew.

'Welcome,' says the Jew, extending a hand. 'Shmuel Jacobsen. I'm the rabbi here. Are you new to the area, or visiting?'

'Visiting,' the man replies absently.

'Would you like to come inside?'

'I don't know.'

The rabbi has business elsewhere, but is reluctant to leave if this person who has found the synagogue needs his help in some way. Eventually the visitor breaks the silence.

'A friend of mine is dying. Cancer. I feel very bad about it. I don't know what to do.'

The rabbi gives a reassuring smile. 'Why do you feel bad about it? You are not the cause of his cancer. You should perhaps do your best to bring him comfort during his last days, and when he is gone you should rejoice in his memory, but you should not feel bad about it. It is the will of God.'

'I can't help it. The last time a friend of mine died I was not the cause of it then either, but I have carried the guilt of his death with me ever since. It has been a heavy burden. I do not wish to carry it twice over.'

'Would you like to come inside? Talking about it might help.'

The visitor shakes his head. 'No. Thank you. I've been talking about it for days already. So far it hasn't helped. I was drawn to this place, but now I'm here it doesn't feel right.'

The rabbi brings his hands together, his fingers steepled, like a Catholic saying a prayer. He taps his lips with the tips of his fingers, wondering. The man is obviously troubled. 'Doesn't feel right?' he asks. 'That's quite something for a Jew to say about the synagogue.'

For long moments the man looks away: at his feet, up the street, searching the trees for birds, anything but meet the rabbi's calm gaze. 'It's complicated,' he replies.

'Complicated?' The rabbi's eyebrows lift and he smiles. 'Everything about being a Jew is complicated.'

The man shakes his head. Slowly, he rolls up the left sleeve of his coat to reveal a tattoo on his arm. Six numbers: 163291.

The rabbi sighs. Understanding dawns. 'Which one?' he asks.

'Auschwitz.' In his mind's eye, the man sees the concrete posts and barbed wire of the camp standing between them, a barrier that is all the more impenetrable because its physical presence is long gone.

'We should talk,' the rabbi says. He puts a hand on the man's upper arm and guides him inside.

June 1944
Konzentrationslager Auschwitz-III, Monowitz
It is two days since Yves was executed. Now everybody knows what happened. With two others, he had stolen a basketful of bread from the kitchen and was taking it around the camp to the *Muselmänner*, those prisoners who had yielded to despair. It was a plan doomed because of its crazy folly. Nearly every *Muselmann* ignored the bread that was held out to them: they did not know what it was they were being offered. They were beyond any help that an extra ration of bread might bring.

It was inevitable that the three men would be caught and punished. Emil wonders if that was why Yves did it: determined to hold fast to the last threads of his dignity, refusing to allow another to decide whether he lived or died. Emil aches with guilt. If he had not made the bargain with the Hauptsturmführer in the first place...

A voice tells him that Yves would be dead anyway: one more day of hard labour would have finished him off. He would have been carried back to the camp by his workmates, already dead or destined for the next *Selektion*. But Emil cannot listen to this voice. The voice of reason has no place in Auschwitz. It is overwhelmed by the twisted logic that tells him that, in addition to his mother and his children, he is now responsible for the death of his friend and he must carry the burden of it to his grave.

Emil has been summoned to see the Hauptsturmführer again. He does not wish to go but cannot refuse. A *Kapo* he does not know marches him to the building and the two of them wait in a corridor, Emil with his face to the wall. After a while the orderly arrives. He gives the *Kapo* a cigarette and tells him to smoke it outside.

Once the *Kapo* has gone, the orderly speaks to Emil. 'I don't know that I should be speaking to you,' he says. His voice sounds harsh to Emil, rough and uneducated. 'Seeing you are nothing but a stinking Yid. But my boss is interested in you. Why, I don't know, but he is, and he's my boss, so I've got to go along with it. But he's a good sort, my boss, so I don't like to see anyone trying to put one over on him. He says you struggled to beat Hauptscharführer Frommhagen. Tell me, is he right? Did you struggle or did you make it look harder than it was?'

'I struggled,' Emil replies, speaking to the wall.

'So how d'you think you'll manage playing one of the officers? 'Cause that's what the boss has got in store for you next.'

'I–I don't know,' Emil stammers. 'It depends.'

'Depends, does it? What exactly does it depend on?'

'If I told you, you wouldn't believe me.'

'Try me.'

'It depends on whether the angels speak to me.'

The SS man bangs Emil's face against the wall, making his nose bleed. 'Fuckin' Kike,' he says angrily. 'I should have known I was wasting my time.'

1962

Gerard Doustraat, Amsterdam

The rabbi leaves Emil to wait in a small room furnished with a couch, chairs and a coffee table. It is a place where couples come to talk about their wedding arrangements and the bereaved make plans for funerals. He returns with two cups of tea and hands one to Emil. 'Tell me about your friend,' he says.

'Which one? The one who is dead or the one who is dying?'

'Does it matter? Either of them; both of them. Whatever you think is important.'

'My friend who died,' Emil says, 'was my bunk mate in Auschwitz. We arrived on the same transport. He was starving to death. I tried to save him. I made a pact with a German, one of the SS, but still they killed him. It was 1944, a summer's day. For him there was no *chevra kadisha* to care for his body, no *tahara*, no readings from the Torah, no *kevura*. His body was thrown into an incinerator. There were no seven days of mourning and no *matzevah* to mark his passing. As far as I know, he has no relatives to light the *yahrzeit* candle. I am the only one who remembers him.'

The rabbi lays a hand on Emil's arm. It is a gesture of consolation, of shared grief, of natural compassion. 'And your friend who is dying now,' he says, gently. 'Is he also someone from Auschwitz?'

Emil raises his eyes to the rabbi's. 'Yes,' he says, 'but not in the way you think.'

'How then?'

It is too easy for Emil to revisit this sorrow: if the sky has a certain colour to it, especially at dusk; or if he finds himself in a large crowd; an orchestra playing Mozart; or something as simple as stale bread: all these things can trigger the memories that surge forward, uninvited. He sees three suspended bodies silhouetted against the sky, the ropes seemingly as insubstantial as silken thread. He sees Meissner talking to a fellow SS officer; he sees the multitude of prisoners surrounding him, subdued by yet another savage demonstration of the power of the SS; he sees the barbed wire that surrounds the *Appelplatz* and the SS barracks beyond. His vision of all of these things has remained crystal-clear, as if he were still there, yet he cannot recall the faces of his own children. He sees them only as he saw them for the last time, as they walked into the shadows, hand in hand with their grandmother, not looking back, and he remembers his last words to them: '*Be good for Granny.*'

'It is the SS officer with whom I made the unholy pact.'

The rabbi's hand falls away from Emil's arm. 'And your survival – was that a result of this pact?'

'Yes.'

'But not your friend?'

'No.'

'And did this officer have anything to do with your friend's death?'

Emil shakes his head.

'But neither did he prevent it?'

'No.'

'I can see how you may owe a debt of gratitude to this man for your life. But friendship – that is a different matter.'

'As you say, a different matter.' Emil gets to his feet. The memories are threatening to overwhelm him. 'Thank you, rabbi,' he says.'

'I hope I have been of some help.'

'I hope so too.'

There is no quick route from Gerard Doustraat to the Singel Canal and the Kerk de Krijtberg, and the walk takes Emil some time. He is not alone on his journey. For companions he has both the living and the dead; voices he cannot quieten, words that howl in his consciousness.

Friendship – that is a different matter.

The rabbi is right. There can be no friendship with Meissner. How could there be?

There is no forgiveness. I cannot forgive.

No. There are some things that are beyond forgiveness; some things that are beyond redemption. Sometimes it takes courage not to forgive because it is easier to forgive, but it is not the right thing to do.

Your forgiveness cannot help me, Watchmaker.

Damn Meissner. What had possessed him to interfere? He had no right.

I would rather make a pact with the Devil.

These words ring in his mind like the bell of an ancient church tolling for the souls of the departed. Yves had seen everything with extraordinary clarity. He would never have countenanced an accommodation with the Nazis and their henchmen.

There is no why.

But there is. The why is Auschwitz and the tens upon tens of thousands who starved, suffered and were murdered. If the dead could speak, would they forgive? And he can almost hear them: all those who waited patiently to go down into the gas chambers, those who collapsed from starvation or who were beaten to death, those who succumbed to the depths of winter or the bullets of the SS on the death marches: their voices clamour to be heard.

I can help you to understand that the power of forgiveness will bring healing for you.

No. I do not need to be forgiven. I did nothing wrong.

My life is not yours to bargain with.

The memory of those words is like a betrayal. They cut through all the familiar certainties he has erected to protect himself.

Forgive me.

Two simple words that are etched into his memory, diamond bright, never dimming. Now they call to him: remote voices broadcast on a Tannoy, a choir singing a lamentation, a crowd at a football match, cheering; no one voice is discernible, until he finds himself again at his wife's bedside in the days before she died. The voice is hers. *You have nothing to be forgiven for*, he tells her, helplessly; *you are blameless*.

How did she understand what he did not?

He finds himself on the bridge that crosses Vondelpark and realizes he is not far from Leidseplein. He has no idea how much time has passed since leaving the synagogue. It feels like hours. He stops, his hands gripping the metal railings that line the bridge, holding tightly. He wants to shout, to the cars and vans going past, to the cyclists, to the people strolling in the park below. He wants to shout, 'Enough! Leave me be! Let me have some peace. Haven't I suffered enough?'

Suddenly, the wind that has been shrieking through his mind stops. The clamour of the voices ceases. The only sound is the breeze soughing through the trees nearby. He is left with a single thought: the *why* of Auschwitz. The dead are waiting. He has a duty to serve them, but their suffering is at an end. He cannot suffer for them. Nor would they want him to. They would want him to live.

He does not consciously come to any decision. It simply happens. What he said unwittingly to the rabbi is true: *A friend of mine is dying*. Since Auschwitz, he has been afraid to allow any bonds of friendship to grow, but now they have taken him by surprise. Emil is engulfed by a surge of emotion: he feels lighter, certain, free. He cannot say how it has happened, but he knows it to be true.

Paul Meissner is his friend.

1962

Kerk de Krijtberg, Amsterdam

The housekeeper showed Emil into the bishop's room. The curtains were pulled closed and the room was in semi-darkness.

'He's quite weak,' she said in a low voice. 'He wakes for a short while and then falls asleep again. I think it's the laudanum.' She turned to go. 'Try not to get him too excited. If you need anything, I'll be in the kitchen.'

Emil pulled a chair up to the bed and sat down. Meissner's eyes were closed. He seemed to be in a deep sleep. Emil bowed his head. Understanding dawned on him: *this* was the place for him to pray, not the synagogue.

He started to speak, quietly. 'I went to a synagogue today, the first time in years. I thought I had questions for which only God would have an answer. I was wrong. I had the answers myself, only I did not know it. I found the answer in a word I spoke without thinking – I told somebody that you were my friend. Such a small word for such a big thing. As soon as the word was uttered I knew the truth of it, like a shaft of light that pierces a dark sky.

'I had a friend who died in Auschwitz, the best friend I ever had. I tried to save his life but he would not let me, he would not abandon his dignity. He was hanged as punishment for stealing food. Do you remember? You were present at his execution; I saw you. Do you remember what we spoke of the next time you summoned me to your presence? It was not an easy exchange of words.

'I remember being marched into your office. I had blood dripping from my nose. You saw it and glared at your orderly. "He fell," the orderly said. I could see from the look on your face that you did not believe him. You dismissed the orderly and offered me your own handkerchief.' Emil fell silent for a moment. 'You would not have known how beautiful it was to feel again clean, white linen between my fingers. I was reluctant to soil its purity by using it to wipe away the blood. I wanted to keep it so I could take it out occasionally as a reminder of what it was like to be clean. And I remember what you said—'

'I am sorry about your friend.' The words came out in a hoarse whisper as Meissner reached a trembling hand across the bedspread to take Emil's. 'That's what I said, didn't I?'

Tears clouded Emil's eyes. 'Yes, Paul. That's what you said.'

June 1944
Konzentrationslager Auschwitz-III, Monowitz
'I am sorry about your friend,' the officer says, for a second time.

Emil says nothing. He holds the handkerchief to his nose.

'I did not break my word to you,' the officer continues. 'It seems there was an administrative error.'

'Pardon me – an administrative error?'

'Quite so. It is unfortunate, but these things happen in times of war. I'm sure you can understand.' The officer's speech is stiff and formal, as if he is aware how hollow his words must sound. 'But you must have something to show for your victory. I will see to it that the status of protective custody is entered in your record instead.'

'Unfortunate? Is that all you can say? My friend is *dead*.' Emil looks to see if the orderly is listening, but he is gone. 'You make it sound as if I had been playing for a toy at a fairground. I was playing to save my friend's life and now he is dead.'

The officer's voice remains tightly controlled. 'I kept my side of our bargain. Your friend knew what he was doing. I am not to blame if he was so careless with his life. I have treated you fairly.'

Emil cannot believe what he is hearing. Does this officer not know that they are in Auschwitz and that there is no such thing as being treated fairly?

'May I have permission to speak honestly?'

The officer gives a slight nod.

'You say you have treated me fairly. If you were treating me fairly you would have greeted me with respect, offered me coffee, a cigarette. There is a gulf between us that is impossible to bridge. Why am I even here? I have been convicted of no crime, yet my children were taken from me and are most likely dead; my wife, too, may be dead. I am a slave forced to live and work in the most primitive conditions in return for starvation rations, and you say you have treated me *fairly*—? You are indifferent to me and to my fate and to the fate of all the thousands who suffer and die every day.'

Meissner can see the truth in Emil's rebuke, but to admit as much is impossible. 'I did everything I could, but the matter is now closed. No purpose can be served by discussing it further.'

'Then why did you summon me?'

'I want you to play another game of chess.'

'Why? So you can dupe me again?'

'Do not provoke me, Watchmaker. I did not dupe you the last time. The matter was out of my hands. I have almost been accused of being a Jew-lover.'

Emil does not reply. His nose has stopped bleeding. He folds the handkerchief and tries to hand it back. Meissner waves it away.

'About this other game of chess,' he says. 'This time you will play against one of the officers.'

Emil will not be taken in a second time. 'I will not do it.'

'I offer you the same terms as before. If you win, you will save a life.'

Emil's head snaps up. 'My wife,' he says. 'I will play for my wife.'

Meissner frowns. 'I've already told you – I have no authority in Birkenau, only here in Monowitz. You must choose someone else.'

'But there is no one else.'

'Nobody whose life is worth saving?'

'I did not say that. I don't know anyone else well enough to choose.'

'Then choose somebody at random. You could draw lots. I don't care how or who you choose, but I want it done quickly.'

Emil knows he has no choice in the matter. Win or lose, he will be forced to play, as he was before. 'How can I be sure that whoever I pick this time will be protected?'

'I will supervise the entry in their camp record myself.'

Emil is beaten. 'How will you know who I have chosen?'

'Tell your *Blockältester*. He will get word to me.'

'I'm thirsty,' the bishop said, hoarsely.

A glass of water stood on the cabinet next to the bed. Emil went to pass it across but Meissner shook his head. 'Help me to sit up.' He grimaced with pain as Emil gripped his arms and pulled him upright. 'I don't like this laudanum,' he said. 'It clouds my thinking.'

Emil offered the glass again. Meissner took it and drank thirstily. 'You tell it exactly as I remember. I have reflected many times on our conversations in Auschwitz.' He paused, collecting his thoughts. 'You remember I told you the other day I thought God had a final purpose for my life?'

'Yes. You said that purpose was me.'

'I did not say so then, but I'm also sure that although He had no part in sending you to Auschwitz, once you were there, God also had a purpose for you.' He looked searchingly at Emil. 'No matter how you might try, you cannot evade God's purpose.'

'What purpose can He possibly have had for me in that place?'

'It was me.' Meissner saw the look of incredulity on Emil's face. 'Please, do not think me so egotistical. Catholics believe that there is more rejoicing in Heaven over one sinner who repents, than over ninety-nine righteous persons who do not need to repent. I was that sinner, and it was you who set me on the path to repentance.'

Emil stared at him. 'Now I am confused. Before, we talked of forgiveness but now you add something else. Which is more important – forgiveness or repentance?'

Meissner took another sip of water. 'For a sinner such as me, without repentance there can be no forgiveness. After the war, when I was awaiting my trial for war crimes, I realized it would not have been possible to seek forgiveness of God in Auschwitz because He had been shut out as surely as all of us were shut in. Auschwitz was a fortress designed to keep God and mercy and compassion as far away as humanly possible.'

'So you repented, and God forgave you.' Emil closed his eyes for a moment, to reflect on what Paul had said. He was missing something. 'But you said that was not enough. What else did you need?'

'There was – and is – only myself.'

Emil rubbed a hand over his face. He felt drained. *My life is not yours to bargain with.* 'And have you been able to forgive yourself?' he asked.

'Not yet. Perhaps never. But I must hope. Otherwise, I am lost.'

'That is what I used to tell myself every day in Auschwitz.'

'And now?'

'Now I wonder whether the hope I held on to so fiercely was worth the price I have had to pay for it ever since.'

'I'm sorry to hear that.'

'There's that word again. And it's still too small, too feeble, for what you need it to do.'

Meissner fell back exhausted. Emil stayed with him for a few minutes and then went down to the kitchen.

The housekeeper was at the stove, stirring the contents of a large pan. 'I'm making some broth for the bishop,' she said. 'The doctor said it was important to try and keep his strength up. Would you like some?'

'Thank you, that's very kind of you.'

'Mijnheer Willi came back while you were talking to the bishop. He said he didn't want to disturb you. Would you mind finding him and telling him that lunch is ready?'

Emil climbed the stairs again in search of Willi's bedroom. He tried two empty rooms before he found the right one. Inside, Schweninger was seated at a small table, writing. He looked up when Emil entered the room.

'Good afternoon,' he said brightly. 'How is the patient?'

'As well as can be expected, I suppose. Lunch is ready if you would like some.'

By the time they got down to the kitchen, Father Scholten had returned from saying the midday Mass. Mrs Brinckvoort ladled generous portions of steaming broth into three bowls and they seated themselves around the table. The priest said grace, and a second prayer for the recovery of Paul Meissner.

'Father,' Emil said hesitantly, 'a day or so ago, the bishop asked if I would like to stay here. At the time I said no, but if it's all right with you, I have changed my mind. While he's so ill, I would like to be close by.'

'Of course,' the priest replied. He turned to the housekeeper, who was setting a bowl of broth on a tray. 'Mrs Brinckvoort, could you make up a room for Mijnheer Clément?' He turned back to Emil. 'If you don't mind my asking, how is that you and the bishop came to be such good friends?'

With a wan smile Emil replied, 'I'm not sure you could call us "good" friends. But friends, certainly. As to how, I have been asking myself the same question. I suppose it's because we went through quite a lot together during the war.'

Before the priest could reply there was a loud crash from upstairs. Mrs Brinckvoort was first out of the door.

They found the bishop on his knees on the landing, the housekeeper trying to help him up. 'He fell,' she announced, unnecessarily.

'Please,' Meissner said weakly, 'don't make a fuss. I needed the toilet, that's all, and I thought I could make it on my own.'

'Here, let me,' Emil offered, taking Meissner's arm and hoisting it around his shoulder. He spoke to the others. 'I'll shout if we need help.'

The two of them edged along the landing to the bathroom. Emil eased the sick man into the lavatory and helped him to unfasten his pyjamas. 'I'll wait outside the door,' he said. 'Shout when you're finished.'

It was a struggle getting Meissner back to bed, but he insisted Emil should not call the others for help.

When he was settled on his pillows again, gasping with pain, Meissner reached across to grasp Emil's arm. 'Thank you,' he murmured. 'I know things look bad, but I'm not finished yet. These episodes come and go. I will be up and about again before you know it. In the meantime, keep talking to Willi. He is not so bad as you think.'

Later, Willi offered to help Emil move his things across to the Krijtberg. In Emil's hotel room, he noticed the small ivory tiles inscribed with Hebrew letters. 'What are these?' he asked.

Emil put them into a soft leather pouch. 'I'll tell you later.'

Afterwards they went to a bar and ordered beer. They sat in an uncomfortable silence, sipping occasionally at their drinks. After a while Emil asked, 'Before we played, did you analyse any of my previous games?'

'Of course. I obtained the records of many of your games, looking for the moves you favour, trying to discern any pattern to your play.'

Emil took a sip of beer. 'And did you? Find any pattern, I mean.'

The German shook his head. 'It was strange. Your play seemed very methodical. I was convinced you must play to a system, but I couldn't work out what it was – every time I thought I could detect a pattern of play, it vanished. It seemed to be taunting me. "Here I am," it was saying. "Look closer." It was like a wisp of smoke from a cigarette – it hangs in the air and then a door opens and it is gone.'

Emil smiled. 'Of course I have a system – perhaps more of a philosophy than a system. But I learned in Auschwitz to keep things to myself. It's hard to break the habit.'

'A philosophy? That's even more intriguing, but you should not keep it to yourself.' Willi regarded him earnestly. 'The game of chess is bigger than either of us. You should tell people about your philosophy, and see what happens when they add their own ways of thinking to it.'

'That's the problem. I don't really understand how it works myself. When I draw on it, it doesn't tell me what moves to make – it's more what my mental approach should be.'

'Is it a form of meditation?'

Emil did not answer. Instead, he reached into his jacket pocket for some cigarettes and, taking one, lit it. Exhaling a cloud of smoke upwards, he offered the pack to Willi and said, 'I suppose you could say it was something like that, yes.'

Willi took a cigarette. 'Look,' he said, holding it loosely between his fingers, 'if you think it's none of my business, all you have to do is say so.' He put the cigarette to his lips.

'No, it's not that, not exactly.' Emil ran a hand through his hair. 'It's just that I've never told anyone before...'

With his good hand, Willi lit up and inhaled deeply. 'Fine. I'm not trying to pry. It was you that mentioned it.'

'My system is based on the Kabbalah.'

'The Kabbalah?'

'Yes. It's a Jewish mystical science based on the Hebrew alphabet. You remember the tiles you found earlier? On each of them is inscribed a letter that signifies one of the powers of the orders of angels. In some way I feel as if I am able to connect with the power and I don't have to think about what moves I should make. I simply know.'

Schweninger gave a wry smile. 'You're playing with the hand of God. That doesn't seem fair.'

Emil shook his head. 'Not the hand of God – the power of angels. It's a little different.'

'But still hardly fair.'

'No, I suppose not.'

'Some people might say you were deluded.'

'Yes. And they might be right.'

'How does it work then, this Kabbalah?'

Emil took a moment to gather his thoughts. 'The night before an important game, I cast the alphabet tiles with the letters facing down and arrange them in a pattern. I pick the one that feels right. The letter that is revealed represents the order of angels I should call on.'

Willi's eyes narrowed. 'What letter was I?'

'The fifth letter, He.'

'And what did that mean to you?'

'"He" signifies the sword of the Almighty and the strength which flows from the limitless power of God. To me it meant I could be confident of victory.'

'But how did it influence the way you played?'

'I sensed it meant I should appear to play cautiously. I already knew of your reputation for aggressive play and thought that if I held back, you would think me timid and press all the harder and not see the trap I set for you. And it worked, did it not?'

Willi grinned, shaking his head. 'That's too subtle for me.' He drained his glass. 'Another beer?'

25.

THE COLLE SYSTEM

June 1944

Konzentrationslager Auschwitz-III, Monowitz

Bodo Brack had a conundrum. Its name was Widmann.

Brack had little liking for the *Blockschreiber*, but he was useful. Widmann knew people, influential people on the outside. He had been convicted of attempted murder, but before that he had made his living as a pimp, and it had been a good living. He had not been one to hang around street corners stumping up business for cheap whores; his girls were high class and catered to a rather exclusive clientele: senior military officers and civil servants. All had gone well until a low-ranking Gestapo type had decided Widmann was doing a little too well, and that he should share his good fortune with others. Thinking he would be able to rely on his clients to protect him, Widmann had shot the Gestapo man and left him for dead. The problem had been that Widmann was not much of a killer and his intended victim survived to testify. Soon after Widmann's arrival in Auschwitz he had started plying his trade again, sucking up to the guards and quickly becoming the leading dealer in *Mahorca*, the adulterated tobacco that he traded for the coupons the SS gave out for the camp brothel.

Brack cared little for Widmann's enterprise, but he knew that the war could not last indefinitely and that to have such contacts outside the camp could prove invaluable. Widmann had been a *Kapo* in charge of a construction *Kommando*. It was brutal work, not at all to his liking, and so Brack had seduced him simply by asking him to be his *Blockschreiber*. The duties were light and did not involve marching to the Buna factory in the driving rain of a Polish winter: Widmann had accepted without hesitation.

However, Brack was now realizing, it was one thing to keep Widmann close in Auschwitz but another to rely on him when the war was over. He needed to find a way to tie Widmann to him, but so far the answer had eluded him.

His musings were interrupted by the arrival of Eidenmüller. He handed a bottle of Schnapps to Brack, and gestured for the *Blockältester* to follow him outside.

'Don't you like the sunshine?' Eidenmüller asked.

'Not really. Anyway, not much of a view, is there?' They laughed. 'What do you want this time?'

'It's the Watchmaker.'

'What's the little bastard done now?'

'Nothing. My boss wants him to play another game. Against an officer this time.'

'And the stupid fuck has refused to play again, is that it?'

'No, he's agreed to play.'

'Then what?'

Eidenmüller stopped in the shade of a birch tree. 'It's like this, Brack. I run a bit of a betting syndicate and I lost a packet on the last game.'

'Because the Yid won?'

'Yeah. Made a bit of a miscalculation. I said to myself, nobody's unbeatable, especially not a runt of a Jew watchmaker. And Frommhagen, the one he beat, he's not half bad. So what I need to know is this – how good is this Watchmaker really?'

'It wasn't me who said the Watchmaker was unbeatable,' Brack said. 'It was a Pole who said he played in some big-shot chess tournament in Munich back in '36. According to him, the Watchmaker would have beaten anybody who played in the tournament. He said he reckoned the Watchmaker had supernatural powers he was so good.'

Eidenmüller hawked and spat. 'Bullshit.'

Brack shrugged. 'Maybe. Who knows?'

'He'll be playing an SS officer next time. Who would you put your money on?'

Brack sniggered. 'Who do you think?'

Eidenmüller glanced at the sun and grimaced. 'Thought as much.' He started to walk away.

'Hang on,' Brack called after him. 'What's he get if he wins this time?'

'Same as before – he gets to save somebody's life.'

'How?'

Eidenmüller stopped and gave Brack a puzzled look. 'I thought you knew – when there's a *Selektion*, they'll be protected.'

Understanding registered on Brack's face. 'Right. So – whose life?'

'Anyone he likes.'

Anyone he likes . . . Eidenmüller's words set the cogs whirring in Brack's brain. By the time he got back to the block he was beaming.

He had found the answer to his conundrum.

Word of Emil's victory over one of the all-powerful SS has circulated around his block, and some of his fellow prisoners have had the audacity to mention it to the *Kapos* in their work *Kommandos*. Most are rewarded with a kicking or a sharp blow from a knotted rope, but this has not prevented the whispers from spreading: the Nazis are not unbeatable.

When Emil returned to the block that evening, Brack was waiting for him.

Seeing him, Emil's stomach contracted to a tight knot of anxiety: the fearful beating he had received at the hands of the block elder remained an acutely painful memory. Why would Brack be waiting for him? The only thing he could think of was that Brack had been told to stop the whispers at their source.

To Emil's alarm, Brack put an arm around his shoulder as if they were the best of friends, and led him away from the block so they could not be overheard.

'You know, Watchmaker, I think you and me got off on the wrong foot. I said to myself, Bodo, you and the Watchmaker ought to be friends, good friends. You'd like that, wouldn't you? Fact is, I've got a bit of a proposition for you.' He patted Emil's shoulder clumsily. 'We both know this war ain't going to last for ever, don't we? Well, I reckon if you help me and I help you, the both of us will live to survive it.'

Emil eyed the *Blockältester* suspiciously. 'What do you want?'

'I want us to help each other, that's all. Look, I've been doing a bit of digging around. I know a lot about you. I know you got a wife in the camp, for example.'

The expression on Emil's face told Brack that he had hit his target.

'She's dead,' Emil muttered. 'I'm sure of it.'

'What if she's not? What if I was in a position to help her? What would you do for me in return?'

Emil searched Brack's face, trying to fathom whether the *Blockältester* was sincere. 'Anything,' he said, his mouth suddenly dry. 'I'd do anything.

Is she still alive?'

'She is. At least, her name hasn't appeared on any of the death reports.'

'Where is she?'

'In Birkenau.'

'Can you get a message to her?'

Slowly Brack shook his head. 'It's chaos there. There's a big *Aktion* going on. Thousands of Jews arriving from Hungary every day, and all of them going straight up the chimney.'

'If it's chaos, how can you help her?'

'I might be able to get her extra rations.'

'What do you want me to do?'

'Simple. Keep playing – and winning – at chess. I know about your deal with that SS officer – I get to choose whose life you are playing for, and I will do what I can for your wife.'

'You want to choose whose life I play for? What if I say no?'

Brack smiled, an unctuous leer. 'You wouldn't want to do that, Watch-maker. Think about your poor wife. Besides, that's not the only way I can help you.' He stepped away, expecting Emil to follow, but the Watchmaker did not move. Brack jerked his head in the direction of their block. 'Come on,' he said.

Brack led Emil to the line for the evening soup ration. He took Emil straight to the front and said to the inmate who was doling out the soup: 'In case you didn't know, this is the Watchmaker and he's a friend of mine. In future he's to get his soup ration from the bottom of the pot, not the top, got that?' He gestured for Emil to hold out his bowl. The ladle dipped to the bottom and came up heavy with chunks of potato and turnip. 'Give him two,' Brack ordered. He winked at Emil. 'So, Watchmaker. Do we have an understanding?'

Like a drowning man, Emil's hunger rose instantly to the surface, gasping for air.

He gave a little bob of his head.

Later, Widmann asked Brack what he was up to. 'Insurance,' came the reply. 'I've got a proposition for you. Some of the Yids in here are bound to have rich relatives in England or America, only they can't get word out to them. But *we* can.' He stepped closer to Widmann and lowered his voice, explaining the deal he had just struck. 'Every time the Watchmaker wins a game, I've fixed it so that I get to choose which life he saves. So, we're going to have an auction – the Yids can bid against each other for their lives. We get word to their relatives in return for a large deposit into a Swiss bank account.'

Widmann grinned. 'I like the sound of it. What exactly are you proposing?'

Brack passed a bottle of Schnapps over. 'A 70–30 split. I've got the Watchmaker, you've got the contacts. All you have to do is get word out to the relatives. What do you say – deal?'

Schnapps or no Schnapps, Widmann was not to be bought so cheaply. He took a large mouthful of liquor and gasped appreciatively as it went down. '70–30 doesn't sound like such a good deal to me. 60–40 sounds better.'

Brack laughed and spat on the palm of his hand, extending it to Widmann. 'It's a deal. If we play this right, there'll be plenty for both of us. By the time we get out of here, we'll have made ourselves some serious money. But' – he pulled Widmann close, his strong, heavy hand closing around the *Blockschreiber*'s, squeezing it until the other man winced. 'Don't ever think of double-crossing me,' he growled. 'If you do, you'll wake up one day trussed like a goose ready for the oven – 'cause that's where you'll be going.'

Widmann pulled his hand away, rubbing it gingerly, eyeing Brack with alarm. 'Don't worry, Bodo. You can trust me.'

'Trust you? I don't think so. But as long as you remember which side your bread's buttered, we'll get along fine.'

1962

Kerk de Krijtberg, Amsterdam

After supper, the bishop insisted on coming down to the sitting room. The housekeeper fussed and muttered but Meissner would not be denied.

'The doctor—' she objected.

'—has been wrong before, Mrs Brinckvoort, and will no doubt be wrong again. It makes me feel much better if I am able to sit and have a civilized conversation with my friends.' He pointed at the antique cabinet that stood against the wall. 'If you look in there, you will find what's left of the bottle of Kümmel. I should be very grateful if you would pour me a large one.'

'But the doctor—'

'To hell with the doctor. If you won't get it…' He looked pointedly at Willi.

Schweninger stood. 'It will be my pleasure.'

Not used to being on the receiving end of harsh words from the bishop, the housekeeper stalked out of the room.

'A toast,' Meissner said, raising his glass, an ironic smile playing on his lips: 'To life.'

*

The next morning, Emil and Willi set off for the Krasnapolsky and the next game of the tournament.

'Did you cast your tiles last night?' Willi asked. When Emil nodded he asked, 'What was the result?'

Emil shook his head. 'The tiles do not always give a clear answer. Last night was one of those occasions. I could not understand what they were trying to tell me. Today I will have nobody to rely on but myself.'

'How does that make you feel?'

'It usually makes me feel quite alone, but perhaps today not quite so much.'

'You will win,' Willi stated confidently. 'I have a feeling about it.'

This time Emil's opponent drew white. He started innocuously enough, advancing his king's pawn one square and his queen's pawn two squares before bringing out his king's knight.

Schweninger had found a chair from where he could see the game. Half an hour later, Lijsbeth Pietersen sat beside him. 'What's happening?' she whispered.

'It's very different from the last game,' he told her. 'The Hungarian is playing defensively, right from his first move. It's as if he knows he can't win but wants to avoid being humiliated. In my opinion, Herr Clément is certain to win.'

'Mijnheer Schweninger, do you mind if I ask you a personal question?'

'It depends on what the question is.'

'Last week, you and Mijnheer Clément were at each other's throats. Now you seem always to be together. What has brought about this transformation?'

Schweninger leaned back in his chair, smiling. 'Chess. That is what has brought us together.'

Miss Pietersen pursed her lips primly. 'Mijnheer Schweninger, if you didn't want to tell me, all you had to do was say so. Please don't mock me.'

'I'm not mocking you, I promise. I don't understand it myself but, for the first time in my life, I have been given a glimpse of the real power of this game.'

'By Mijnheer Clément?'

'Yes. By Mijnheer Clément.'

Although the game dragged on for over two hours, its end was never in doubt. Afterwards, Emil and Willi walked without speaking along the Singel Canal. When they reached the Krijtberg, Willi walked straight up the steps but Emil loitered on the street.

'If you don't mind,' Emil said, 'I need to spend a little time alone.'

'Of course. Are you going to the Leidseplein?'

'Yes, I think so.'

'I should have known.'

Back at the Krijtberg, Meissner was in the sitting room, a shawl wrapped around his shoulders. He seemed to have aged years in a matter of days, though his eyes were bright and alert. 'How did it go today?' he asked, as soon as Willi entered the room.

'Emil won.'

'Naturally.' Meissner twisted stiffly in his chair and peered down the corridor, like a naughty schoolboy keeping a look out for the teacher. 'Willi, could I trouble you for a cigarette? Mrs Brinckvoort has hidden mine.'

They sat in companionable silence, staring at the hearth and blowing smoke at the ceiling.

'You know, if Mrs Brinckvoort catches us, there'll be hell to pay.' Meissner laughed and started to cough.

'I suppose.' Willi flicked his cigarette butt into the fire. He looked troubled.

'Is everything all right, Willi?' Meissner asked.

'No. It's not – not really.' He paused, then announced: 'I'm thinking of giving up chess.'

'Giving up chess? In the name of God, why?'

'Until a few days ago I thought chess was simply a game, a game with rules that could be understood and which, with sufficient dedication, could be mastered. I thought I was a master; fellow players in my own country honoured me by calling me "Master". But it is an empty title.' He raised his head to give Paul a quizzical look. 'I wonder how well you really know Emil Clément. To him, chess is not a game or even an art – it is an act of worship. It is not something to be mastered, it is something to be *lived*. I do not think I can compete with that.'

26.

THE TROMPOWSKY ATTACK

June 1944

Konzentrationslager Auschwitz-I

Unterscharführer Eidenmüller was fuming. Brack had been told to make sure the Watchmaker had taken a shower and was in a clean uniform. He had done neither. The prisoner stank; he could not be taken to the officers' mess in that state – Meissner would have apoplexy. But Brack had insisted it was not his fault: there was no water in the prisoner showers and clean uniforms were unobtainable. Eidenmüller's solution had been to use the showers in the enlisted men's barracks, but there was nothing to be done about the uniform. He promised himself he would give Brack hell for dropping him in it like this.

The Watchmaker stood facing the wall outside the entrance to the officers' mess waiting for the Unterscharführer. He could scarcely believe his luck: a shower with hot water – and soap. It was as if he had been per-mitted to indulge himself in the most decadent of luxuries. For the first time in months he felt clean, and when he breathed in, it was the tang of soap he could smell, not the sourness of the *Häftlinge*. It was almost criminal that he had had to put his filthy rags back on.

Inside, the Unterscharführer found his officer. Meissner looked at his watch. He spoke sharply. 'Why are you so late? You should have been here a quarter of an hour ago.'

Eidenmüller looked straight ahead. He could take no liberties here, in front of so many officers. 'Beg pardon, sir. I had to take the prisoner to the enlisted men's barracks for a shower.'

An officer standing next to Meissner grimaced. 'A Jew having a shower in SS barracks? I'm surprised you didn't cause a riot.'

'Me too, sir. But the Hauptsturmführer's orders were that the Jew should be cleaned up before being brought here and the water in the prisoner washrooms has been cut off.'

'Where is he?' Meissner asked.

'Outside, sir. Waiting for permission to come in.'

'What are you waiting for? Bring him in.'

The murmur of conversation stopped abruptly when Emil entered. SS officers lined the walls; most had been drinking. Malevolent eyes followed the Watchmaker's progress to a table that had been set up in the middle of the room. Emil stopped close to Meissner and stood to attention. The silence was broken by a snigger. Meissner gave an angry look.

Somebody spoke. 'Well, for Christ's sake, what are we coming to? A fucking Yid – in here?'

Then there was a shouted '*Achtung!*' and all eyes turned to the door where the Kommandant, Sturmbannführer Bär, was now standing.

'Gentlemen,' he said, loudly, 'what we are about to witness is evidence of the truth of National Socialist principles in practice – a practical demonstration of the superiority of Aryans over the Jews. For that we must tolerate this unpleasant intrusion.' He wrinkled his nose as if offended by a smell. He looked directly at Meissner. 'Herr Hauptsturmführer, I'd like to get this over with as quickly as possible.'

The Watchmaker was given a small bench to sit on. He drew black.

His opponent wore on his left collar patch the three silver pips of an

Untersturmführer. He waited with an air of nonchalance until Emil had settled himself, then ground out his half-smoked cigarette beneath the heel of his boot before advancing his queen's pawn. The Watchmaker responded by bringing his king's knight to sit in front of its bishop's pawn. The SS man brought out his queen's bishop to threaten the knight.

Meissner watched impassively. He could not see much of an advantage in what his fellow officer had done. If the Watchmaker did not move his knight, the white bishop would take it, but would then itself be taken. It seemed a careless move on the SS man's part.

Before the Watchmaker's arrival, Meissner had tried to counsel the junior officer against being overconfident – in vain. Only six months before, Untersturmführer Kurt Dorn had been in the SS officer-training school; after two months in the *Hundstaffel* at Mauthausen he was sent to Auschwitz. Dorn was typical of the new breed of concentration camp officers: what he lacked in intelligence he more than made up for with unconditional obedience. Meissner did not think he had emerged so brainwashed after his time in officer school. Perhaps it was different for the Waffen-SS: they had to be able to think – their enemies could fight back. Dorn's arrogance was monumental. He was delighted to play, he told Meissner; it gave him the opportunity to show a Jew pig where he belonged – in the dirt with all the other pigs.

It is one of the cardinal rules of chess theory that the same piece should not be moved twice in succession in the opening phase of a game. Emil violated that rule now, and with his second move placed his knight to threaten the bishop. In only two moves Dorn had contrived to lose the initiative and was on the defensive. The game was already as good as lost.

The last moves of the game were played in oppressive silence. Emil did not dare to take his eyes off the board so hostile had the air around him become.

With a surly flick of a finger Dorn tipped over his king to concede defeat. 'A fluke,' he said, sulkily. He stared menacingly at the Watchmaker. 'Either that, or you cheated.' Emil said nothing. He dared not meet the SS man's gaze. 'Set up the board and we'll play again,' the officer ordered.

Meissner strode over. 'Are you quite sure you want to do that, Herr Untersturmführer? I saw no evidence of cheating. Perhaps you…'

'There will be no second game.' It was the Kommandant. 'Get the Jew out of here.'

Eidenmüller hustled the Watchmaker away. The Kommandant glared at Meissner. 'Herr Hauptsturmführer, you will report to me first thing on Monday morning.'

1962

Kerk de Krijtberg, Amsterdam

'So,' Willi said, 'you won your second game with ease. No wonder the SS officers were angry. You gave their noses quite a tweaking. You could at least have made it look difficult.'

Emil pushed the remains of his breakfast away and reached for a cigarette. 'It was not so easy as that,' he replied. 'For a start I was very afraid. It's quite daunting to be in a room where every person really does want you dead. I could sense their eyes on me, imagining a pistol held to the back of my head. That's all it would take, they were telling themselves, and this inconvenient Jew could be forgotten.' He paused, unconsciously rolling the cigarette between his fingers. 'If I had been matched against an experienced player, there might have been some pattern to his play which I could have used to delay the inevitable conclusion, but this man had little real idea of chess and there was no thought behind his moves. For him to have reached the final of the camp contest must have been sheer luck, no more. He was the author of his own defeat.'

'He lost because of his own arrogant carelessness,' Meissner said. 'There were many like him in the Totenkopfverbände. What else would you expect, when all they had to do was watch over starving prisoners and herd women and children to their deaths?'

His words had a sobering effect and for a while they sat in silence, until Willi asked, 'What about the angels – did they come to your aid on that occasion?'

'Angels?' Meissner rasped.

Willi levelled a finger at Emil. 'Our Watchmaker believes he is able to call on angels for guidance. A most unfair advantage, I would say.' He smacked his leg and laughed.

Meissner gave Emil a curious look. 'I always sensed there was more to you than meets the eye. Tell me about your angels.'

With an unlit cigarette dangling from his lips Emil stood, picked up the kettle and carried it to the tap. He filled it and waved it at the others, spilling a few drops of water on the tiles. 'Anyone else want more tea?'

'Yes,' Meissner said, 'but stop avoiding the question.'

Emil struck a match to light the gas. Setting the kettle on the flame he stooped to get a light for his cigarette, blowing out a cloud of blue smoke after it caught. 'It's not such a mystery,' he said. 'I have created a system based on the Kabbalah. Each of the orders of angels has a specific attribute. I meditate on the attribute and it guides my style of play.'

Meissner nodded, as if he had stumbled on an insight that had long eluded him. 'Going back to Willi's question, what did the angels tell you on that occasion?'

'It was not so easy to summon them in Auschwitz; I had no tiles to cast.'

Willi leaned forward, eager to hear what Emil had to say. 'So, what did you do?'

'I had to find a number at random, to correspond with a letter from the Hebrew alphabet. I was with your orderly…'

'Eidenmüller?'

'Yes. I counted the number of times Eidenmüller called me a Yid. The number corresponded to Zebaoth, the God of hosts whose power is represented by the order of angels called Principalities. I knew immediately I should sweep my opponent aside without regard for any other consideration.'

The whistle on the kettle started to shriek. Emil turned off the gas and made the tea, stirring the leaves to make it strong. He looked over at Meissner as he did so. 'After seeing how angry the Kommandant was at the result, I could not understand why he let you continue with more games,' he said, adding milk to their cups and, for the bishop, sugar.

'Yes. That proved to be an interesting conversation.'

June 1944

Konzentrationslager Auschwitz-I

Meissner was outside the Kommandant's office at 7 a.m. He had spent most of Sunday working out what he was going to say, though what he couldn't admit to his superior, or perhaps even to himself, was that he had started to feel a grudging respect for the Watchmaker.

It was almost nine when Bär turned up, accompanied by a senior officer who followed Bär into his office. The Kommandant seemed preoccupied until he said, 'Ah, Meissner. There you are. Good of you to come.' He pointed at the other officer. 'I don't think you've met

Obersturmbannführer Höss, have you?' Meissner clicked his heels and brought his arm up in a salute. 'The Obersturmbannführer was the original Kommandant of Auschwitz. He's back temporarily to oversee the *Aktion* involving the Hungarian Jews. The results have been really quite impressive.'

'A privilege, sir,' Meissner said, with a deferential dip of his head towards Höss, wondering whether the Kommandant had completely forgotten the chess game.

'So impressive,' Bär continued, 'that the Obersturmbannführer has proposed the *Aktion* be intensified. Eichmann tells us he can send an additional transport every day, but we don't have sufficient men at this end to process them. Yours is the only section with any men to spare. You have such a genius for organization I'm confident you'll be able to manage if we take, say, fifty men and their NCOs off you. We wouldn't need their officers – would we?' he concluded, with a questioning look at the senior officer.

'Sir,' Meissner objected, 'may I respectfully remind you that the order to give priority to armaments production came from the Reichsführer-SS himself? I don't see how we can maintain capacity if you take so many men.'

'Nonsense. Where's that never-say-die spirit the SS is famed for?' The Kommandant gave his subordinate a condescending smile. 'Anyway, after the stunt you pulled on Saturday I'd have thought you'd want to do something to try and retrieve your reputation.'

'My reputation, sir?'

'Let's not mince words, Meissner. You're a bloody good officer – too good to be true, some are beginning to say. You don't want people to start thinking you're a Jew-lover.'

Meissner was indignant. 'Sir, I protest. It's not a question of loving or hating Jews. It's a question of duty. And my duty has been – and I assume still is – to produce as many bullets, shells and steel helmets as possible.'

Höss joined in. 'You are quite right, Meissner,' he said, mildly. 'It is indeed a question of duty. Your duty – *our* duty – is to follow orders without question. The orders to intensify the *Sonderbehandlung* of the Jews from Hungary come from the very highest level. I'm sure I don't need to elaborate. Time is short; the Hungarians are wavering. They may surrender to the Bolsheviks at any time. So this takes precedence over all other considerations, wouldn't you agree?'

There was only one acceptable answer. 'Naturally, sir.'

'Good. That's settled then.'

'Now, about the Jew chess player,' Bär added.

'Ah, yes, as I was saying on the way over, such an interesting idea,' Höss said. 'Though it doesn't seem to have worked terribly well so far.'

'Sir,' Meissner said, 'I think I can explain why things have not gone as expected.'

Bär took a seat and invited the senior officer to do likewise. 'Please do,' he said, acidly.

'In the first game, it was clear that Hauptscharführer Frommhagen was reluctant to take part. The Jew must have been able to discern this and take an advantage from it.'

'You can hardly blame the Hauptscharführer for being reluctant to play a Jew,' Höss remarked. 'One can understand it could have been quite distasteful to him.'

'Then how do you explain what happened with Dorn?' Bär demanded. 'He was more than eager to teach the Jew a lesson.'

'Quite so, but he underestimated his opponent. A fatal mistake when dealing with Jews in my experience, sir.'

'Nonetheless, I think you should bring this experiment to an end,' the Kommandant said. 'Immediately.'

'As you wish, sir, naturally.'

'I'm not sure I would agree,' Höss intervened. 'This Dorn, the one whose overconfidence led to his defeat – has it not occurred to you that in what he did there is a potent metaphor for the kind of difficulties that beset the Party?'* Meissner and Bär exchanged a puzzled glance. 'Consider,' Höss continued, 'although chess is a serious intellectual duel, Dorn was foolish enough to take his victory for granted. Don't you see? National Socialism suffers from the same problem. If it is not constantly confronted, it will grow complacent and die of hardening of the arteries. And the SS – as the Party's natural protector – should be in the vanguard of this challenge.'

Bär shifted in his chair, his discomfort at the senior officer's words only too evident.

'Don't pretend to be so shocked,' Höss continued. 'It's hardly heresy – one sees these kinds of ideas expressed almost every week in the *Schwarze Korps*.† In my opinion, what Hauptsturmführer Meissner is doing should be applauded as a bold experiment designed to challenge complacency within the SS and at the same time expose the very real danger posed by the Jews, who will take advantage of any weakness they perceive on our part. With the Jew taking full advantage of his natural slyness, it is working exactly as one would expect, and should continue to its natural conclusion.'

'Which will be?' the Kommandant asked.

* Nationalsozialistische Deutsche Arbeiterpartei – National Socialist German Workers Party – the full name of the Nazi Party.
† The official newspaper of the SS.

'The defeat of the Jew at the hands of the SS, of course. But only when we begin to take him seriously.'

There was no mistaking the look Bär gave Meissner: *This had better work*. 'Very well,' he said. 'But from now on, Meissner, it will be your responsibility to make sure our men do not underestimate the cunning of their opponent.'

'That should hardly be necessary,' Höss observed.

'No, sir,' Bär replied, 'but if it's all the same to you, I would prefer to leave nothing to chance.'

27.

THE ENGLISH OPENING

June 1944

Cologne

The rail lines running west from Kraków had been repaired, so Meissner was at last able to go home on leave. He had written to his parents to let them know he was coming, but they hadn't replied; indeed, it was over a month since he had last heard from them, but he wasn't unduly worried: Allied bombing was still severely disrupting all but the most urgent communication throughout Germany.

The devastation that met him in Cologne shocked him to his core: as a living organism, the city had all but ceased to exist. He was used to the carnage of battle, but this was different: it was his home, the place that had nurtured his hopes and dreams. For as far as he could see, apart from the cathedral, all that remained of the city was rubble and the skeletons of buildings gutted by fire that had fallen from the sky in an avenging hail. It was only eight years since he had left to go to university. Then it had been a bustling metropolis of over three-quarters of a million inhabitants; now it was a ghost-town, reeking of the stench of a dead city: escaping gas, smoke and exposed sewers.

His childhood home on Friedrichstrasse was a charred ruin. Of his parents and his fiancée there was no sign. He knew he should have been frantic for news of them, but the sheer scale of the desolation overwhelmed him, numbing his emotions. They could not have survived.

The Reich records bureau had no information, and all he could discover from the civilian defence centre was that the area had been hit by incendiary bombs about six weeks earlier. Now all that remained was the blackened form of the cathedral with its twin spires still reaching upwards to Heaven, miraculously preserved in the very midst of the inferno as if by the will of God Himself.

Meissner stood on the cathedral steps and watched a small number of people as they straggled in for Sunday Mass. The world had become incomprehensible to him. What kind of faith, he wondered, could draw people to this place on such a day: the desperate devotion of those who prayed for salvation before they too were consumed by fire, or the hubris of those who could not believe that they were deserving of God's wrath and who begged fervently for Him to send this rain of destruction elsewhere? And what had happened to his own faith? Was it lost, or simply hiding? The Lord knew he had seen enough for it to shrink to nothingness: the horrors of the Eastern Front and Auschwitz were more than any man should be asked to witness. But to see hell visited upon his own home, on his own family – that was too much to bear. He knew should have been feeling grief, anger, sorrow, fury, but the truth was he felt nothing. He was empty.

The only certainty was that nothing remained for him there.

He took a last drag on his cigarette and flicked it to the ground before turning his back on the cathedral doors.

Meissner had been ordered to report to the WVHA, the SS economic and administrative HQ, on his way back from leave, to give a first-hand report to Glücks on the status of the armaments factories within the Auschwitz sphere of control. It was the last thing he felt like doing. After the devastation he had just witnessed, it seemed pointless.

There was a tension within the higher echelons of the SS, with the RSHA* and its fixer, Eichmann, set on the extermination of as many Jews as possible, and the WVHA wanting workers for its slave factories. The war situation was becoming increasingly desperate, but nobody seemed willing to make a decision as to which of these contradictory demands should take precedence. Of all the actors in the drama, Meissner understood least the role of Höss. In the WVHA he was second in authority only to Glücks, yet he was carrying out the mandate of the RSHA with quiet yet unstoppable efficiency.

There were no trains to be had to Berlin, but Meissner managed to hitch a ride to Potsdam with two SS officers. They were both SIPO† officials and besieged the Waffen-SS man with questions about his experiences on the Eastern front and in Auschwitz.

'I intended to go to the east myself, to serve in the Einsatzgrüppen,'‡ one of the SIPO men confided, 'but I was told the quota for this region was already full. Then we began to hear the stories of how the work was affecting the men who did go – how they had to be plied with drink in order to carry on and how many were driven to suicide. I was glad in a way that I was spared all that.'

'That's why the extermination camps were set up,' the other added. 'To find a cleaner way of eliminating the Jews.'

---

* Reichssichserheitshauptamt: SS Reich Main Security Office. The delivery of the 'Final Solution of the Jewish Question' was in their remit.
† Sicherheitspolizei: the State Security Police. Its officers were members of the SS.
‡ SS death squads that followed the army into Poland and Russia and conducted mass killings of Communists and Jews.

'And it seems to have worked,' the first one said. 'Look at you – being in Auschwitz doesn't seem to have done you much harm.'

'I'm not involved in the liquidations,' Meissner replied, trying to keep his tone neutral. The SIPO was notorious for finding dissent and sedition in the most unlikely places, even among war heroes. 'I'm based at the main work camp. My responsibility is to keep the armaments factories running, so you could say I am more interested in keeping Jews alive than in killing them.'

'Does that not bring you into conflict with your fellow officers?'

Meissner frowned. 'Yes, from time to time.'

'And how do you deal with it?'

'I tell them I'm following orders, same as they are.'

From Potsdam he got a train into the centre of Berlin, and from there begged a ride with the daily courier between SS headquarters and the WVHA offices in Oranienburg.

Gruppenführer Glücks seemed less interested in the state of the slave factories than he was in the performance of Obersturmbannführer Höss. Meissner sensed the Gruppenführer disliked his deputy and wanted information that would undermine him. It was not an intrigue in which Meissner wanted to become embroiled, and he kept his answers short and evasive. He knew it would not commend him to the head of the concentration camps but, as he saw it, unless a miracle happened to save Germany from total defeat, this was hardly something he needed to worry about.

The final leg of Meissner's journey back to Kraków found him alone in a train compartment. He had had plenty of time since leaving Cologne to reflect on where his fate had led him. The Nazis had lied. The whole edifice was built on lies. Mentally he ticked off the lies of which he had personal evidence: the Bolsheviks were sub-humans who would be defeated easily; no enemy bombs would fall on German cities; Germany would never be asked to fight on two fronts again. And then, there were the Jews. How many lies had been told about them? They were beyond counting. And he had swallowed those lies, all of them. What did that make him? A fool or an accomplice – or both?

In Berlin he had obtained writing materials and, using his valise as a table, he started to compose a letter that he hoped would help him make his escape.

Abteilung 1

Konzentrationslager Auschwitz

30 June 1944

Dear Peter,

It seems an age since we faced the Ivans together at Voronezh, but it's actually been less than a year. Hard to believe, I know. Do you remember how we said we would laugh in the teeth of death? That was a lifetime ago. Duty in the K-Z is much less dramatic than fighting in the front line, but it has to be done. The amount of material we are able to contribute to the war effort is quite staggering. The workshops for which I am responsible produce thousands of steel helmets, bullets and shells every week – imagine how you would fare without them – and I am told that the first production of synthetic oil in the Buna *Werke* here at Auschwitz is only weeks off. Your Panzers will need that oil, so don't be too quick to look down your nose at me, even if all I have become is a glorified factory manager.

I have to confess I have not found life easy in Auschwitz. Most of the officers in the Totenkopfverbände look down on the Waffen-SS as brainless apes who can hold a rifle, but not much else. The way they see things, theirs is the more difficult and more important task. They have been entrusted with the struggle against the eternal enemy of Germany, even though they can't fight back. I'm talking about the Jews, of course. When you're facing a squadron of enemy tanks, everything is simple. It's a case of kill or be killed. The Ivans know that as well as we do – no quarter expected, and none given. When we were indoctrinated in officer training, I accepted what we were told about the danger posed by the Jews, but I never dreamed it would come to what I have witnessed here. Do not doubt me when I tell you that thousands of Jews – men, women and even children – are killed every day. There is no let-up in the slaughter.

I tell myself that I am fortunate. I am not in the camp where the killing is done and I am not involved in this brutality. In fact, I am quite insulated from it. But that does not absolve me from the guilt in which I must share because I am here and do nothing to prevent it. I tell myself that it would be futile – what would I achieve other than getting myself shot by the Gestapo? But the little rats' teeth of remorse are gnawing at me without mercy. The absurdity of it came to me recently. I got a lift from a couple of SIPO men and I told them that because I was involved in armament production I wanted to see Jews spared for work in the factories, not killed as soon as they arrive. That's what my life has come to – an SS officer in a death camp who is trying to keep the prisoners alive when everybody else wants them dead. Behind my back it is being said that I am a Jew-lover.

I must get away before I become like the rest of them. My honour is all that is left to me now. I have just returned from Cologne. Mother and Father and Maria were killed in an air raid. Do you think there is any way in which I could return to the regiment? At least then I could hope to be killed in action.

The compartment door was pulled open. A railway conductor stood in the opening, a hand extended for Meissner's ticket. The SS man turned over the page so the conductor would not see what he had written before reaching into his breast pocket for his travel authorization. The conductor gave it no more than a cursory glance before clipping its edge and passing it back with an apology for disturbing the Hauptsturmführer.

When the man had gone, Meissner read the pages through. With a shake of his head he tore them up. Everything was wrong. All except one thing. He must find a way to escape.

1962

Kerk de Krijtberg, Amsterdam

Emil awoke not remembering where he was. It took a few moments to orientate himself. His room was unlike anywhere he had ever stayed before. It was furnished simply, with a narrow bed, a wardrobe, some drawers, a writing table and chair, and in a corner, a prie-dieu with a crucifix affixed to the wall above it. Emil knew of the Catholic devotion to the cross, but still, its presence in the room unsettled him: the suffering Saviour with His promise of redemption among whose last words were, '*Father forgive them, for they know not what they do.*' Every time the cross caught his eye, it brought those words back to him. After a moment or two, he could not stop himself from glancing in its direction every few minutes, as if daring it to utter the words aloud.

It is not the Jewish way to kneel to pray, but Emil did so now, lowering himself onto the prie-dieu. He was unsure of what shape his prayer should take. Before his encounter with Meissner in the Leidseplein his life had been simple but certain. He carried the burden of Auschwitz with him everywhere and had become used to its grim companionship. He had long known that the camp was a living, breathing organism, painfully conscious that an outpost of hell had been planted in the fragment of earth on which it stood. The camp was both a victim and a witness: watching, waiting, weeping: keeping a tally of the crimes that were visited within its boundaries, yet powerless to prevent or punish them. It was this certainty that had given direction to Emil's existence for nearly twenty years. It was his duty to bear witness, never to forget, never to forgive. But it had made his life a bitter one, something to be endured, not relished.

Something Meissner had said the other night came back to him now. *But I must hope. Otherwise, I am lost.*

It dawned on Emil that *he* was lost. The rules of Auschwitz had blinded him, especially the rule that forbade hope. Even at so great a distance in time, he was unable to tell where he was or see where he was going. His life was meaningless. His devotion to chess had kept him going, but it had become mechanical, something against which he could measure himself, a disguise for the true condition of his soul.

He raised his eyes to the figure on the cross. 'Is that it?' he mouthed silently. 'Is that how a Christian prays – by listening?'

The bronze eyes stared sightlessly back at him. Emil shook his head and pushed himself up from the prie-dieu.

He found Meissner in the kitchen. His cheeks were brighter and he seemed a little less frail than the day before.

As Emil took a seat at the table, opposite Meissner, he decided to tell him about his encounter with the crucified Christ. He was not sure how he expected the priest to respond – perhaps with a discourse on the nature of the redeemer and redemption. After all, Meissner had been a missionary: it was his job to win souls for Christ.

Instead, Paul asked, 'What was it you wanted when you knelt before the cross?'

Emil was taken aback by the question. 'What makes you think I wanted anything?'

Meissner smiled. 'In my experience, prayer is something that most people reserve for times of great need. They stand before God as a supplicant, begging for His intervention.' He sighed. 'That's not how it works, I'm afraid. Most of the time, the best you can hope for is an insight of some sort – a revelation, I suppose you could say. It seems to me that is what has happened to you. Something has been revealed to you, but it is up to you to decide what to do about it.'

Emil shook his head. 'I think I was hoping for more than that.'

'Like what?'

'I don't know. I thought that someone like you – a priest – would be on more intimate terms with God; that you would know what He wanted you to say.'

'But there's the very problem, don't you see? It is not God's way to be so direct. Both of us are searching for the same thing – forgiveness – but it seems determined to elude us. And when we turn to God for an answer, He is silent – but why? Since I met you again I have thought of little else.' He leaned over and took Emil's arm, looking at him intently. 'But there is something I have come to understand. Forgiveness is bound up with hope. If you cannot hope, you cannot forgive. In my faith, to abandon hope is a grievous sin. It is hope that we must both rediscover, before we run out of time. And my time is running out.'

28.

THE KING'S PAWN GAME

July 1944

Konzentrationslager Auschwitz-III, Monowitz

Nobody knows how news travels so quickly, but the atmosphere in the camp is transformed by the Watchmaker's defeat of a second SS officer – for a few days, at least. There is a whiff of pride among some of the inmates, especially those in Emil's block: one of their number has taken on the invincible SS and beaten them – again. And, as if good news is contagious, there is also a rumour that has spread around the camp – that there will be no more *Selektionen*. But it is no more than a cruel delusion.

Such false prophecies are common currency, but the Watchmaker is real and those Jewish prisoners who still harbour secret hope in their souls speak of him in a wistful manner, like some past glory that has all but been forgotten but which is suddenly remembered. It is no secret that when he wins a chess match against the SS, a prisoner – a Jewish prisoner – will cheat the gas chamber. Now, wherever he goes, he is hounded by a straggle of inmates who shamble in his footsteps, as if following their messiah, some of them bold enough to tug at his sleeve, hoping to attract his attention and become the next one to be nominated. He is their champion; his is the solitary act of defiance against the indignities that are heaped on them every day. He is even said by some to possess magical powers. Shouts of encouragement follow his every step. Even some of the

244

Kapos greet him respectfully when he passes by, an unheard-of privilege for a Jew.

Brack is delighted with his protégé. Emil is given a bunk to himself, with clean straw and an extra blanket. When he leaves the block in the mornings, the *Stubendienst* inspects Emil's tunic to ensure it has the prescribed number of buttons.

Emil is troubled by all the attention. Almost since he first entered the camp he has had a companion in whom he could confide, but now he is alone. He does not trust Brack. There is no honour among thieves, even less among murderers. He is only too familiar with Brack's reputation for casual brutality. He knows of the incident last year when one of the newly arrived politicals pushed back angrily when the Ältester shoved him out of the soup queue. A red triangle on a prison tunic denotes a far higher status than does the crude star worn by the Jews, but that did not stop Brack from ordering his minions to hold the Communist's head in the soup until he drowned. The soup men then continued to dole out the ration as if nothing had happened.

No, Brack's newfound concern for Emil's welfare is a patent pretence. His life has improved immeasurably, but for how long? Emil is still not sure exactly what Brack is getting out of this, but there must be some advantage to him or he would not be doing it. As soon as Emil's usefulness is over, he knows he will be abandoned.

Emil is also more than a little worried that, since the game against Untersturmführer Dorn, he has heard nothing from Meissner.

One evening, Emil is stopped on the way back to his block from roll call by a Dutch Jew. He tries to give Emil his bread ration. When Emil refuses it, he says, 'But there must be something I can do to thank you.'

'Thank me? For what?'

'For saving my life. I am the one whose life you won from the Germans in your last game of chess.'

Appalled, Emil steps back. 'Do not try to thank me. Do not think for one moment that this is something I am doing willingly. I have been forced into this as with everything else in this place. As far as I am concerned, it is just another of the cruel tricks that the Germans like to play on us.'

The man shakes his head. 'I cannot agree with you, my friend. Your courage strikes at the heart of this evil regime. According to the Torah, he who saves one life saves a thousand, and that is the truth of it.'

'Courage?' Emil says. 'Please, do not mistake coercion for courage. When I entered the place where I played against the SS officer I was so full of fear that I almost lost control of my bowels. I do not know how I managed to win. That somebody's life should depend on my performance in a game of chess is an outrage.' He stops and raises his hand to point at the *Kommandantur* building beyond the electrified fence. 'Only the SS could devise a scheme so monstrous that we, its victims, would consider ourselves its beneficiaries.'

But the Dutchman is adamant. 'You are wrong, my friend. The very existence of this place is a contradiction. Every aspect of life here is the opposite of what it is on the outside. We cannot judge what happens here according to the rules of a civilized society. Here there is no right or wrong, only survival. It is a duty to survive, and every life that is saved is a victory.'

Emil can see that the man is not open to argument and tries to move past him, but the Dutchman catches Emil by his sleeve and holds fast to it. 'I do not know your name, my friend – I only know they call you the Watchmaker. My name is Kastein, Avram Kastein, of Rotterdam. Before the war I was a wealthy man. When this is over, if you survive, come to Rotterdam and look for me. I will not be hard to find. You will find me more than generous.'

In his zeal to show his gratitude he tries to take Emil's hand, but Emil is horrified by the Dutchman's words. He cannot bring himself to collude in such a bargain. For him to accept payment would be an act of betrayal. How could he profit from the place where his family was exterminated? How has this man permitted himself to be so corrupted by the perversion that is Auschwitz to even think of making such an offer? Without a word he pulls out of the Dutchman's grip and turns to run away. But Kastein calls after him: 'Herr Brack said you might be difficult, but my word is my bond. If we survive this, remember, no matter what, no matter when; I pay my debts.'

But Emil is no longer listening. He understands now how Brack is choosing the people whose lives will be put at hazard during his games, and the knowledge chills him.

An orderly stepped into Sturmbannführer Bär's office and waited for the Kommandant to acknowledge his presence. After some minutes, he was eventually forced to say, 'I'm sorry to disturb you, sir. Hauptsturmführer Meissner is here. He's asking to speak to you.'

Bär closed the file he had been reading. 'Meissner? I thought he was still on leave.' When the orderly made no reply he said, 'Very well, show him in. And have that Bible-worm bring us some coffee.'

Bär observed Meissner closely as he limped into the office, leaning purposefully on his walking stick. He did not stand to greet his subordinate, but waved him towards a chair.

'I wasn't expecting you back so soon,' he said. 'Anything wrong?'

'Nothing more than thousands of other Germans have had to put up with, sir.' When Bär gave a quizzical look Meissner continued: 'I went home on leave. It's been bombed. There's nothing left.'

'Nothing?'

A muscle twitched in Meissner's jaw. He shook his head.

A prisoner wearing the violet triangle of a Jehovah's Witness entered bearing a tray with a jug and two cups. The Kommandant waited until he had put it down, then told him to get out.

'How are you doing?'

'I'll manage.'

The terse tone of Meissner's response prompted the Kommandant to scrutinize his officer more closely. He could not help but notice how tightly Meissner was gripping his walking stick and wondered whether it was to stop his hands from trembling. 'I can arrange for more leave if it would help.'

'No. Thank you, sir. But there is something else you can do for me.'

The Kommandant raised a cup to his lips and took a sip before replying. 'Yes? What?'

'You can approve my request for a transfer back to active service.'

Bär narrowed his eyes and leaned back in his chair. 'There are many, including the Reichsführer-SS, who would say that what you do here *is* active service, and essential to the war effort.' He shook his head. 'I'm sorry, Meissner, but it's out of the question. The Hungarian *Aktion* is in full swing. You simply can't be spared.' He took another sip of his coffee, as if to indicate that the subject was closed, but Meissner was not deterred.

'With respect, sir, I don't really care what Reichsheini* might have to

---

* Himmler's nickname among the SS. It was not used in an affectionate way, especially among the Waffen-SS, where respect for Himmler was often scant.

say on the matter. It is my prerogative to request a transfer, and you have no good grounds for refusing it.'

'No good grounds? You think so?' Bär frowned. Meissner's obstinacy was verging on impertinence. 'Face facts, Meissner. Even if you could find a unit to accept you – bearing in mind that you are not fully able-bodied – have you any idea how difficult it would be to get a replacement for you? On the rare occasions I can get an officer sent here, all I get are the dregs – office clerks, schoolmasters and postmen with a grudge, who only want to wear a uniform to impress the women back home. They're unreliable and ill disciplined. I'm sorry, but I cannot support your request. You're far too good an officer for me to let go.'

Meissner stiffened. He had set his mind on getting away from Auschwitz. 'I am an officer in the Waffen-SS,' he said through gritted teeth. 'I enlisted to fight the enemies of the Reich, not to play nursemaid to Jews.'

'If you're referring to the problem of the chess player you seem to have adopted, there's a simple answer: get rid of him. Make sure he is included in the next *Selektion*, then forget about him.'

'I can't do that, sir. It is a question of honour.'

There was a brief silence. 'In that case, I can do nothing to help you.'

1962

Leidseplein, Amsterdam

Meissner had rallied and insisted he needed to get some fresh air. He said he would like to go with Emil to what he smilingly referred to as 'the best chess club in Amsterdam'. He was not up to walking, so they took a taxi to the Leidseplein. Willi had some business to take care of and said he would meet them there.

When they arrived, Emil ordered coffee and rolls and then they went through to the lounge at the rear of the bar. Meissner eased himself into a chair at one of the tables with chessboards sitting on them and leaned his walking stick on the wall behind. Emil took a seat opposite and started to set out the pieces.

'Would you like to play?'

'Me?' Meissner said. 'Against you?' He laughed.

'Why not?'

'I won't give you much of a game, will I?'

'It doesn't matter. We're playing for the love of it.'

'In that case, yes. I would like to very much.'

Meissner drew white and moved his king's pawn forward two spaces. 'It's hard to believe that, after all these years, I'm actually playing the famous Watchmaker at chess,' he said.

'Yes, who would have thought that a humble Jewish *Häftling* would come so far?' Emil mirrored Meissner's move.

As he did so, Willi came in, carrying a tray with their order. 'The barman asked me to bring this through,' he said, glancing at the board as he deposited the tray on a nearby table. 'Aha. A double king's pawn opening. Interesting.' He pulled up a seat beside Meissner. 'Did you know, Paul, that there are only twenty opening moves that white can make? The king's pawn game is a powerful opening. You have a dominating position in the centre of the board and both the queen and the bishop are set free.'

'That's a nice thought,' Meissner said.

'What is?'

'That a bishop could be set free.'

Willi smiled self-consciously. 'I was thinking,' he said. 'We should get on with the story.'

'In case I don't make it to the end?' Emil and Willi exchanged a worried look. Paul started to laugh but it quickly turned into a cough.

'No, of course not,' Willi said. 'I want to know how our friend fares when he has the entire weight of the SS thrown at him.'

'Well,' Emil said with a grin, 'as you can see, I'm still here, and the SS isn't, so I suppose that must tell you something.'

'It's interesting,' Meissner said, 'the notion of freedom. It's something I've spent a lot of time thinking about since the war, and not because of the years I spent in prison.' His voice caught and he cleared his throat. 'It's not something I speak about much, but after Emil won his second game I went home on leave, to Cologne. It changed my life.'

Willi took a bite of a ham-filled roll. 'Really? In what way?'

'It set me free,' Meissner replied simply, reaching for his coffee. 'You must bear in mind,' he continued, moving his king-side knight, 'that I was no stranger to devastation. I fought at Kursk, perhaps the bloodiest of all the battles in the east. I saw plenty of action – real action – but nothing prepared me for what I found at home. I thought I had already seen hell on earth, but I was wrong. Cologne was the real hell, because it was my home. I have never seen anything like it. The destruction was terrible. Terrible.'

Paul's voice had fallen to a whisper, so Willi said quietly, 'And your home?'

'Gone.' Paul sighed heavily. He delved into a pocket, brought out a handkerchief and blew his nose loudly. When he continued, his voice was thick with emotion. 'Everything – everyone – had been taken from me. I had nothing. No, that's not quite true. I still had the SS. That was my home then. But not the SS of the camps – they were a disgrace, a squalid bunch of petty crooks out to make as much as they could out of the "Final

Solution".' He winced at his own words. 'I wanted no company with *them*, you understand. I wanted to make my escape, back to the Waffen-SS, back to my old regiment, back to where once again I could serve with honour.'

'Honour?' Emil broke in. 'It seems incomprehensible to me that someone should talk about serving with honour in an organization like the SS.'

Meissner reached across the board to squeeze Emil's hand. 'I can understand why you would think that, Emil; and my service in Auschwitz does me little credit, I know. I confess I was convinced that National Socialism, with its values of order and unity and obedience, was the salvation of the German people. I thought I could contribute to the struggle without becoming tainted by it.' He looked away. 'I was wrong. I thought the SS was an elect order carrying out the work of Providence. I was wrong about that too, but I hoped that if I could get back to my old unit, I would be able to regain my self-respect.'

'And is that how it worked out?' Emil asked, coolly.

Meissner bowed his head. 'No.'

29.

GIUOCO PIANO

Friday, 21 July 1944
Konzentrationslager Auschwitz-III, Monowitz

Rejoice, rejoice! Hitler is dead, assassinated in his field headquarters in East Prussia. For the first time anyone can remember, the inmates are not marched off in their work *Kommandos* after morning roll call, but are returned to barracks. The SS guards are out in force, patrolling the camp perimeter with dogs. Their weapons are not slung over their shoulders, but are held at the ready, fingers hovering over the triggers. They look jumpy and wary. The rumour mill is grinding away, its stories becoming more fantastic with every hour: Hitler was shot by his own guards, Göring has been killed by a bomb, Goebbels has been strung up in the street by an angry mob. Gradually the inmates come out into the sunlight and congregate along the wire, watching the guards, wondering.

Hours pass. The noon soup ration is delivered. This serves to pull the prisoners back into the body of the camp, for nobody can ignore the call of hunger, but they eat quickly, too curious about this unprecedented state of affairs to stay away from the wire for long.

They do not know that in Berlin a battle has been fought at army headquarters between soldiers loyal to the officers who plotted to kill Hitler, and Waffen-SS units whose allegiance to the Führer is beyond question. But now it seems that nobody is above suspicion: even senior members of the SS have been implicated.

The camp guards do not know any of this, either. They have been told they are on high alert for fear that Polish partisans may attempt to break into the camp and free the prisoners. Naturally, the guards regard the milling thousands along the perimeter fence with suspicion.

As the day lengthens, even though no prisoner has been permitted to exit the camp, the order is given for evening roll call. But the prisoners do not stray from the wire. A day spent in idleness scanning the horizon has given many an itch for freedom. By now they have heard the rumour that an attack by partisans is imminent and they do not want to let slip the chance to escape. They tell themselves the partisans must be concealed in the trees to the south, waiting until they are at full strength before they launch their attack, or perhaps they are waiting for nightfall, for it would be foolish to risk an assault in broad daylight.

The camp bell is rung, a signal for the inmates to return to their blocks. Some automatically start to walk back. Others turn their heads for a moment but are unwilling to relinquish the positions they have occupied. This day is like no other. They do not want it to end in another capitulation. Now a group of guards is walking towards the fence. They are waving their arms and shouting furiously for the prisoners to disperse, threatening them with dire consequences if they do not obey. Dogs are barking, straining at their leashes, fangs bared. Some prisoners, emboldened by the rumours, dare to shout back, hurling obscenities and curses. If words could kill, no guard would be left standing.

Without warning a machine pistol is fired, a long burst of automatic gunfire that does not finish until a metallic click indicates that the magazine is empty. The noise echoes through the camp, alerting prisoners, officers, and guards alike, but it is not the partisans attacking. Where the shots have been fired, men lie dead or wounded, some screaming, blood spreading across the patchy grass. A few prisoners run, but most look on stupidly, frozen into inaction. With an angry grimace, the guard who has fired his weapon releases the empty magazine and replaces it. In a deliberate gesture he tilts back his helmet and wipes his brow with his sleeve, as if he has completed a difficult task to his satisfaction. He turns to his companions and jerks his head in the direction of the remaining prisoners. With approving smiles the rest of them raise their weapons.

There is no need to give any order: when he fires again the others follow suit, a lethal hail that hits the defenceless mass and fells them instantly. Now all the prisoners are running for their lives without a backward glance to see how many have fallen.

In a matter of seconds, it is over.

The guards are laughing. 'Fucking Kikes,' one says, reloading his weapon as they walk away, leaving the carnage behind them. 'They never learn.'

In his office, alerted by the sound of gunfire, Hauptsturmführer Meissner is inspecting his pistol, making sure there is a bullet in the chamber, before putting it into its holster. Calmly, he puts on his service cap, collects his walking stick and limps quickly to the outer office. Bewildered NCOs and men are away from their desks, peering out of the windows. None is armed or ready for action.

'All of you,' Meissner barks, 'get away from the windows.' Sheepishly the men return to their desks. 'Who's the senior rank here?'

A Scharführer calls out. 'Me, sir.'

'Grawitz, isn't it? Send a runner to Hauptsturmführer Brossman. Tell him we're ready to assist and await his orders. Then get the men armed and assembled downstairs. Quickly. I'll be back in five minutes. Eiden-müller, you're with me.'

Without another word Meissner heads for the stairs, the call to action too strong to resist, his orderly following in his wake. They reach the guard room next to the main gate without incident. There they find Obersturmführer Schottl, the Lagerführer. He is shouting into the mouthpiece of a telephone.

'What's happening?' Meissner demands.

Schottl regards his superior with contempt. He has not forgotten their exchange at the hangings. 'Nothing that you need to worry about, *sir*.'

'Thank you, Obersturmführer,' Meissner replies coldly, 'but I think I'll be the judge of that. It sounded to me like automatic fire, several weapons. Do you know where it came from?'

When Schottl does not reply, Meissner turns to an NCO. 'You, Ober-scharführer – where did it come from?'

'The southern perimeter, sir, as far as we can tell.'

'Thank you.' Meissner turns to Schottl and gestures to the door. 'Shall we?'

With a glare at the Oberscharführer, Schottl says, 'Don't you think it would be better to stay here, to have a central post of command?'

'In my experience,' Meissner replies, 'nothing beats an on-the-spot assessment. But if *you* think...'

Schottl immediately grasps the veiled implication of the Hauptsturm-führer's words, as do the rest of the men in the guard room. 'No, sir. Of course not. After you.'

It does not take long to reach the site. It is a massacre. A squad of four guards and an Unterscharführer are already there.

'Do you know what happened?' Meissner calls.

'No, sir. We only just got here ourselves.'

Meissner rolls a corpse over with the toe of his boot. There are three bloody entry wounds across its chest. 'Better see if any of them is still alive.'

But Schottl objects. 'Sir, don't you think we should be preparing for an attack? We were put on alert to expect a partisan raid. This could be part of it.'

'I doubt it,' Meissner observes. 'If it were partisans, it would be dead Germans lying here, not prisoners. I think somebody has been a little trigger-happy.'

'Sir,' one of the guards shouts, 'here's one still alive. What shall I do with him?'

'If he's able to talk, ask him what happened, then get him to the infirmary.'

But Schottl will hear none of it. 'There's no point asking a prisoner what happened – all they know how to do is lie. And we'll not waste our time taking them to the sick bay.' He pulls out his pistol and strides over to where the wounded man is lying. Without a word he puts it to the man's head and pulls the trigger.

Meissner is disgusted, but there is nothing he can do. He is only an administrator and Schottl is the Lagerführer. He turns away. He is not squeamish; he has seen many men killed, but never before in such a casual manner. 'Let's go,' he says to Eidenmüller, 'before I do something I'm bound to regret later.'

On their way back, Eidenmüller asks, 'Is it true, sir? Has somebody tried to kill the Führer?'

'I'm afraid it is. And from what I've been told, it seems there were many involved in the conspiracy. No doubt the details will come out over the next few days, but I am assured that although he has been injured, the Führer lives.'

They run into the guards commander, Brossman, leading a platoon of men. 'I don't suppose you have any idea what's happened?' Meissner asks.

Brossman stops, letting an NCO lead the men on. 'It seems there's been an unfortunate accident,' he says, flinching as a shot rings out. 'A loose finger on an over-sensitive trigger, shall we say?'

'More than one loose finger, I would have said,' Meissner replies, as another shot pierces the evening air.

'What's happening now?' Brossman asks, referring to the gunshots.

'More "unfortunate accidents". Obersturmführer Schottl is proving to be particularly accident-prone.'

'Little shit,' Brossman says.

'Yes.' Meissner turns to Eidenmüller. 'We've left the men waiting. You'd better go and tell them the panic is over. I'll be back soon.'

As Eidenmüller hurries off, Brossman jerks his head in the direction of the sporadic gunshots. 'Do I need to see it for myself?'

Meissner shakes his head. 'No, not unless you want to see the scale of the carnage.'

'How many?'

'At least a hundred, and Schottl is doing his level best to add to the count.' Meissner reaches into his tunic pocket and extracts his cigarette case. Opening it, he takes one and offers the case to Brossman, who pulls out a lighter. Both men inhale deeply, enjoying the bite of the smoke as it hits their lungs. They turn their backs on the slaughter and head back towards the SS buildings.

'How did you manage to end up here, Otto?'

Brossman puckers his lips and puts a finger to them to remove a strand of tobacco. 'Fucked if I know,' he says. 'I was a Scharführer in Mauthausen. They sent me there because I was qualified as a mining engineer. But once I got there that didn't seem to matter. I was put in the guard detail and the next thing I know, I've been sent to the *Junkerschule* in Bad Tölz.'*

'Really? I was there myself. When were you there?'

'1940. And you?'

'Not until the autumn of '41.' Meissner takes up the thread again. 'And after officer training, you came here?'

'No. I was sent to Poland. Until September '41 I was on Globocnik's staff in Lublin. God, he was a vicious bastard, I can tell you. With the invasion of Russia I expected to be sent east with the Einsatzgrüppen, but luckily for me, I suppose, I found myself posted here. At that time there was only the *Stammlager*, and a few thousand Russian POWs that we put to work constructing the camp at Birkenau. I was put in charge of the guard company, and I've been here ever since. How about you?'

Meissner grins self-consciously. 'I only ever wanted to be in the Waffen-SS. Death or glory, that's me. I contemplated a career in the Luftwaffe, but in my last year at university a Waffen-SS officer came to speak to us. They were the Führer's shock troops, he said, the imperial guard of National Socialism. That was good enough for me.' He was silent for a moment. 'Everything was so much clearer then than it is now.' He let his cigarette butt fall from his fingers. 'Otto,' he continued, 'I've been meaning to speak to you about this damned Jewish chess player. Will you take him on? I should warn you – he's good. He struggled against Frommhagen, but I think it was only because of nerves. He beat Dorn easily.'

---

* Bad Tölz was one of three SS *Junkerschules* – officer training schools.

It is a warm evening. Brossman takes off his cap and wipes the sweat-band with a handkerchief. 'Dorn? He's worse than Schottl. I don't know what the SS is coming to when they let pricks like those two in.'

'So, how about it? Will you play against the Jew? Only make sure you beat him, or Bär will have me shot.'

Brossman glances at the sky and sniffs. 'Can you smell that? It's the crematoria at Birkenau. Never quite get used to the smell, do you? Between you and me, Paul, I'm sick of it. Sick of the war, sick of all the killing. I think we may have made a mistake about the Jews. We're never going to get rid of them all, so why are we even bothering?' He shakes his head. 'Yes, I'll play your Jew, and I'll even do my best to beat him, but I'm not making any promises.'

'For his sake I hope you do beat him.'

'Why?'

'Because after you he would face Hustek.'

'Christ. I wouldn't wish that on anybody. Not even a poxy Yid.'

'Quite. But on the other hand...'

'Yes?'

'I've seen the Jew play. I'm no expert, but I think he may be quite exceptional. What if he beats you and Hustek, too? Then what?'

The sound of another shot breaks the calm. Brossman scowls. 'Luckily for me,' he says, 'that's not something I'm going to have to worry about.'

1962

Leidseplein, Amsterdam

'I remember that night very clearly,' Willi said. 'Talk about panic. We didn't know what was going on. The ministry building was surrounded by soldiers and we were told we couldn't leave. Joey the Cripple was frantic, expecting to be hauled out and shot any minute. Then, at about seven o'clock, there was a telephone call from the Führer. The officer in charge of the men outside came into the building and spoke to him. Everything changed after that. We were ordered to tune in to the radio for an emergency broadcast. That's when we learned what had happened. There had been a bomb, but Hitler had survived. The traitors were holed up at the General Army HQ. The people of Berlin were ordered to stay off the streets. We weren't far from the army headquarters and, a little while afterwards, we could hear the gunfire, very clearly. Then, shortly after midnight, Skorzeny arrived with SS troops and it was all over.'

'I have often wondered what would have happened if Hitler had not survived,' Paul said.

Willi pondered for a moment. 'The obvious thing would have been for the army to take over and negotiate a peace,' he said wistfully. 'We probably wouldn't have been occupied by the Russians.'

'Perhaps, then,' Emil said, 'it was better that he did survive. If Germany had not experienced such a catastrophic defeat as she did, it would have been only a matter of time before another Hitler emerged and the whole disaster was enacted again.'

'I do not think we would have let such a thing happen.'

'I wish, Willi' – Emil's voice was suddenly harsh – 'that I could share your confidence, but having experienced what a person like Hitler and his henchmen could inflict first-hand, you'll forgive me if I say that no price would be too high to make sure it could never happen again.'

30.

THE CHIGORIN DEFENCE

August 1944

Konzentrationslager Auschwitz-III, Monowitz

It is not the place of a *Häftling* to seek an audience with an officer in the SS, but nearly two months have gone by since the game against Dorn, and still there is no word from Meissner. Even Brack is showing signs of unease. It is some relief then, when, finally, word reaches them that the Watchmaker must report to the Hauptsturmführer without delay.

A *Kapo* escorts Emil to Meissner's office. Meissner is alone – even Eidenmüller is absent. The SS man seems distracted. He sends the *Kapo* away, and Emil stands at attention, waiting. Meissner limps to the outer office and returns bearing a pot of coffee and two cups. 'Please take a seat,' he says, and, filling a cup, hands it to the dumbfounded prisoner.

'Thank you,' Emil manages to say, as he sits. He takes a sip from the cup. It is too hot, but the smell of it is intoxicating. It is *coffee*, real coffee.

'Cigarette?' A pack is handed over. 'Keep it.'

Emil's hands tremble as he tears the pack open and puts a cigarette between his lips. He has nothing to light it with and waits, until the officer points to a box of matches on the desk.

Emil inhales deeply, savouring the first rush of nicotine. It is some moments before he realizes he is being watched. 'Why are you doing this?' he asks.

'The last time we spoke you accused me of being uncivilized. That is far from the truth. Germans are a civilized people. But we have allowed ourselves to come under the control of a bunch of gangsters. That is our disgrace and your great misfortune. There is little I can do about that, but I have decided I can put up with it no longer. I am not permitted to leave my post, but I will no longer play the game according to their rules.'

'*Their* rules?'

'They used to be my rules too, but no longer.'

Emil looks away, stunned. He wonders if he is dreaming. For an SS officer to talk to him in this way is unthinkable.

'Are you playing some kind of game with me?'

There is an edge to Meissner's voice when he replies. 'No. No more games, Watchmaker.'

Emil searches for a reply but can find nothing. He feels as if he is alone in a deep cave, groping blindly, trying desperately to understand the words that flit around him, like bats, in the darkness. He wonders if he is being tested and responds by saying, bitterly: 'It does not matter whether you are playing a game with me or not – nothing can change my situation. Not until you Nazis and all you stand for have been utterly destroyed.'

The SS officer stiffens. For a moment his eyes rest on a photograph of Hitler that adorns the wall. 'I know,' he says. 'I'm sorry. Truly.'

Meissner's words are shocking, astounding. They hit the Watchmaker with the force of an earthquake: whole cities topple and fall into dust.

Emil is bewildered by the transformation that has come over the SS man. He hears his own voice as if it were coming from the next room: 'Sorry? Dear God. Do you expect me to believe that? You give the impression of being sincere, but for all I know this is simply some new and refined cruelty that you have dreamed up. How do I know there will not

263

be some bolt from the blue – that all of a sudden, some punishment will descend on me without warning?'

Meissner does not reply. Instead, he pushes himself up and walks to the hat stand where his belt is hung. Taking his pistol from its holster he pulls back the action and puts a cartridge into the chamber. Then he hands it to Emil.

'It's loaded,' he says, 'so be careful with it.'

'What do you want me to do with this?'

'Whatever you like.'

'But why?'

'I want us to pretend, for a while, that this is not one of the circles of hell and that we are two civilized men having a civilized conversation.'

'And which circle of hell do you think we are in?'

'Isn't it obvious? The ninth one.'

'The ninth one? Heresy?'

Meissner shakes his head. 'No. Treachery.'

Treachery. The word rumbles like an aftershock. Emil becomes aware of the pistol in his hand. It feels strange. It is heavy, its black metal smooth to the touch, and cool. He sees it as though through a magnifying glass: there are traces of grease around the moving parts and blemishes on the handgrip where it has been damaged, perhaps in battle. Gingerly, he rests a finger on the trigger. It would be child's play to shoot the SS man; at this range he could not miss.

If Yves were alive, what would *he* do? The answer is certain: he would kill the German. But Emil is not Yves and the certainties that once guided his life have all been torn away: if he killed Meissner, would that mean he had descended to the same level? And – the most uncertain of all his uncertainties – what if Meissner is sincere?

There is a clock on the wall above the door. The Watchmaker glances at it. He has been here for thirty minutes and there has been no bolt from the blue.

Gently, he puts the pistol on the desk.

Meissner smiles, but it seems out of place.

'What do you want from me?'

'I want you to fulfil the Führer's direst warnings about the Jews.'

'I don't understand what you're talking about.'

'Watchmaker, you are one of the most dangerous prisoners in the camp. I'm surprised the Gestapo hasn't taken an interest in you.'

A look of alarm crosses Emil's face. 'Why would they? I'm not political.'

'Of course you are. Every Jew is political, because, according to the Führer, every Jew is part of the international conspiracy against Germany.'

'Ah, yes. The international conspiracy,' Emil says scathingly. 'I was an ordinary person doing what I could to make my way in the world, a watchmaker with a tiny shop in Paris. What danger did I pose to Germany? How could you even think that I could be part of a worldwide conspiracy? The idea doesn't stand up to any rational examination.'

'You would say that, wouldn't you?' Meissner opens a desk drawer and lifts out a bottle. 'Cognac?'

'No, thank you. In my state it would probably kill me.' Emil inhales deeply, catching the warm aroma of the spirit as the officer pours himself a generous measure. 'All right, then,' he continues, 'what about the poor, uneducated peasants in the Ukraine? Most of them have never set foot outside their villages. How could they be part of an international conspiracy?'

Meissner taps his nose with a finger. 'Ah. That's the clever part. *They* were an enormous Fifth Column. For years they have been lying dormant, waiting patiently, lulling us into a false sense of security. But when they got the word, they would rise up and overwhelm the German people.'

'How can you believe that?' Emil asks in wonderment. 'It's nothing more than a hate-filled fantasy.'

'I agree. But don't you think it's strange that among the nine circles of Dante's hell, not one of them represents Hatred?'

Emil's eyes stray to the half-empty bottle of cognac. Meissner catches the look and smiles wryly. 'I've not been drinking, Watchmaker. Not yet.'

'I would like more coffee, if there is any left.'

'Of course. Help yourself.'

While the Watchmaker refills his cup, Meissner picks up the pistol and resets the safety catch. 'I almost wish that you had shot me,' he says.

'Shoot you? Why would I do that?'

'Because I am your enemy.'

1962

Kerk de Krijtberg, Amsterdam

Emil brought the coffee pot from the stove and refilled their cups. 'Every time I have coffee it reminds me of that time in your office,' he said. 'I have never known coffee to taste so good, before or since. It was exquisite.'

'But what was it,' Willi asked Meissner, 'that you wanted Emil to do?'

'It was quite straightforward, though I hadn't thought it through fully at the time.' Meissner's face relaxed as he thought back, retrieving the memories. 'It took a while to sink in how rattled the Kommandant was by Emil's victories. As Höss said, this was a test of National Socialism, and a challenge to the complacency of the SS. Bär didn't see it that way – he considered it a dangerous experiment that should be brought to an end. Then I realized they were both right. I knew that Emil had an extraordinary gift and that, no matter what we did, he would win. This would expose one of the fault lines in Nazism – that the idea of the master race was a myth; a fantasy built on nothing more solid than the sinister delusions of a megalomaniac. I remembered the ideological lectures we had in the SS training school. We were told that the Russians were sub-human, but then we saw what they were like on the Eastern front: they were the same as us. We had been lied to. What if we had also been lied to about the Jews? I think it was in Cologne that I realized none of it made any sense. That was when I knew I wanted Emil to win.'

Meissner took a sip of coffee, putting his thoughts in order. 'The next game was to be played in the middle of August. I wanted it to be in the officers' mess again, but Bär vetoed that. He wanted it played in the prison block in the *Stammlager*, where nobody would see it. Hardly fair to Emil of course, but that was the intention – to intimidate him – all the prisoners knew what went on inside its walls. Naturally, none of this prevented Eidenmüller from taking bets' – Meissner smiled briefly at the recollection – 'which he told me were heavier than ever. But what came as a complete surprise was who turned up to watch.'

August 1944
Konzentrationslager Auschwitz-I
A room on the upper floor of the prison block in the *Stammlager* has been emptied.

Otto Brossman has heard tales of this place, though he has never been inside before: of cells below ground so narrow that it is possible only to stand in them; of prisoners locked in basement cells and left to starve to death in the darkness. It is said that some cells have been bricked up to entomb their occupants.

The room itself is intimidating. The plaster on the walls is painted a pale creamy colour, but it is discoloured in many places by dark stains. It is not difficult to imagine what goes on in there.

A single table and two wooden chairs have been set up in the middle of the room. A chessboard stands waiting for the players to arrive.

'I think the Jew is going to find this place more than a little daunting,' Brossman says in a low voice.

'That'll make two of us,' Meissner replies.

The Watchmaker is escorted in by Eidenmüller. Meissner nods to his orderly but pointedly ignores the prisoner.

'Is that it?' Brossman asks.

'Yes. The Kommandant did not want any spectators. He also insisted that you have an advantage. There will be no draw to see who gets which colour. You get to choose.'

'Then I choose white.'

The SS man advances his queen's pawn two spaces. Without hesitation the prisoner makes the same move. The SS man brings up his queenside bishop's pawn to stand beside its companion. The prisoner brings out his queenside knight. The SS man brings out his kingside knight. The prisoner moves his queen's bishop across the board. White pawn takes black pawn and the prisoner retaliates by taking the white knight with his bishop. Black bishop falls to a white pawn and with that the black queen is out to take the white pawn in the centre of the board. All this has taken place with almost unthinking rapidity.

White is ahead, just, and Meissner is holding his breath.

Play is interrupted by the sound of a heavy footfall on the stairs. A shadow looms on the landing and in walks Oberscharführer Hustek.

'Oh,' he says in mock surprise. 'I didn't think you would have started already. I'm sorry to be late, but then I didn't receive an official invitation.'

'What are you doing here, Hustek?' Meissner asks, already knowing the answer. 'The Kommandant wanted this game to be a quiet affair, not a crowd-puller.'

'But I'm not a crowd, am I?' Hustek replies. 'I'm only me. When I heard what trouble you had gone to over this little game, I thought to myself it's about time I took a closer look at this unbeatable Jew. So here I am.'

'Clear off, Hustek. That's an order.'

But Hustek is not to be deterred. With a smile sweetly laden with disdain he says, 'I thought we had already agreed, Herr Hauptsturm-führer, that since I'm Gestapo, I'm not answerable to you. Besides,' he says, almost as an afterthought, 'seeing as how I will be the next person to play the Jew, unless by some miracle he manages to lose tonight' – he sniggers – 'I have Sturmbannführer Bär's permission to be here. If that's all right with you, Herr Hauptsturmführer?'

Meissner fixes his eyes on the Gestapo man, taking in the cocky smile and pose of casual insubordination. He glances at Brossman to catch a look of resignation as it flits across the other officer's face.

The prisoner keeps his attention fixed on the chessboard.

'Don't worry about me,' Hustek adds. 'I'll be quiet as a mouse. Pretend I'm not here.'

'Fine,' Meissner says, making a tactical retreat. For now.

Hustek takes up position against a wall, lights a cigarette and says not another word; but he watches. Unblinkingly.

Before the game, Emil had sought out Brack. 'I want to know whose life I'm playing for this time.'

'None of your business,' Brack says.

'I think it is. I need to know the person who will go up the chimney if I'm unlucky enough to lose. I want him to look me in the eye and tell me he understands what a risk he's taking.'

'Oh, he understands all right,' Brack says. 'Same as every other Yid in this place. On the one hand, there is the certain knowledge that, sooner or later, one of the *Selektionen* will get them and they will never be seen again; or, on the other hand, they can gamble that you really are unbeatable – which is what they all think anyway – and that for reasons that frankly are beyond their comprehension, a life will be saved.'

'I still want to see him.'

'Afterwards,' Brack insists. 'You can see him afterwards.'

1962

Kerk de Krijtberg, Amsterdam

'Those early moves were played at a breathtaking pace,' Paul remembered.

'I can imagine,' Willi replied. 'Such an unconventional response. The SS officer must have come with a well-prepared game plan, yet you took him by surprise. When did you pause for breath?'

'Only after he took my bishop.'

'It must have been a terrifying ordeal. In my wildest dreams I would never have thought of a game of chess being played in a torture chamber, with a man's life at stake.'

'It was very tense,' Meissner said. 'The stakes were extremely high – more so than we realized at the time. I knew that if Emil won it would create more trouble for me, but at the same time in my mind I was urging him on. Brossman gained the early advantage and I was more nervous than I would have been facing a Russian tank. I can't speak for Emil, but the spectre of the Gestapo witnessing the whole affair made it difficult to draw breath. I could guess what Hustek usually got up to in that room. Eidenmüller had asked around about him, and what he discovered was not flattering, even by the standards of the Gestapo.'

Willi shuddered. 'I never met anyone from the Gestapo – not that I know of, at least,' he said.

'Lucky you. But Hustek...simply being in the same room with him made you feel uneasy. If you had met him on the street you would have known immediately that he was someone to avoid.'

'I agree,' Emil added. 'I never felt such malice in any of the other Gestapo I encountered.'

'Other Gestapo? You never mentioned that,' Meissner said, with some surprise.

'Why would I? You never asked me how I came to be in Auschwitz.'

'I assumed you were sent there because you were a Jew. I'm afraid I never thought beyond that.'

'No, I don't suppose you would. There must have been ten thousand Jews in Monowitz, with ten thousand tales of how they came to be there. You had no reason to ask me about my story.'

October 1943
Annecy

Emil returned from the town dripping wet from the downpour: another fruitless errand. Every time he went he ran the risk of being picked up. Annecy was not a large town and strangers were soon noticed.

In the confusion following the fall of France, Emil had taken his family south, to Rosa's parents in Périgueux. In late 1942, when the Germans moved to occupy the Vichy territories, Emil managed to get a letter to

Meister Nohel in Basle asking for sanctuary. His old master had replied quickly: 'Come at once,' he had written, 'before the round-up of Jews gathers pace.' But Emil's mother was ill. Her ankles were swollen and she had been feverish. The doctor said she could not possibly travel. So they had delayed until the following summer. Even then it had not been an easy journey, heading for the Swiss border shepherding two young children and an ageing mother, trying to avoid attention.

Near Annecy, they had come upon a farmer out early to bring in his cows. Emil told him they were heading for Geneva. The farmer said they did not have far to go, perhaps fifty kilometres, but the border was heavily guarded. He offered them shelter in his barn and told Emil of a café in town where he could make contact with the Resistance, who might be able to guide them. He told Emil to ask for Jacques. If, in reply, he was told that Jacques had gone away to care for his sick mother, he should then say that he had heard that Madame Blanchard was making a good recovery and that he hoped Jacques would be back soon.

Every day for four days Emil had returned to the café, asking its patrons if they knew Jacques. All he had got were blank looks. It did not bode well. They would have to move soon, before somebody told the Germans about the persistent stranger asking for a man he did not seem to know.

When he got back to the barn, it was empty.

Trying to bring his pounding heart under control, Emil inched around to the farmhouse. There were two vehicles in the yard: a small military car of the type used by the Germans and a black Renault. Emil smelt the acrid tang of cigarette smoke. A German soldier was lounging against one of the farm buildings, blowing smoke rings to ease his boredom.

From inside the house Emil could hear his children crying. He had two choices: to save himself, or to try and bluff his way out of the situation.

Ignoring the soldier, he strode into the house.

The ground floor consisted of a single room, with a large fireplace and cooking range along one wall and a table opposite; in the corner was an ancient dresser crammed with various items of crockery.

Although the room was large, it seemed crowded. In one corner was his mother, his wife and their two sons; in another, the farmer and his wife. Around the fire were four men: two in military uniform, one in civilian clothes and a French gendarme.

'What the hell is going on?' Emil demanded.

The answer came from the man in civilian clothes. His French was adequate, though his accent was execrable. 'Who are you, monsieur?'

'My name is Emil Clément.' He looked anxiously at his wife. The brave face that Rosa had been wearing for the sake of the two boys fidgeting nervously with her skirt, crumpled. Her eyes pleaded silently for him to find a way to rescue them. His mother was beside herself, her lips trembling and her hands twisting and re-twisting her handkerchief. The sound of Emil's voice startled his children and they started to cry again. 'And this is my family. I demand to know what is going on.'

The gendarme intervened. 'Monsieur,' he said, almost apologetically, 'this is Herr Hefelmann. I'm afraid you must go with him.'

'Why? I have done nothing wrong.'

The gendarme shrugged. 'Nonetheless, monsieur...'

'I *demand* to know what is happening!'

Emil's outburst brought a smile to the face of the man in civilian clothes: a mocking, insincere smile. 'I am Obersturmführer Hefelmann. Gestapo,' he added, with a touch of malice. 'You, monsieur, are under arrest.'

'On what charge?' Emil appealed to the gendarme. 'I have a right to know.'

'You have no rights,' the Gestapo man snapped. 'You are a Jew.'

1962

Kerk de Krijtberg, Amsterdam

'For nearly a week, off and on, we were interrogated by the Gestapo. Where had we come from? How had we travelled? Where had we stayed? Who had helped us? The same questions, over and over and over. First me, then my wife, then my mother. I think it hit my wife the hardest. She had never experienced anti-Semitism and simply could not comprehend what was happening. "Why?" she kept asking – over and over.' Emil looked up. 'To this day, if she were to walk in and ask me that question, still I would not be able to answer her.'

'We were conditioned,' Meissner said quietly. 'Brainwashed, lied to and conditioned to obedience.'

'But why were you conditioned? How did such a hatred of Jews arise?'

'It was not only Jews. The Nazis hated Communists, homosexuals, Gypsies.'

'You still have not answered my question.'

'That is because I do not know the answer.'

Willi interrupted. 'Were you tortured?'

Slowly Emil shook his head. 'There was no need. They had my children. I told them everything I could.'

'What were their names? Your sons, I mean.'

'Louis and Marcel. Louis had his fifth birthday while we were in the prison in Annecy. Marcel was three.'

Emil lowered his head into his hands, unable to continue.

The Janowski Variation

1962

Amsterdam

In the morning the three of them took a taxi to the Krasnapolsky.

Reaching the top of the hotel steps, Meissner pulled on Willi's sleeve. 'Hang on,' he gasped. 'I need a moment to get my breath.'

Willi eyed him warily. 'Are you sure you're well enough to be out like this? The doctor said…'

Meissner's face creased – Willi could not tell if it was with pain or irritation. 'If the doctor had his way, he would have me in an invalid's chair in a sanatorium somewhere. I'm fine, really, so please stop fussing.'

In the next round of the tournament Emil was drawn against an Englishman, David Abramson.

'Is he a Jew?' Willi asked.

'I have no idea,' Emil replied. 'Does it matter?'

Willi shrugged. 'I was wondering whether your Kabbalah would be effective against another Jew.'

The game was tough. The Englishman drew white and, in keeping with his nationality, played the English Opening, advancing his queenside bishop's pawn two spaces.

'Good. An orthodox first move,' Willi whispered in Meissner's ear.

Emil's response was not: he brought out his kingside knight's pawn.

275

Willi smiled. 'I should have expected this by now,' he said. 'Once again he knows his opponent will have a well-structured game plan, so he sets out to stymie it immediately with an unconventional move.'

Two hours later, the game was still in progress. The two spectators moved to the hotel lounge for coffee and sandwiches. 'Don't the players get a break?' Meissner asked.

'Of course, if they request it. But Emil would not dream of joining us – he will want to maintain his concentration.'

The game continued almost to the time limits imposed by the competition and ended in a draw. The players parted amicably and would play again the next morning.

'How many more rounds are there to play?' Paul asked Emil, as the three of them waited on the hotel steps for a taxi.

'If I beat Abramson? Only two.'

'So this is a quarter-final?'

'I suppose it is, yes.'

'I hadn't realized.'

'Me neither.'

Back at the Krijtberg, Mrs Brinckvoort had left a stew for them to warm through for supper. Hungry after missing lunch, Emil wolfed his meal. After doing the washing up, he excused himself.

'Where are you off to?' Meissner asked.

'It's obvious, isn't it?' Willi called from the pantry, where he was drying the dishes. 'He's going to cast his tiles.'

'Are you?' Meissner asked. He continued in a mildly amused tone: 'You know the Church has a strict injunction against fortune-telling and the like?'

'It's not really a question of simply casting the tiles,' Emil tried to explain. 'It's not like a witchdoctor throwing bones or a fortune-teller reading tea leaves. It involves meditating on the will of God. I have to be open to the Divine will. If I'm not, then no amount of casting of tiles will help.'

'I think I understand,' Meissner replied. 'And I would really like to see how it's done sometime.'

'More to the point,' Willi said, 'how did you do it before your match with Brossman? And how did the game end? I've been waiting all day to hear.'

'It's getting late, Willi,' Meissner said. 'It's a long story and Emil has an important game tomorrow. Perhaps that should wait until after Emil has won this round.' He glanced slyly at Emil. 'But I should still like to see how you do it.'

Emil brought the tiles down from his room and placed them face down on the kitchen table. He arranged them vertically in a column of three, then a column of four then another column of three. 'This is the shape of the Sephiroth,' he said. 'Put simply, each of the ten placements represents a different manifestation of the infinite will. But the different manifestations do not signify that God's will might change or has changed; rather, it is our ability to perceive the Divine will that changes. The highest point corresponds to the infinite creative will. The others are aligned with wisdom, understanding, knowledge, compassion, judgement, beauty, eternity, submission and accomplishment. After I have meditated, I decide which of the tiles I should turn.'

'Which one will you choose tonight?' Willi asked.

'None of them.' He turned to Paul. 'I would like you to choose.'

Paul had not expected this. 'Are you sure? What if . . .'

'I'm sure, Paul.'

Meissner stood over the table, pondering his decision. 'Which one signifies compassion?'

Emil pointed to the third tile in the central column. 'That is called Tif'eret,' he said. 'It balances the two positions above – Gevurah, signifying severity and Hesed, which is unconditional kindness.'

Meissner turned the tile. 'What letter is that?'

'Beth.'

'What does it mean?'

'It belongs to the order of angels called the Ophanim. In its most literal sense, it denotes the selflessness of wisdom. What it means tonight, I have no idea.'

August 1944

Konzentrationslager Auschwitz-I

Brossman was unable to maintain his early advantage. Once the opening flurry of moves was over, the Watchmaker found a way to strike deep into his opponent's territory. At checkmate, Brossman stared at the board for several minutes, trying to work out where he had gone wrong.

At a gesture from Meissner, he and Brossman left the room. Eidenmüller followed with the Watchmaker. Not a word was spoken.

Oberscharführer Klaus Hustek stayed behind, musing over what he had witnessed. He did not share Meissner's opinion of Brossman's ability as a chess player, but there was no doubt the Jew was good. Well, he would have to do something about that. Hustek prided himself on being methodical. He did not prejudge the wretches who were brought to him for interrogation – that was merely a charade to put them off balance. Even so, in his estimation Meissner had been taken in by the Jew and would do his utmost to protect him. He would have to find a way to neutralize the Hauptsturmführer.

The next morning Hustek asked to speak to the Kommandant. He sensed that Bär was extremely uneasy about the chess games with the Watchmaker and adjusted his own attitude accordingly, making it almost the complete reverse of what it had been at the final of the SS championship: he was respectful and deferential.

'Don't get me wrong, sir,' he said. 'It's not that I don't want to play the Jew – I do. I want to put him in his place, good and proper. It's just that I want to prepare thoroughly and, what with all the rumours flying around after the attempt on the Führer's life, I need to be able to devote myself to hunting out any conspirators who may be hiding here. So what I suggest is that the game against the Jew is delayed for a month, or perhaps longer.'

Bär agreed. 'Do you have a date in mind?'

'Yes, sir. October the thirteenth. And I would like the game to be played at the Solahütte, with your permission, of course.'

When the news was relayed to him, Meissner was baffled. 'Delayed until October?' He checked the calendar. 'Friday the thirteenth? What's he playing at?'

Eidenmüller had noticed the change that had come about in his commanding officer since his return from leave: he was pensive and kept to himself much more. Eidenmüller had tried in his clumsy way to discover what was troubling his boss, but had been rebuffed.

About a week after the game between the Watchmaker and Brossman, Eidenmüller was in the SS barracks in Monowitz looking for Unterscharführer Hoven, one of the few SS men who had bet on the

Watchmaker to win. Eidenmüller owed him money and he never welched on his bets.

Hoven was a hopeless gossip who was in charge of prisoner records for the Monowitz camp. As he watched his winnings being counted out, he could not suppress the urge to pass on his latest titbit: 'Bet you don't know who's been taking an interest in your Watchmaker,' he said, with a knowing smirk.

Eidenmüller looked up sharply. 'He's not my Watchmaker.'

'But you've made a packet out of him, haven't you?'

'Business, purely business. Anyway, who is it that's taking an interest in him?'

'That Gestapo creep, Hustek.'

'Hustek?' Eidenmüller said, raising an eyebrow. 'That's not so surprising. He's next in line to play the Watchmaker.'

'I'd say the bastard's been doing more than taking an interest, if you get my meaning.' Hoven tapped a bony finger against his nose.

'Bastard—?' Eidenmüller asked, curious.

'You've never been interrogated by the Gestapo, have you?' When Eidenmüller shook his head, Hoven continued: 'I have – by Hustek. Calling him a bastard is too good for him in my book. It was because of him I got demoted and sent here. I had a cushy little number, with benefits, you might say, before he shoved his nose in.' He curled his lip in disgust. 'Fucking Gestapo. They're all of them bastards, if you ask me.'

Minutes later, a frantic Eidenmüller was outside Meissner's office. But he couldn't go in – the Kommandant had arrived before him, and Eidenmüller could easily guess what he was saying. He could not have been more wrong.

'The planes,' Bär was saying, 'are American, apparently from bases in

Italy. Now that we're within their range, we can expect more than reconnaissance flights in future. What arrangements are in place for air-raid protection?'

Meissner stumped across to a filing cabinet and extracted a thick file. 'The shelters for all the camps are listed and designated on maps in here, sir,' he said, passing it across. 'We have given priority to the Buna *Werke*, with concrete blast walls and underground shelters sufficient for the civilian and SS personnel.'

'But not the prisoners?'

'No, sir. In accordance with policy, they are considered expendable. With more shipments arriving daily, it is a simple matter to replace any casualties.'

'Good. And what about your Watchmaker?'

'*My* Watchmaker, sir?' Meissner watched the Kommandant's face carefully for what it might reveal, but his expression was stony. 'Naturally, there is no special provision for him. In the event of an air raid he will have to take his chances, same as all the other prisoners.'

'Good.' The Kommandant stood and put on his cap. When he reached the door he said, 'It would be ironic, would it not, if the Watchmaker became a casualty of what he might consider "friendly" fire?'

As soon as the Kommandant had left, Eidenmüller entered. Meissner was peering at a large map of the Buna complex pinned to one of the walls. He barely looked up.

'Sir. Something important you should know.'

'It'll have to wait. I have to make an inspection of the air-raid-protection installations in Buna. If it's urgent, get Untersturmführer Schneider to deal with it.'

'I can't, sir. It's about the Watchmaker.'

*

Hustek had wasted no time getting on with his plan, and he was pleased with the progress he had made. What he had told the Kommandant about the need to hunt for anti-Hitler renegades within the camp was nonsense, of course – if they had been included in the conspirators' calculations at all, the camps were no more than an embarrassment to them. What Hustek wanted was time to find ways to put pressure on the Watchmaker. And he thought he had found the perfect way.

Employing the simplest of police investigative procedures, he went to the archive of prisoner records. All slave-labourers in the camp were registered; when they died, that was also recorded and cross-referenced to the original entry. It would be easy for Hustek to discover the Watch-maker's real name, the date he had entered the camp and where he had come from. Then all he had to do was to look for another prisoner with the same surname who had arrived on the same transport. They were almost certain to be related.

Unterscharführer Hoven had good reason to be wary of Hustek. A year earlier, he had been among those assigned to work in Kanada, where he had fallen under suspicion of misappropriating items of jewellery. He had been interrogated by Hustek. While it was out of the question that violence would be used against a fellow SS officer, still, the Gestapo man had frightened him. Hoven had indeed been purloining choice items for months, but he kept his mouth shut, and in the end nothing was proven. On Hustek's recommendation, however, he had been demoted and trans-ferred away from the source of temptation. Since then, he had nursed a grudge against the Gestapo in general and Hustek in particular, though he had been able to do nothing about it – yet.

When Hustek walked through his door, Hoven was so startled that it had registered immediately in Hustek's finely tuned index of suspicion. Did Hoven have something to hide – again? It was possible – probable, even. Hustek made a mental note to follow it up.

'I'm looking for information about the Watchmaker,' Hustek said.

'The Watchmaker?'

'Don't pretend you don't know who I'm talking about.'

'No. Of course not.' Hoven licked his lips. 'Everyone in Monowitz knows the Watchmaker. What did you want to know?'

'Just get me his record and then forget I was ever here.'

'What are you going on about?' Meissner demanded irritably.

'It's Hustek, sir. Unterscharführer Hoven in the records section told me. Hustek has been nosing around for information about the Watchmaker.'

'I don't see what's so shocking about that. Hustek's Gestapo. It's exactly what I'd expect him to do.'

'Yes, sir. I mean, it's more than that. Hustek wanted to know what his name was, where he came from, what transport he arrived on – everything. It's not the Watchmaker he's interested in, it's who came to the camp with him.'

Realization dawned. 'His wife.'

'Exactly, sir. And I wouldn't give much for her chances if Hustek finds her.'

'No,' Meissner reasoned, 'that's not what he's up to. If he finds her, he'll use her to make the Watchmaker throw the game.' Angrily, the officer slammed his hand against the wall. 'So obvious! Why didn't I think of that?' He gave his orderly an appraising look. 'And what about your friend, Hoven – did he give Hustek the information he wanted?'

Eidenmüller had never seen his boss so agitated. 'No, sir. Not yet. He said it would take a few hours to retrieve it from the archive. Hustek said he would go back tomorrow.'

'Do you know where she is?'

'That's where we might be able to pull a flanker, sir. Hustek didn't ask Hoven anything about the wife – must have his own way of finding out where she is. But Hoven has the records of all the prisoners assigned to the satellite camps – which come under your jurisdiction, sir.'

'And?'

'We found her. She's in the munitions factory at Rajsko. If we move quickly, we can get to her before Hustek.'

Rosa Clément is not in the munitions factory. She is in the *Krankenbau* in the women's camp in Birkenau. She has the *durchfall* – starvation-induced diarrhoea – and she is not fit for work. She will have rest and extra rations for two weeks in the hope that she will become fit for work again; if not, she will be selected for the gas chamber. Her fate is uncertain at best. Even if the *durchfall* resolves, the killing factories might be short of their daily quota and she will be selected anyway.

Rosa does not want to die, but she no longer fears it. She has seen too much death in the camp to be afraid any longer. Her overwhelming feeling is not of fear, but of weariness. When she first arrived she was employed in the *Krankenbau*, but after a few months somebody decided there were too many nurses and not enough munitions workers, so now she is assigned to a *Kommando* that is taken every day to a poorly venti-lated factory where she and perhaps a thousand other women make shells for the artillery. It is summer and the heat inside is stifling. The air is dry and thick with dust from the gun-cotton, which gives all the women hacking coughs. Rosa is better off than many. Handling gun-cotton is not her job. She inserts fuses into the ends of the shells. At first, whenever she twisted a fuse into its mounting she would say a prayer that it would fail to go off. It was as far as she was able to take any attempts at sabotage. Now she is indifferent: her actions are purely mechanical; she saves her prayers for herself.

In the K-B Rosa knows she has a much better chance of recovering if she is able to wash her hands after she uses the slop bucket, but although the doctors and nurses have asked repeatedly for a supply of water, there is none for washing. If she wants that, she must struggle all the way to the latrine. Even then it is not certain there will be any water. It is easier for the camp authorities to assign new arrivals to work than it is to connect a supply of clean water.

There is a commotion at the entrance to the K-B. An SS officer has arrived and is demanding a roll call. Everybody – doctors, nurses and patients – must show their tattoo with their camp registration number. It takes time to check off every prisoner.

When Rosa holds out her arm to reveal her number, the SS man smiles triumphantly.

'You,' he says, 'will come with me.'

32.

THE PHILIDOR POSITION

1962

Kerk de Krijtberg, Amsterdam

During the night Meissner's condition deteriorated. He endured a fever without complaining, but as soon as Mrs Brinckvoort saw him the next morning she summoned the doctor.

'How is he?' Willi asked the doctor when he came downstairs.

'Not good. It's like I said – he will have good days and bad days, but gradually he will have more bad days than good days until all he has left to him are bad days. All I can do is to make him as comfortable as possible. His main problem at the moment is pain in his bones and also in his abdomen, where his spleen has swollen. You will need to change his sheets – they are wet with perspiration. I will leave something for the pain, but it is only a matter of time before we have to take him into hospital.'

'Can we see him?' Emil asked.

'You can go up, but only for a few minutes. He's very tired.' He looked at the housekeeper. 'Mrs Brinckvoort, I expect you to make sure that the bishop follows instructions this time. If he insists on going out in his condition, I cannot answer for the consequences.'

They went up, but Meissner was sleeping. Back in the kitchen Emil pulled on his coat, for the walk to the Krasnapolsky.

'I'll come with you,' Willi said.

'No. It's all right. I'm not intending to play. I'm going to ask for a post-ponement.'

'What if they won't agree to it?'

'I don't know. I haven't decided.'

Willi reached into the closet for his own coat. 'Then I'm definitely coming with you.'

By the afternoon, Meissner was sitting up in bed drinking sweet milky tea and gently scolding Mrs Brinckvoort for fussing over him. It was well into the evening before Emil and Willi returned.

Standing beside the bed Emil seemed subdued, but Willi was jubilant.

'I take it,' Meissner said between coughs, 'that you beat the Englishman?'

'Beat him?' Willi smiled broadly. 'Paul, you should have seen it. The Englishman is good – very good, as you saw for yourself, but Emil? Pah. Let me tell you, I have never seen such nuanced play. The way he forced the Englishman to concede was magnificent. This is Emil's tournament, and, if he wants it, the world championship is his for the taking.'

Meissner turned to Emil. 'A man who has done so well should look more pleased with himself, no?'

'I am pleased, of course I am. But somehow it seems less important to me now.'

Mrs Brinckvoort put her head around the door. 'There's a fish pie and potatoes in the oven, if you haven't eaten,' she said.

'Thank you,' Willi replied. 'We haven't. We came straight here.'

'I'll come down,' Meissner said, hopefully.

One look from Mrs Brinckvoort was enough to tell them she would not permit it.

'The doctor said you must rest,' Emil said.

'The doctor is a lunatic. He knows I don't have much time left but instead of letting me make the most of it, he wants me to sleep or dribble the rest of my days away. Well, I won't have it.'

'I can bring food up on a tray,' the housekeeper offered.

'Good. And please, stop acting as if you have to protect me from knowing the worst. I know it already. I've known it for months. The only question is when. I've received absolution, and I'm ready to meet my maker so let's stop pretending, and talk about what's important.'

'Which is?' Emil asked.

Meissner looked him straight in the eye. 'Your wife.'

August 1944
Konzentrationslager Auschwitz-I
Rosa Clément is in a solitary confinement cell in the prison block. She has been there for days with no idea of why she was taken there. Ordered to follow the SS man from the K-B, she was made to climb onto the back of an open-topped lorry and driven away from the stark chimneys and the death stench of Birkenau to another camp, where the blocks are tall and made of brick and the prisoners do not have quite the same look of starved hopelessness.

Nobody speaks to her. Three times a day her cell door opens and the normal rations given to the *Häftlinge* are pushed in: for breakfast, the bitter liquid that passes for coffee, coarse black bread and a smear of margarine; and noon and evening, a bowl of soup made from cabbage and potato peelings. In the morning she carries her slop bucket to a latrine and pours its contents in. At least she is not made to work. After a few days the *durchfall* stops, but she is no closer to knowing why she is there.

'She's disappeared,' Eidenmüller said, mystified. 'According to my pal,

Connie Lammers, she was taken from the K-B in the women's camp by an unknown SS officer. It has to be Hustek. But where she is now, he has no idea.'

'She's in the prison block in the *Stammlager*,' Meissner said, 'She has to be.'

'You can't just take someone and put them in there, sir,' Eidenmüller objected. 'There are procedures that have to be followed – grounds for detention, records that have to be completed. Even Hustek couldn't get away without sticking to at least some of the rules.'

'You want to bet? The Watchmaker is a Jew. That means his wife is, too. They have no rights. So what if Hustek has broken the rules? Who's going to discipline him over it? Bär? I think not. But that gives us an advantage. Hustek thinks he's safe. He has no idea that we know what he's done, and in war, as he's about to find out, intelligence is the key to victory. We'll have her out of there in no time.'

'We?'

Meissner was smiling. The adrenaline of battle was already coursing through his veins. 'Yes, Ernst, *we*.' Eidenmüller looked at him askance; the Hauptsturmführer had never called him by his first name before. 'Look,' Meissner continued, 'we have to face facts. The war is lost. Anyone with half a brain knows it. And what do you think the Allies will do when they discover what we've done at Auschwitz? Pin a medal on us? We all of us need to think about what's going to happen to us after the war. We are going to need friends. Friends who will be prepared to testify that we weren't the ones herding helpless Jews into the gas chambers. Friends who will testify that, on the contrary, we tried to help them. If we rescue his wife from Hustek's clutches, don't you think the Watchmaker might be grateful?'

Eidenmüller shook his head. 'But Hustek? He's Gestapo. It doesn't do to cross those bastards. What if we get caught?'

'I'll take full responsibility. You were only following orders. But it won't come to that. Brossman despises Hustek too, and he's promised to help. Between us we can do it. Trust me.'

Night watch in the prison block is easy duty. A Scharführer is in overall command, plus two troopers on each floor, making a total of seven. Nothing ever happens at night. Apart from whimpers and occasional howls, there is not a sound to disturb the balmy August air. The SS men take it in turns to sleep – strictly against standing orders – but this is Auschwitz, and all its enemies are contained within its electrified fences. There is simply nothing to fear.

Hauptsturmführer Brossman's night inspection is a complete surprise. He arrives with a squad of ten troopers and angrily demands an explanation for why the Scharführer is asleep on duty, along with three of his men. Brushing aside the Scharführer's protestations, he insists on conducting an impromptu inspection.

The Scharführer protests. 'I'll have to get permission first.'

Brossman feigns outrage. 'Permission? From whom?'

The officer nominally in charge of the prison block is a Gestapo Obersturmführer, but everybody knows it is Oberscharführer Hustek who calls the shots.

'Oberscharführer Hustek, sir.'

'If I have anything to do with it,' Brossman growls, 'you've just signed your request for a transfer to the Eastern front.'

Despite the subdued light, the Scharführer pales visibly. To hell with Hustek. 'At y-your service, H-Herr Hauptsturmführer,' he stammers.

'What can I do to assist you?'

Brossman actually smiles. 'That's better. Now, it has come to my attention that a prisoner is missing from the women's camp. The Rapportführer concerned has been somewhat dilatory in bringing it to my notice and has been disciplined. According to him, the prisoner was brought here, but I cannot ignore the possibility that she has escaped. As I'm sure you're aware, the Kommandant takes a very dim view of escapes, and it's my responsibility to prevent them. So I want to see the paperwork for every prisoner detained here, while my men inspect the cells.'

'I assure you, sir,' the Scharführer says solemnly, 'at this moment, there are no women in the cells.'

'I hope you're right, Scharführer, for your sake.'

It takes only minutes to go through the detention records. The Scharführer has spoken the truth. There is no record of any female prisoner.

'Thank you, Scharführer,' Brossman says. 'It looks like we've been sent on a fool's errand.' Then a shout comes up from the lower level.

'There's a door down here, sir, but nobody seems to have the key.'

'A door with no key?' Brossman looks at the Scharführer, who shrugs. 'That doesn't seem right. Let's take a look, shall we?'

The door is solid wood and is set flush into a metal frame. There is a peephole near the top, and hinges and a lock made of what looks like cast iron.

'Who's in there?' Brossman asks.

'According to the records, nobody, sir.'

'Then why is it locked? Unlock it at once.'

'I don't have the key, sir.'

'Who does?'

'Oberscharführer Hustek.'

Brossman nods, as if the answer to an elusive mystery has been revealed.

At the end of the lane that leads to the prison block, Meissner and Eidenmüller are waiting in an SS staff car. Eidenmüller is on edge, but Meissner is feeling better than he has for months.

'If we get caught, sir, we'll both be for the high jump, I know it,' Eidenmüller says, through clenched teeth.

'Relax. What's the worst that can happen?'

'We could be sent to the Eastern front.'

'Don't worry about it. I've been there. It's better than here, I promise you. Someone with your talents would be a godsend. You would be in your element.'

Eidenmüller cannot believe what he is hearing. 'In my element? Getting shot to fuck by the fucking Bolshies? Not on your life – sir.'

'Get down,' Meissner hisses. The two men sink low in the car as one of Brossman's troopers jogs by.

'Where's he going?' Eidenmüller whispers.

Meissner does not answer. Moments later, the trooper runs back carrying a sledgehammer.

Inside her cell, Rosa Clément is listening to the commotion in the corridor with mounting apprehension. Suddenly somebody hammers on her cell door. 'Who's in there?' a voice yells. 'Answer me.'

Rosa does not know how to reply. She is not sure who she is any more. The light goes on. She blinks, trying to adjust to the brightness. Then she sees an eye at the peephole.

'Take a look for yourself,' Brossman says to the Scharführer, who is beginning to realize how much trouble Hustek has landed him in.

'According to your records, there is nobody in the cell, but quite clearly there's a woman in there. Even the Gestapo cannot imprison people without due process. I can only conclude that Oberscharführer Hustek has abused his authority with regard to this prisoner for his own personal reasons.'

'There'll be hell to pay over this.'

'How right you are,' Brossman agrees. He turns his attention to the door again. 'You, in there – what is your name?'

They can barely hear the reply. 'Rosa Clément.'

'How long have you been in there?'

'I'm not sure. A week, perhaps longer.'

It takes the trooper only a few minutes to return with a sledgehammer. The lock is smashed off and the door opened. The woman seems confused that her rescuers are SS men. 'Be silent,' Brossman orders. 'Follow me.'

He leads her to the waiting car. 'You took your time,' Meissner says.

'A slight problem with the door.'

'How long will it take to get to Mauthausen?'

'Ten or eleven hours, I would guess. But take your time.' Brossman looks back towards the prison block. 'I'll keep these beauties out of harm's way until you return.'

They headed south and east, towards Austria. In the back of the car, Rosa struggled to understand what was happening. Everything seemed unreal, as if she were in a dream. Her senses were heightened: voices too loud, lights bright, colours vivid. The glass of the window against which she rested her face seemed strangely cool and yielding. She tried to focus on the blur of shadows that streamed past but everything was moving too quickly. Until a week ago, her life in the camp had been brutal but mostly predictable; then the SS had put her in a cell and now other SS men had taken her out. It made no sense. Questions raced through her mind: was she to be freed? Or, more likely, was she simply a puppet in some game the Germans were playing? She wondered where she would be by morning, whether she would still be alive.

It was some time before she asked, 'Where are you taking me?'

The SS man in the passenger seat did not turn around when he answered: 'We are going to the K-Z at Mauthausen, in Austria. It's a work camp. You will be safer there.'

'Safer? How?'

'There are no gas chambers in Mauthausen.'

'Why are you doing this?'

'I can't tell you. It is better that you do not know.'

The answer made Rosa feel a little calmer. Wherever she was going, it could not conceivably be worse than the horror that was Birkenau.

The SS man offered her coffee from a thermos and a hunk of bread. This small act astonished her; tears rose to her eyes. Saying nothing, she blinked them back and reached hungrily for the bread.

It was the second miracle of the night, as unexpected as the first: real bread, soft and white, aromatic; not the hard, sawdust-filled pig-food that she had become used to. She held it, hardly daring to believe what she possessed. It was like treasure – if only there were somewhere safe she could hide it . . . but she was too hungry for that. Still she hesitated. It was such a simple, everyday thing, yet so utterly out of reach; if she put it in her mouth it would be gone . . . Then she was chewing ravenously, her heart beating quickly and her breathing heavy, as if she were with a lover. The bread was soft, moist and delicious; she wanted it to stay in her mouth for ever. As long as she had bread in her mouth she would never be hungry again. And the taste … she had never tasted anything so good. It tasted of breakfast in her favourite café on the corner of the Rue de Maine, of a rich dark sauce mopped up from a plate, of the sharpness of mustard spread thick on roast beef; it tasted of before the war, of summer evenings when she would promenade with friends along the Tuileries, of the heady scents from the perfumerie on the corner of the Rue Danton, of coffee in Montmartre, of champagne in Le Chat Noir.

It tasted of freedom.

'More bread?' Meissner asked.

She stared suspiciously as he passed the loaf, stiffening herself like a cat ready to pounce in case he was playing with her, teasing only to snatch it back.

Now it tasted of the south, of a bright spring day strolling along a river path with Emil and Louis and Marcel, the boys yelling with delight as they threw bits of stale bread to the ducks.

The spell was broken. The bread congealed in her mouth to a claggy dough, which she had no saliva to soften. A wave of nausea threatened to overwhelm her, and she had to spit the bread out into her hands, coughing and spluttering. She had come back to the real world, to this car with its booming engine and two SS men headed for God alone knew where.

Dawn found them on the outskirts of Brno. 'We take the road south,' Meissner said, consulting a map on his knee.

Eidenmüller, at the wheel, disagreed. 'Don't you think we'd be better sticking to the main roads, sir? Less likely to be stopped.'

'You think so?' Meissner examined the map again. 'Possibly, but it would take us too far out of our way.'

'If we get caught with her, we've had it.'

'What are you saying? That we should ditch her and run?'

'No, sir. That's not what I'm saying. What I'm saying is...'

Rosa lifted her head. 'I need to pee,' she said.

They pulled off the road into a copse of trees.

Rosa got out of the car, making for the trees. Meissner followed. 'I'm sorry,' he said, 'but I must insist on going with you. I cannot take the risk that you might run away. Please do not try. It would give me no pleasure to shoot you.'

Rosa squatted behind a bush. To pass water is such a basic human act, but this was the first time since her arrest that she had been able to do it in a place that was not surrounded by barbed wire. It gave her a strange feeling of liberty, as if she could simply get up and walk away from this place and never stop until she reached the ends of the earth.

It was almost exhilarating, but it was short-lived.

'What's she doing in there?' she heard Eidenmüller muttering.

The men relieved themselves, then Meissner took over at the wheel, determined that they would follow the southern route.

From the back seat Rosa looked out on the countryside, mesmerized. The road was lined with trees in full leaf, swaying gently in the morning light; hedgerows brimmed with flowers; and fields were heavy with produce, nearly ready for harvest. She tried to think back to the last time she had been able to look upon such a landscape – was it really only a year ago?

She dozed on the back seat and woke only when they stopped to fill the petrol tank from the jerry cans strapped to the side of the car. 'Where are we now?' she asked.

They had been passing through hamlets with German place-names for some time. 'In Austria, heading for Linz.' Eidenmüller took the wheel again. Towns passed by: Hagenberg, Pregarten, Altenhaus.

Meissner was staring out over the countryside, trying to keep his eyes open, when Eidenmüller gave an almost inaudible groan: 'Oh, shit.'

Ahead was a patrol of soldiers, one of them waving a hand for them to stop.

'Get down, right down into the foot well,' Meissner ordered Rosa. Hurriedly, he pulled a blanket over her.

As they drew closer they could see it was a squad of four Feldgendarmerie, led by an Obergefreiter. 'Relax,' Meissner told Eidenmüller, 'even you outrank him. Besides, we're SS. He has no jurisdiction over us.'

'Thank Christ for small miracles,' Eidenmüller muttered, pulling the car to a halt.

Meissner rolled the window down. 'Yes?' he snapped.

The Obergefreiter jerked to attention and saluted. He was barely out of his teens.

Meissner raised his right hand, palm outwards. '*Heil Hitler*. Now what is it? I haven't got all day.'

'Beg pardon, Herr Hauptsturmführer, we are looking for some deserters. Somebody reported seeing them in this area.'

'Army deserters?'

'Yes, Herr Hauptsturmführer.'

'Then you're wasting your time with us, aren't you?'

The Feldgendarmerie NCO swallowed. 'Beg pardon, Herr Hauptsturmführer, but I must ask to see your papers.'

The NCO was rewarded with a look of disdain. 'Eidenmüller, show him your papers.' Mcissner made no attempt to retrieve his own. Instead, he reached for a cigarette and popped it between his lips. He gave the

NCO the full force of a glare from his ice-blue eyes. 'Well? What are you waiting for? Don't you have any matches?'

'Of course, Herr Hauptsturmführer. At once.' A match flared. Meissner reached out to steady the NCO's hand as he puffed to light the cigarette.

Eidenmüller passed his identity card over. The NCO perused it nervously. For long moments it seemed they were cocooned in a bubble of silence, but the slow ticking of the car's engine penetrated, louder and louder until, to Eidenmüller, it seemed as deafening as a steam-hammer. From the hedges along the road, the cheerful chirping of sparrows seemed unreal and out of place.

Meissner recognized the electricity that fills the air before battle, yet he drew steadily on his cigarette, with an air of irritation at the unnecessary and intolerable delay.

'Auschwitz?' the NCO eventually said. 'You're a long way from home. What are you doing here?'

Meissner reacted angrily. 'That is none of your business and I have had enough of this nonsense.' He flicked the cigarette at the NCO's feet and turned to Eidenmüller. 'Take this man's name and unit number.'

Eidenmüller was sweating. His head was pounding. He fumbled in his tunic pocket, but the Feldgendarmerie NCO knew when he was beaten. 'No need for that, Herr Hauptsturmführer.' He handed back Eidenmüller's papers. 'You're clear to proceed. I'm sorry we detained you.'

Meissner did not even glance at the NCO as he pointed a finger at the road ahead. Eidenmüller put the car into gear, gunning the engine to put as much distance between them as he could.

Meissner placed a hand on his orderly's forearm. 'Not too fast, Ernst,' he said, 'or they'll suspect they've been had.'

'Beggin' your pardon, sir, but you're mad.'

'Why do you say that?'

'All you had to do was show them your papers.'

'No. That was too great a risk. Nobody must know we were here.'

'But it was OK for them to see *my* papers?'

'In an hour they'll have forgotten your name, but an SS-Hauptsturm-führer? That's something they would remember and would be bound to report.'

'And they won't report what happened anyway?'

A gleeful smile appeared on Meissner's face. 'Not likely. They would have to report that they let me go without seeing my papers. They'd prob-ably end up on the Eastern front.'

They had been told to look for a hamlet called Grünau. There, they would be met by an SS officer, a friend of Brossman's from his days in Lublin. They concealed the car in a small wood and waited.

At the appointed hour, they saw a *Kübelwagon* slowly making its way towards them. Meissner stepped out from behind the trees and waved it down. When the car stopped he called out, 'Otto Brossman sends regards from Lublin.'

The voice that came back was high-pitched and anxious. 'Brossman? I think I may know him. Where did he do his training?'

'Bad Tölz.'

'When was he there?'

'1940.'

A harsh grinding sound came from the *Kübelwagon* as the driver botched putting it into gear again, then the car crept forward until it was almost touching theirs.

The driver got out: an SS-Obersturmführer wearing thick-lensed glasses, which he took off and started to polish nervously. 'Quickly,' he hissed. 'There's not much time.' He used the glasses to point at what looked like a heap of ragged clothing lying on the back seat. 'I have to get back before this one is missed.'

Eidenmüller bent to pull out the rags and grunted. They were heavier than he expected. His hands met resistance, cold and clammy. 'Shit.' He let go instantly and stood upright. 'What is this?'

'A body of course – one in, one out. That's the only way it can work.'

Eidenmüller looked aghast at the corpse. 'Is it a woman?'

'Of course it's a fucking woman. What did you expect, a monkey?'

'What happened to her?'

'Died of a fever.'

'Christ. Was it anything contagious?'

Meissner brought Rosa Clément over. 'How will you get her in?'

'Easy. She'll be passed off as this one.' He jerked his head at the body that Eidenmüller was pulling out of the *Kübelwagon*. 'Nobody knows she's dead yet. I'll have the new one allocated to a work *Kommando* in a different part of the camp. The prisoner count will tally and nobody will be any the wiser.' The Obersturmführer peered short-sightedly at Rosa. 'She's about the same size. We'll need to get their clothes switched.'

With a rapid gesture Meissner indicated to Eidenmüller that he should remove the clothes from the cadaver. With obvious distaste he set to his task, rolling it onto its back to unfasten the jacket buttons. The corpse's eyes were open and they stared at him accusingly. 'Holy Mother of God…' He jumped back, almost toppling over in his desire to get away from the body. Instinctively, he crossed himself. 'Sorry, sir, I can't do this. I really…'

Rosa was there, a hand on his arm. She crouched down beside the woman's body. Its limbs were stiff and the skin had a waxy quality, making it difficult to get the clothes off. Finally it was naked; she looked vulnerable and pitiable, like a lost child. A tear slid from Rosa's eye and fell on the woman's face, a connection between their two existences that crossed the barrier that death had put between them. Under her breath, Rosa said a quick prayer, the first in months: 'Eternal rest give unto her, O Lord, and let perpetual light shine upon her...'

'Well?' the Obersturmführer demanded, looking at his watch.

It was Rosa's turn. In her months at Auschwitz she had suffered the humiliation of being forced to undress many times, not least during the frequent *Selektionen*. She had been stripped of her dignity along with her clothes to the unpleasant remarks of leering SS guards who openly ogled the women lined up for their inspection like vegetables on a market stall: 'Nice tits for a Jew...too hairy...too bony...' She had learned to make her mind go elsewhere so that she was not the one they were staring at, slavering over. But now, being told to undress by these men, this was different. These were her rescuers – had they restored her dignity, or was it only a loan that they could call in whenever they wanted?

'Come on, you stupid Jewish bitch.' The Obersturmführer was polishing his glasses again. The anger in his voice was palpable – or was it anxiety? 'Get your fucking clothes off and get hers on so I can be on my way.'

Rosa's hand moved to the top button of her jacket. 'Turn around,' she said, not knowing where the courage to say these two small words came from.

When Rosa was hidden in the foot well of the *Kübelwagon*, Meissner held out a hand to the other officer. 'Thank you. I know you're taking quite a risk over this.'

'I only hope it's worth it.'

'It will be. After the war you can say you were one of the few SS who saved the life of a Jew.'

'What now?' Eidenmüller said, once the *Kübelwagon* had departed.

'Back to Auschwitz, where our friend Brossman will have filed a report that, after freeing the unknown prisoner in the prison block, she was tragically shot trying to escape. And, lucky for us, we'll have a body and the paperwork to prove it. Unfortunately, an administrative error will send the body to the crematorium before Hustek has the chance to see it. Shame, eh?'

'What'll happen to her?'

'The Watchmaker's wife? She'll have to make do as best she can, same as all the other prisoners. But at least we've given her a fighting chance.'

1962

Kerk de Krijtberg, Amsterdam

It had taken Meissner some time to get his story told, between frequent bouts of coughing.

Emil sat transfixed, his supper untouched. 'So that's how she got to Mauthausen,' he said finally.

'You didn't know?' Willi asked.

'I never told him,' Meissner said. 'If Hustek had found out, it would have been the end of her and everyone involved.'

'I assumed that she had left Auschwitz with everyone else in January '45. Quite a few prisoners ended up in Mauthausen,' Emil said. 'When I found her in the autumn, she was ill and confused. When she told me that an SS officer had broken into the prison at Auschwitz in the middle of the night and taken her away, I thought she was delirious.'

'I have always wondered,' Meissner said, 'whether she survived. I'm glad she did, God be praised.'

Emil could not hold back the wave of bitterness that broke over him. 'Why would you praise your god for such a thing?' he spat. 'I cursed his name for what he did to her.'

'But I thought you and she were—?'

Emil stood, shaking his head, not bothering to wipe away the tears that had started down his cheeks. 'Oh, yes, we were reunited. For six days. Then she was taken from me a second time.'

Willi reached out to grasp Emil's wrist but Emil pulled his hand away.

'I'm so sorry,' Willi said. 'Truly. How—?'

Emil slumped back into his chair, the anger leaving him as quickly as it had come. 'Scarlet fever. She was too weak, you see, and by then she had lost the will to go on.'

'Dear God, dear God,' Meissner whispered, beating his chest. '*Mea culpa, mea culpa, mea maxima culpa.*'

33.

KING'S INDIAN ATTACK

1962

Kerk de Krijtberg, Amsterdam

The next morning Emil woke early. He wasn't sure what time it was but daylight was filtering around the edges of the curtains. He had not slept well. His night had been spent wrestling with memories. He had wanted to recall the good times he'd had with Rosa, but his mind had refused to cooperate. Instead, it had taken him to the miraculous day he had found her name on a Red Cross list, then to all the bureaucrats in their petty fiefdoms whom he had had to fight in order to get to her; then how he had found her, in bed number 117 in the makeshift hospital in Sankt Georgen an der Gusen: such a pretty name to disguise the enormity of what had happened there.* He remembered holding her hand, white and bloodless, so frail, like an old woman's. At first she hadn't recognized him; later, she could not trust herself to believe that he had also found a way to survive and that now he had found her. He had told her that he would never leave her side again. A smile had flickered across her face only to be replaced by pain. 'Forgive me,' she had said.

He remembered his last words to her. 'Louis and Marcel,' she had asked, her eyes wide but not seeing, her fingers suddenly locking his

---

* Sankt Georgen an der Gusen was very close to the Mauthusen concentration camp.

hand in hers. 'How are they?' He hadn't been able to bear telling her the truth. 'They're fine,' he had whispered. 'You'll see them soon, very soon.'

Another lie that had emanated from the kingdom of lies. Its intentions were good, but it was still a lie. He had vowed then that there would be no more lies in his life.

Emil got up. Quietly he looked into Paul's room, but he was in a deep sleep. He decided to go down to the kitchen, put on some coffee and have the first cigarette of the day on the bench overlooking the canal.

Willi was already at the kitchen table, smoking and staring vacantly ahead, a half-empty cup in front of him. He looked as if he hadn't slept, either.

'Is everything all right, Willi?'

'No. In fact, nothing is right at the moment.' He spoke in a dull monotone.

'What are you talking about?'

'It finally hit me last night.' Willi raised his head to look directly at Emil. 'What you and Paul have been talking about. It's all real, isn't it? It's not a story. It's not ancient history. It happened, and you and Paul were in the thick of it. And now I find myself caught in it too, and I realize how horrific it was, how cold and calculating and evil it was, and that it was done by Germans and that the victims were innocent women and children, and I don't know what to think about it and I don't know if I can deal with it.'

Emil sighed. 'What you are feeling is the legacy of Auschwitz. It is a burden that Paul and I must carry for the rest of our lives, and now I think that it has fallen upon your shoulders too. There is nothing you can do but bear it as best you can.'

Willi did not seem convinced. He ground out the stub of his cigarette in an ashtray and immediately took another from the packet. His hands shook as he lit it. 'The thing is,' he said, 'when you were playing chess against the SS it was not like other games, with only an intellectual duel at stake – they were the most real and vital games that have ever been played. Only a few years ago there was a game so extraordinary it was dubbed the game of the century. You must know it – the American master, Byrne, against the young prodigy, Fischer. It was a masterpiece of sacrificial play. Breathtaking. But it is insignificant beside your games in Auschwitz, and yet the world will never know of them.' He turned to look squarely at Emil. 'And if Paul had not almost knocked down my hotel room door, I would not have learned of them either, nor would I have come to know you, and so I would have continued to convince myself that what you had to say about Auschwitz was the product of the embittered imaginings of a man who feels guilty because he survived.'

Emil pulled out a chair and lit a cigarette for himself. 'Surely enough evidence about the death camps has emerged since the war to convince you they were more than imaginings, Willi?'

Willi stared at his hands, avoiding Emil's gaze. 'During the war I worked in the propaganda ministry. One heard things. We all knew that something was happening. We knew that the Jews of Germany had been sent east – but then they disappeared. Where could they have gone? Tens of thousands of people don't just disappear into thin air. We were told they were sent to work camps. Then stories about the camps began to circulate. They were not told openly, you understand – that was not possible, the Gestapo had ears everywhere. But behind closed doors, between people who trusted one other, things were said.' He drew deeply on his cigarette and let the butt fall from his fingers into the dregs of his coffee. 'It's not possible to keep such a secret. Men come home on leave and tell their families, and word gets out. I knew what was happening; everybody did.' Absently, he reached for the cigarette pack again only to find it empty. He crushed it in his hand and dropped it onto the table top. 'I told myself it could not be true,' he continued, 'it was too wicked, too incredible. Conditions in the work camps were harsh, but that was to be expected – we were at war with the Bolsheviks, a war to the death. Casualties could not be avoided. War is cruel... but death camps? It was not only unbelievable, it did not make sense – so much better to put the Jews to work than to kill them. Why kill them? There was no profit in it for the Reich. So I told myself the stories were not true. Could not be true.'

'And now?'

Willi bowed his head. Silent tears streamed down his face. When he spoke, his voice was tremulous. 'Now I am ashamed. Ashamed of myself, ashamed of my country. For the rest of my life, I must live with the knowledge that we are a nation of murderers.'

Willi's hands were still shaking. Emil felt a swell of pity for him. 'You're right, Willi. And it's painful to realize and difficult to bear.'

'You said that no German who lived through the war could claim to be innocent of the death camps... that there were no good Germans.'

Slowly, Emil shook his head. 'Yes, I did say that, didn't I?' He stood and picked up the kettle, walking to the sink to fill it. 'You're not the only one who is learning how wrong he can be.'

September 1944
Political Section, Konzentrationslager Auschwitz-I
The Buna *Werke* has been bombed. The bombers came in daylight, but instead of running for shelter as fast as their legs would take them, many of the prisoners waved their caps and cheered. The effect on prisoner

morale is extraordinary: now they talk endlessly about how the Allies will bomb the gas chambers and crematoria in Birkenau.

The Gestapo is convinced that the factory has become a target because Polish partisans have managed to get information to the Allies. Oberscharführer Hustek has been ordered to find the prisoners who are communicating with the partisans, and it has presented him with an opportunity. In the technical workshop where the Watchmaker works, he has daily contact with Polish workers; that makes him a suspect.

Two of Hustek's men have been sent to bring him for questioning.

Hauptsturmführer Meissner is in the Kommandant's office. For twenty minutes he has been on the receiving end of a barrage of questions about the midnight 'inspection' of the prison block. Sturmbannführer Bär is not convinced by Meissner's insistence that he had nothing to do with it.

'Sir. I wasn't there. I wasn't even in the camp at the time.'

'Where the hell were you then?'

'I told you, sir. I had a couple of days' leave. You authorized it. I went to Kraków.'

'Then why can't you say where you went in Kraków, or who you saw? In fact, anything at all about your leave in Kraków?'

'Because, sir, as I've already explained, I took a wrong turning and then my car broke down. I spent the night in the forest. The next day it took me hours to walk to where I could find a telephone and call for help.'

'Hours? You could have walked to Kraków in a day if you had to.'

Meissner holds up his walking stick.

'Don't get clever with me, Meissner.' His superior's voice is sharp. 'How did you manage to find out the woman was in the prison block?'

Meissner shakes his head wearily. 'I knew nothing about it until after I got back. From what I have been told, Hauptsturmführer Brossman decided to check the block on the off-chance she might be there. That he found her was pure luck.'

The Kommandant scowled. 'Brossman, yes. I don't know how you managed to involve him in your scheme, but I'll find out.'

'Sir, I'm sure you'll find Hauptsturmführer Brossman's motives were entirely genuine. The woman had gone missing. Brossman was duty-bound to search for her, and Hustek was holding her without authorization and for no legitimate reason. She wasn't even entered into the log as being there. Holding a prisoner for personal reasons flies in the face of all sorts of regulations, and it's against the law.'

'Don't be so ridiculous,' Bär snaps. 'Hustek's Gestapo. He's above the law.'

Meissner can feel his anger rising. 'But with the woman as his prisoner, he would have had a hold over the Watchmaker. Surely you can see that?'

'Does it matter, as long as he wins?'

'It matters to me, sir,' Meissner retorts. 'Hustek is a disgrace to the SS. He's not fit to wear the uniform.'

'That's not for you to say, Meissner. I'm satisfied that Oberscharführer Hustek's work makes a significant contribution to the war effort.'

Before Meissner can stop them, the words are out: 'If you think kidnapping a helpless woman makes a significant contribution to the war effort, then you're as bad as he is. Don't you understand? The war is over. Germany has lost. It is only a matter of time before the Russians are in Berlin. I've fought them, I know. There's no holding them back. Not any more.'

Bär's face pales with anger. 'You forget who you are talking to, Meissner. I *won't* have defeatist talk here. You are an officer in the SS. You should be ashamed of yourself.'

Bär's words break the thread that has been holding Meissner's temper in check. Before he knows it, he is shouting: 'I won't take that from you, sir, or from anyone else who's spent *their* war lording it over women and children, herding them from cattle trucks into gas chambers at the point of a rifle. Only someone who's seen the enemy close enough to smell them knows the truth of this war. The Waffen-SS know the truth of it, and we'll carry on fighting until our last breath; but, by God, we know the truth of it.'

When Meissner stops, he realizes the Kommandant is staring coldly at him. 'Finished? Good. Do you still want that transfer? If you can find a unit desperate enough to take you, then you can have it. Now get out.'

Meissner was shaking as he walked down the administrative building steps. Walking stick or not, going back to Monowitz on foot would help him to calm down.

He had not gone as far as the main gate when he found Eidenmüller waiting for him.

'What are you doing here?' Meissner asked, sharply.

'Sorry, sir, but you need to get back quickly.'

'Why?'

'Hustek's after the Watchmaker, sir. His men are in the camp now.'

Hustek had sent two agents to the Buna factory. Neither of them had been there before. It was vast: pipes ran everywhere in a seemingly inextricable tangle; some were suspended from overhead gantries, others ran at ground level. In the distance, the agents could see a large, square building with a row of tall, black chimneys pushing into the sky.

The bomb damage was extensive. At various points they could see men in civilian clothes carrying clip-boards, assessing the destruction; around them gangs of men in striped uniforms were clearing away rubble or removing damaged piping or machinery. Others scurried backwards and forwards, some heavily laden, still more pushing trucks along narrow-gauge rails or pulling hand-carts; others were digging. Everywhere, the furious activity was being driven by the clubs or thick, knotted ropes wielded by the *Kapos*.

'This is hopeless,' one said. 'We'll never find him here. It's chaos.'

'We should ask someone,' replied the other. 'The Rapportführer might know where he is.'

'Forget it. I know the Rapportführer here. Gessner. No point asking him. Him and Hustek don't get on.'

'Does anyone get on with Hustek?'

The first one rolled his eyes. 'Let's go to the camp. Bound to have better luck there.'

In the records office they found Unterscharführer Hoven.

'We're looking for the prisoner called the Watchmaker.'

Hoven looked up from the file on his desk that he was studying. 'Really? And who exactly is "we"?'

'Gestapo.'

The word alone was sufficient to generate a spasm of anxiety in Hoven's bowels.

'What exactly is it you want?'

The two men exchanged a knowing glance. They had the measure of Hoven. 'Just tell us where to find him.'

Hoven turned back to his file. 'Block 27,' he said, without looking up.

As soon as they were gone Hoven closed the file and left his office. Eidenmüller was in the next building along. He would want to know that the Gestapo was after the Watchmaker.

*

311

The two Gestapo men threw open the door to Block 27 and, unannounced, entered the day room. Two men were sprawled on wooden benches along the wall, asleep. Both had green triangles on their jackets. Without ceremony, the first Gestapo man pulled their legs up, tipping them onto the floor. With a rush of expletives the prisoners picked themselves up, rubbing gingerly at flesh that would soon bear bruises.

'Who the fucking hell are you?' one of them demanded angrily.

'Gestapo.'

Sullenly, the prisoners glared at their tormentors.

'We're looking for the Watchmaker. We were told he is in this block. Where is he?'

Neither prisoner spoke.

The Gestapo man pulled a cosh from his pocket and slammed it onto a table. 'We don't want to make life difficult for you. Just tell us where he is.'

The prisoners maintained their silence.

This time the cosh was waved beneath the chin of one of them. 'Only we haven't got too much time, see?'

'He's in the Buna *Werke*,' one of the prisoners said. 'They're all in the Buna *Werke*. They'll be back tonight.'

There were chairs around the table. The Gestapo men settled themselves down to wait. 'What have you got to eat?' one asked.

The prisoners shook their heads. 'Nothing. We had the soup ration at noon. There's nothing now until after roll call.'

'Shit,' the Gestapo man said. 'I'm fucking starving.'

Eidenmüller took the road from the *Stammlager* towards Oświęcim. Meissner was deep in thought. At length he said, 'This friend of yours, Hoven – do you trust him?'

'I don't really know him that well, sir. He doesn't like Hustek, I know that much. He's frightened of him.' Meissner went back to his thoughts. 'What are we going to do, sir? If Hustek gets hold of the Watchmaker, we'll never see him again.'

'Yes, I know that,' Meissner said irritably, 'but I don't know what we're going to do. I'm trying to think of something.'

By the time they got to Monowitz, a plan was starting to form. The problem was one of organization. There was no way a prisoner could be hidden for more than a few hours: the twice-daily roll call would immediately reveal he was missing. No, if Hustek wanted the Watchmaker he would find a way to get him.

Hustek had to be distracted by something bigger.

When they arrived they went straight to Hoven's office. 'Shut the door,' Meissner ordered. The Unterscharführer looked alarmed.

'What can I do for you, sir?'

'Where do you stand regarding the Watchmaker?' Meissner asked.

'The Watchmaker? I don't know what you mean, sir.'

'Hustek's men have come for him. You know what that means.'

'Yes, sir.'

'Do you want to let Hustek get him? Or do you want to stop him?'

'Yes, sir. I mean, no, I don't want that bastard to get his hands on him. But what can I do?'

'It's very simple. Forget you ever saw Hustek's men. They were never here. Understood?'

Understanding registered on the Unterscharführer's face.

'But—'

'No buts, Unterscharführer. Just stick to your story. You never saw them. If you keep to that you'll be safe. If you waver, you're a dead man.'

The opportunity to get back at Hustek beckoned. It was now or never. 'Yes, sir. I never saw anyone, sir.'

'What next, sir?' Eidenmüller asked, when they were outside again.

'Into the camp. We need to find Brack.'

Brack was near the kitchens, watching a couple of prisoners tending the vegetable plot. The harvest looked bountiful: beans, tomatoes and cucumbers – luxuries the prisoners could only dream of.

Brack pulled himself to attention when he saw Meissner.

'Don't bother,' Meissner said, 'this isn't a formal visit, and you haven't seen us. Is there anywhere we can talk privately?'

Brack smiled and pointed to a nearby block. 'In there. I'll see you in five minutes.'

Brack had sent them to the camp brothel. It was empty. Meissner explained the situation, adding, 'For all we know, Hustek's men are in your block right now.'

Brack's dream of a fortune amassed in a Swiss bank started to dissolve. His face creased into an angry frown. 'Hustek is a pig. He won't get away with this. Not if I can help it.'

'I didn't know you knew Hustek,' Eidenmüller said.

'Oh, yeah, I know him all right. I've got a score or two to settle with Hustek.'

Block 27 was on the northern perimeter of the camp, next to the wire.* It took little time for Brack to gather a few cronies, though Widmann was

---

* The Monowitz camp was divided into two sections, north and south. Between them, a service road ran east to west, bordered by a double fence of barbed wire, with the inner fence electrified for good measure, and a gate at each end. The service road did not extend all the way to the eastern perimeter, so at this point it was possible to walk between the sections.

nowhere to be found. In ones and twos they met behind the block, hidden from the guard towers.

'Right,' Brack said. 'Everybody ready?' He waited for everyone to show a weapon. 'No knives, remember. And no messing about. Straight in. Right,' he said again. He was feeling nervous. This was new territory. 'Let's get in there and do this.'

The Gestapo men were surprised when four men in prisoner garb came from the dormitory into the day room and took up positions barring the main door. More men followed. They were all carrying heavy wooden clubs.

A glance was all it took for the Gestapo men to work out what was going to happen to them. One of them, his face a mask of shocked disbelief, tried to bluster: 'If you know what's good for you, you'll leave now,' he said loudly.

'Well, that's the problem, isn't it?' Brack said menacingly, as he pushed the door closed. 'I've never known what's good for me.'

The other Gestapo man pulled out a pistol. With an angry yell Brack brought his club down on the Gestapo man's wrist. There was a momentary howl of pain before a blow to the head silenced him.

The first Gestapo man held his hands up in a gesture of supplication. 'No!' he begged. 'No, please—'

It was over quickly.

'Jesus,' one of Brack's men said, licking lips that had suddenly become parched. 'You realize what we've done, don't you?'

'Stop whining,' Brack said. 'There's no going back now. I know Hustek. He's an evil bastard. If he gets wind of this he'll have us thrown into the ovens while we're still alive.' He pointed at the bodies with his bloody club. 'These two were never here. None of us knows anything about them.' He glared at the two who had been caught in the block by the Gestapo men. 'That includes you. Unless you want to join them—?'

For an hour they worked harder than they had worked in all their time at Auschwitz. The room was scrubbed and the corpses were stripped and swung into a handcart outside.

One of Brack's men looked longingly at the pile of discarded clothing. 'Pity,' he said. 'Specially the boots – almost new.'

'Into the stove with them,' Brack ordered. 'I want no traces left.' The pistol could not be disposed of so easily. He would have to think about what to do with that.

'What about the bodies?'

'Don't worry, it's taken care of.'

Every day prisoners died in the Buna factory. They were hauled back by their fellow inmates to be counted in the roll call. Afterwards, their remains were thrown onto a lorry and taken to Birkenau for cremation. They were not counted again. Today would be no different, except that there would be two more. If anyone had bothered to look, they might have noticed two freshly cropped heads and physiques that were not skeletal. That might have aroused suspicions, and a closer examination would have revealed hands that were not calloused from hard labour, and feet that had not been rubbed raw by the wooden clogs that the inmates wore. But who would look? Two more among thousands were neither here nor there. Besides, the only people who would handle them were the Birkenau *Sonderkommando*, prisoners whose job it was to empty the gas chambers and put the carcasses into the crematoria.

They would have rejoiced to know they were putting the bodies of Gestapo men into the furnace.

*

Two days later, Meissner had a visitor.

He was announced by Eidenmüller. 'Oberscharführer Hustek to see you, sir.'

Meissner looked up from the papers that were spread across his desk. 'Take a seat, Oberscharführer,' he said. 'What can I do for you?'

'Two of my men have gone missing,' Hustek said, as he sat down. 'I was wondering whether you might know where they are.'

'Me? Why would I know where they are?'

'They were here, in Monowitz. They were here on my instructions. They were here to pick up the Watchmaker.'

Meissner leaned back and steepled his fingers. 'I still don't understand why you might think I would know where they are. I'm not in charge here: Obersturmführer Schottl is the Lagerführer. You should speak to him.'

'I already have. Nobody saw either of my men. Nobody. Don't you think that's strange? You would have thought *somebody* would have seen them.'

'I don't know.' Meissner concentrated hard on keeping his expression deadpan. 'There are always people coming and going, in and out of the camp. Someone might have seen them, but taken no notice of them. That wouldn't be so strange, would it?'

'Look, Herr Hauptsturmführer.' The Gestapo man tried giving a friendly smile, as if he were taking Meissner into his confidence. 'I know we got off on the wrong foot, and I know you see yourself as the Watchmaker's protector, but I do have a genuine reason for wanting to question him.'

'Really? What about?'

'About the bombing raids on the Buna *Werke*.'

Meissner laughed. 'You think the Watchmaker is working for the Americans? Oh, that's priceless.'

Hustek compressed his lips into a sneer. 'It's only recently that Buna has become a target. We're convinced the Polish underground have passed information about it to the Allies. But they must have had someone on the inside to tell them about the factory in the first place. The Watchmaker works in one of the instrument shops. He speaks to Polish workers every day. He's an obvious suspect.'

'For God's sake, man! Buna is full of Polish workers. Thousands of them pass through the factory gates every day. They don't need the Watchmaker to tell them what's going on inside. Besides, if you knew him as I do, you'd know it couldn't be him.'

'Why's that?'

'Because the only thing that interests him is chess. Nothing else matters to him any more.'

'But I still have two men missing.'

'They're bound to turn up eventually. Men go absent without leave all the time, even in the SS.'

'Not in the Gestapo.'

'I take it you've checked with their families?'

Hustek responded with a disdainful look.

'I'm afraid I really can't help you.'

'Can't or won't?'

Meissner ignored the question. 'If there's nothing more, I have work to do.'

Hustek stood and strode to the door. Putting his hand on the handle, he turned back. 'Do I have to play against the Kike?'

'If you don't, you lose by default.'

Hustek nodded, with a look that said he had known that this was how it would be. 'Well,' he said, 'far be it from me to be the one who saves a Yid from the gas chamber.' A sinister smile formed on his face. 'You know, Herr Hauptsturmführer, you should pay a visit to Birkenau yourself sometime, see what it's like. It's quite something to see the gassing – hundreds of people so alive one minute and so still, like a tableau in a waxworks, the next. And the screams, you should hear the screams. Gives you a real sense of a job well done.'

The mask of impassivity that Meissner had been wearing fell away. 'I wouldn't know,' he replied, his voice tight with suppressed rage. 'The only death I've ever seen is the kind where men get blown to pieces or roast to death in a burning tank. And the more I think of it, the more I realize what a fitting end that would be for you.'

Hustek was determined to have the last word: 'A word to the wise, Herr Hauptsturmführer. That journal of yours ... I would keep it in a safe place if I were you. You wouldn't want the wrong people to know what was written in it.'

'How do you—?'

But Hustek had gone, leaving Meissner with the answer to a question that had been eating at him for months.

1962

Kerk de Krijtberg, Amsterdam

'I realized then,' Meissner said, 'that I could not put off applying for my transfer any longer. I immediately wrote to my comrade, Peter Sommer, in my old regiment. By then they were back on the Eastern front, so it took nearly a month before I got his reply.'

'What did he say?' Willi wanted to know.

'That the fighting was as brutal as ever, that he had been promoted again, and that yes, if I wanted it, there was a place for me as an adjutant in the staff HQ.'

'When would that have been?' Emil asked.

'Early October, perhaps a week before your game with Hustek. I had thought he would have been back for you, but he never came near. And then there was the uprising in Birkenau.'

'An uprising? By the prisoners?'

'Yes. The *Sonderkommando* at one of the crematoria rebelled. There was a small battle. They killed several guards and NCOs, and blew up the crematorium. Then they broke through the wire and ran off.'

'What happened to them?'

'I don't think many of them escaped. Those who were caught were brought back and executed. But the question on everyone's lips was how could Jewish prisoners in Auschwitz have managed to get hold of weapons and explosives? It was inconceivable. Bär was apoplectic with rage, and Hustek bore the brunt of it. He'd been so distracted by his determination to neutralize Emil that he'd completely missed what had been going on under his very nose. He was told in no uncertain terms to get to the bottom of it. I think he even forgot about his missing men.'

'So everything went quiet in the run-up to the game?'

'Not quite. Oberscharführer Hustek still had one roll of the dice left.'

34.

THE GRÜNFELD DEFENCE

October 1944

Konzentrationslager Auschwitz-III, Monowitz

The camp is subdued. At daybreak the sun in the east is red, a sure sign that bad weather is on its way. The camp has been trying to ignore the creeping approach of winter, for it knows the majority of the inmates will not live to see the spring and that, for all of them, each day will be purchased in suffering, and measured in icy clouds of breath, the stamping of feet on the ground, and the hunching of shoulders against the chill wind.

Among the inmates there is a growing unease – it is like a caged tiger, pacing restlessly from side to side, snarling. By now everyone knows of the uprising by the *Sonderkommando* in Birkenau and of how it was suppressed with a savagery that was notable even by the savage standards of Auschwitz. Now the inmates watch the SS in their towers around the camp and their patrols along the wire, wondering whether this same savagery will be turned upon them as well.

But that is not the main source of the unease. In the summer, to boost construction in the Buna factory, 2,000 extra prisoners were brought into the Monowitz camp. They were housed in tents near the parade ground. Now that winter is near, these men have been moved into the blocks, making the already overcrowded quarters even more squalid.

During the summer, *Selektionen* among the prisoners had come to a standstill while the gas chambers and crematoria of Birkenau had worked overtime on the slaughter of the Hungarian Jews. Now that the Hungarian *Aktion* is over, the old hands among the prisoners predict that the *Selektionen* will begin again: although it is of their own making, the SS will not tolerate such overcrowding for long.

Each inmate assures his neighbour that they will not be among the ones selected: only the old and the weak and the sickly will go. It does not matter if the neighbour is old or weak or sickly, they are told they are not old enough or weak enough or sickly enough. Everybody knows that these are empty words. The Germans are very thorough.

The *Selektion* comes without warning on a Sunday afternoon. The inmates are lining up for the soup ration. The bell sounds. All must return to their blocks.

Brack knows it is coming – he has gone through the procedure many times. Only Jews are selected, and he has their *Häftling-Karten* ready with their number, name, nationality and age and whether they are a specialist worker.

Brack wants everything to go quietly. He tells everyone to undress, and get into their bunks. He strolls to bunk number three, where the Watchmaker has a new companion to share his sleeping space.

'You know what's coming, eh?' Brack says.

Emil nods. 'Of course.'

'Don't worry, you're safe. Even if your card wasn't marked "protected", you are a specialist, and in good health.'

It is perhaps two hours later when an SS doctor and guards arrive at the block and the *Selektion* begins.

Starting at the furthest end of the dormitory, Brack and his minions move along the rows of bunks, striking them with wooden clubs, driving the fearful prisoners into the day room. Soon more than 200 naked men, each holding a card tightly in his hand, are herded into a space that is too small for them.

Now, the door to the outside is opened. Waiting there is an SS doctor. Brack stands to his right, and on his left the *Blockschreiber*, Widmann. Along the alley between the blocks, the outside door to the dormitory is opened. One by one, each prisoner must exit the day room, give his card to the *Blockschreiber* and then, naked, run along the alley and back into the dormitory. During these few seconds, the doctor decides whether each man will live or die.

After it is finished, Brack looks with disbelief at one of the cards. He takes it back to the SS doctor.

'Herr Obersturmführer,' he says, 'I think there has been a mistake.'

The doctor looks coldly at the prisoner with his green triangle and his all-too-clean uniform. 'Mistake? How so?'

'*Häftling* 163291. He is a specialist and in good health. Also, he has *Schutzhäftling* status. He is not for *Selektion*.'

The doctor hesitates for a moment, then says: 'Show me.'

Brack passes him the Watchmaker's card. The doctor looks closely at it.

'Where does it specify that this prisoner is a specialist or that he is in protective custody? He is for *Selektion*. Now get on with it.'

Brack stares at the card. It is not the one he prepared earlier. He goes back into the block to find the original. There is no trace of it. With an oath he goes in search of the *Blockschreiber* but he is nowhere to be found.

He finds one of his cronies. 'Where is Widmann?' he asks.

'I don't know. I haven't seen him since the *Selektion*. Maybe he's gone to the latrine.'

'I bet he's gone a lot further than that. Get the word out. I want him, and I want him *now*.'

But Widmann is not to be found. He is on his way to the *Stammlager* and freedom. In return for doctoring the Watchmaker's record card, Hustek has promised Widmann his liberty. Tomorrow, when the selected prisoners are sent to Birkenau, Widmann will be on a train to Stuttgart, and from there, with luck, to Switzerland.

But there is nothing Brack can do about Widmann now: he has a far more pressing problem. At dawn the next day, trucks will come to take the selected prisoners to the gas chambers. Before that happens, Haupt-sturmführer Meissner must be told what has happened. But it is Sunday. He will not be in his office and there is no way to contact him. There is only one thing to be done.

The Watchmaker must be hidden.

It will not be easy. In the morning, after the work *Kommandos* have departed for the day, there will be a second roll call for the selected inmates. It will take time to conduct two roll calls, giving Brack a little breathing space to find Meissner. But when the roll call count does not tally, the SS guards will search the camp. It will not take long: the dogs will soon sniff out the hidden prisoner.

Two hiding places come to Brack's mind: the camp brothel and the forge. The brothel because it is the last place the Germans will look, and the forge because the smell of the place may put the dogs off.

If the Watchmaker is found before Brack can get to Meissner, it is likely he will be shot on the spot.

But the Watchmaker is reluctant to cooperate.

'It is Hustek's doing,' he says. 'Why fight it? He will get me in the end, anyhow. I have nothing left. My family is gone; the only friend I had is gone. At least this way I won't have to go through another winter watching the people around me dropping like flies.'

Brack is appalled. For years he has lived in a world where moral values have been extinguished; but in the Watchmaker he has seen something rare. It is more than his incomprehensible devotion to chess: it lies in his dogged determination not to succumb to the dead weight of indifference that Auschwitz hangs around every inmate's neck, and in his rejection of the idea that he might profit from the lives he has saved. Above all, it is evident in the way that the Watchmaker has refused to surrender his dignity. None of these things is clear in Brack's mind, nor does he conceive of any of them as 'good', for in Auschwitz there is no good; but, as he struggles to understand, he sees it as something that is *right*, how the world ought to be if it were not for the barbed wire within which they are all confined. A quiet voice within tells him that this is something he must fight for.

Brack cannot articulate any of this. His response is to slap the Watchmaker and bellow: 'Do you want to die?'

'Of course not,' Emil replies, rubbing his cheek.

'Then do as I say.'

'No.'

Exasperated, Brack raises a hand to strike Emil again, but he knows that Emil will not respond to violence so he lets it fall.

Abruptly, Brack leaves the block and steps into the cold evening air. He does not go far – just past the punishment block to Block 30. He is looking for somebody.

A short time later he is back. 'There is someone I want you to meet,' he says. He pushes a prisoner towards the Watchmaker.

'Who is this?'

'This is the life you will save when you win against Hustek. Talk to him. I want you to understand that if you throw away your own life, you will almost certainly be taking this one with you.'

The Watchmaker refuses to look at the prisoner; he fixes his gaze on Brack. 'No. You cannot put this responsibility on me. This scheme was not of my devising.'

'It doesn't matter. All that matters is that it is within your power to save this man's life. I want you to look him in the eye and tell him why you won't do it.'

Emil reluctantly contemplates the man. He is short, his head is shaven, and his face is riddled with sores, perhaps the result of vitamin deficiency. Like everybody, his uniform is patched and filthy, but he does not have the defeated look that many of the prisoners have. His eyes are alert and searching.

'What is your name?' Emil asks.

'Daniel. Daniel Farhi.'

'You are French?'

The man shrugs. 'Not exactly. My wife is French and my father is French-Egyptian. I'm from Cairo. In 1940 we were visiting my wife's family in Paris when we got caught by the German advance. It's a long story, m'sieur, but here I am.'

'What did you do in Cairo?'

'I was a dealer in gold.'

Emil nods. That explains Brack's interest in this man. 'What about your family?'

'My wife escaped to Spain. My children are in Egypt. As far as I know, they are well.'

'Do you understand the risk you are running? The man I'm up against in this game has no scruples. None. If I lose, he won't be satisfied with waiting until you are taken by a *Selektion* – he's the kind to take you to the gas chamber himself and laugh all the way home afterwards.'

Farhi smiles. 'But you will not lose. You are the Watchmaker.'

Emil sighs. He turns to Brack. 'And how much have you extorted from this one?'

Farhi interrupts. 'If it is a question of money, m'sieur...'

'Monsieur Farhi, it is not a question of money. But don't let yourself be fooled into thinking that our esteemed *Blockältester* is doing this because he cares for your welfare. He cares about himself.'

Emil bows his head, defeated by the inescapable logic of Auschwitz. 'All right then, tell me what I must do.'

The brothel is constructed of wood, the same as every other building in the camp. In one of the rooms on the upper level there is a hollow space beneath the floorboards. It is a hiding place for various items of contraband that are smuggled in and out of the camp. Using it to conceal the Watchmaker is likely to mean the end of its usefulness, but that cannot be helped.

It is a tight fit, but Emil manages to squeeze in.

'No matter what,' Brack says, 'make no sound.'

At 6:50 a.m. the sun rises. Brack immediately sends one of his trusted lieutenants to find a friendly SS guard. He must get a message to Eidenmüller. The prisoners are not allowed to march to Buna in the dark so they do not set off until 7:15. Ten minutes later, the prisoners picked out in the *Selektion* start to assemble on the *Appelplatz*. They are slow to form ranks – understandably so. They can see the trucks waiting for them on the service road, between the gates that are locked at both ends.

Despite the cold wind the SS guards are in no hurry, and it is nearly eight o'clock before the Rapportführer is told they are one short. He orders a recount. This time the count is done briskly, and the guards pay closer attention. The result is the same. The prisoners are left shivering in the cold while a search of the camp is mounted.

Meanwhile, Eidenmüller is waiting anxiously outside Meissner's office. On Mondays Meissner is in the habit of coming in early. But not today. The night before, Meissner was in Solahütte talking to Brossman about his plans to rejoin his unit, and urging his fellow officer to go with him. He sees no reason to pursue his duties with the same diligence as before. He does not arrive until shortly after eight.

'It's the Watchmaker,' Eidenmüller tells him breathlessly. 'There was a *Selektion* yesterday. I don't know how, but he was included. Brack's hidden him, but it won't be long before he's found.'

Lips tight with anger, Meissner storms outside, Eidenmüller following in his wake. At the gate they are let through under the watchful eye of the Lagerführer, Obersturmführer Schottl. He goes into the guard room and picks up the telephone.

Meissner and Eidenmüller hurry past the parked trucks and through the second gate. Brack is leaning against the wall of the sick bay, watching for them.

'What the hell happened?' Meissner asks.

Brack explains as they walk to the brothel. Through the wire they can see two teams of guards with dogs searching the clothing store on the north side of the camp.

'This way,' says Brack.

THE DEATH'S HEAD CHESS CLUB

Inside, he pushes aside a bed and pulls up a floorboard to reveal the Watchmaker.

Meissner nods. 'Follow me,' he says.

Together, they take the path past the kitchens to the *Appelplatz* where Meissner presents the prisoner to the Rapportführer. 'I believe this is the one you are looking for.'

The Rapportführer is under the command of Obersturmführer Schottl. He is about to order the Watchmaker to join the ranks of other prisoners when the Lagerführer arrives.

'Thank you, Herr Hauptsturmführer,' Schottl says to Meissner, 'for finding our escaped prisoner. I don't know how we would have managed without you. Now we can get on with sending these scum where they belong.'

'Not this one,' Meissner says. 'This prisoner is in protective custody and is not for *Selektion*.'

'Of course,' Schottl says silkily. 'He can go back to his block as soon as you show me his *Häftling-Karte*. Until then...' He gives a pointed look at the Rapportführer.

Meissner looks at Brack. 'Do you have his card?'

Brack shakes his head. 'It's been switched. Otherwise I would have got this sorted last night.'

Meissner turns to Eidenmüller. 'On my order. Take the prisoner to my office. Now.'

'Yes, sir.'

Schottl is no longer smiling. 'I can't permit that, sir. This prisoner has been selected for liquidation.' He gives an order to the Rapportführer. 'Get that stinking Yid onto the transports – now.'

*

329

1962

Kerk de Krijtberg, Amsterdam

'Dear God,' Willi said. 'Then what?'

Emil glanced at Paul. 'What happened next took everyone by surprise, especially me. It was unbelievable.'

'What?'

Meissner grinned. 'I pulled my gun on him.'

Willi was stunned. 'You pulled your gun on a fellow SS officer?'

'Yes. You should have seen the look on his face.' Paul started to laugh.

'How did you think you would get away with that?'

Paul's laughter turned into a coughing fit. It took a while to subside. 'I had no idea,' he said, between coughs, 'but it was the only thing I could think of. It would've taken hours to do what Schottl was telling us to do, and by then it would have been too late.'

'What did he do?'

'What could he do? He looked at me in total and utter amazement. "Put the gun away," he said. "You're not going to use it."'

'What did you say?'

'I think I said, "Are you sure you want to take the risk?"'

'And he let you take Emil away, just like that?'

'No,' Emil said. 'That's not how it ended. While you and the other SS officer were having your stand-off, somebody else came over.'

Paul remembered. 'My God, you're right. Hustek.'

'What did he do?' Willi asked.

'Nothing,' Paul answered. 'It was very strange. Afterwards, I realized he must have been behind it all along. At first he did not appear angry or even disappointed that his scheme had failed; on the contrary, he seemed to have expected it. Then he saw Brack. In an instant his manner changed.

He looked thunderous. "Brack," he said, "I wondered where you had got to. I never thought you of all people would become a Jew-lover." Then without another word he turned and walked away. Schottl shouted after him, "What should I do with the Jew?" Without looking back Hustek called over his shoulder, "Let him go with his new friends."

'So,' Willi said, 'out of all those men who were selected, you were the only one to survive.'

The three suddenly became very solemn. 'Yes,' Emil said. 'Out of them all, I was the only one.'

35.

THE CARO-KANN COUNTERBLOW

1962

Kerk de Krijtberg, Amsterdam

The next morning, Meissner was ailing badly. He had to be supported by pillows to sit upright, and his breathing was raspy and laboured; when he tried to shift his weight, his face contorted with pain. The doctor was called and a nurse was arranged to come and administer morphine, but after only one injection the patient refused to cooperate: the morphine clouded his thinking. The doctor tried to insist, but he reckoned without Meissner's tenacity. In the end he had no choice but to relent: if Mrs Brinckvoort would leave a measuring phial and the bottle of laudanum next to the bed, the bishop could help himself whenever the pain became too much.

Emil was restless. He played with his lunch, prodding the food on his plate aimlessly until, with a clatter, he let his fork drop.

'What's the matter?' Willi asked.

Emil didn't answer. He pushed his chair back and walked to the door. 'I'll see you later,' he said.

Willi sat at Paul's bedside for most of the afternoon, chatting or reading to him. When Emil returned, Willi was in the kitchen.

'How's Paul?' Emil asked.

'He's asleep. But he was awake on and off most of the time you were out.'

'That's good. He should rest while he can.'

'He's been asking for you. He wanted to know where you were. I told him I didn't know.'

'I've withdrawn from the competition.'

There was a short silence. 'I had a hunch that's what you were going to do,' Willi said. He stood up and laid a hand on Emil's shoulder. 'It's a big decision. You could have won. I think you would have. You would have had your shot at the World Championship.'

'Perhaps. But my heart's no longer in it.' Emil moved towards the door. 'I'll look in on Paul,' he said. 'There are more important things than chess.'

When Meissner awoke, the two men took their places at his bedside. Emil told him of his decision.

'It was the right thing to do,' Meissner said, his voice weak and thready.

'You think so? I thought you would have been disappointed.'

Meissner shook his head. 'No. You've already played the most import-ant game of your life.'

'You mean the one against Hustek?'

'What else? How could anything ever come close to that?' Wincing with pain, Meissner pushed himself up on his pillows. He looked ashen. The laudanum was untouched. 'I'm so tired,' he whispered. 'You'll have to tell Willi about it. But don't leave anything out – I'll be listening.'

'The first thing to tell,' Emil said, 'is about the place where the game was played. It was the SS country club and, after nearly a year in the camp, it seemed I had been transported to paradise.

'I was taken there by Eidenmüller. He had been promoted to Scharführer.

His attitude towards me had changed quite a lot and he treated me quite decently. Whether this was due to Paul's influence, or for some other reason, I really don't know. Before we left he had me showered and given fresh clothes, and brought me some food – white bread and a little cheese and sausage. For a short while I felt better than I could ever remember. Then he drove me into the forest and up to the SS summer retreat.

'It was built on the side of a hill above a river and looked out across a valley. You came upon it quite suddenly – one second you were in thick woodland, and the next there was this marvellous view. Eidenmüller escorted me inside and told me not to respond to anything that was said to me unless it was a direct and sensible question.'

The bed creaked; Paul had moved to shift his weight, his face creasing with pain. Emil looked pointedly from Willi to the bottle of laudanum, but Paul motioned with a finger for him to carry on.

'You should understand,' Emil continued, 'that after three games in which I had beaten their SS comrades, emotions were running high. I was not permitted to wait in the room where the game would be played. Instead, I was taken to a balcony and left there alone until it was time to start. The weather was glorious, not a cloud in the sky, but bitterly cold. As I stood there, it struck me as a cruel irony that there could be such an idyll so close to so much suffering and death.

'After a while Eidenmüller came out. "It's time," he said. He seemed subdued, or perhaps he was angry. Inside, there was an air of almost desperate defiance, as if everyone knew the end was not far off but were determined to go out with a bang. After the previous games I thought I knew what to expect. I had steeled myself against the hostility, the jostling and the jeering, but nothing could have prepared me for the sight that confronted me.'

Friday, 13 October 1944
Solahütte, SS country club, German-occupied Silesia

The country club lounge was packed. Standing room only, the air thick with cigarette smoke. Waiters in white jackets made their way to and fro carrying trays laden with drinks. The only space was at the centre, where a table and two chairs had been set up. On the table was a simple wooden chess set; only the players were missing.

When the Watchmaker appeared in the doorway, a hush fell on the room. Emil hadn't expected that – he had expected to be assailed with shouts of *Kike, StinkJude, Jewish scum*. The silence was worse. He followed Eidenmüller across the room, his head bowed and his eyes fixed on the floor. Still, the oppressive silence; the whole room waiting, holding its breath.

He stopped at the table. Still no shouts, no threats, no sounds. Then, a snigger. Slowly, the Watchmaker raised his head. The SS men were struggling to hold back laughter. Emil followed their gaze; what he saw made his stomach churn.

It was another prisoner. He was in heavy manacles and around his neck somebody had strung a cardboard placard that read: *Don't speak to me. I am already dead.*

With a start, Emil realized who the prisoner was: it was Daniel Farhi. He looked terrified.

The room exploded in hoots of laughter and applause, and glasses were banged on tables in appreciation of the joke.

Unseen by the Watchmaker, Hustek was on the margin of the crowd, watching his reaction, a scornful smirk on his face.

Meissner was on the porch outside to greet the Kommandant. On his arrival, Meissner asked him to take a prominent place among the crowd, but Bär refused. He would observe proceedings, he said, from a distance.

When Meissner entered the lounge he saw the Watchmaker standing next to the chess table. Hustek was speaking to him, but he couldn't hear what was being said. Determined to prevent the Gestapo man from intimidating the Watchmaker any further, Meissner put all his weight into pushing through the crowd.

'Take a good look, you piece of Kike shit,' Hustek was saying, jerking his head towards Farhi. 'You know who he is, don't you? Aren't you wondering how I know about the little scheme you and Brack have got going together? How you're going to get rich after the war is over…? Listen carefully – I'm going to beat you, and when I do, I'm going to take that one over there and put him into the gas chamber myself. Then I'm coming for you.' He paused to let his words take effect. 'You're not so cocky now, are you?'

'What's going on?' Meissner demanded.

'I was merely spelling out a few home truths for your Jew friend, Herr Hauptsturmführer,' Hustek replied.

'Ignore him,' Meissner said to the Watchmaker. 'Your protected status has been confirmed by the Kommandant. There's nothing he can do about it.'

Hustek grinned, a self-assured leer. 'As you say, Herr Hauptsturmführer, but there's more than one way to skin a cat, if you know what I mean.' He took his seat.

Meissner indicated the Watchmaker should do the same, and waited for the noise in the room to subside.

As in the previous game, the Kommandant had insisted that Hustek be given choice of colour. He chose white and moved his king's pawn forward two spaces. Immediately he lit a cigarette, inhaled deeply and blew smoke into the Watchmaker's face. 'Oh, pardon me,' he said, before doing it again.

The Watchmaker showed no reaction and calmly moved his queenside bishop's pawn forward one square. The pulse pounding in his ears was deafening.

Hustek advanced his queen's pawn to stand next to its brother. The black queen's pawn moved forward two spaces to meet it. Ignoring the gambit, Hustek advanced his king's pawn one space. Emil brought out his queen's bishop to the middle of the board. The white king's bishop advanced to the third row. The black bishop swooped to take it.

'Thought that was clever, didn't you?' Hustek said, and moved his queen forward to capture the black bishop.

Emil said nothing. He moved his king's pawn forward one square.

Hustek responded by staring at Emil. He knew few people could bear the pressure of that gaze. But Emil looked back without flinching. At the front of his mind burned the Hebrew letter Zayin, representing the order of angels called Principalities and whose essence is in conquering. This was his shield against Hustek's viciousness.

The Gestapo man turned away, flicking ash from his cigarette onto the floor before advancing his kingside bishop's pawn two squares. Emil brought forward his bishop's pawn one more space. Again, Hustek ignored the sacrifice. Instead, he moved his queenside bishop's pawn one space. Emil's fingers hovered over his queenside knight.

'I know about your wife,' Hustek said, almost amiably, as if this were the most ordinary conversation imaginable. Emil looked at him sharply, but remained silent, advancing the knight so that with the next move he would threaten the white queen.

Hustek responded by bringing out his kingside knight. 'Did Meissner tell you – she was shot trying to escape.' He sniggered. 'At least that's what the report said.'

Emil closed his eyes, forcing Zayin back to the centre of his consciousness. Seemingly of its own volition, the black queen moved diagonally three spaces.

Hustek castled, pushing his king into a corner and releasing his kingside rook. 'I did what I could to help her. I had her in protective custody, but your chum, Meissner, got wind of it and decided she needed to be rescued. Bungled it, of course.'

Emil brought out the second black knight.

Hustek seemed to have been leading up to a concerted attack, but now all he did was to advance his queenside knight's pawn one space. Black bishop's pawn took white queen's pawn, stopping ahead of the white queen. With a contemptuous shake of his head, Hustek took the black bishop's pawn.

'She'd still be alive now if he hadn't interfered.'

Emil brought his kingside knight forward.

Hustek moved his queenside bishop one square on the left diagonal. His attack was taking shape, with a phalanx of pawns dominating the centre of the board and a formidable triplet of queen, knight and bishop behind. Black's position seemed disorganized and purposeless in comparison. Emil moved his queenside rook sideways two spaces.

Hustek advanced his own queenside rook's pawn one space. 'Has he told you he's applied for a transfer away from Auschwitz?' Emil tried to keep his features impassive, but Hustek saw immediately that his words had struck home. 'Oh, I see he hasn't. No, it seems he craves a return to active service. Life in our little camp is not exciting enough for the good Hauptsturmführer. But if you ask my opinion, I'd say he was running away from something.' He ground out his cigarette and lit another. Again he blew smoke into Emil's face.

Emil brought up his queenside knight to take the pawn standing before the white queen. The board now seemed set for a quick-fire exchange of pieces.

Hustek lifted his kingside knight. 'I wonder why he didn't tell you. Do you think it's because he knows he won't be able to protect you when he's gone?' With a disdainful flick of his fingers he took the black knight.

Emil brought up his kingside bishop to threaten the white knight. Hustek could not move it: it would put his king in check. For a moment his confidence slipped, then he smiled. 'A little obvious, don't you think?'

He moved his kingside rook sideways until it stood behind his queen. Emil took the knight that was protecting the king. Hustek scowled. Without pausing to think, he advanced his remaining bishop to take the knight. Despite the loss of the knight he was still in a strong position, with his queen behind his bishop, and a rook in a direct line behind to support it.

Black bishop immediately took the white bishop.

'Check.'

Angrily, Hustek took the bishop with his queen. Only then did he see the danger.

The Watchmaker's strategy had been masterful. He had made his moves look disjointed, disorganized, as if there was no real thought behind them, as if all along all he had been able to do was react to Hustek's superior strategy. But now, out of nothing, he had conjured a winning move.

The black rook moved the length of the board to the back row on the white side.

Frantically, Hustek looked for a way to counter this move, but there was nothing. He did not understand. Only moments ago his had been the stronger position. How had the Watchmaker managed to reverse their positions without him seeing it?

Meissner, seated to the side, sensed something momentous had happened.

The Watchmaker spoke. 'It's your move, Herr Oberscharführer.'

36.

THE GREEK GIFT

Kerk de Krijtberg, Amsterdam

'Extraordinary,' Willi breathed. 'I was with you every move. So you beat the champion of the SS, and you won another life. But you must have known that Hustek would not honour the bargain that Paul had made with you. Was it true that Paul had requested a transfer?'

Meissner raised a hand from the bed. 'I'm afraid it's true,' he said, his voice frayed from coughing. 'And I knew it was selfish of me: I was running away, but I did not expect to survive the war. Casualty rates in the Waffen-SS were horrific, much higher than in the Wehrmacht, and I thought that in death my honour would be restored.' He was taken by another spasm of coughing. Willi helped him to sit up and Emil passed him a glass of water. After a few sips the spasm eased, but Meissner's face was grey with pain.

'Do you want some laudanum?' Willi asked. 'The doctor said it would help the coughing as well as the pain.'

Meissner shook his head. 'It was the Kommandant who, quite unwittingly, gave Emil the protection he needed after I had gone. And it was through him that the final character entered the Watchmaker's story.'

'Another character, so late in the game? Who?'

Meissner took another sip of water before replying. 'It was you, Willi. You also had a part to play, and you were probably instrumental in saving Emil's life.'

'Me?' spluttered Willi. 'It would be nice to think so, but I don't see how. I never went near Auschwitz.'

'Precisely.'

Friday, 13 October 1944
Solahütte, SS country club, German-occupied Silesia
With a furious shout, Hustek up-ended the board. Chess pieces flew into the air and scattered across the floor. In the stunned silence that followed they could be heard rolling to a halt. Hustek was standing, with his arm extended and his pistol pointing at the Watchmaker's head but, suddenly, the Gestapo man forced a smile and lowered the gun. 'No,' he said, his voice quietly menacing. 'Shooting is too good for you, Watchmaker.'

Without another word he forced his way through the packed ranks of spectators, not caring whom he pushed out of his path.

Then there was uproar.

Harsh words were shouted, and angry looks directed at the Watchmaker. One man spat at him; a woman threw her drink over him. Some stood, looking as if they intended to give him a beating, or worse.

Emil tried not to look at them. He was scanning the room for Daniel Farhi, who seemed to have disappeared. Then he saw him – crouched down in a corner, his hands clasped over the top of a head, trying to hide. It was the best thing he could have done: the crowd continued to direct its fury at Emil until Meissner placed himself in front of him.

Meissner stared down the crowd, daring them to include him in their invective.

Across the room, Eidenmüller steered Farhi along the front of the bar towards the exit.

'Let's go,' Meissner said softly, to Emil. Holding his walking stick before him, as if threatening to use it if necessary, Meissner edged his way through the crowd, the Watchmaker on his coattails.

The doorway was blocked by the Kommandant, his face red with anger. 'Well?'

'Sir,' Meissner replied, 'I think this is not the time. We should wait until tempers have calmed.' He glanced behind. The noise had not abated. Somebody yelled, 'Jew-lover!'

'I don't think we have the luxury of *that* much time, Meissner. I will see you in my office first thing on Monday.'

'Yes, sir. *Heil Hitler.*'

Monday, 16 October 1944
Kommandantur building, Konzentrationslager Auschwitz-I
Sturmbannführer Richard Bär read and reread the file on the desk before him. He was searching for anything that would provide a clue to Meissner's disloyalty. Before July there was no doubt that the Hauptsturmführer had been one of his best officers: conscientious, and capable; but he had changed. Where, Bär wondered, had Meissner's defeatist attitude come from? More importantly, what had happened to transform him into a Jew-lover?

Absentmindedly, he scratched a pimple that had erupted on the end of his nose and winced as he took the top off. A drop of blood fell onto the open page. He pulled out a handkerchief and dabbed at it, but all he managed to do was smear blood across the neat, type-written words. It was Meissner's request for a transfer: Bär took his pen and signed it.

There was a knock at the door.

'Hauptsturmführer Meissner, sir,' his orderly said.

Bär was much calmer than he had been on Friday night: he thought he had found a solution to the problem of the unbeatable Jew. It would be Meissner's last duty before he left.

'Send him in.'

Meissner entered and brought his heels together, raising his arm in salute. '*Heil Hitler.*'

The Kommandant ignored the salute, and did not invite Meissner to sit down. Instead, he leaned back and observed his troublesome officer closely, as if by doing so he could discover the cause of his disaffection. 'That was quite a stunt you pulled on Friday night,' he said eventually.

'You'll pardon me for pointing it out, Herr Sturmbannführer, but it was not my idea for the game to be played at Solahütte, nor was I the one who arranged for a prisoner to be manacled in the corner. If anyone is to be accused of pulling a stunt, surely it is Oberscharführer Hustek.'

'The funny thing is, Meissner, now that I've had time to think about it, I find I'm much less concerned with the uproar you caused than I am with your disloyalty.'

Meissner was indignant. 'Disloyalty? How have I been disloyal?'

'You have been disloyal to your fellow SS officers, to the SS, and to the Führer; and above all, disloyal to the blood of the German *Volk.*'

'Why? Because I arranged a few chess games against a Jew?'

Bär pursed his lips and shook his head. 'Of course not. You are disloyal because you have taken the Jew's side.'

Meissner's eyes narrowed in anger, then he did a double take – was that blood on the Kommandant's nose? 'Sir, no. I will not take that,' he replied. 'I have never taken the Jew's side.'

A drop of blood fell onto the Kommandant's tunic. He seemed not to notice. 'No? Then prove it to me: have him liquidated. I don't care if you do it yourself, or have him sent to the gas chamber.'

Meissner's reply was immediate. 'No, sir. I can't do that.'

Another drop. 'That's what I thought.'

'Sir. All I have ever sought was to maintain my honour in my dealings with him. I gave him guarantees if he won his games. Surely you would not have me break my word?'

Only now did the Kommandant seem to notice the blood. Irritated, he held the handkerchief to his nose. 'I don't expect you to break your word, Meissner, but you helped him to win, didn't you? That's what is so unforgivable.'

Meissner watched, fascinated, as the rich, dark blood of the German *Volk* seeped through the Kommandant's handkerchief. He made himself look away, to the photograph of Himmler on the wall, so fond of invoking the *Volksblut* himself. 'How?' he replied, evenly, trying not to rise to the Kommandant's provocation. 'How did I help him win?'

Bär removed the handkerchief from his nose to examine it. Meissner caught himself staring again. *Yes*, he thought, *take a good look – it's blood; and it's about as close as you will ever come to being wounded in action.*

The Kommandant's words cut across his musings. 'You can't deny that it was your actions, Meissner, that prevented Oberscharführer Hustek from beating the Jew.'

'With respect, sir, I did nothing to prevent Hustek from winning. All I did was to stop him cheating. Look what he managed to do with me trying to stop him – what would he have done if he'd had a free hand?'

The Kommandant dabbed at his nose again. The bleeding seemed to have stopped. He turned his attention back to Meissner. 'I've seen this

345

happen before, Meissner, where an unscrupulous Jew corrupts an other-wise blameless German. What you need to do is recognize what he's done to you and get yourself out from under his influence.'

Meissner had to work hard not to show his exasperation. 'Sir, I protest. I am under no Jewish influence. If anything, my fault was having too much faith in the supremacy of the SS.'

Bär regarded his subordinate coolly. 'This is getting us nowhere.' He picked up a sheet of paper from the desk and passed it across. 'I've made my decision – two, actually. Here is your transfer request. I've author-ized it. As soon as you've been assigned to a new unit you can leave. However, before you go, we must have a solution to our little local Jewish question.'

There was a book on the desk. The Kommandant pushed it over to Meissner. 'Do you know what this is?' Meissner shook his head. 'It's a copy of the register of the Grossdeutscher Schachbund – the German Chess Federation. It contains the names and addresses of all its members. What I've decided is this – we will invite the chess champion of Germany to Auschwitz. He will play our unbeatable Jew and put an end to his pre-tensions once and for all.'

Meissner was appalled. 'That's hardly fair, sir. The Watchmaker has never played chess at that level.'

Bär slammed his fist down on the desk. 'Fair?' he roared. 'I don't care whether it's fucking *fair*, Meissner! This thing has gone too far, so now I must put an end to it.' He paused for breath before continuing more calmly: 'Don't you understand? Here in Auschwitz we are the front line fighting international Jewry. We cannot afford to lose a single battle, or we will be devoured. In war, everything is fair.'

Meissner knew he had to choose his words carefully. 'Don't you think you're taking this a bit too seriously, sir? Don't forget, Obersturmbann-führer Höss himself supported the idea. He said it was good for the SS to be challenged, that it would keep us from becoming complacent.'

'I'm not interested in what Höss or anyone else has to say,' the Kom-mandant said angrily. 'I'm the one who will be held to account if anything goes wrong. I'm concerned only with the good order of this camp, which your ridiculous ideas and your notions of fair play have disrupted. We've already had to put down one rebellion this year – this Watchmaker has given the prisoners hope. They've seen him beat the previously unbeat-able SS. Well, I have to take that hope away and remove their illusions. So you will find this chess champion and bring him here. That is an order.'

October 1944
Ministry of Public Enlightenment and Propaganda, Berlin
Willi was late back from lunch. He was late for everything these days. With the relentless Allied bombing and all the shortages, even the Min-istry of Propaganda could not guarantee food in the canteen. Besides, nobody cared any more, least of all him. The war was as good as lost, though nobody dared to say so.

His colleague, Georg, was gone: an English bomb had taken out his apartment block one moonless night about two months ago. At first, Willi had missed the older man's harping about his being late and how important it was to look busy, but that had passed. Now there was merely a pretence of work in the department, and the only men left were the cripples: Willi and others like him who weren't capable of holding a rifle. He hadn't had a woman in months. Women looked askance at men his age wearing civilian clothes. They would taunt him: 'Why aren't *you* at the front?' He had been tempted, once or twice, to pull off the glove that covered his artificial hand and wave it at them, but in the end he couldn't be bothered. What was the point? The war was getting to everyone. All he wanted now was for it to be over.

There was a scrap of paper on his desk – a note from his boss, Falthauser. As Willi scanned the note, he mused sourly, *Why hasn't an Allied bomb taken* him *out, instead of Georg? There's no justice.*

It made no sense. Apparently an SS officer had been looking for him. What could the SS possibly want with him? Pocketing the note, he set off to find his supervisor.

The increased intensity of the bombing had not improved Falthauser's temper. 'I have no idea what they want with you,' he told Willi, 'but you are ordered to report to the SS economic-administrative sub-office on Prinz Albrecht Strasse, immediately.'

Willi did not delay his visit. It wasn't as if he had any work that couldn't wait.

The SS headquarters had been hit by the bombing, but people were still working inside. He was directed to a young Untersturmführer, whose office consisted of a desk in a passageway.

'Are you Wilhelm Schweninger?' the officer intoned.

'Yes, that's me.'

'Wilhelm Schweninger the Reich chess champion?'

Willi rolled his eyes. Like many in the Propaganda Ministry, he did not like the SS – perhaps a reflection of the prejudices of his master, Goebbels. 'Yes,' he replied. 'I am Wilhelm Schweninger, the Reich chess champion.'

The SS officer peered at him as if he found it hard to believe that such a poor specimen could be champion of anything. 'We have received a rather unusual request,' he said, 'from the Kommandant of K-Z Auschwitz. I have instructions to induct you as an honorary member of the SS, and arrange transportation to the camp.'

'Auschwitz? What possible reason could there be for me to go to Auschwitz?'

'Apparently your presence is required for a game of chess.'

1962

Kerk de Krijtberg, Amsterdam

'I couldn't believe my luck.' Willi chuckled. 'At last I had a uniform. True, it was an SS uniform, and people in my building would look down their noses at it, but outside the ministry it would stop all those sneers and muttered comments. I might even get a woman or two again, especially seeing as I was given the honorary rank of Sturmbannführer.'

'When did this happen?' Emil asked.

'The end of October, beginning of November.'

'But you never got to Auschwitz, did you?' Emil asked. Willi shook his head. 'Why not? Were you reluctant to come?'

'Not at all – I would have done almost anything to get away from the bombing, even if it was only for a short time. No, every couple of days I would go back to the SS building – in my new uniform, of course – only to be told there was no transport.'

Meissner lifted a hand from the counterpane, waving it feebly. 'And it was because you were not able to come that Emil survived, of that I am sure,' he said, his voice barely audible.

'But why?'

Meissner's breathing was laboured and he struggled to reply. 'My transfer was overdue. My old comrade, Peter Sommer, was now the Division commander's chief of staff. I had been ordered to go west and take up duties as his adjutant in Koblenz in preparation for the *Ardennenoffensive* in December, but like you, Willi, I too was delayed by a lack of transport.'

Emil didn't understand the point Paul was making. 'Why would Willi's failure to reach Auschwitz have had any bearing on what happened to me?'

Meissner tried to push himself up on the bed and groaned with pain.

'Here,' Willi said, reaching for the bottle. 'For God's sake, man, have some laudanum.'

'Later. I'll have some when it's time for me to sleep.' Meissner waved the bottle away. 'Don't you see, my friend?' he continued. 'Once I had left the camp, I could no longer protect you. But you were not harmed because Bär was waiting for Willi to arrive and teach you a lesson: the only way to destroy the legend of the unbeatable Watchmaker was for you to be defeated by one of the SS.'

'When did you finally leave to rejoin your old unit?' Willi asked.

'Not until the tenth of November. It was a time of great confusion. Bär even asked me to reconsider my transfer request. The Russians had reached the suburbs of Budapest, which was only about four hundred kilometres away. I think by then even he could see what was coming. But I couldn't stay. I knew Hitler would never give in, and I wanted to face the end with my old comrades, not a shameful surrender in a camp surrounded by thousands of starving prisoners.' He took a ragged breath. 'But there was one last thing I was able to do to protect Emil.'

'What was that?'

'Something I gave to Eidenmüller.'

'What did you give him?'

But all Meissner could do was to shake his head. He was exhausted and, with a muted gasp, fell back into the pillows.

Emil and Willi exchanged a worried glance.

'I wish he would take the bloody laudanum,' Willi whispered.

Emil nodded, but said, 'I can understand why he won't.'

Meissner did not open his eyes but croaked hoarsely, 'I can still hear you, you know.'

Willi grinned. 'Don't worry, old man, we're not going to force it on you. But you need to rest. We'll come back later.'

'Give me some now, before you go,' Meissner whispered. 'But promise me you'll be back. I want to know how it ends.'

Emil helped Paul to sit up while Willi measured a dose of the narcotic. Meissner choked on the bitter liquid, and a little dribbled down his chin. Emil took a handkerchief to wipe it off. Meissner reached up a hand to grasp Emil's arm. The strength of his grip took Emil by surprise.

'Promise me,' Meissner hissed.

'Don't worry, Paul. I promise.'

A minute later, Willi reached across to touch Paul's arm.

'I think he's asleep,' he whispered. He stood and crept towards the door. Emil followed.

But Paul is not asleep. He is striding through the Buna *Werke* frantically searching for somebody, though he doesn't know who. Then it comes to him: the Watchmaker. He must speak to him urgently. He calls to everyone he sees: 'Where is the Watchmaker?' Nobody has seen him. He should be in the instrument workshop, but he is not there. Paul turns into a blind alley. Facing him is one of the wooden watchtowers that are usually spaced at intervals along the camp perimeter. There is a man standing on the platform at its top; a man in a long black leather coat and wearing a SS cap. Paul shouts to him: 'Where is the Watchmaker?' The man turns to face him. It takes a moment for Paul to recognize him. It is Hustek, but not Hustek. His face has turned into a death's head, its lidless eyes staring, and the teeth and jaws locked in a hideous grin. 'The Watchmaker?' it says. Hustek's voice echoes along the alley, filling the air, as if coming from a loudspeaker. 'He is not here; he has gone up the chimney. Where he belongs.'

37.

ENDGAME: FOUR KNIGHTS

1962

Kerk de Krijtberg, Amsterdam

Though his bedroom is warm, Meissner cannot stop shivering. He is not sure where he is. He raises his head expecting to see the familiar items that define his life: the prie-dieu, the crucifix, his breviary at the side of the bed, but there are none of these things. He is in a large room where the walls are covered in maps, with arcane symbols drawn across their surface. Light comes from antique crystal chandeliers suspended from the ceiling and through large mullioned windows, where each small pane of glass is taped to prevent it from splintering in the event of an explosion. He can hear the shrill sound of telephones ringing and all around there are men in military uniform. Now he knows where he is. All night he has been trying to get through to the logistics command in Dietrich's VI Panzer Army HQ. The Second SS Panzer Division has performed miracles: they have broken through the Allied lines and are advancing fast, but now, less than forty kilometres from Namur, they are running out of fuel. The field telephone is down. No matter what he does Meissner cannot get through, yet he must get fuel for the Panzers.

There is only one thing for it: he will have to go in person. He looks for Sturmscharführer Schratt, who'd saved his life at Voronezh. Like him, Schratt is a survivor, wounded and then assigned to administrative duties.

Schratt hates it; he tells everyone it is like serving a prison sentence.

'Schratt!' Meissner yells. The NCO appears out of nowhere. 'Find us some transport. We're going to Dietrich's HQ.'

The only available vehicle is a motorcycle and sidecar. Schratt drives it through the freezing mud like a man possessed. Meissner crouches low in the sidecar, a machine pistol cradled across his knee in case they meet the enemy. But the enemy they encounter is not one that can be fought off so easily: an American Mustang fighter zooms in low over the trees and strafes them with a long machine-gun burst. Schratt veers from side to side and Meissner empties the magazine of his weapon ineffectually. The aeroplane turns for a second pass. This time Schratt cannot avoid the hail of bullets. His body is cut almost in two and the bike somersaults into a ditch. Meissner is thrown clear and comes to hours later in a field hospital.

Miraculously, Meissner's injuries are superficial. The doctor says he can go. But there is no transport. Meissner is furious. The outcome of the offensive depends on getting fuel for the Panzers. Eventually he manages to reach his division on a field telephone.

'I was trying to get through to the logistics group at Dietrich's HQ,' he says, 'but I didn't get there. We were strafed by an American plane.' Then he remembers. 'Schratt is dead.' Old Schratt – old, indestructible Schratt. No time now to mourn. 'Somebody must get through to them. Without fuel, the attack will grind to a halt.'

'Calm yourself, Paul.' It is Peter Sommer. 'I'm sorry Schratt is dead. We'll have to manage without the fuel. There's none to be had.'

'Manage without ... but how?'

'Just get yourself back here, Paul. You're needed.'

*

Emil jerked awake to find himself still in the chair beside Paul's bed.

Father Scholten was at its foot, quietly telling his beads. 'He's delirious,' Scholten said.

Paul was shivering with fever, muttering and mumbling. He cried out: 'Schratt!'

'What time is it?' Emil asked, blinking away sleep.

'Late.'

'It's all right, Father,' Emil said. 'I'll look after him. Just give me a minute to wake Willi. I'm sure he would want to be here too.' He went to Willi's room and knocked. 'Willi? Paul's not too good. I think you'd better come.' He went back into Meissner's room.

Willi arrived, pulling a robe around his rotund stomach.

'Dead...' Meissner muttered. '...manage...needed here...'

'What's he talking about?' Willi asked.

'I have no idea.'

'He's raving. How much laudanum did he have?'

The next morning Meissner was pale, and his skin had taken on a waxy hue. His breathing was laboured and he could speak only with great effort. Mrs Brinckvoort insisted he take more laudanum. He was too weak to argue, but would not take all that she measured out.

'Emil,' he murmured, 'my part in your tale is done. But I want to know what happened in the last days of the camp, and on the death march.'

'Death march?' Willi asked.

'The SS did not want the prisoners to fall into the hands of the Russians,' Emil explained. 'As far as they were concerned, we were still capable of work. So, days before the Russians arrived, the prisoners were marched out of the camp.'

'In the middle of winter? How did they manage to survive?'

'Thousands didn't. They either fell by the wayside and froze to death or were shot if they couldn't keep up.' Emil stopped. The air in the room suddenly seemed stale. He crossed to the window to raise the sash a little. 'Nobody knows how anyone managed to survive,' he said, resuming his seat. 'Least of all the survivors.'

'And you were on this death march?'

Meissner reached out a hand to tug feebly at Willi's sleeve. 'Why don't you let him tell his story?'

16 January 1945
Konzentrationslager Auschwitz-III, Monowitz
It is cold. In the three years he has spent at Auschwitz, Eidenmüller cannot remember it being so cold. A thick blanket of white hoar frost covers the trees, and icicles hang from eaves and window ledges. It snowed a couple of days ago and the roads and paths are covered in dirty slush. They are short of everything: food, fuel, even coal, and Eidenmüller is getting sick of tinned beef or pork. In the distance he can hear the booming of guns. He is not sure how close they are, but he is getting nervous; he does not want to hang around to meet the Russians. Meissner has told him that when they encounter the SS they do not take prisoners.

A new officer, Untersturmführer Walter, has taken over Meissner's duties, but he is fresh from the Hitler Jügende* and has no idea of anything apart from shouting and throwing his weight around. Fortunately, it is not difficult for Eidenmüller to keep out of his way.

Even the prisoners know the end is near. The gas chambers have been

---

* Hitler Youth.

shut down and explosive charges have been placed ready to demolish them.

The Buna factory is a deserted wasteland. It was bombed repeatedly in the autumn and, with the Russians so near, there is no point attempting repairs. Until a week ago, work *Kommandos* were sent every day to salvage what could easily be dismantled and shipped out, but no longer. Even if it were possible to remove more material, there is no transport. The prisoners are shut up in their blocks in enforced idleness, an intolerable situation for the camp authorities but one they are powerless to remedy. The SS have their belongings packed, awaiting only the command to abandon the camp. But though they have been expecting the order for days, it has not come.

The SS barracks have become like the front line: most of the NCOs are drinking heavily, and arguments are frequent occurrences. Eidenmüller seeks refuge in the empty Monowitz administration offices. The files have all been burned and most of the equipment removed. All that remains is the furniture – desks and chairs – which he has been breaking up and putting into the stove for fuel. He wonders how Hauptsturmführer Meissner is getting on. He has heard about the offensive in the Ardennes that will throw the Allies back to the coast, and he knows that the Hauptsturmführer's division is in the thick of it. He hopes Meissner does not get killed. He is the best officer Eidenmüller has ever had.

He hears footsteps on the stairs. Quickly he folds a cloth over the pistol he has been cleaning and puts it into a drawer. It was a parting gift from the Hauptsturmführer – a Russian Tokarev T-33 semi-automatic, a souvenir from the Eastern Front. It is a simpler design than the Luger, the standard handgun of the SS. It has a solid feel, and its weight in his hand is reassuring, as if to tell him he can trust it never to misfire. When Eidenmüller had asked why the Hauptsturmführer was giving him such a thing, he had replied only that he had a feeling it might come in useful one day.

The steps are coming closer. A board creaks outside the door and Untersturmführer Walter walks in.

'Eidenmüller,' he says. 'What are you doing here?'

'Not much, sir. I was making sure that we hadn't missed any of the files that were supposed to have been destroyed.'

'Very commendable,' says the Untersturmführer. 'Now come with me.'

'Yes, sir. I just need the latrine. I'll meet you downstairs.'

The Untersturmführer retraces his steps. Not knowing when he'll be able to return, Eidenmüller retrieves the pistol and puts it in his pocket.

Outside, the officer tells Eidenmüller of the plans to evacuate the camp: the prisoners will be distributed among other concentration camps in Germany and Austria; the sick will be left behind to fend for themselves. Eidenmüller asks how transport will be provided for so many prisoners. 'They will have to march,' the officer says.

The plan is foolishness. The recent snowfall was heavy and it seems likely more will come soon. How will prisoners in their ill-fitting wooden clogs and threadbare uniforms be able to march in such conditions? But that is not the Untersturmführer's problem. His only concern is to ensure his men are ready for the journey. When? The day after tomorrow.

Walter does not stay long: he is anxious to be seen to be performing his duties diligently, and the best place to do that is in the vicinity of a superior officer.

When he is sure Walter is gone, Eidenmüller enters the camp and walks to the Watchmaker's block. In the day room, Brack and his cronies are gathered around the stove. Most of the inmates are in their bunks trying to keep warm.

'Anywhere we can talk?' Eidenmüller asks Brack.

Brack follows him outside and they walk briskly along the slush-covered paths, great clouds of vapour billowing from their mouths.

'We've got our marching orders.'

Brack raises an eyebrow. 'Yeah?' he says. 'When?'

'Not just us. Everybody. Day after tomorrow.'

Brack stops. 'Everybody? No. It's not possible. These men won't make it far in this weather – it'll kill them. It's bad enough walking to the Buna factory and back.'

Eidenmüller agrees. 'Look,' he says, 'there's a chance for some of them to survive. I know about the deals you've done with a few of the Yids – but if they die, I'm guessing all bets are off.'

'What do you suggest?'

'Get them into the *Krankenbau*. You, the Watchmaker, and a few others. The sick are going to be left behind. The officers think the cold will finish most of them off, but once we're gone, you can start breaking the barracks apart for fuel. What do you say?'

'It sounds like a good plan, but what's in it for you?'

'I've been thinking. After the war, people like me, you know – ex-SS – are going to find it hard. I'll get you into the sick bay too and keep any nosy parkers out of your hair when our men come to empty the camp. After the war's over, I'll find you and we can come to an arrangement.'

Brack smiled. 'Funny, I never took you for the trusting type.'

'I'm not. If you don't play fair with me, you won't like the consequences, I promise.' Eidenmüller spat on his palm and held out his hand. 'Deal?'

Brack did the same. 'Deal.'

*

1962

Kerk de Krijtberg, Amsterdam

'Of course I didn't know any of this at first,' Emil said. 'Brack told me, later, when we were in the infirmary.'

'Brack,' Meissner wheezed. 'He was a complicated character. Out for number one. But there was more to him than that, I think.' His eyes closed.

'Next morning we went to the *Krankenbau*. Obviously we were not ill, but Eidenmüller had concocted a story about an SS doctor who suspected us of having typhus. The Jewish doctor was unconvinced until a packet of cigarettes appeared and with that, his concerns seemed to vanish.'

'So you and Brack and these others went into the sick bay and waited for the Russians to arrive?'

'If only it had been that simple, Willi.' Emil turned to Meissner. 'Are you still listening, Paul?' A squeeze of a hand showed that he was.

'That night we had a visitor.'

'Who?'

'Hustek.' Emil felt Meissner stiffen at the mention of this name. 'He was looking for me. Brack tried to stall him by telling him I had typhus. "Bring him out here then," Hustek said. "If he's got typhus, he's as good as dead anyway; better to let the cold finish him off, it'll be kinder in the end." But Brack shook his head. "Nothing doing," he said. But his words were empty and he knew it.

'When I came out, Hustek was there holding a pistol. I almost expected him to shoot me there and then, but he waved the gun and said, "This way." I had hardly moved when he had second thoughts and pointed the gun at Brack. "You as well," he said.

'He walked us at gunpoint through the camp, up the service road, through the gates and into the SS administrative building. It was empty, and he marched us up the stairs into Paul's old office.'

Hustek made Brack and the Watchmaker stand in the two corners furthest from the door. There was a paraffin lamp on the desk. He lit it, then settled himself astride a chair with his back to the door, and took out a pack of cigarettes.

'Smoke, Brack?' he said. When he got no reply he shrugged and put the cigarettes back in his pocket.

'Why have you brought us here?' Brack demanded.

'I would have thought that was obvious.' Hustek used his unlit cigarette to point at the Watchmaker. 'Killing your Jew friend here – that wouldn't cause me any problems at all. But killing you, Brack? Questions might be asked. I could hardly say you were shot trying to escape, could I? No, I needed somewhere where you wouldn't be found until it was too late to matter.' He smirked, struck a match and inhaled deeply, blowing the smoke at the ceiling. 'I suppose,' he continued, 'I should ask if you have any last requests.' He seemed to find that very funny, and laughed so hard he started to cough. When he had recovered, he said, 'By the way, Brack, I thought you would want to know that Widmann told me all about the deal the two of you cooked up. Your idea, of course – Widmann wasn't clever enough for that, but he was clever enough to realize he needed a new partner. Me.'

Brack glowered at Hustek, but said nothing. His brain was working feverishly: there was a slim chance he might survive, providing Hustek fired at the Jew first. Then, in the corridor outside, a floorboard creaked.

*

Eidenmüller hadn't wanted to spend the night in the SS barracks – it had been bad enough the night before, with most of his fellow NCOs drunk and whining repeatedly about having to escort prisoners in this weather; so he had brought a cot up to his old office.

He had been awoken by the sound of someone laughing. There was a light on in the Hauptsturmführer's office. Quietly, he had eased himself up and crept to the door.

In the flickering light, Eidenmüller could see the Watchmaker in the far corner. Holding the Soviet handgun tightly, he took a step forward.

Hustek spun round, peering into the darkness.

'Put the gun down, Hustek,' Eidenmüller said.

Hustek recovered quickly. He swung his gun to point it at the Watchmaker. 'You won't shoot me,' he said. 'Not for the sake of a stinking Yid.'

'I wouldn't be so sure.' Eidenmüller's face glistened in the lamplight. 'I've sort of taken to him. He's not a bad sort – for a Jew. On the other hand, nobody likes you Gestapo scum – not even your own mothers.'

Hustek did not waver. He kept the pistol aimed at the Watchmaker. 'Don't be so fucking stupid. You might win – for now. But in the morning, I'll be back with a squad of my men and I'll have him, whether you like it or not. It'll be a lot easier for you if you walk away now. I'll forget you were even here.'

Eidenmüller shook his head. 'You are a cocky bastard, aren't you? I knew that's what you would say, and I knew what I would have to do as soon as I saw it was you.'

Hustek's mind was raging. Why hadn't he checked the other rooms? The chances were the SS arse-wipe couldn't hit the side of a barn from five metres, but it was a sure thing that Brack and the Yid would be on him before he could say *Heil* fucking *Hitler*.

'You can shoot me,' he said, trying to keep his voice even. 'But as soon as I sense your finger squeezing that trigger I'll kill your precious Yid. No matter what you do, he'll be dead, so let's be sensible, eh?'

Hustek sensed a flicker of movement. With a snarl of rage, he pulled the trigger.

Within a fraction of a second, three shots were fired and two men fell to the floor. One was Hustek: Eidenmüller's bullet had taken him cleanly in the head. The other was Brack.

Brack had had a pistol of his own, nestled in the waistband of his trousers: it was the Luger he had taken from the Gestapo man that he and his cronies had murdered. He had known that Hustek intended to kill him, but he was no Jew to go to his death meekly.

Watching the exchange between Hustek and Eidenmüller, he detected a momentary hesitation as the Gestapo man's gaze wavered and pulled out his pistol. Seeing the danger, Hustek switched his aim. They fired at each other almost simultaneously. Brack missed his shot, but took a bullet in the stomach.

Emil felt a sudden pressure on his hand. 'Eidenmüller,' Paul murmured, struggling to rouse himself. 'What happened to Eidenmüller?'

'As far as I know, Eidenmüller is alive and living somewhere under the name of Leon Nadelmann.' He caught Willi's dubious glance, but continued. 'Brack wasn't dead, but he was in pain and bleeding heavily. We stripped off Hustek's shirt and used it to try and staunch the flow of blood. Then, between us, we carried him back to the infirmary.

'He died about an hour later. There was nobody to mourn him and, as was usual, his body was dumped outside to be sent for cremation. By morning it would have been frozen solid. Eidenmüller saw his chance – "One out, one in," he said. Several prisoners died that night. He assumed the identity of one of them.

'The next day the camp was evacuated. The prisoners were lined up in the snow and marched off. I never saw any of them again. A week or so later, the Russians arrived.'

The Watchmaker's story had reached its end. A ragged breath passed Meissner's lips. 'Thank you,' he whispered, so quietly Emil could barely hear him. 'The last time we parted I neglected to say goodbye. Not this time. Go with God, Watchmaker.'

The artillery battery – three self-propelled Wespe light howitzers com- manded by a young SS-Obersturmführer – had taken position behind the Russian village to shell Soviet positions about three kilometres distant. The officer had sited the guns behind a low ridge, which was why nobody saw the approach of a squadron of Russian T-34 tanks as they advanced through the village. If not for a gust of wind that had carried the sound of their engines, the surprise would have been complete.

In an instant, the officer's remarkably blue eyes took in everything. Calmly he ordered a retreat and mounted the rear-most vehicle. 'Call HQ,' he shouted to the radio operator. 'Tell them we need a Stuka strike or we're done for.'

The first tank came over the ridge. With a loud *crump*, its gun fired. A mound of earth flew into the air beside the first Wespe. The Russian's tactics were sound: if the first Wespe was disabled, the others would have to slow down to get around it. A second tank appeared and fired at the retreating Wespes. Another miss. But the Obersturmführer knew their luck could not hold for long, the tanks were faster than they were. Then a third and a fourth tank appeared. They did not continue the chase but halted.

'Fuck,' the Scharführer commanding the Wespe said. 'They don't need to chase us. They'll pick us off before we reach the next ridge.'

Two shots were fired almost in unison. One kicked up a shower of earth in front of the first Wespe; the other hit the second. The howitzers were only lightly armoured and the shell from the T-34 gouged a hole in its side and tore away the track below. Amid shrieks of pain from the crew, the Wespe ground to a halt.

'Schratt,' the Obersturmführer yelled to his second in command, 'get to gun number two! Help them get out. I'll take over here.' The officer squeezed into his place. 'Driver,' he shouted, 'turn this thing around. Aim us at the first tank.' He turned to the gunners. 'Get the gun loaded and depress the barrel fully. As soon as you're done, we'll shoot over open sights.'

The driver locked the left track and turned the Wespe. The manoeuvre took the Russians by surprise. The Wespe fired at point blank range and blew the turret off the first Russian tank, detonating the ammunition within, creating a maelstrom of fire and smoke.

'Next one,' the officer ordered. The driver peered through the smoke, trying to line up his vehicle with the next T-34.

'Fire.' Another hit: not a killing hit, but the tank was immobilized.

Then – an explosion beside the T-34s that had halted. The first Wespe had followed their example and had also turned upon their attackers.

The officer whooped, the joy of battle upon him.

And then his world was torn apart. There was a thunderclap so loud it made his ears ring and the Wespe was tossed up from the ground as if by a giant's hand. He was thrown clear – when he looked up, he saw the Wespe was on its side and burning. *Christ*, he thought. He had better move before the flames reached the ammunition.

He tried to stand but where his left foot should have been, all that remained was a bloody stump; oddly, he felt no pain. Around him the battle raged: two Tigers had crested the hill and had started firing on the T-34s. He was in the centre of a whirlwind of white-hot metal, but seemed immune. Everything appeared to be moving in slow motion.

Then he saw Schratt walking towards him. The Scharführer was waving. When he got close he was smiling, his hand extended to help him up. Meissner took it; Schratt's grip was firm and cool. He pulled Meissner to his feet.

To Meissner's amazement, his foot was no longer injured.

'Obersturmführer Meissner,' Schratt said, 'I've been sent to get you.'

'Get me?' Meissner said. 'How is this happening? I thought you were dead.'

Schratt shook his head. 'Old soldiers never die,' he said.

Meissner did not seem able to grasp the idea. 'Never?'

'No, sir. Never.'

37.

The Immortal Game*

1963

Konzentrationslager Auschwitz-II, Birkenau

It is early. Beyond a long line of concrete fence posts, rows of barrack blocks rise like dark, primeval creatures out of the morning mist. Crumbling chimney stacks stand stark against a pale sky, like the masts of stranded ships.

Emil rubs condensation off the car window to peer out. They are on a narrow road that runs beside the remains of a long fence. Every so often he can see the stumps of a watchtower sticking up out of the ground like broken teeth, black and rotten.

This is not the Auschwitz he remembers. He had thought the Monowitz camp was big, but this is *vast*.

The driver brings the car to a halt beside a red-brick tower that stands above an arch, through which a railway spur runs. He points to the building beside it. A man is waiting there, stamping his feet in the cold.

'*Dzień dobry*,' Emil says, trying to remember the little Polish he picked up in the camp. '*Nazywam się Emil Clément.*'

---

* 'The Immortal Game' was played by Adolf Anderssen and Lionel Kieseritzky in London in 1851. In a series of seemingly rash moves, Anderssen sacrificed most of his major pieces – queen, both rooks and a bishop – but then achieved checkmate with his remaining bishop and knights. It is considered to be a chess game without peer.

'Good morning,' the man replies. 'Fortunately, I speak German.'

The man is a professor from the University of Kraków, the supervisor of the preservation work that is being carried out. Birkenau is to become a museum. Monowitz is all but gone. The Buna factory is being run by the Polish government.

The professor is not at all happy that Emil and his companions have arrived to disturb his work. 'Could we hurry, please?' he says. 'All this is most irregular.'

Everything since Paul's death has been irregular. According to the Catholic authorities in the Netherlands, it was irregular for a German priest to be sent 'home' to die in Amsterdam. Then there was the question of the will. Paul had had few possessions, apart from his beloved coffee set – which he left to Mrs Brinckvoort – and his journals, which he bequeathed to Emil.

His desire to be cremated caused consternation.

'The Catholic Church does not hold with cremation,' Father Scholten explained, stiffly.

'But it is what Paul wanted,' Emil insisted.

'But he was a priest,' Scholten objected, in turn.

Willi intervened. 'Exactly,' he said. 'He understood what he was asking for. Surely the Church would not deny his dying wish?'

In the end, it was Paul's final request that caused the greatest problems.

Emil and Willi made enquiries through the Polish Consulate in Amsterdam. It was out of the question, they were told. As for visas, obtaining them was rarely straightforward, even less so with what they had in mind.

For several days Emil and Willi racked their brains for a solution. 'What we need is a fixer,' Willi said, after a few drinks.

Emil slapped his hand to his forehead. 'That's it, Willi! You've got it. And who did Paul say was the best fixer he ever knew?'

'Eidenmüller.'

They found him in a bar in the small Dutch town of Simpelveld, only two kilometres from the German border, near Aachen.

The barman looked up from polishing a glass as two men walked in. 'Good afternoon,' he said. 'What can I get you gentlemen?'

Emil recognized him at once. He extended a hand. 'Eidenmüller,' he said, quietly, in German. 'It's been a long time.'

A shadow crossed the barman's face. 'I think you must be mistaken,' he said quickly. 'My name is Nadelmann. I've never heard of this... what was his name?'

'Eidenmüller,' Willi said, then, more loudly: 'We're friends of Hauptsturmführer Paul Meissner.'

A look of alarm crossed the barman's face. 'Keep your voice down,' he hissed. 'Who are you?'

'Do you really not recognize me?' Emil asked.

The barman shook his head. 'Should I?'

'Yes. I'm the Watchmaker.'

The barman stopped his polishing. 'My God,' he said. 'Why have you come?'

'We're trying to carry out the dying wish of an old friend, and we're hoping you will be able to help us.'

Eidenmüller seemed confused. 'Old friend? Who?'

'Paul Meissner. He died a few weeks ago.'

The news took Eidenmüller by surprise. 'Really? Paul Meissner? He was in the Das Reich Division, you know. Hard bastards they were – not many of them left after the Russians finished with them. But my old Hauptsturmführer made it. Well, I'll be…' He nodded to himself. 'Still, I'm sorry to hear he's dead. He was a good sort – for an officer.' He looked up. 'But hang on. You said he was an old friend. I wouldn't have thought…'

'Nor me,' Emil said. 'But he helped me find something precious that I thought was lost for ever.'

'Oh? What was that, then?'

'Myself.'

Fortunately the bar was empty. Eidenmüller flipped the sign on the door to *Closed*. 'What exactly is it you think I can do?' he asked.

'We're not exactly sure,' Willi replied. 'But Paul said you were the best fixer in the SS.'

Eidenmüller smiled self-consciously. 'Please don't let anyone hear you saying that,' he said. 'I've tried to put those days behind me.'

The solution to their problem, Eidenmüller decided, was twofold: first, they needed a story that was plausible and would stand up to cursory scrutiny; second, they needed money.

'Money? Why do we need money?'

'Communism,' Eidenmüller replied. 'It seems wrong, I know, but what Communists want more than anything is money. I bet there aren't many real Communists in Poland, but you can be damned sure there's an awful lot of poor people. We used to say a Pole is always good for a bribe. I bet that hasn't changed since the war – worse, if anything, I would have thought. But we might need to bribe a lot of people, so we'll probably need a lot of money.'

'We're finished then,' Willi said. 'I wouldn't say I was badly off, but I don't have much to spare.'

'That makes two of us,' Emil said.

'Three,' Eidenmüller added. 'All I've got is this place. And there's not only me to think of.'

'You're married?' Emil asked. Eidenmüller nodded. 'Does she know, about, you know...?'

'Yes. I told her everything.'

'Children?'

'Yes. Two boys.'

'What did you call them?'

'Paul...and Freddy. That was the Hauptsturmführer's second name.'

'I didn't know.'

'I once had a peek at his service record. He was a brave man.'

'Yes, he was,' Willi said. 'Right to the end. So,' he continued, 'we need money, but we don't have any. Short of robbing a bank, where are we going to get it?'

'I think I might know where,' Emil said.

The house seemed out of place. The street – Oudedijk – was pleasant enough, with trees along its length and broad pavements, but in the midst of ranks of modern apartment blocks, the large, detached, nineteenth-century villa seemed to have been planted on an anarchic whim. However, the name on the brass plate below the bell was the one that Emil remembered: *Kastein*.

'May I speak to Mijnheer Kastein?' he asked, when a maid in an old-fashioned black uniform with white collar and cuffs answered the door.

'Who shall I say is calling?'

'Tell him...Tell him it's the Watchmaker.'

Kastein was as good as his word of nearly twenty years ago: he almost hurtled through the door to drag Emil inside, shaking his hand and refusing to let go.

Coffee was served in a sumptuous lounge. 'I'm sorry I lost contact with you, Watchmaker,' he said. 'But now that you're here, we must make sure not to let it happen again.'

'If you had followed the world of chess you would have found me easily enough.'

'I never knew there was a world of chess to follow. All I knew was our little chess club in Auschwitz. You, me, Brack, and that SS officer and his flunky.'

'It may seem a little strange, but that's why I'm here.'

Kastein was a godsend. Not only did his money smooth their path, he had contacts. Within days, four visas had been arranged.

'Four?' said Emil, surprised.

'I'm going with you.'

Kastein offered to charter a private plane for them, but on this point Emil was adamant. A plane was not right, he said. This was not merely a journey; it was a pilgrimage. They would go by train.

And now they are standing at the gates of Birkenau.

'Which of you has the money?' the professor asks. This is why they have come so early – so there are no witnesses. Kastein is to make a substantial donation to fund the restoration work: US$10,000. If it goes through official channels it will disappear; corruption is as endemic among the Communists as typhus was in the camp. The professor promises it will be spent wisely.

Now he leads them along the side of the railway track to the ruins of the crematoria. Ground mist swirls like phantoms around their feet as they walk.

They enter a grove of birch trees. It is very quiet, almost silent; even the singing of birds is absent.

To their right is a jumble of shattered concrete and bricks – a building that has been demolished and abandoned.

'It was blown up by the Germans. You see it exactly as they left it,' the professor explains. 'There are some who say it should be restored so that people can see what went on inside. There are others, including me, who think it should be left as it is as a monument to those who died.'

For Emil, the answer is obvious. 'It should be left as it is. Everyone knows what went on inside.'

'I'll leave you to do what you came for,' the professor says. 'I'll see you back at the gate. But don't take too long.'

Don't take too long... The professor's words seem misplaced. He doesn't understand that time has no meaning for the inmates of Auschwitz, living or dead.

Emil walks apart from the others, to the edge of the trees, wondering at the unearthly quiet. The silence is oppressive, not peaceful. If he listens very hard, will he be able to hear the screams of the ghosts who inhabit this place? Will he hear the last utterances of his mother and his children? He tries to listen to the voices that mill about him in the silence. But they are all talking at once, and he cannot hear what any of them is saying.

And, now he is here, a new uncertainty pushes itself forward – an unwelcome addition to the many he has nurtured since leaving Auschwitz. This grotto is a sacred place. It is home to the thousands who perished here. What right does he have to add to their numbers one who was among their oppressors?

He had wondered what it would be like to return, but now he is here, he is not sure what he feels. He is back, but he is not back. Nothing about this place is familiar.

This is a different Auschwitz, and the memories that permeate this place are not his.

All that is left is his conviction that he must honour Meissner's last request. From his rucksack he takes a metal canister. Hands trembling, he pulls at the lid and some fine, light-coloured powder spills onto the ground.

For long moments, Emil holds the canister as if not knowing what he should do with it. Then he walks into the birch grove, scattering the ashes as he goes. He does it hurriedly, far more quickly than he had intended, as if fearing he might change his mind before he has finished. When the canister is empty he stands there, following with his eyes the patterns the ashes have made upon the ground. They will not be there for long: a strong breeze or a shower of rain and they will be gone.

There will be no memorial stone for Paul Meissner. The only trace that his ashes have been laid here will be in the memories of four men. Emil feels a pang of guilt: he should have scattered the ashes slowly; it would have been more respectful, but it is too late now. The others – Willi, Eidenmüller and Kastein – are silent witnesses. Nothing is said until Emil rejoins them.

'I suppose one of us should say something,' Willi suggests.

Eidenmüller cannot. Tears are streaming from his eyes.

'We should say Kaddish,' Emil says.

But this is too much for Kastein. 'I made a promise to you, Watchmaker, and I have kept my word, but this—' He walks apart to stand next to the ruins of the crematorium. When he speaks again his voice seems to shout into the silence. 'Not for him. I cannot say Kaddish for *him.*'

'Not only for him,' Emil says, mildly. 'For all of them.'

It is a great deal to ask. Kastein's memories are not Emil's memories. He has no knowledge of the journey Meissner has made. He has only his own recollections – of death, of loss, of privation and suffering, injustice and hatred, and, for him, it is among these that the memory of Meissner belongs.

Reluctantly, he turns away from the ruins, and rejoins the others.

'Thank you,' Emil murmurs. From his bag he takes a book. Reading from it, in a sonorous voice he starts to chant in Hebrew. The others bow their heads. It does not take long.

'What does it mean?' Eidenmüller asks, when it is over.

'It is the prayer for the dead. It's not easy to translate exactly, but it's something like: "*May the name of God be lifted up and praised by all creation according to His will. May His reign be established and may His saving grace be made manifest and His anointed one be found among you during the days of your life and during the days of the house of Israel, quickly and without delay. Amen and Amen.*"'

'What I don't understand,' Kastein says, struggling to keep his voice even, 'is why an SS officer would want to have his ashes scattered here. I would have thought it would be the last thing he'd want.'

'Meissner was a changed man,' Emil says. 'He said that he could think of no more fitting place on earth. He said he would spend eternity asking for forgiveness.'

Kastein raises his eyes to look wonderingly at the iron-grey clouds overhead. Eternity is beyond his ability to imagine.

Eidenmüller pulls back his sleeve to glance at his watch. 'We should go before the professor comes looking for us.'

'There's one more thing we have to do,' Emil says. He reaches into his bag, pulls out a small box, and passes it to Willi.

'What is it?' Kastein asks.

'It's pocket chess,' Willi says, starting to smile. 'Are we going to play here?'

'We are. The game we should have played all those years ago. Can you think of a better way to honour him?'

'No. We had better make sure it is a good one.'

Willi picked white. He moved his king's pawn forward two spaces. Emil did the same. A faint breeze stirred the trees. Willi glanced over his shoulder to where Emil had scattered Meissner's ashes. 'Do you think he's here now, watching us?'

Emil smiled. 'I'm sure of it.'

SS Ranks used in
The Death's Head Chess Club

SS Rank	British Army Equivalent
Reichsführer-SS	None. Throughout the war, this position was held by Heinrich Himmler
SS-Gruppenführer	Lieutenant General
SS-Standartenführer	Colonel
SS-Obersturmbannführer	Lieutenant Colonel
SS-Sturmbannführer	Major
SS-Hauptsturmführer	Captain
SS-Obersturmführer	1st Lieutenant
SS-Untersturmführer	2nd Lieutenant
SS-Sturmscharführer	Regimental Sergeant Major
SS-Hauptscharführer	Battalion Sergeant Major
SS-Oberscharführer	Company Sergeant Major
SS-Scharführer	Sergeant
SS-Unterscharführer	Corporal
SS-Rottenführer	Lance-Corporal

HISTORICAL NOTE

Introduction

The Death's Head Chess Club is a work of fiction, but its setting is the worst crime against humanity in recorded history. Hans Frank, the governor-general of Nazi-occupied Poland during the Second World War, said, 'Jews are a race that must be completely exterminated.'

Of all the death camps, Auschwitz had the biggest role to play in this genocide. An estimated 1.1 million people died in Auschwitz during its four and a half years as a concentration and death camp, the vast majority of them Jews from across Europe.

Auschwitz – the camp

Auschwitz was originally conceived of as a concentration camp, a place where the enemies of the Nazi state could be incarcerated away from public view. These included political enemies (mainly Communists), homosexuals, gypsies, Jehovah's Witnesses and Jews.

Concentration camps in Germany (such as Dachau and Sachsenhausen) and the principles on which they were run were long established. Prisoners were subject to brutal, sometimes capricious discipline, housed in primitive conditions with inadequate nutrition, and hard labour was imposed mercilessly. This was what was expected when SS-Hauptsturmführer Rudolf Höss was appointed as the first Kommandant of Auschwitz to establish one of the first concentration camps in the newly conquered territories (Silesia), arriving on 30 April 1940.

Auschwitz was established as a penal work camp on the site of a former Polish army barracks. Its beginnings were inauspicious: the barracks were extremely dilapidated and infested with vermin, and the resources available to Höss were meagre, but his appointment as Kommandant was well judged: he was resourceful, hard working and completely dedicated to his task.

As the number of camps included in the Auschwitz umbrella expanded, this first camp would be designated Auschwitz I, the *Stammlager*. Eventually, there would be three main camps: Auschwitz-I, Auschwitz-II Birkenau and Auschwitz-III Monowitz.

It was with the expansion into Birkenau that the role of Auschwitz evolved to become a combined work camp and death camp (unlike other sites in Poland, such as Chełmno, Sobibór and Treblinka, which were solely extermination camps). In the late summer of 1941, while Höss was away from the camp, his deputy, Fritzsch, conducted an experiment, killing Russian prisoners of war using the pesticide *Zyklon Blausäure* (Cyclone cyanide) which until then had been used to kill infestations of insects. When Höss returned, Fritzsch demonstrated the new method of killing, of which Höss approved whole-heartedly, writing later that he was relieved that this method had been found as it would spare him a 'bloodbath'. Between then and the summer of 1942, Höss supervised the construction of the first purpose-built gas chambers in Birkenau for mass murder using Zyklon-B.

During this time, the German industrial giant IG Farben put forward a proposal to build a factory in Silesia to manufacture synthetic rubber and oil from the poor-grade coal that was abundant in the area. The factory would be part of the Auschwitz complex and would be built using slave labour from the camp. This was designated Auschwitz-III Monowitz.

It is here that the Watchmaker's story unfolds.

The life of Auschwitz as a concentration camp came to an end in January 1945. On 18 January, with Red Army units within a few miles, the SS force-marched around 60,000 prisoners who were considered fit enough out of the camp, westwards, on foot, in appalling weather conditions. This was the infamous death march. Already debilitated by starvation rations and wearing only their ragged camp clothing and camp-issue clogs, thousands died: some collapsed and froze to death, others were shot if they lagged behind. When Russian soldiers arrived at the camp on 27 January they found nearly 8,000 prisoners who had been left behind: close to 6,000 in Birkenau, a little more than 1,000 in the *Stammlager* and about 600 in Monowitz. Among the Monowitz survivors was Primo Levi. Orders had, in fact, been given by the SS area commander, Obergruppenführer Schmauser, that prisoners considered too weak to be included in the mass exodus should be shot, but the rapid advance of the Russians had made the camp SS nervous and, in the end, they had been more concerned with saving their own skins than with the fate of a few prisoners who they thought were likely to die of disease or starvation anyway.

Historical characters in The Death's Head Chess Club
The main characters – Emil, Paul, Willi, Bodo Brack – are fictitious. Some of the supporting characters are historical figures. These are:

- Rudolf Höss – first Kommandant of Auschwitz
- Arthur Liebehenschel – his successor
- Richard Bär – the third (and last) Auschwitz Kommandant
- Otto Brossman – guard commander

- Eduard Wirths – chief garrison physician at Auschwitz
- Vinzenz Schottl – Lagerführer of the Monowitz camp
- Richard Glücks – head of the Concentration Camps Inspectorate

Klaus Hustek's character is based on SS (Gestapo) Oberscharführer Josef Erber.

After the war, a series of war crimes trials took place. Between 1946 and 1948 about 1,000 former members of the Auschwitz SS were extradited to Poland where a number of special courts were set up, including the Supreme National Tribunal which tried the most important criminals. In March 1947, the first Auschwitz Kommandant, Rudolf Höss, was tried in Warsaw and sentenced to death. In November and December of the same year, in Kraków, forty former members of the Auschwitz SS were tried. Of these, twenty-three were sentenced to death, including the second Auschwitz Kommandant, Arthur Liebehenschel. Others received sentences ranging from three years to life imprisonment. In 1950, following numerous appeals, the former SS Hauptsturmführer Otto Brossman was acquitted of war crimes by the Kraków court.

Some former SS personnel from Auschwitz were tried and convicted for crimes other than those that were committed at Auschwitz, including Vinzenz Schottl who, as early as 1945, was convicted by a US war crimes tribunal and sentenced to death.

Eduard Wirths and Richard Glücks committed suicide.

Between 1949 and 1980 other former SS personnel were tried in the Federal Republic of Germany. The last Auschwitz Kommandant, Richard Bär, was arrested in 1960 and died in detention awaiting trial. Former SS Oberscharführer Josef Erber (who had changed his name from Houstek) was arrested in 1962 and brought to trial in Frankfurt in December 1965. He was sentenced to life imprisonment and released in 1986. He died one year later.

Chess

Most of the chapter headings relate to chess moves. The moves were chosen to reflect some aspect of the chapter content. I do not know whether or not there was a chess club for the SS in Auschwitz, and in my research I have found no evidence to confirm it either way. The unofficial Chess Olympiad did take place in Munich in 1936, in circumstances as described in Chapter 21, though, of course, Wilhelm Schweninger's involvement is fictitious. The teams from Poland and Hungary were made up of Jews, and they both beat the German team. Hungary won the tournament with ease with twenty wins in a row, something that wasn't repeated until 1960. Poland finished second, with Najdorf winning an individual gold medal.

ACKNOWLEDGEMENTS

I am indebted to many who have inspired or helped me on this journey.

I found great inspiration in the harrowing and courageous personal accounts of those who survived Auschwitz, particularly Primo Levi, Filip Müller and Elie Wiesel, and also of those who did not survive and whose names are all but forgotten today: Zalman Gradowski, Dayan Langfus and Zalman Leventhal were among the numbers of the *Sonderkommando*; their diaries were unearthed after the war. In addition, I could never have written this book without the meticulous scholarship of numerous historians who have documented various aspects of the Nazi state, the SS, the Holocaust and Auschwitz.

I would like to express my thanks to the people who helped to make this book a reality: my agent, Carolyn Whitaker, for having faith, Ravi Mirchandani, for giving me a hearing and James Roxburgh, Belinda Jones and Ileene Smith for their endless patience and constructive editing suggestions.

And to my family – Barbara, Hannah, Laura, Andrew and Jack – thank you always for your constant love and understanding.

To all those who suffered or died as a result of the Holocaust, this book is respectfully dedicated.

Note on the Author

John Donoghue has worked in mental health for over twenty years and written numerous articles about the treatment of mental illness in a variety of medical journals. He is married and lives in Liverpool.

CONTEMPORARY PORCELAIN

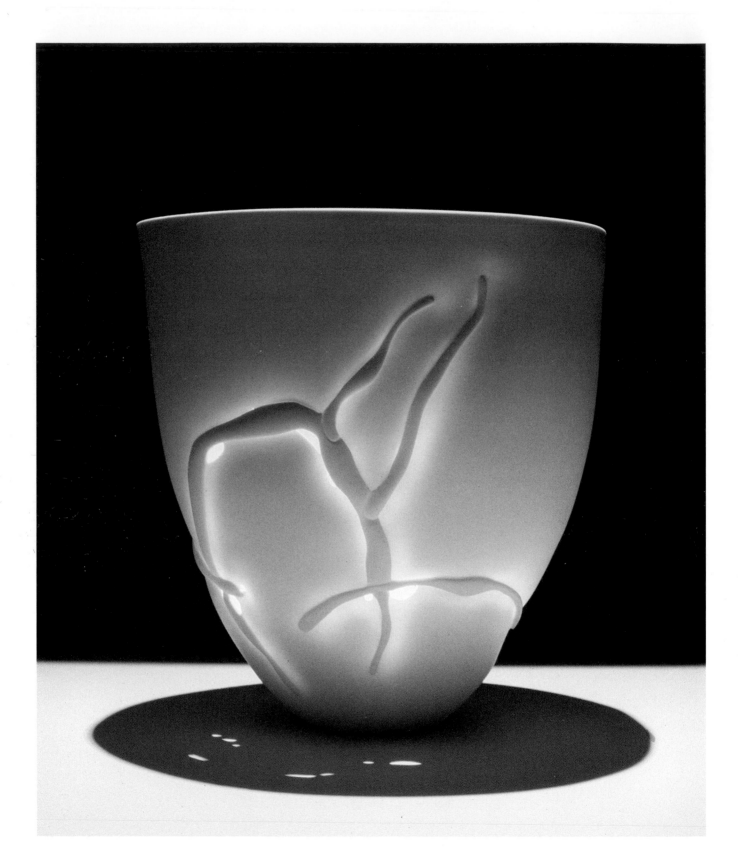

CONTEMPORARY
PORCELAIN

MATERIALS, TECHNIQUES
AND EXPRESSIONS

PETER LANE

A & C Black · London   Chilton Book Company · Radnor, Pennsylvania

Dedication

To the memory of my mother, Freda Margaret Lane (1906–1994), whose courage, fortitude and caring good humour was a shining example to everyone during her final, painful illness.

First published in Great Britain 1995
A & C Black (Publishers) Limited
35 Bedford Row, London WC1R 4JH

ISBN 0-7136-3956-3

A CIP catalogue record for this book is available from the British Library.

First published in the USA by Chilton Book Company, Radnor, Pennsylvania 19089
ISBN 0-8019-8635-4

Jacket illustrations
Porcelain Vessel, wheel-thrown carved and pierced, by Horst Göbbels. *Photograph by Wolf Böwig.*

Frontispiece
Vessel form in bone china, slipcast, carved and altered, 20 cm high, by Angela Verdon, 1992.

Designed by Bob Eames
Typeset by August Filmsetting, St Helens
Printed in Singapore by Tien Wah Press (Pte.) Ltd

'Sphere Protrusion', porcelain, 45 cm high by Peter Masters, 1991. The strong rhythmic raised pattern is built up from individually applied elements; sodium vapour glaze fired to 1280°C in a natural gas kiln.

CONTENTS

Acknowledgements

Any author of a book of this kind must rely heavily upon the goodwill and cooperation of many people. I am deeply indebted to all the porcelain makers who have so generously given of their time and expertise in helping me to gather material for this book. I am especially grateful for the loan of photographs willingly provided by so many potters around the world and to the photographers for allowing their reproduction as illustrations for the text. In particular, I would like to thank Wolf Böwig, of the Keramik Galerie Böwig in Hannover for taking great care in photographing the work of several important artists for me. Hein Severijns (Holland), Jan Schachter (California), Curtis Benzle (Ohio), Bill Hunt (Editor of *Ceramics Monthly*), Janet Mansfield (Editor of *Ceramics: Art and Perception*), Sandra Black (Western Australia), Erik Pløen (Norway), and others were all extremely helpful in providing me with addresses of potters working in porcelain. My sincere thanks are due also to Chris Hogg and Harry Fraser for their helpful technical notes on the search for porcelain and bone china bodies with good working properties. Many potters, gallery owners and collectors at home and abroad have all given me the encouragement needed to produce a completely new book on contemporary studio porcelain. My thanks are also due to my editor, Linda Lambert, who persuaded me that it was time to address the subject again. To my wife, Jean, for her patience and tolerance while I spent long hours communicating only with my word processor, and who regularly interrupted her own creative work to keep me supplied with good food and endless cups of coffee, a very special thank you.

Peter Lane, 1994
New Alresford, Hampshire

INTRODUCTION

There have been many exciting developments in the field of contemporary ceramics since my first book on the subject was published in 1980 under the title of *Studio Porcelain*. This was an attempt to examine an area of the discipline which, despite its long history, had been largely neglected by studio potters. This new book endeavours to address the subject afresh and to investigate what changes in attitude or in approaches to design and making, if any, may have occurred during the intervening years. In the course of my research, I have consulted a large number of ceramicists who regularly work with porcelain and tried to discover something of their personal philosophy towards their art and its place in modern society. Particular emphasis is given in the book to the enormous diversity and rapid development which has taken place over the latter part of the 20th century in international studio porcelain and considers some of the aesthetic concerns, technical achievements and working methods of these ceramicists working with porcelain and its close relative, bone china.

Porcelain offers a far wider range of options and applications than those most popularly perceived for it. The basic qualities usually associated with or required of high-fired porcelain such as delicacy, translucency, fineness, whiteness, density and purity remain available, of course, but many potters have chosen to break with traditional expectations of the medium. Their primary concern is more likely to be the exploration and realisation of three-dimensional form, using porcelain as the most appropriate plastic material, and incorporating various techniques for their purposes. Often, those singular physical properties will be still evident in a porcelain object but the emphasis on any or all of these will depend upon the manipulative processes employed at various stages from wet to dry; the thickness of sections; the application of colour in oxides, stains, slips or glazes; and on the final firing.

It has generally been accepted that porcelain, as a material, can be somewhat daunting both to use and control until one becomes familiar with certain unique aspects of its character. In *Studio Porcelain* I tried to clear away much of the fog and mystique surrounding the successful making of

porcelain and to offer advice and suggestions for its imaginative use. Today, there appear to be virtually no boundaries which cannot be stretched and few rules that can remain inviolate in this area of human invention as can be seen by the immense variety of forms and surface treatments in the work of porcelain potters from around the world which have been assembled together in this book. Originality, flair and skill combine in the best work to present us with numerous stimulating images: vessels, tiles, wall panels, figurative sculptures, and abstract objects all

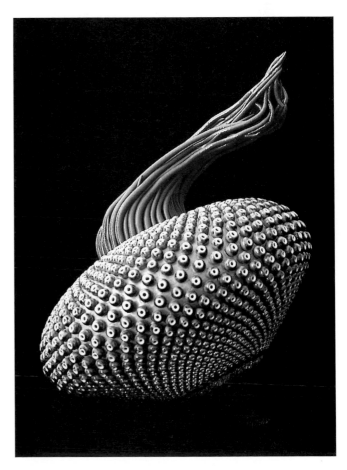

'Sphere Protrusion', porcelain, 45 cm high by Peter Masters, 1991. The strong rhythmic raised pattern is built up from individually applied elements; sodium vapour glaze fired to 1280°C in a natural gas kiln.

created in an unusually 'unforgiving' medium. It must be acknowledged that a number of potters who became well-known after several successful years working with porcelain have turned to earthenware clays because they found that the lower firing temperatures presented them with greater control, but others have preferred to continue using this fine, white body while gaining fresh inspiration through pushing the material to the very limits of their ability.

Not all the pieces illustrated will be immediately recognisable as porcelain because they seem not to fit into any of the familiarly held perceptions. One might question, therefore, whether porcelain was the proper medium to use for them, but for one reason or another, it was decided that a different clay body would fail to satisfy all the practical and aesthetic requirements which the artist deemed essential for his/her personal expression. In each case, porcelain acts as the common denominator linking all the works chosen to illustrate this book. Techniques and processes described are, in many instances, similar to those identified with other branches of ceramics adapted, where necessary, to suit individual needs.

The work of the contemporary ceramicist has grown out of a long and glorious history. It seems that countless generations of potters have already explored every practical, technical, social, cultural and aesthetic aspect from the preparation and composition of clay bodies and glazes to the construction and firing of many different types of kilns in producing the vast wealth of ceramics which we all inherit. In truth, it is often stated that since so much has gone before, there is little scope for truly fresh invention.

Goblet form on tall, angular stem made from wheel-thrown and handbuilt elements and fired to 1280°C in a gas kiln with a reducing atmosphere, 38.5 cm high, by Maria Bofill, 1993.

Second left   Porcelain pot, 11 cm high, by Geoffrey Swindell, 1989. Wheel-thrown, with textured surface made at the leatherhard stage by imprinting marks with a wire brush. This texture is enhanced later by a feldspathic glaze overloaded with vanadium. Fired to 1250°C in an oxidising atmosphere.

Second right   Slipcast porcelain vessel form with carved rim by David Fink (USA), 1993. Colour glazed inside but with the exterior polished. The inspiration for this piece came from eroded rock formations.

Far right   Porcelain Vase with 'gosu' brush decoration in blue, 28 cm × 15 cm, by Alistair Whyte, 1993.
Photograph by Avon Colour Studio.

Nevertheless, ceramics continues to offer us the appropriate, and universally understood, visual and tactile means to express individual thoughts, ideas and feelings. In this respect one can make an analogy with words or with musical notes in that they, also, are infinitely reworked to communicate anew.

Few clays can be used 'as dug' in the making of refined ceramics. Therefore we refer to the clay mixtures as bodies. Varying amounts of clays and certain other materials such as quartz, flint, feldspar, nepheline syenite, Cornish stone, whiting, silica sand and talc are combined together to make workable plastic bodies to suit a whole range of purposes and firing temperatures. Porcelain bodies, however, are usually composed of just three main ingredients: kaolin (China clay), feldspar and quartz with smaller amounts of ball clay or bentonite added to ensure plasticity. Unfortunately, ball clays can impair the whiteness and affect translucency whereas bentonite is less likely to do so. However, bentonite (a highly plastic, colloidal substance with a very fine grain size), which is widely used for preparing porcelain with good throwing properties, can increase problems of shrinking and cracking if more than six per cent exists in the composition.

Porcelain is simply a composition of fine, relatively similar sized particles of kaolin, silica and feldspar which achieves a more complete fusion than stoneware or earthenware clays that tend to be made up with additional ingredients including sands or grog. It is the extra silica content of porcelain which contributes its glassy translucent quality but, at the same time, makes it more susceptible to stress due to its high rate of expansion and contraction. All potters are aware of the importance of slow cooling following a kiln firing but porcelain is especially vulnerable to dunting, if cooled too quickly, at those points where the silica inversion take place at 570°C and 226°C respectively.

Despite differences in composition, most porcelain bodies possess the potential to be translucent but the degree to which that state is achieved depends on the thickness, or rather thinness, of the clay. Nevertheless, if translucency alone is held to be the key to defining 'true' porcelain, it may be argued that many of the bodies currently available are no more than white porcellanous stonewares. Therefore, the definition of porcelain is open to question. However, this is not an issue that concerns us here. My researches have discovered an extremely wide range of applications for white, porcellanous bodies having a very high content of the essential kaolin, feldspar and silica supplying the main qualities expected of porcelain. Some body compositions are considerably more translucent than others but that particular property may be of little interest to the ceramicist for whom form, surface, colour or texture is sufficient for their expression and communication. Porcelain bodies generally become vitrified when fired to temperatures well above 1200°C and the higher this is, the greater the proportion of glass that will be formed in the body. This is the main factor assisting the passage of light through it, although complete vitrification is not necessary for this to occur.

There are many potters for whom those delicate and varying degrees of translucency, which can only be revealed after the final firing, will be the supreme attraction and ultimate goal. The interplay of light onto and through a finely-made piece provides one of the most satisfying experiences in both seeing and touching. Yet this aspect may not appeal to everyone. Instead, some ceramicists

Porcelain bowl with extremely thin walls, thrown, turned, and decorated with brushed and trailed slip over latex resist, 44 cm diameter, by Arnold Annen, 1992.
Photograph by Reto Bernhardt.

may be attracted to porcelain more for its smooth, dense texture which allows it to accept the finest incising, piercing and carving at various stages from wet to dry. Others will prefer to exploit whiteness for its own sake or as a 'canvas' for colour. For there is no doubt that much of the appeal of porcelain (and even more so with bone china) as a material in which to produce forms of diverse kinds owes a good deal to that particular quality of clean brightness uncontaminated by iron or other impurities. The full, unblemished colour spectrum is thus made available for unhampered use.

Often, porcelain has been chosen to form the whole or a significant proportion of the body composition for making quite low-fired ceramic objects. In such instances, the potters are not concerned with meeting the normal requirements for domestic use (e.g. to hold liquids) so they do not need the extra strength and durability afforded by firing the body to maturity. All porcelain bodies must be fired to temperatures in excess of 1200°C if they are to become impervious to water. But, even, when fired as low as 1000°C, porcelain still offers an extra-fine, smooth, white body, superior to most others, that provides such excellent opportunities for surface treatments that they compensate for any physical weakness. In some cases, potters have chosen to use porcelain in the form of slips to coat and conceal any coarser clays they have used to create the piece. Porcelain-based slip gives them a good, white ground for colour while a thicker application can be compacted and burnished to a silky-smooth sheen.

Potters, perhaps, are more intimately occupied with and, to a certain extent conditioned by, the materials, techniques and processes of their discipline than any other artist-craftsmen. They have to understand sufficient of the practical physics and chemistry involved if they are to avoid frequent frustrations. Even the most experienced suffer disappointments from time to time when results are not quite what had been intended. The search for personal ideals is continuous and, in most cases, their appetite for

Top Jug and bowl forms slipcast in bone china and decorated with airbrushed ceramic stains by Sasha Wardell, 1992.

Middle Vase, 'Autumn', 35 cm high, by Judith de Vries, 1992. Constructed from separately made 'leaves' of laminated, coloured porcelain built up piece by piece. Fired to 1200°C in an electric kiln. *Photograph by Claude Crommelin.*

Bottom 'Desert Night', porcelain bowl, 29 cm diameter × 18 cm high, by Pippin Drysdale, 1993. Wheel-thrown, with painted coloured stains on top of a white (tin/zirconium) glaze, fired to 1200°C in an electric kiln.

Opposite 'Chalice of Promise', handbuilt porcelain, wood-fired in an anagama type kiln, 26.5 cm high, by Catharine Hiersoux, 1990.

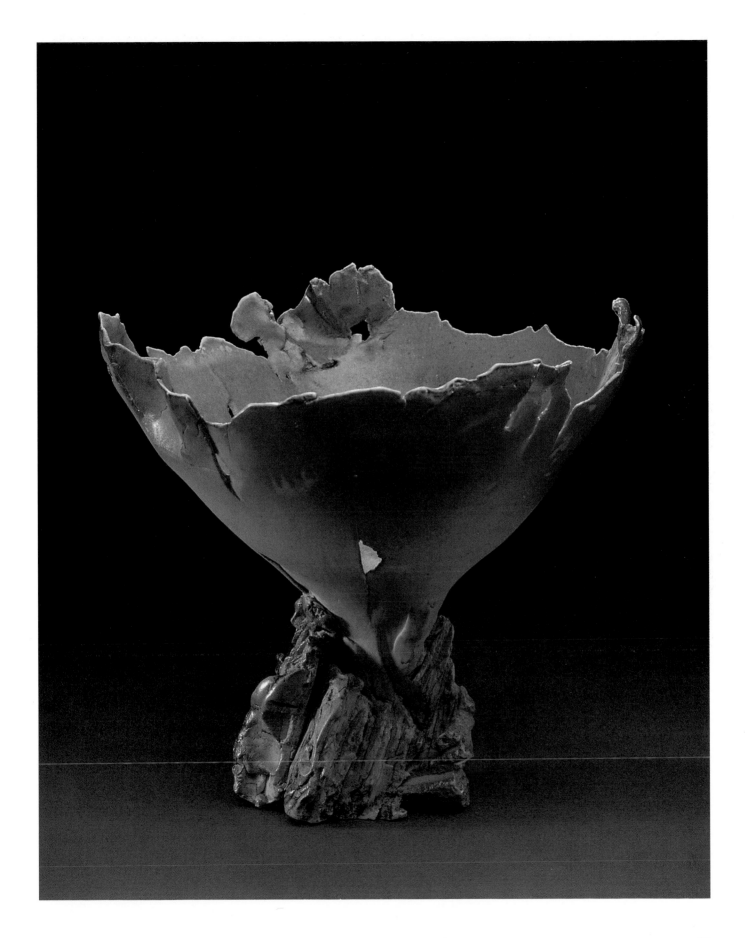

technical understanding is voracious. This interest has spawned an enormous number of books which have been published on every aspect of ceramics during the years following the Second Word War but the demand for yet more information about technicalities remains undiminished.

Despite the inveterate curiosity of most potters, I have discovered a surprising number who admitted that they have little or no interest in ceramic chemistry for its own sake. They obtain all their commercially-prepared materials from reliable sources knowing how they will perform in use so that they can concentrate all their creative energies to procure fairly predictable results. Above all it is the expression that matters. During more than 30 years of making and teaching ceramics, my own interest in and respect for the diverse ways in which individual artists around the world resolve technical as well as aesthetic problems of design remains strong. I firmly believe that as experience grows so does the realisation that there is so much more than anyone can possibly comprehend in a single lifetime. Therefore, we have to be selective, concentrating upon particular aspects that appeal to us and, in that continuous enquiry, we are limited only by the time we can devote to it and by our own capacity to understand. This

fact, for me, contributes to the continuing excitement of ceramics and of porcelain in particular. The main aim of this book, therefore, is to examine and explain some of the personal thoughts, feelings, approaches and techniques currently employed by individual ceramicists in the specialised field of porcelain. However, it is important to stress that those techniques can never be a satisfying end in themselves. They are only the *means* employed to achieve that end. Any discussion about techniques, therefore, must be directly related to the more significant aesthetic achievements of the work illustrated.

It is highly unlikely that the reader will find that *all* the works depicted in this book appeal to his or her personal taste. Nor has it been possible to include reference to every notable potter working in porcelain at the time of writing. Nevertheless, I believe that, as an author, it is essential to exercise a broadly catholic choice which gives a reasonably wide representation of studio porcelain in the late 20th century. I have consulted a great number of ceramicists working in porcelain and bone china around the world all of whom have been most generous in providing me with information about their thoughts, feelings, aims and processes. Direct quotations from them are frequently used to amplify the text. In this way, I have been able to include

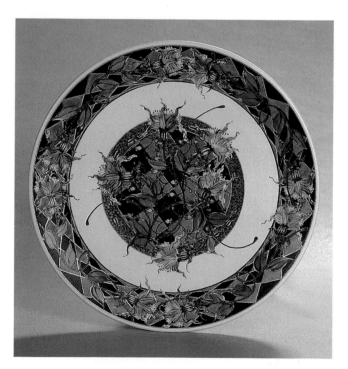

'Huntly', porcelain plate, 29.5 cm diameter, by Peter Minko (Australia), 1993. Wheel-thrown and burnished at the leatherhard stage before bisque firing to 920°C. Hand painted with finely ground pigments (mainly metallic oxides) and fired twice to 1280°–1300°C in oxidation to fuse the colours to the unglazed surface. Gold lustre is then applied in a further firing to 760°C.

Porcelain Bowl, 38 cm × 7 cm, by Russell Coates, 1993. Wheel-thrown, with painted underglaze blue decoration under a clear/white glaze fired to 1270°C and then enamelled with the design of a cross in a red circle surrounded by paired cormorants, geometric border and dolphins.

details of the working methods of many potters from different social and cultural backgrounds. These are illustrated and discussed throughout the book. The materials potters use in the execution of their art are common to all, but their stimuli, influences, approaches and objectives cover a very wide spectrum.

My own personal preference is for making 'vessel' forms, especially bowls, since they are open to infinite variation both subtle and extreme and whether or not concerned with function. Although countless millions of container forms have been produced in ceramics to serve a multitude of purposes from the humble to the sublime,

Bowl in multi-coloured (yellow, blue, black and brown), laminated porcelain, fired to 1320°C in a reducing atmosphere, 16 cm diameter, by Rainer Doss, 1993.

Porcelain Sculpture, untitled, with aluminium tubes and steel wire, 19 cm × 19 cm × 15 cm, by Wil Broekema, 1991. *Photograph by Dick Huizinga.*

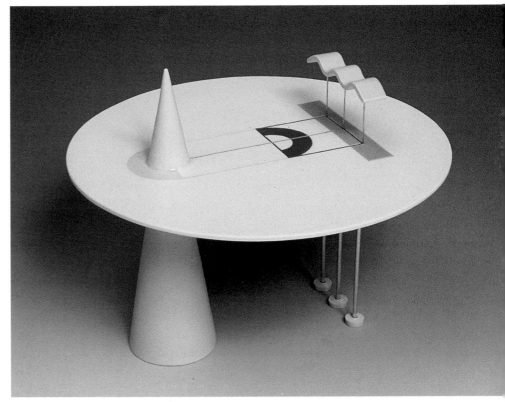

there will never be an end to their aesthetic possibilities. The best of these objects transcend utilitarian needs to become the purest form of three-dimensional art.

Throughout history, ceramics presents us with a magnificent kaleidoscope of human expression, functional, figurative and abstract. But too many art critics tend to dismiss sculptural work executed in clay as being of little relevance to the field of 'fine' art and arguments concerning its status remain unresolved. Uncompromising attitudes raise questions as to whether criticism of any ceramic work can be truly objective other than in matters of fact, that can be judged in those measurable, quantifiable aspects such as

pure craftsmanship? Indeed, to what extent can critical criteria remain constant in the face of continuing development? the unrelenting speed of change affects us all. What one generation adores the next often *abhors* as in other areas of visual expression. It would seem virtually impossible to identify a definitive kind of 'public' taste that might indicate what should be expected of ceramic art today. We do not *need* individually produced, handmade ceramics. They are not essential for everyday, practical purposes. Of course, there will always be those who prefer not to use industrially-made ceramics, or glass, or plastics, etc. in a domestic situation and, doubtless, their needs will continue

to be supplied, but the modern potter is not *bound* to cater for them. Therefore, the only certain restrictions, apart from economics or individual sensibilities, are those imposed by the potters's own ability to control the material processes of his or her art. One can choose to build upon tradition or fly in the face of it. Above all else, contemporary ceramics should be accepted as a prime vehicle for tactile, visual expression.

Many questions came to mind during my enquiry into contemporary studio porcelain, some of which relate to ceramics in general. Although some answers may be found in the following pages, most will remain open to discussion and reassessment. It is extremely difficult to attempt a definitive analysis of a discipline in a state of constant flux, but by questioning, examining and observing developments around the world one can arrive at some small understanding and appreciation of the wonderful diversity to be found in modern ceramics. We can look at a piece and ask ourselves in what way it relates to traditional ceramics or how it fits within the context of the late 20th century? Whether it has the power to evoke a sympathetic or antipathetic response in us? Are there references to, or influences from, any other branches of the visual arts? Does it seem to reflect a moment in time like the present or does it echo past moods, expressions or cultures? How 'original' is it and does it matter if it is not? Is it so esoteric that it only belongs in an exclusive gallery setting?

Two slipcast and altered bone china vases with sprayed ceramic stains and fired to 1240°C in an electric kiln, 20 cm high, by Angela Mellor, 1993.

'Bloom', handbuilt, wood-fired porcelain, 33 cm high, by Catharine Hiersoux, 1992.
Photograph by Richard Sargent.

Porcelain Bowl, 30 cm diameter, by Greg Daly, 1993. With etched surface and lustre decoration. This piece has just one glaze containing copper carbonate, but one half is green where the kiln atmosphere was predominately oxidising and the other is red where a reduction has taken place. This is caused when one burner out of four has a reducing flame resulting in a localised reduction occurring.

We are constantly bombarded with images from so many different sources that few can fail to be affected by them. The natural world has long provided inspirational material for creative expression in ceramics but experiences of travel, transport, architecture, urban environments, etc. in addition to aspects of the human condition such as war, famine, social injustice and even family relationships can also act as trigger points for intensely personal work.

I have been fortunate in being able to select examples of porcelain ceramics to illustrate the text from ceramicists whose earlier work has been included in my previous books and to have discovered and made contact with many others whom I did not previously know. For my part, I found the research involved to be both invigorating and frustrating. The frustrations were constant because the gathering and collating of material together with the concentrated effort of writing allowed no time for me to respond in my own ceramic work to the surge of creative energy aroused by such an amazing diversity of images, or the richness of invention and ingenuity, demonstrated in the work of so many ceramicists included in this book. It is my hope that the selection presented will prove both stimulating and thought provoking. In an ideal world all the illustrations would be published in full colour but, where this has not been possible, dimensions, colours or other detailed information has been provided in the captions to enable the reader to visualise the objects as they really are.

As can be seen in this broad survey of contemporary studio porcelain, there are at least as many women as there are men engaged in ceramics at every level but, for reasons of economy throughout this book, terms such as potter, artist, craftsman, ceramicist should be read as synonymous and applicable equally to either gender.

Porcelain sculpture (unglazed), 'Zone Series 12', thrown, altered and assembled, 18 cm by 12.8 cm approximately, by Margaret Realica, 1990. The slabs are made from finely thrown cylinders which are cut open when they have stiffened slightly. Electric kiln fired to 1260°–1300°C.
Photograph by Robert Aude.

'Container Form', by Lara Scobie, 42 cm × 37 cm × 21 cm. Constructed by building up layers of thinly rolled porcelain (Harry Fraser porcelain body). The textures are achieved by pressing the clay into Indian printing blocks. Oxides and underglaze stains are applied to the texture and then sponged off to leave a residue of colour in the impressions. Fired to 1300°C in a reduction atmosphere.

Laminated and assembled porcelain bowl, 15 cm × 17.5 cm × 17 cm approx., by Thomas Hoadley, 1993.
Photograph by Paul Rocheleau.

QUALITIES AND PROPERTIES OF PORCELAIN

Composition of porcelain bodies

Despite an abundance of fairly reliable materials available from commercial sources, the search for the ultimate porcelain body free from any disadvantages continues. The ideal would probably be a supremely white body which would be very plastic, easy to throw or handbuild, be able to support itself when wet, have minimal shrinkage, resist cracking or splitting at every stage from wet to dry, be translucent when relatively thick, be strong when fired, and to mature around 1200°C while performing to perfection in any kind of kiln or atmosphere. Even with the advanced technology available to the ceramics industry today, it is unlikely that all these requirements can ever be met but we continue to explore possibilities.

A translucent porcelain body recipe, specially developed for use by the late Audrey Blackman (well-known for her rolled modelled porcelain figures), was published in *Ceramic Review* (No. 100) in 1986. It remains popular with a number of British potters and is as follows:

Porcelain Bowl, diameter 12 cm × 10 cm high, by Karl Scheid, 1992. Wheel-thrown porcelain with diagonal relief carving under a feldspar-petalite copper red glaze fired to 1360°C in reduction.
Photograph by Tomoki Fujii.

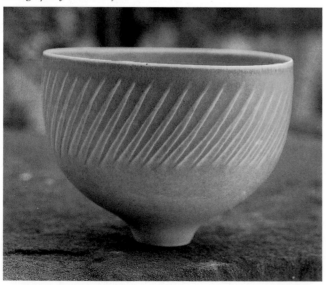

Standard Porcelain China Clay (English China Clays)	50%
Westone – H (sodium activated white Texas bentonite)	5%
FFF Feldspar	27%
Quartz (300s mesh)	17%
Whiting	1%

Another recipe for a throwable bone china body was made for Anne Hogg (see page 46) and this, also, appeared in *Ceramic Review* (No. 113) in 1988.

Bone ash	50%
Super Standard Porcelain China clay	25%
MF4 flux	25%

2.5% Westone – H white bentonite is added to this recipe.

Both these bodies were developed by Anne's husband, Dr Christopher Hogg, and I am indebted to him for the following information.

Both of these bodies use a particularly white and pure bentonite from Texas. The company producing it was owned by English China Clays, but it was sold to Laporte at Redhill in Surrey a couple of years ago. Whether they still import the bentonite into England, I do not know, but it is now called Bentolite H (yes, with an 'l').

From a scientific point of view, whiteness and translucency of porcelain are well understood to the extent of being calculable, given the right information. The properties are dependent on two fundamental properties: light absorption and light scatter. (I am here ignoring the influence of thickness, which, although very important, I take as being obvious.)

Light is absorbed by colouring metal ions, usually iron and titanium in clay bodies. Light is scattered at interfaces between the glassy matrix and the crystalline phases present such as mullite from the clay, and undissolved quartz. Colouring metal ions reduce both translucency and whiteness. Crystalline phases reduce translucence but increase whiteness. The whiteness and translucency actually achieved are the result of the balance between these two parameters.

To make a porcelain that is both white and translucent requires the minimum of colouring metal ions and a fairly low level of crystalline phases. This means using pure clays, no ball clay for example, and a high feldspar content to give plenty of glass on firing and only a small quantity of crystalline phases. Needless to say, these requirements conflict with the plasticity required for throwing, and stability during firing. Compromises are inevitable.

Firing porcelain in reduction helps, converting yellow ferric iron to pale blue ferrous iron that is less strongly colouring, provided that no titania is present to interact with it. Cornish china clays contain little titania, but many china clays from other parts of the world can contain as much as in many English ball clays.

Another technique is to add something that reacts with the iron and bleaches it. This is what happens in bone china, where the phosphate from the bone ash in effect bleaches the iron. The result is an almost pure white body that is very translucent. Unfortunately, a lot of bone ash is needed to ensure that all the iron is combined with the phosphate, and a bone china body can be described as a porcelain body mixed with an equal weight of bone ash. This halves the clay content and so greatly impairs the plasticity.

Bowl in multi-coloured laminated porcelain, fired to 1320°C in a reducing atmosphere, 15 cm diameter, by Rainer Doss, 1993.

Three vessel forms, 'Composition', handbuilt with laminated, multi-coloured porcelain, fired to 1280°C in an electric kiln, 22 cm, 20 cm and 15 cm diameter, by Mieke Everaet, 1992.

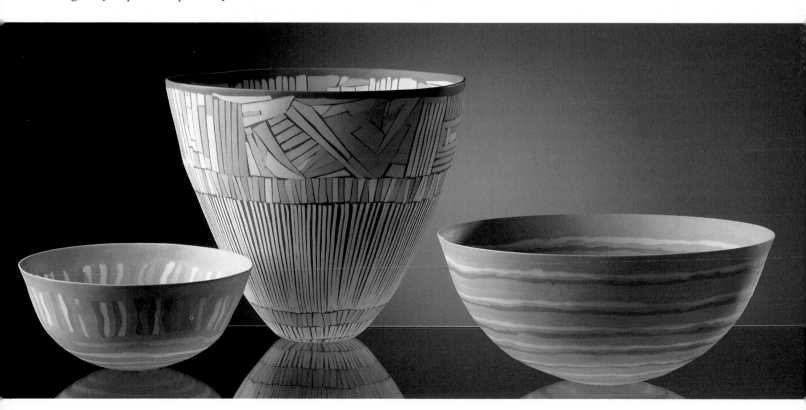

In the extreme, the two properties of whiteness and translucency are conflicting: a material is either extremely white and opaque or extremely translucent and not white. If nearly all the light is reflected back to you, there is none left to pass through, and conversely if much of the light passes through, less is reflected back. White opaque glazes are opaque because they are white; window glass is very translucent but not at all white. In practice, things are not that extreme, and most people have an appreciation of what is white and translucent in porcelain, compared to what is not.

In addition to all that, there is the property of plasticity that I have mentioned only in passing. Here, I'm afraid science has still a long way to go in understanding the fundamentals. There is plenty of practical experience and many empirical tests for plasticity, but not much science. The simplest solution to poor plasticity is to add a little bentonite, and use the purest you can get. A sodium-activated bentonite is best, acidified after mixing it in to ensure good flocculation. Preferably use an organic acid that burns away, such as acetic acid (vinegar). Mineral acids give off unpleasant fumes during firing. An alternative method of flocculating is to add a very little slaked lime (and I mean a very little, if you value the skin on your hands). Some China clays produced in Czechoslovakia and much used in German porcelain are flocculated this way.

A good, reliable porcelain body introduced to many potters in Britain during the 1960s and 1970s and which became extremely popular was the David Leach Porcelain Body. I used it almost exclusively for several years. This body is still available from commercial sources today and can be obtained in many parts of the world as indeed, can most other prepared bodies. The porcelain from Limoges in France is the preferred vehicle for the work of several potters whose work is illustrated in this book. Others use a porcelain based on the Zettlitz kaolin from Czechoslovakia. My own current preference is the the Harry Fraser Porcelain Body produced by Potclays Limited in Etruria, Stoke-on-Trent, England. I have found this body to be generally most reliable to use. It throws well, fires white and, although it has a reasonably wide firing range, it is translucent when potted thinly enough at temperatures as low as 1220°C. Harry Fraser explained the process of developing this particular porcelain for me as in the following notes.

There are many recipes for porcelain bodies. Most of them are blends of kaolin with a flux (usually feldspar) and free silica in the form of flint or quartz. Some recipes include additions of ball clays, bentonite or other plasticisers. The incorporation of ball clay is very desirable from a plasticity viewpoint but, if present in any significant amounts, tends to prevent translucency. Consequently, its use in porcelain bodies is usually confined to recipes where translucency is not a requirement – for example, in porcelain insulators.

Development of a plastic, throwable but white firing and translucent porcelain is very dependent upon the type of kaolin used. Grolleg features in many recipes and indeed was the basis of the well-known David Leach Porcelain Body formulation in the 1960s and 1970s. However, an even more plastic kaolin was then produced by English China Clays and known as Standard Porcelain China Clay. This China clay has a very slightly lower iron content than Grolleg and thus fires slightly whiter as well as being slightly more plastic. I, therefore, selected it as the basis for a new porcelain body, using FFF Feldspar as the flux and 200s mesh quartz to develop thermal expansion. Preliminary mixes were not sufficiently plastic and so Quest white bentonite was progressively introduced until the plasticity seemed to be reasonably good – and certainly as good as any other porcelains then available.

A problem is that we all know what plasticity is but nobody has yet succeeded in devising an instrument that can properly measure it. Plasticity is closely linked to green strength and that we can measure by means of a Modulus of Rupture machine. MOR tests done on clay samples of the new body showed that green strength was well up to that of other porcelains. However, previous experience had indicated that the handling properties could, perhaps, be further improved by slight flocculation. This also would enable filter pressing times to be significantly reduced and thus lower production costs.

Trials were done using whiting and other flocculants as a part replacement for feldspar in the body recipe. Whiting does, however, become a very vigorous flux at high temperatures – especially where a glassy matrix is developed – and so refractoriness tests had to be carried out to quantify the extra fluxing effect. In this way, an optimum flocculant addition was incorporated which produced a slightly better throwing body, the clay

Three Vessel Forms, tallest piece is approximately 25 cm high, by Anne Hogg, 1993. Wheel-thrown bone china with carved decoration. Rust particles were kneaded into the plastic body used for two of these pieces to provide the black speckles. Fired in an electric kiln to 1270°C.

Two porcelain bowls, 12 cm and 6 cm high, by Suzanne Bergne, 1993. Thrown and altered on the wheel, with poured glazes and fired twice to 1220°C in an electric kiln.
Photograph by Andra Nelki, Indigo Studio.

Handbuilt ceramic form combining an earthenware base with supporting a porcelain vessel decorated using the neriage technique. 60 cm high. This piece is the result of collaboration in design and execution by two Belgian artists, Frank Steyaert and Chris Scholliers in 1993.

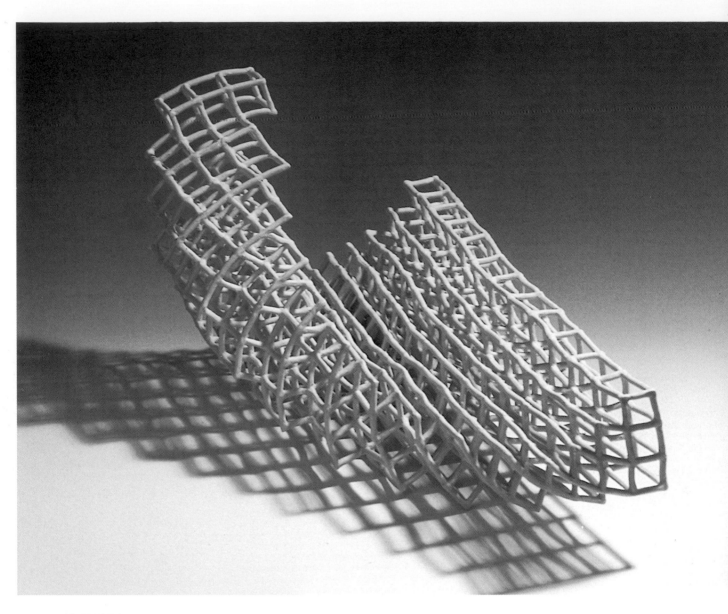

Porcelain sculpture 'Zonder Titel', constructed from extruded coils of Limoges porcelain body (TM10) fired in reduction to 1260°C to obtain a colder, more bluish white colour, 70 cm × 40 cm, by Netty Van Den Heuvel, 1992.

'Bird of Paradise', 28 cm diameter, by Rolf Bartz, 1990. Porcelain platter, wheel-thrown and carved, with airbrushed underglaze colours (orange and pale blue). Fired 1260°C in an electric kiln, unglazed but polished with silicon carbide paper after the final firing.

seeming more flexible and standing up better. It was incidentally interesting that the improvement in throwing properties of the clay body could not be detected on the MOR machine. Flocculation also reduced the filter pressing time from around ten hours to about seven, enabling production in the normal working day.

The quartz grain size was also important. In porcelain bodies, the effect of the quartz content on thermal expansion depends on its particle size, and this is influenced by the firing temperature and amount of glass formation which takes place. Glass formation dissolves the free silica, converting it to silicate which lowers thermal expansion and thus has an opposite effect to free quartz. The finer the particle size the more effective free silica becomes in promoting thermal expansion but also the more easily it can be taken into glaze solution by the solvent action of the fluxes. A 200s mesh grade of quartz was selected which, in trials, gave the best combination of craze resistance and fineness.

The new porcelain body was then sampled to porcelain users whose production trials confirmed that it threw exceptionally well and fired to a good colour and translucency.

A most important consideration was the production plant upon which to produce the new porcelain. Hitherto, production of studio porcelain bodies had been by slotting the production in between batches of other white firing bodies, e.g. white earthenware and white stoneware types. In a sliphouse system one can clean out blungers, agitation arks and pugmills but not very easily, and it is impractical to clean out interconnecting pipework to the pumps etc. In a factory, therefore, it is likely that when switching from one body to another

there will be some degree of contamination with what was previously processed. For this reason, the practice of rejecting the initial production and progressively feeding it back into the system is generally used to minimise any contamination with the previous body. Nevertheless, this procedure cannot be as good as the use of plant dedicated only to porcelain production.

Production of the new body was, therefore, withheld until dedicated plant could be made available. Two years later, suitable plant became available at Potclays Limited and the body was launched into production.

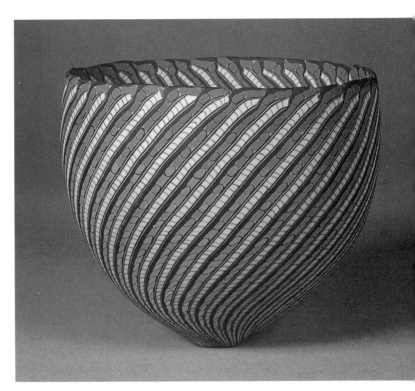

Bowl Form, 15 cm × 12.5 cm, by Dorothy Feibleman. Laminated parian, built as a flat slab, pressed in to a mould and then 'thrown' upside down to close the foot and compress the laminations. Fired to 1120°C in an electric kiln.
Photograph by Thomas Ward, courtesy of Bonhams, London. This piece is in the collection of Galerie Hunteregger St. Polten, Austria.

Porcelain 'Yo Yo' Jar, freely decorated with metallic oxides and wash and lines drawn through the glaze, 25 cm × 17.5 cm, by Tom Coleman, 1993.

Body recipes

Many potters choose to make their own porcelain bodies to recipes with which they have become familiar over a long period of time. In this way, they can avoid some of the problems encountered in the use of commercially-prepared bodies when ingredients are altered for one reason or another. **Tom Turner** (USA) uses a body which he has made up from the following recipe for more than 18 years:

Tom Turner Porcelain (cone 9–10)

Vee Gum-T	4
OM4 ball clay	12
Tile 6 kaolin	75
Kaopaque-20	38
Custer feldspar	60
Silica (200s mesh)	70
Epsom salts	0.25

Translucent porcelain bowl, by Patrick Piccarelle (Belgium), 1993. Wheel-thrown and trimmed several times, carved and bisque fired and then engraved with dental tools. The holes are filled with a high viscosity glaze (Cornish stone 85, whiting 15) and then glazed overall with a palette of feldspathic glazes. Fired in reduction to 1280°–1300°C (gas kiln).

Porcelain Sculpture, untitled, with glass marbles, and steel wire and steel tops applied to the tapering porcelain column, 34 cm × 30 cm × 15 cm, by Wil Broekema, 1993. The porcelain is fired to 1240°C in an electric kiln before assembling with adhesive.
Photograph by Wil Broekema.

Vessel Form, with resist pattern towards the rim sponged away in relief, and the lower section painted in colour, 8.5 cm × 11 cm diameter, by Astrid Gerhartz (Germany), 1993.
Photograph by Wolf Böwig.

'Vee Gum-T is the whitest and most plastic material I've ever found. It is a plasticiser and lubricant that doesn't burn out. The Epsom salts are essential for throwing as a flocculated body will stand up and a deflocculated body will not.'

Turner mixes the above body in a particular order. Firstly, the Vee Gum-T is blunged in warm water or hot water and then he proceeds down the list of ingredients and, by adding the most plastic materials first, maximum plasticity is achieved. This body matures at cone 9 and will survive up to cone 10 but then begins to deform. For handbuilding, the Vee Gum-T content should be increased to between 2% and 3%. To lower the maturation point, 1% of talc is added for each lower cone number required.

Two triangular vessel forms, by Sandra Black. Slipcast porcelain, carved and pierced at the leatherhard stage and cleaned up when dry. Fired to cone 7 in an electric kiln.
Photograph by Victor France.

Sandra Black (Australia) suggests a porcelain body recipe developed by Mike Kusnik in Western Australia:

No. 1	Cresta B.B. kaolin	60
	Potash feldspar	40
	Zinc oxide	3

She altered this recipe in 1983 in order to improve the whiteness as follows:

No. 2	Cresta B.B. kaolin	30
	Eckalite No. 1 kaolin	30
	Potash feldspar	40
	Zinc oxide	3
	Zircon	2.5

Another variation provided by Black also comes from Mike Kusnik:

Cresta B.B. kaolin	40
Eckalite No. 1 kaolin	32
Zinc oxide	3
Silica	26
Bentonite	3

'This clay is a very white and plastic porcelain. The feldspar, zinc oxide, silica and bentonite are milled for 12 hours. After 12 hours, add the kaolin and mill for a further four hours.'

Black prepares her porcelain in batches of ten kilos dry weight, firstly making it into a slip which is stirred and sieved through a 100s mesh. 'The clay is then ball milled for between 16–24 hours. This removes any iron spots and grinds the clay to a fine consistency before it is poured into cloth bags to be hung up to dry in a shaded area. When the right consistency is obtained, the bags are dampened down with a water hose to remove dirt and to soften hardened slip around the opening. The clay is removed from the bags and wedged before storage. It is usable after its first wedging but storage is recommended to improve plasticity.'

Derek Clarkson (UK) uses the 'Audrey Blackman' porcelain body referred to earlier in this chapter for his very translucent bowls with incised decoration. For his crystalline glazes, however, he prefers to use the Special Porcelain body (firing range 1300°–1400°C) from Limoges (available in Britain from Reward-Clayglaze) because it combines well with the glaze recipes and firing cycles he has developed. (This is described in greater detail in Chapter Five.) He reclaims the trimmings produced when turning his pots by putting them into a plastic bucket and moistening them with water from a fine hand sprayer to bring them to a soft, throwing consistency. The full bucket is left for two or three weeks and then the contents are thoroughly wedged to a good condition for throwing.

I have found it essential not to allow porcelain clay trimmings to dry out completely if I intend to re-use them for thrown work. When reconstituting the clay by hand wedging, it is difficult to rid it completely of air pockets which can prove fatal in thinly thrown bowls. My preferred method is to let the trimmings fall into my wheel tray containing slip from the previous throwing session and then mix this up thoroughly before removing it to stiffen on a large, two inch thick plaster batt resting on the bench beside my wheel. After one or two hours this reclaimed clay is turned over on the batt to stiffen further. It is then kneaded and wedged ready for throwing. I do not possess a de-airing pugmill but, although this method does work for me, the reclaimed body cannot compare with fresh clay. As a consequence, I often prefer to mix the 'old' clay with an open textured, stoneware clay and use it for hand-building.

Paper porcelain

An increasing number of ceramicists have been experimenting with porcelain bodies mixed with other materials such as paper or textiles. Soaking textile fabric in slip enables them to wrap thin flexible sheets around a form and the organic matter is burnt away in the kiln to leave the 'skin' of fired clay behind. Cotton paper pulp mixed 50/50 with dry clay produces a heavy slip that can be poured on to plaster batts to make flat sheets or it can be cast to shape in plaster moulds. Stiffened sheets can be rolled out so that the surface resembles leather. These sheets can be torn or cut with scissors and assembled into various forms in the normal way. Firing should be carried out in a well-

'Pots with Minoan Influences, (Pots No.51)', 20 cm × 6 cm, by Paul Scott, 1993. Etching printed on paper porcelain with cobalt oxide under a transparent glaze fired to 1200°C.
Photograph by Andrew Morris.

ventilated area to allow for the pungent gases that the mixture releases. **Paul Scott** (UK) is one who has explored the possibilities offered by mixing paper pulp with porcelain. He uses a mixture consisting of two parts porcelain to one part paper pulp. This proportion gives the material

remarkable strength in both the leatherhard and dry states and it is possible to produce literally paper-thin sheets with it. Although Scott uses these ceramic sheets rather like a printmaker would use ordinary paper for making etchings (see page 143 for a description of this technique), others have created sculptural expressions with similar material.

Translucency

The translucency of porcelain is an essential ingredient in the work of a number of ceramic artists including **Arnold Annen** (Switzerland). Having worked with different clays and firing processes in Switzerland, France, Japan, Holland and Germany between 1970 and 1989, he returned to set up his studio in Basel. There he began to develop a unique technique for making his distinctive, paper-thin porcelain bowls in 1991. His methods demand a disciplined approach and an extremely high standard of craftsmanship. Initially, bowls are thrown with walls at least twice their final thickness. Accumulated slip is removed with steel ribs inside and out and then Annen uses two hand-held gas burners to dry the piece until leatherhard. The burners are held opposite each other, one inside and one outside, and the wheel revolves. A chuck is thrown with the same porcelain body and turned precisely to match the diameter of the bowl's rim. Inverting the bowl onto the chuck, Annen gently taps it as the wheel rotates until it is properly centred and trimming can commence. Sharpened metal strip tools are used to shave away successive layers from the outer surface of the bowl. Then the bowl is placed upright in another chuck so that the inside of the bowl can be worked on with sharp, kidney-shaped steel tools, thinning the wall still further. The abrasive action of the clay makes it essential that tools are sharpened regularly as the work proceeds. The bowl is inverted once again for the footring to be opened up and, with care, shaped approximately but left thick enough to withstand the stress of further handling. Annen checks the greatly reduced thickness of walls and base by shining a torch through them. At this stage they are little more than 1 mm thick. The rim is then refined with the same steel tools prior to decorating the outer surface of the bowl.

Annen re-centres the bowl upside down on the wheel to paint latex resist onto and around the foot and a little way up the side from the base. He holds the bowl by the resist protected foot while he squirts narrow lines of latex diagonally across the form, working from the foot towards the rim, and force dries the latex with his gas burner. The emerging design is constantly checked and assessed. When satisfied, Annen takes a large Chinese brush to apply separate, sweeping strokes of porcelain slip over the latex, using the gas burner to dry the slip instantly. The lines of latex are then peeled away and, with a fine nozzle, he trails lines of slip selectively across the form and immediately dries them with the burner flame.

The extreme fragility of these bowls requires them to be fired upside down in a chuck made to fit from the same porcelain body. Annen makes his chucks with as much care as he gives to the bowls so that they can correctly support them in the kiln. Alumina is mixed with water and painted around the rim of the chuck to ensure that the bowl will be easy to release on removal from the kiln. The pieces are once-fired in a gas kiln to a maximum of 1260°C under a reducing atmosphere with spectacularly translucent results (see photograph below).

Porcelain bowl with extremely thin, translucent walls, by Arnold Annen, 1993. This piece was wheel-thrown and turned. Decoration was produced by using latex resist brushed over and trailed with porcelain slip. Unglazed. 17.5 cm high × 26.5 cm diameter. *Photograph by Reto Bernhardt.*

Arnold Annen trimming a wheel-thrown bowl with sharp tools in order to reduce the wall thickness to just 1 mm.

Arnold Annen decorating a porcelain bowl with brushed slip over latex resist.

Arnold Annen trailing porcelain slip on a latex-resisted bowl.

Arnold Annen removing latex resist after decorating a porcelain bowl with brushed and trailed slip.

25

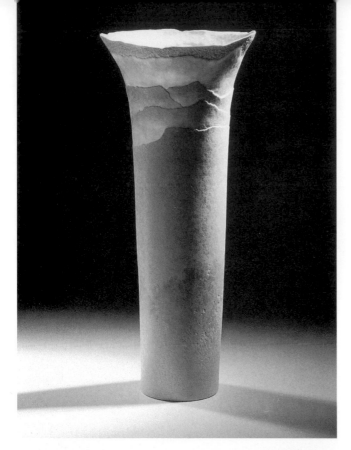

Annen uses a porcelain body from Limoges (TM 10) which is a popular choice among several of the European potters represented in this book. It takes him four days of concentrated effort to complete each piece together with its supporting chuck. Due to the extreme thinness of his bowls it is impossible to rectify any mistakes and even the slightest air bubble will ruin the work. Everything must be done at exactly the right stage and this demands absolute concentration throughout the whole process. He fires his unglazed bowls in a gas kiln under reducing conditions in order to obtain a cold, white colour as the body would

Left Flared, cylindrical vessel form, slipcast in two layers, by Jeroen Bechtold, 1993. The outer layer has been partially removed to reveal greater translucency. 34 cm high. In order to distinguish between the two white layers, Bechtold mixes organic colouring compounds (food colouring) with the second layer.
Photograph by R. Gerritsen

Below Eggshell porcelain vessel form slipcast in layers with decorative surface carved away to increase translucency, 21 cm high and 32 cm wide, by Jeroen Bechtold, 1992.
Photograph by R. Gerritsen.

Above Wheel-thrown 'supporters' made from the same porcelain body as the bowls they will support, upside down, during the high temperature firing, by Arne Åse.

Below Unglazed, translucent porcelain bowl, 38 cm diameter, fired in reduction to 1250°C by Arne Åse. The decorative surface detail is produced by painting a shellac resist pattern and then sponging away the unprotected areas of the design.

Above Unglazed, translucent porcelain bowl, 20 cm diameter, fired in reduction to 1250°C by Arne Åse. The decorative surface detail is produced by painting a shellac resist pattern and then sponging away the unprotected areas of the design.

Porcelain slab form, unglazed, pierced, fired in reduction to 1280°C, and mounted on a painted, wood base, 54 cm high, by Horst Göbbels. *Photograph by C. Struck.*

have a rather warmer tint when oxidised. He built his kiln well-insulated with ceramic fibre and controlled by computer so that he could fire quickly, taking only one and a half hours between 900°C and 1250°C and, thus, avoid risking deformation.

Translucency can have a bewitching effect on the observer and many other potters also make use of this exceptional quality, although it does require directional lighting if it is to be fully exploited. **Jeroen Bechtold** (Holland), for example, carves away parts of the outside in varying layers from some of his pieces. Multiple glazes are applied and fired in oxidising conditions (see photograph on page 26). Again, it is necessary for light to be shining into the pieces from directly overhead if they are to be properly appreciated. **Arne Åse** (Norway) uses a different method to vary the thickness and thus the degree of translucency of his porcelain plates and bowl forms. He paints a design onto the raw pot with a shellac solution and allows it to dry before thinning the wall by carefully sponging away unprotected areas. His sensitive brushwork with the shellac resist helps him to achieve a richly textured surface whose delicate, translucent quality is revealed by the passage of light through the piece (see photograph on page 27).

Horst Göbbels (Germany) also exploits the full potential of translucent porcelain and gives extra emphasis to its exquisite refinement by incorporating precisely pierced holes in some of his sculptural objects. Thinly rolled sheets of porcelain stand unwaveringly straight alone or in formal ranks behind one another, minimally incised or pierced with strictly controlled designs. In some cases, additional linear elements are provided by coloured strings or wires which pass through the slab and appear to act as guy ropes holding the piece upright. The quiet, understated purity of these pieces achieves a sense of perfection that would be destroyed by unnecessary ornamentation.

Smoothness, whiteness and precision

One of the greatest attractions of the medium for those potters who choose to work in porcelain is its smooth grain and dense body. This invites a degree of precision in design and execution that would be difficult to achieve in a more granular clay. Clear, sharp profiles, positive shapes, crisply defined patterns and fine linear drawing seem to be completely appropriate to porcelain. Of course, strict control of the material, tools and processes is absolutely necessary by those who would work in this way and it will not suit any craftsman who prefers potting more freely and

Above Porcelain sculpture made from six incised slabs mounted together. This piece has been fired in a reducing atmosphere to 1280°C, 36 cm high, by Horst Göbbels.
Photograph by C. Struck.

Above right Unglazed porcelain vase, thrown and turned, incised and inlaid with stained slips (pink and black), fired to 1280°C and then polished with silicon carbide paper, 11 cm diameter, by Anne Leclercq, 1990. *Photograph by Peter Bors.*

leaving more to chance. Often, it is a matter of personality. Ceramics, as in any other art form, reveals something of its maker's feelings and character. I must confess that much of the appeal of porcelain to me in my own work is the opportunity that it allows for preciseness. I like to be in control, to make things exact so that they fit as close as possible to a personal concept of perfection. Of course, I recognise that my ideal will not necessarily be the same as another would choose but I find great difficulty in working any other way. I can enjoy and admire asymmetry in the work of others but I am always searching to establish some kind of visual

balance in my own. I feel sure that any conscious attempt to adjust my attitude or approach would appear contrived and fail dismally. This does not mean that precise forms lack sensitivity. Expressive qualities are not the sole prerogative of wild abandon!

The vessels by **Anne Leclercq** (Belgium) are beautifully controlled in the throwing and turning. This precision is matched by the equally exact placement of lines inlaid with slips with which she decorates the surface. Thin lines around the inner and outer edges of the top of her flanged pot, illustrated overleaf, are totally in character with the

Bottom Unglazed, blue (cobalt oxide) porcelain bowl, thrown and turned, incised and inlaid with pink and black lines of stained slips to define a triangular section. This piece was bisque fired and then polished before refiring to 1280°C and then re-polishing, 13 cm diameter, by Anne Leclercq, 1991.
Photograph by P. Goossens.

Top Unglazed, white porcelain bowl with incised and inlaid slips in grey and pink, 15 cm diameter, by Anne Leclercq, 1990.
Photograph by Peter Bors.

severity of the form beneath. These lines, together with similar bands around the base, mark the boundaries of the piece. Her flared bowl also has narrow inlaid bands that define positive changes in the profile but they also confine shorter, coloured strips which appear to float freely between them.

A similar degree of control is evident in the vessel forms by **Johan Broekema** (Holland). Strongly defined horizontal bands, alternately light and dark, draw attention to the circular section of his wheel-thrown pieces. Using the wheel exclusively, he aims explicitly for ultimate perfection in his geometrical vessel shapes and, with a judicious use of glaze, bands them with contrasting lines in black and white to achieve a harmony between form and glaze. His work exhibits the same precise mastery of form when he uses other glazes like the traditional celadons, tenmokus, oilspots, or copper reds on his vessels and which often have narrow lines encircling them at strategic points to mark directional changes of profile. Geometric designs require exact placement of each element if they are to succeed. This degree of control does present the risk of producing a rather cold, clinical feeling which will not be attractive to everyone. However, such an approach is likely to be extremely successful when both form and surface treatment are composed in complete harmony. (Broekema's glaze recipes are listed on pages 188–9.)

Most potters will agree with **Caroline Whyman** (UK) when she says that, 'form, for me, is the most fundamental consideration for my ceramics. If the form is weak, I don't think that it can be redeemed by decoration. Finish is my next obsession, that is why I use porcelain because for me, it demands care and attention to detail. Nuance is what I look for in form, and subtlety.' She often uses grid patterns in her decoration and can draw them, without measuring beforehand, by banding guidelines (vertical and horizontal) on to the pots with a blue or red stain used in colouring food. This shows up well on raw porcelain for any kind of decorating and it burns away in the bisque firing. 'It's great for trying out various ideas directly on the forms.'

Whyman uses a series of tools with tiny loops for carving into porcelain preparatory to inlaying coloured slips. She also uses porcelain stamps to impress dots for inlay rather than drill bits because it is much quicker. Other stamps have been made with carved designs to impress into the clay. Her favoured slip is made from the porcelain body with the addition of one per cent cobalt carbonate which is cheaper and produces less speckling than the oxide. This is a simple recipe but she always adds a deflocculant so that she has the advantage of a fluid slip without excess water wetting the leatherhard porcelain too much as she works. 'This is especially important on plates with lots of decoration because they would just 'pancake' from the effect of so much slip!' To save time, she applies the slip over the whole surface and lets it dry to a *hard* leatherhard condition before turning it away with a flexible metal 'kidney' tool. She lines her wheel tray with plastic sheet to catch and save the trimmings to be used to make more coloured slip. This precaution also prevents her wheel tray

Lidded vessel form with precisely placed bands of black and white giving further emphasis to the shape and sharply defined profile, 10 cm high, by Johan Broekema, 1993.

Top left   Porcelain bowl, with high foot, wheel-thrown and turned to create a very positive profile and banded with sharply defined black and white lines, 13 cm diameter, by Johan Broekema, 1993.

Lidded box, porcelain, thrown and turned, painted with bands of colour to accentuate the form, 13 cm diameter, by Johan Broekema, 1993.
Photograph by Frankot.

from becoming contaminated. 'Occasionally, smudging occurs even when the pieces are quite dry, but I can deal with that more easily with *wet and dry* silicon carbide paper after bisque firing.'

Grids have always fascinated Whyman, 'they are *so* simple but offer *infinite* possibilities and I quickly found a

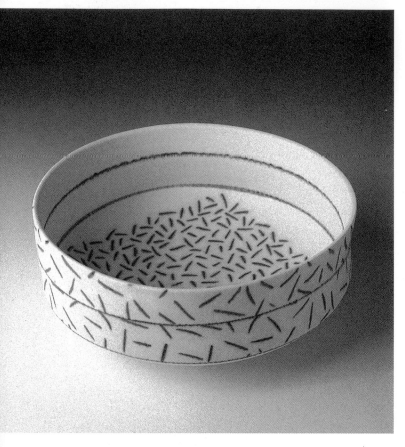

Porcelain bowl, wheel-thrown and turned, incised and inlaid with blue slip, 26 cm diameter, by Caroline Whyman, 1993.

Right Porcelain plate, 'Eternal Triangle' series, wheel-thrown, incised and inlaid with blue stained slip and then sprayed with blue and turquoise, barium/lithium based glazes, 27.5 cm diameter, by Caroline Whyman, 1993. This piece was made in the 'Audrey Blackman' porcelain (see recipe on page 16).

Opposite Porcelain plate, incised and inlaid with blue stained slip under a barium/lithium-based turquoise glaze, 29 cm diameter, by Caroline Whyman, 1993. This method of decorating the surface allows precise placement of all elements of the design.

connection between grid patterns and woven textiles. You either place something on the grid or below it; you either *add* decoration to the grid or leave it blank.' Much of her inspiration comes from geometric textiles and also from basket weaving, especially those from early civilisations. Similar patterns appear, she says, due to a basic grid framework that can be seen in work from South America, native North America, Maori carvings, African textiles, early Greek work, Indian/Asian weaving and Japanese textiles.

Another area of influence identified by Whyman is philosophy and, in particular, Eastern philosophy. 'I study a Chinese form of meditation and philosophy called *Qi ging*, and I find that I have used symbols, often universal, like triangles, dots and squares when I review my work over 20 years or so.'

She rarely uses images from nature and prefers the abstract to the concrete. 'Dots in grids were a symbol of the universe for the Chinese. These can be seen as spiralled dots on their jade *bi* or *pi* as they used to be called. I think that I could continue working with these symbols indefinitely, trying to create harmony and balance. The space in and around the design plays a vital role in the dynamic of the overall appearance. When I feel that a design *really* works it is because there is a dynamic tension between the decorated and undecorated area.

The physical properties of porcelain in its plastic and leatherhard state does, undoubtedly, have a profound effect on the approach to working with it for many potters. It seems to encourage them to work with a high degree of precision – crisp, uncluttered profiles, sharply turned with a

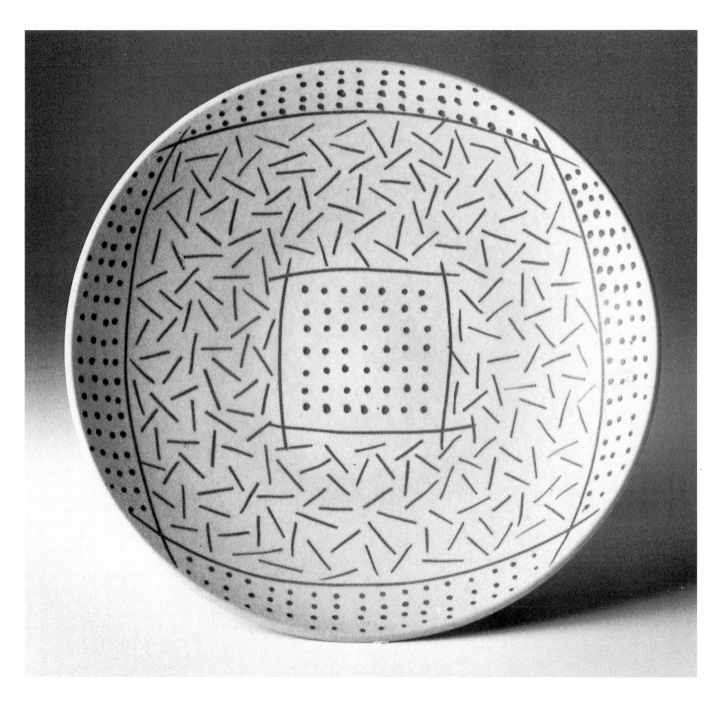

positive and critical attention to detail. Often for those who work in this way, it is a reflection of their own personality.

Neatness in one's character need not be inhibiting although it contributes towards an ordered attitude to the material and to an individual's desire to remain fully in control of the form and its surface treatment. Clearly, there will be others whose nature will not permit them to work within such confines and they will approach porcelain making with greater freedom, as can be seen in later chapters of this book.

The extremely fine grain, whiteness and density of porcelain invites precise treatment in a way that would be utterly alien to coarser clay bodies. Cutting into the surface of sandy textured clays gives the potter a completely different feeling. My own work is mainly in porcelain but I find that my attitude immediately becomes looser and more vigorous when working in even a fairly smooth stoneware. Likewise, the work will appear more rugged than anything produced in porcelain.

FORM AND FORMING PROCESSES

Throwing and turning porcelain

It is a delight to watch any accomplished craftsman at work and to observe a skilled potter throwing on the wheel is particularly fascinating. The seemingly effortless rise and fall of the spinning lump of clay as it is coaxed towards the still centre and then opened up and raised so fluently. The stretching and swelling of the wet clay walls as they respond to the pressure of the potter's fingers to grow as if organic, magically into a new hollow form. This becomes a natural, intuitive process of making and one in which a feeling for the soft, plastic material flows through the potter's fingers as a sensitive expression of him or herself.

Porcelain is not the easiest of bodies with which to throw but it does have its special attraction. It does demand an acute sensitivity towards its condition at all stages of working. It can suddenly collapse if too much water is absorbed while throwing or if the thickness of the

Cup and Saucer, porcelain, 6.5 cm × 6 cm, by Susanna Fagermo, 1993. The cup has a transparent glaze fired to 1400°C with cobalt chloride and vanadium pentoxide decal fired to 1280°C. The saucer has an opaque glaze fired to 1400°C in reduction with vanadium pentoxide decal fired to 1280°C.

walls is irregular. Some potters illustrated in this book prefer to use slip rather than water as a lubricant. However, there is an element of risk attached to this practice if one allows slip to build up on the surface. It is wise to remove any surplus slip with a steel kidney or other tool from time to time during the throwing process.

An experienced thrower can produce large numbers of pots much more quickly than anyone who builds with slabs or coils. The wheel allowed me to make enough pieces to explore a variety of surface treatments during the period when I was a full-time teacher without the opportunity to devote long sessions to working on my own. Following several years developing thrown forms in earthenware and stoneware bodies my conversion to working almost exclusively with porcelain took place in the early 1970s when one of my students expressed a desire to formulate a porcelain body for a special project. I discovered a satisfying affinity with the nature of porcelain despite difficulties experienced with throwing it initially. Its smooth character and whiteness first appealed and then, as my ability to control it improved to the point where I could throw thinly enough to achieve a delicate translucency, I was completely seduced by it.

I have always enjoyed throwing with porcelain that has been properly prepared and is of even consistency, but I am less happy with material which has been reconstituted from previously used porcelain trimmings. I do not have access to a good de-airing pugmill and reclaiming 'old' porcelain effectively takes such an inordinate amount of precious time that I frequently mix it with stoneware bodies or use it for handbuilding where the danger of air bubbles appearing in thinly thrown walls does not apply.

Careful preparation of the plastic porcelain body is essential before commencing to throw. Unless all air bubbles are eliminated and an even texture achieved, porcelain is much more difficult to throw fluently and efficiently than stoneware or earthenware clays which have similar deficiencies. This is because the more open texture and larger particle size of coarser clays provides them with greater wet strength. In the right condition, however, porcelain is a delight to throw. The clay creams smoothly, sensuously through the fingers in a way that can be best appreciated after a period of throwing with stoneware material. This is because the open, sandy texture of most stoneware bodies feels decidedly gritty in comparison with porcelain. Porcelain potters are aware that their material is, undoubtedly, far less tolerant of insensitive treatment at any stage of throwing than coarser clays. Certainly with porcelain a deeper level of concentration is necessary. The thrower must be able to adjust pressure, movement and speed intuitively as the wheel revolves and should try to acquire a particular sensitivity to the changing condition of the clay. Porcelain can quickly become overworked and 'tired' and this makes it prone to collapse without warning. Some porcelain potters allow for the inevitable absorption of water during throwing by working with the clay in a slightly stiffer condition from the beginning because, unless they are kept sufficiently lubricated with water to prevent from them suddenly drying, the point may be reached where hands will stick to the clay and pull the piece out of shape.

When throwing, porcelain bodies can produce a good deal of slurry which should not be allowed to build up too thickly on a pot. It can be removed with a throwing rib or a modelling tool while the wheel is turning. Similarly, excess water must not be left to accumulate and pool inside as this can weaken the base and cause uneven drying. It is wise to apply sufficient pressure on the inside of the base to align the clay particles and reduce the risk of cracking. The way in which porcelain pots are released from the wheel can affect them later. Cutting through the base with an extra thin, stranded wire on a slowly revolving wheel helps to equalise the stress.

Right Miniature porcelain pots (maximum height 3.5 cm) thrown on a full size potter's wheel by Andrea Fabrega (USA).

Right 'Conical Vessel with Handles', by Andrea Hylands, 1993. Bone china, slipcast and assembled, decorated with airbrushed colours and fired to 1240°C in an electric kiln.

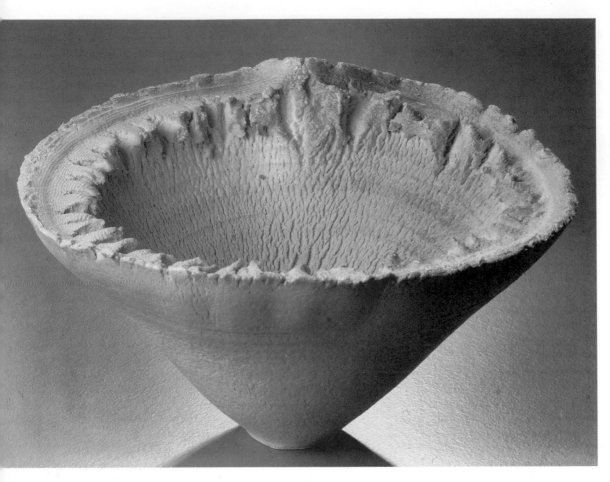

Vessel form, wheel-thrown porcelain, by Fritz Rossmann (Germany), 1993. With part kaolin engobe. 23 cm diameter. Salt glaze fired to 1250°C. This piece was thrown and then 'rolled on the ground or on a table' to produce the unusual texture which is given further emphasis by salt glazing.
Photograph by Baumann Fotostudio.

Caroline Whyman (UK) uses the 'Audrey Blackman' porcelain body referred to on page 16 but she has experienced an unusual number of problems with cracks forming in the base, both 'S' cracks and others in parallel series. She combats these faults by compressing the bases with a rib as she throws, and allows the pots to dry slowly and evenly. She says that she

always lets all my work equalise in dampness, before I do any turning, by wrapping it up in polythene sheet. This slows down the whole making process but ensures less cracks either in the base or the rims if I turn them when the tops are dryish and the bases damp. I throw by using slip instead of water, sometimes adding a minute amount of Fairy Liquid (dishwashing detergent soap) which makes a wetter lubricant and allows me to throw for longer. I also stretch the pots from the inside using wooden spoons modified to a Japanese egote shape. Turning and trimming is always done with very sharp metal tools and I take great pleasure in sharpening them on an oil stone each time I use them.

Two Jugs, 10 cm × 8cm and 14 cm × 7 cm, by Prue Venables (Australia), 1993. Wheel-thrown and altered porcelain. The bases of these pieces were removed when they had stiffened slightly and the sides pushed into the new shapes away from the circular section. New bases are attached when they have stiffened further. 'The intention is to introduce a sprung tension to the forms while retaining the softness of the throwing'.

'From the Sea', porcelain form, handbuilt with impressed texture inlaid with ceramic stains, unglazed but polished, fired to 1320°C in reduction, 30 cm high, by Erik Pløen, 1993.
Photograph by Jan Enoksen.

'Madame No No', porcelain sculpture, assembled entirely from wheel-thrown sections which are then altered and carved to complete the image, 20.5 cm high, by Dalit Tayar (Israel), 1993.
Photograph by Wolf Böwig.

Righi Porcelain dish, decorated with latex resist pattern and copper red, fired to cone 10 (1300°C) in a ceramic fibre kiln with a reducing atmosphere, 35 cm × 10 cm, by Alistair Whyte, 1993.
Photograph by Avon Colour Studio.

Cups and saucers, wheel-thrown porcelain, 15 cm × 8 cm, by Prue Venables (Australia), 1993.

Some potters use the facility of the wheel only to make shapes which are then altered away from the circular cross-section or cut and reassemble them into new forms. Often, this leaves little evidence of the throwing process visible in the finished piece. The Australian potter, **Prue Venables**, enjoys making small, functional vessels which she finds provides her with constant challenges and excitement. All her work is thrown and turned. Much of her latest work has developed through an interest in altering simple thrown shapes. Their bases are removed and the side walls bent into new shapes. New bases are added when the forms have stiffened. She tries to introduce a 'sprung tension' to the piece while retaining the softness of the throwing. The

bending is often severe enough to cause cracking if the timing is not accurately judged. She finds that porcelain tolerates such movement only when precisely ready. If this pressure is applied too early in the drying it can collapse, while adjustments made to the form too late leads to cracking.

When **Alistair Whyte** (Australia) went to study in Japan soon after completing his ceramics diploma at the Bendigo Institute in Victoria, he had to make considerable adjustments to his throwing technique. Writing about his experiences in *Pottery in Australia* (Vol. 27, No. 4), he explained that all throwing of porcelain, apart from extremely large pots, is done off the hump. Many of the wheels used in Kyoto are fixed speed wheels and so the work is taken off the wheel while it is still spinning, and potters sit cross-legged in front of their wheels. The direction of the wheel spin is also opposite to Western potters, i.e. clockwise. Having initially learned to throw in Australia, most of these habits were too radical for me to change in a hurry, so I chose compromise and throw my own way using Japanese throwing techniques.

He goes on to emphasise the importance of making specific tools for a particular function in the throwing process.

When making a set of tools for, say, a saucer, the first tool made is the *tonbo* (or dragonfly) measure. This is made of bamboo and measures the inside depth and width of what is being made. It is to this measure that the throwing ribs are made. There are usually two, these being the *dango* (which is made from fine grained, softer wood) and the *hera* (usually made from *sakura* or *nashi* i.e. cherry or pear) which is the finishing rib. The *sanfo* is the throwing rib, being about the thickness of a finger, and is used to draw the clay up to the correct height and thickness. The *hera* is carved back to a fine edge and is purely a final shaping and finishing tool.

Making a new set of tools for each item proved to be an excellent learning experience for Whyte. It was also an essential practice because his master's tools were designed for throwing with the wheel spinning in the opposite direction.

Slipcasting

Slipcasting multiples is the method of production mostly associated with industry but it is also used with great success by studio potters, in particular those who choose to work with those white clay bodies which are lacking in plasticity. The prime concern of such potters is less likely to be mass production than the opportunity to prepare basic forms for further treatment such as by carving, piercing, individually decorating or altering in some other way. Porcelain lends itself as well to this process as does any fine-particled clay but it is especially appropriate for working with its close relation, bone china.

Bone china is renowned for its supreme whiteness and translucency. It differs from so-called 'true' porcelain both

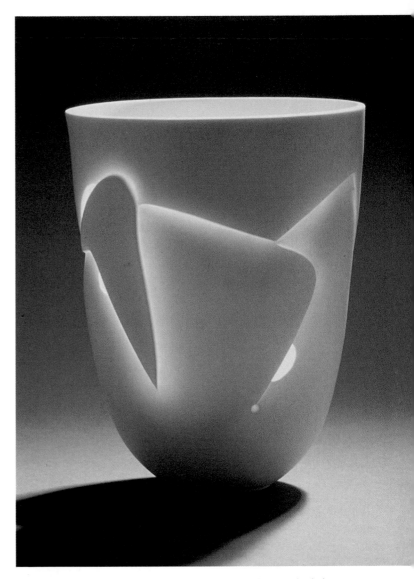

Vessel form in bone china, slipcast, carved and altered, 20 cm high, by Angela Verdon, 1992.

Bowl in bone china, slipcast, carved and altered, 20 cm diameter, by Angela Verdon, 1992.

in its composition, which includes approximately 50 per cent bone ash (calcium phosphate produced from calcined cattle bones), and in its relationship with glaze. Whereas, normally, the porcelain body and glaze fuse together as one at high temperatures, bone china is fired to maturity in the bisque firing around 1250°C and a 'skin' of glaze is fired on at a much lower temperature. Bone china first appeared in England towards the end of the 18th century. It was the result of experiments attempting to match the translucent properties and refinement of Chinese porcelains which had captivated and defeated European potters for many years. Its manufacture was confined almost exclusively to England and factories in Stoke-on-Trent and elsewhere made great quantities of wares in this material.

Sandra Black (Australia) piercing bone china bowl forms with an electric drill, 1989.

Industrially-produced English bone china remains in popular demand all over the world but it is a medium that presents the studio potter with particular problems. Due to the necessarily high proportion of bone ash in a typical bone china body, it lacks the plasticity of porcelain and it is, therefore, mainly slipcast in plaster moulds. Models for casting moulds can be made in clay but plaster makes better original models. Solid lumps of plaster can be turned on a horizontal lathe to give a perfectly smooth surface or rectangular shapes can be cast between sheets of glass. Facets, twists and other details are introduced by hand carving or planing the plaster model. Careful attention must be paid to the profile when modelling for a one-piece mould to ensure it will release the eventual slipcast form. Multi-part moulds can also be used but seams are difficult to conceal unless the mould can be designed so that the seam runs along the edge of the model or where positive changes of direction occur. This is because seams will show up as raised lines on cast bone china after firing no matter how well they have been fettled away before placing in the kiln. Newly made moulds should be allowed to dry naturally because they can crack if exposed to excessive heat.

A few potters, notably Glenys Barton and Jacqueline Poncelet in England during the 1970s, attempted to explore the potential of slipcast bone china for individual work. In the following decades others, attracted by its response to light, were persuaded to experiment and develop their own answers to the inherent practical problems encountered. The scale of the work tended to be small, mainly slipcast vessels of various simple shapes made in one piece dropout moulds. **Angela Verdon** (UK) began working with bone china in the 1970s and over the years she has skilfully worked in this medium, having devised her own, somewhat time-consuming methods in order to creatively exploit its translucent properties. Her extremely thin, slipcast vessels are often pierced with intricate patterns of tracery so that they resemble lace. Occasionally, different colours of bone china slip were cast in layers through which she then carved her designs. Later work is less geometrically treated and the carving has assumed a more organic, linear character with patterns that flow around simple bowl shapes. When illuminated from above, light passes easily through the piece and gives extra brilliant emphasis to these sinuous lines so that the piece takes on a quilted appearance. Although Verdon is still very much concerned with luminosity and purity in her work, she now executes most of it in a slipcast porcelain body from Limoges and her current developments with this are more fully described on page 109.

The first contact that **Sandra Black** (Australia) had with bone china was at Canberra School of Art in 1983. She worked, initially, with a casting body fired to 1280°C but changed to using another which required a lower temperature in 1984 because it offered a better response to colour and the advantage of cheaper fuel costs. Later, having resolved problems previously experienced with colour, she returned to using the higher firing bone china. She prepares her casting slip with great care and describes the procedure as follows:

1. Measure the water at 600 ml to every kilo of dry material.
2. Add deflocculent to water. Dispex, sodium silicate or soda ash are used singly, or in combination.
3. Mix dry ingredients together, add to the water and stir using a power drill with a paint mixer attachment to ensure even dispersal. At this point a little more deflocculent may be added to increase fluidity if the slip is too thick. Care is essential because if there is too much deflocculent it will have the reverse effect.
4. The slip is then sieved and, if required, ball milled for 2–6 hours.
5. The slip is then tested by casting a small mould. Its condition is correct if it fulfills the following two parameters:

(a) casting time between 5–10 minutes = 2–4 mm in thickness.

(b) it should drain cleanly away without shaking the mould.

Teapot, 'Thai Memories', made in black bone china with applied gold leaf by Sandra Black, 1991. The bone china slip is stained with iron chromate 7%, black iron oxide 7% and cobalt carbonate 3.5% and, as these are strong fluxes, the normal firing temperature is lowered to cone 4–cone 5 depending on the firing schedule.
Photograph by Victor France.

Left 'Wrapped Vessel Form' in black bone china, 70 cm high, by Sandra Black, 1990.
Photograph by Victor France.

The slip is stored in an airtight container and then left to settle for 24 hours before use. It must be thoroughly stirred (being careful not to trap air bubbles which causes pinholes to develop) before each cast is taken.

Ready-made slips can be obtained from pottery suppliers for potters who find their preparation tedious. **Sasha Wardell** (UK and France) is one who feels that the material is difficult enough to cast and fire and she welcomes the opportunity to use prepared slips that help to simplify the process of working with bone china. She still finds it necessary to pass the slip through a 60s mesh sieve and to adjust its fluidity with a few drops of sodium Dispex deflocculant. Her pieces are cast for 1–2 minutes before draining the mould. Spare clay is then cut away and the cast left to

White 'wrapped vessel form' in bone china, 20 cm high, by Sandra Black, 1986. Muslin, nets and other textile fabrics soaked in slip can be wrapped or draped around clay forms and fired to retain its appearance. The organic fibres burn away to leave the fragile 'skin' of fired slip in place.
Photograph by Victor France.

Below   Three stoppered vases in slipcast bone china decorated with airbrushed ceramic stains, 15 cm and 21 cm high, by Sasha Wardell, 1990.

stiffen overnight (in order to reduce the risk of distortion) before removing it from the mould.

Normally, it is important to ensure that the mould is clean and dry for casting but, if it is so very dry that the cast releases while draining excess slip, then it can be dampened slightly beforehand. In any case, casts will release at different rates according to the dryness of the mould and the atmospheric conditions at the time. On no account should attempts be made to dry the cast too quickly. Sandra Black stresses the need for patience at this stage because bone china has a notorious 'memory'. Sasha Wardell also speaks of this problem which she describes as the 'idiosyncratic nature of bone china' not only in coming to terms with its high shrinkage rate but also with its tendency to warp alarmingly. Wardell finds this 'both intriguing and frustrating' at the same time. She referred me to an article she wrote for *Ceramic Review* Vol. 111 (1988) in which she described this memory manifesting itself when a cast has been knocked or dented in the green state. This will be 'remembered', despite any attempt to repair the damage, and revert to its distorted form in the high firing. This is a feature of other thinly potted porcelain bodies but its effects are more exaggerated in bone china. It is a characteristic which Wardell believes 'could be exploited and

Pair of jugs, with blue/pink/white or grey/black/white airbrushed decoration, in slipcast bone china, 12.5 cm high, by Sasha Wardell, 1992.

Teapot with cups and saucers in slipcast bone china, with airbrushed ceramic stains under a clear glaze, teapot 19 cm high, cups 8 cm high, by Sasha Wardell 1988.
Photograph by Hedges Wright.

Wide-based vase in slipcast bone china, made from two sections, with airbrushed decoration in yellows/orange/blue-grey/white, 19 cm high, by Sasha Wardell, 1988.

therefore open up a whole new way of working with china, if the "surprise" element is desired'. However, she prefers to remain more fully in control in order to secure reliable results.

Sasha Wardell's thinly cast forms are fired three times with, firstly, a 'soft' firing to 1000°C after which the work is sanded with fine grade *wet 'n dry* paper. Originally, she omitted this preliminary stage but too many pieces were lost when being handled and cleaned up while still in the raw state. The next firing is taken to 1260°C and soaked at that temperature for one and a half hours. This allows the body to mature and achieve perfect whiteness and translucency before decoration is applied. Finally, the work is fired to 1080°C to fix the coloured stains.

Sandra Black, on the other hand, uses an even lower bisque firing to only 750°C before sanding the carved surface decoration of her particular bone china pieces. If they are taken to a temperature above 800°C the bisque ware becomes too hard. She has fired bone china in both electric and gas kilns but warns that a heavy reducing atmosphere can cause grey areas to appear. However, further firing in oxidation overcomes this problem. She has found that bone china will withstand rapid temperature changes in the initial part of the firing cycle and in the latter stages of cooling. 'I have fired up to 720°C in one and a half hours for lustres and then opened the kiln at 600°C while cooling. One piece was fired three times in one day without cracking.' Such work is on a very small scale so pieces will accept these thermal stresses more easily. Her larger forms with

various draped elements have also survived fast glaze firings to 1260°C in 3½ to 4½ hours without cracking.

Among Sandra Black's more impressive pieces are a number of tall vessels wrapped in textile bandages soaked in slip. The taller pieces, mounted on thrown porcelain bases, have an air of mystery and appear almost threatening. Coloured slips are airbrushed on to these forms while they are leatherhard and then fired to cones 7–8. Other pieces are assembled from slipcast elements and airbrushed with a black slip at the bisque stage and then given a fast firing to cones 7–8 in six hours.

Recipes

Sandra Black relies on two different recipes for making her bone china casting slips. The first of these was developed by Dr Owen Rye at Canberra School of Art. It is normally fired to cones 8–9 and consists of the following materials:

(B6 Body)			
Eckalite No. 1 kaolin	30	parts by weight	
Bone ash (natural)	40	"	" "
Potash feldspar	22.8	"	" "
Silica	2.2	"	" "

These ingredients are mixed with 600 ml of water together with 2 g Dispex and 1 g sodium silicate to each kilogram of dry material. In making her black stained bone

Large based vase, with delicate blues/pinks/white airbrushed decoration, in slipcast bone china made from two sections joined together, 21 cm high, by Sasha Wardell, 1990.

Three Vessel Forms, tallest vase 25 cm high, by Anne Hogg, 1993. Wheel-thrown bone china with carved decoration. The black spots in two of the pieces are from rust particles kneaded into the body in order to relieve the extreme whiteness. Fired in an electric kiln to 1270°C.

Teapot with overhead handle, porcelain with dry ash glaze fired to cone 10 with salt, 28 cm high, by Neil Moss (USA), 1993. *Photograph by Brian Goodman.*

china slip she adds 7 per cent iron chromate, 7 per cent black iron oxide and 3.5 per cent cobalt carbonate to the mixture. However, it should be noted that these oxides act as powerful fluxes so the firing temperature may need to be lowered to around cones 4–5 according to the firing pattern adopted. As with all ceramic materials, great care should be exercised during their preparation and use. Danger from ingested dust and toxic elements can be avoided by wearing protective clothing such as masks and rubber gloves.

The second slip is a recipe devised by Mike Kusnik at the Western Australia Institute of Technology in Perth. It is fired to cones 6–7.

Cresta BB kaolin	40 parts by weight	⎫ mixed with water and
		deflocculents
Bone ash (natural) 40	" " "	⎬ in the same proportions
Nepheline syenite 20	" " "	⎭ as above.

Casting slip can be recycled but care should be taken to avoid contaminating the new batch. Sandra Black suggests adding no more than 20 per cent scrap to any new mix of slip and recommends including 0.1 per cent barium car-

bonate in order to neutralise sulphates which can cause peeling faults.

Bone china is generally acknowledged to be very difficult, if not impossible, to throw because it lacks plasticity due to the low percentage of clay in the body. However, **Anne Hogg** (UK) has been using a throwable bone china for several years. It is prepared to a recipe developed by her husband, Chris. They live and work in a quiet Cornish village close to some of the finest china clay deposits in the world. The recipe for this plastic body is based on traditional ingredients as follows:

Bone ash	50
Super Standard Porcelain china clay* (kaolin)	25
MF4 flux**	25
Westone-H white bentonite	2.5%
	added to the above.

Anne Hogg has found no real disadvantage throwing with this bone china body. Experience has taught her how best to come to terms with its individual character and so to anticipate the results. She has found that thrown shapes which are tall and narrow survive better than those which are more open. Shorter, wider pots having a V-shaped section are less likely to slump or warp in the kiln than those having a U-shaped profile. Throwing, turning, trimming, carving and reshaping in the pre-bisque state can be carried out in much the same way as with a standard porcelain. She kneads the plastic china body in a spiral motion before making it into a very round ball and *placing* it on a batt on the wheel. Centring is done quickly with hands and clay well lubricated with water because the clay must not be allowed to drag or spirals will appear in the fired pot. Sudden movements are to be avoided. Drying must be slow and gradual. The bisque firing is only to 840°C so that the pieces can be polished smooth with wet 'n dry silicon carbide paper ('any higher makes sanding hard work').

Firing is conducted in either gas or electric kilns to 1270°C in about ten hours. The temperature rise between 1170°C and 1270°C is carefully monitored to take an hour (to minimise the risk of distortion) because it is at this stage

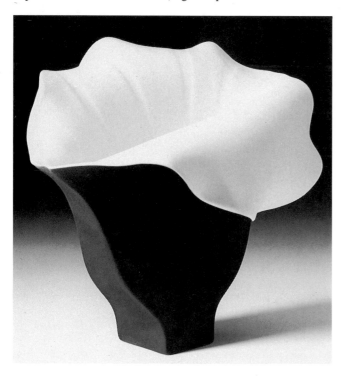

Slipcast and altered bone china vessel inspired by natural form, 20 cm high, Angela Mellor, 1990. Fired in an electric kiln to 1240°C, the form has been encouraged to deform gradually during the firing by reshaping part of the rim.
Photograph by James Austin.

*This special china clay, produced by English China Clays, is strong and plastic with a low iron content. It is distributed by Whitfield and Son, 23 Albert Street, Newcastle, Staffordshire, England. This company also markets the Westone-H white bentonite.
**The commercially prepared MF4 flux could be substituted by either Cornish stone or a combination of 15 per cent soda feldspar and 10 per cent quartz.

Slab-built porcelain vases with impressed decoration and ceramic stains fired in an electric kiln to 1240°C, 27 cm and 14 cm high, by Angela Mellor.

that 20 per cent shrinkage occurs. Kiln shelves coated with Molochite (a china clay grog made by English China Clays) allow the pot bases to shrink and move without snagging. The kiln is held at the top temperature for a soaking period of half an hour to improve the translucency of the china but the pieces can suddenly melt and collapse like glass if that temperature is exceeded.

Having been given a small sample of this bone china body with which to experiment, I discovered that it is creamily smooth while throwing. Small shapes can be made with very thin walls if the approach to throwing is direct and uncomplicated. I found that larger forms needed to be left with rather more thickness but any excess material can be pared away by turning later.

It was the ultimate whiteness, thinness and translucency of bone china that attracted **Angela Mellor** (UK) to experiment with slipcast forms based on similar shapes that she had previously produced by slab building with porcelain. She finds that the

tactile quality of bone china is very appealing and its marble-like surface has a warm sensuality about it. Slip casting bone china allows me to make ultra thin shapes which are extremely translucent, pure and so white that ordinary porcelain seems almost grey in comparison. The supreme whiteness makes colours so much more vibrant.

A part of Ole Lislerud's studio showing some large porcelain panels, inscribed with the Norwegian Constitution, waiting to be made up into a section of the architectural piece commissioned for the new Supreme Court Building in Oslo. The final work consists of two columns 32 metres high by 4 metres wide covered with thin porcelain slabs with a total area of 250 square metres. 1993.

She prefers to make asymmetric forms and does not use 'setters' to support the pieces in the kiln because she encourages the forms to 'move', to become more fluid during the firing and thus closer in character to the organic forms of nature that inspire much of her work. Alumina is packed inside her pots and around the base to prevent them sticking to the shelf.

Architectural applications of porcelain

The large sculptural works of **Ole Lislerud** (Norway) provide convincing evidence of the confident expertise with which modern studio potters have exorcised those peculiar problems, real or imagined, in handling porcelain. To be able to make, manipulate, decorate and successfully fire a flat sheet of porcelain no more than 3 mm thick and with a surface area up to one metre long by 80 cm wide is no mean feat. But to complete an architectural commission for the Supreme Court building in Oslo, which entailed the production of 250 square metres of equally thin porcelain slabs inscribed with the full text of the Norwegian Constitution, is a remarkable achievement. Lislerud was awarded this commission when he won an open competition for the

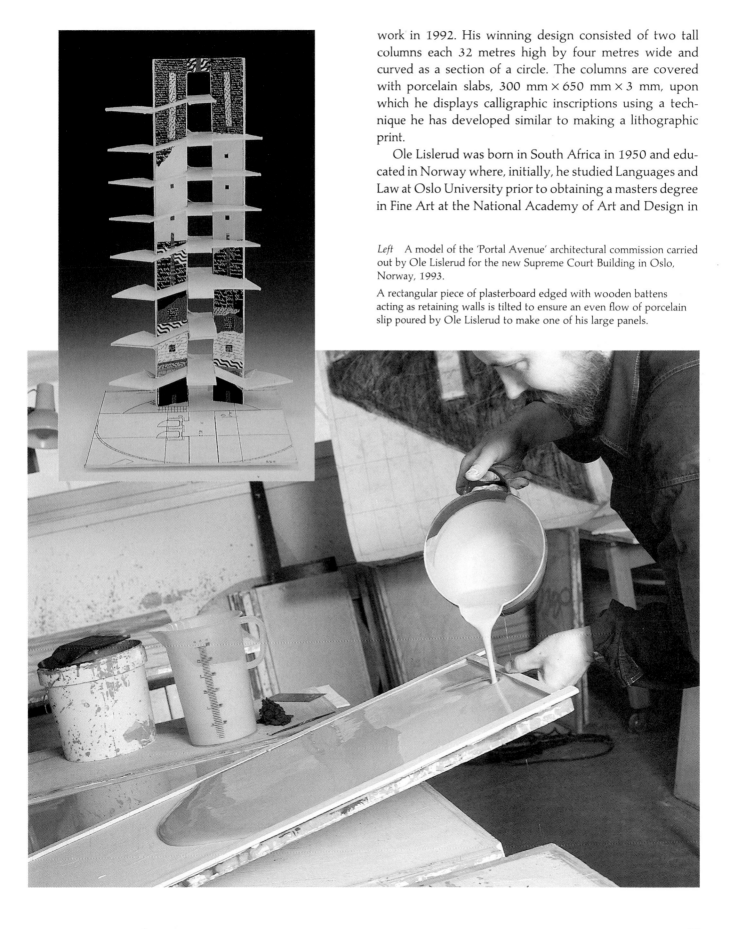

work in 1992. His winning design consisted of two tall columns each 32 metres high by four metres wide and curved as a section of a circle. The columns are covered with porcelain slabs, 300 mm × 650 mm × 3 mm, upon which he displays calligraphic inscriptions using a technique he has developed similar to making a lithographic print.

Ole Lislerud was born in South Africa in 1950 and educated in Norway where, initially, he studied Languages and Law at Oslo University prior to obtaining a masters degree in Fine Art at the National Academy of Art and Design in

Left A model of the 'Portal Avenue' architectural commission carried out by Ole Lislerud for the new Supreme Court Building in Oslo, Norway, 1993.

A rectangular piece of plasterboard edged with wooden battens acting as retaining walls is tilted to ensure an even flow of porcelain slip poured by Ole Lislerud to make one of his large panels.

49

Oslo where he now teaches. He explains the inspiration for his work as arising from his study of archaic forms and symbolism. His continuous search for appropriate aesthetic criteria to interpret and express his response to this interest led him to experiment with tablets or slabs and composite forms built up into columns and portals. Combining sculptural and graphic elements together in his search for artistic expression fascinates him. He feels that manipulating the smooth porcelain surface with lines and marks like calligraphy is essential to the process of emphasising his symbolic intentions. He states that, 'despite the minimalistic form, there is constant experimentation regarding surface treatment which is expressive and spontaneous in character. Thus a tension is created between form and surface — between the archaic and the contemporary.'

Lislerud firmly believes in the importance of acquiring knowledge and understanding through systematic research. The methods used to make the components to construct his sculptural installations were developed during a ten-year period of intensive experiment. Casting plaster on polished marble produces extremely smooth boards 25 mm thick. These plasterboards are then used to cast porcelain by pouring slip on them from one position while they are inclined at a sufficient angle for the slip to flow evenly. The size of the plasterboards matches that of the shelves in Lislerud's kiln. The procedure of actually casting thin slabs of porcelain is the most difficult part of the whole process of manufacture because small mistakes can create big problems. The most common faults resulting from incorrect casting are: cracking, warping and distortion with corners curling to destroy the flatness. Tilting the plasterboard while pouring slip from the top edge helps to avoid subsequent cracking. Lislerud discovered that pouring slip in a more random way shows up the drying process as cracks appear along the joins and overlaps as the

Top left Ole Lislerud pours a thin layer of porcelain slip containing titanium dioxide on to a plasterboard previously coated with a black stained slip through which calligraphy has been inscribed. This results in a yellow linear inscription on a black ground. Many layers can be added in this way to build up a composition. 1993.

Centre Ole Lislerud unloading one of his large (100 cm × 80 cm) porcelain panels, fired to 1300°C, from the kiln. He can fire as many as three of these stacked on top of each other without warping. 1993.

Bottom left Ole Lislerud painting a heraldic device on a once-fired porcelain panel with a red glaze to be re-fired to 800°C. 1993.

Right 'Script', a monoprinted porcelain tile 300 mm × 600 mm × 3 mm, by Ole Lislerud, 1993. With the colour and texture built up from several layers of porcelain slips containing rutile, titanium, iron oxide, and black stains. This piece is fired in reduction to 1280°C but left unglazed.
Photograph by Lislerud.

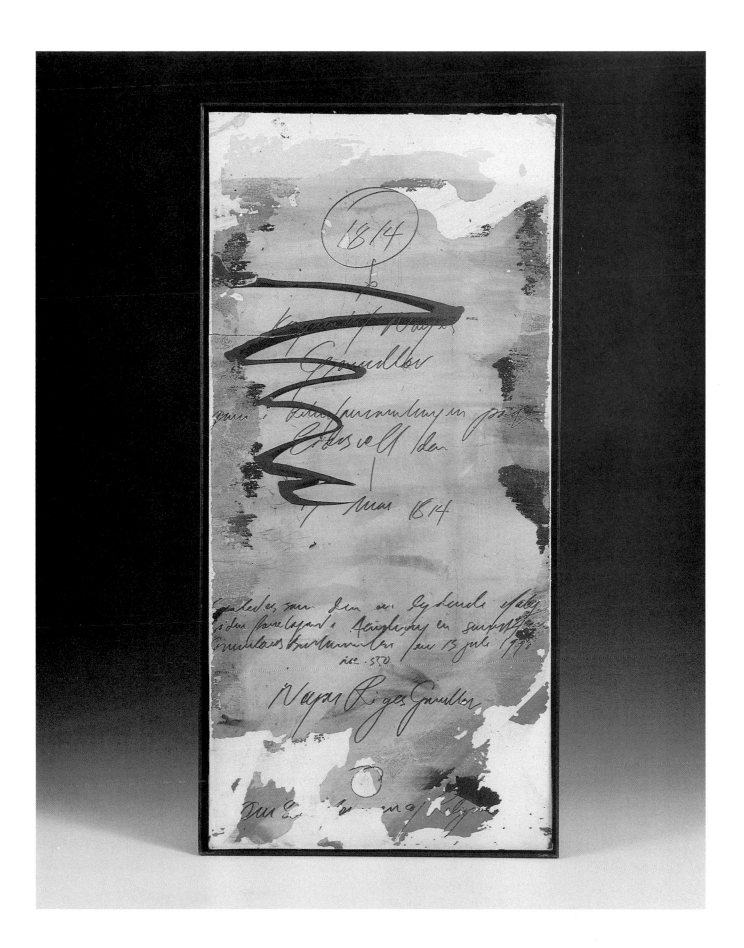

porcelain dries rapidly in contact with the plaster. Hence the need to ensure an uninterrupted flow of slip to cover the board. Wooden battens are placed around the edges of the plasterboard to contain the slip to a depth of 3 mm. The battens are not fixed to the board because he finds that they will maintain their position without moving while the slip is poured. After ten minutes the slip has dried sufficiently for the battens to be removed. A thin-bladed knife slices between the batten and the porcelain and also under the slab to loosen it. 'If this is not done carefully it will definitely warp.' Ten minutes later the slab is pulled gently away from the plaster, first one end and then lifting from the other. The newly loosened slabs are then placed on paper-lined plasterboard (as used for ceilings and partitions in the building trade. 'Fantastic for drying porcelain and keeping it flat!) of the same size and left to dry.

When trying to speed the production of his porcelain slabs, Lislerud abandoned the normal drying procedure and found that he could transport the newly cast slabs directly into the kiln. By applying a thin coating of aluminium oxide dust to the leatherhard slabs before turning them over onto the 'builders' plasterboard' they would slide easily onto the kiln shelves. 'These slabs turned out to be completely flat and, because they were leatherhard and only 3 mm thick, none were broken when stacking and sliding into position.' On the other hand, completely dry slabs are sometimes 'so fragile that they can crack just by looking at them!'

By carving into the plaster slab before pouring slip, precise, surface relief marks and patterns are produced on the smooth porcelain. Another technique is to incise through a very thin layer of coloured porcelain (e.g. black) slip applied to the surface of the plaster. A different coloured slip (e.g. yellow) is then painted over those incised marks before the final thickness of porcelain is poured. The first layer of thin slip tends to stick partially to the plaster ('which can produce very interesting visual effects') when the slab is released while a thicker layer of slip gives a more even colour. Multiple layers with different colours can be applied and scraped through to form quite complex designs. Lislerud is able, also, to change the scale and character of his calligraphy by 'writing' with a slip trailer, drawing directly on to the plaster with either coloured slips or specially formulated glazes prior to casting the porcelain slab. These designs trailed on to plaster will release completely with the cast slip. If necessary, he will leave such compositions to dry and be cast hours or even days later.

Lislerud's porcelain is fired to 1280°C in a reducing atmosphere. He obtains the raw material from Porsgrund

Dale Zheutlin working with large porcelain slabs in her studio. She avoids distorting the slabs by working on top of boards covered with plastic and newspaper. 1993.
Photograph by Nick Saraco.

Porselaensfabrikk, the only porcelain factory in Norway and which fires this same body to 1400°C. Occasionally he has fired as many as three of his thin porcelain slabs on top of each other without suffering any loss through cracking or warping. However, warping can happen from time to time and his remedy is to refire the slabs with pieces of broken kiln shelf on top to act as weights and, combined with a higher temperature, they will flatten out. Where there is no glazed area on the slab, it can be fired upside down to accomplish the same end. Some of the slabs are subjected to a final firing of 800°C with low temperature glazes giving bright colours.

Large-scale wall sculptures in porcelain are by no means the sole prerogative of European ceramicists and at least one American, **Dale Zheutlin**, has completed a number of important architectural commissions in this medium. Designing for specific sites involves collaborating closely with architects, interior designers, art consultants and

'Archisites' porcelain wall sculpture 420 cm × 420 cm (14' × 14'), by Dale Zheutlin, 1993. Decorated with coloured stains and glazes, commissioned by JMB Properties, New York. Fired in oxidation.
Photograph by Paul Warchol

'Twin Spans', porcelain wall panel by Dale Zheutlin, 1991,
450 cm × 180 cm (15' × 6') (fired in oxidation). Commissioned
by the Delaware River and Bay Authority, Wilmington. The image
is abstracted from the Delaware River Bridge.
Photograph by Andrew Bordwin.

clients representing public agencies and large corporations.
However, she says that it is important for the artist to
retain creative control. She described her experiences in
this kind of work in an article for *Ceramics Monthly* (June
1993) and I am indebted to her and to the magazine for
allowing me to quote some of the salient features involved.
She was awarded a financial grant in 1986 and this allowed
her to experiment and develop the necessary technology
to accomplish the kind of large-scale projects that
interested her.

Handling oversized slabs before they are fired presents
a problem. They are difficult to turn without stretching
or bending, so I dry them on boards covered with plastic and newspaper. Working directly on the floor, I
change the top layer of newspaper every six hours. The
clay is weighed down with boards for the first 24 hours,
then air dried.

In order to avoid firing difficulties, Zheutlin found that it
was necessary to work out her design in segments to be
fired together on site.

I started with slabs $\frac{3}{8}$ inch thick and no more than
18 × 24 inches overall, because that was the maximum
size that could fit into my 28 inch, octagonal kiln. These
segments were fired on edge, four at a time, then
regrouped as wall units. I now have a top loader, rectangular electric kiln, which offers flexibility in experimentation and a degree of economy, plus it will fire
larger slabs.

As her work evolved, Zheutlin changed from concentrating on 'flat, planar surfaces without colour to more
dimensional construction with colour developed from a
variety of glazes and stains. I began to cut the slabs, then
put them back together by overlapping, tilting, inter-
secting and reassembling.

Experiments and glaze tests were conducted with the
help of an assistant to establish a palette of 32 colours.
Taking into account a five per cent shrinkage rate, the slabs
were rolled out and allowed to stiffen before laying them
on the floor in preparation for carving, incising, the appli-

'Twin Span', porcelain wall panel designed and made by Dale Zheutlin, 1991. Mounted in the headquarters building of the Delaware River and Bay Authority.
Photograph by Andrew Bordwin.

cation of stains and glazes, and to be cut into manageable sections. They were left covered and weighted until dry and then stored in vertical racks. 'After firing, the sections were assembled on armatures so that a template could be made to serve as a hanging guide. I always try to do a trial hanging in my studio, although this is not always possible for very large projects.'

One of Zheutlin's most exciting commissions was a 15 feet wide abstract interpretation of the Delaware River Bridge for the Delaware River and Bay Authority.

It did not begin auspiciously. I was happy to receive an invitation from the art consultant to submit a competitive proposal for a sculpture to hang on the wall at authority headquarters. But the committee of architects and engineers who had designed the Delaware River Bridge had expressed a preference for something representational, whereas I normally work in the abstract. The only way I would stand a chance for such a project

'Time Slice', translucent, inlaid porcelain mosaic panels with lights mounted behind, 120 cm × 60 cm × 240 cm approximately, by Curtis Benzle, 1980.
Photograph by Curtis Benzle.

'Night Landscape', porcelain panel with inlaid coloured porcelains mounted with silver on brass, fired to 1260°C in reduction, 55 cm × 30 cm, by Sony Manning (Australia), 1994.
Photograph by David McArthur.

'Weaving a Carpet' translucent porcelain tiles pierced and 'stitched' together to create a larger image, by Arne Åse.

Black and white tile panel in porcelain and mounted on wood, 78cm × 58 cm, fired to 1250°C, by Mary White.

would be to make sketches (not slides) and a model of my concept, which I express-mailed to the art consultant. Imagine my shock to learn that my package had arrived the day *after* her initial presentation to the committee. Nevertheless, she was interested enough to show it at her second presentation and I was asked to meet with the committee to explain my proposal.

Following what she describes as 'a probing and stressful interview', Zheutlin was awarded the commission and was invited to view the bridge 'from the top down'. Donning a hard hat and protective clothing she ascended to the small elevator 440 feet to the top of the south east tower. 'Its gently swaying motion was in rhythmic harmony with my shaking knees and euphoric head.'

She discovered that working for a public body was quite unlike anything she had previously experienced. 'It required a lengthy contract, $1 million in liability insurance and month by month documentation of my progress (including such details as how many pounds of clay I was using, and the firing schedules).' In addition, her proposal had been complicated by the fact that she was intending 'to work in a clearly unclaylike fashion'. Although she had submitted several options, the committee had chosen the most difficult and most sculptural of the models presented.

The sculpture needed to be understood from a distance of 100 feet by people entering the building but when seen at close quarters 'it had to be as precise and accurate as the bridge itself.' Zheutlin wanted to select a position as if in the middle of the twin spans of the bridge and she set about

'Pots No:45', porcelain panel (60 cm × 40 cm) with pen and 'ceramic ink' wash and underglaze colours, fired to 1200°C, by Paul Scott, 1993.
Photograph by Andrew Morris.

preparing preliminary studies using archival photographs and then a computer to re-plot the image in perspective. 'Ultimately, it required five sculptural elements fitted together to create the dynamic tension of the bridge.'

The architects and engineers monitored Zheutlin's progress and she felt that she wanted 'to compliment their achievement with a wall sculpture that captured the blue light, the wind, the reflection off the water, the strength and beauty of the span, and my own unforgettable experience at the top of the tower'.

Smaller tiles have long been used to cover extremely large and often complex architectural structures but porcelain is a less familiar material for this purpose than either earthenware or stoneware. One of the most amazing uses of stoneware tiles is that of clothing the multiple arching roof of the Sydney Opera House. Porcelain is being increasingly used for more decorative purposes despite its inherent difficulties. **Paul Scott** (UK), for example, uses combinations of porcelain tiles to create panels and murals rather like a painter might use a white surface for drawing and painting. He prepares a mixture of ceramic stains suspended in water and proceeds to draw directly on to the porcelain bisque with a pen. This method produces fine linear drawings which he supplements with thin washes of similar ceramic 'inks'.

INSPIRATION IN THE DESIGN OF FORM

Sculptural objects

Potters have long exploited the marvellous versatility of porcelain for fashioning intricate, smoothly finished shapes from the whimsical to the more provocative and esoteric of three-dimensional expressions. **Carrol Swan** (New Zealand) has always worked with white clays but she enjoys the plasticity and extra fine smoothness of porcelain that allows her to pinch it into thin sheets or to build open mesh forms woven from rolls of clay. She made a series of grid-like basket pieces suggested by the kind of metal grids used to reinforce concrete in building construction. Her aim was to recreate an image of that encrusted metal in an open 'vessel' to which she could add 'precious objects, such as saggar fired eggs, rods

and spheres, in gleaming gold, platinum and copper, as a contrast between the old and rusting and the bright and new'. She began by actually coating a metallic mesh with porcelain slip but found that the metal slumped at about 1000°C and the slip had a tendency to chip off. The problem was solved by using extruded porcelain coils which could be easily bent and joined without cracking 'as long as you work quickly' and which became hard and strong at high mid-range temperatures. The unglazed grid baskets cradle slipcast spheres lustred in gold and platinum and whose 'polished' surfaces display curving linear patterns in

'Porcelain Basket', handbuilt from extruded, stained black porcelain, with spheres and rods marbled with gold and platinum lustres, fired in an electric kiln to 1180°C (final lustre glaze firing to 750°C), 15 cm high, 32 cm wide, 26 cm deep, by Carrol Swan, 1993.

reflecting the surrounding grid. Some pieces mimic other materials like paper and boiled sweets. These last were first produced in response to an invitation to participate in a Halloween exhibition. 'Paper' bags sprawl invitingly open spilling their contents across the table. The convincing 'sweets' are finished with underglaze and onglaze colours, enamels and lustres. Some are inlaid with body stains or are made of unglazed agateware.

Porcelain lends itself to working in such extremely fine detail that it has been used for modelling figures, animals, plants etc. for centuries. Victorian dolls often had porcelain heads so delicately modelled and coloured as to appear almost lifelike. Modern potters also have enjoyed this facility to imitate or recreate nature in porcelain. When increasing numbers began to rediscover porcelain in the second half of the 20th century, it seemed appropriate that they should work in small scale. This was due in part to the

Top left 'Minties', a 'bag of sweets', handbuilt, painted with underglazes and with onglaze enamels, by Carrol Swan, 1993. The 'bag' was fired to 1140°C bisque, painted with underglaze colours and then fired to 1020°C. The 'sweets' were fired to 1280°C and painted with onglaze enamels. Base size 10 cm × 23 cm.

Top right 'V Grid Basket', handbuilt with extruded porcelain coils stained black, by Carrol Swan. Fired in oxidation to 1180°C. The spheres and rods are lustre glazed with gold and platinum or with red crackle glaze fired to 750°C. 29 cm high, 33 cm wide.

Right Porcelain 'Head', 43 cm × 24 cm excluding the pedestal, by Gyorgy Fusz (Hungary), 1992. Made by preparing a plaster cast taken from a live model. The cast is then altered before plastic porcelain is pressed into it. The piece is fired, unglazed, to 1260°C in a wood burning kiln. *Photograph by Wolf Böwig.*

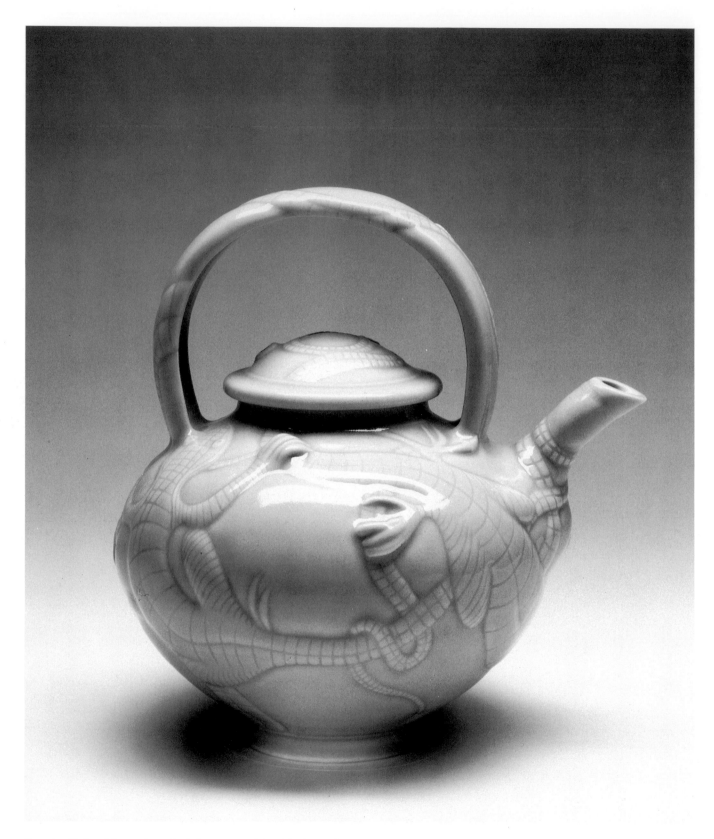

Teapot with lizard decoration, wheel-thrown porcelain with pieces of
porcelain added to the surface and then carved, turquoise celadon
glaze, 25.5 cm high, by Elaine Coleman, 1993.

perceived technical difficulties and partly in deference to it. The material was so different from the coarse, heavy-looking stonewares which had dominated the field of studio ceramics since the Second World War that it demanded a new approach. It could be easily pinched into paper-thin pieces and then manipulated and twisted into shapes that resembled natural forms whose delicate appearance belied their fired strength. From the 1960s onward natural forms like flowers, fungi, birds, fish, and a cavalcade of fantasy creatures have been produced in great numbers. Most are little more than shallow, decorative objects of no artistic significance destined to join the multitude of twee kitsch from previous generations.

'Seated Woman', porcelain sculpture, assembled entirely from wheel-thrown sections which are then altered and carved to complete the form, 29 cm high excluding the pedestal, by Dalit Tayar (Israel), 1993. *Photograph by Wolf Böwig.*

Slab-built porcelain pot with impressed texture and green glaze, by Peter Beard.

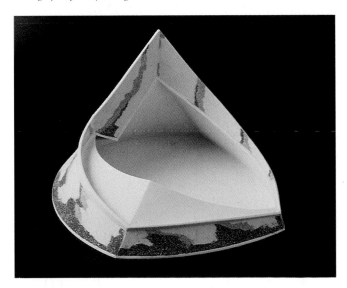

Sculptural Form, handbuilt from multi-coloured, laminated and inlaid porcelain slabs and fired to 1280°C in an electric kiln, approximately 25 cm within the square base, by Saskia Koster, 1991.

61

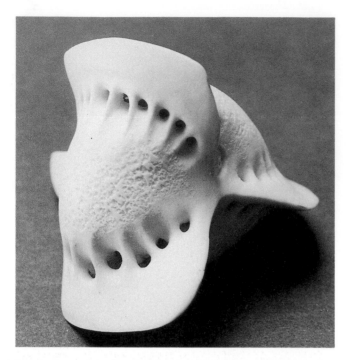

A number of distinguished English potters, attracted to porcelain by its fine working properties, proceeded to exploit it with imagination and distinctive flair. Foremost among them were Peter Simpson and Mary Rogers. Although their work was inspired by, or made reference to, organic forms, it rose far above the mere imitation of nature. Simpson's work in the mid-1970s evoked ripe fruits and seed pods with smooth spherical forms split apart to reveal interiors tightly packed with wafer-thin sheets. This contrast between simple exterior and crowded contents was an exploration not only of the aesthetics of form but also of the very nature of porcelain itself. Similarly, Mary Rogers pinch-built a series small bowls with walls so thin that they could be coaxed into folds and layers to orchestrate the quality of light passing through them rather like the petals of a poppy flower. They were as much a response to the plastic purity and translucency of the material and the process of making as they were a comment on the natural world. These expressions prompted many

Handbuilt porcelain object, unglazed and polished, carved and pierced, fired to 1260°C in oxidation 10 cm long, by Maggie Barnes, 1991.
Private collection in Germany. Photograph by Maggie Barnes.

'Bow Form', slab-built porcelain carved and pierced, with textured slip decoration, unglazed but polished, by Maggie Barnes, 1987.
Collection Wolf Böwig. Photograph by Wolf Böwig.

imitators, especially among students many of whom produced clusters of frilly, fungoid objects often lacking in understanding, sensitivity or purpose. Other potters chose to combine the contrasting character of heavily grogged stoneware bodies and that of porcelain within one object. Peter Beard (UK) developed a memorable series of pieces incorporating delicately pinched, conglomerate 'growths' of translucent, glazed porcelain erupting from geometrically-shaped black stoneware in a way that gave added emphasis to their respective natures.

Maggie Barnes (UK) worked initially in stoneware but, as her interest focused onto particular areas of the natural world which she found especially inspiring, she realised that only porcelain could provide the means that would enable her to express her feelings about them. 'The material both disciplines and rewards the maker, it is a demand-

Porcelain Bowl, by Maggie Barnes, 1989. Thrown, carved and pierced with the exterior surface covered with textured slip. Unglazed but polished. 12 cm diameter. Fired in an electric kiln to 1260°C. This piece was inspired by a prolonged study of dried, bracket fungus. *Photograph by Hans Friedrichs.*

'Marine Form', unglazed porcelain (polished), with textured slip decoration over the dome, fired to 1260°C in oxidation, 13 cm diameter, by Maggie Barnes.
Collection of Dr Wido Parczyk. Photograph by Maggie Barnes.

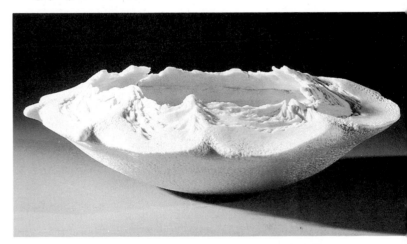

'Crater Bowl', handbuilt porcelain with textured slip, carved, 131 cm × 80 cm, by Maggie Barnes.

ing and seductive clay, responding better to coaxing than to a more forceful approach.'

Her fascination with natural objects began early in life.

Since a small child wandering around the beaches and waterways of East Coast with my father, who was a passionate fisherman, I have gathered from the natural world. The child's habit of collecting 'treasures' to hoard at home stayed with me, grew into adulthood with me, delights me still, and is the foundation from which creativity is fed to this day. I was fortunate to have a teacher in those formative years who encouraged me to explore the natural world of my childhood environment, to

'Crater Form', unglazed porcelain with slab base, textured with slip, and coiled, pinched and carved walls, 23 cm × 11 cm, fired to 1260°C in an electric kiln while cradled in a bed of silver sand to support the wide outer rim, by Maggie Barnes, 1992.
Photograph by Wolf Böwig.

'Fan Bowl', wheel-thrown and carved porcelain vessel, fired in an electric kiln to 1260°C, unglazed and polished, 18 cm high by Rolf Bartz, 1988.

make drawings and to use words to record my findings. He remained my dear friend until he died and took pleasure in watching my obsession evolve until it found its natural expression in clay many years later. It has never been my intention to 'copy' nature but to somehow capture and express, through the medium of porcelain, some of that initial wonder and pleasure experienced with eyes and fingers when the 'found object' is first encountered. When someone says *it feels like a . . .* or *it reminds me of . . .* as they turn the porcelain piece in their hands, then I know that part of my own delight has been communicated and shared. It does not matter too much whether we are reminded of the same things or not; the fact that these are echoes of the natural sources which inspired the piece is enough. There is then a kind of dialogue between maker and those who encounter the work.

A series of 'Marine Forms' developed as a result of

Barnes' explorations and these were made with two thinly rolled slabs of porcelain which were allowed to stiffen slightly in a curved mould and then joined at the rim to create a slim, hollow form. When leatherhard, the rims are reshaped with a scalpel to define the form and these edges are pared away with a stainless steel blade to thin them further. The main body of the piece is then carved and pierced on one or both sides and the openings gently cleaned up and smoothed with a very fine, damp brush. Sometimes the carving extends into and over the rims, altering the form and producing a less symmetrical shape. Pinching and/or paddling with a small wooden spoon helps to extend the narrow edge where the two rims meet before they are refined until they become wafer thin and translucent when fired. These pieces are textured by sponging and brushing thick slip onto selected areas, creating contrasting surfaces and adding tactile and visual interest. Following bisque firing, the pieces are polished with carborundum paper and the process repeated after the final firing. In these small sculptures that fit within the palm of one's hand, Barnes has managed to capture the *essence* of the found objects which inspired them.

Another, more recent development in Barnes' work is a series of pieces which she calls 'Crater Forms'. She describes these as a comment on the raw, more rugged beauty to be observed when elemental forces destroy with far greater energy than the more gradual and gentle process of decay. Because she was 'pushing porcelain to its extremes of tolerance' and encountering difficulties of splitting, cracking and, even, collapse, considerable technical problems had to be resolved before she was able to exercise some degree of control.

The bases of these pieces are made from slabs to which coils of clay are added forming the profiles and contours 'whilst allowing the natural movement of the piece to evolve'. Crumpled kitchen paper is used to pack inside the developing crater and to support the soft walls. Several pieces are tackled at the same time to permit the walls of each to stiffen while work continues on another. Carving around the edges of the 'craters' begins when the forms are leatherhard. The texture of the base form and the outer rim is built up with many layers of smooth and grogged porcelain slip by sponging and brushing. The unglazed porcelain contributes its own special qualities to the final effect.

The vocabulary of visual art often involves the organisation or adjustments in the relationship of opposites such as light to dark, rough to smooth, pattern to plain, colour to non-colour (i.e. to black, white or neutral tones), 'hot' to 'cold' colours, line to mass, positive to negative, open to

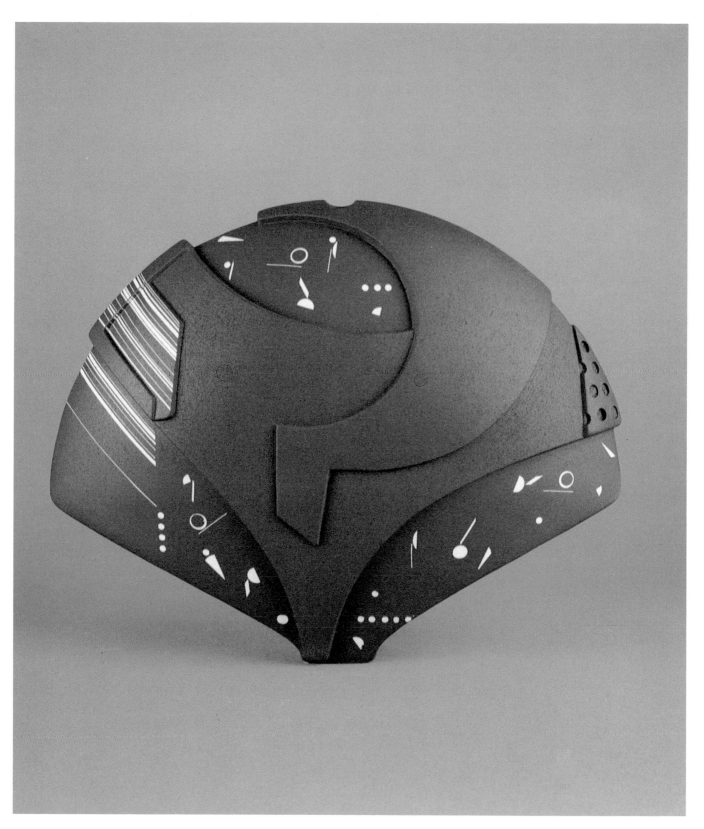

Porcelain Form, decorated with black slip and gold lustre, 23 cm high × 24 cm wide × 8 cm deep, by Brigitte Enders (Australia), 1986. *Photograph by Klaus Moje.*

Three Cats made from individually thrown segments of porcelain and assembled by hand, approximately 17 cm high, glaze fired in reduction (gas kiln) to 1360°C, by Beate Kuhn, 1993.
Photograph by Peter Lane.

closed, inner to outer, tall to short, wide to narrow, horizontal to vertical, etc., etc. We are usually more aware of these elements of design when viewing sculpture or two-dimensional art because 'function', in the sense of domestic application, is no longer part of the equation. On that basis, any three-dimensional sculptural object in ceramic should be judged to stand or fall on its own criteria because the *material* used in its manufacture has no bearing on its acceptance or rejection. However, the position of ceramic sculpture in the world of 'fine' as opposed to 'decorative' art, irrespective of scale or method of manufacture, is subject to continuing debate.

Beate Kuhn (Germany) is well-known for her imaginative sculptural vessel and animal forms constructed from multiple wheel-thrown sections which are assembled and fired to 1340°C in a gas kiln. She displays a mastery of technique that few can rival. As many as 50 separate pieces may be used to build one of her amusing cats but, despite the complexity of their construction, the artist has managed to capture the 'essence' of the animal with a touch of humour. Even the smallest features such as the eyes, ears

Porcelain Cat, handbuilt from individually thrown segments and fired in a reducing atmosphere to 1360°C, by Beate Kuhn, 1993.
Photograph by Bernd Gobbels.

and paws are wheel made. Sympathetic observation has enabled her to translate her feelings for the animal and for her chosen medium in a way that pays tribute to both. Although they are instantly recognisable, these objects are in no sense *realistic* models of cats. Apart from the natural softening effect of the glaze, no attempt has been made to disguise the individual segments which make up the form. Porcelain contributes a sumptuous quality to these very personal expressions that cannot be equalled by other clays.

Continuous exploration and re-examination of a recurring theme, whether it be of a particular form, an aspect of design, or an abstract concept is a fruitful exercise for anyone who responds to the necessary discipline involved. **Jeroen Bechtold** (Holland) is fascinated by vestiges of history that stimulate creative thought. He refers to the way his imagination is triggered by visits to museums where a simple cooking pot prompts questions about the hands that made it and the lives of those who used it. The tumbled, broken remains of once mighty buildings also promotes reverie. Bechtold likes to sit down by ruined castles and contemplate the decay of such symbols of

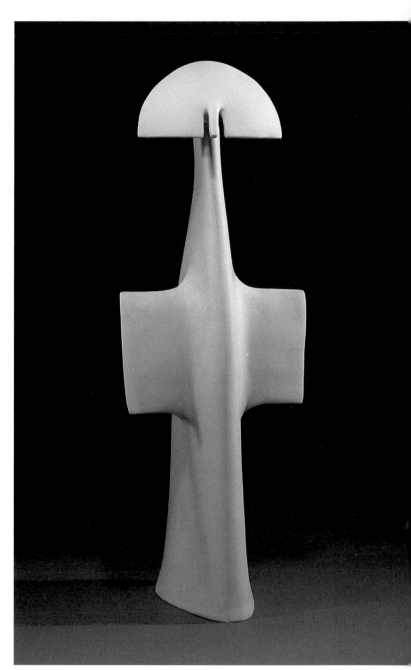

Porcelain sculpture by Ruth Duckworth.
Photograph by Wolf Böwig.

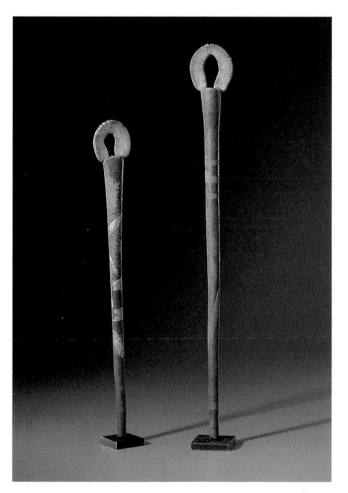

'Companions' porcelain sculpture, slab-built and painted with oxides, fired to 1250°C in oxidation and reduction, 39 cm to 65 cm high, by Fritz Rossmann, 1992–3.
Photograph by Baumann Fotostudio.

'82nd Reconstruction of the remains of the Holy Grail', (rear view) porcelain sculpture made from slipcast and press-moulded elements, with multiple glazes and firing under oxidising conditions. The interior of the form is covered with a 22 ct gold lustre. 48.5 cm × 48 cm, by Jeroen Bechtold, 1992.
Photograph by Rene Gerritsen

Front view of sculpture on p. 68.

sculpture, you can explain different things at the same time, like a Mozart opera where six people can sing different tunes and text, each and everyone of equal importance, but together in one sound. As you learn to listen to opera so you have to learn to "read" my grails, for explanations can be found in layers.'

Slipcasting is the main technique used by Bechtold because it allows him to easily control the wall thickness. He finds that casting is also best for the cut and assemble method he uses because the clay particles are not forced into alignment as they are when throwing and this reduces the risk of cracking. Originally, he graduated from art school intending to work as an industrial designer and was thus drawn to the casting process. He believes that 'it is better to be master of only one technique than to be average in many'.

power and wealth. 'Behind those walls, kings, princes, dukes and cardinals plotted, schemed and played their games. You can imagine their armies marching past. With the same eyes you can look at modern buildings of concrete and glass and wonder what will remain of our own civilisation.' He questions how much of the material wealth and power man values today actually remains when he dies?

A continuing body of work has been born of these musings. This is a series entitled 'The Reconstruction of the Holy Grail' of which each piece is individually numbered. He talks of reconstructing the remains of something that exists only in legend. The fact that people need what he calls 'myths' to be able to make sense of their existence intrigues him. He makes hollow forms having heavily textured walls, 'battered and weathered', with one side torn open to reveal the treasure of an inner purity. 'With a

'Time Well' series bone china sculpture (mounted on a thrown porcelain base), slipcast and assembled, with additions of slip impregnated fabric wrapped around the form and once fired to cone 7–8 to burn away the organic matter. This piece was airbrushed with coloured slips at the leatherhard stage, 75 cm high, by Sandra Black, 1990.

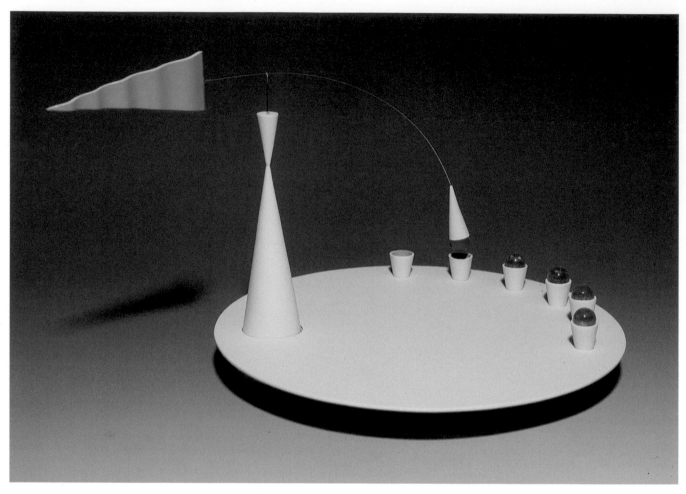

Porcelain Sculpture, untitled, with glass marbles and steel wire, 38 cm × 29 cm × 23 cm, by Wil Broekema, 1993. The porcelain is fired to 1240°C in an electric kiln before assembling this piece.
Photograph by Dick Huizinga.

Bechtold begins by filling several moulds with porcelain slip which he leaves for half an hour or more, depending on the humidity in his studio. After draining the moulds the pots are left to dry naturally for a few hours. When he removes them from the moulds he selects one to become the main form which he cuts and folds open. 'This action helps to determine the final appearance.' Parts are cut away from the other casts and joined onto the first to increase its size and visual impact. 'In this way, I am able to free myself from the limitations of slipcasting.' Some of the remaining sections of clay are used as temporary 'architectural' supports to hold the opened form, 'usually, I open the pot so far that this is essential'. Similarly, further supports are required while in the kiln to prevent distortion. These must be made from the same material to equalise shrinkage. Smaller casts are made of figures and decorative elements

Porcelain sculpture, untitled, with steel wire, by Wil Broekema, 1990. This piece is made from handrolled slabs with the surface relief pressed into it by a cardboard stamp. The pieces are fired separately in an electric kiln to 1240°C and then assembled with an adhesive. cm × 4 cm × 24 cm.
Photograph by Dick Huizinga.

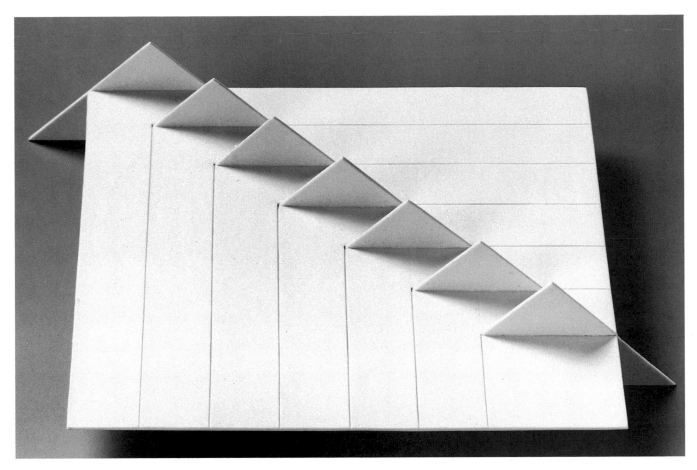

which are sprigged on to the main form as the work proceeds. 'I always keep my eyes open for small objects or
interesting reliefs which I can use as models for casts
because I need a whole "library" of plaster moulds when
working on a series of my grails.'

Final adjustments are carried out when the piece is
leatherhard and able to stand without physical support and
the inside is sanded until perfectly smooth. Then it is fired
four or more times with successive layers of glaze ('I use
glaze purely as a medium to apply pigments and stains').
The inside is coated with a clear glaze and often covered in
a final firing with gold, platinum or mother of pearl lustres.
Rather like a seashell whose rough exterior contrasts with
its smooth inner face, these pieces evoke a feeling of precious quality, but with an added sense of mystery.

The emotional response to natural phenomenon or the
human condition has been well-documented in my previous books. It will remain a constant source of inspiration
for countless generations of potters but there are many
others whose approach is more of an intellectual exercise
which results in an abstract arrangement of shapes possessing no obvious points of reference. The Dutch potter,
Wil Broekema (Holland), for example, works almost

Porcelain Sculpture, untitled, slab built from thin, handrolled sheets,
and fired in an electric kiln to 1240°C, 30 cm × 25 cm × 6 cm, by
Wil Broekema, 1986.
Photograph by John Stoel.

Porcelain Sculpture, untitled and unglazed, handbuilt and with added
glass marbles, brass wire and tops to tapering columns, 35 cm × 25 cm
× 13 cm, by Wil Broekema, 1993. The porcelain elements are fired to
1240°C in an electric kiln before assembling the work.
Photograph by Wil Broekema.

71

Porcelain Object, unglazed, made from thinly rolled slabs, pierced and incised, 32 cm high, fired in reduction to 1280°C in a gas kiln, by Horst Göbbels.
Photograph by Faahsen.

Porcelain Sculpture made from rolled slabs (Limoges porcelain body KPCL), perforated and painted to graphically define specific areas, fired in reduction to 1280°C in a gas kiln, by Horst Göbbels, 1992. This and similar works by Göbbels are often architectural symbols for towers, keeps, gates, pylons, etc. The perforations are intended to 'include the environment into the process of creating'.
Photograph by Wolf Böwig.

exclusively with precise geometric shapes made from thin, perfectly finished sheets of porcelain. A recurring theme is concerned with the subject of 'balance', physical, visual and aesthetic. Porcelain is the ideal material for her to use because, she says, it has a dense grain structure that allows her to make ultra thin sheets that are relatively strong and which become translucent when backlit. Linear elements, incised or in relief are drawn on the clay to complement the formal composition. The addition of wires and glass beads in some of Broekema's sculptures increases the impression of three-dimensional drawings in space. Feeling that some of her pieces seemed too severe she decided to introduce limited colour in an attempt to 'make them more dynamic' and light-hearted. Her paramount concern is to achieve 'harmony in form, composition and colour'.

Broekema rolls her slabs of porcelain by hand and cuts them into various geometric shapes. Surface reliefs are made by pressing cardboard 'stamps' into the thin sheets. Individual pieces that make up her sculptures are fired separately to 1240°C and then assembled and joined together with adhesives. Coloured lines and other selected areas are glazed with a mixture of frit and body stains. Her finished pieces have an air of cool, reserved, understated elegance about them. This is a sensation also generated by the slab sculptures of Horst Göbbels who constructs his pieces with tall, rectangular sheets which stand alone or quietly ranked beside each other as objects for contemplation. Sometimes his slabs are pierced with holes regularly spaced to define selected areas. The spectator's attention becomes focused on the material, the form and the action of light in equal measure.

Ceramics is a wonderfully versatile medium but the nature of clay is such that the size of any form made and fired in one piece has to be quite small when compared to objects fashioned from wood or metal. Greater scale can only be achieved by making and assembling a number of separate components. The possibilities then become infinite. The process of making and handling, the need to ensure the clay is completely dry before firing and, finally, the capacity of the kiln all impose restrictions on scale. Therefore, the impact of much sculptural work in ceramics is diminished due to its small size. If we do not know the true scale of some of the porcelain assemblages by **Margaret Realica** (USA) and illustrated in this book, for example, we can imagine them to be several metres high. We are aided in this respect by seeing them as photographs rather than the objects themselves. They could, indeed, serve as maquettes for more substantial constructions. Realica was born in England but now lives and works in California. 'Deconstruction and reconstruction' is a recurring theme in

73

much of her recent work. She draws on personal experiences in making these composite sculptures including images of bombed out buildings explored as a child. Giving an explanatory title to such works may help one to understand something of their origin and of the artist's intent. However, the objects are powerful enough to stand and be judged in their own right despite their small scale. She says that 'a piece of art should be able to stand alone, stripped of any verbal intervention. It should appeal to the eye, mind and spirit. Words should not be necessary.'

In Realica's 'Zone' series, angular structures pierce, define and dominate space with girder-like pieces of clay leaning against and supporting each other from opposing directions. Given no indication of actual size and seen only in illustration they assume magnificent proportions. Broader slabs set among the 'girders' suggest fragments of broken buildings precariously balanced between strong diagonals. These increase the feeling of violent destruction rather than gradual decay.

> My thinking and vision revolve around nature, the machine, the environment, human conditions, and experiences past and present. I work with the broken and the whole of these, the conflicts and incongruities, a world where the differences between the organic and

the mechanical have broken down. The challenge is still within the theme of opposites (like) past and present, but working towards a harmony of the two and reaching for the unexpected.

Incredibly, every single piece of Realica's work in porcelain is initially thrown on the wheel. Even the slabs are made from thrown cylinders. These are allowed to set slightly and the walls are further compressed with a rubber kidney tool while the wheel rotates. When the cylinders have stiffened to the point where they are no longer sticky to touch but still fairly soft they are removed from the

Porcelain Sculpture, 'Zone Series', thrown, altered and assembled, 20.4 cm by 18.5 cm approximately, by Margaret Realica, 1991. The slabs used in constructing this piece were thrown as thin-walled cylinders before being cut open and rolled out. This method helps to prevent warping. Glazes are sprayed on and parts airbrushed with metallic lustre. The individual pieces are assembled and cemented together after the firing to 1260°–1300°C in an electric kiln.
Photograph by Robert Aude.

'T/Pot' porcelain sculpture, thrown, altered and assembled, 28.5 cm by 17.7 cm, by Margaret Realica, 1988. The slabs are made from finely thrown cylinders which are cut with a sharp surgical knife and opened out when they have stiffened slightly. The various elements of the sculpture are cemented together after the final firing (1260°C–1300°C).
Photograph by Robert Aude.

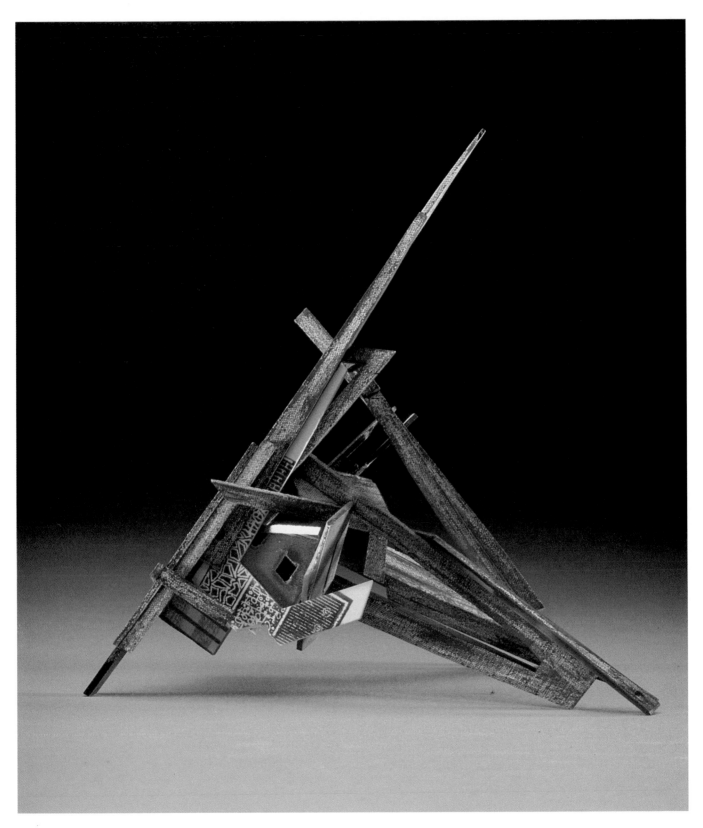

Porcelain Sculpture, 'Zone Series', thrown altered and assembled, 20.4 cm by 15 cm approximately, by Margaret Realica, 1990. The artist makes her slabs from cylinders thrown, using slip rather than water as a lubricant, which she cuts open and rolls out when slightly stiffened, in order to reduce the risk of warping. The pieces are fired separately and assembled after the final firing (electric kiln 1260°–1300°C) with adhesive.
Photograph by Robert Aude.

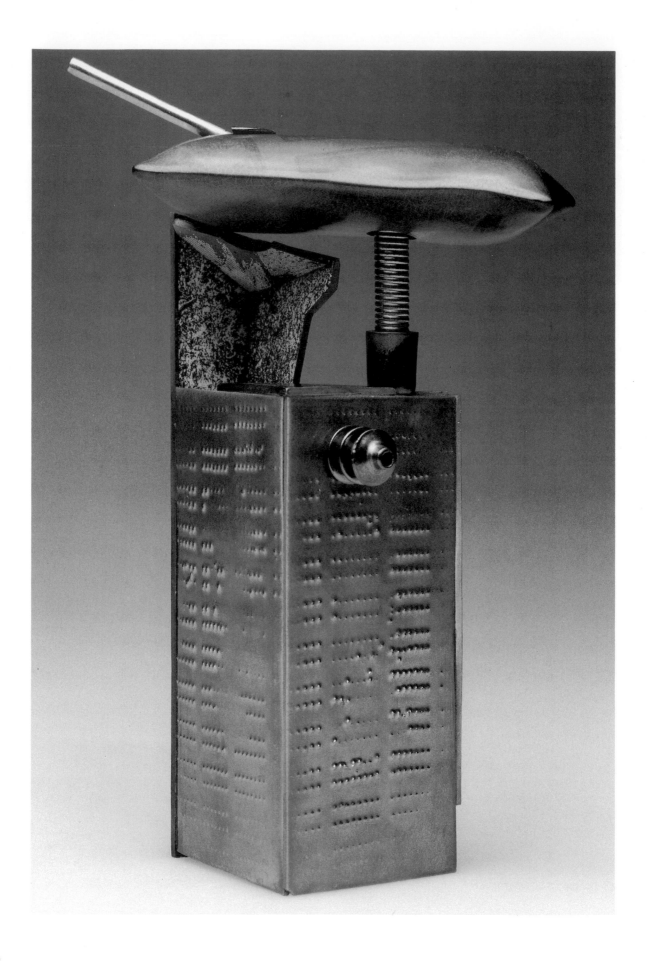

wheel, cut open with a surgical knife and rolled out flat. 'Rolling out thrown pieces produces finer slabs that warp much less and can hold their shape.' She finds that fewer stress cracks occur in slabs made this way and then combined with other thrown pieces. 'The procedure may seem a little lengthy but I find it actually saves time and it gives me a more polished, machined-like finish.' She feels that the action of pulling up the clay when throwing is more suited to the way she works rather than the heavier compression obtained by normal slab rolling.

In some of her porcelain sculptures, especially those based on the notional idea of teapots, Realica demonstrates the range of her technical skill by introducing convincing reproductions of machined metal objects like screws, threaded tubes and nut and bolts. The illusion is strengthened further by airbrushed metallic lustres. Her pieces are burnished with rubber when leatherhard and with a stone when dry. Bisque to 1060°C. Some parts are then glazed with either an opaque matt white or a bright white lithium glaze and fired in an electric kiln to between 1260° and 1300°C.

The porcelain sculptures of **Ruth Duckworth** (USA) cannot be easily classified. They grow out of a rich ceramic tradition but they stand alone being unlike other ceramic expressions from either the past or the present. Their subtlety and coolness owes something, perhaps, to her European background. Having fled Nazi Germany in 1936, she first studied sculpture, working mainly in wood and stone, in London. That previous experience as a sculptor was to stand her in good stead when she later made the transition into working with clay. In 1964 she moved to America to take up a teaching post at the University of Chicago and she has lived and worked in that city ever since. She managed to purchase an old factory building in 1982 and this was converted into a home with plenty of space for a large studio. This allowed her to work on a much larger scale. Several important architectural commissions soon followed and some of these have been illustrated in my previous books. However, it is her smaller pieces in unglazed white porcelain which, for the purposes of my current research, are worthy of particular attention. Some of these consist of an open topped, barrel-shaped form supporting a vertical slab which bisects the top and

'Crated Teapot', porcelain sculpture, 16.5 cm by 12.5 cm approximately by Margaret Realica, 1993. Each part of this work was first thrown as thin-walled cylinders and then cut and rolled out when stiffened slightly. Elements are fired separately and assembled after glaze firing in an electric kiln. Glazes are sprayed and lustres airbrushed.
Photograph by Robert Aude.

cuts part way down into the vessel walls. Another small bowl has one side cut away as a semicircular section to reveal a bulbous form split vertically into two parts, each of which sprouts a horizontal wing with subtle changes of plane. This piece may suggest plant growth or bones (especially vertebrae or ball and socket joints) and it would succeed equally if executed in bronze or polished brass but the smooth white surface of porcelain responds particularly well to the soft modelling action of light falling across it. Duckworth manages to distil the very essence of morphological experience and sensation into these undemonstrative abstract sculptures.

A different kind of expressive action is demonstrated by the work of **Wilma Selten** (Holland). She responds to the plastic properties of porcelain itself in producing a series of pieces made from finger-grooved sheets which she cuts

'Electric Teapot', porcelain sculpture, 24 cm by 17.5 cm by 7.5 cm approximately, by Margaret Realica, 1993. The elements which make up this work are all made from thrown pieces. Even the slabs are cut from thinly thrown cylinders, rolled out, and press moulded onto a 'found' computer board. Sprayed glazes and airbrushed metallic lustres are applied. The various parts are assembled and cemented together following the final firing.
Photograph by Robert Aude

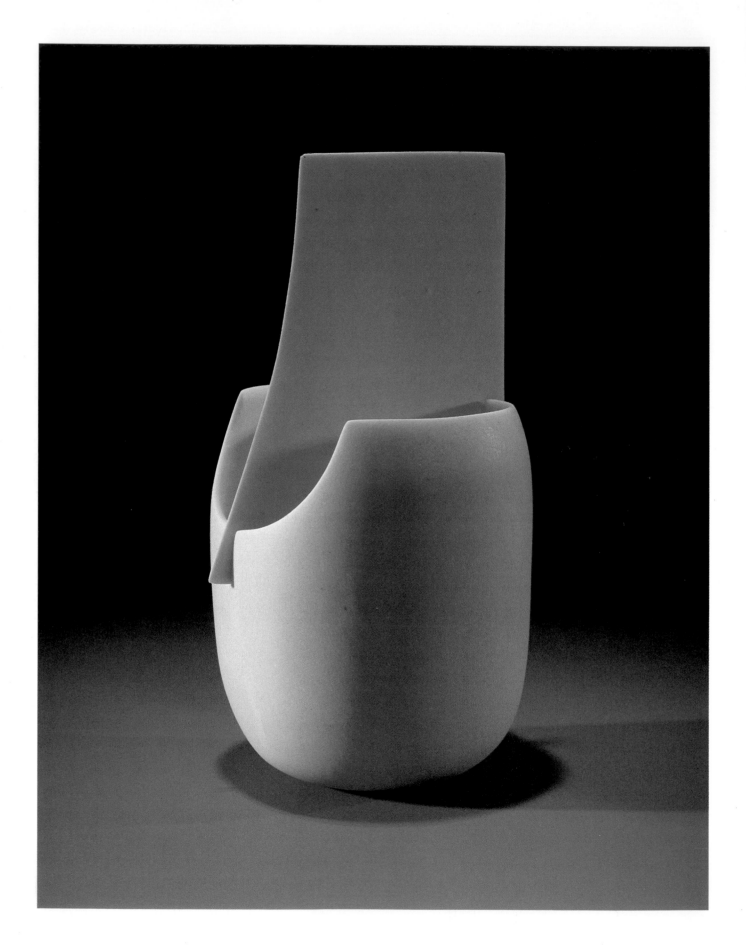

into strips and bends round spontaneously to link with others to create new forms.

Altering the physical properties of porcelain by mixing it with other materials has often provided a rich source of inspiration in itself. Stains and oxides are commonly used for coloured porcelain and grogs of various sizes are often added to strengthen the body for larger pieces or to supply textural interest, but mixing paper pulp 50/50 with the plastic clay offers exciting possibilities which several potters and sculptors are now exploiting. In Belgium, the sculptor, **Emile Desmedt**, uses 'porcelain paper' either on its own in smaller works or combined with other materials

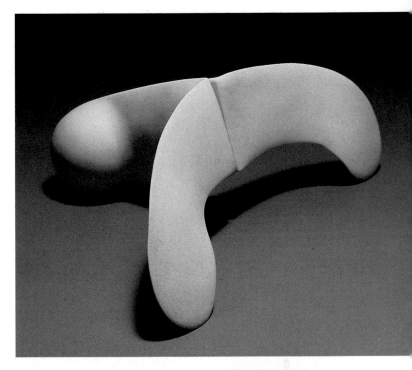

Porcelain sculpture (17 cm × 9 cm) by Ruth Duckworth, 1992.
Collection of Henry Rothschild. Photograph by Wolf Böwig.

Porcelain sculpture (10.5 cm × 29 cm × 19 cm) by Ruth Duckworth, 1993.
Photograph by Wolf Böwig.

Porcelain sculpture (17 cm × 20 cm) in three pieces by Ruth Duckworth, 1992.
Photograph by Wolf Böwig.

'Pink and Yellow Coiling', porcelain sculpture made from finger-grooved sheets sliced into straps and interlinked, by Wilma Selten Holland, 1992.

Spiral sculpture made from 'paper porcelain', 30 cm, by Emile Desjmedt, 1993. Porcelain slip is mixed with paper pulp to provide the basic material with which this piece was made.
Photograph by courtesy of Galerie La Main, Brussels.

in larger ones. His 'spiral' sculpture demonstrates the versatility of this adaption of the porcelain body.

Order and unpredictability come together in some of **Mary White's** sculptural work. In the early 1980s, she began to make organic forms in porcelain using the material rather like torn paper to be assembled in layers. Her ideas come from 'layers of rock on the seashore, shells, waves rippling over sand, and colours in the sea and sky. I like geometric forms which need skill in making and also freer organic forms which require imagination and even accident for their freshness. Sometimes, I can manage to combine these in one piece'. She returns again and again to the idea concept of 'craters'. She began making flanged bowls with cratered centres. These were followed by globe forms set into open-sided pyramids revealing craters which had coloured glass or mirrors at the bottom. 'Mystery fascinates me. I like to give people surprises. They see a simple shape, hold it in their hands and find something that involves them, perhaps a mirror that reflects their eye, or remove a lid from a box to find something unexpected inside.' The piece illustrated on page 81 is contained within a wooden box frame. The formality of the square frame draws attention to the irregular, cratered centre. We are invited to look into and past several separate, thin layers leading to the colour and reflections deep inside. A German quotation, beautifully lettered is visible beneath the top layer and encircling the crater. All her work is made from the well-known 'David Leach' porcelain body (which she colours with body stains to provide herself with a palette of almost 30 different shades) and fired to 1250°C in a small, top loading electric kiln.

Porcelain is an important constituent of the special body mixtures prepared by a number of ceramic sculptors who, rather than use porcelain alone, choose to combine it with white stonewares for one reason or another. Although this practice loses certain of those qualities we might reasonably expect to find in pure porcelain, its addition to other bodies can make a significant contribution to the character and appearance of a piece. **Mal Magson** (UK) has used porcelain in conjunction with 'T' material (a grogged white stoneware) or another white stoneware body which she colours with stains and oxides. The coloured clay and porcelain are laminated by repeatedly rolling and folding them together. Then the resulting agate slab is cut into slices and used to inlay patterns into other slabs of clay. Sometimes the agate becomes part of the wall so that the colours can be seen on both sides of the piece. 'Initially, I included porcelain in the mixture for its whiteness but that, for me, is the least interesting characteristic compared with the quality and nature of the surface it can produce. Vitrified

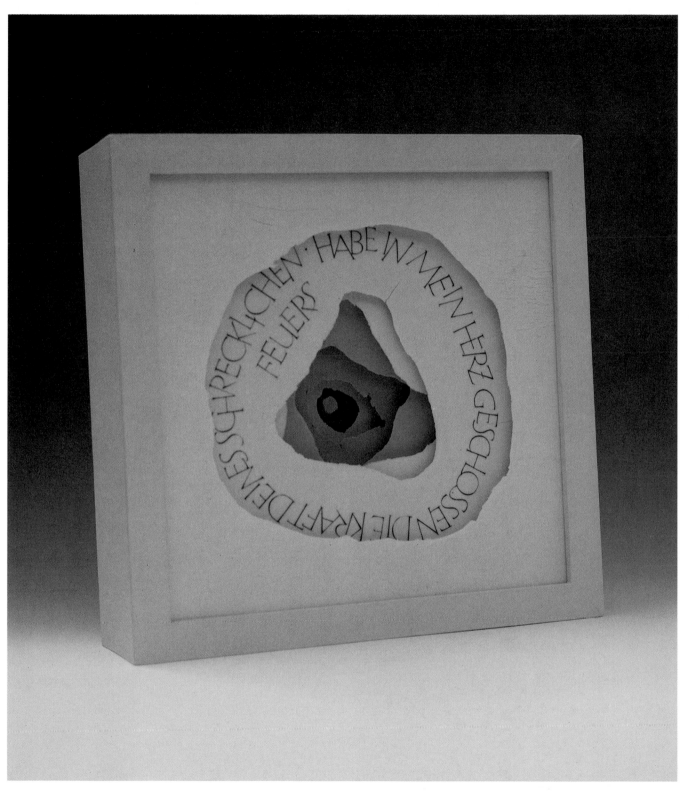

'Crater' sculpture made from thin sheets of unglazed porcelain in a wooden box frame, 26 cm × 26.3 cm, by Mary White, 1993. The centre of the crater is in coloured porcelain with a mirror mounted in the middle. The crater is inscribed with calligraphy, a quotation in German. Fired to 1250°C in an electric kiln.

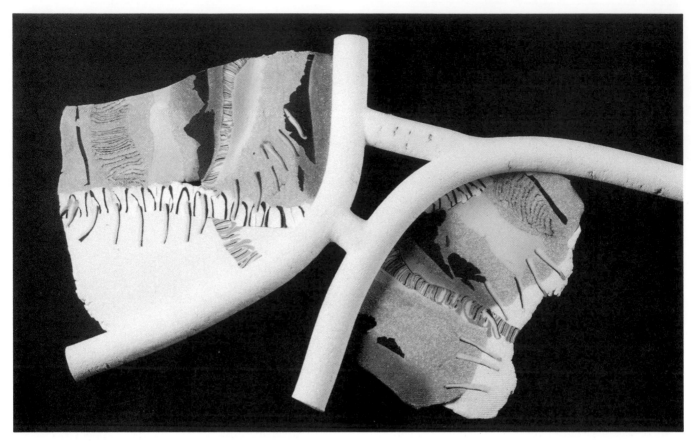

'Wall Piece', handbuilt in 'T' material with stoneware and porcelain inlay (elongated patches of porcelain is 'shadow' stained by copper contamination), 41 cm by 24 cm, fired to 1260°C, by Mal Magson, 1993.
Photograph by Andrew Morris.

porcelain has a slight sheen and a compact smoothness: a sensuous, tactile quality.' She says that she takes advantage of the way porcelain reacts when placed under, over or next to certain coloured clays to become 'suffused with shadows and dark haloes'. An extra depth is given to this suffusion of colour by the translucency of the porcelain which she finds especially appealing.

The most obvious and well-known problem experienced with the lamination of different clays i.e. splitting and separation, is manipulated and controlled by Magson to 'create a low relief across the surface of patterned areas similar to braille'. She has learnt which stains and oxides cause the greatest shrinkage to occur and which coloured bodies should not be placed next to one another to avoid splits and separation, although occasionally, splitting is encouraged to become part of the design.

Magson works on flat slabs using a roller to make a pattern surface or a laminated colour composition. These then become the basis for free-standing or press-moulded bowls. After drying thoroughly, the work is fired to a low bisque of 750°–800°C, so that it can be rubbed down with

'Wall Piece', handbuilt in stained stoneware and 'T' material with porcelain inlay, fired to 1260°C, 64 cm by 40 cm, by Mal Magson, 1993.
Photograph by Andrew Morris.

a fine grade of silicon carbide paper, followed by a final firing to between 1250°–1260°C according to the intensity or brightness of the colours required. 'The very special and characteristic qualities of porcelain are major elements in the aesthetic impact of my work.'

Porcelain is being increasingly used to make panels and wall sculptures some of which are quite substantial. Often, they are made up of a number of smaller elements for ease of handling and to avoid problems in drying and firing which can result in cracks appearing, but large panels can be made in one piece when the body recipe includes a proportion of bisqued porcelain ground into small particles as a grog to open up and to give support to the plastic material while working. Shrinkage and drying difficulties are thereby reduced.

Patchwork arrangements of flat porcelain tiles mounted on plywood cut to match the overall shape is the chosen method used by **Sylvia Hyman** (USA) to resolve some of her wall sculptures. Strong colours and positive patterns are organised by her so that they appear to overlap and counterchange and seem to be three-dimensional. To what extent these panels gain extra credence by virtue of being made from porcelain tiles rather than by direct painting in oils or acrylic on to board might be open to question but the artist has *chosen* to work in clay and to concentrate all her energies into controlling its behaviour. Hyman was trained originally as an art teacher specialising in painting and, like so many ceramicists who began working in other art disciplines, she found that 'clay was more enticing than paint' and she has remained with it ever since. The absence of a more formal training in ceramics encouraged her to discover how best to handle the medium as necessity demanded and, at the same time, she enjoyed the freedom to find her own means of expression. The more obviously organic nature of much of her earlier work in porcelain, some of which was illustrated in *Studio Porcelain*, arose out of the need to experiment with materials and techniques. Porcelain especially lent itself to a succession of sculptures inspired by 'spores and sperm and sexual selection' and which she called her *Sporophore and Sporophyll* series. These were composed of multiple sheets of thinly rolled porcelain mounted like wings on top of pedestals or bursting out of rounded, soft-looking forms in convoluted frills as if from a fruiting body. Some of her lively, tiled panels are made in white, unglazed porcelain reliefs with flowing ribbons of clay entangled with spiky growths casting complex shadows of varying depth. More recent work has given way to the exploration of new forms concerned with emotional aspects of human relationships and interpersonal communication. These consist of two or three separ-

'Patchwork' (Mixed Message Series), glazed porcelain tiles mounted on plywood, 41.5 cm × 47.5 cm, by Sylvia Hyman, 1989.
Photograph by John Cummings.

'Fading Memories' (Relationship Series), 45 cm × 37.5 cm × 26 cm, by Sylvia Hyman, 1992. Slab-built porcelain sculpture, bisque fired to cone 06 and then sanded smooth. Onglazes are sprayed directly on to unglazed areas over masks to produce the pattern before a final firing to 1200°C.
Photograph by John Cummings.

'Something in Common', slab-built porcelain sculpture sprayed with **overglazes**, 40 cm × 39.5 cm × 26.5 cm, fired to 1200°C in oxidation, by Sylvia Hyman, 1992.
Photograph by John Cummings.

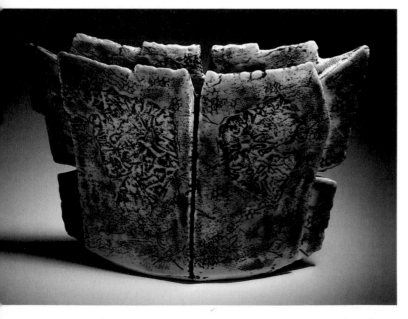

Handbuilt porcelain with impressed textures inlaid with coloured **ceramic** stains, unglazed by polished, reduction fired to 1320°C, 20 cm **high,** by Erik Pløen, 1993.
Photograph by Jan Enoksen.

ate but related forms grouped together on a flat base. The outer profile of the major pieces describes a simple and complete entity while the inner ones are individually contoured to express an aspect of communication or, in some cases, non-communication between them.

Hyman's sculptures are handbuilt from slabs of porcelain, bisque fired to cone 06 (approx. 1000°C) and sanded until absolutely smooth. They are mostly left unglazed with only small areas of glaze for accents and fired again to cones 5–6 (approx. 1190°C–1215°C) before spraying onglaze enamels directly on to unglazed areas (with some parts masked to remain white) and refiring, finally, at low temperature.

Handbuilding is the method preferred by **Erik Pløen** (Norway) for his richly textured slab-sided forms. The distinctive surfaces of his porcelain objects are impressed and inlaid with ceramic stains of different colours to emphasise the texture. The pieces are left unglazed and fired to 1320°C before 'polishing' with silicon carbide paper. A reduction atmosphere is induced when the kiln temperature has reached 950°C and continued until the end of the firing. This process gives the porcelain an attractive, bone-like finish which is pleasant to touch. Pløen has not used glazes on his work for some time because he finds that the Limoges porcelain (HPB) is well-suited for his coloured textural pieces. He is not concerned with translucency and he improves the body further for sculptural work by adding five per cent Molochite (passed through an 80s mesh sieve) to prevent cracking and excessive shrinkage. This addition has no effect on the whiteness but he stresses the importance of firing it in a reduction atmosphere.

Pløen has two workshops, both by the sea. The main one is in Son, a small fishing village by Oslo Fiord while the other is on a skerry (a small island) in the North Sea, so nature has a great influence upon the way he thinks and works. Pebbles on the beach, rock strata with its cracks and cavities, and conglomerates of shells provided the stimulus which led to the pieces illustrated here. Sea creatures are also a rich source for ideas and it was a flounder, with its flattened form and strong pattern, that prompted the piece on page 37.

A combination of throwing and handbuilding is used by **Ingvil Havrevold** (Norway) to create her sculptural objects and, like her partner Pløen, she also adds textural interest to her work but in a different way. She applies layers of porcelain slip to enliven the surface which is then covered with a coloured glaze based on nepheline syenite. The pieces are fired in oxidation to 1280°C. The body used is exactly the same as Pløen's including the addition of Molochite. She can sometimes trace the source of a particu-

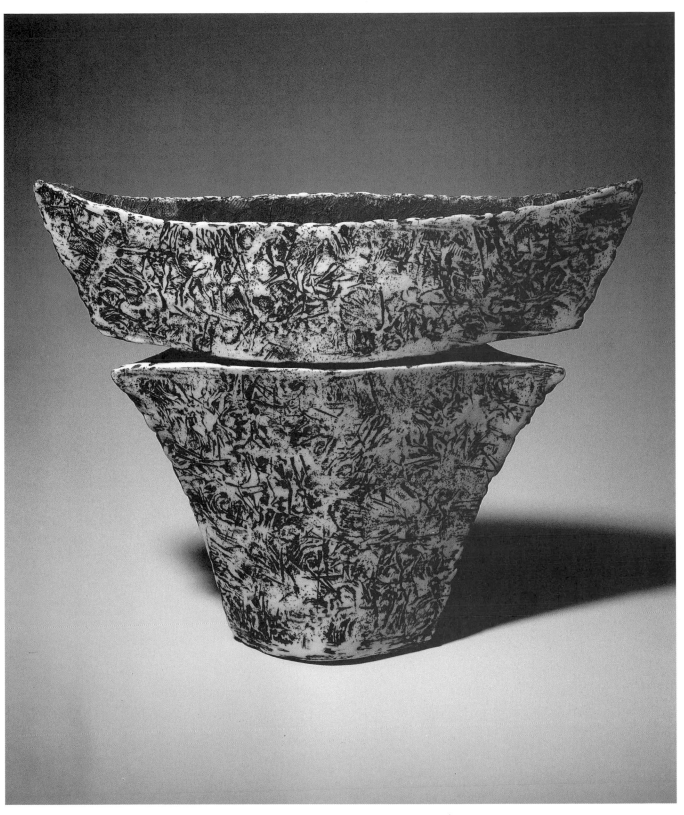

Vessel Form, handbuilt porcelain with impressed texture inlaid with ceramic stains, unglazed but polished, fired to 1320°C in reduction, 30 cm high, by Erik Pløen, 1993.
Photograph by Jan Enoksen.

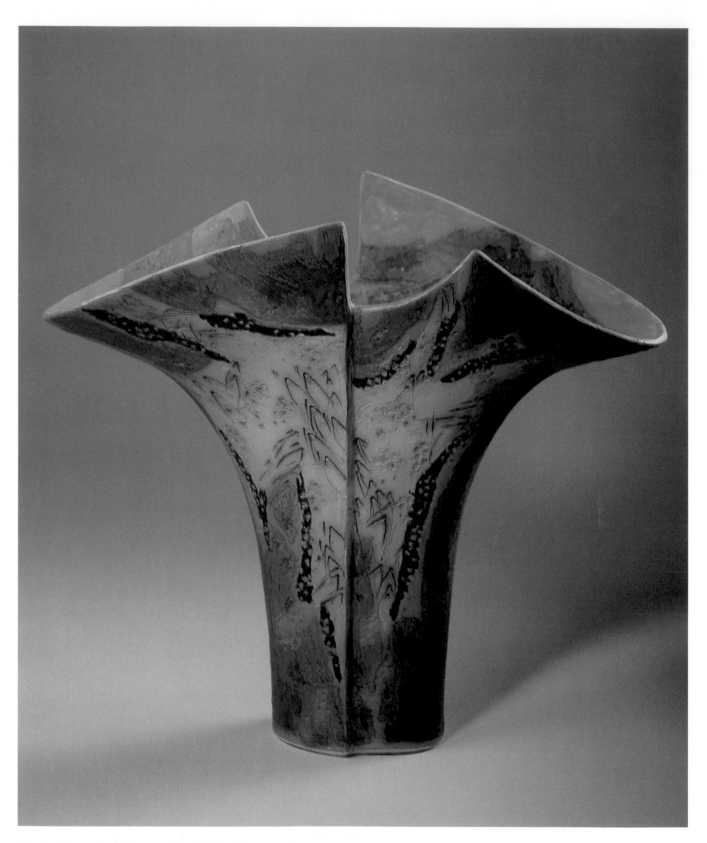

Porcelain Form, wheel-thrown and handbuilt, with impressed texture
inlaid with coloured nepheline syenite glazes and parts left unglazed,
fired to 1280°C in oxidation, 28 cm high, by Ingvil Havrevold, 1993.
Photograph by Jan Enoksen.

lar idea developed in clay but much of her work is intuitive. Like Pløen she too looks constantly to nature. 'I enjoy sitting on a rock looking out to sea, especially in a stormy wind with the sea and clouds in constant motion' (see illustration opposite). She also refers to the influence of landscapes and trees upon her thinking. 'In early spring, the birch has a fascinating lilac shimmer around the stem and branches' (see illustration on this page). 'I can remember the first photograph of the earth taken from space in 1968. It was very impressive and it has given me much inspiration'.

Unusual and exciting porcelain sculptural pieces, possessing elements of the kind of rhythmic geometry often found in natural forms, have been developed by **Peter Masters** (Australia). These pieces, which have no other function but to occupy space while delighting the eye, are executed with a high degree of mathematical precision that gives them a strong, tactile appeal. Despite the strict organisation necessary to achieve the precise placement of the individually applied clay balls or spikes, Masters works intuitively, relying solely upon the accuracy of his eye to judge the exact relationship of each to the others within the overall pattern. The spiral movements created with these additions energise the forms and call to mind similar patterns in nature such as cacti and sunflower seedheads without being in any sense imitative. He explains his concept of these forms as having a basic volume resembling, perhaps, a turnip or a bean, but he has 'attempted to transcend any association with recognisable species. Thus the environments in which these forms might exist may be earthly, but certainly not domesticated. However, a viewer may still feel that these forms are not of this world, and this is perfectly acceptable, because their origins could indeed be cosmic.'

The basic spheres and ovoids are either wheel-thrown (for smaller pieces than 50 cm (approx. 20 in.) in diameter) or coiled, to produce a domed 'onion' shape with thick walls that can be turned when leatherhard and refined to fit the precise curvature required for each piece. The spikes are made separately by rolling between forefinger and thumb, grading their sizes and spacing according to where they

Porcelain Form, made from wheel-thrown and slab-built elements. 23 cm high, by Ingvil Havrevold, 1993. Texture is created by the application of slip in various ways. Coloured nepheline syenite-based glaze fired to 1280°C in an oxidising atmosphere.
Photograph by Jan Eriksen.

Goblet, wheel-thrown, with handbuilt stem, 22 cm high, by Peter Masters, 1989.

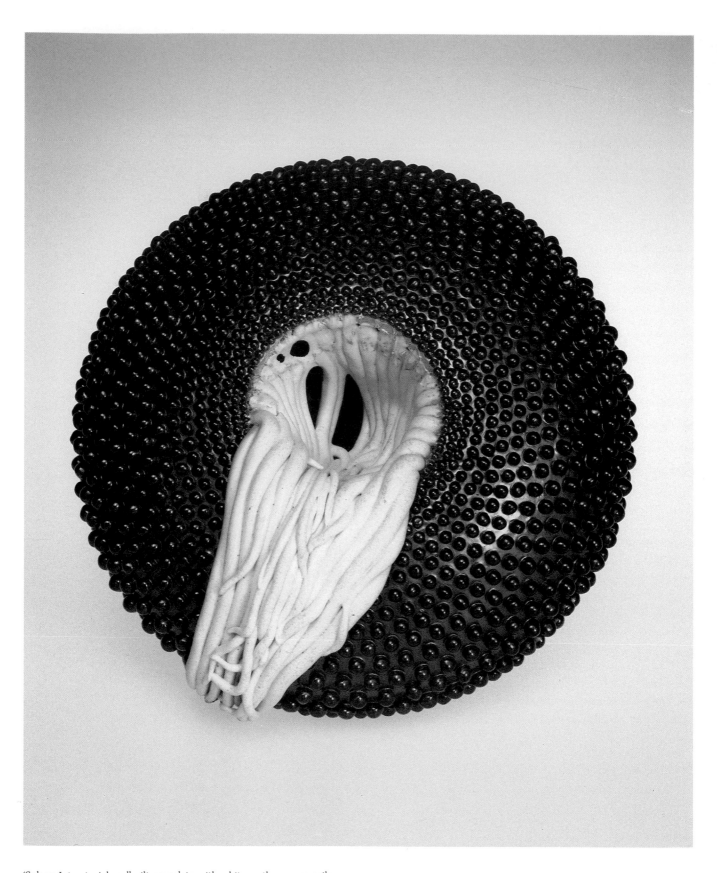

'Sphere Intrusion', handbuilt porcelain with white earthernware coils,
30 cm diameter, saltglazed, 1990, by Peter Masters.

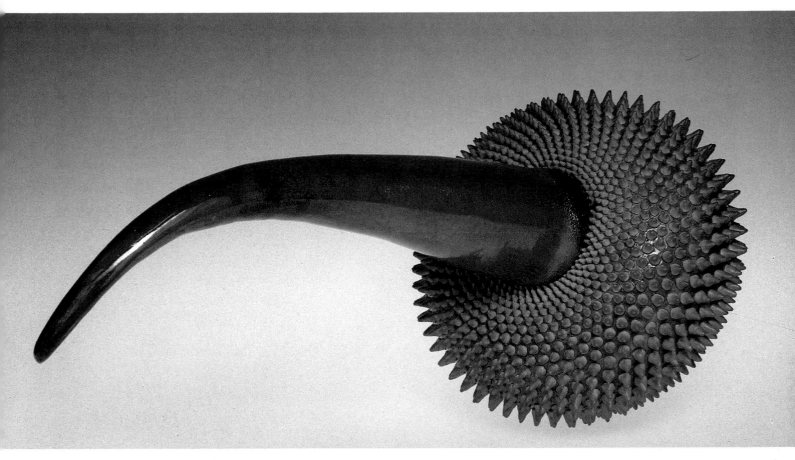

are to be arranged on the main form, becoming smaller and more tightly packed towards the top and bottom. The repetition of so many small units produces an appearance of considerable complexity.

Masters has created many 'growth' forms incorporating patterned surfaces which have evolved intuitively. He has always been fascinated by the sea and sea life and by growth patterns in nature, and he is 'awed by gigantic vegetables like marrows and squash'. He describes the forms he makes as

consisting of a spherical shell with a relatively short, tapered extension referred to as the 'ovoid' (resembling perhaps the subterranean part of a turnip) and a singular projection, either extending into free space or rejoining the ovoid. Having only two contact points with the supporting surface, they are very dynamic, primary forms with visual rotational instability. They vary in size from about 20 cm to 60 cm (8 in. to 24 in.) in diameter. The ovoids have a high relief surface pattern of balls or spikes. Thus, there is a very active secondary

Bowl constructed in a complex open mesh pattern from extruded coils of porcelain, 47 cm × 40 cm, by Netty Van Den Heuvel, 1991.

'Protrusion' handbuilt porcelain sphere with earthenware spike (approximately 67 cm) by Peter Masters, 1990. The surface is enriched with individually applied pieces built up into a strong pattern resembling growth progressions developed in nature. Slips and oxides are sprayed on with an airbrush or an atomiser. The piece is salt glaze fired in a natural gas downdraught kiln. The atmosphere is oxidised to give brighter colours.

movement. With some patterns, incorporating holes or additional inserts in the balls or spikes, a tertiary movement takes place. The forms are high-fired and sodium vapour glazed giving them very luminous, and contrasting, matt surfaces with brightness or colour. The main hues are yellows, greens, blues, browns and pinks on a white porcelain ground.

The kiln is often cooled slowly to encourage crystallisation to take place in rutile slips and oxides.

Although he believed that nothing could be totally new, and had often suggested to his students that generating ideas for design was rather like taking water from an eternal source such as a mountain stream ('the same water but always fresh'), Masters had felt, initially, that his 'protrusions and intrusions' were in some way 'original'. However, he was 'not surprised to find several historical examples of pots including more contemporary work of noted ceramicists like France's Francine del Pierre and Emile Decoeur which employ similar use of pattern'. Further research led him to the mathematical work of Leonardo and others relating to numerical sequences to be found in nature.

Repeated linear elements form the basis of the amazingly complicated grid-like structures by **Netty Van den Heuvel** (Holland). Building constructions and the geometry of micro-organisms provide her with a constant

'Wall Ball', press-moulded sculpture in Limoges porcelain body (TM10) fired to 1260°C in a reducing atmosphere, 22 cm × 11 cm, by Netty Van Den Heuvel, 1991.

Porcelain sculpture 'Zonder Titel', constructed, layer by layer, from extruded coils of Limoges porcelain body (TM10) fired in reduction to 1260°C to obtain the colder bluish-white, 37 cm × 36 cm × 36 cm, by Netty Van Den Heuvel, 1992.

'Sailing Vessel' by Lara Scobie 1993, 58 cm × 27 cm × 20 cm. Handbuilt from layers of thinly rolled sheets of porcelain. The texture is enhanced by brushing oxides and underglaze stains over it and then sponging the surplus away to leave a residue in the depressions.

source of reference and fascination. She begins by preparing a drawn plan to work out a pattern for the grid. The three-dimensional form is built up with individual units or ribs of extruded porcelain attached to specific points to create a complex, but highly ordered, arrangement of connecting lines defining space. These pieces are made with Limoges porcelain body (LM10) and fired in reduction to 1260°C in order to obtain a bluish white colour.

The multiplication of units of similar shape but varying in size contribute to the imaginative porcelain sculptural objects by **Lara Scobie** (UK). Her forms are intricately constructed by building up complex layers of thinly rolled clay. Small strips are torn from thin sheets of porcelain and then pressed into an Indian printing block, of which she has a small collection, so that the resulting textured piece is incorporated into the design. Ropes and scrolls of clay are added to the assemblage, each unit helping to create a three-dimensional composition rich in texture, pattern and visual interest. These wonderfully evocative sculptures are bisque fired to 1000°C before oxides and underglaze stains are applied in broad washes of colour with a large brush. Sponging some of the colour away subsequently leaves deposits to pick out and give emphasis to the impressed textures. Several layers of colour are built up in this process. Finally, a large brush dipped into a transparent glaze is swept over the form and fired to 1300°C . Earlier pieces were subjected to a reduction atmosphere but she experienced increasing problems with cracking and warping

'Basket', by Lara Scobie 1993. Constructed by building up layers of thinly rolled porcelain. Texture is produced by pressing the clay into old Indian printing blocks. Colour is inlaid into the textures by brushing oxides and underglaze stains into it and then sponging away to leave a residue in the depressions.

which have been overcome to a large extent by changing to electric kiln firing. Scobie says that this has had an added bonus in that the porcelain retains its pure whiteness 'which gives it a lovely sparkle'.

Scobie's involvement with the material is somewhat unconventional but she was attracted to its use by its inherent fragility and its response to working in fine detail. Whilst she wanted to incorporate these qualities in her work she also felt a need to react against 'much of what is stands for'. Her ideas have evolved through the working processes.

> The suppleness and plasticity allows me to stretch and bend each tiny element, and to build up many layers of delicately patterned clay. The works are my interpretations of various objects both real and imaginary while incorporating relative symbols into the design to give the piece a unique identity and a true sense of worth and meaning.

The unique porcelain figures by **Richard Shaw** (USA) are skilfully assembled from slipcast elements that imitate a wide range of found objects. The transfer-printed, individ-

Top 'Steamship Jar', slipcast porcelain, 53 cm × 15 cm × 10 cm, by Richard Shaw, 1993.

Left 'Seated Figure with Grey Head', slipcast porcelain, 52.5 cm high, by Richard Shaw, 1985.

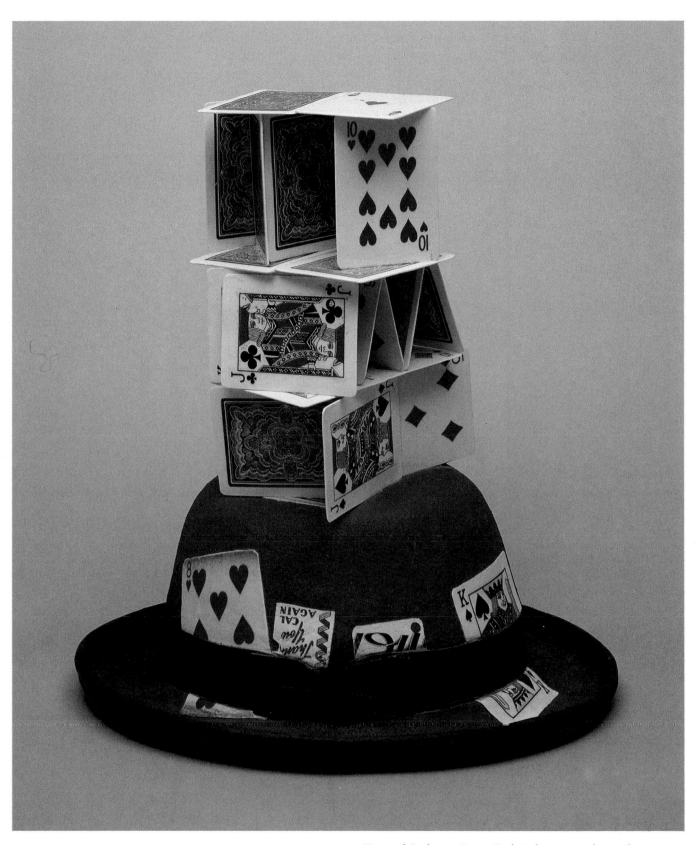

'House of Cards on a Brown Derby', slipcast porcelain with ceramic
decals, 40 cm × 25.5 cm × 28 cm, by Richard Shaw, 1993.
Photograph by Lewis Watts.

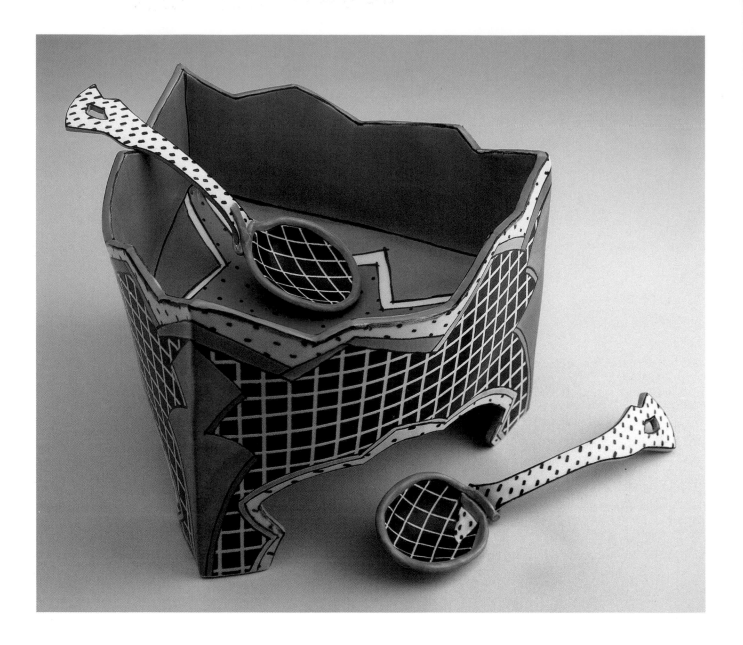

ual parts which he uses to make up his forms are disturbingly realistic representations of familiar domestic items like jars, tins, books, chairs, twigs and other pieces of wood. He explains that

> ceramic decals offer several advantages which can't be obtained with hand decoration of a ceramic piece. Most obvious is the ability to make two or more copies of a particular design. Another advantage is the possibility of doing a drawing on paper, reproducing it through a printing process, and applying it to the work as a decal instead of drawing directly on the piece. Reproduction of photographs and found two-dimensional material can be obtained through the use of ceramic decals.

(See page 143 for further information on the preparation of ceramic decals.)

Vessel forms

Ceramicists frequently take a vessel form as their starting point to develop ideas. In some instances, the functional aspect of the form as a container remains, in others it may have completely disappeared. The teapot towers made by **Jane Smith** (UK) are sculptural, decorative *and* functional objects. They are partly thrown with handbuilt additions. The example illustrated shows four teapots stacked one upon another in ever decreasing size with spouts and hand-

Left 'Pasta Server with Two Spoons', porcelain with underglaze decoration, by Dorothy Hafner (USA), 1984.
Photograph by S. Baker Vail.

Above 'Teapot Tower', four 'dragon' teapots, wheel-thrown porcelain, carved and incised under a celadon glaze, mounted on a carved plinth and stacked one upon another to a total height of 25 cm with the largest being 19 cm wide, by Jane Smith, 1993.
Photograph by Andrew Morris.

pots equipped with spouts, handles and lids attached to a larger shape is merely the inception for the exploration and resolution of a new three-dimensional form. Their flat sides present broad areas for pattern or texture but Peach chooses to treat them boldly in geometric arrangements of colour outlined with narrow strips of white. The division of these flat areas is almost architectural in appearance with strong linear elements strategically placed at positive angles as if lending structural support to the piece. The colours are applied as underglazes and glazes by brushwork and then fired at a relatively low temperature in an electric kiln to cone 5 (around 1190°C).

The whiteness of porcelain holds attractions for those potters who do not necessarily wish to fire it to its traditional and more usual high-maturing temperature. Firing porcelain bodies in sawdust at relatively low temperatures well under 1000°C (after an initial bisque firing around 1040°C) appeals to some because certain colour effects and surface flashing from smoke and the reaction with metallic salts can be obtained. A fair amount is inevitably left to chance in this process and the ware is usually only decorative due to its comparative fragility. **Shellie Jacobson** (USA) makes sculptural vessel forms by handbuilding from slabs of porcelain and firing in a simple sawdust kiln. She tries to obtain the maximum effect from the simplest applications. She says that

for glazes, I use both raku and low fire recipes, especially ones with copper as they respond well to the reduction atmosphere in the sawdust fire. I also use a moderate solution of sulfates (about 5 g in half a cup of warm

Teapot and stand, semi-functional. 18 cm × 13 cm × 12 cm by Dianne Peach, 1993. Slipcast porcelain assembly with underglaze colours and glaze brushwork. Fired in an electric kiln to cone 5.
Photograph by Dianne Peach.

les aligned. The spouts are fashioned into the necks and heads of mythical dragons whose tails curl round to act as handles. The 'tower' is supported by a pierced and carved stand made from an inverted bowl. A pale blue celadon-type glaze gathers in the depressions and enhances the delicate modelling and impressed textures. Smith's delight in both her subject and in the use of porcelain shines through this piece and brings a smile to most observers.

The teapots by **Dianne Peach** (Australia) are very different in character. They are assembled from slipcast porcelain sections and she describes them as either semi-functional or non-functional. The notion of traditional tea-

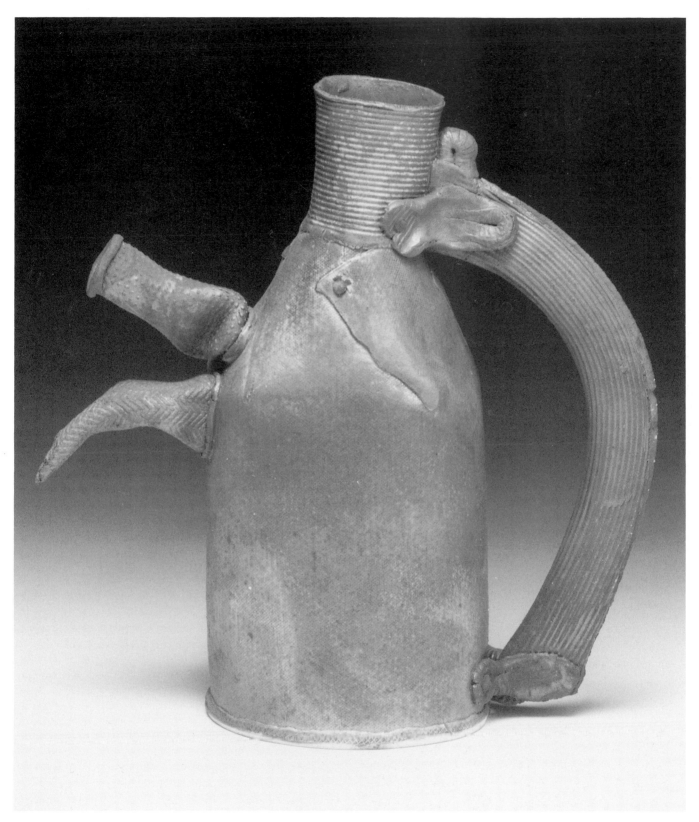

Left 'Viking II' by Shellie Jacobson, 1993. Handbuilt porcelain body with glazes, stains and metal additions. Bisque and glaze fired to cone 04 and reduced in sawdust, 14.5 high.
Photograph by Philip W. Smith.

Above Ewer, handbuilt porcelain body with glazes, stains and metal additions, bisque and glaze fired to cone 04 and reduced in sawdust, 19.5 cm high, by Shellie Jacobson, 1993.
Photograph by Philip W. Smith.

water) which can be brushed or sprayed. My cone 04 firing temperature is the same for both bisque and glaze. This leaves the body open for the subsequent reduction fire, but still strong enough to withstand the thermal extremes of it.

A completely different approach to the *concept* of functionality as the starting point for creating forms in clay can be seen in the work by **David Jones** (UK). In this case, porcelain is merely a constituent part of the plastic body which can contain anything between 15 per cent and 50 per cent of Molochite (a porcelain grog) or 'T' material. Porcelain, as a clay body, he says has always held a special fascination for him

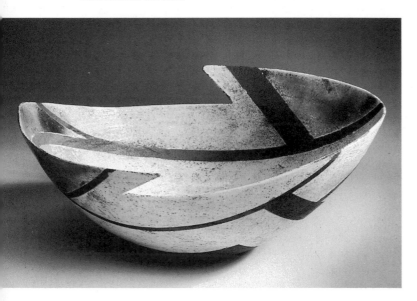

Raku fired porcelain bowls (1100°C) with lustres containing gold, silver and copper, by David Jones.

because it brings with it an aura of purity and refinement. This gives an axis on which to build and from which to rebel. My work has always been concerned with precision and the precious, or their opposites. Thus, a fine white body which will accept pure colours and lustres is very valuable. Originally, I was fascinated by a clay that would become translucent with heat, and I evolved a dialogue on the surface between a painted pattern and a revealed (thin) skin of translucent clay. I was dissatisfied with the (technically) superficial lustre on top of the glaze and was very excited by the opportunity to create in-glaze lustres using the raku process. I have slightly modified the body by using a mix of porcelain and molochite or 'T' material. The clay is still pyroplastic at the relatively low temperatures at which I now fire, and it is possible to deform the bowls by firing

them on their edge in order to hint at the transforming experience undergone by the pot in the kiln.

I have tried to establish a balance in my work between expressing a set of ideas in clay, i.e. comments on the material, and *the ceramic tradition*; that is the line from primitive utensils for everyday consumption of food and drink to objects for the court, for museums, or for the contemporary collector to whom function is not a necessary quality. The themes that I have used are very much centred on the Far Eastern ceramic tradition and the bowls that I make are a comment upon a Sung bowl or one from Arita. This has been mediated in recent years by a growing fascination with raku and, thereby, the vessels of the Japanese Tea Ceremony. In many respects, this tradition sets out to be the antithesis of court porcelain. It is a celebration of crude and spontaneous handling of clay, of directness and of accident. It is a naturalness that is highly refined. The attention given to the undulating rim and to the carving of the foot places this activity in exactly the same category as other court arts in demanding a highly educated audience to appreciate the nuances of the pots. In my raku work, although I start with a white porcellanous body (which is ideal for colour development) the unglazed areas of the pots end up black as a result of secondary reduction. Thus the colour of the body of a bowl is in complete contrast to that of a Ming bowl. It is important to me that this difference should be so dramatic.

Jones is now attempting to address another tradition through his work, that of industrially-made porcelain and bone china of the 18th and 19th centuries, while casting 'an oblique glance at the products of Wedgwood and Thomas'. He describes them as 'vessels associated with the "English Tea Ceremony". I use this phrase to deliberately echo the Japanese for it had a code of behaviour, equally as rigorous, regarding how the beverage should be served and consumed. Indeed, the arcane natures of both traditions as to the steeping of the leaves seem very similar in their pernicketiness.'

The 'Fin Pot' by **Eileen Lewenstein** (UK) illustrated on page 100, has more than a passing resemblance to the traditional teapot but the winged additions serve no other purpose than to extend the basic form of the spherical container and thus alter its character. For her 'Triptych' she has again taken a simple form, the cylinder, which is thrown and altered in an unusual way. Three cylindrical pots have been adjusted to a flattened oval section and then pressure is applied alternately inwards and outwards along vertical edges so that the pots complement and relate to each other when they are placed in a line (see page 100).

Emmanuel Cooper (UK) also refers to vessel forms for continuing inspiration, in particular, a series of teapots, jugs, bowls, vases and lidded boxes, all of which are related to domestic function and to the traditional role of the potter as artisan. Cooper stresses the idea that a vessel should be an object of interest in its own right in addition to any purpose it may serve as a container. In discussing his work, he mentions 'anthropomorhic references' and his feelings for his jug forms and flared vases that 'seem to be

Above 'Deconstructed Tea Set', porcelain mixed with 'T' material, thrown and altered with slab additions and raku fired lustres (1100°C), by David Jones.

Right Teapot, 20 cm high, by Pam Korte (USA), 1993. Porcelain, thrown and handbuilt elements, with impressed decoration. Fired to 1280°C in an electric kiln.
Photograph by Ron Forth.

like people or animals. Some are tall and skinny, reminiscent of greyhounds or athletes while others are more sturdy and approachable, but all assert their own personality.' These pieces are partly handbuilt and assembled from several parts to break away from the complete domination of the wheel'. He uses glazes 'whether smooth and "wet" or with crusty, textured, dry surfaces in an attempt to form one seamless whole'. He is attracted to porcelain whether it is used alone or opened up with fine alumina hydrate because it allows him to produce a variety of intense colours that would not be possible in stoneware.

Top
'Triptych', three related pots, porcelain, thrown and altered, 20 cm high, fired in an electric kiln to 1250°C, by Eileen Lewenstein, 1988. *Collection of International Academy of Ceramics, Geneva.*

Left 'Fin Pot' vessel in the form of a teapot, thrown and handbuilt porcelain, with dark blue glaze fired to 1250°C in an electric kiln, by Eileen Lewenstein, 1990.

Porcelain vessels with undulating profiles, blue glaze fired to 1250°C in an electric kiln, tallest 40 cm, by Eileen Lewenstein, 1990.

Above 'Night Sky' (back) and 'Winter Sky' (front) by Emmanuel Cooper, 1993. Porcelain jug forms thrown in two sections and joined together. 'Night Sky' (28 cm high) has a dolomite glaze with painted oxide decoration, 'Winter Sky' (20.5 cm high) has zinc oxide/porcelain slip under a barium carbonate/zinc oxide with nickel oxide glaze. Fired in an electric kiln to 1260°C.

Opposite 'Folded Bowl', by Andrea Hylands, 1992. Bone china, slipcast and handbuilt, with airbrushed colour. 27 cm high × 31 cm wide. Fired in an electric kiln to 1240°C. The piece is 'wet and dry polished after firing to achieve a sheen'. This piece is one of a series in which lines and edges are of aesthetic and tactile importance.

Some of the most unusual and exciting work currently being produced in porcelain and bone china with reference to vessels is that by **Andrea Hylands** (Australia). She was born in Britain but studied at Latrobe University College in Northern Victoria where she obtained her BA (ceramics) degree and her present studio was established in 1984 at Chewton in central Victoria. The originality and high quality of her work was duly acknowledged in 1992 when she was the Joint Grand Prize winner at the 13th Biennale Internationale de Ceramique d'Art at Vallauris in France. Apart from its obvious visual relationship to vessels, Hylands' work is almost impossible to categorise. It can be analysed, of course, in terms of geometric shapes assembled in various proportions and combinations while their surfaces can be appreciated for their colours, patterns and textures, but, beyond that, her works have more eloquence than can be expressed merely in words. They seem to be of an unreality given concrete form.

Hylands describes the absolute whiteness of bone china as being 'ideal for the application of colour'. She combines both slipcasting and handbuilding in the construction of her pots but few clues remain to inform us of their origins or of the techniques used to arrive at the finished piece. Ceramic stains are mixed with frits or with porcelain and bone china slip and airbrushed to give a flat expanse of colour before bisque firing. Further colours are then applied over stencils in preparation for the final firing which is conducted in an electric kiln to around 1220°C with a half hour soak at the top temperature. Then the work is polished with silicon carbide paper, wet and dry, to achieve a surface sheen.

She explains that most of her work still relates to a vessel:

The vessel has an important physical function: that is one of containing. This function, owing to its familiarity, has a strong point of contact with an audience. The folded bowls are a series I am still continuing to make. Lines and edges are prominent qualities in my work and I allude to feeling and touching. The starting point for basic shapes depends on previous work. I do not jump around from shape to shape arbitrarily, but simply evolve and modify ideas for forms. I enjoy making them look as if they have not been made from clay.

The latest series is about reinterpreting the pot in an abstract way. These vessels are the products of an intricate process and they have been complicated and enriched with decoration and embellishment. Using distortion and deception places them between the ordinary and extraordinary, revealing some ambiguity of purpose. There is no overt symbolism in my pieces, but the familiar is turned into surprise, exaggerating the surreal aspect of a pot as opposed to a pot as a commonplace object. In the later series of abstract vessels, I have

Above Two porcelain jug forms with 'insert' spouts, by Sandy Simon (USA), 1986.

Left 'Cup on Pedestal', porcelain, slipcast and handbuilt, 32 cm high, fired in an electric kiln to 1240°C, by Andrea Hylands.

Right 'Vessel with Handles', by Andrea Hylands, 1992. Porcelain, slipcast and handbuilt. The first layer of colour is applied and bisque fired before stencils and airbrushed colours are used to complete the surface design. 52 cm high. Fired to 1240°C in an electric kiln.

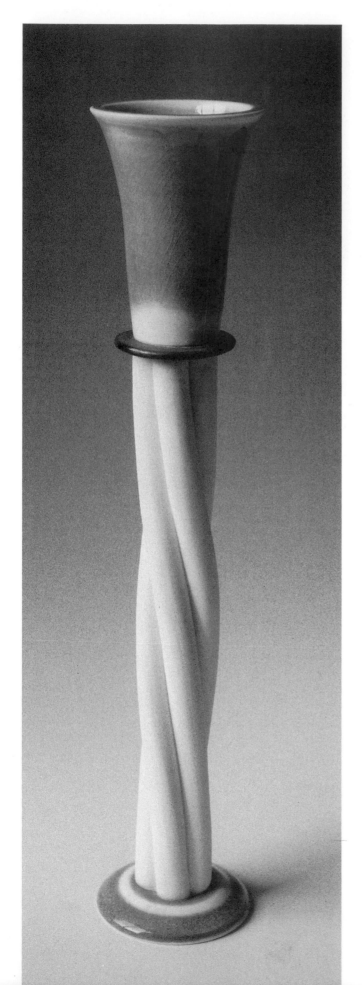

increased the scale of the work and some of my new forms are a metre high.

Maria Bofill (Spain) is another porcelain potter who uses distortion and exaggeration in her forms which claim only tenuous association with traditional vessels. Elevated cup shapes balance precariously on tall, undulating or twisted stems whose tiny bases seem barely capable of holding them still. She creates objects 'without function; it is a search fluctuating between the classical and the contemporary. I do not want to attain perfection: on the contrary, I love natural and living things.' She likes to make forms that appear to be in motion and she considers her pieces to be 'small, Mediterranean architectonic objects'. She is particularly interested in goblets, columns and capi-

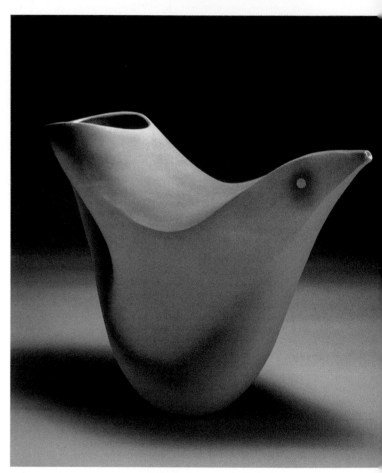

Porcelain jug in the form of a bird by Peter Lane, 25 cm high, 1991. Wheel-thrown and altered while still wet, airbrushed with underglaze stains on the bisque and fired to 1240°C in an electric kiln.

Left   Goblet form with a tall stem of twisted coils, porcelain, 38 cm high, reduction fired to 1280°C in a gas kiln, by Maria Bofill, 1993.

Right   Two tall 'goblet' forms, porcelain, wheel-thrown with handbuilt additions, 39 cm and 28.5 cm high, fired in reduction (gas kiln) to 1280°C, by Maria Bofill, 1993.

A group of slipcast porcelain vessels with carved rims, glazed inside but with polished exteriors by David Fink (USA), 1993. Tallest approximately 31 cm.

tals and often starts work with a clear idea of the form in mind but this may undergo modification during the creative process.

Bofill uses the wheel and, also, slabs to produce her pieces.

After an idea has taken shape, I make each of the various elements separately. I am always working on several pieces at the same time. Firing of these elements is also done separately and it is only after the second firing that I decide on the definitive shape of the piece. Mounting them is complicated. It is, in a way, the creation of an architectural structure: placing and removing the parts,

examining and combining the different elements until a satisfactory shape is achieved. This may be the original idea or not. Problems arising during the work with porcelain often give me new ideas for further pieces.

Glazed work is fired in a gas kiln and subjected to a reducing atmosphere to 1280°C , while those pieces which are decorated with engobes are fired in an electric kiln in oxidation to 1240°C.

Working to a particular theme concentrates the mind wonderfully. This may involve examining a certain form and trying to discover various options and nuances that give it fresh life and interest. Changing between techniques of making, decorating, glazing or firing may spark off new ideas or inspiration may be stimulated by the struggle to resolve problems of design or those judged to be inherent in the material itself. Certainly, it was an invitation to take part in an exhibition entitled '101 Jugs' that made me address myself freely to a vessel form that rarely figured in my repertoire. I approached the subject in a light-hearted way with function as only a minor consideration. Having decided to work in porcelain, I threw a tall V-shaped bowl about 30 cm (12 in.) high with walls no more than 4 mm ($\frac{1}{4}$ in.) thick. Realising that the piece was close to collapse towards the end of the throwing cycle, I encouraged opposing sides to fall inwards until they met in the middle while the clay was still very wet. Without adding any extra clay, the original piece was flattened slightly into an oval section and further adjustments were made to define the 'tail' and these act as a kind of handle. Meanwhile the 'beak' became the spout with the larger opening by the 'tail' giving easy access to the volume inside. Airbrushed ceramic stains were shaded to accent the 'bird' shape and add to the allusion. Although pure function was not uppermost in my mind, the pot actually works as a jug. It holds liquids and pours well with one hand under the 'tail' and the other beneath the 'throat'! (see illustration on page 106).

Natural rock formations, especially concretions like stalactites and stalagmites or sandstone and igneous rocks eroded by wind and water into convoluted shapes provide ample reference points for the work of **David Fink** (USA). He arrives at his forms by carving plaster models in an attempt to capture some of the sculptural qualities produced by natural forces of erosion over millions of years. The models are used to make plaster moulds for his slipcast porcelain. The rims are hand carved when the casts have stiffened to give greater individuality to repeated shapes. The interiors are glazed but the outer wall surfaces are polished after the final firing taken to cone 5 (almost 1200°C). Visual interest is increased when light falls across the white surface creating hard and soft shadows that articulate the form.

Nature provides much of the stimuli for the exotic vessels by **Curtis Benzle** (USA). His pieces are made up of multiple layers of coloured and patterned porcelain sheets laminated together and compressed while the clay is at the wet stage. In any one piece there may be up to six different layers.

The intended result is for the viewer to be confronted with a constantly changing imagery dependent on the available light. For me, this represents the reality of mentally processing the many elements of my environment simultaneously. For instance, when I gaze out of my studio window I see certain objects immediately brought into focus: trees, grass, flowers. As I continue to look, I bring into focus dew, mist, birds passing and a

'Landscape', porcelain plate, handbuilt, incised and coloured with black ceramic stain, fired to 1280°C in reduction, 50 cm, by Ole Lislerud.

subtle shifting of light and shadow. To all this is added the remembered images relevant to the same scene: days of rain, snow, children playing, leaves changing and on and on. It is this 'layering' of imagery that encourages *my* layering of translucent porcelain surfaces.

After many years working exclusively with slipcast bone china, **Angela Verdon** (UK) decided that it was no longer acceptable to suffer the very large number of pieces that were lost in the making process. The loss rate had always been high, especially when she worked with paper-thin clay

but the desire, almost an obsession, to create forms which utilised and exploited the maximum amount of light, to create vessels so fragile and translucent as to be almost unbelievable overcame the disappointment. However, later, the restrictions of the medium proved too limiting for me and the work became sterile and mechanical. There seemed to be nowhere else I could go with bone china.

She had completed a series of extremely thin forms; some very thick black and white laminated pieces; she had also

'Passage', handbuilt porcelain, inlaid and incised, 20.5 cm × 45 cm × 10 cm, by Curtis Benzle, 1990.

Slipcast and carved porcelain vessel, first bisque fired to 900°C and then further refined and sanded before firing up to 1260°C in oxidation, 34 cm × 26 cm, by Angela Verdon, 1993.

want the medium to dictate the message and, hopefully, this is the state I am moving towards'. She feels that she is just beginning to understand and appreciate the differences between bone china and porcelain but is enjoying the opportunity to make much larger pieces. More of the actual work is carried out in the 'green' state and she has discovered a strength and plasticity that was lacking in the china (which she had always fired to a soft bisque 'before I had hardly touched it').

Verdon now draws marks and images directly on the clay cast and carves them out or around, leaving certain parts prominently raised and surrounded by very thin areas. 'I want to draw the eye in and towards an image by the light and colour in a subtle way to create a sense of calm stillness in the piece.' The concept of 'less is more' is what she strives to achieve in these works, to move away from what she feels is her almost obsessive attention to carving pierced detail and to 'really simplify'. Her current work in Limoges porcelain is first fired to 900°C and then thoroughly sanded smooth before refiring up to 1260°C in an oxidising atmosphere. A final polish during which she pays special attention to the raised areas of the surface relief completes the process.

Another potter who prefers to retain the white appear-

tried staining the body with rich, dark blues, greens and blacks and inlaid gold and silver but it was with 'considerable relief' that she obtained a residency in Cleveland that allowed her time to experiment widely for two years. (It was during this period that she won the Inax Prize which enabled her to work for three months in Japan.)

Verdon worked with many different clays and made countless tests with various materials while attempting to rediscover her true sense of purpose, without the attendant problems experienced with bone china, only to find that she came back to the realisation that light, purity, simplicity and all the other qualities that had captivated her in earlier work remained dominant. 'I realised that stoneware, "T" material, brightly coloured glazes, etc., were not for me.' She decided to switch her efforts to slipcasting with a more reliable porcelain body from Limoges in her search for greater spontaneity and freedom in her work without the labour-intensive involvement of bone china. 'I don't

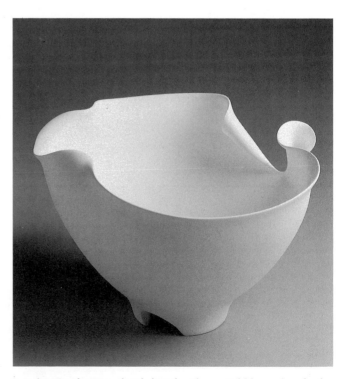

Porcelain Bowl, trimmed and altered, with a matt feldspar glaze fired to cone 9 (1280°C) in an electric kiln, by Gwen Heffner, 1993.
Photograph by Ron Forth.

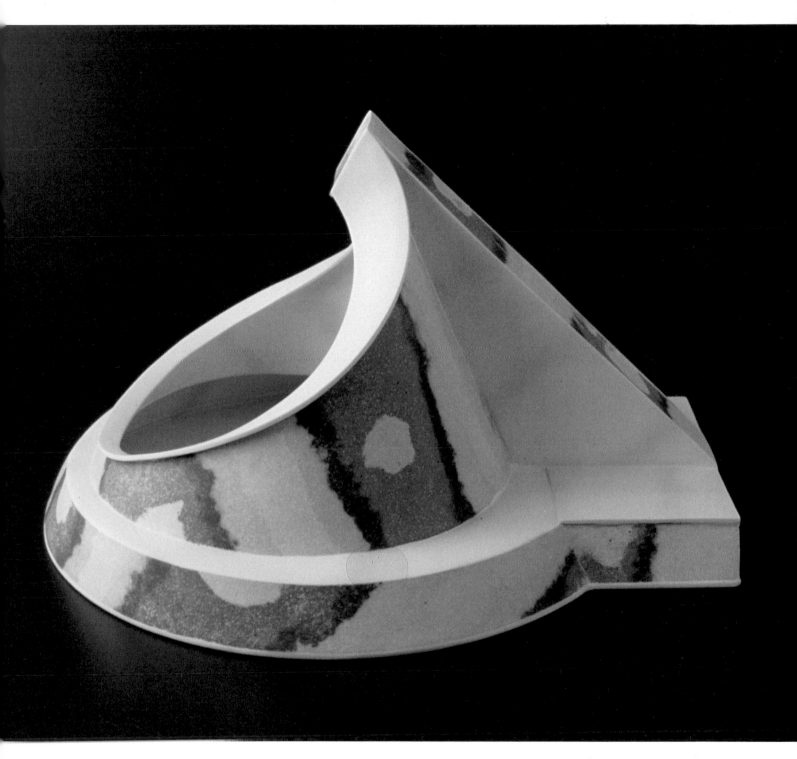

Porcelain Form, 33 cm × 28.5 cm, by Saskia Koster, 1990. Handbuilt
with slabs of laminated and inlaid, multi-coloured porcelain. Fired to
1280°C in an electric kiln. The artist plans her pieces first by making
them in paper and then deciding which colours and patterns are the
most appropriate to complement the form.

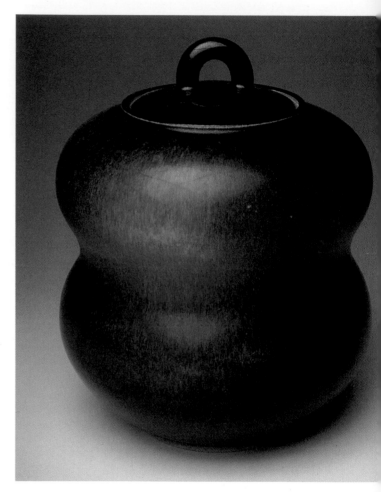

Lidded jar with richly coloured blue and red feldspathic glaze containing copper, cobalt, iron, and manganese, fired to cone 10 (1300°C) in reduction, by Christopher Sanders (Australia), 1993. *Photograph by Terence Bogue.*

'Ripple Jar' with red feldspathic glaze containing iron and copper, fired to cone 10 (1300°C) in a reducing atmosphere, 32 cm high, by Christopher Sanders (Australia), 1993. *Photograph by Terence Bogue.*

ance of porcelain or to use fairly matt glazes is **Gwen Heffner** (USA). All her vessel forms are wheel-thrown and turned while still quite wet. 'Since form is my main focus, I throw with an inside rib and a flexible metal outside rib to get a clean form without throwing rings.' She pushes her bowls into an oval form after trimming them 'thus creating the symmetry of the wheel and allowing an easy trim on a round pot'. She cuts into and alters the rims of her pieces with a fettling knife and then uses a sponge to wet and stroke the edges 'much in the way that one *pulls* a handle', coaxing them into new shapes. In order to overcome

uneven drying problems with altered rims and forms, she inverts them onto pieces of plastic 'bubble wrap' which protects them from damage while they dry more evenly.

One porcelain potter who became well-known for her strongly thrown, classical shapes (and whose work was included in two of my previous books, *Studio Ceramics* and *Ceramic Form*) but who felt an urgent need to pursue new directions in her vessel forms is **Catharine Hiersoux** (USA). She mentioned a moment when she was unpacking her kiln and discovered a beautiful, narrow necked vase, with a copper red glaze, that had become separated around

'Abyss', handbuilt, wood-fired porcelain, by Catharine Hiersoux, 1990.
Photograph by Richard Sargent.

its widest point. When she lifted the top of the vase, the bottom remained 'open like a cracked eggshell.' This stimulated her into searching for new means of expression with looser forms. She knew then that she wanted to free the clay and herself from 'strict, formal bonds and to open up the forms, to push the translucency of the porcelain and work more with the inner space, both literally and metaphorically'. Loose, altered forms were placed on more clay which she sculpted, beat, shaved and pierced for freer movement between inside and outside. 'I wanted translucency, but needed structural support . . . maybe the whole piece did not need to be that thin.' She began trying to establish a balance between translucent and opaque areas, between fragility and toughness (thin, high-fired porcelain is much stronger than any similar piece made in earthenware). 'There was a sense of either having endured time or of *being new growth*, an ambivalence that still exists. The challenge was for me to explore the dimensions.' She remains committed to the vessel as a point of departure in her exploration of form but is prepared to adapt to any future changes that may develop. She built a wood-burning kiln to fire these new pieces because she wanted to use a process that 'just "touched" the forms, enhancing, highlighting them . . . these pieces were still of the earth but not just natural. There are lots of problems with wood firing . . . it's not very predictable . . . but the chance for magic is much greater.'

'Teapot', slipcast porcelain with painted decoration, 15 cm high × 27 cm × 7 cm, by Sandor Dobany (Hungary), 1992. *Photograph by Wolf Böwig.*

Left 'A piece that works', handbuilt porcelain, wood-fired in an anagama type kiln, 40 cm high, by Catharine Hiersoux, 1990. *Photograph by Richard Sargent.*

Porcelain vessel forms by Fritz Rossmann (Germany), 1993. Made by initially throwing shapes on the wheel and then rolling them on the ground in a spontaneous way. 20 cm and 27 cm diameter. Fired in salt glaze to 1250°C. *Photograph by Baumann Fotostudio.*

SURFACE TREATMENTS FOR PORCELAIN

Painted decoration

The pure white porcelain body lends itself especially well to surface designs applied as stains, oxides, slips, glazes, lustres or enamels. Tools used may be paintbrushes of various sizes and shapes, sponges, rubber stamps, transfers, slip trailers, or spray guns and airbrushes. Colours can be overlaid and the piece fired and re-fired several times to different temperatures, and in all kinds of kiln atmospheres until the desired result is achieved. Resists and masks of paper, card, tapes, nets, latex and wax are often employed to widen the range of creative possibilities. Sources of both figurative and abstract imagery are infinite.

Arne Åse painting an inverted porcelain bowl with shellac resist and water soluble colourants. The shellac burns away in the firing.

Water-soluble colourants

One of the more unusual methods of applying colours to porcelain has been comprehensively explored by **Arne Åse** in Norway. His book, *Water Colour on Porcelain* (published in 1989 by the Norwegian University Press) deals with this in considerable detail. Rather than use the heavier pigments made from metallic oxides, Åse has conducted an enormous number of experiments with water-soluble colourants such as iron chloride, nickel chloride, ferrous sulphate, potassium dichromate and many others. He points out that most, if not all, of these materials are extremely poisonous and hazardous to health. They must be stored, handled and fired with great care. Åse compares the softer, gentler colours given by water-soluble metallic salts with effects achieved by using oxides and offers an analogy with watercolour and oil paints. Certainly, the spectrum of colours developed by him is unusually delicate and distinctive. He expresses the view that 'ceramics is a pictorial art, artists relate to the world of visible phenomena from which they draw their inspiration and which governs their main modes of expression'. He refers to the changing role of contemporary ceramics and believes that the subject reveals evidence of 'a completely new branch of the fine arts on the verge of breaking through in all parts of the Western world'. He feels, as do I and many others, that ceramic art bears no direct relationship with traditional criteria of usefulness and function. Its more important purpose in a contemporary setting is the communication of thoughts, feelings and impressions through visual means.

Arne Åse has specialised in studying the effects of water-soluble colourants when used on unglazed porcelain fired to 1280°C in a reduction atmosphere. Concentrating his efforts in this way he has managed to produce a reliable palette of stable colours mixed in various solutions and combinations. Shellac is often used as a resist medium on his painted porcelain bowls. Sometimes, colourants are dis-

Right
The finished porcelain bowl after once-firing in a reducing atmosphere, unglazed to 1250°C. This bowl was fired upside down on a porcelain ring to prevent any distortion. By Arne Åse, 1993.

Porcelain Plate, unglazed, 65 cm diameter, by Arne Åse, 1993. Decorated by painting a shellac resist and washing away part of the unresisted surface (the shellac burns away in the firing). Some parts also painted with water soluble colourants. Fired to 1250°C in reduction.

solved in glycerine or syrup to improve their workability. Occasionally, he combines phosphoric acid with the soluble salts or, possibly, a thickening agent may be added to the mixture to be painted under or over other colours. Solubles added to oxides extends the options even further so that the subtlety and range of colour effects appear to be infinite.

Using precious metals

Greg Daly (Australia) is another potter who has developed an unusual and expressive technique using colour. His current work is an exploration of light and illusion with images which 'are abstractions of landscape and objects I have experienced in and around my environment'. Wheel-thrown plates, dishes, bowls and spherical forms with richly glowing glazes have long been a feature of his ceramics. Porcelain is a material perfectly suited to accept the high gloss glazes he favours. Coloured glazes are used as the base or background for painted additions of lustres made from gold, cobalt, bismuth and zinc in different combinations. The addition of gold and silver leaf helps to enrich the surface imagery even further. Linear patterns

Above Lidded Pot, 15 cm × 12 cm, by Greg Daly, 1992. Porcelain, decorated with gold and silver leaf. Glaze fired to 1280°C. The leaf is then attached to the surface, prior to refiring (between 720°C–800°C), with a medium made from pine resin mixed with a light oil such as lavender or eucalyptus (approximately 10 g of resin to 50–70 mls of oil).

Porcelain Vase, 35 cm high, by Greg Daly, 1993. Wheel-thrown, with resist lustre decoration. Fired to cones 9–10 (1280°–1300°C) with a high gloss glaze and then subjected to further firings to apply lustres at 760°C. The surface was prepared with wax resist over which acid is painted to etch into the surface.

Right Porcelain Vase, with bright blue, glossy glaze and gold lustre decoration, 20 cm high, by Greg Daly, 1993.

are etched into the coloured areas making a silky matt surface that acts as a foil for the lustres. Daly aims in this way to create illusions of colour and light that flow over the surface (drawing the viewer) into the depth of the glaze. The intensity of tones and colours changes when viewed from different angles and light sources.

Daly has had considerable experience of working with precious metals on ceramics and he says that he finds the application of gold and silver leaf is relatively simple to accomplish. The best results are usually produced when used on a glossy glaze but leaf can also be applied to ceramics for 'black firing' or on to a satin matt surface for different effects and with varying degrees of success. It is important to use the correct medium to attach the leaf

Porcelain Platter, 80 cm diameter, by Greg Daly, 1991. Wheel-thrown, with resist lustre decoration. Fired to cone 9–10 (1280°–1300°C) with a high gloss glaze. Lustres are then applied over a hot wax resist and refired to 760°C one or more times. Finally, acid is painted over wax resists and allowed to etch into the surface.

leaf and, in the case of gold, that it should be as pure as possible '22 ct at least'. When dry, a piece of paper is held over the leaf and light pressure applied to ensure consolidation with the ceramic surface.

Metallic lustres and onglaze enamels

Daly sometimes makes up his metallic lustres in a similar way to those used in conjunction with gold or silver leaf and these can be painted on together with enamels if required after applying the leaf and the whole is then fixed in the same firing. In some instances the leaf is placed on top of a previously fired lustre. Firing temperatures vary to allow for the different softening points of glazes used. Earthenware glazes soften at lower temperatures than

because ordinary glues can leave scumming on the glaze or a layer between the glaze and the leaf which prevents proper fusion taking place. The medium he uses is made from pine resin melted with a light oil such as lavender or eucalyptus with approximately 10 g of resin to 50–70 ml of oil. This produces an oily, sticky medium that may also be used as a base for enamel painting. This medium is painted on to the surface to be decorated with the leaf which can then be manoeuvred into position quite easily to define a pattern. Daly recommends the use of high quality

Three Porcelain Vases with resisted lustre decoration painted over previously fired lustres, 10 cm diameter, by Greg Daly, 1993.

stoneware or porcelain but generally the lustre and leaf firings are conducted between 720°C – 800°C.

Daly prepares his lustres by melting 10 g of pine resin and then adds metallic salts in the form of nitrates or acetates. For a 'mother of pearl' effect, he adds 3 g of bismuth nitrate and 2 g of zinc acetate by constantly stirring 'until the mixture takes on a glossy appearance, slowly adding lavender or eucalyptus oils (pure turpentine can also be used with the oils). Other lustre colours can be made in a similar way. Gold, in combination with other metals can give reds, pinks, blues and copper colours.' The lustrous coloured surface of these ceramics develops as the resin is burnt away *reducing* the constituent salts to a metallic state. This local reduction can take place in an electric kiln without causing damage to the elements but good ventilation should be ensured by leaving spyholes open with the bungs out.

Another highly effective technique imaginatively used by Daly is that of etching glazes with acid. An acid-etched surface provides an excellent foil for the lustre surface or a glossy glaze. In this case, more than one glaze may be used. If a solid lustre is applied over them, it will block out the underlying colour but etching through this reveals varying colours with a satin matt surface. In the lustred bowl (illustrated on page 14) two different glazes have been used and gold and silver leaf applied as previously described. Resin-based lustres were then airbrushed over the surface followed by an enamel colour. When the bowl has been fired, latex, wax and/or tapes can be used as resists for the acid which is to be painted over the surface. Daly emphasises the attention he pays to safety when working with acids.

Porcelain pot, 11 cm high, by Geoffrey Swindell, 1989. Wheel-thrown, fired to 1250°C in an oxidising atmosphere (electric kiln) and then decorated with onglaze lustres, the surface of which has been marbled and broken by painting or spraying a medium selectively (paraffin or detergents will beak the surface of resin/oil based lustres) before the lustre has fully dried and prior to firing to 750°C in an electric kiln.

Rubber gloves should always be worn and the process must be carried out in a well-ventilated area. 'The straight hydrofluoric acid is not very safe for this work but another form has bifluoride as an active ingredient. This may take a little longer to etch the surface but it is a little safer to use.' The time needed for the acid to take effect depends upon

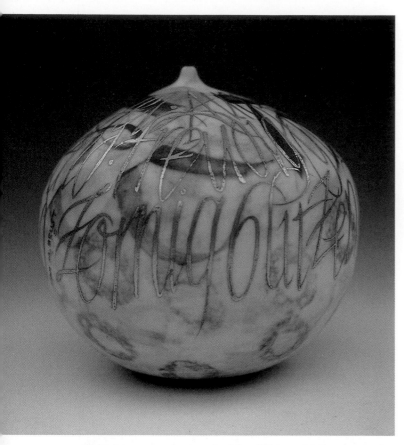

Globe form, 14 cm diameter, by Mary White, 1993. Porcelain, with a white, barium glaze, fired to 1250°C in an electric kiln and then decorated with calligraphy in black oxide and gold lustre and refired.

'Vanitas' container form, wheel-thrown porcelain with underglaze and high fired painted glazes and gold lustre, 21 cm diameter, by Olaf Stevens, 1990.

the hardness of the glaze and the requirements of the design. Hot water is used to wash the piece and remove any wax resist followed by further washing with liquid soap to neutralise the acid and prevent any scumming from spoiling the surface.

Acid etching of ceramic glazes creates a surface which is very smooth to the touch and quite unlike anything achieved by sand blasting. Daly has discovered that 'the combination of different coloured glazes and finishes with lustres, gold and silver leaf, enamels and etched surfaces can lead to surface decoration which has great depth, illusion, colour, pattern and design. The exploration of these techniques releases the imagination through its countless subtle variations.'

I have discussed the painted lustres of **Geoffrey Swindell** (UK) at some length in my previous books and, although his many commitments in other areas have greatly reduced the amount of time he is able to devote to his own creative ceramics, the answers he gave in response to my questions precisely echo those of so many ceramicists who choose to work in porcelain. Like Arne Åse, Swindell is not concerned with functional applications in the way that a teapot, for example, might be used for making and serving tea. 'But there are practical considerations like fired strength, stability and durability. However, the main function I aim for is that the "presence" of the form should affect the senses and give pleasure by its beauty as do many natural objects.' He admits that, for him, the nature of the materials used in his work have a profound effect on the finished image. Combined with the techniques and the concept they are 'inseparable' elements in any good work of art or craft. Swindell says that the whiteness of porcelain gives him a perfect ground as it does not interfere with the purity of applied colours. He likes to make 'well-engineered, precise forms – almost mechanical – and then soften the appearance with a more "organic" quality of surface' with glazes that are textured with marbled lustres. It is through this image of 'precision and looseness' that he attempts to communicate his interests in other objects that he collects, thus presenting a 'synthesis' of both man-made and natural qualities.

Swindell paints commercially-prepared lustres on to glazed pots and then breaks the surface tension of the medium with solvents such as paraffin or detergents brushed or sprayed selectively on to it. This action causes the lustres to retreat away from the solvent spot or line with a halo of concentrated colour around the edge. Further colours can be added and the piece might be fired several times with successive treatments until the visual texture and colour fully fits and complements the form.

Gold, silver and platinum lustres are very expensive

'Container with Circles', wheel-thrown porcelain, with yellow glaze and gold circles (23 ct gold), 25 cm diameter, by Olaf Stevens, 1993.

Porcelain Plate with high-fired painted glazes, and bees painted in gold lustre, 53 cm diameter, by Olaf Stevens, 1990.

'Horizons', porcelain bowl, 59.5 cm diameter × 17.5 cm high, by Pippin Drysdale, 1990. Wheel-thrown, painted with layered, prepared glaze stains on top of a white tin glaze using latex resist as a drawing agent in producing the design.

items in the potter's palette. Therefore, the traditional and more familiar use of precious metals in ceramics is to apply them sparingly as banding or outlining or to highlight details of the design. **Mary White** (Germany) makes good use of her training in calligraphy to paint gold lettering on some of her porcelain bowls and pots. Her calligraphic script is fluently executed encircling the forms as a fully integrated part of the design. **Olaf Stevens** (Holland) is more extravagant with the application of gold lustre. The inner surfaces of some of his simple bowl shapes are completely covered with shimmering gold. His bowls are all thrown with unusually thick walls but he refines their surfaces until they are perfectly smooth and ready for painting. These rather severe forms might easily appear dull but Stevens enlivens their surfaces with generous discs and ovals of gleaming gold, loosely placed, around their circumferences. The first colours are applied as underglazes on the bisque to be covered with a translucent yellow glaze. Onglaze enamels are painted before a third firing and, finally, the gold lustre and a fourth firing. This bold approach to decoration is very different to the elaborate, crowded ornamentation he has applied to other vessel forms of similar shape. A skull and crossbones symbol makes an incongruous appearance among a multitude of colourful flowers and insects jostling for space around the outside of one bowl while the inside glows with plain gold

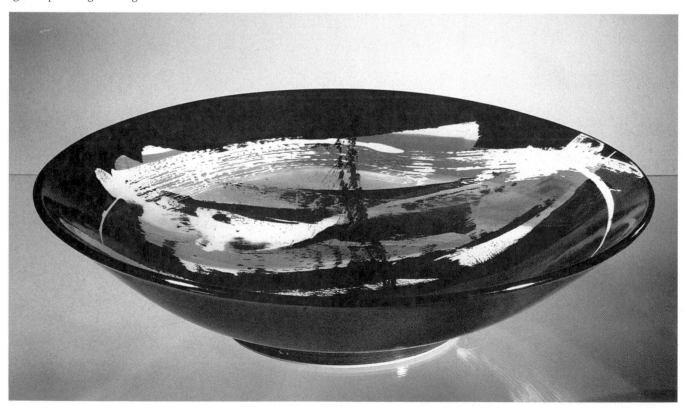

lustre. The result fits uncomfortably close to becoming kitsch for, apart from its technical excellence, it bears little relation to mainstream studio ceramics at the time of writing. But Stevens' intentional note of discord is intended to shock, to draw attention to the transitory nature of human life. He quotes 'all is vanity' in describing this aspect of his work which closely follows a similar allegorical theme in 17th century Dutch painting.

Right 'Logging Series', porcelain plate, 60 cm diameter, by Pippin Drysdale, 1990. Wheel-thrown, painted with layered, prepared glaze stains on top of a white tin glaze using latex resist as a drawing agent in producing the design.

Porcelain Bowl, 'Russian Series', 20.5 cm diameter × 13 cm high, by Pippin Drysdale, 1993. Wheel-thrown, with painted coloured stains on top of a white (tin/zirconium) glaze fired to 1200°C in an electric kiln, followed by lustre firings to 780°C. The lustres are applied as an 'extra skin' on the fired stains to add richness to the colours.

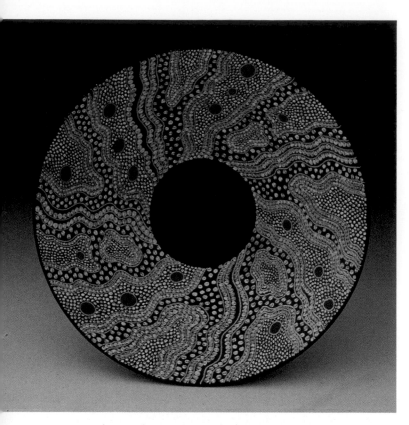

Porcelain Bowl, 'Australian Outback Series', diameter 35 cm, by Marianne Cole. Wheel-thrown, with shiny black glaze fired to Orton cone 9 in an electric kiln, and then decorated with painted liquid bright gold lustre and coloured enamels and refired to cone 018. *Photograph by Michal Kluvanek.*

Freely painted brushwork in both lustres and under-glaze stains is a strong feature of the work by **Pippin Drysdale** from Western Australia. She lives in Perth which she describes as 'the most isolated city in the world – surrounded by desert and the Indian Ocean'. This feeling of isolation is reflected in her artistic endeavours giving it a regional identity. She states that all her life she has been surrounded by wide open land and seascapes and she has always been fascinated by contrasts of light, colour, space, texture and spirituality. Her work is directly inspired by her experience of that environment. She is noted particularly for her large, painterly platters which incorporate each of those elements expressed in terms of colour. All her pieces are individually made and decorated in wheel-thrown porcelain, bisqued to 1000°C and then painted with stains mixed in equal parts with frit 4712. Bentonite from the USA (three per cent) is added and the mixture is put first through a 150s and then a 200s mesh sieve to ensure even dispersal. The stains are applied in layers, hand-painted, sprayed and dipped on top of a white glaze using latex resist as a drawing agent. The base glaze has a

wide firing range and contains tin oxide and zirconium silicate with zinc oxide and barium carbonate. This is fired to Orton cone 4 or 5 (1180°–1200°C) while lustres are often applied for the third, fourth and, sometimes, fifth firings to Orton cone 016 (780°C) on top of the previously painted and fired stains 'to add an extra skin which gives a rich dimension to the colours'.

Pippin Drysdale's painted designs are confident, bold and vigorously executed. Colours and shapes swirl over and around her pots as if in constant motion. She feels that the essence of her vessel forms is a 'solitary explanation of celebration' … an embodiment of refreshed emotional response to my unique Western Australian environment, depicting subtle landforms and colours expressing light, skies, deserts, oceans and horizons'. She travelled extensively during the early 1990s to further widen her experience by working in a traditional Italian majolica factory and teaching in Britain, Siberia and the United States. This has provided her with new influences, 'from Russian icon paintings to the flamboyance of Italian carnivals', which are beginning to appear in her work.

The bowls, elaborately decorated with gold lustre and coloured enamels, by **Marianne Cole** (Australia) are inspired by aboriginal painting and the Australian Outback. She describes her work as 'an ongoing experiment with ideas derived from many sources, in particular, the vast ceramic legacy left to us from ancient cultures'. Extensive foreign travel has enabled her to see such works in their environmental and cultural contexts. Their 'physical presence exudes an aura reflecting each culture's passion for form and decoration' and these influences are in tune with her own 'unabashed zest for rich and complex surfaces'.

The painted decoration on top of a shiny, black glaze which has been fired to 1280°C in an electric kiln is undertaken in a dust-free room. It is a lengthy process, using commercial enamels and liquid bright gold. A special pen (a miniature version of a batik pen) is used to draw the network of fine gold lines. Gold 'thinners' can be added to allow the liquid gold to flow freely. 'It is a precise process requiring a steady hand, good light and good eyesight.' Although she has a *general* concept in mind when she begins decorating, the design actually develops on the bowl as she works.

Mary Rich (UK) prefers to cover her porcelain vessel forms with underglaze stains and coloured slips to provide

Porcelain Teapot, wheel-thrown, decorated with coloured glazes and gold lustre brushwork, by Mary Rich (UK), 1992. *Photograph by Jon Furley.*

Porcelain Bowl, 26.5 cm × 10.5 cm, by Mary Rich, 1993. Wheel-thrown and banded with purple slip under a barium carbonate glaze which has been fired in reducing conditions to cone 10. With painted decoration in liquid bright gold with purple and black lustre. *Photograph by Roger Slack.*

Porcelain bowl, 38 cm × 7 cm, by Russell Coates, 1993. Wheel-thrown, with underglaze blue and enamelled design of square cross with paired cormorants and a geometric border surrounded by sealions swimming amongst seaweed.

a dark ground which is then fired with a clear, satin matt glaze prior to painting her intricate, decorative designs in gold lustre. Much of her work is small in scale from jewel-like, miniature bottles and bowls to cane-handled teapots, banded and crosshatched with fine gold lines to make complicated, geometric patterns. Similarly involved patterning features in the work of **Russell Coates** (UK). Having won a scholarship to study ceramics in Japan, he spent a fruitful period during the 1980s learning about the art of underglaze blue painting and enamelling on porcelain (Kutani ware). His work remains strongly influenced by that experience and it still demands very careful planning and rigorous preparation. Designs are worked out in detail on paper first and then transferred on to his dishes using tissue paper and charcoal. Colours are chosen as the work progresses.

Coates likes porcelain, especially for throwing. One of the bodies he uses is a natural porcelain from Japan similar to that first found at Arita where Imari ware is made. He says that the use of this clay 'tends to shift the emphasis away from translucency', a quality which has been so important in Western porcelain, due to its iron content. He bisque fires between 800°C and 1000°C and then outlines his patterns in underglaze blue which is eventually covered with a clear, white glaze and fired again to Orton cone 9 (1270°C) in a reducing atmosphere. (The plates and bowls are supported on setters in the gas kiln.) Further decoration is accomplished with five enamel colours, red, yellow, green, blue and purple, underpainted with black. Burnished gold may be included also and the final firing is taken to a temperature of 830°C. Stylised birds, animals, fish, dolphins or plants encircle the rims of his decorative plates surrounding an elaborate centrepiece reminiscent of Celtic designs. Describing his choice of subject matter for his painted designs, Coates says,

> Dolphins are liked by all and they introduce environmental and conservation themes. Creatures and plants look well painted in enamels which can be too hard and shiny for purely abstract or geometric patterns. In the last few years, I have been inspired by Cretan, Celtic, Anglo-Saxon and Mediaeval themes. Unfortunately, they take a long time to do.

Porcelain Bowl, 41 cm diameter × 8 cm high, by Russell Coates, 1993. Wheel-thrown, with underglaze blue and enamelled design rose window surrounded by fish and a geometric border. The underglaze pattern is covered with a clear/white glaze and fired in reduction to 1270°C before applying the enamel colours and refired to 870°C.

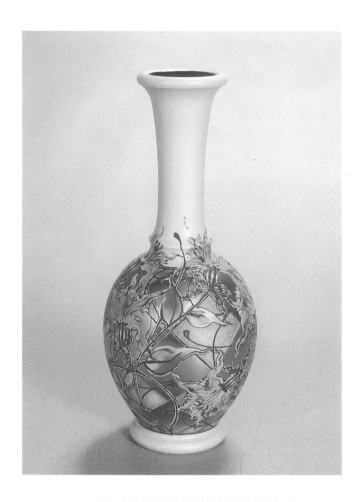

He explains that the lengthiest part of the making process is the enamelling on the fired glaze, at a point 'where the work of most potters has finished'.

Coates admits that enamelled porcelain may have a limited appeal. 'It seems that although many people have heard of Imari ware, few potters even know much about "Kakiemon" or "Dovetailed Colours" which are the roots of the tradition that I studied in Japan.' He feels it is unfortunate that 'the level of boredom bequeathed by Western transfer printed enamels is such that most potters lose interest at mention of the word'.

There is certainly an appreciative audience for highly patterned wares at the time of writing but such detailed painting requires careful, thorough planning and great discipline in its execution. **Peter Minko** is an Australian potter working in the Bendigo region of central Victoria who gains much of his inspiration from the wealth and variety of the natural flora in the surrounding bush. Con-

'Goldfields' porcelain vase, 18 cm high, by Peter Minko (Australia), 1993. Wheel-thrown and burnished at the leatherhard stage, bisque fired to 920°C and then painted with finely ground pigments made mainly from metallic oxides. Fired twice more to 1280°–1300°C to fuse the colours to the unglazed surface.

Porcelain Bowl, wheel-thrown and altered while still soft, with painted decoration, 20 cm diameter, by Kevin White, 1990.

'Goldfields 2', porcelain plate, 30.6 cm diameter, by Peter Minko (Australia), 1992. Wheel-thrown and burnished at the leatherhard stage. Bisque fired to 920°C and then individually handpainted with finely ground pigments (mainly metallic oxides). Two firings up to 1280°–1300°C in oxidation conditions fuse the colours with the unglazed porcelain surface. Gold lustre is applied in a further firing to 760°C.

Porcelain Bowl, wheel-thrown and altered while still soft, with painted decoration, 20 cm diameter, by Kevin White, 1990.

Porcelain Dish painted with underglaze blue (cobalt) fired to cone 11 and then onglaze enamel added and refired, 26.5 cm diameter, by Kevin White, 1989.

centrating on fairly simple vessel forms, he has been able to embellish them with an exotic range of richly coloured patterns. Each piece is wheel-thrown in a fine porcelain body and burnished at the leatherhard state to ensure the surface is smoothly compacted. Bisque fired to 920°C they are then individually painted with finely ground pigments (predominantly metallic oxides) and fired twice more to between 1280°–1300°C in oxidation to fuse the colours on the unglazed surface. Only the inside surfaces are glazed. Those pieces with gold lustre applied in parts are fired again to 760°C. Minko says that he chose to work with this particular porcelain and technique because it was the only way in which he could obtain the kind of finish to display his detailed painting with complete clarity. His fluent draughtsmanship is well-illustrated in the pieces on pages 132 and 133.

Brushwork

Kevin White is another Australian potter who makes decorative bowls and plates decorated with brushwork which is rather more abstract but still clearly based on plant growth. These pieces are obviously functional although not specifically utilitarian. He manipulates and alters wheel-thrown forms while they are still soft 'to impart structure and movement' and uses decoration to emphasise their dynamic aspects. In commenting on his objectives, White states 'whilst at rest the work seeks to act as the custodian of ceremony and through use to celebrate it'.

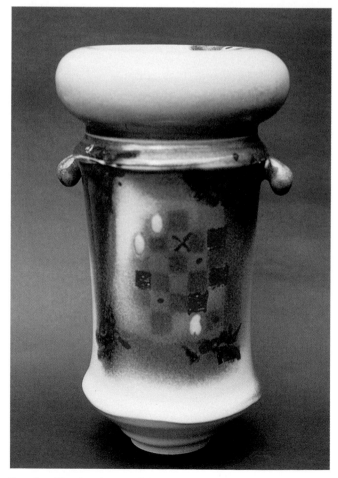

Porcelain Vessel with painted decoration by Paul Davis, 1989.

Shallow, porcelain bowl, 45 cm diameter, by Paul Davis, 1993.
Decorated with maiolica type glaze coloured with ceramic stains
painted over a sandy textured high fired glaze containing a large
mount of calcined alumina.

Porcelain Bowl, 45 cm diameter × 15 cm high, by Paul Davis, 1993.
Wheel-thrown with slab additions, with a very 'dry' glaze (1320°C
reduction fired) and painted with coloured maiolica type glazes and
refired to 1100°C.

Above   Porcelain Vase, wheel-thrown in two parts, with slab additions, decorated with brushwork, by Paul Davis, 1989.

Top left   Porcelain vessel, 45 cm diameter, by Paul Davis, 1993. Wheel-thrown with slab additions. The very 'dry' glaze (1320°C in reduction) has a high proportion of calcined alumina producing a sandy texture. Painted colours provided by ceramic stains in a maiolica type glaze and refired (1100°C).

Left   Bottle Form, by Derek Clarkson. Wheel-thrown porcelain, with brushwork motif painted in a diagonal rhythm (this motif is repeated four times up the pot). Fired in reduction to 1300°C.

Right   Porcelain Bottle, 30 cm × 18 cm, by Alistair Whyte, 1993. With leaf decoration in latex resist and copper pigment under a clear glaze. Reduction fired to produce the copper red colour.
Photograph by Avon Colour Studio.

Three incense burners, porcelain decorated with painted gold and silver decoration, approximately 12 cm × 12 cm, by Alistair Whyte, 1993.
Photograph by Avon Colour Studio.

Large Lidded Jar, wheel-thrown porcelain, with brush decoration, by John Takehara (USA), 1993.

Some earlier work by **Paul Davis** (Australia) also is freely decorated with brushwork motifs developed from plant design (see page 136) but it is his latest pieces that are more unusual in their treatment. He uses mainly an insulator porcelain made by a local manufacturer. This clay is not particularly white but it is milled to an extremely fine particle size. Most porcelain glazes fit this body well. (See the glaze recipes listed on page 187.) Excellent white clays are available in Australia, he says, but industry does not seem to have a need for translucent porcelain. Davis' brightly coloured pieces are produced by a fairly complex process. After a normal bisque firing they are coated with a glaze containing a large quantity of calcined alumina which develops a sandy texture on the surface when fired to cone 11 (1320°C) in a reduction kiln atmosphere. Then he reworks the surface with a majolica-type glaze stained with various colours that is refired to 1100°C. 'This method provides me with a chance to use a wide range of colours which would otherwise be difficult to achieve at 1320°C.'

Alistair Whyte (Australia) spent several years studying porcelain ceramics in Japan and he acknowledges that oriental influences remain strong in his work although he does not try to produce 'Japanese' pots. 'Apart from making use of learned techniques, I try to be true to my own feelings of design and decoration. I am strongly drawn to the use of blue and white on porcelain because I feel that it enhances the whiteness and purity of the material.' It was while he was in Japan that Whyte first began to use *gosu*, the natural cobalt blue colour to be found in

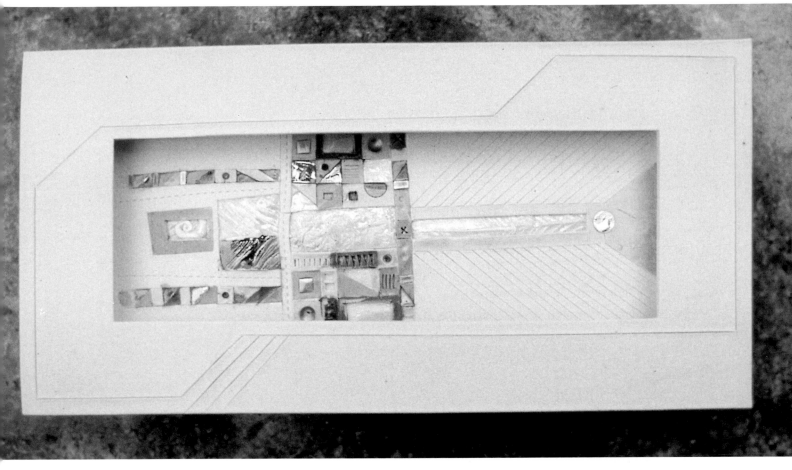

Porcelain tray, 19 cm × 9.5 cm, by Gordon Cooke, 1993. Slab-built, carved and stamped surface with low fired glaze and lustres. Bisque fired to 1250°C before glaze is applied and refired to 1100°C. Onglaze lustre colours are then painted and fired to 750°C in an electric kiln.

Kiyomizu sometsuke (blue and white ware), which is a familiar aspect of much of his own work. At the present time, he is slowly exploring the use of a variety of glazes and more and more colour but he would probably regard himself as 'something of a purist'. He talks of

the meditative aspect of designing and carving the tools in the making process and of the patience that has to be learnt from the time of making and drying to the final firing of the kiln. The sense of satisfaction when, having created an object of beauty in porcelain, the light shines through between your fingers.

As with so many of the potters I have met, **Gordon Cooke** (UK) uses porcelain for its whiteness and close grain, and the opportunities offered by this to work in very fine detail. His unusual method for manipulating surface texture was fully described in *Studio Porcelain* but his latest work is rather different in character and treatment. He aims to create a unity between form, surface and colour. He says that he is motivated by many things ('not least the necessity to pay the mortgage!') but he thinks that the endless

Two porcelain boxes, by Gordon Cooke, 1993. Handbuilt, carved and stamped surface with low fired glaze and lustres. Bisque fired to 1250°C before glazing and refiring to 1100°C and decorating with colour on top of the glaze. larger box is 10 cm × 13 cm.

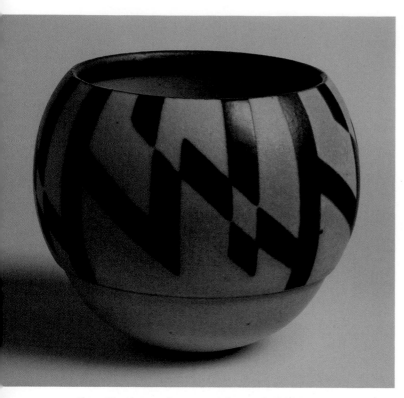

Open Vessel, 14.9 cm × 12.8 cm, by Ursula Scheid, 1992. Porcelain with paper resist design in black slip applied by brush under a feldspar/barium glaze and fired to 1360°C in a gas kiln with a reducing atmosphere.
Photograph by Rolf Zwillsperger.

permutations that are possible in arrangements of texture, pattern and colours that appeals to him most of all. He especially likes the 'secretive nature of boxes and the element of surprise when the lid is lifted to reveal inner decoration'. His present work is influenced by African fabric patterns, natural form and the paintings of Gustav Klimt and Friedrich Hundertwasser. He is also fascinated by certain architectural details which he records constantly in drawings and photographs. His pots are fired to a high bisque at cone 8. An earthenware glaze fired to 1100°C is applied to those areas which he wants to shine. Onglaze lustres are painted on to this as well as on some unglazed sections adding extra visual interest.

Painting with coloured slips enables the ceramicist to define precise areas with completely flat and opaque colour. They can be matt or shiny according to their composition. Normally, the same body provides the base material for making the slip but small additions of flux to this will encourage greater fusion and give the surface a sheen. **Ursula Scheid** (Germany) uses slips on some of her porcelain vessels in conjunction with intricate, geometric designs made from arrangements of cut masking tape which encircles and complements the forms with positive vertical and diagonal elements. The precise placement of the masking tapes is worked out directly on each unique piece before coloured slips are applied by painting. It is a

Lidded Box, slab-built porcelain with tape, resist design in coloured slips under a matt glaze, fired to 1360°C in reduction by Ursula Scheid

Vessel form, porcelain with resist design in coloured slips under a matt glaze, by Ursula Scheid, 1992.

Vessel Form, 30 cm high, by Kristin Andreassen, 1991. Handbuilt porcelain, with multi-layered slip decoration, fired to 1260°C in reduction.
Photograph by Teigens Fotoatelier A.S.

'Autumn Landscape', porcelain vessel, handbuilt, decorated with layered slips of various colours, fired to 1260°C in reduction, 32 cm high, by Kristin Andreassen, 1990.

firmly into the shape of the mould. The top of the pot is covered with a polythene sheet for an hour or so to allow the pot to stiffen further before 'stretching' the walls outwards with the bowl of a large, old-fashioned, egg-shaped, kitchen spoon. The curvature of the spoon fits most shapes and is easy to hold. A cardboard paddle is then used to refine the outer surface of the form.

Since I make my pieces by handbuilding, there is no reason why my pieces should have perfect symmetry. As I work on the shape, I look for lines and directions in the surface which I can use to make changes in the form. I often start by creating an imbalance, and try to recreate a balance by altering other parts of the 'cylinder'. Working with wet clay, the material itself will tell me by collapsing when I have crossed the boundary because a shape that stands well while wet can also survive a high-firing temperature without collapsing.

Andreassen uses a wide variety of coloured porcelain and slips for her decorated surfaces. Many layers of coloured porcelain covering each other partially or totally comprise the patterns.

Usually the bottom layer is black because other colours are intensified by its presence. Since the black contains much cobalt oxide, it may shine through other colours as a soft blue shade. I usually have an idea about the pattern before I start working, deciding which colours and techniques to employ and the main direction of the design. The rest is improvised. I try to make the vessels express different moods. The inspiration comes from erosion, nature and the material itself. I try to take advantage of any happy coincidence. The base layers may be added in various ways depending on their softness or plasticity. I can roll out very thin coloured slabs between two sheets of linen, scratch and draw on them, and stretch them carefully before attaching them to the base slab. I may paint or pour liquid slips directly on to the slab, dry it out with a piece of linen and fix it with a rolling pin.

Another, more unusual method used by Andreassen is to paint slips and water-based stains on to canvas attached to plywood or plasterboard. According to the tools used and the fluidity of the colours, she can make soft shades or precise line drawings to be applied, once the moisture *shine* has gone, to the base slab as a kind of 'transfer' pattern and the design is fixed by rolling. The vessel can then be constructed in the usual way with its pattern already in place.

fairly complex process. Finally, the slip decoration is covered by a transparent, matt glaze based on feldspar and barium, reduction fired to 1360°C in a gas kiln. The globular, swelling shapes of her bowls in particular seem as if they are stretching these patterns almost to bursting point, adding to their feeling of tension.

Kristin Andreassen (Norway) handbuilds using a porcelain body from Limoges (TM 10/LPB). She begins by pinching out a base and pressing this into a plaster mould to ensure it has a steady bottom and leaves it to stiffen until leatherhard. A cylinder made from a previously decorated, rolled out slab is then attached to the pinched section in the mould. Pressure is applied from the inside to fit the clay

Printed decoration

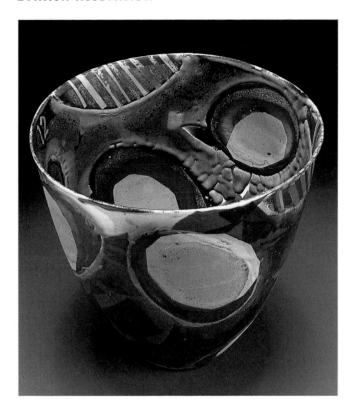

Ceramic transfers and printing methods have long been used in decorating pots for mass consumption but it is an aspect that has received only scant attention from studio potters. However, the techniques do present opportunities for painting or printing extremely detailed designs on to porcelain either in the leatherhard and the bisque state or on top of glaze. **Paul Scott** (UK) is one who has exploited this method on both tile panels and vessel forms. He uses a photocopier to make transparencies of drawings which he intends to reproduce as a ceramic print and then transfers this image on to a silk screen coated with a light sensitive film. The silk screen, with its light sensitive face, is placed down on to the transparency drawing and exposed to light from a mercury vapour lamp for about five minutes, making a contact print to fix the image. Then the screen is washed out with warm water to remove the areas not fixed by the exposure, i.e. the drawn images, and checked to ensure that the mesh is cleared of gel ready for printing. Screens made in this way can be used for printing directly on to tiles and slabs (Scott prefers to print on porcelain when the clay is becoming leatherhard) or for producing ceramic transfers for use on glazed pieces.

For printing underglazes on unfired clay, Scott mixes an 'ink' consisting of 10 parts of stain with 5 parts of powdered porcelain body (finely sieved) to 10 parts of a water-based print medium using a palette knife to blend the material thoroughly on a flat glass plate. The mixture is thinned slightly to increase its volume with the addition of between 5 and 10 parts of a textile printing medium. He points out that the consistency of the prepared 'ink' is critical to printing successfully but this can only be judged through a process of trial and error. Finally, the 'ink' is forced through the mesh of the silk screen and printed on to the leatherhard tiles. Powdered glaze replaces the clay for making transfers and this is mixed with an oil-based medium and printed on to decal paper, a special paper coated with gum. When the printed images have dried, they are covered with a layer of transparent solvent-based resin applied through a blank silk screen. The transfers can be cut up when the 'covercoat' is dry. Soaking them in

Porcelain Bowl, 30 cm × 26 cm, by Susanne Fagermo (Norway), 1993. Slipcast, with transparent glaze coloured with vanadium pentoxide, fired to 1400°C in reduction. Decorated with silkscreen decals containing cerium oxide, vanadium pentoxide, uranium pentoxide, cobalt oxide and black ceramic stain and refired to 1280°C.

Below 'Pots No.32', porcelain panel with pen and ceramic 'ink' and underglaze colours, 60 cm × 40 cm, by Paul Scott, 1993. *Photograph by Andrew Morris.*

Porcelain Bowl, slipcast, with silk screened decal decoration
containing uranium pentoxide and opaque glaze, fired to 1280°C in
oxidation (multiple firings), 30 cm × 26 cm, by Susanne Fagermo,
1993.

warm water allows the transfers to float off the paper ready
for immediate application to glazed ware. Detailing his
processes in an article written for *Ceramic Review* No. 140,
Scott places great emphasis on safety when handling these
materials. 'If you do make ceramic transfers, ensure that
you get safety datasheets on the oil-based medium and the
covercoat. Use good ventilation at all times, and store
products safely.'

Airbrushing

The airbrush is a wonderfully versatile tool. There are
many different types available from which to choose one
best-suited to the work in hand. The most basic models
provide a constant spray pattern but far greater control is
obtained with those having a trigger action. The latter
model can produce an infinitely variable spray from very
thin lines to the coverage of broad areas and with textures
anywhere between coarse and fine. Passing ceramic materials at quite high pressure through these instruments

does have a more abrasive effect than used with inks etc.
and they require careful maintenance. It is necessary also to
keep them meticulously clean while the work is in progress
as well as after work is finished for they can easily clog up
with compacted pigments, slips, lustres or glazes which
stop them functioning correctly. Perhaps the most annoy-
ing and frustrating thing that can happen when pigment
accumulates around the needle or when solid particles
build up within the nozzle, is the sudden splattering of
uncontrolled colour. This will most often occur, in my
experience, when I have become so absorbed in the more
expressive design aspects that I have neglected this ele-
mentary precaution and am approaching the final stage of
the work! Since the main attraction of airbrushed colour is
the smooth graduations that can be achieved, uninten-
tional splatters or blobs will destroy the effect and illusion
for which one aims.

I take the precaution of putting all my stains, whether
commercially-prepared or mixed myself with an underglaze medium, through a 200s mesh cup sieve to ensure
even dispersal with no lumps. The airbrush is dismantled
and thoroughly cleaned after each session. While the work
is in progress, also, clean water is frequently passed
through the instrument so that no build up of hardened
material is allowed to impede the free flow of colour. The
nozzle cap must be regularly removed and the aperture
checked for the same reason. Great care is necessary during
this procedure because the needle point is so fine that it can
be easily damaged. A bent needle will affect the performance of the airbrush quite badly and delicate work will be
ruined by uneven splattering of colour. It is advisable to
always keep a spare needle handy as a replacement. A bent
needle can sometimes be repaired by gently rotating the
point against a smooth board in a stroking movement.

Underglaze stains are well-suited to airbrushing on to
porcelain at any stage from dry to bisque or over unfired
glaze. Bright coloured stains that will withstand high temperatures and remain close to their appearance when first
applied have become readily available over recent years.
Colours and patterns can be applied freehand but, more
frequently, masks of one kind or another are used to control the exact placement of the medium. Hand-held shapes
cut from paper or card are simple masks to use. They can be
oversprayed repeatedly as they are moved about the surface to build up multiple marks having a distinctive quality.
Rich visual textures and tonal variations are thus possible
with economy of means, provided that the mask does not
become too wet so that the medium runs off and mars the
design. Similarly, fixed masks made from paper tapes or
other material must be dried out between successive appli-

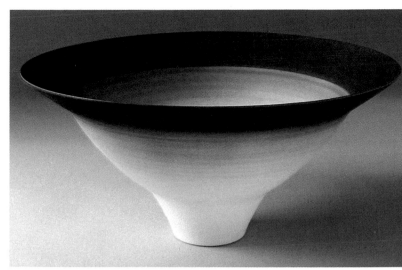

Porcelain Bowl, 'Skies Series', 11 cm high × 27.5 cm diameter, by Peter Lane, 1993. Wheel-thrown and airbrushed with ceramic stains on the bisque. Fired to 1260°C in an electric kiln.

'Mountain Dawn' (Skies Series), wheel-thrown, translucent porcelain, airbrushed on the bisque with underglaze stains, fired to 1260°C in an electric kiln and polished, 13 cm high, by Peter Lane, 1993.

cations if bleeding of one colour into another at the edges is to be avoided.

Masking tape of the kind used in the automobile industry and for protecting window glass when the frames are painted is ideal for use with an airbrush and I, and many other potters, have used it extensively. It can be purchased in different widths which can be cut and reshaped to suit most aims. Some brands are slightly less adhesive than others and this is an undoubted advantage when applying tape to areas previously sprayed with underglaze stains so that another colour can be added. Coloured stains are best prepared with a good binding medium which fixes the colour firmly to the pot and prevents smudging. A number of excellent underglazes mixed with a suitable medium are commercially available for this purpose. My own preference is to work directly on bisqued ware (previously sanded smooth) by airbrushing the lightest colours first and to proceed with progressively darker colours until finally, perhaps, black is reached. This may mean that the piece is almost completely covered with tape, obscuring the design, until peeled away. I use a hot air gun to dry the colours and stop the tape from becoming saturated to overflowing with liquid medium when building up complex patterns with tapes. (Tapes made from any kind of plastics must be used with discretion because they quickly become too wet. They have the added disadvantage that they will shrink under excessive heat and so cannot be force dried.) With care, the colour remains clear and unblemished when, eventually, the tape is removed. Working in this way from light to dark rather than the reverse process avoids the problems encountered when removing a tape that leaves a residue of adhesive on an area still to be oversprayed. (Sasha Wardell works in the opposite direction, from dark to light colours when decorating her bone china with underglaze stains and she refers to the risk of pigment or glaze particles settling on traces of glue to become fixed in the final firing. See page 44.)

Unless masks of one kind or another are used with the airbrush, the spray pattern will always produce a soft edge even when the needle is set at the smallest aperture. This can be turned to advantage by combining soft and hard edges within the overall design. Colours can be merged gradually into one another so that the hues alter in the transition. Underglaze stains also offer the added convenience of remaining fairly true to their unfired colour when applied to pure white porcelain. It is easier, therefore, to assess the success or otherwise of the surface design before committing it to the kiln.

Translucent porcelain bowl mounted on an earthenware base by Patrick Piccarelle (Belgium), 1993. The bowl is thrown and trimmed to a very thin section, carved, bisque fired and then engraved and pierced using dental tools. The holes are filled with a high viscosity glaze and then glazed overall with various feldspathic glazes and fired to 1300°C in a gas kiln. The bases for this series of pieces are fired between 850°C and 950°C depending upon the kind of black surface required.

slight irregularities that appear after bisque firing can be done with a fine grade of sandpaper (I use a zinc-based type) and the surface is sponged clean of dust so that airbrushing can begin. (Sandra Black prefers to polish her porcelain bisque, after soaking it in water to avoid the usual build up of dust, by using firstly a 300 grade of wet and dry sandpaper and then the finer 600 grade.) Following the final firing to 1220°C or above, the work is thoroughly polished with a very fine grade of silicon carbide paper, 'wet 'n dry'. This action removes any hard particles which may have emerged as the clay contracted further in the kiln, spoiling the smooth surface.

Carving and piercing

Porcelain is especially amenable to carving and piercing at various stages of making but, perhaps, it is at its most seductive when the clay has lost some of its moisture. Carving when the clay has dried out completely has its attractions for some potters but it does present a very real risk to health through inhalation of clay dust. For this reason I would not recommend carving unless a degree of moisture remains and that it is sufficient to bind the cut waste together as it is removed. *This waste clay should not be permitted to fall on the floor and be trodden to dust as it dries.* Another important reason for working the clay while it is still damp is that it retains a certain flexibility and is thus less likely to crack or split under the pressure of carving tools.

I frequently left pieces to dry out completely when I first began carving porcelain in the early 1970s and often suffered considerable frustrations as a result. It is much more difficult to cut smoothly into bone-dry porcelain even with the sharpest of tools. I have found that the perfect condition for most carving applications in my own work is when the clay has dried to a rather stiff, 'leatherhard' state. Distortion is far less likely to occur when this point is reached.

Many different tools can be used and each will impart its own character to the work. Bent wire loop tools having a round section produce a slightly softer edge to cut channels than those made with a flatter section. Solid blades, whether metal or wooden, meet with greater resistance in the clay and can leave more obvious chatter marks. Both open and solid tools can be used to carve channels of varying width and depth in one movement in a rather calligraphic manner. Needle points give thinner linear marks which usually remain constant in width. Multiple, repetitive marks made in the surface of a pot with any tool produces a strong rhythmic texture. I have made some of

Slips and glazes are less amenable to airbrushing, although not impossible to use successfully, due to their nature and larger particle size. They tend to take longer to dry naturally. The hot air gun speeds this process but glazes usually remain friable to some extent and liable to disturbance while handling. Handheld masks are more appropriate in this case since tapes cannot be applied to unfired glaze. Resin-based lustres can also be used to good effect providing that the airbrush is thoroughly cleaned between each application of colour.

Clear glazes over stains make the colours appear brighter but many people find that a glossy, reflective surface lessens the visual impact while matt glazes tend to mute the colours. High-fired porcelain, therefore, is frequently left unglazed. Instead, pieces are polished smooth at several stages in the making process. Rubbing down any

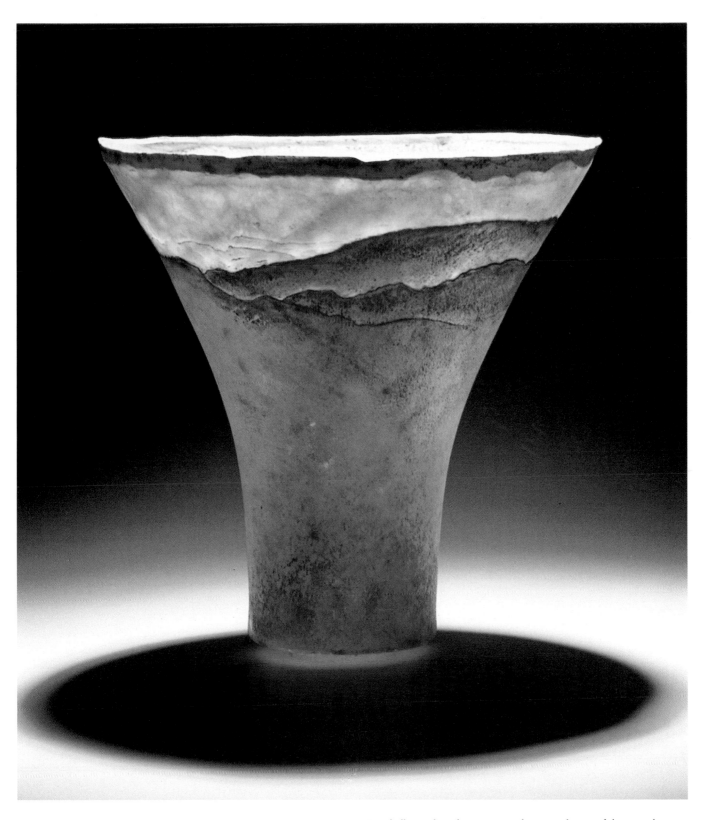

Eggshell porcelain slipcast in two layers with part of the outer layer
carved away to increase translucency. Multiple glazes were applied
and fired several times in an oxidising atmosphere. 26 cm diameter.
By Jeroen Bechtold, 1993.
Photograph by R. Gerritsen.

walls were pierced proved critical for their physical survival. If too much clay was removed below a certain level relative to any given profile, the walls would be weakened and unable to maintain their shape. It is always of the utmost importance to give sufficient support to the wall of a bowl with one hand while the other applies pressure in carving. This is especially so when working from the inside outwards because all the stress is centred over very small area. Carving from the outside inwards is slightly less risky because, to some extent, the pressure is distributed more evenly around the circumference. I had to work fairly rapidly in order to counter the problem of the clay drying out as I worked. I have never liked to see carving which merely pierces through the wall leaving a crude cut edge as a sharp

'Ring of Trees', porcelain bowl, wheel-thrown, carved and pierced, with satin matt white glaze, fired to 1260°C in an electric kiln, 16 cm diameter, by Peter Lane, 1982.

Vessel Form with carved top and pierced decoration, reduction fired to 1280°C in a gas kiln, 16 cm high, by Horst Göbbels.
Photograph by Wolf Böwig.

my favourite tools from metal strips used in the building industry to bind parcels of bricks to a wooden pallet. These strips can often be found lying around on building sites or dumped in skips. Reduced into short lengths (10–15 cm) (4–6 in.) and cut across diagonally at one end, they can be sharpened on a grindstone to make ideal tools for incising porcelain. Vee-shaped linear incisions with one side of the vee longer than the other can produce surface effects rather like those to be seen on beautifully carved Chinese vessels with celadon glazes from the 10th and 11th centuries.

Greater care is necessary when piercing right through the clay wall not only in its execution but with proper regard to the fired strength of the finished piece. If piercing is done without sufficient understanding of the stresses which the form will suffer in the kiln, serious deformation can occur. The risk of slumping is reduced where the wall of the piece is vertical but special care is necessary where holes are cut through on sharply curved sections which have to support the weight of the clay above. Faults of this nature are more likely to be revealed in large forms. I well remember problems I had to overcome with a series of porcelain bowls I used to make on the theme of 'Trees'. This entailed cutting away a fairly extensive part around the circumference of a bowl. Each of those thinly-thrown bowls stood on quite narrow footrings from which they swelled up and outwards to the rim. The point at which the

Cylindrical Vessel Form, porcelain, carved and pierced and fired to 1280°C in reduction in a gas kiln, 13 cm high, by Horst Göbbels.

Translucent porcelain slab sculpture, pierced and threaded with red strings. Reduction fired to 1280°C in a gas kiln, 38 cm high, by Horst Göbbels, 1991.
Photograph by Wolf Böwig.

right angle within its thickness so I would always bevel the edges with the narrow-bladed scalpel immediately after completing the pierced shapes. These would be softened further with a fine grade of steel wool when the piece was completely dry (see illustration on page 148).

Some of the finest filigree carving of porcelain in recent years has been done by the German potter, **Horst Göbbels**. He has produced work of great delicacy and with much intricate, highly-ordered detail. Many of his vessel forms have only minimal contact with the surface on which they stand. Bottoms are rounded or raised on small foot-rings or elevated on integral pedestals. These devices contribute even more to the appearance of weightlessness and ethereality. At the same time, the mathematical precision

of both the design and of the carving conveys a feeling of strength as much as fragility. There is little sense of fragmentation because that which has been removed is balanced by and of equal value to that which remains. The relationship of the inside and outside surfaces is accentuated. Colour and glaze are of secondary importance in such pieces and many are left unglazed. All his vessel forms are thrown using the KPCL porcelain from Limoges in France. Carved and perforated sections of the design are done with a broken saw blade when the piece has dried to the consistency of hard leather. The work is fired to 1280°C in a gas kiln with a reduction atmosphere.

'Deco Bowl' and 'Bird and Fish Bowl', porcelain carved and pierced with surgical blades, fired to cone 10 (1300°C) in an electric kiln, by Sandra Black.

Sandra Black from Western Australia has long been recognised for her carved and pierced porcelain and bone china vessels. Her designs are sometimes reminiscent of the angular patterns of the Art Deco period. Geometric carving in relief often has elements of the pattern cut away completely, giving emphasis to the rhythmic decoration and revealing the inner wall. Such pieces are frequently polished smooth but left unglazed. Her chosen motifs (e.g. 'fish and birds') are often interlinked or juxtaposed rather like an Escher drawing without the transmutation (see illustration above). She likes to make about 20 or more pots on the wheel and stores them in an old refrigerator to keep them damp. She stresses the importance of turning or trimming them to an even thickness of about 2 mm ($\frac{1}{16}$ in.) rather than leaving them too thick so that they lose translucency or making them so thin that they risk being cracked while carving or slump in the kiln. Black restricts herself to just four tools in the carving process. There are a surgical blade in a cane holder, a soft brush, a sponge and a water sprayer. Designs are first drawn on to the pot with the tip of the blade and then cut into about half the wall

Teapot, 'Time Gate', series made in black bone china with applied gold leaf by Sandra Black, 1990. The bone china slip is stained with iron chromate 7%, black iron oxide 7% and cobalt carbonate 3.5% and, as these are strong fluxes, the normal firing temperature is lowered to cone 4–cone 5 depending on the firing schedule.
Photograph by Victor France.

Bowl, slipcast porcelain, carved and pierced at the leatherhard stage and cleaned up when dry, fired to cone 7 in an electric kiln, by Sandra Black.
Photograph by Victor France.

'Deco Vase', by Sandra Black. Wheel-thrown porcelain, carved with surgical blades, lightly sanded at the dry stage and polished after bisque and final firings with silicon carbide pads. Fired to cone 10 in an electric kiln.
Photograph by Victor France.

thickness. The same blade is used on its side to remove excess clay and establish the relief. The soft brush is used to dislodge small particles without damaging the design and, finally, a damp sponge softens the edges and smooths the surface. The work is bisque fired to 950°C and those that are to remain unglazed are soaked in water and sanded down, first with a 300 grade then a 600 grade of silicon carbide paper until they are completely smooth. Polishing the pieces while they are wet prevents dust flying around and from clogging the silicon carbide grit.

Karl Scheid's carving shares the control and precision that is evident in the work of Horst Göbbels and Sandra Black but, although abstract, it is usually more organic in nature. His vessel forms are not pierced but instead the carving flows around and embraces his forms making them objects for quiet reflection. Glazes pool in the depressions. Ridges, although crisply cut, are softened and less severe. Repeated, rhythmic movements with the carving tool endows his work with an unforced, naturally rhythmic pattern that encompasses and complements the form in an expressive way that makes it unique.

A more powerfully demonstrative kind of carving can be seen in the porcelain pieces by **Rolf Bartz** (Australia). His interest in carving was aroused initially by the work of prominent ceramicists using this technique and being heavily influenced by products of the Art Nouveau and

Oval Shaped Vessel, 14 cm high, by Karl Scheid, 1989. Porcelain with cobalt slip and relief decoration under a copper red, feldspar/petalite glaze. Fired to 1360°C in a gas kiln with a reducing atmosphere.
Photograph by Rolf Zwillsperger.

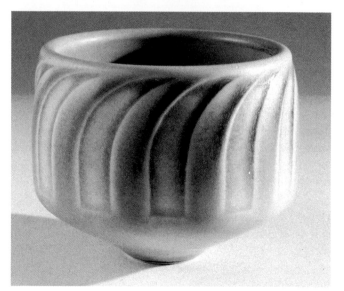

Slab-built vessel form 20 cm high with the top square 9 cm × 9 cm, by Karl Scheid, 1993. Mounted on a square base, porcelain, painted with green slip, partly unglazed and part with copper red feldspathic glaze fired to 1360°C in reduction atmosphere (gas kiln).
Photograph by Rolf Zwillsperger.

Bowl, wheel-thrown porcelain with diagonally carved relief decoration on copper slip under a feldspar-petalite glaze, fired to 1360°C in a reducing atmosphere. 10.9 cm diameter × 7.2 cm high, by Karl Scheid, 1990.
Photograph by Bernd Gobbels.

Bottom right Porcelain bowl with fluted carving under a copper red glaze, fired to 1360°C in a reducing atmosphere, diameter 11.9 cm × 9.8 cm high, by Karl Scheid, 1989.
Photograph by Peter Lane.

Art Deco movements. The growth and shapes of plants provide him with ample subject matter to embellish a variety of vessel forms. Pieces are wheel-thrown with unusually thick walls because he likes to carve deeply and to suggest different layers and overlapping shapes. No further clay is added to these pieces and the eventual form is decided purely by the amount of clay which is removed during the carving process. Having thrown a piece and allowed it to become firm and easy to handle, he trims it to perfect the shape, especially for his vase forms. Normally, he throws about six pieces in one session and this provides him with enough basic material for carving to keep him fully occupied for two weeks or more depending on the complexity of the design. Incising and excising is carried out when the clay has dried to a fairly hard state. Various tools are used for this work but his favourite for carving is a nib-shaped tool with a curved head and shaft, sharpened on the edges and fitted into a handle. The abrasive action of the clay causes this to wear down very quickly. The flat wire type of modelling tools are particularly useful for smoothing and scraping between raised areas of the design. He has found that some dental tools are excellent for dealing with tight corners and narrow sections while flexible aluminium scrapers are ideal for smoothing away unwanted carving marks on larger areas. It can take anything between four and ten hours to complete a single carved form. 'Probably the hardest part of all is handling the pot while carving, especially in the latter stages as it becomes more fragile. On a number of occasions I have cracked a piece while carving the last part and seen several hours of work come to nothing.'

When the pieces have been thoroughly dried, Bartz uses a fine grade of steel wool to finish smoothing the whole surface and then applies colours (commercially-prepared underglaze stains) painted with a brush or sprayed through an airbrush. The work is once-fired to 1260°C in an electric kiln before being given a final polish with wet 'n dry emery paper. This gives the work a smooth, tactile finish which he feels is more sympathetic to the carved design than a glaze.

Most potters who choose to carve porcelain refer to the problems experienced in the latter stages when the pieces are drying rapidly and too much pressure applied while carving or piercing the thin walls can cause cracks which may not be evident until the work has been fired. **Margaret Frith** (UK) mentions losses suffered in this way and also other frustrations encountered in several commercially-prepared bodies when iron specks appeared in the otherwise pure white surface. This encouraged her to prepare her own porcelain body, made by the 'slop' method, and that particular problem has now been eliminated. She throws all her bowls and then turns them upside down on the wheel to obtain an even thickness throughout the length of the wall before adding a thickly thrown ring to the base. This is re-thrown *in situ* to match the pot. 'This method has stopped any 'S' cracks appearing in the base of the bowls.'

Potters often complain about 'S' shaped cracking in the

'Lily Bowl', 14 cm high, by Rolf Bartz, 1991. Wheel-thrown and carved porcelain, with airbrushed and painted underglaze colours. This piece is unglazed but it has been polished with silicon carbide paper after firing to 1260°C in an electric kiln. *Photograph by Grant Hancock.*

'Lily Plate', 23 cm diameter, by Rolf Bartz, 1992. Wheel-thrown and carved porcelain with airbrushed and painted underglaze colours and once-fired to 1260°C in an electric kiln. Unglazed but polished with wet and dry silicon carbide paper. *Photograph by Michal Kluvanek.*

153

'Lily Vase and Plate', wheel-thrown and carved porcelain with airbrushed underglaze stain in pale blue, fired in an electric kiln to 1260°C, unglazed but polished, by Rolf Bartz, 1989.

bases of their porcelain pots but this is a problem that I am rarely troubled by in my own work. I find that bowls, especially, can be thrown while leaving sufficient thickness in the base to provide a footring which can be turned out from the inverted pot at the leatherhard stage. The pressure of the turning tools (I always use small, strapwire tools for this purpose) helps to compress and align the clay particles sufficiently to avoid cracking occurring. Bowls are usually left to dry naturally, inverted on their rims. However, on occasions when time is of the essence, I have dried out quite damp bowls with their footrings in direct contact with our Rayburn cooker-cum-central heating boiler in the kitchen without loss. I check the state of dampness in each piece by holding its foot against a mirror which reveals a ring of condensation until completely dry.

Porcelain Bowl, 28 cm diameter, by Margaret Frith, 1993. Wheel-thrown, with wax resist decoration and painted with coloured pigments and glazes (blue, black, purple, orange and white). Fired to 1280°C in a reducing atmosphere (gas kiln).
Photograph by Nick Broomhead.

Porcelain Bowl, 24 cm diameter, by Margaret Frith, 1993. Wheel-thrown and carved with floral design under a blue celadon glaze which pools in the depressions to emphasise the carving. Fired to 1280°C in a reducing atmosphere.

'Fan Vase', 22 cm high, by Rolf Bartz, 1986. Wheel-thrown porcelain, deeply carved, unglazed but polished with wet and dry silicon carbide paper after firing to 1260°C in an electric kiln.
Photograph by Grant Hancock.

Margaret Frith likes to commence carving while the clay is at the softer end of leatherhard because she says that 'after handling for an hour or two it dries quickly and you have to be very careful not to break it as you near the end of the work'. She carves with metal tools made from old hacksaw blades by her husband, David, who is a stoneware potter. The blades are given wooden handles to make them more comfortable to work with.

I like to use them like drawing with a pencil so they must be nice to hold. The smoothness of the porcelain body makes it ideal for carving on open bowls and jars. These designs are mainly floral. I draw beforehand but I like to work directly on to the clay without copying so that I can achieve greater spontaneity and flow. Every imperfection shows on a pale blue celadon, carved piece and losses can be frustratingly high. A piece of soft, malleable clay, nurtured through all its processes and carefully placed in the fire and coached to orange heat, never ceases to amaze me at the cooling of the kiln. A wonderful transformation takes place which can last for thousands of years. This is the force that drives me on!

Lidded Ginger jar with Bird Knob, by Margaret Frith, 1993. Wheel-thrown porcelain, wax resist decoration with coloured pigments and glazes (blue, black, pink, white and orange). Fired to 1280°C in reduction (gas kiln).
Photograph by Nick Broomhead.

Incising

Traditional celadon-type glazes have long been favoured by those who incise and carve porcelain. Every mark, even the smallest scratch in the clay surface is emphasised and revealed under these delicately coloured, transparent glazes. In the hands of a skilled carver today, pieces made in this way still possess the same seductive qualities that have charmed countless numbers over hundreds of years. Some of the most expressive incised work being produced in porcelain in the 1990s comes from the American potter, **Elaine Coleman**. Her fluent drawing of cranes incised on a large porcelain plate under a pale, turquoise blue celadon

'Two Jars with Elephant Lids', 14 cm and 12 cm high, by Margaret Frith, 1993. Wheel-thrown porcelain with carved decoration under a blue celadon glaze, fired to 1280°C in a reducing atmosphere.

Surface detail of a laminated agateware dish 'Rocks and Minerals Series (1988–1989), porcelain, unglazed but polished, by Maggie Barnes.

Porcelain Plate, wheel-thrown and incised with a pattern of cranes under a turquoise blue celadon glaze, 40 cm diameter × 6.5 cm high, by Elaine Coleman, 1993.

158

'Mediterranean Mosaic', handbuilt from multi-coloured, laminated and inlaid porcelain slabs and fired to 1280°C in an electric kiln, 41.5 cm × 31 cm, by Saskia Koster, 1991.

glaze demonstrates the possibilities of the technique extremely well. It is essential to make positive movements with any tools used for incising because a tentative or hesitant approach results in clumsy, awkward work that will be ruthlessly exposed under the glaze.

Neriage and inlaid techniques

Porcelain can be easily coloured with commercially-prepared stains or combinations of metallic oxides to povide the potter with a reliable and scintillating palette. Marbling is the simplest way of using compound mixtures of coloured clays but the patterns produced are fairly random. Such mixtures are usually wedged together before use and they inevitably develop linear patterns in a spiral formation around a wheel-thrown pot. If the potter wishes

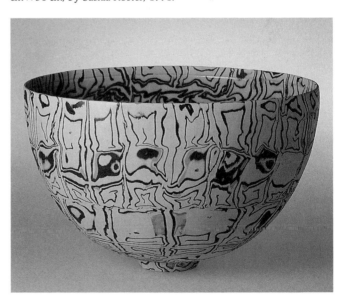

Porcelain Vase, wheel-thrown and incised with 'leaf' decoration completely covering the surface, under a dark green, celadon glaze, 45 cm high, by Elaine Coleman, 1993.

Bowl made from mainly white and blue/black-stained porcelain laminated and pressed into a mould, 23 cm × 16cm, by May An Go 1993.

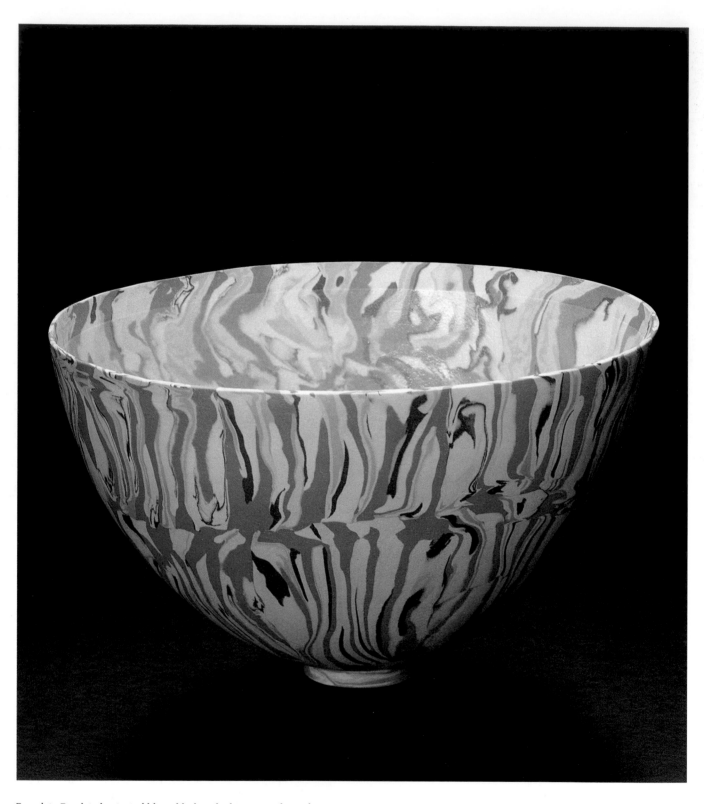

Porcelain Bowl, in laminated blues, black and white, press formed in a
mould, 26 cm × 20 cm wide and 17 cm high, by May An Go, 1992.
In the collection of Boymans Museum, Rotterdam.

to keep the inner surface white while the outside becomes a striated pattern of inlaid clays the white porcelain 'host' body is first centred on the wheel and then sliced open in two or three places around the circumference for coloured clays of the same plastic consistency to be inserted. The form is then opened up in the normal way and pulled up to the required height and shape. Any 'muddy' slip created in the process of throwing is carefully removed from the surface with a sharp tool (flexible kidney-shaped steel tools are ideal for this purpose) towards the end of the throwing process. Subsequent turning will help to increase the clarity of the colours. Further visual interest can be given to pots thrown in this manner by rhythmic, vertical fluting with a wire tool when leatherhard.

When researching my first book *Studio Porcelain* in 1979, I found only a few potters specialising in the technique of neriage or marquetry which entails the use of multi-coloured porcelain sliced up and assembled so that the pattern becomes an integral part of the form. This method allows the potter much greater control than is possible in marbling. It also requires far more care in the construction and a great deal of patience. Drying of forms made this way must be extremely gradual if cracking and separation of the constituent pieces is to be avoided. The slow building process has a certain advantage in that the maker can

'Flying Home', 20 cm high × 45 cm wide × 10 cm deep, by Curtis Benzle, 1992. Vessel form with inlaid and incised, multi-coloured porcelain. The extremely thin walls of this piece allow light to pass through enhancing and revealing both inner and outer decorated surfaces at the same time.
In the collection of The University of Miami.

Bowl in porcelain stained yellow, black and white, laminated and pressed into a mould, 23 cm × 19 cm, by May An Go, 1992.

161

adjust the design as work proceeds. In addition, what you see is what you get, allowing for slight variations in the intensity of the colours in the final firing. Problems can arise, however, where stains or oxides cause uneven fluxing of the body so that some pieces shrink more than others pulling the joints apart. This can be overcome by (a) carefully testing the proportions of colour stain added to the base body to ensure compatibility and (b) firing very slowly to the optimum temperature. Some forms may need to be supported in bisque moulds during firing to help them keep their shape without distortion due to the different fluxing effects of added stains.

Potters such as **Dorothy Feibleman** (UK), **Curtis Benzle** (USA) and **Thomas Hoadley** (USA), whose work has been featured in my previous books, have continued to refine the art of neriage while many others are now producing exciting and high quality work by the same method. In particular, three Dutch potters, **Saskia Koster**, **May An Go**, and **Judith de Vries**, and **Mieke Everaet** from Belgium have all chosen to use variations of this technique with considerable success.

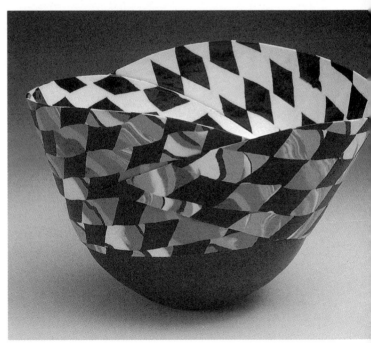

Bowl Form, porcelain, 29 cm × 19 cm × 19 cm, by Judith de Vries, 1993. The base is wheel-thrown and then pushed into an oval form and slabs of laminated and inlaid coloured porcelain are added to it. The inside has a transparent glaze but the outside is polished with very fine silicon carbide paper. Fired to 1200°C in an electric kiln.

Left Bottle Form inlaid with coloured porcelains, evoking a landscape theme, burnished exterior with glaze only on the inside. Fired to 1280°C in reduction, 30 cm high, by Sony Manning (Australia), 1994. *Photograph by David McArthur.*

Vase, 'Spring', approximately 35 cm high, by Judith de Vries, 1993. Constructed from separately made 'leaves' of laminated, coloured porcelain built up piece by piece. Fired to 1200°C in an electric kiln.

Vase form, 42 cm high, by Judith de Vries, 1992. Made from laminated strips of coloured porcelain. A multi-coloured, laminated slab is laid on top of a white porcelain slab and the two are joined together by rolling. The inside is glazed but the outside is polished. Fired to 1200°C in an electric kiln.

Vase, 'Bluebird', 35 cm high, by Judith de Vries, 1992. Constructed partly in a mould and partly by handbuilding with slabs of laminated, coloured porcelain. Two layers of clay are rolled out together (so that the inside remains white and without pattern) and then cut into strips and assembled, overlapping each other, with slip. The lower part outside is sprayed with a porcelain engobe mixed with 6% bodystain (blue) while the inside is celadon. Fired to 1200°C in an electric kiln. *Photograph by Claude Crommelin.*

165

Above
Laminated Parian vessel form, 20 cm × 11 cm approx., by Dorothy
Feibleman. Built as a flat slab and then put in to a mould. Distortion
and further changes in shape take place in the firing (1120°C in an
electric kiln) due to overloading with chemicals.
Photograph by Thomas Ward, courtesy of Bonhams, London.

(a) Pair of earrings, laminated and carved porcelain mounted on cast
and constructed 18 ct gold. Ceramic beads made by forming around a
needle and cutting with a surgical scalpel. The gold beads are cut from
18 ct gold tube on a lathe, the arrows are cast 18 ct gold. 4.5 cm.
(b) Multi-strand necklace with cast 18 ct gold arrows and had cut
ceramic arrows. Ceramic beads made around a needle and cut with a
surgical scalpel. 18 ct gold beads cut and carved on a lathe. Spacers of
18 ct gold and carved and ground agate porcelain. Side slide clasp
constructed of 18 ct gold and cut and ground agate turquoise
porcelain set in bezels. 30 cm.
(c) Single strand porcelain necklace with laminated and carved beads
and end pieces with 18ct gold cast beads and 18 ct hinged, moveable
clasp. 'The end pieces are meant to be worn at the back but people
tend to wear them at the front.' 30 cm. By Dorothy Feibleman.
Photograph courtesy of Christies, London.

Three vessel forms, 'L'Afrique', handbuilt with laminated, multi-coloured porcelain, fired to 1280°C in an electric kiln, 23 cm, 22 cm and 22 cm diameter, by Mieke Everaet, 1993.

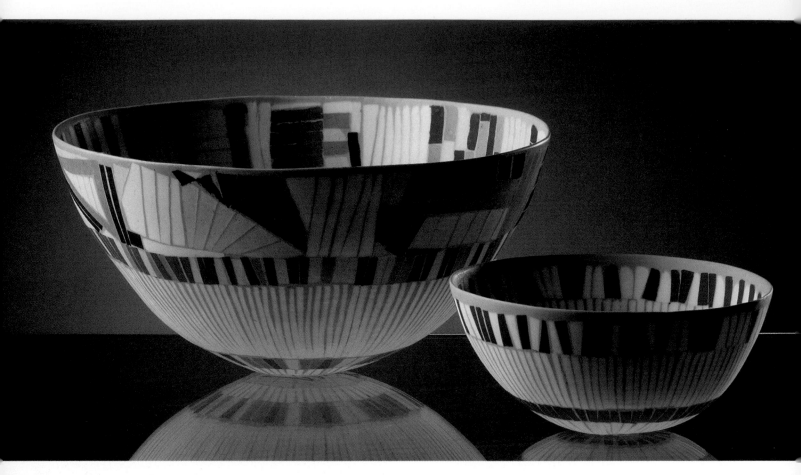

Two Bowl Forms, 20 cm and 7.5 cm diameter, by Mieke Everaet, 1992. Handbuilt with laminated, multi-coloured porcelain with their translucency enhanced by 'eggshell thin' walls. Fired to 1280°C in an electric kiln.

Saskia Koster makes architectural 'vessel' forms in which she tries to impart a sense of harmony through 'space and silence'. Inspiration for much of her work comes from the flat, empty and rather monotonous landscape around Groningen in the north west of Holland. She makes many sketches and describes attempting to translate her feeling for the 'extensive space and silence of my flat country' with its patchwork and stripes of fields and dykes, the movement of clouds across the landscape, and atmospheric conditions generated by the changing seasons. Form and colour are inseparable in her work. Colour contrasts with and accentuates elements within the object. Her abstract vessel forms are often based on combinations of circles and squares because she wants to 'create unity between forms of different qualities' and this offers opportunities 'to make unexpected objects with a tension' through their interaction. Koster makes models of part or all of her pieces in paper first. This is necessary for her to determine how slabs will fit together. Generating and rearranging geometric

forms she is always conscious of her wish to 'design an individual (three-dimensional) object having no direct reference to existing shapes'.

She introduces colour into the white porcelain two different ways. Sometimes colours are mixed thoroughly throughout the body which allows her to produce well-defined patterns. The other method requires the preparation of coloured porcelain which is then dried completely and ground into powder. A slab of plastic white porcelain is then covered with the coloured powder and rolled into the surface. The powder absorbs moisture from the damp clay and ensures a perfect marriage between the two.

The method of joining strips and slabs of porcelain with slip is common to all handbuilding, but where coloured stains are likely to cause varying rates of shrinkage, and this problem is further compounded by using slabs made up of many different elements, then drying becomes the most critical stage of the whole process. Koster says that experience has taught her 'to be very patient, *very, very* patient' and this statement is echoed by others. She says that the drying period can take as long as four months to one year according to the form and whether it is constructed as a single or double walled piece.

The extremely complex decorative patterns seen in the work of **Judith de Vries** are made piece by piece with multiple strips of coloured clays. These are rhythmically arranged in overlapping layers which, to some extent, dictate the evolution of the forms and produce a strong sensation of movement. The coloured stains and oxides are mixed with water before kneading and wedging into the white porcelain. Occasionally, she uses moulds to support the bottom, or bottles or cans as props inside vertical vessels while she is working on them. Some of the forms also require supporting in moulds while in the kiln if they are not to suffer deformation.

Dorothy Feibleman refers to her particular technique of assembling sections of poly-coloured porcelain as millefiore. In one of her methods she rolls out, separately, several thin, even slabs of clay of different colours on finely textured cloth. The slabs are coated with thin layers of slip between them and then bonded together using a rolling pin. A sharp knife is used to cut a slice vertically through the layered slab and each strip is then turned on its side to reveal the striped surface. These are rejoined with slip (often of a contrasting colour) and pushed tightly together to make into a new slab which can itself be re-cut in a variety of directions and reassembled until a particular design is achieved. Eventually, the new slab with its pattern appearing on both sides can be cut to fit a plaster mould into which it is gently coaxed. The whole is then wrapped in polythene to allow gradual drying to take place. Any smudging of the colours occurring during assembly are scraped carefully away when dried to a leatherhard state and, finally, smoothed when the pot is bone dry.

Glazes are rarely used by potters using neriage techniques because the clarity of the patterned surface could be obscured or become too reflective. The crisp designs and bright colours to be seen in the work of **Mieke Everaet**, for example, would be, in a sense, cheapened by a covering of shiny, transparent glaze. This young potter, born in 1963, has developed a uniquely personal style that brought her international recognition soon after completing her studies in Antwerp. Despite some unexpected results and failures caused by technical difficulties with uneven shrinkage of porcelain mixed in different colours, she has produced many exquisitely beautiful designs. Her pieces are well-conceived and executed with a remarkable liveliness considering their graphic complexity, while colours are carefully coordinated to unify pattern and form.

Everaet speaks of the forms, composition and colours of her pieces as evoking 'exotic influences, emotions inspired by nature or the memories of recent styles transcribed into

Bowl with strong, diagonal pattern in lines of different coloured porcelain laminated together and fired to 1320°C in a reducing atmosphere, 15 cm diameter × 8 cm high, by Rainer Doss, 1993.

Bowl with strong diagonal pattern of multi-coloured, laminated porcelain, fired to 1320°C in a reducing atmosphere, 17.5 cm diameter × 15 cm high, by Rainer Doss, 1993.

Rectangular Dish form made from press-moulded, laminated, coloured porcelain, fired to cone 8 (1250°C), 34 cm × 34 cm, by Anne Mercer, 1993.

artistic language'. The bowl is a favoured shape with its open character offering both inner and outer surfaces to view and, since the design is echoed precisely within and without, there is little room for confusion. The simplicity of these basic forms can support complex graphical imagery to a degree that would overwhelm a more consciously articulated shape. Light, especially when strategically placed, is gathered and diffused through extremely thin walls, and adds a certain magical quality. Black slip used to join the fragments of coloured porcelain appears as black boundary lines of varying thickness. The density of the black contrasts delightfully with the variable translucency of the coloured areas. Many of her bowls have thin strips of colour alternating with thinner black lines rising up vertically and radially from a small base to form a broad encircling band. This often constitutes a large part of the bowl which supports another band with contrasting colours and

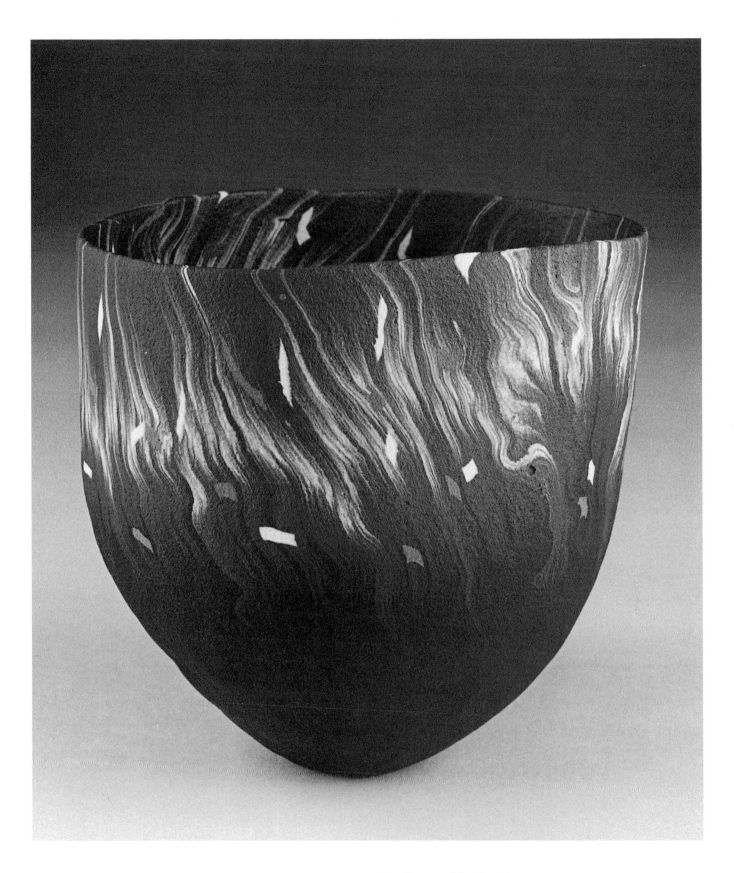

Porcelain Vessel, handbuilt from different coloured clays laminated together, by Thomas Hoadley, 1987.

Three handbuilt bowls with laminated sections, porcelain, tallest 25 cm high, by Thomas Hoadley, 1993.
Photograph by Paul Rocheleau.

tones around the rim which defines the personality of the piece. The work is fired in an electric kiln to 1280°C.

Rainer Doss (Germany) exploits diagonal rhythms in many of his inlaid bowls. Stripes of different colours and widths from wide to narrow swirl upwards, sharply angled around the forms in a strong pattern mirrored inside and out.

Of course, another way to make precise placements of colour is to inlay slips and stained plastic clay made from the same body to ensure compatibility. I use some of the dried trimmings from my wheel-thrown work as the base material. This is thoroughly dried and reduced to fine powder ready to be weighed for the additions of carefully measured percentages of stains or colouring oxides. After mixing with water this is then sieved several times through an 80s and 100s mesh to obtain even dispersal of colour throughout the mix. Unless the mixture is required to be used as a slip for painting, spraying or inlaying, I pour the

slip mixture into a plaster mould previously lined with a fine muslin cloth and leave it to stiffen to a plastic state. The cloth enables the clay to be easily removed from the mould without sticking. It can then be kneaded to a workable consistency as a coloured body for inlaying or assembling into neriage-type patterns or for making one-piece forms.

Coloured porcelain can be placed directly on top of slabs of the same body and in the same condition, whether white or coloured, and then pressed into the parent slab by rolling. This method causes the applied pieces to spread under pressure of the roller and allowances must be made for that in the design. The inlaid slabs may be used in various ways to build any kind of form but one of the most suitable is to lay the rolled slab face down over a plaster or bisque hump mould to create a dish or bowl with its decorated surface uppermost. An example of this technique can be seen in the 'Bug Plate' by **Anne Mercer** (Australia).

Inlaid slabs made by the rolling method offer other possibilities when they are stretched in the opposite direction. Instead of bending the decorated surface inwards as described above, the slab can be bent round into a cylindrical shape with the pattern outside. This movement causes the inlaid elements to separate slightly from the parent slab so that a narrow crevice appears around the outline. This fissure can itself be inlaid with slip, oxides or stains. Rolling white into white porcelain and painting a dark colour in the cracks is particularly effective. Any excess colour is removed with a metal scraper or steel wool when the work is dry.

For even greater control of the placement of colour, the completed object can be incised (up to half the thickness of the wall) or areas removed from the surface and then inlaid with slips or with plastic clay only slightly damper than the underlying form. Slow drying is usually necessary to prevent separation or cracking. Again, excess clay is cleaned up when the piece is dry. Slips must be applied until the inlay stands proud of the surface to allow for shrinkage as it dries out. Compressing the slip into the incisions when it has stiffened helps to ensure a good bond.

Tom Hoadley (USA) cites the countless variety of patterns to be found in nature as providing his primary source of inspiration but other influences 'range from fabric designs to styles of contemporary music, to painting and graphic design'. His distinctive bowl forms are begun by draping a disc of soft clay, whether patterned or a solid colour, over a bisqued hump mould. When it has stiffened enough to hold its shape, it is removed from the mould and turned upright on to a batt with the outer edge supported by wads of clay. The rim is then moistened and scored so

that slices taken from variously patterned, laminated blocks can be attached and built up into the main walls of the pot. The sides are then paddled on the outside while a cloth-covered wad is used for support on the inside. Gently beating the pot in this way helps to strengthen the seams, compressing the patterns, and also stretches the form into the required shape. This forming process is followed by slow drying, scraping with a metal rib at the leatherhard stage, and several sandings both before and after the bisque and high firings.

Inlaid coloured porcelains which are polished with silicon carbide grits rather than glazed have a special visual and tactile appeal. Without a 'skin' of glaze distancing the observer from direct contact with the piece, the colours remain clean and clear. Matt glazes tend to obscure the patterns while transparent glossy ones produce reflections which disturb the form. It is hardly surprising to find so many potters in the 1990s who are attracted to working with techniques such as neriage and inlays do so because their work in most respects is little changed in appearance after firing. They have reduced the number of variables due to glaze composition and body fit or the uncertain effects of atmosphere adjustments in the kiln during firing. An electric kiln may not give them those delightful surprises (and occasional disasters!) which can be the reward of reduction firing in a live flame kiln but it does provide them with an enviable degree of reliability.

'Bug Plate', made from press-moulded, laminated, coloured porcelain, fired to 1250°C (cone 8), 22 cm × 22 cm, by Anne Mercer, 1993.

GLAZES FOR PORCELAIN

The chemistry of glazes is a vast subject and open to limitless possibilities far beyond the scope of this book to deal with in any detail but a suggested reading list will be found at the end of the book. It is a subject that is of only passing interest to those ceramicists who either use no glaze at all or who prefer to rely on commercially-prepared glazes that they know will perform reliably for their purposes. However, it is an area of ceramics which, despite many publications covering every aspect of the technology involved, continues to fascinate or mystify many.

The colour response of white porcelain has been previously mentioned with regard to stains, oxides and slips but even the most simple of glazes on porcelain can have unequalled luminosity. A classic example is a glaze composed of just two natural materials:

Cornish stone	85 parts by weight
Whiting	15 parts by weight

Cornish stone is a feldspathoid containing feldspar, quartz, kaolinite, mica and a small amount of fluorspar so it consists of enough of the right constituents to melt into a glassy state on its own but to produce a reliable glaze other materials are normally added. A number of alkalis such as potash, soda, calcia and magnesia are introduced into a glaze composition by Cornish stone but in the above recipe further calcia is added in the form of whiting (calcium carbonate) to act as a flux. This well-known glaze is one which I have used extensively for its ability to craze evenly over porcelain. The resulting fine network of lines can be stained in various ways to emphasise the crackle pattern. Experience has taught me that the thickness of the glaze coating dictates the nature of the crackle. The more thickly glaze is applied, the wider apart the (initial) crackle lines will be. The converse is also true but if the glaze is too thin no noticeable crazing will occur. However, if the combined thicknesses of glaze on inner and outer surfaces exceeds that of the body wall it can cause cracks and splits around the rim of a bowl. Crazing is likely to continue for a while and so the resulting crackles can be stained with one or more colours. Ink is normally used for this purpose but finely ground oxides of iron, copper, cobalt or manganese can be mixed with a medium and rubbed into the lines and the piece refired to produce further visual texture. New crackle patterns occur on cooling and these can then be stained with inks for extra interest. This glaze has a fairly wide firing range and I have used it successfully at temperatures between 1220°C and 1300°C. Without additions of colouring elements and in the relatively clean atmosphere of an electric kiln, the glaze becomes a glossy, slightly warm white, but under reduction conditions in a live flame kiln, it is affected by minute traces of iron present in the materials making up body and glaze which produces a cooler, bluish tint. This simple glaze offers many possibilities for use under or over other coloured glazes, over coloured slips or when stains are added to it. One can take it as a starting point for further development and experi-

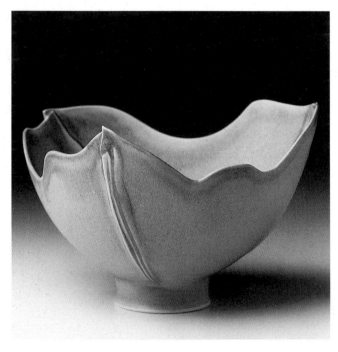

Porcelain Bowl, trimmed and altered, with a matt feldspar glaze fired to cone 9 (1280°C) in an electric kiln, by Gwen Heffner, 1993. *Photograph by Ron Forth.*

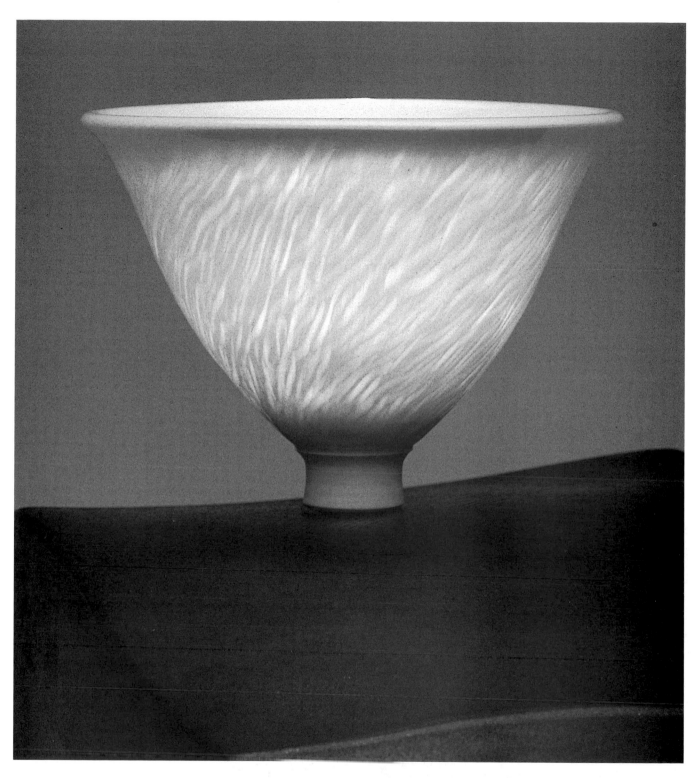

Translucent porcelain bowl, by Patrick Piccarelle (Belgium), 1993.
Wheel-thrown and trimmed several times, carved and bisque fired and
then engraved with dental tools. The holes are filled with a high
viscosity glaze (Cornish stone 85, whiting 15) and then glazed overall
with a palette of feldspathic glazes. Fired in reduction to 1280°–
1300°C (gas kiln).

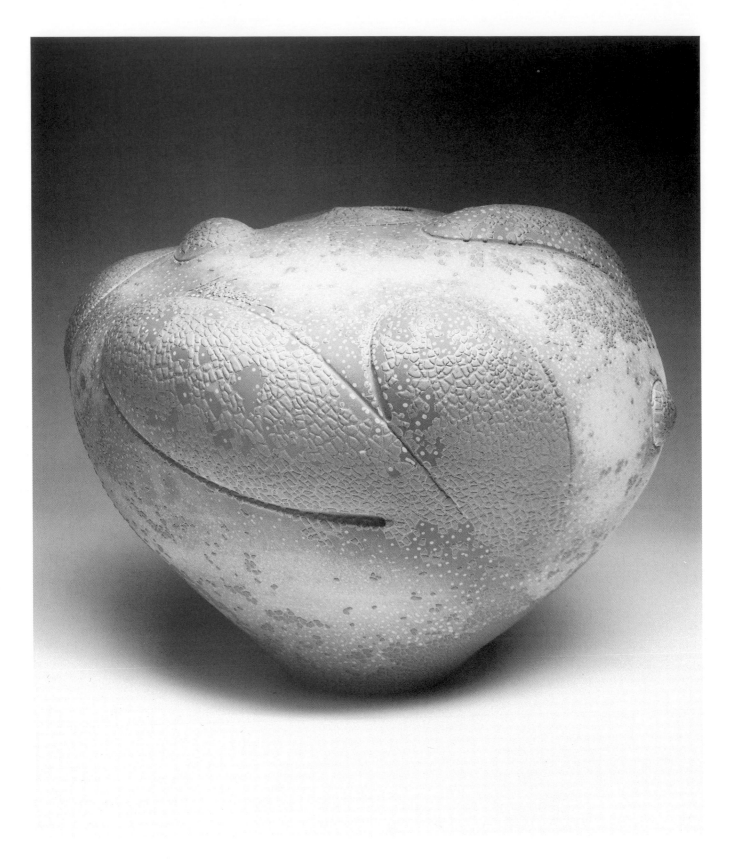

Loosely thrown porcelain vase with a crackle glaze applied over a
different, solid glaze and fired to cone 10 in a reduction atmosphere,
30 cm high × 40 cm wide, by Tom Coleman, 1993.

ment. Adjustments can be made by progressively substituting small amounts of china clay for some of the Cornish stone, for example, to produce a satin rather than a glossy surface. Natural oils in human skin can impede the application of water-based inks into the crackled glaze so pots destined to be stained should be handled carefully and protected with cloth until the process of inking has been completed.

Glaze chemistry is something of a mystery to many amateur potters and there is also a surprising number of professionals who admit to having little knowledge or interest in the subject. The search for an ideal, reliable glaze that will transform pots with its magical qualities certainly occupies a large proportion of pottery students around the world. Glaze tests are often fitted into odd spaces in the kiln as part of this quest. Ultimately, most sensible potters rely on very few glazes which they get to know and understand intimately.

Crystalline glaze experiments

A great deal of effort is sometimes put into trying to grow crystals in glazes. The oxides which act as crystallisers and opacifiers in a glaze are provided by baria (BaO), calcia (CaO), magnesia (MgO), tin (SnO_2), titania (TiO_2), zinc (ZnO) and zirconia (ZrO_2). Porcelain bodies are particularly well-suited to crystalline glazes, which can have a kind of mystical quality, but they are not universally popular. Large, flamboyant crystals spreading over the surface of a pot can tend to dominate and distract from the form. The maker's satisfaction is often in achieving these random effects irrespective of whether they properly complement the form. The nature of the glaze composition and the degree of control exercised during the firing cycle will, to some extent, condition the results but a good deal must be left, inevitably to chance. **Hein Severijns** (Holland) has had extensive experience of crystalline glazes over many years and he warns ceramicists who do not fully comprehend glaze technology against adventuring into the crystalline field. It is not his intention to discourage experiments with such glazes but he feels that it is too easy to be seduced by them and that too often excellent crystalline effects are used in the 'embellishment of imperfect inappropriate pots'.

Severijns has studied many articles dealing with the subject and has been surprised to find the same glaze recipes appearing in which the main component is an American Ferro-frit, difficult to obtain in Europe, without suggesting alternatives. He rarely uses the brighter, shiny

Bottle Vase, 43 cm high × 20 cm diameter, by Hein Severijns, 1993. Wheel-thrown porcelain, with matt crystalline glazes coloured with cobalt, iron and titanium and fired to 1280°C in an electric kiln. The kiln is cooled slowly for 12 hours for the temperature to drop to 980°C to encourage crystal growth.
Photograph by Peter Bors.

179

'Bottle Vase', 43 cm high, by Hein Severijns, 1993. Wheel-thrown porcelain with matt crystalline glazes fired in an electric kiln to 1280°C and cooled slowly for 12 hours down to 980°C to encourage crystal growth.
Photograph by Hein Severijns.

crystalline glazes because he prefers the silky touch of satin matt surfaces even though they provide more of a challenge to produce. They are more unreliable and, he says, their success depends on many more factors than those that influence the glossy types. They are more aesthetically appealing to him with their smaller, rounder crystals embedded within the surface 'like a starry sky'.

The development of crystals within a glaze is dependent upon (a) the chemical composition and its physical properties and (b) the temperature and duration of the firing and cooling cycles. In his excellent book on *Ceramic Glazes* (see bibliography), Parmelee stresses the important role played by the nature of the glaze.

Chiefly because it must serve as a solvent for the silicates which are later separated during cooling and because its physical properties, notably the viscosity during that period, must be favourable to the growth of the crystals. This is shown by the widely different types of glazes in which zinc silicate, for example, may be induced to crystallise. The reaction of the glaze and the body, in so far as the solution from the latter is concerned, may be important in some instances since a fundamental relationship is thereby disturbed

Severijns' glazes are based on 'the crystallisation of zinc-barium-silicates with quite complex crystal structures whereas the shinier glaze crystals are mainly composed of willemite Zn_2SiO_4 with colouring oxides taken into the crystal matrix'. The basic formula for his glazes varies within the following limits based on the molecular or unity method devised by Seger:

KNaO	0.15−0.20				
ZnO	0.35−0.50				
BaO	0.20−0.40	Al_2O_3	0.15−0.20	SiO_2	1.5−2.2
CaO	0.05−0.15				
MgO	0.05−0.10				

His glazes are applied in several layers.

For the first layer of glaze I add 5% of SnO_2 and 5% of TiO_2 plus some quartz to make it somewhat stiffer and reduce the risk of running. (I always fire my pieces on a thin disc of soft refractory brick to absorb any glaze runs which can be ground away and polished later if necessary.) This layer is applied quite thickly. Subsequently, glaze is put on with a brush or by spraying very thin layers of the base glaze coloured with natural oxides from cobalt, copper, iron, manganese and titanium. Up to six layers may be used. It is interesting to note that base glazes with less than 0.35 ZnO and more than 0.35 BaO give rose-red colours with 2% nickel oxide, while the same percentage of nickel oxide in a glaze containing less than 0.20 BaO and more than 0.45 ZnO produces blue crystals against a light brown background. Thin layers of glaze rich in zinc silicates are applied in between and the final layer contains compounds of molybdenum, tungsten or vanadium to influence and improve the crystallisation.

Limoges porcelain bodies (mixtures of TM10, TM18 and 45937) are used for Severijns' wheel-thrown vessels. Bisque firing is taken to the slightly higher than usual temperature of 1100°C to reduce the eventual reaction between body and glaze. The final glaze firing is first taken up to 1260°–1280°C and then the kiln is rapidly cooled to 1080°C to assist the formation of nuclei before raising the temperature again to be held at 1150°C for three hours. This is followed by a gradual firing down process which involves dropping the temperature in a series of cooling steps to 1120°C, 1100°C, 1050°C, then back up to 1100°C, 1070°C, 1040°C and 1000°C for periods each varying between half an hour and three-quarters of an hour. He has found that the firing cycle contributes as much as the glaze composition to the ultimate success of crystalline glaze development but he insists that it is for every potter to discover his own personal 'signature' through the many variables involved.

I prefer to work empirically with dry batches of glaze materials measured by weight rather than to work out formulae by molecular equivalents. As long as careful and thorough records are kept, not only of the materials used but also concerning the placement of pots in the kiln, the kiln atmosphere, the pattern of firing and cooling and the temperature reached, this method can suffice for most potters. A crystalline glaze recipe, which resulted from such practical experiments I conducted several years ago, has a silky smooth surface similar to those favoured by Hein Severijns. This glaze proved well-suited to porcelain, providing that it was applied to the right thickness, without such a lengthy cooling programme. Doubtless it would have produced more consistent crystalline results had I not lacked sufficient patience to watch over the kiln and had

'Drop Form', 22 cm high, by Hein Severijns, 1993. Wheel-thrown porcelain with matt crystalline glazes fired in an electric kiln to 1280°C and cooled slowly to 980°C in 12 hours to encourage crystal growth.
Photograph by Hein Severijns.

attempted a longer period of cooling to allow time for the crystals to grow! The recipe for my glaze could be used as a starting point for further exploration so I give the details as follows:

Nepheline syenite	50	parts by weight
Barium carbonate	15	parts by weight
Zinc oxide	20	parts by weight
Flint	15	parts by weight
	100	

Up to four per cent light rutile should be added to the above (or titanium dioxide which gives slightly different results) to 'seed' the crystals. Colouring carbonates of copper (0.5 per cent–2 per cent) or cobalt (0.25 per cent–1 per cent), or oxides of iron (2 per cent–4 per cent), manganese (up to 4 per cent) or nickel (up to 2 per cent) can be added also singly or in combination (to a suggested total maximum of 4 per cent colourant) for a variety of coloured crystal formations when fired in an electric kiln to 1260°C. Bungs and spyholes should be left closed and the kiln unopened until completely cold. Crystalline glazes are under a great deal of compression and if the above glaze is applied too thickly, it can cause thinly thrown porcelain to fracture, but if too thin few crystals will appear. This is very much a matter for trial and error experiments as with all the recipes printed in this book.

Another potter who has conducted extensive tests and experiments with crystalline glazes, **Derek Clarkson** (UK), differs in his approach to the subject from that of Severijns although they share much common ground. Clarkson wrote an article published in *Ceramic Review* (No. 137 in 1992) describing his methods in some detail and he has generously supplied further information for the purposes of this book. He declares that he can offer no rational explanation for the attraction crystalline glazes holds for him. 'It can be a passionate, obsessive affair overriding one's good sense!' His practical work, after several years, is still experimental with each glaze having a different firing cycle. The use of a fairly small (2 cu. ft.) electric kiln with a programme controller and containing no more than six to

Porcelain Vase, 20 cm high, by Derek Clarkson, 1993. Wheel-thrown, with crystalline glaze producing large green crystals (copper carbonate with titanium dioxide). Fired to 1280°C and cooled slowly from 1078°C to 1030°C in five and a half hours.

Porcelain Bottle, wheel-thrown, with dark green crystalline glaze (refer to text for details of recipe and firing programme), 21.5 cm high, by Derek Clarkson, 1993.
Photograph by David Seed.

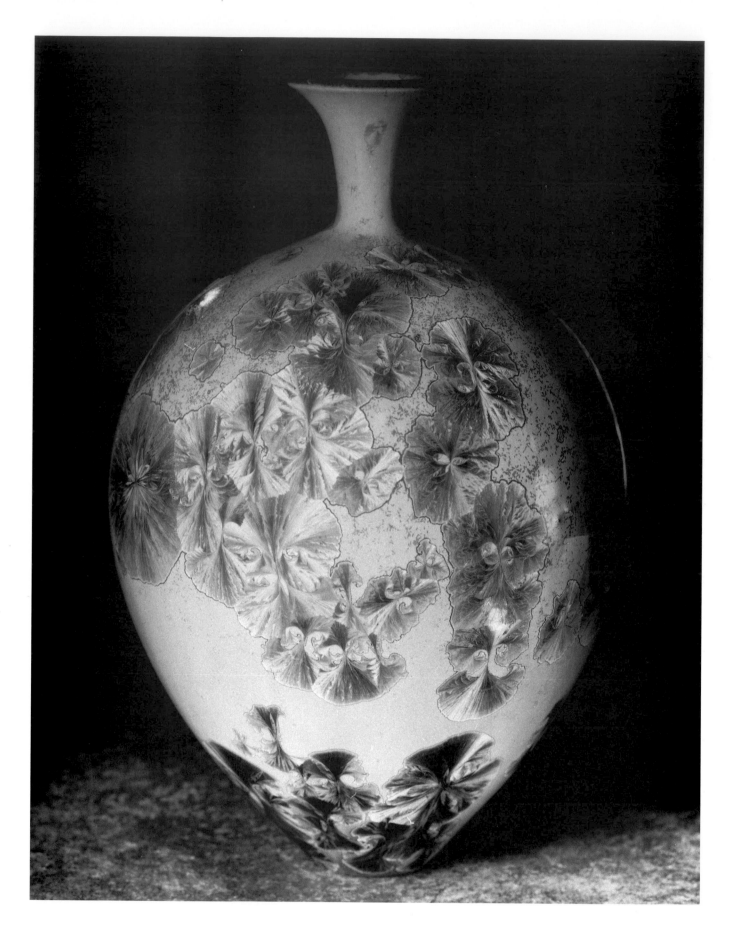

eight pots per firing makes this a practical, economical proposition. His 12 cu. ft. gas kiln is 'much more inhibiting' for these experiments.

Clarkson uses a chemical balance to accurately measure and make up just sufficient glaze for each pot. Colouring oxides are sieved through a 120s mesh cup sieve before adding to the glaze, and the complete mixture is twice passed through an 80s mesh sieve to ensure even dispersal. The glaze, mixed to a creamy consistency, is brushed on to the pot with a one inch brush, applying the bulk of it on to the top third (most of his crystalline glazes are used on narrow necked 'bottle' forms and approximately 100 g dry weight is used to coat a bottle form 26 cm high with the inside left unglazed). Wider necked forms are glazed inside with a non-crystalline glaze in order to avoid cracking the piece by the pooling of glaze in the bottom were a crystalline type to be used. A further layer of crystalline glaze is applied by brush over the first for 5–6 cm down the neck of the piece. 'This glaze flows down over the first giving a linking crystalline effect.'

For the development of large crystals on a plain background, the glaze has to be quite fluid. This can create problems with glaze running off the pot and on to the kiln shelf. In order to deal with this occurrence, Clarkson uses a flat-bottomed saucer (bisque fired from the same porcelain body to equalise the shrinkage) to contain any excess glaze, and a pedestal about 3 cm high is also made from the same body to lift the pot above that pooled glaze in the saucer. The pedestal is made to fit *exactly* to the diameter of the footring in the base of the pot. After bisque firing, a mixture of 2/3 flint and 1/3 china clay is generously applied between the pot and its pedestal to assist separation after the glaze firing. Separation is then achieved by first scratching through the glaze surface all the way around the junction with a glass or tile cutter and then tapping gently with a chisel around this line. The footring is then smoothed with a flint tungsten carbide disc mounted in an electric drill and finished off with carborundum paper or block.

The colouring oxides mainly used by Clarkson are cobalt carbonate, copper carbonate, manganese dioxide and red iron oxide in different combinations using all four or just one in amounts from 0.05 per cent to 6 per cent. A limitless range of colours, varying in subtlety, are possible

Covered Jar, porcelain with dry, wood ash glaze, salt fired to cone 10, height 18 cm × 20 cm wide, by Neil Moss (USA), 1993.

and which can be repeated accurately. He finds that there need be no end to experimenting in the search for more matt glazes, more muted colours, the introduction of a wider range of materials into the glazes, and in 'seeding' to obtain the crystal formations. 'The number of crystals forming in the glaze and their location on the pot cannot be controlled precisely. However, with careful attention to every detail of the making process, some repetition of fairly similar characteristics can be achieved. The clay, the glaze composition, its application and the firing cycle all play a vital part.'

Clarkson conducts the usual bisque firing but takes his glaze kiln up to 900°C as for a normal glost and proceeds from that point to fire up to around 1260°–1290°C as quickly as possible before switching off the kiln. The temperature is then encouraged to drop rapidly by opening vents and spyholes (to prevent glaze running too much) until 'somewhere between 1150°C and 1020°C at which temperature crystals develop'. All openings in the kiln are then closed and the electricity switched on again to hold the temperature steady within this range for up to five hours. The kiln is then switched off and allowed to cool naturally. 'Periods of moving to higher and/or lower temperatures will produce concentric bands within the crystals.'

Titanium dioxide is an important ingredient for aiding crystal formations in glazes. Amounts about five per cent

Porcelain Bottle, 26 cm high, by Derek Clarkson, 1993. Wheel-thrown, with crystalline glaze (silvery blue crystals on a speckled tan background). Details of this glaze recipe and its firing programme are given in the text.
Photograph by David Seed.

tend to make the glaze less shiny and the background becomes a darker, opaque tan colour and above 10 per cent larger crystals begin to beak up into the more familiar mottled surface obtained in many glazes with titanium/rutile compositions.

Zinc oxide also encourages crystal growth and it often contributes about 25 per cent of the glaze recipe. Clarkson has found that the high shrinkage problems associated with zinc oxide can be reduced by calcining it in a bisque-fired bowl to about 1000°C. Its volume will decrease but its weight will be reduced only slightly by calcining.

Crystalline glaze recipes

The glaze recipe and firing cycle used by Derek Clarkson for the porcelain bottle illustrated on page 183 is as follows:

Ferro Frit 3110	42.0	*This glaze was fired in 2 hrs. 5 min from 900°C to*
Calcined zinc oxide	31.5	*1260°C, then cooled to 1095°C and held there for*
Flint	20.0	*1 hr. 25 mins, then cooled to 1065°C and held there for*
Titanium dioxide	5.5	*1 hr. 30 mins, then cooled to 1055°C and held there for*
Alumina hydrate	0.4	*15 mins, then cooled to 1045°C and held there for*
China clay	0.6	*15 mins, and allowed to cool completely.*

+ 6% Copper carbonate

The recipe and firing cycle for the porcelain bottle illustrated on page 184 was:

Ferro Frit 3110	43.0	*This glaze was fired in 1 hr. 50 mins from 900°C to*
Calcined zinc oxide	29.0	*1260°C then cooled to 1093°C and held there for*
Flint	19.0	*1 hr. 25 mins then cooled to 1069°C and held there for*
Titanium dioxide	8.0	*1 hr. 45 mins then cooled to 1053°C and then held there for*
Alumina hydrate	0.5	*1 hr 30 mins then cooled to 1041°C and held there for*
China clay	0.5	*25 mins and then allowed to cool completely.*

+ 0.4% Copper carbonate
1.2% Manganese dioxide

The variables are infinite but the meticulous record-keeping shown in these two examples by Derek Clarkson indicate the importance he attaches to noting every detail of the process involved in the successful creation of crystalline glazes.

Further glaze recipes for porcelain

Sandra Black uses the following glaze for 1260°–1280°C which has a 'dry' surface:

Whiting	50 parts by weight of dry material
China clay	50 parts by weight of dry material
Feldspar	50 parts by weight of dry material

Colours are produced by adding different glaze stains up to a maximum of 10 per cent to obtain the intensity of colour required. Glazes are sieved through at least an 80s mesh. For her carved pieces where she wishes to give greater emphasis to the design, she used a clear glaze 'originally developed for hotel china' with a firing range of 1220°–1300°C but which performs best between 1260°–1280°C. This glaze has proved to be very reliable and it has a low

Large porcelain pot, 75 cm diameter, by Paul Davis, 1993. Wheel-thrown, with a black crystalline glaze composed of feldspar, the local Albury slip (similar in nature to the well known Albany slip from the USA) and a high proportion of manganese dioxide. Fired to between cones 10 and 11 in a reducing atmosphere. (The full recipe for this glaze is potash feldspar 67.3; whiting 2.79; talc 1.35, kaolin 4.45; silica 3.6, red iron oxide .76; manganese dioxide 20.5, all parts by weight.)

rate of thermal expansion. Its quality can be improved further by ball milling and, of course, it can be coloured in the usual way or made opaque by the addition of five per cent tin oxide:

Nepheline syenite	29.3	parts by weight
Whiting	9.7	
Barium carbonate	6.4	
Zinc oxide	7.9	
Talc	3.9	
China clay	10.1	
Ball clay	5.0	
Silica	27.7	

Paul Davis offers the following recipes which he uses for reduction firings to 1300°–1320°C:

Celadon Glaze (for cone 10)

Potash feldspar	61.26
Talc	.04
Whiting	10.22
China clay	2.57
Silica	26.41
Iron silicate	4.00
Red iron oxide	.02

Apricot Lustre Shino Glaze (for cone 10)

Nepheline syenite	50.9	
Potash feldspar	39.2	Spray over top of glaze
Terracotta clay	6.1	with pine ash for rich
China clay	9.2	lustrous orange.
Salt	3.6	

Porcelain Vase, 30 cm high × 42.5 cm diameter, by Elaine Coleman, 1993. Wheel-thrown and incised (using dental tools) with cranes around the upper part under a green, celadon glaze which pools in the depressions giving emphasis to the design.

Porcelain Bowl, 45 cm diameter, by Paul Davis, 1993. Brightly coloured, with glaze containing a large proportion of calcined alumina which produces a sandy textured surface. This is fired to 1320°C in a reduction atmosphere and then reworked with a maiolica type glaze, stained with various colours and refired to 1100°C.

Chun Glaze (*for cone 10*)

Potash feldspar	61.25
Soda feldspar	1.70
Talc	1.24
Whiting	18.29
Bone ash	.57
Silica	16.90
Red iron oxide	.28
Yellow ochre	1.60

Johan Broekema offers the following glazes for reduction firing at 1320°C:

(a) *Matt black glaze:*

Feldspar	25	
Whiting	11	
Magnesite	15	add 8% black body stain
China clay	14	
Quartz	25	

Vessel Form, wheel-thrown porcelain with copper red glaze fired in
reduction, 16 cm high × 11 cm wide, by Johan Broekema, 1993.

(b) Clear porcelain glaze:

Feldspar	24.5
Whiting	24.0
Magnesite	3.0
China clay	19.0
Quartz	29.5

(c) Copper red glaze:

Soda feldspar	42
China clay	8
Whiting	15
Quartz	33
Calcium borate	5

+ zinc oxide 2%, tin oxide 2%, copper cabonate 1%.

Left   Lidded Vessel, wheel-thrown porcelain with black and white banded glazes, 13 cm high × 8 cm wide, by Johan Broekema, 1993.

Right   Porcelain Vase, 36 cm high × 21 cm diameter, by Hein Severijns, 1993. Wheel-thrown, with matt crystalline glazes coloured with cobalt, titanium, nickel, copper and iron. Fired to 1280°C in an electric kiln and cooled very slowly to encourage crystal growth. *Photograph by Peter Bors.*

Below   Cone-shaped vessel form with domed lid, wheel-thrown porcelain banded with various colour stains on a satin white glaze, 9 cm high × 9 cm wide, by Johan Broekema, 1993.

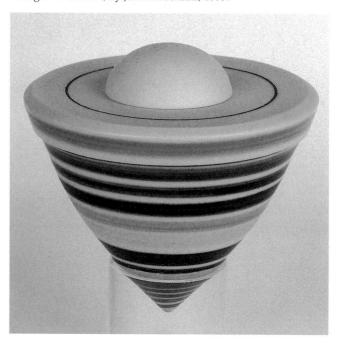

Hein Severijns offers two crystalline glaze recipes with the amounts given as percentages for quick reference. Both are for 1260°–1280°C.

Matt–semi matt base glaze

Potash feldspar FFF or B411	33	
Soda feldspar F7 Ventilato	12	'Add colouring oxides and apply
Zinc oxide	15	many layers. In between these, very thin
Barium carbonate	18	layers of glaze having 80 per cent $2ZnO.SiO_2$
Lead bisilicate frit	5	(zinc silicate), quartz, whiting and talc,
China clay	3	eventually with 5% iron oxide.'
Talc	5	
Quartz	5	
Whiting	4	
	100	

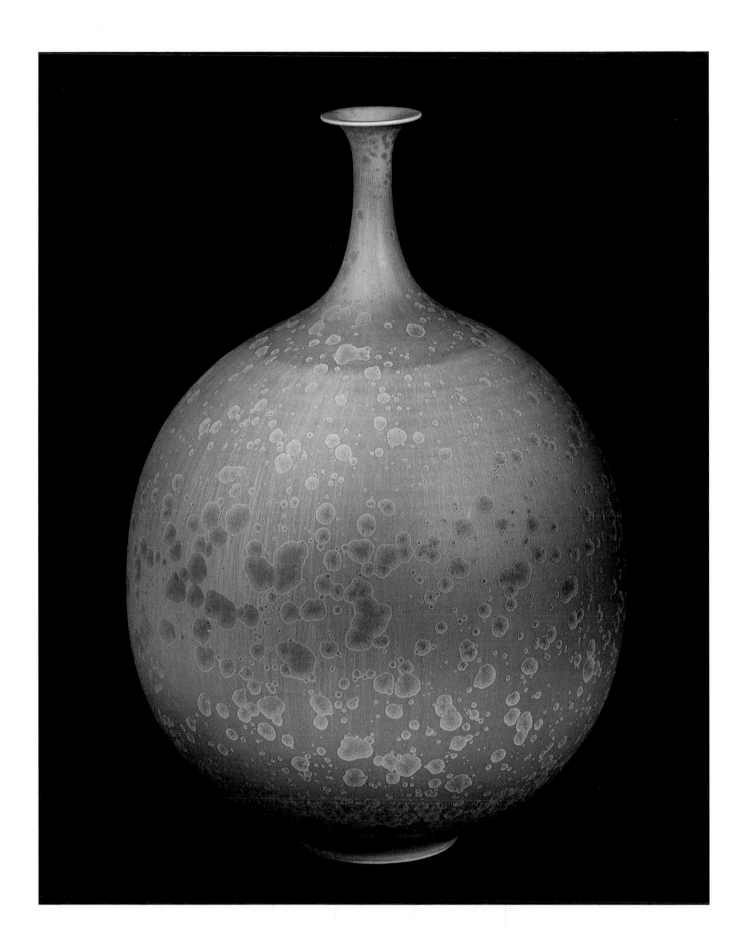

Shiny–brilliant base glaze

Frit (Reimbold & Strick A2120)	34	
Frit (Reimbold & Strick A3389)	16	'Add colouring
Zinc oxide	25	oxides and
China clay	2	apply thickly!'
Titanium dioxide	5	
Quartz	18	
	100	

Glaze application

Derek Clarkson gives the following recipe for his favourite celadon glaze:

Cornwall stone	80
Ball clay AT	5
Molochite	5
Wollastonite	10
Talc	6
Bentonite	1
Red iron oxide	1

Clarkson applies his crystalline glazes by brushing but dips pots into his ash glaze. This glaze needs a generous thickness but requires careful application because any

Porcelain Mug, 10 cm high × 12.5 cm wide, by Gail Russell, 1993. Wheel-thrown, with applied sprigging taken from antique lace and a press-moulded handle from a silver tray. Green celadon glaze.

unevenness in the glaze will remain after firing. He holds his bottles at the rim/neck and dips them, base first, into the glaze up to the narrowest part of the shoulder. As soon as the glaze is dry enough to touch (almost immediately) the top of the bottle is then glazed down to meet up with the previously glazed area. The inside is left unglazed. Brush decoration is carried out whilst the applied glaze is still damp because dry glaze on the porous porcelain body sucks the water-mixed oxide pigment too quickly from the brush, thus making long thin brush strokes difficult. 'Inadequate brush strokes cannot be "touched up" but it is possible to scrape off a little pigment (shortening a too long brush stroke or slimming one too fat). However, this should be kept to a minimum.'

I prefer to spray all my glazes because I want to have an even layer with no 'runs' or fingermarks to mar the surface. It is essential to do this in a properly vented spray booth. Porcelain bisque is notoriously difficult to dip glaze because it can become easily saturated and take a very long time to dry. Some potters try to overcome this problem by dampening the bisque slightly to lessen the absorption, but it is better either to adjust the glaze suspension with the right amount of water or to fire the bisque to a higher temperature to reduce its porosity. Double dipping of glazes is much easier to accomplish on stoneware bisque. Overlaying one or more glazes offers interesting possibilities. This is especially true when, for example, a 'dry' or matt glaze is applied on top of a more fluid one. The first glaze melts and begins to flow dragging and breaking the surface of the drier glaze. When one glaze is dark in colour and the other light, even greater visual interest can develop. One method which I have found very rewarding to explore is a kind of glaze sgraffito. This entails spraying one glaze which, can be drawn into, as soon as it is dry, with a sharp tool (not necessarily pointed, almost any shape will do) right through to the underlying body. Traces of glaze will be left and, even with a white glaze, there will be a marked difference between the sgraffito and the glaze when fired. The first layer of glaze and sgraffito can itself be oversprayed (preferably before it is *completely* dry in order to lessen the risk of lifting off the first layer which can cause 'crawling'), with another glaze different in character, colour or tone and the two will interact but the design will remain clear to see. This is a very direct way of working that can be extremely satisfying (see examples on page 193). I have achieved some of my best results when using this glazing method with a clear, transparent glaze under a matt, or even dry, glaze stained with various oxides. Rich blues, greens and reds (from cobalt and copper in combination or with other oxides) can appear where the

Porcelain Teaset by Joanna Howells (UK). Each piece is wheel-thrown as a complete sphere and then altered into the various forms. Celadon glaze fired to 1280°C.

two glazes merge together and the more linear sgraffito design is picked out with contrasting, darker colour.

I rarely do more than make simple, experimental 'line blends' when working out new glaze compositions. Since I use a spray booth to apply all my glazes, the 'waste' glaze which gathers on the inner walls is added to that which is fettled from the bases of pots to mix together into new glazes. These are usually fairly predictable in colour and texture but I make regular tests, nevertheless, and am occasionally surprised by the results. More often, adjustments are made to each batch of any size until I am satisfied with its appearance and performance. It is a simple matter to increase the flux content of any glaze which is too dry, or to add china clay to those which would benefit from a more matt surface. This seemingly haphazard procedure reduces the waste that would otherwise occur when sprayed glazes of different kinds are in constant use in a small workshop.

Porcelain Bowl, 13 cm high × 29 cm diameter, by Peter Lane, 1990. Wheel-thrown porcelain, with glossy, transparent glaze incised through to the body and then oversprayed with a matt barium glaze containing cobalt carbonate and iron oxide. Fired to 1280°C in a reducing atmosphere (Liquid Propane Gas kiln).

193

Bottle Form, wheel-thrown porcelain, with satin matt white glaze incised through to the body prior to firing to 1260°C in an electric kiln 20.5 cm high, by Peter Lane, 1991.

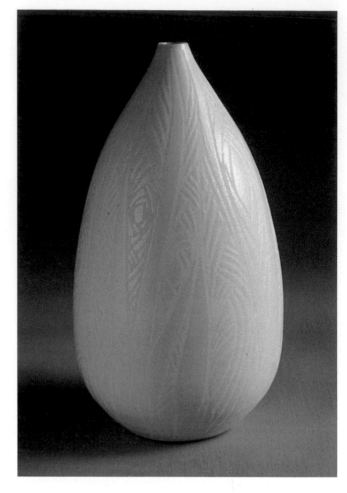

One of my favourite glazes works equally well for porcelain in both oxidation and reduction firings and the recipe and also for others better-suited to oxidation are as follows:

1260°C–1280°C

Potash feldspar	65
China clay	5
Barium carbonate	20
Dolomite	10

Add (a) 0.75% copper carbonate and 0.25% cobalt carbonate or (b) 0.25% cobalt carbonate and 2% red iron oxide or (c) 0.75% copper carbonate and 2.5% rutile or other combinations for colour.

Smooth matt 1250°C (Oxidation)

Nepheline syenite	45
Barium carbonate	13
Zinc oxide	20
Flint	20
Lithium carbonate	3

Smooth matt surface with crystal inclusions. Interesting variegated colour from additions of 3–4% rutile together with up to 2% copper carbonate or up to 1% cobalt carbonate. Titanium dioxide may be used in place of rutile with slightly different results. Slow cooling will aid the growth of crystals. *Too thick an application of glaze can cause runs and risks cracking thinly made porcelain.*

Shiny porcelain glaze 1260°C. (Oxidation)

Nepheline syenite	70
Whiting	9
Zinc oxide	9
Flint	10
Lithium carbonate	2

Shiny glaze studded with tiny crystals. Inclined to run above 1260°C if applied too thickly. The addition of 2–4% rutile or titanium dioxide in combination with up to 2% copper carbonate gives good results but it is worth experimenting with small amounts of cobalt, iron, manganese also.

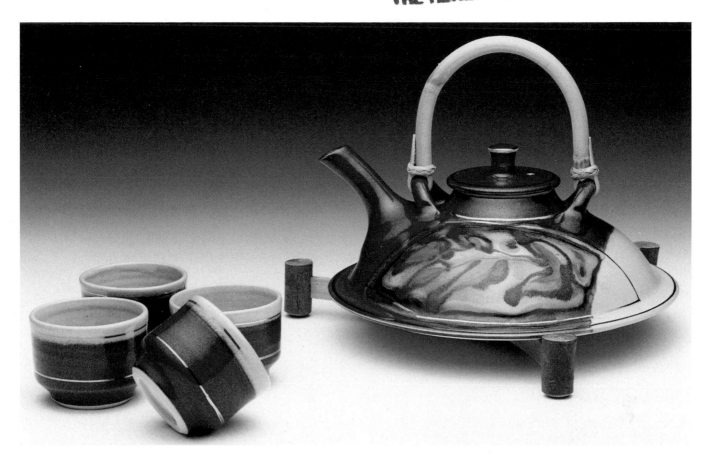

Cane-handled Teapot with wooden stand and four cups, 26 cm diameter, by Bryan Trueman, 1992. Wheel-thrown porcelain with wax resisted glazes (Chun, copper, iron and chrome) fired in reduction to 1300°C and the gold lustre applied and refired to 740°C in oxidation. *Photograph by Uffe Schulze.*

Bryan Trueman (UK) uses a variety of overlaid glazes with wax resists to produce rich visual textures. He has always tried to use glazes in a very personal way, calling upon his previous experience in painting and printmaking, with masking techniques that allow him

to convey my sensory responses to things around me. By orchestrating an exotic collection of high temperature glazes and anticipating their movement, distortion and interaction with each other and experimenting with different temperatures and kiln atmospheres have been the most significant aspects of my work. The challenge has always been the 'freeze frame' effect of shutting down the kiln at the precise moment when all the melting and colour maturation has taken place and you think that you have achieved what you had set out to do. These refined critical judgements are the results of numerous firings in which failures as well as successes combine to establish parameters that enable me to develop greater understanding of the process.

'Frederick Henry Bay Window Series', 45 cm diameter, by Bryan Trueman (UK), 1992. Large porcelain platter, wheel-thrown, decorated with multiple glazes (Chun, copper, iron, rutile and chrome) poured over wax resist design. Fired to 1300°C in reduction atmosphere (ceramic fibre, downdraught LPG kiln). *In the collection of University of Tasmania. Photograph by Bryan Trueman.*

195

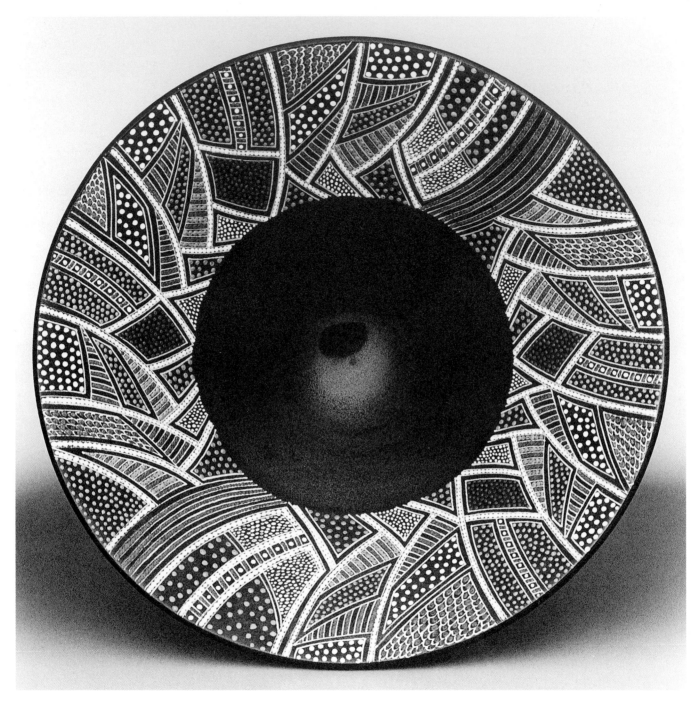

Porcelain Bowl, 'Australian Outback Series', diameter 45 cm, by
Marianne Cole, 1993. Wheel-thrown, with shiny black glaze fired to
Orton cone 9 in an electric kiln, and then decorated with painted
liquid bright gold lustre and coloured enamels and refired to cone
018.
Photograph by Michal Kluvanek.

Trueman's images are produced by using opalescent and opaque glazes overlapping and interlapping (edge to edge) over a black glaze. The base glaze is a dark tenmoku formulated to remain stable at cone 10. This stability prevents subsequent glaze layers from running and distorting too much. A wax resist is brushed over parts of the tenmoku prior to pouring more fluid glazes. Interlapping parts of the design are controlled by painting wax to mask areas of one glaze where it is due to meet another edge to edge. The unwanted section of glaze can then be sponged off and left to dry before pouring another glaze in its place. This method ensures a clearly defined boundary between the two glazes.

The two main opalescent glazes used by Trueman are a pale blue Chun and a copper red.

The Chun glaze is responsive to various oxides applied over images painted in wax resist, particularly chrome and cobalt. Rutile over the tenmoku provides an opaque effect which can be controlled by the thickness of the rutile painted on. I use several methods of applying glaze over the wax images but pouring, brushing, sponging and slip trailing are the most common. Each provides different linear and textural qualities to the finished piece.

Bryan Trueman offers the following glaze recipes for cone 10 reduction firing:

'Novelty II', 21 cm × 6 cm × 18.5 cm, by Dianne Peach, 1993. Semi-functional teapot, slipcast porcelain assembly with thrown knob. Decorated with underglaze colours and glaze brushwork, fired to cone 5 in an electric kiln.

Chun glaze 1

Potash feldspar	52.40
China clay	.75
Magnesium carbonate	2.55
Whiting	3.55
Silica	24.00
Zinc oxide	5.50
Bone ash	.90
Red iron oxide	.75

Chun glaze 2

Potash feldspar	50
Silica	23
Whiting	14
Zinc oxide	11

Tenmoku glaze:

Potash feldspar	46.50
Whiting	14.25
China clay	8.75
Silica	19.50
Red iron oxide	8.50

Copper red glaze:

Potash feldspar	36
Silica	36
Borax frit	10
Whiting	15
Tin oxide	2
Bentonite	1
Black copper oxide	0.5

Tom Turner (USA) has experimented with crystalline inclusions in his copper red 'oxblood' and 'flambé' glazes. He tries to encourage the growth of crystals in the glaze in his normal reduction firing schedule without a special cooling programme. Another glaze which has proved to be of considerable interest is made from a natural clay found beneath his house in Delaware, Ohio. The clay is ball-milled and one per cent iron oxide is added to it. 'It's a gorgeous, natural *hare's fur* glaze with crystals where thick.' He has named this slip glaze 'Peachblow' after the road in which he lives. All his pots are wheel-thrown porcelain and reduction fired to cone 10 in ten hours. 'The reduction period starts at 1850°F (1010°C) with an ACI oxy-probe reading of .70 and no changes or adjustments are made until the kiln is turned off and the damper closed.

We use no clean up period nor do we quick cool. The kiln is cooled in about forty hours and unloaded without gloves.'

Tom Turner suggests the following glaze recipes as *starting points* for experiment ('never before published because chemicals and kilns vary so much. I doubt whether they will work for anyone else. When I lived in Florida, I did not protect the copper red pots during firing but when I moved to Ohio and put my kiln inside tall barns, the taller chimneys required that we semi-saggar them. By this I mean that soft bricks are set alongside the pots on the fire side (*to act as baffles to divert the direct action of the flames*). Other formulae don't require this adjustment either BUT MINE DOES. My copper red is a product of years of experiment with the Chun base glaze given in Carlton Ball's books.'):

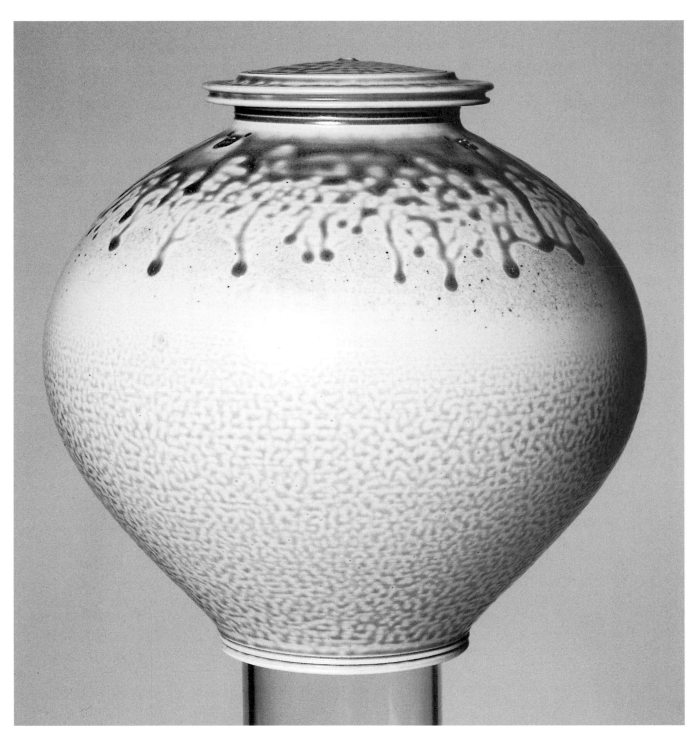

'Dome Jar', 25.5 cm × 15 cm, by Tom Turner, 1993. Wheel-thrown porcelain, with copper red glaze and zinc glaze with rutile inlaid on the lid. Fired to cone 10 in reduction with no special cooling cycle.

Covered Jar, 25.5 cm high × 17.5 cm wide, by Tom Turner, 1993. Wheel-thrown porcelain with assimilated wood ash glaze, part thick and part thin, fired to cone 10 in a reducing atmosphere.

Satin celadon glaze:

Cornish stone	25	'This is a variation of the David Leach
Silica	25	recipe with additional clay and some
EPK china clay	34	alumina hydrate to promote a satin
Whiting	25	surface that appears frosted. VeeGum T
Alumina hydrate	1	is the whitest and most plastic material I've
VeeGum T	1	ever found. It's a plasticiser and lubricant
Iron oxide	1.7	that does not burn out.'

Teapot, wheel-thrown porcelain with faceted sides and copper handle, with 'Peachblow' glaze (refer to text for details of this glaze), fired to cone 10 in a reducing atmosphere, by Tom Turner, 1993.

Lidded Casserole, diameter 19 cm × 15 cm high approx., by Gail Russell, 1993. Wheel-thrown porcelain with satin celadon glaze and blue ash glaze brushed over. Then an iron/rutile wash decoration brushed on top and dots of white glaze applied. Reduction fired to cone 10.

Tom Turner oxblood glaze:

Kingman feldspar	72
Silica (325 mesh)	45
Whiting (low Mg)	25
Kaolin	4
Gerstley borate	8
Magnesium carbonate	7
Barium carbonate	7
Zink oxide	3
Tin oxide	1.5
Copper carbonate	.75
Frit 3134	1.25

Tom Turner flambe glaze:

Kona A3 feldspar	150
Silica	90
Whiting	30
Kaolin	6
Gerstley borate	40
Dolomite	20
Barium carbonate	14
Zinc oxide	6
Tin oxide	3
Copper carbonate	1.5

Firing methods

Reducing atmospheres can be introduced into live flame kilns extremely easily by altering the ratio of fuel and air. Cutting back on the air supply alone encourages the excess carbon from unburnt fuel to search out oxygen from the metallic elements contained in bodies, slips and glazes and thus altering the colour and appearance of the pots. The drama and additional involvement experienced by potters working with reduction glazes in live flame kilns is quite different from the more detached, almost clinical, practice

Above 'Dragon Teapot', 28 cm high, by Marianne Cole, 1993. Wheel-thrown Limoges porcelain with pulled handle, fired in an anagama kiln for 72 hours to Orton cone 13/14. *Photograph by Michal Kluvanek.*

Left Porcelain Vessel, 35 cm high, by Emil Heger (Germany), 1993. Wheel-thrown, painted with ceramic stains and reduction fired in a gas kiln to cone 7 (1230°C approx.) with saltglaze.

Right Porcelain Vase, 39 cm high, by Masamichi Yoshikawa, 1991. Slab-built, incised decoration stained with cobalt under a satin glaze with a pale blue tint. Fired in a reducing atmosphere. *Photograph by Wolf Böwig.*

'Architecture II', slab-built porcelain with pale blue, celadon-type glaze, 14 cm high × 26 cm × 26 cm, by Masamichi Yoshikawa, 1991. *Photograph by Wolf Böwig.*

'Architecture I', 16 cm high × 19 cm × 38 cm, by Masamichi Yoshikawa, 1992. Slab-built porcelain with pale blue, celadon-type glaze. This artist makes all his pieces from assembled slabs of varying thickness. Most pieces are quite thick and solidly built in asymmetrical way. He aims at a 'well-balanced irregularity'. *Photograph by Wolf Böwig.*

of firing with electricity. It is possible to introduce similar conditions in electric kilns for short periods but with some risk to the life of the wire elements and this is not normally advisable. However, one method used by Derek Clarkson to achieve respectable copper reds in some of his crystal-line glazes, without the same degree of risk to the elements, is worthy of mention. He discovered that he could obtain fine copper red glazes (containing between 0.25 per cent and two per cent copper carbonate) just by pouring old or used vegetable cooking oil from a tablespoon through the top central vent of his kiln. The vent was restricted to a hole no more than $1\frac{1}{2}$ in. (10 cm) wide (closed with a bung) and a bisque saucer was placed on the floor of the kiln directly under the hole with pots arranged around it. A spoonful of oil in every few minutes, and the bung replaced, over a period of an hour and a half while the temperature was dropping from 850°C to 650°C. At this stage the kiln is no longer switched on but is cooling natur-ally. Approximately half a litre of cooking oil was used in the process. The main disadvantages to this method appear to be, firstly the constant attention required during the

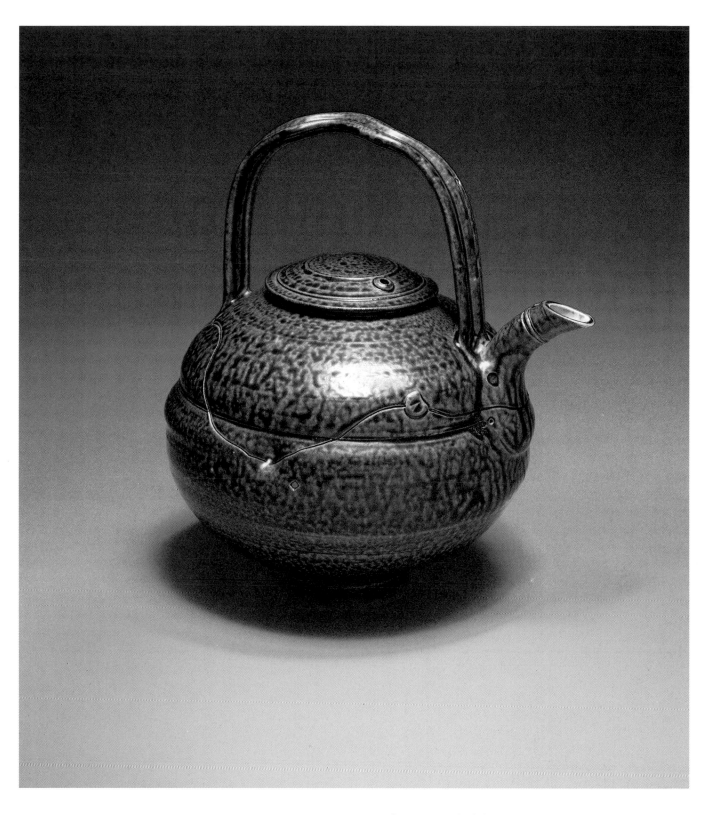

Porcelain Teapot, wheel-thrown and altered, with yellow wood ash glaze fired to cone 10 in reduction 28 cm × 26.5 cm, by Tom Coleman, 1993.

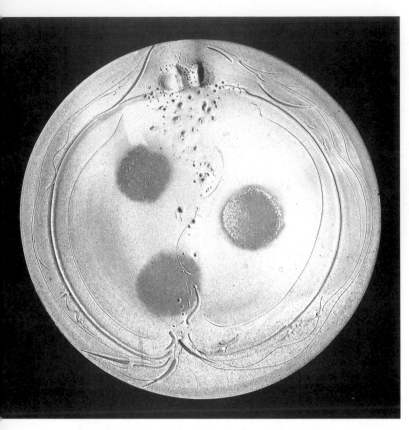

'Flatfish Dish', porcelain with incised decoration, fired in an anagama kiln, 35 cm diameter, by Terry Davies (Australia), 1993.
Photograph by Michal Kluvanek.

period of reduction and, secondly, the unpleasant smell that clings to the workshop for several days afterwards!

Nothing can quite match the excitement of firing with living flames. When we moved to our present address in Hampshire, it proved impossible to take my excellent gas kiln with me and the glazes which I had perfected for reduction firing lacked the attraction and element of surprise when transferred to the more detached and predictable firing by electricity. There seems little point in trying to imitate those uniquely attractive effects of reduction firing in an electric kiln, although many potters try to do so. Both oxidation and reduction offer ample opportunities to experiment and to achieve very satisfactory results with or without glazes. In either case, it requires a supreme act of faith on the part of the potter to commit the result of his or her labours, perhaps the work of several months, to be transformed by such intense heat. The most radical changes, of course, are wrought by the glazes which will be no more than dull, powdery coverings to the underlying ceramic objects. Hence the excited anticipation which accompanies many glaze firings, especially when experimental work is involved.

The most simple of familiar, traditional, oriental porcelain glazes can acquire a fresh and exciting appearance when applied to contemporary ceramic forms. Copper reds of different shades have long been a challenging and popular choice for many potters. Likewise, celadons ranging from the palest blues through greys to pale and deeper olive greens are frequently chosen to enhance incised work and surface carving. The grey-green version of this glaze, so revered by the Chinese from the T'ang period onward for its jade-like appearance, is generally accepted as the original and, therefore, proper colour for 'celadon', although there is some confusion over the origin of the name. The delicate colour variations and soft luminous quality of Chinese celadons comes from differing amounts of iron present in the glaze and/or body together with countless undissolved particles and tiny bubbles held in suspension within the glaze. Fired in a reducing atmosphere, even small amounts of iron are sufficient to contribute colour to the glaze. The Japanese potter, **Masamichi Yoshikawa**, clothes his monumental slab-built pieces with a particularly sumptuous, pale blue celadon glaze. Made from very thick slabs of porcelain, his work is sometimes decorated with incised, linear drawing picked out with cobalt. The visual power of these forms is in complete harmony with the glaze that seems to flow with great depth over them.

Reduction firing, however, is not always possible for those who live in an urban conurbation. The greater predictability of electric kiln firing has proven perfectly satisfactory for the needs of a considerable number of potters whose work is illustrated in this book. Porcelain bodies are relatively inert compared to those more commonly associated with stoneware and which rely for effect on their positive contribution to the final results achieved through the reaction between body and glaze. Iron spots burning out from stoneware bodies to enliven even the dullest reduction glaze would, in most cases, be inappropriate blemishes on porcelain.

Without the need to make ceramics that must conform to fit functional, domestic requirements, potters are no longer bound to make vessels watertight. In this book are illustrations of the work of potters who have chosen to dispense with firing porcelain to the high temperatures necessary to mature the body. This liberty has allowed them to produce objects of beauty and interest serving purely decorative purposes. Others may fire their pieces many times with multiple glazes at both high and low temperatures. The options are infinite and the directions chosen for exploration are the decision of each individual. That which appeals to one will be anathema to another.

The freedom from any traditional constraints has encouraged fresh, adventurous approaches to working with clay. There can be little doubt that the enormous variety of forms, surfaces and expressions which we see today in porcelain and ceramics generally, will continue growing, enriching our environment and adding to our cultural heritage with each succeeding generation.

Porcelain Form, by Ingvil Havrevold, 1993. Wheel-thrown and handbuilt, with impressed texture inlaid with coloured nepheline syenite glazes and parts left unglazed. Fired to 1280°C in oxidation. *Photograph by Jan Enoksen.*

CONCLUSION

It is never easy to evaluate the true worth of works of art created in one's own time because it is virtually impossible to become detached enough to appraise them with a totally objective eye. The inevitable question that arises when assessing works which may be held in high regard today or which grab the attention for one reason or another is *will they survive the test of time*? So often in the past that which seemed so fresh and exciting soon palls through lack of substance. Contemporary work preserved in museums and in serious private collections does acquire a certain status by association. In this respect the selection policies followed by public institutions, especially, present them with an enormous responsibility. Auction houses too, by their approval and increasing sales of work by living ceramicists, have the opportunity to influence public taste as well as the standing of individual artists and the commercial value of their works. Recent prices at auction of pieces by Hans Coper or Lucie Rie, and others in England have been so high that increasing numbers of collectors have been encouraged to look upon contemporary ceramics as worthy of serious investment. Nevertheless, in comparison with other branches of the art market, ceramics still offers a relatively inexpensive purchase for anyone wanting to possess original works.

For many people the term 'pottery' implies the making of functional vessels intended primarily for domestic use

Bowl form, 52 cm diameter, by Thomas Naethe (Germany), 1993.
This piece is a composite form made in a *stoneware* clay with painted coloured slip banding. Porcelain slip is sprayed over the bisque and then a white feldspathic glaze reduction fired to 1250°C in a gas kiln.
Photograph by Foto Strenger.

Porcelain Plate, wheel-thrown, decorated with metallic oxides and a chun glaze (cone 10 approximately 1300°C), 40 cm diameter, by Tom Coleman, 1993.

Porcelain Form, with black slip and gold lustre decoration, 31 cm
35 cm × 10 cm, by Brigitte Enders, 1992.
Photograph by Klaus Moje.

Left
Vessel form, 21 cm high, by Thomas Naethe (Germany), 1993. This
piece is a composite form made from wheel-thrown sections in a
stoneware clay, partly painted with coloured slip. Porcelain slip is
sprayed over the bisque and then a white feldspathic glaze reduction
fired to 1250°C in a gas kiln.
Photograph by Gros-Photographie.

but we have seen that the majority of those individuals
whose work is represented in this book are more concerned with expressing personal feelings in response to the
various stimuli that impinge upon their lives. In some cases
'function', in the recognised sense, remains an important
element. In others, vessel forms provide a springboard for
fresh explorations and invention. The reworking of traditional forms in porcelain like bowls, vases or teapots etc.,
need never be a dull exercise, especially when translucency, delicacy and purity contribute their cherished
qualities to the final appearance. Expressions possessing
subtlety and sensitivity can create long-lasting impressions
while demonstrations of extrovert flamboyance may soon
be forgotten. Anyone who takes an interest in ceramics

Raku fired porcelain bowls (1100°C) with lustres containing gold,
silver and copper, by David Jones.

learns to recognise even the simplest objects as being from
the hand of a particular craftsman or woman. Their identity
may be revealed through extremely subtle visual clues.
Slight nuances in the profile, the way in which the form
rises up from its base, perhaps the style of decoration or
maybe just the choice and arrangement of colours will
provide enough information for instant recognition. No
more than a quiet, restrained elegance may suffice. Recog-
nising the indefinable quality that gives a ceramic object a
kind of 'presence' irrespective of any label or category
assigned to it is an ability which becomes more refined as
experience in the field grows. In *Studio Porcelain* (1980) I
wrote that, 'a simple bowl may possess a quiet, unassuming
"presence", no less impressive than the most complex
sculpture, whether designed for use or otherwise. The best
solutions to aesthetic problems are often remarkable for
their simplicity.' But, whatever form the work may take, it
can express the very essence of considered ideas as well as

revealing something of the emotional involvement of the individual who made it.

Unusual images or surprising uses of a traditional material may capture the imagination but without substance or, perhaps, further development, they are unlikely to prove much more than a passing fancy. Sculptural objects created in ceramics by modern potters have often been underrated or dismissed as being of little significance. In part this may be because they are difficult to categorise. Should they be labelled as 'fine art' or *merely* pottery? Indeed, does it really matter? Undoubtedly, it is often easier to accept and absorb that which conforms to traditional concepts. Anything which appears to violate normal boundaries may need more time to become familiar and, therefore, acceptable. The new can excite but it may also offend sensibilities. Therein lies a dilemma, for entrenched attitudes impede the progress of thought, ideas and expression. One can cultivate an 'open' mind without necessarily conceding personal principles or granting *carte blanche* approval to a work merely on the basis of its 'originality'. Each object whether as a vessel form or as a figurative or abstract sculpture is the concrete realisation of multiple and complex strands of human feeling. The reso-

Handbuilt ceramic forms combining earthenware bases surmounted by porcelain cups decorated using the neriage technique, 26 cm and 32 cm high. These pieces were produced through the collaboration in design and execution by two Belgian artists, Frank Steyaert and Chris Scholliers in 1994.

A group of four related slab-built vessel forms 20 cm high, by Karl Scheid, 1992. With angled top sections, porcelain, decorated with different coloured slips applied by brush. Glaze fired to 1360°C in a gas kiln (reduction).

lution and production of each ceramic piece requires the artist to work with ingenuity and sensitivity, to have a thorough understanding of materials and processes, and a sincerity of purpose if it is to successfully appeal to a wide audience. We may choose to deny *any* worth in work which does not happen to coincide with our own personal taste or does not conform to some perceived ideal but if we try to value any genuine human endeavour we can learn to judge each piece on its individual merit and become enriched in the experience.

GLOSSARY

Agateware
Ceramics assembled from layers of different coloured clays (usually prepared with body stains or metallic oxides), laminated and sliced through.

Airbrush
An instrument which operates with compressed air to propel a fine, adjustable spray of coloured material (stains, slips, glazes, lustres) onto the ceramic.

Albany clay
An American clay from Albany, New York, containing a high proportion of fluxes and a fine grain size, which is used as a brown/black slip glaze at temperatures above 1240°C.

Albury clay
An Australian clay having similar characteristics as Albany clay.

Alkali
Opposite to acid. Potash, soda and lithia are strong fluxes. Potters also use alkaline earths such as calcium, barium, magnesium and strontium as fluxes.

Alumina
Aluminium oxide. An important ingredient in clays and glazes. It provides the plasticity in clay and acts as an opacifier, stiffener and matting agent in glazes. Usually added in the form of china clay.

Applied decoration
Often describes additions of pieces of clay to the main form. Can also be decoration with slips, oxides, stains and glazes used in various ways.

Ash glaze
A glaze containing a proportion of ash from burnt organic material, mainly trees, straw, grasses, etc.

Ball clay
An extremely fine-grained, light coloured. sedimentary clay, sometimes used as a plasticiser in porcelain bodies.

Ball mill
A porcelain jar filled with pebbles and used to grind minerals and glazes to a fine particle size.

Banding
The application of horizontal stripes of oxide, stain, slip, glaze or lustre to pots on a rotating wheel.

Barium
An alkaline earth. Barium carbonate (poisonous) is used in glaze recipes for particular surface and colour effects (notably with copper and nickel).

Batt
This can be a kiln shelf, a removable wooden disk attached to the wheelhead for throwing making it easier to remove freshly thrown pots, or a slab of plaster or low-fired bisque used to dry wet clay.

Bentonite
A clay with a very fine grain, used to plasticise porcelain and added to glazes in small amounts around two per cent to aid suspension in the slop state.

Bisque
Unglazed ware, usually porous.

Bisque firing
The first firing of clay into ceramic. Usually conducted prior to glazing or other treatment because it is easier to handle than in the raw state.

Blunging
Mixing clay with water in a blunger to produce a smooth slip.

Bodies
Any clay or mixture of clays. Few clays are used by potters 'as dug'. Normally they use mixed clay bodies with different qualities for specific purposes.

Body stains
Colours prepared from metallic oxides to mix into slips and clay bodies.

Bone ash
Calcium phosphate made from calcining cattle bones. It is used in certain glazes to give a milky quality and is a major constituent of bone china.

Bone china
A very translucent white ware with a high proportion of bone ash.

Bung
A ceramic stopper to fit in the spyhole of a kiln.

Calcine
To heat materials to a sufficiently high temperature to drive off chemically combined water.

Calcium
The carbonate form is extensively used as a flux in glazes.

Carborundum
The trade name for silicon carbide, a hard grit used for polishing ceramic and, occasionally, added to glazes to cause local reduction in electric kilns.

Carving
Cutting into and removing clay from the surface of (usually) leatherhard clay.

Casting slip
Deflocculated mixture of clay and water in suspension for pouring into moulds.

Celadon glaze
A high-fired, grey-green glaze often used over incised or carved decoration. Blue and grey glazes having similar characteristics are sometimes described as 'celadon' types.

China clay
Kaolin, a pure form of primary clay, high in alumina and extremely refractory.

Chun glaze
A thick, opalescent glaze and bluish tint caused by scattered blue light waves.

Cobalt
Small amounts of the oxide and carbonate forms of this mineral give strong blue slips, bodies and glazes.

Coiling
Coils are made by rolling clay between the fingers or by extruding through a machine. Forms can be built up with coils joined together.

Cones
Elongated, three-sided pyramids composed of ceramic materials graded to measure the actual 'heat work' in a kiln and designed to collapse at specific temperatures. Cones can be observed through the spyhole during the firing.

Copper
The oxide and carbonate forms are used to give greens, blues and reds in slips and glazes according to their composition and the kiln atmosphere.

Copper red glazes
In reduction firing small amounts of copper produces red in reduction.

Crackle glaze
A glaze designed to craze by shrinking more than the body. The pattern of crackle lines is often stained after firing to give them greater emphasis.

Crazing
This occurs when the glaze does not fit the body due to uneven expansion and contraction. Either can be adjusted by the addition of silica.

Crystalline glaze
Glaze with crystals visible in and on the surface. Usually 'seeded' with titania, zinc or zirconium to encourage the growth of crystals. Slow cooling also helps.

Cup lawn
A small, cup-shaped sieve with a fine mesh.

De-airing
The removal of all air bubbles in a plastic clay prior to working.

Deflocculation
The dispersal of fine clay particles suspended in a slip prepared for casting. Soluble alkalis are added so that the slip can contain a high proportion of clay to a small amount of water without loss of fluidity.

Dolomite
A natural mineral, containing calcium and magnesium, used as a flux and crystalliser in high temperature glazes.

Dunting
Cracking of the body during firing or cooling.

Earthenware
Porous pottery usually fired to temperatures under 1100°C.

Engobe
Slip applied to pots at either the unfired or the bisque stage.

Engraving
Shallow incisions made into the surface of a ceramic at any stage.

Extruded
Plastic clay can be shaped into various sections by forcing it through a metal dye.

Feldspar
One of the most useful material in ceramics. Used as a flux in bodies and as a natural frit in glazes.

Feldspathoid
Mineral with similar properties to feldspar e.g. Cornish stone and nepheline syenite.

Fettling
Trimming away excess clay, slip or glaze before firing.

Flambé
A bright, glossy glaze streaked with reds produced by the use of copper in reduction.

Flint
Silica for bodies and glazes.

Fluting
Cutting vertical or diagonal grooves in the surface of a pot.

Flux
An oxide which lowers the melting point of a glaze mixture and aids vitrification in bodies.

Footring
The thrown or turned ring of clay supporting a bowl.

Frit
Glass or glaze which has been ground to be added to a glaze or body recipe. Frits are often prepared to make soluble materials insoluble for use in glaze mixtures.

Fusion
The melting of ceramic materials.

Glaze stain
Pigments made from oxides and added to give colour to glazes.

Grog
Fired clay body ground and graded to pass through various mesh sizes. It is added to bodies to provide extra wet strength and reduce shrinkage.

Inlay
Clays and slips, usually of different colours, inlaid into the porcelain body.

Iron
An important source of colour in ceramics. Rust reds, browns, tans, blues, greens and blacks can all be produced from different forms of iron oxide in various compositions and kiln atmospheres.

Kaolin
China clay.

Kidney steel
A small piece of flexible steel shaped like a kidney and used for shaping and scraping clay.

Kneading
Mixing plastic clay to an even consistency by hand.

Latex resist
A liquid rubber solution which can be painted or trailed on to a pot. When dry it resists water-based mixtures of colour, slip or glaze.

Lawn
A fine mesh of wire or fibre for sieving wet materials like slip or glaze etc.

Leatherhard
Clay in a stiffened condition but with sufficient moisture content to accept carving, piercing, inlaying and slipping.

Lithium carbonate
A strong alkaline flux used in glazes.

Lustre
Metallic salts of copper, gold, silver, platinum, bismuth and tin are mixed with resin and oils to deposit pure metal on the surface of pots in a localised reduction firing at a relatively low temperature around 750°C.

Magnesia
Used in bodies and glazes. Contributes opacity and mattness when percentages between 20%–30% are used in high temperature glazes. Often added in the form of dolomite.

Manganese (carbonate or dioxide)
Used as a colourant in bodies and glazes giving browns, blacks and purples.

Molochite
A refractory grog made by English China Clays in Cornwall.

Neriage
A form of decoration where slabs of contrasting coloured clays are laminated together, cut into strips and reassembled into patterns pressed into moulds.

Onglaze enamels
Soft, coloured glass with a low melting point for painting on top of fired glaze.

Opacifier
Materials in a glaze composition which remain suspended in the fired glaze. Tin, oxide, titanium dioxide, zinc oxide and zirconium dioxide are the principal agents.

Oxidation

This occurs when there is an ample air supply in the kiln during firing.

Oxide

A chemical compound formed between oxygen and another element.

Oxidising atmosphere

A clean kiln atmosphere where plenty of oxygen is present.

Paper porcelain

Porcelain slip mixed together with paper pulp and cast and rolled into sheets.

Plasticity

The essential property that allows clay to be shaped and reformed, but excess plasticity can make a clay unworkable or increase the amount of shrinkage when fired.

Polishing

This term is used to described the method of smoothing fired porcelain with silicon carbide 'sandpaper'.

Potash (potassium oxide or carbonate)

A strong alkaline flux and an important constituent of porcelain bodies and glazes.

Press mould

A hollow mould, made from plaster or from fired clay, used to form clay pressed into it.

Pyrometer

An instrument to measure temperature in the kiln.

Quartz

Silica. Used in body and glaze composition.

Raku

A Japanese word used to describe a particular type of low-fired ware made from a refractory clay able to withstand the shock of removal from a red hot kiln with tongs and rapidly cooled in water, or covered with combustible materials to create reducing conditions for special effects.

Reducing atmosphere

An excess of carbon is introduced into the kiln, usually about 900°C, so that oxygen atoms are extracted from the oxides present in the ceramics to produce often radical colour changes in glazes, notably from copper and iron.

Reduction firing

See reducing atmosphere.

Refractory

Resistant to high temperatures.

Rib

A tool usually made of wood or metal and used in throwing or for shaping.

Rutile

A natural titanium dioxide used to modify other colouring oxides. Alone, it has small traces of iron which produce tan colours. It is also used to give mottled colour effects in glazes. It is often used in crystalline glazes.

Salt glaze

Common salt thrown into the kiln fire at high temperatures decomposes and volatilises to combine with the alumina and silica in the clay body to produce an uneven glaze surface resembling orange peel in texture.

Satin glaze

A semi-matt glaze.

Sgraffito

Decoration scratched through the surface of slips or glazes or painted oxides.

Silica

All ceramics contain silica. It occurs as flint or quartz or sand. It is the essential ingredient of glass and glazes. Clay is a combination of silica, alumina, and water.

Silicon carbide

A compound of silica and coke used for its refractory properties and in grit form, as a powerful abrasive.

Slip

A creamy mixture of clay and water. The potter's *glue*. Can be coloured and used to completely cover a pot, or used for inlay and other decorative purposes.

Slip glaze

A fusible clay which melts to form a glaze at high temperatures.

Soak

A period during which the kiln temperature is kept constant to allow glazes and body to mature.

Soluble salts

Chlorides, nitrates and sulphates of metals commonly used as colourants in ceramics.

Sprigging

Adding pieces of clay as relief decoration.

Stannic oxide

White tin oxide, used as an opacifier in glazes.

Stoneware
A vitrified ware, usually fired to temperatures in excess of 1200°C with low porosity (no more than 5%).

Talc
Magnesium silicate. Used as an insoluble form of magnesia in bodies and glazes.

Tape resist
Paper masking tape used to protect areas of a design when painting, spraying and dipping slips, glazes and coloured stains.

Tenmoku
A high-fired glaze containing a large amount of iron oxide. It is usually brown to black in colour with streaks of rust, especially where thin on rims and carved edges.

Throwing
Making hollow pottery forms by hand on a rotating wheel.

Tin glaze
An opaque, white glaze containing tin oxide. This glaze forms the base for painting coloured pigments as seen in maiolica and delftwares.

Titanium
A creamy coloured opacifying agent which also produces crystals in a glaze.

Trimming
Turning or trimming waste clay away from a pot rotating on the wheel. This is usually done at the leatherhard stage.

Turning
See *Trimming* above.

Underglaze stains
Prepared ceramic pigments applied to the raw clay or bisque and normally covered with a transparent glaze. Colours which are capable of withstanding high temperatures are often used on porcelain without a glaze coat.

Vanadium oxide
A rare metallic oxide used to produce yellow pigments with tin oxide or zirconia, and blue pigments when combined with zirconium silicate.

Viscosity
Without the property of viscosity, glaze runs off a pot as molten glass. Viscous glazes hold their position due to internal friction between the particles of their composition. The alumina content in a glaze is one of the factors affecting viscosity.

Vitrification
The point at which the glassy materials within a body melt and flow into and fill the spaces between the clay particles and interact with them fusing them together. The vitrified state is the furthest point at which the body will hold its shape prior to deformation.

Wax resist
Molten wax or a wax emulsion design painted or trailed onto unfired clay, bisque, or glaze, resists water-based colours, slips and glazes with great clarity.

Wedging
The preparation, or restoration, of plastic clay by kneading into a smooth, homogeneous mass, free of air bubbles ready for use.

Whiting
Calcium carbonate. A material which is frequently used as a flux in glazes and as a source of calcia in clay bodies.

Wollastonite
Calcium silicate. A natural mineral used in glazes as a source of calcia.

Zinc oxide
Used as an auxiliary flux in glazes. It has a strong effect on certain colouring oxides and is generally best with copper or cobalt. Zinc oxide is often an important constituent of crystalline glazes.

Zirconium oxide
Used as an opacifier in glazes, often as a substitute for the more expensive tin oxide. Helps to promote crystal formation and mottled colours in glazes.

Suggested Further Reading

Books

Åse, Arne, *Water Colour on Porcelain* (Norwegian University Press, 1989)

Axel, Jan and Karen McCready, *Porcelain: Traditions and New Visions* (Watson Guptill, 1981)

Billington, Dora, *The Technique of Pottery*, (Batsford, London, 1966)

Blackman, Audrey, *Rolled Pottery Figures* (Pitman/A&C Black, London, 1978)

Casson, Michael, *The Craft of the Potter* (BBC Publications, London, 1977)

Clark, Kenneth, *The Potter's Manual*, (Macdonald, 1983)

Clays and Glazes (The Ceramic Review Book of Clay Bodies and Glaze Recipes, 1988)

Colbeck, John, *Pottery: Techniques of Decoration* (Batsford, London, 1983)

Cooper, Emmanuel, *Electric Kiln Pottery* (Batsford, London, 1982)

Cosentino, Peter, *The Encyclopaedia of Pottery Techniques* (Headline Book Publishing, 1990)

Flight, Graham, *Ceramics Manual* (Collins, London, 1990)

Fournier, Robert, *Illustrated Dictionary of Practical Pottery* (A&C Black, 1973, 1977, 1992)

Fraser, Harry, *Glazes for the Craft Potter* (Pitman/A&C Black, London, 1973)

Gibson, John, *Pottery Decoration: Contemporary Approaches* (A&C Black, London, 1987)

Godden, Geoffrey, *Encyclopaedia of British Porcelain Manufacturers* (Barrie & Jenkins, London, 1988)

Gompertz, G. St. G. M., *Chinese Celadon Wares* (Faber and Faber, London, 1968)

Grebanier, Joseph, *Chinese Stoneware Glazes* (Pitman, London, 1975)

Green, David, *Understanding Pottery Glazes* (Faber and Faber, London, 1963)

Green, David, *A Handbook of Pottery Glazes* (Faber and Faber, London, 1978)

Hamer, Frank and Janet *The Potter's Dictionary of Materials and Techniques* (A&C Black, London, 1975, 1986, 1991, 1993)

Hamilton, David *Stoneware and Porcelain* (Thames and Hudson, London, 1982)

Hopper, Robin, *The Ceramic Spectrum* (Chilton Book Company, USA, 1984)

Lane, Peter, *Studio Porcelain* (Pitman/A&C Black, London and Chilton Book Company, USA, 1980)

Lane, Peter, *Studio Ceramics* (Collins, London and Chilton Book Company, USA, 1983)

Lane, Peter, *Ceramic Form: Design & Decoration* (Collins, London and Rizzoli, New York, 1988)

Leach, Bernard, *A Potter's Book* (Faber and Faber, London, 1945)

Medley, Margaret, *The Chinese Potter* (Phaidon, Oxford, 1976)

Nelson, Glenn C., *Ceramics* (Holt, Rinehart & Winston, New York, 1978)

Parmelee, Cullen W., *Ceramic Glazes* (Industrial Publications, Chicago, 1951)

Rhodes, Daniel, *Clay and Glazes for the Potter* (Chilton, USA and Pitman/A&C Black, London, 1973)

Rhodes, Daniel, *Stoneware and Porcelain* (Chilton, USA and Pitman, London, 1960)

Rhodes, Daniel, *Kilns: Design, Construction and Operation* (Chilton, USA, 1969)

Savage, George, *Porcelain through the Ages* (Penguin, London, 1954)

Scott, Paul, *Ceramics and Print* (A&C Black, London, 1994).

Wood, Nigel, *Oriental Glazes* (Pitman/A&C Black, London, 1978)

Periodicals

American Craft (Published by the American Crafts Council, New York)

Ceramics: Art and Perception (35 William Street, Paddington, Sydney NSW 2021, Australia)

Ceramics Monthly (Columbus, Ohio, USA)

Ceramic Review (Published by The Craft Potters' Association, London)

Crafts Magazine (Published by the Crafts Council, London)

Pottery in Australia (Published by The Potters' Society of Australia, Sydney)

La Revue de la Ceramique et du Verre, (France)

INDEX